DARK VOYAGE TRILOGY

THE CHILDREN OF THE GODS SERIES BOOKS 77-79

I. T. LUCAS

Dark Voyage Trilogy is a work of fiction! Names, characters, places and incidents are products of the author's imagination or are used fictitiously and are not to be construed as real. Any similarity to actual persons, organizations and/or events is purely coincidental.

Published by Evening Star Press, LLC.

EveningStarPress.com

ISBN: 978-1-962067-43-0

MATTERS OF THE HEART

1

FRANKIE

Frankie regarded her boss with a wide-eyed stare and a sinking sensation in the pit of her stomach. "Are you serious? You're not even giving me two weeks' notice? You want me to leave right now?"

Who fired people on a Monday afternoon, right after the lunch break?

Scumbags like Vernon. That's who.

He nodded. "I've found that it's best to make a clean cut and not drag things out. I will pay you for the next two weeks, of course." He gave her one of the fake smiles he usually reserved for customers. "Consider it a paid vacation."

The finality in his tone didn't leave room for argument.

"Can I at least know the reason for my termination?"

Frankie had a feeling it had to do with the 'niece' he'd brought to the office the other day and paraded around like a prize horse, introducing her to everyone. What was her name?

Was it Ashley?

Frankie couldn't remember and didn't care.

The thing was, no one's niece looked like that or clung to her uncle's arm like a panda to a tree branch.

Did Vernon need to set his mistress up with a job?

The guy was so cheap that he couldn't even be a proper sugar daddy.

Vernon sighed dramatically. "Where should I start?" He braced his elbows on the desk and steepled his fingers. "Let's see. You are often late, you make typos in the emails I dictate to you, and you don't bother to run them through a spellchecker. Do you know how embarrassing that is for me? People assume that I wrote those emails myself."

Frankie squirmed in the uncomfortable chair. Everything he'd said was true, but it didn't happen as often as he'd made it sound. Everyone was late once in a while, and everyone misspelled a word here and there, and the spellchecker didn't catch every mistake.

His 'niece' wouldn't do any better, that was for sure.

Well, at least Vernon hadn't told her that she had a big mouth and an attitude. That was the reason Frankie had been fired from her previous job.

The problem was that if he fired her for a cause, she wouldn't get unemployment benefits, especially if he exaggerated her supposed misconduct, which the scumbag would certainly do.

"What if I promise to do better?" She was fighting tears. The money in her bank account wouldn't cover next month's rent. "Can you give me another chance?"

"It's not conducive to a good office environment to have a disgruntled employee spreading discord." Vernon leaned forward, giving her a surprisingly earnest look. "You are not happy here, Francesca, and you let everyone know that. You might be happier somewhere else."

So, that was supposed to be the reason for her sudden and totally unprovoked termination?

But, no one working for Vernon was happy. He and his partners expected each of their employees to do the work of two or three people, and on top of that, the pay sucked. Still, the others might have been better at keeping their discontent to themselves, while Frankie had a big mouth and no filter.

She might have blabbed to the wrong person.

Was it the barista at the coffee shop across the street?

Or maybe someone had overheard her talking shit on her lunch break about Vernon and his sleazy partners?

At least he was going to pay her for the next two weeks. That might be enough time to find another job with less stress and better pay.

Heck, she could probably make more money taking care of kids and cleaning houses, and she might even enjoy that, but Frankie had a college degree for Pete's sake. Her parents would be mortified if she didn't use it after all the effort and sacrifice they had made so she could get the education they never had.

Besides, Frankie liked dressing elegantly and working in an office.

That said, the office attire at the dream job Mia had promised her was probably super casual. Beta testers for the Perfect Match Virtual Fantasy Studios couldn't wear anything form-fitting while performing their duties, and they had to take their shoes off.

Mia had promised her the job months ago, but nothing had come out of it so far. Supposedly, the machines weren't ready because of production delays, but Frankie had a feeling that Mia might have promised something that she couldn't deliver.

"Will you at least write me a reference letter?" she pleaded, hating herself for having to beg Vernon for anything.

But what else could she do?

If he wrote her a reference, he couldn't later claim that she was a horrible employee and wasn't entitled to unemployment benefits.

"Of course." Vernon Hoffesommer III looked relieved. "In fact, you can write whatever you want, and I'll sign it."

That was better than Frankie had expected, but knowing Vernon, she'd better write it and get his signature before she left, or he would later claim he'd never promised to do it. Right now, he obviously wanted to get rid of her as fast as possible, and she needed to take advantage of that.

"Thank you." She gave him a dazzling smile. "I'll type it up right now, so I don't need to return for it."

Vernon's expression soured, confirming her suspicion that he was desperate to get rid of her, but he nodded. "Make it short."

Was his 'niece' in the waiting room? Ready to jump into Frankie's seat or onto Vernon's lap?

Probably.

"I'll be right back." She rose to her high-heeled feet and walked out of his office holding her chin up, even though she was faking it big time.

After typing up a glowing reference letter, she actually checked it for spelling mistakes before printing it out and striding back into Vernon's office.

He read through the letter with a grimace, twisting his fleshy lips, and when he shook his head, Frankie held her breath, but then he reached for his pen and signed it.

"Good luck, Francesca."

Unbelievable.

Frankie hadn't thought he would actually sign the thing. She'd made herself sound like the best assistant an executive could ever hope for.

To sign that, Vernon must have felt guilty for kicking her out to make room for his 'niece.'

Relief washing over her, she took the printed page from his hairy fingers and offered him her hand. "Thank you, Mr. Hoffesommer."

In exchange for his signature on the letter, she was willing to suffer his gross touch one last time.

Vernon had never done anything more than put his sweaty paw on her shoulder or her upper arm while passing by her desk, so it wasn't enough to sue his ass for sexual harassment, but to say that it had been unwelcome was to put it mildly.

Dreading his slimy touch, she'd stopped wearing outfits that exposed her shoulders or arms to the office.

Back at her desk, Frankie collected the one picture of her family and the tiny cactus she'd brought to decorate her space. Lifting her eyes, she scanned the rest of the staff working in the office's main room. She searched for one face that she would miss, but none of them even bothered to look up.

Hell, she'd made some friends during the eighteen months she'd worked there. They could at least wish her luck.

Turning around, she saw why no one dared to lift their heads.

Vernon stood at the doorway with his arms crossed over his chest and resting on his large belly.

Was he worried that she would steal a pen? Or maybe a book of stamps?

Plastering on a smile, she waved at her former coworkers. "Goodbye, everyone." She turned to Vernon with that smile still affixed to her face. "Goodbye, Mr. Hoffesommer. I hope your 'niece' will like it here better than I did."

2

DAGOR

"What do you think?" Negal pointed with his chin at the two women walking through the door of the coffee shop that had become their refuge over the weekend.

The females were pretty, for young humans that is, but neither had the poise, elegance, and self-assurance that Dagor appreciated in his companions.

Sneakers and jeans just did not do it for him, and neither did all the skin decorations that were so fashionable among the young humans in this city.

Gods couldn't get tattoos because their bodies healed the punctures faster than the artists could make them, and Dagor was thankful for that. Who wanted to be stuck with crappy artwork for eternity?

Or even great artwork, for that matter?

"Not my type." He closed his lips around the paper straw and drew up more of the delicious Frappuccino that had become his favorite drink since he'd discovered it.

"You are too picky." Negal leaned closer to him. "You won't find goddesses here, and you need to compromise. For humans, those two are not bad."

"I'm not picky." Dagor put the Frappuccino down. After spending five years on Earth with him, Negal should have known what type of females interested him. "The attorneys the other day were very pleasant company."

Neither had been beautiful or even pretty, but the conversation was stimulating, and they had been immaculately dressed.

Negal grinned. "Yeah, those two were superb in more ways than one, or at least the one I picked. It's a shame we can't see them again."

After spending the night with them in the hotel, the ladies had been more than eager to provide their phone numbers, but Dagor and Negal had a rule about being with human companions more than once.

Before meeting Gabi, Aru had obeyed the same rule, but he'd broken it for her without giving it a second thought. At the time, Dagor couldn't understand their commander's odd behavior and his fascination with the human, but as it had turned out, Gabi had not been fully human. She had godly genes in her, which explained the attraction.

Still, Gabi was not a goddess, only an immortal—a hybrid who was considered an abomination in their home world.

Not that Dagor believed in that nonsense. Gabriella was a lovely female, but even more importantly, she was Aru's fated mate. Nevertheless, the union was problematic in the sense that Aru could never take her back to Anumati with him and could never introduce her to his family and friends back home. The resistance would have welcomed her, but there was no way to smuggle her onto the patrol ship, or any other ship for that matter. All the stasis pods were accounted for, and their occupants' biometrics were monitored from Anumati.

If only the resistance could build its own ships somewhere away from Anumati's watchful eyes, but that was impossible. Humans thought their privacy was being eroded, but they had no idea how much worse it could get.

The one good thing about being on Earth was the freedom to do and say whatever he wanted without worrying about the censorship that possibly extended even to thoughts. There was no proof, but there were rumors about the king employing telepaths. Most of them couldn't read actual thoughts, but they could sense intentions, which was dangerous for the resistance.

Rebels had learned how to shield their thoughts and emotions.

The problem was that it didn't mean much when there was so little that he could do with this planet's primitive technology.

Leaning back in his chair, Dagor groaned. "I need something to do that involves using my head for more than people-watching. I'm bored out of my mind, and I'm not even a century old yet."

A guy sitting at the table next to theirs turned to him and nodded. "I get it, bro. Sometimes I feel ancient, too."

Forcing a smile, Dagor lifted the plastic cup and saluted the guy.

He'd found out that humans responded well to noncommittal gestures that could mean many different things.

Negal glared at him. "You need to keep your voice down."

"I know. My bad."

That was another human expression Dagor had adopted that worked very well for a variety of situations.

Leaning even closer to him, Negal whispered in his ear, "You are too young to suffer from the affliction of boredom. Perhaps you should contact the ship's counselor."

Dagor wasn't losing his mind, and he had no intention of talking to the counselor, but to get Negal off his back, he had to acquiesce.

"Perhaps I will go to see her after this mission is over. You know that empaths need skin-to-skin contact to be able to provide real help. She can't do much for me through the communicator."

"By the time we get picked up, it might be too late," Negal said in their native tongue. "A hundred and fifteen years is not long in the life of a god, but if you are already showing signs of mental fatigue, you should not delay seeking help. Even talking with the counselor might be beneficial. She might give you advice on how to combat these early signs of decline."

Dagor didn't wish to offend Negal, but he'd had enough of the insinuations that he was going insane. It was a major concern for Anumatians, but he was too young to be showing even early symptoms.

"My mental faculties are intact. It's just that we are stuck here doing nothing while Aru takes care of his mate. I am tired of sitting in this blasted coffee shop and watching humans come and go." He lifted the venti Frappuccino cup. "That's the only saving grace of this place."

Arching a brow, Negal leaned back. "I quite enjoy the respite we have been given. Sitting here and hunting for suitable bed companions is far more enjoyable than trekking through Tibet and sleeping on the cold ground. I am not looking forward to the day Aru decides that Gabriella is strong enough to travel, and we will be back on the road, searching for the missing Kra-ell pods."

Sometimes, Dagor wondered whether Negal's linear way of thinking was an inborn tendency or a product of his many years in the service.

"The pods are not the only thing we should be searching for."

The immortals were hiding gods among them, and Aru knew about it. He just didn't seem to think that his teammates were trustworthy enough to tell them about what he had discovered.

No matter how Dagor tried to excuse his leader's motives, the insult stung.

The smirk slid off Negal's face. "We are not supposed to know about the gods, and I feel conflicted about not telling Aru that we do."

The guy at the other table looked at them with curiosity in his eyes. "What language are you two speaking?"

"It's a dialect of Hungarian," Dagor said. "We are from a small village high up in the mountains, and our people are the only ones who speak this particular form of the language."

The guy nodded sagely. "I thought that it sounded European."

Dagor wasn't sure whether Hungarian sounded like their native tongue or even if the country had mountains, but this explanation had worked before, so he used it again.

Negal shook his head. "If you want to keep talking, we should get out of here."

"And go where? To the penthouse where Gabi and Aru might be frolicking amorously on every available surface?"

He didn't begrudge Aru his happiness, but he wished the guy would get over the honeymoon phase so they could get moving again.

They had a mission to complete.

Negal released a sigh. "We could go to a museum or to a library. There is so much we still don't know about these humans, and we can use this idle time to learn more about them."

"The humans are of no interest to me. I want to find out who the gods are that Gabi's brother talked about. Perhaps we should just confront Aru and tell him that we know."

The conversation between Gabi and her brother had been recorded by the spy bug they had attached to the brother, and Aru had later erased it. Their leader wasn't familiar enough with human tech and didn't realize how primitive it still was. He couldn't have guessed that deleting the recording wouldn't do the trick.

Dagor's intention hadn't been to spy on their leader when he'd checked the trash folder. Suspecting that Aru had messed with the laptop, he had checked it just to make sure that nothing important had been deleted by mistake.

Listening to the recording, he'd realized what Aru had been trying to hide, but not why he had done it. They were supposed to be a team, and they were all members of the resistance.

Aru should have trusted him and Negal with the information, and it was disturbing that he hadn't.

What else was he hiding from them?

3

ANNANI

After spending the weekend in atypical solitary contemplation, Annani had a little more clarity about the information they had learned from the three gods who claimed to belong to the resistance. Regrettably, it was not enough to help Kian form a strategy regarding the threat of the Eternal King.

Her paternal grandfather.

Her greatest nemesis.

It was funny how inconsequential Mortdh and Navuh seemed in comparison.

Mortdh had been a bully with delusions of grandeur, a powerful compeller, but a mediocre politician at best. He had not been difficult to outmaneuver, but in the end the law of unintended consequences had prevailed, resulting in a disaster that had eclipsed anything Mortdh had in mind for her and the future of the gods.

Perhaps things would have ended the same way regardless of her role in shaping the events, but Annani would always carry the guilt of inadvertently being responsible for her people's demise.

For Khiann's death.

His murder at the hands of Mortdh.

If she could have seen the future, she would never have pursued him. It would have been better to have never known the great love they had shared than to mourn his death.

Mortdh was dead, and his successor, her current arch-nemesis, was not as delusional and not as powerful as his father, but Navuh was smarter and a better politician. It took more than his incredible compulsion ability to lead an army of immortal warriors dedicated to the cause and eager to do his bidding.

Her clan could deal with Navuh and his Brotherhood of murderers, but just barely so, while the Eternal King was in a league of his own.

He had been ruling over the gods, the rulers of the galaxy, for hundreds of thousands of years, and according to Aru, a large number of his subjects were not opposed to his rule. They were satisfied with their lives on Anumati.

Her grandfather was brilliant, a true master of propaganda, but then even the gods were easy to manipulate. As long as there was prosperity and something to strive for, people were willing to overlook things like the gradual erosion of their personal freedoms, especially when such things took place ever so slowly over eons.

So what if saying things that did not agree with the official line could get them in trouble?

Remaining silent was easier than becoming part of the resistance and actively doing something against the censorship.

Not everyone had what it took to be a rebel, but she must have inherited her father's rebellious character because no one could accuse her of being complicit.

Annani was an idealist and a fighter.

Or had been.

Now that she had a clan comprised of her descendants, their chosen mates, and two other groups of people to protect, she was much less hasty to rise to the challenge than she had been in her youth.

Still, she was keenly aware that Earth was uniquely positioned to host the rebellion against her grandfather. Come to think of it, her father had laid the groundwork, either anticipating this or just as a result of following his moral compass and building a community based on the ideals he had pursued on Anumati.

Had Ahn envisioned Earth becoming the place where gods, immortals, humans, and Kra-ell, both purebloods and hybrids, could coexist in harmony and equality?

Had he foreseen that Kra-ell and immortals could someday form fated bonds and produce uniquely gifted hybrid children?

The tapestry the Fates had woven on Earth was unlike anything else in the universe. Had they done it to show the gods a model of a civilization that did not discriminate between the different species?

A society that did not place taboos on mating between gods and Kra-ell, immortals and humans?

Had they foreseen the new species of hybrid children that would be unlike anything the galaxy had seen before?

Right now, Earth was far from utopia, and humans overwhelmingly outnumbered all the other alien species living among them, but that was just the beginning. It could become the crown jewel of the resistance, the place they could point to for people to see what was possible.

The problem was protecting this precious jewel from the Eternal King and also from self-destruction.

Thanks to technology, the world's economy was so interconnected that it did not make sense for one superpower to launch a military attack against another, but humans did not always do what made sense, and the threat of a third world war was not as far outside the realm of probability as many believed.

Regrettably, the vast majority of the world's leadership was not concerned with the well-being of its citizenry. The elites looked after their own, filling both their pockets and those of their associates, while the young died in senseless wars and families died of plagues and famines that could have been avoided.

There was nothing new under the sun. Generations came and went, but the dynamic never changed.

With a sigh, Annani walked over to her favorite armchair and sat down.

Would things ever get better?

She had spent her entire life, over five thousand years, working on improving the human condition, and the fruits of her labors were evident, but there was still so much to do, and now it seemed like she was running out of time.

Lifting her arm, she examined her luminous skin and wondered whether it looked dimmer because of her melancholy mood or if it was her imagination.

The mystery of the commoner gods on Anumati lacking glow still had not been satisfactorily answered, and perhaps the simplest and easiest explanation was lack of energy. Perhaps they lacked luminosity because they were suppressed and their freedoms were limited. Maybe positive energy was needed to fuel the glow, and the commoner gods on Anumati did not have enough of it, while all the gods she had known on Earth had a healthy glow, and not all of them had been nobility.

Annani shook her head.

That could not be the explanation.

She had not met Aru and his friends yet, but if finding his fated mate did not make Aru burst with positive energy and activate his glow, then he did not have the ability.

When her phone rang, Annani pulled it out of the pocket of her gown and smiled at Kian's handsome face filling the screen.

"Hello, my darling son," she answered.

"Good evening, Mother. Are you busy?"

"Not at all."

"Are you in the mood for receiving guests?"

Annani chuckled. "That will depend on who the guests are."

"Syssi and I would like to share a vision that Syssi had and ask your opinion about it."

Excitement bubbled in Annani's chest, and as she lifted her arm to look at her glow, it was much brighter than before. Perhaps there was a connection between mood and luminosity after all.

"I would love a visit from you whatever the reason." She had to admit that the vision added a level of excitement. "Are you bringing Allegra along?"

"She is asleep. I'll leave Okidu to watch her, and if she gets fussy, he can bring her over."

Annani laughed. "Am I a bad grandmother for wishing her to get fussy just so I can see her?"

"You are the best grandma," Syssi said in the background. "We will put her in the stroller and bring her over."

"She is sleeping!" Kian protested. "You know what happens when we wake her when she doesn't want to be up. She becomes a terror."

"I'll be careful," Syssi said. "Perhaps she should be there when I share my vision."

To Annani's great surprise, Kian agreed.

"Yeah, you might be right."

She could not stifle her curiosity. "Why would you need Allegra with you to tell me about your vision?"

"Syssi will explain when we get there," Kian said. "We will be on our way shortly."

4

KIAN

"You're incredible," Kian whispered after Syssi had somehow managed the impossible and transferred Allegra from the crib to the stroller without waking her up.

"I know." Smiling smugly, Syssi packed several bottles and pacifiers in the baby bag.

Allegra wasn't a great fan of pacifiers, mostly using them as projectiles to throw at people when she wanted their attention, but occasionally they helped her fall asleep.

The soft pink blanket she had gotten from Anita was also a necessary sleeping aid. It was surprising that Syssi's mother even knew how to knit, let alone found the time to knit a blanket for her granddaughter.

Which reminded Kian. "Did you talk to your parents about the cruise?"

"I did." Syssi transferred the command of the stroller to him. "Surprisingly, my mother was excited about joining and said that she would try to get a replacement. If she finds a doctor to take over for her, she'll let me know so we can make the flight arrangements." She smiled. "It's not like we are giving my parents ample notice to plan. You only decided to go ahead with the cruise yesterday, and we are sailing in two and a half weeks."

It wouldn't have mattered if her parents had months to prepare. Most of the time, Anita just didn't want to leave her clinic, and not being able to find a replacement was always a convenient excuse for why she couldn't come to this or that event.

And yet, Syssi never made a fuss about it or showed her disappointment, and it wasn't because she didn't want to see her parents. She was just selfless and accepted that her mother's work always came first.

His wife was the most understanding person on the planet, and he was the luckiest guy to have her.

"Let's take a little stroll up the street," Syssi said.

It was only a few paces to his mother's house, and it was a pleasant evening for a stroll, but he had promised that they would be there shortly.

"Just for a few minutes." He passed his mother's house and kept walking. "Are you excited?"

Syssi shrugged. "I'm excited about Alena and Orion finally getting married and all the other weddings that will take place on the cruise. As for my parents, I will hold off my excitement until their flight is booked, and even then, I won't allow myself to celebrate until I see them boarding the ship."

"That's a wise attitude." He wrapped his arm around her and pushed the stroller with his free hand. "But then everything you do is wise."

She arched a brow. "Really? Says the guy who was upset about me chasing visions."

"In your infinite wisdom, you convinced me of the futility of my worries."

Syssi's frown deepened. "Who are you, and what did you do with my husband?"

"I am a reformed man." Kian winked. "Most of the time."

"Oh, yeah? And what are you at other times?"

He chuckled. "Sometimes I'm still the alpha-hole you fell in love with and married."

She didn't smile. "I've never called you that. Where did you even hear that expression?" She narrowed her eyes at him. "Have you been reading my romance novels again?"

He pretended to look guilty. "You leave your books in my office, and it's easy to pick one up and start reading a paragraph or two." He smiled. "I need to know how to keep things fresh, and those books are a great source of inspiration." And also a few laughs, but he kept that part to himself.

Sometimes, when he had to work late into the night, Syssi sat on the couch in their home office and read while he worked. He loved having her there and seeing the relaxed expression on her face while she was immersed in the story. She read romance novels to relax at the end of her day, and those types of books guaranteed happily-ever-afters, where nothing truly terrible ever happened to spoil her mood.

There was enough of that in the real world.

Letting out an exasperated sigh, Syssi put her hand on his arm. "Please don't. Those are someone else's fantasies, not mine. If you want inspiration, my Perfect Match scenarios are a better source."

"You haven't written anything new in a while."

"I know." She sighed. "Between taking care of Allegra, working at the university, and dealing with one crisis after another, I don't have the bandwidth left to think creatively." She lifted a hand to her temple. "I used to be able to tune everything out and concentrate on the scenarios, but lately, I can't even bring myself to read through the Perfect Match financial reports or do anything productive at the end of the day."

"You need a vacation." He kissed the top of her head. "That's one of the reasons I accepted my mother's suggestion and made compromises regarding the cruise. The Kra-ell will stay behind with most of Kalugal's men."

Syssi tilted her head. "I hope Jade doesn't feel left out."

He snorted. "I would love to reenact her response for you, but I'm not a good enough actor to do it justice. The gist was that she called me nuts for thinking that her people would ever want to get on that ship again. The Kra-ell hate deep water, and some are still traumatized by the swimming lessons Phinas forced them to take in the ship's freezing pool."

"Yeah, it occurred to me that they might not be overly enthusiastic about going on the cruise. Your mother will be disappointed, though. Knowing her, she thought seeing her presiding over the weddings would be the best way to introduce her to the Kra-ell without making it formal."

Annani had met with Jade and several of the other main Kra-ell players, but there hadn't been a formal meeting with all the newcomers.

Kian trusted Jade, but he didn't yet trust all of the Kra-ell. That was one of the reasons he hadn't lowered the security alert level even after the crisis with the new gods had been resolved. A team of Guardians watched over his mother twenty-four seven.

"I just hope she won't demand a formal meeting with the Kra-ell before we sail."

Syssi arched a brow. "I thought you trusted Jade."

"I do, and she also vowed to protect the village to her last breath, but I'm not sure about all the others, and I need more time to get to know them."

"Did she give you the life vow? You said that you didn't want her to do that."

"It wasn't the life vow per se, and I tried to stop her, but it was no use. Jade is an incredibly stubborn female."

"And yet you like her."

He nodded. "I see a lot of myself in her."

"I'm okay with you admiring Jade, but don't overdo it." Syssi pouted. "You are making me jealous."

Kian stopped and turned to his mate. "You are the person I admire most in the world. You are everything to me." He took her hand and brought it to his lips. "You and our daughter own my heart."

Perhaps he could have come up with something more eloquent, but that was how he felt.

"I know." Syssi smiled. "I was just kidding about Jade. But you can't admire me more than your mother. That's just not right. She's the Clan Mother, the only legitimate heir of the Eternal King, and therefore, the second most important person in the galaxy, or perhaps even the most important one if the resistance takes the Eternal King down."

5

SYSSI

Kian's steps faltered for a moment, but then he let out a sigh and continued walking. "For some reason, hearing you say that has driven it home, and it scares the shit out of me. I was always apprehensive about my mother's safety, paranoid even, but that is mostly because of how reckless she used to be. She and Alena would fly to a random destination with just their Odus for protection, and she wouldn't even tell me. I never knew where she was or what she was doing. Thankfully, she hasn't been doing that lately, but then new worries surfaced. The sanctuary is the safest place for her, but I can't force her to stay there and not go anywhere."

"Right." Syssi nodded. "I don't think it's a good thing. It worries me that your mother seems to have lost some of her mojo. Not having a companion to travel with is the main reason she doesn't go on excursions anymore, but she might also be a little depressed."

That wasn't healthy for the goddess on several levels. She needed adventure and excitement to keep her positive attitude and sharp mind, but as important as that was, it wasn't as critical as the knock her sex life must have taken.

No son wanted to think about his mother's needs as a female, but Annani needed the excursions to pick up bed partners. She couldn't do that while cooped up in the village or the sanctuary.

After losing Alena as her companion, Syssi had hoped Annani would choose a new one from the immortal females in the sanctuary or even in the village or Scotland, but she hadn't, and she wasn't the type who enjoyed hunting for companions alone.

If Annani had lost her libido, it meant that she was depressed, and that was not good.

"Did you notice anything specific?" Kian turned around, heading back toward his mother's house.

"It's nothing major, and there isn't one thing I can point to. It's just that I don't think she is as happy and exuberant as she used to be. It's not like her to be satisfied with her roles as the head of the clan and its matriarch. She needs to get away for at least a little bit, and she hasn't done that in a while."

"I've noticed." Kian let out a breath. "I was happy that I could finally sleep at night without worrying about her shenanigans, but you are right that it's not good for her. Perhaps I need to talk to her."

He looked like he'd just bitten into a lemon.

"I think that your sisters are better suited for that kind of conversation. We should talk with Alena."

The best and safest solution for Annani would be to bring human lovers to her and then thrall them before returning them to where they'd been picked up from, but Annani wouldn't agree to that. Syssi had never spoken to her mother-in-law about matters of the heart, or rather of lust, but given the goddess's personality, she enjoyed choosing her bed companions herself, and she loved the seduction part.

Not that she ever had to work hard on that.

Annani was the most beautiful woman in the world, even when she used shrouding to make herself look more ordinary.

When they were a few feet away from the goddess's front porch, Kian stopped, scanned the area again, and nodded at the Guardians stationed nearby to protect her.

He'd thought Syssi hadn't noticed him doing that when they had passed the house before, but he should have known that there wasn't much he could hide from her. "Your mother doesn't need the extra security. These Guardians can't stop anyone or anything that she's incapable of stopping herself."

"I know." Kian lifted the stroller and carried it up the three steps leading to Annani's front porch. "It's for my peace of mind. Besides, she's as defenseless as any of us when she's asleep, and she can't be constantly alert and scanning for danger when awake. The Guardians are there twenty-four seven, but they rotate, and they are on high alert." He knocked on the door.

It was opened immediately by one of Annani's Odus, who bowed deeply.

"Good evening, Master Kian, Mistress Syssi, and Mistress Allegra. Please, come in."

Syssi wanted to point out that the Odus never slept and that they were the best defense for the goddess, but she knew it wouldn't change anything. Kian had admitted that the Guardians were there mainly for his peace of mind, and she could understand that.

He needed to have an active role in his mother's defense.

Annani smiled from the couch. "Please, join me. I have tea and an assortment of desserts ready."

The spread was on the coffee table, and as Syssi eyed the elegant teapot, she thought about her vision of the luminous goddess and the modern art she'd had in her receiving room.

Details of that vision were starting to fade, but she remembered the golden vase vividly. Or did she?

She was unsure whether it had been a vase or a statue, but given the spotlight above it, the piece was artwork and not something that had utility beyond the beauty of its form.

"Syssi, my dear." The goddess's voice cut through her musings. "Are you having another vision?"

"No, Clan Mother." She dipped her head. "I was thinking about the vision I had before the last one. It was also about a luminous goddess, and although I don't think it was the same one as in my latest vision, I think that the two are connected somehow."

The goddess inclined her head imperiously. "You will tell me all about it after we have tea." She patted the couch cushion next to her. "Come sit with me."

"Yes, Clan Mother."

"Mother or Annani will suffice, dear. I have told you so many times."

Syssi smiled sheepishly. "I know, and I apologize for having difficulty addressing you informally, but can you blame me? No human or immortal can be in your presence and treat you casually."

"Is it the glow?" Annani lifted her arm and looked at her luminous skin. "I can do away with it." The glow disappeared before the last word had left her mouth.

"It's not just the glow. Your power is palpable whether your skin is luminous or not, and you are the second most important person in the galaxy." Syssi smiled. "Possibly, the most important."

6

ANNANI

Unmoved by Syssi's declaration, Annani put her hand on her daughter-in-law's thigh. "Semantics, dear. I am just as important today as I was yesterday or a month ago." She smiled. "I admit to having a big ego, but not so big as to think of myself as the most important person in the galaxy."

"But you are," Syssi insisted. "You're the Eternal King's only legitimate heir."

"So what? That only puts a target on my back. Besides, even if my grandfather did not want me dead, I would not want to be in the position of one day having to step into his shoes. They are too big for my tiny feet."

Annani had always been embarrassed by her child-like feet, but since the idiom fit so aptly, she lifted her leg and let the skirt of her floor-length gown slide up and reveal her foot.

Kian chuckled. "Your feet might be small, but they leave big impressions."

Syssi laughed. "That was a good answer, Kian."

He looked very satisfied with himself. "The thing is, we don't know the size of the Eternal King's shoes. Perhaps he has tiny feet as well. But the size of the impressions they leave, now those are awe-inspiring. I have to keep reminding myself that he's a despicable person who had no qualms about killing his own children, and to stop admiring him."

"Can we change the subject, please?" Annani lifted the teapot and poured tea into the three cups Ogidu had prepared. "I would rather hear about Syssi's visions than talk about my grandfather and his shoes." She handed a teacup to her daughter-in-law.

Syssi glanced at Kian. "Should I start with the first one?"

He nodded. "It's relevant to the second one."

After taking a sip of the tea, Syssi put the cup down. "In the first vision, I saw a goddess of such brilliant glow that I couldn't discern her features. Still, I knew she was exquisitely beautiful in the way dreams tell us things that we don't actually see. She was tall and had long white hair that shimmered like diamonds. Her gown was silver with some delicate pattern on it. Another female entered the room, who was also a stunning goddess, but since she bowed, I figured she was a servant or an underling. She told the other goddess something that I couldn't understand, but the impression I got was that she was delivering exciting news. They were both smiling. I thought she might have been your mother, but Kian told me she was petite, so it couldn't have been her."

And while her mother had also been luminous like the other gods in their community, her glow had not been blinding.

Was it possible that instead of receiving a vision, Syssi had been remote viewing someone on Anumati?

That could be even more valuable than the visions.

"Did you see any details of the room?" Annani asked.

Syssi nodded. "It wasn't large." She waved a hand around the living room. "About this size, and it was decorated in a soft, feminine style. At first glance, I thought I was seeing the past, but then I noticed a gold vase or piece of artwork with an abstract, modern shape. Later, when I thought back on the vision, I also realized that there had been no windows in the room and no torches, but it was well-illuminated and not just because of the glowing goddess. There was overhead lighting, with a spotlight directly over the modern art piece."

"You must have viewed Anumati," Annani said. "If the vision was in real-time, you were remote viewing rather than seeing into the future or the past."

"That has occurred to me." Syssi leaned down and picked up her teacup. "I've never remote viewed before, so I don't know how it differs from a vision."

Annani smiled. "I have never had a vision, so I cannot tell the difference either. I can only describe my experience while remote viewing. It feels like spying—a camera-view lens that allows me to peek. My remote viewing is not strong and usually only allows me to see people I care about. Other remote viewers can see locations and spy on their enemies, but that is not my talent."

Syssi frowned. "Do you get impressions? Like you know what is happening even if it is not part of what you are seeing?"

Annani shook her head. "It is no different than seeing someone through a video call."

"That's the difference." Syssi put her empty cup down. "You see things as they are. I see things as my mind makes them seem. It's kind of like the difference between watching a movie and reading a book. My mind fills in the blanks."

7

SYSSI

It felt awkward to have a talent that seemed superior to Annani's, and Syssi had to remind herself that the goddess had many talents that were more powerful and useful than her vague visions.

Annani could thrall, shroud, and compel immortals, which only gods could do in varying degrees of power. Compulsion was a rare ability, though, even for gods, and Annani's dislike for it meant that she hadn't tested her full powers yet and had probably utilized only a fraction of what she could do.

Could she be as powerful as her grandfather?

Syssi was reluctant to even mention the possibility. Annani seemed determined not to step into the Eternal King's shoes even if they were offered to her on a golden platter.

Hey, maybe that was the symbolism of the golden vase she'd seen in her vision.

Right.

Visions were so damn tricky.

Annani lifted a plate of cookies and offered them to her. "Is there anything else you want to add about that vision?"

Squinting, Syssi tried to remember if she'd forgotten to mention anything of interest. "I can't think of anything, but maybe something will come to me later." She took a cookie and bit a small piece of it.

"It's delicious. Who made it?"

Annani smiled. "Ojidu, but the recipe is courtesy of Lusha." She turned to look at Kian. "She is such a lovely young woman. I wish we could keep her in the village. From what I hear, a certain young pureblood is interested in her."

"It was Lusha's choice to return to Safe Haven." Kian snatched a cookie off the plate. "There is no future for her and Pavel. Not unless we figure out how to activate her recessive Kra-ell genes. He has another thousand years of life ahead of him, while she has less than a century."

Annani sighed. "That is regrettably true." She turned to Syssi. "What was your second vision about?"

Syssi put the teacup down. "What impressed me the most about this vision was its clarity. It was much more cohesive than my other visions, and I think Allegra had something to do with it. I was in her room when I induced the vision. She was asleep, but perhaps her presence was enough to enhance my ability."

Annani smiled proudly. "My granddaughter is special. I have no doubt that she will do great things for the clan one day."

Kian groaned. "I just wish she could have a normal life. I don't want to place the burden of leading the clan on her shoulders."

Annani arched a brow. "Are you angry with me for putting this burden on your shoulders?"

He shook his head. "I accepted it willingly. This is what I was born to do."

"Precisely." Annani nodded. "When Allegra comes of age, she will decide whether she wants to lead. It might be what she was born to do as well."

"I think I know what she will decide, and I'm not happy about it."

Syssi leaned over and put a hand on his knee. "There is plenty of time to worry about that. She might decide to be a musician for all we know."

That got a smile out of Kian. "I hope she does that."

"That would be lovely." Annani turned to Syssi. "Now, tell me about your vision."

Syssi nodded. "The second vision took place in a large reception hall, and by large, I mean cavernous. I estimate it was an area of about three thousand square feet, give or take a couple of hundred, and the ceiling was at least forty feet high. It was supported by thick pillars with fancy capitals but not in any style I'm familiar with. Again, there were no windows, but the illumination came from torches this time. Three torches were attached to each column, so there was plenty of light. A goddess sat on a throne-like chair on top of a low dais. She was as bright as the one from the previous vision, but she wasn't the same female. Her bearing was different, although also regal. She wore a toga-style pure white dress, gathered at the shoulder and secured with a golden clasp."

"Were there any other people with her?" Annani asked.

"A scribe sat next to one of the columns, recording what the petitioners asked for and the goddess's replies. I couldn't understand the language, but I got the impression that they were asking for a blessing. The goddess gave the first couple some good news and put her hands on their heads. I forgot to mention that they had been on their knees in deep obeisance. They seemed very happy with what she told them, but the next petitioner wasn't. Another thing that I forgot to mention was that the petitioners were all gods. I couldn't see the scribe, but I assume she was also a goddess."

Annani tilted her head. "Perhaps this vision was about the past. What did the scribe use for writing?"

"Something that looked like a stylus or a quill, but I didn't see ink. She sat on a pillow on the floor and had a little wooden table to write on. It was the size of a lap desk. She wrote in a book, though, not a scroll. It was bound in some material I didn't recognize and was big."

"What about the gods' glow? Did the petitioners emit any?" Annani asked.

"No, and thank you for reminding me. I forgot that part. All three were exceptionally beautiful, which was how I knew they were gods, but the couple didn't have a glow at all, and the god that came after them had a little. If the vision was from Anumati, then the couple were commoners, and the guy was some minor noble."

"That is possible," Annani said. "Although I still do not understand why the commoners on Anumati have no glow. Are they all depressed?"

"That is not likely," Kian said. "Perhaps it has something to do with nutrition. The nobility might have access to some elixir that the commoners do not."

Syssi chuckled. "Perhaps the stories about the special foods that the gods consumed and humans were prohibited from touching were not myths any more than the existence of the gods."

"I am not aware of any such elixir," Annani said. "But then, I was not privy to most of my father's secrets."

Leaning back, Kian crossed his arms over his chest. "Syssi's visions might be vague, but they usually try to tell us something. We were hoping that you would help us make sense of this one. Anything else you can think of that will make its meaning clearer?"

Annani pursed her lips. "The lack of technology could signal that it was a place of worship, which means that the goddess you saw was a priestess. That would also correspond to her giving the couple a blessing."

"Maybe the shrine was on one of Anumati's colonies," Kian said. "And that was why there was no artificial lighting."

Syssi shook her head. "I doubt the gods living in those colonies would have agreed to forgo such conveniences. They are not exiles like the rebel gods sent to Earth."

8

ANNANI

As Kian and Syssi looked at her, Annani shrugged. "My guess is as good as yours as to the location of your vision and what it tried to show you. Do not forget that I was born on Earth, and as I said before, my father did not share information about Anumati with me." Annani leveled her gaze on Syssi. "You said that you induced the second vision. Did you induce the first one as well?"

"With the first one, I meditated and asked to be shown things that might help us with the newcomer gods. I don't know what the vision was trying to tell me, though."

"And the second time?" Annani prompted.

"I wanted an explanation for the first one." She scrunched her nose. "I just remembered something that I forgot to mention about the first vision. The goddess wore a gold necklace, a medallion with a design I couldn't see, probably because of her intense glow. I wonder if the two goddesses are really as luminous as I saw them or was it the nature of the visions to obscure their features."

"There is obviously a connection between the two goddesses." Annani refilled her teacup and took a sip. "I also think their luminosity in real life is not as bright as in your visions. Since you are not remote viewing, and what you see is not like a movie but an interpretation of the information the vision is feeding your mind, you might have created the glow to symbolize something. Maybe the two goddesses are sisters, or both are royalty, or maybe they are both rebel sympathizers. The only ones who can provide us with any clarity are the three gods currently residing in Kian's old penthouse." She turned to her son. "I want to talk to them."

He shook his head. "That's a very bad idea. What if you look like your grandfather, and they immediately recognize you as his heir?"

She smiled. "Why would that be a bad thing, my son? Only mere moments ago, you and Syssi wanted me to pick up the banner and challenge my grandfather's rule. To do so, I must first be recognized as the legitimate heir."

Kian opened his mouth, closed it, and opened it again. "I didn't say that. I don't want him to know that you exist."

"Of course not. You are always worried about my safety. I appreciate that, and most of the time I humor you, but not this time. I need to speak with these gods."

"Why? You can make a list of questions, and I'll ask them for you. You can even speak with them on the phone and ask them yourself."

She smiled. "I want to see their response to me and my glow. That cannot be done via a phone call or a messenger. It is also why I want to meet all three, not just their leader. Negal and Dagor might be less guarded than Aru."

Kian shook his head. "The moment your grandfather learns of your existence, he might choose to eradicate the entire planet just to get rid of you. Even if Aru and his teammates are trustworthy, they will get picked up in a hundred and fifteen years, and there is very little chance that they will be able to keep you a secret."

Leaning back, Annani regarded her son with an indulgent smile. "You are overthinking everything, Kian. If I had done that when I started out on my mission, there would be no clan, and humans would have been centuries or even thousands of years away from developing the technologies they have today. Sometimes, you need to follow your gut and take a risk. Aru, his teammates, and an entire patrol ship housing thousands of warriors, scientists, and other crew members are part of the resistance, and yet they managed to fly under the radar of the Eternal King."

"We only have Aru's word for that. What if he lied?"

"Andrew can talk to him," Syssi offered. "I don't know whether his gift works on gods, but it's worth a try. You can also get Edna to probe him."

Annani nodded. "Please do both and schedule a meeting. I am sure that Onegus needs time to prepare, and I want to meet them before we sail in two and a half weeks."

Kian was so pale that Annani feared he would faint, but she had to draw a line in the sand somewhere. It was not that she thought his fear for her was exaggerated or uncalled for, but she had not gotten to where she was by living in a panic room.

Well, that was not entirely true.

The sanctuary was the most secure panic room on the planet, but Annani refused to spend her entire life there.

She would perish from boredom.

Unlike Kian, Syssi was grinning. "After the meeting, we can invite Aru, Gabi and his friends on the cruise. It would be a wonderful opportunity for them to meet everyone. I'm so excited."

Kian groaned. "I'm starting to regret this whole thing. The ship is fully armed now and can defend itself from Navuh but not from the might of the gods."

Leaning forward, Annani tried to reach for his hand, but he was sitting too far away and had to meet her halfway. "The Eternal King is many light years away, and by the time any of his forces could get here, our beautiful ship will probably be rusting in the junkyard or wherever they retire old ships to. In the meantime, I refuse to live in fear. I will meet with these three gods and invite them to join us on the cruise myself."

9

KIAN

"Thank you for meeting me here." Kian shook Edna's hand and then Andrew's.

"I'm excited," the judge said. "After hearing so much about these gods, I can't wait to meet them."

Kian had informed the council about the latest developments, and most of them had expressed a wish to meet up with the gods, but he hadn't been ready to do that yet.

His mother had twisted his arm.

"I'm curious about them too." Andrew smiled good-naturedly. "It seems like you and I are here every other week, testing this or that person. It's never boring in our world, so it's all good. I don't mind missing lunch with Tim to come help you out."

The forensic artist was incredibly talented, maybe even paranormally gifted, but his personality left much to be desired.

"How is our dear Tim?" Kian led them toward the elevator. "Weren't we supposed to test whether he's a Dormant?"

His brother-in-law smiled sheepishly. "You didn't seem overly excited about Tim potentially joining the clan, and I couldn't blame you, so I pretended to have forgotten about it. Do you still want to test him?"

Kian motioned for Edna to go ahead before following her into the elevator. "If you can arrange for it to be done away from the village, then sure. I don't want a wasted potential Dormant on my conscience."

"We don't know that Tim is a Dormant, and his case is weak. The only thing that makes him a suspect is his supernatural talent to render almost life-like portraits of people just from how others describe them. No one, human or immortal, ever felt an affinity with Tim, and according to Amanda, that's a stronger indicator than a paranormal talent." Andrew chuckled. "The guy prides himself on being a pain in the ass." Wincing, he glanced at Edna. "Forgive my language, judge."

She chuckled. "I'm mated to Rufsur. I hear much worse."

Kalugal's second-in-command was a little rough around the edges, but he was a good guy, and Kian liked him. If not for him and Edna, the accord between the clan and Kalugal and his people would have never been signed.

"Did you tell Aru that we were coming?" Andrew asked as they got out of the elevator at the penthouse level.

"I told him to expect us, but I didn't tell him what it's about." He let out a breath. "I'm walking a thin line with these gods. On the one hand, I want to establish friendly relationships with them because they are our only link to Anumati and the Eternal King's plans, but on the other hand, I can't bring myself to trust them. They are too powerful, and the story they told us is too convenient, and now my mother insists on meeting them, and I'm desperate for any excuse to tell her that it's not possible."

Andrew patted his shoulder. "I get it. I can't compare my parents to your mother, but I get frustrated with them too. I only want what's best for them, but our opinions differ as to what that entails."

Edna chuckled, which was uncharacteristic of her, but then she had changed a lot since mating Rufsur, who was her exact opposite. "From what I gather, dealing with parents is more difficult than dealing with children. I don't have children yet, but I do have a mother, and she is not easy."

Kian didn't know Edna's mother well, but if the judge said that about her, he had no doubt it was true. Edna was not prone to exaggeration.

"No earpieces?" Andrew asked when they stopped in front of the penthouse door.

Kian grimaced. "My mother had a few things to say about my paranoia, and I decided to take a page out of her book and just go for it. No earpieces and no Okidu to guard me. Anandur and Brundar are already there, though, and they have their earpieces in." There was a limit to how reckless he would allow himself to be, but perhaps it was too much for the judge. He looked at Edna. "Are you okay with that?"

She shrugged. "Even with your new resolution regarding the level of risk aversion you are comfortable with, I know you wouldn't have forgone these safety features if you believed they were needed."

"You know me well, judge."

"Indeed, I do."

This time Kian remembered to knock instead of just walking in.

Anandur opened the door with a big grin on his face. "Hello, boss. We have everything ready."

"Meaning?" Kian asked.

"Come in and see." He threw the door open.

10

DAGOR

As the redhead opened the door for his boss, Dagor emptied the rest of the Snake Venom down his throat and put the bottle down.

The beer was growing on him, and it seemed to please Kian's bodyguards that they had managed to make a convert out of him.

It was funny how alcohol was truly a universal equalizer. Gods, immortals, and humans loved to socialize while drinking. Barriers went down, people felt more at ease with each other, and tongues loosened up.

When Aru pushed to his feet, Dagor and Negal followed, and even Gabi rose to greet the clan leader.

He hadn't arrived alone. One of his companions was a female who looked like an attorney, given her attire and the severe expression on her face, and the other was a male whose posture and confidence spoke of a past in the military.

Was he another guard?

"This is the clan judge, Edna," Kian introduced the female. "And this is my brother-in-law, Andrew."

So Dagor had been right about the female, and he was probably right about the male, but confirmation of that would have to wait.

Aru offered his hand to the judge first. "I'm Aru. Are there any legalities involved with our temporary residence in the penthouse?"

She offered him a barely-there smile. "No, and I'm not here in my capacity as an attorney and a judge."

"Edna is also a council member," Kian said.

The judge turned her eerily penetrating gaze to Dagor and offered him her hand. "Hello."

She had the eyes of an oracle. Was Kian lying about who she was?

Just in case she was one, Dagor bowed his head respectfully. "I am Dagor. It's an honor to meet you, councilwoman."

The smile she gave him was warmer than the one she'd given Aru. "It's nice to make your acquaintance, Dagor."

The greetings were repeated with Gabriella and Negal, and then everyone sat down on whatever piece of furniture was available.

Naturally, the males had waited for the ladies to be seated first.

Kian rubbed the back of his neck. "This is awkward." He let out a breath. "There is no polite way to do this, so I'm just going to say it as it is. Andrew is a truth-reader, and Edna can read your soul. I brought them both to reassure myself that you can be trusted. Please don't take it as an insult. I'm known for being super cautious, and I've used Andrew and Edna's services to test all newcomers."

"What do you mean by reading our souls?" Aru asked the question that was on Dagor's mind.

"She can't read thoughts, so don't worry about that, but she can read intentions and emotions. I need to make absolutely sure that you mean no harm to any of my people."

Dagor stifled a derisive snort. Kian was no doubt concerned about the gods within his clan, the gods that Aru thought he should hide from his companions.

"I understand," Aru said. "But I have my own secrets that I need to keep, and I'm not a hundred percent sure that I can trust you, so we are at an impasse because I don't want Edna inside my soul." He cast her an apologetic look. "No offense, judge."

She dipped her head. "None taken."

"You can test me," Negal volunteered. "I have nothing to hide."

"Neither do I," Dagor said with a pointed look at Aru.

If she discovered that he resented Aru for hiding things from him and Negal, it would be a good thing. It would save him the trouble of confronting their team leader about it.

Kian didn't look happy. "What about Andrew? Do you mind if I ask you a few questions and have Andrew verify the veracity of your answers?"

"I don't mind that, but if you ask me questions I don't wish to answer, I won't."

"Understood." Kian turned to Edna. "Can you take Negal and Dagor to my old home office and test them there while I ask Aru a few questions?"

She hesitated. "I'd rather take one at a time. I need to concentrate, and it's difficult to do with another person in the room. Besides, I thought you wanted Andrew to verify their answers as well."

Dagor would have preferred to stay in the living room while Kian interrogated Aru so he could hear the answers, but he didn't like that the judge seemed afraid to be alone with him and Negal.

Dagor put his hand over his chest. "You have nothing to fear from me or Negal. We mean you no harm." He turned to Kian. "We mean no harm to any of your people, no matter whether they are immortals, Kra-ell, or others."

"Truth," Kian's brother-in-law said.

Kian regarded Andrew for a long moment before returning his gaze to Dagor. "Are you happy here, Dagor?"

"Sure. Why wouldn't I be? The bed is very comfortable."

Andrew chuckled. "That was a lie."

Kian frowned. "The bed is not comfortable?"

Andrew chuckled. "I don't think he meant the bed."

11

ARU

Aru had no intention of letting Edna into his mind, and he hoped she couldn't do that without touching him.

In fact, he regretted shaking her hand.

His secrets were too important to fall into even the friendliest of hands.

"What did you mean?" Kian asked his brother-in-law.

Andrew shrugged and tilted his head toward Dagor. "Ask him."

Dagor cast a quick look at Aru before lowering his eyes. "The penthouse is very comfortable, but being around a honeymooning couple is not easy."

Aru was aware of that, but there wasn't much he could do about it. He and Gabi tried not to act overly amorous in front of Negal and Dagor, but every look they exchanged was laden with the love and desire they had for each other.

"Truth," the brother-in-law said.

The wife was a seer, and her brother was a truth-reader. That was a lot of paranormal talent in one family. Were they related to the gods living in Kian's community?

Syssi and her brother possessed impressive abilities. They were both good-looking but did not possess the near perfection that Kian exhibited, meaning they were not direct descendants of gods. Their godly ancestor must have been formidable, though.

"Okay." Kian let out a breath. "I'm glad that your talent also works on gods." He turned to Aru. "What about you? Can you repeat Dagor's words?"

Aru had no problem doing that, but he was getting tired of Kian second-guessing him. "The bed in the primary bedroom is very comfortable, thank you."

"Truth," Andrew said. "Even though the answer was sarcastic."

"Come on, Aru." Gabi nudged her mate's arm. "Tell them that they have nothing to fear from you."

"I already did, and it's annoying that I was not believed."

"They only want assurances." She took his hand and gave it a squeeze. "It's not personal, Aru. They are facing an existential risk, and they have to take security seriously." She shook her head. "We, not they. I am now part of their community, and my safety is tied to theirs. Remember what they did to me so I couldn't tell anyone about immortals? They are super cautious not because they are paranoid but because it's necessary."

"Thank you," Kian said. "I'm glad to have at least one person understand why I have to be so careful."

"I mean you no harm," Aru said. "Not to you, not to the Kra-ell, and not to anyone else in your community. I'm racking my brains trying to figure out how to keep you all hidden from the Eternal King for as long as possible."

"Truth," Andrew said.

"Is everyone on the patrol ship really part of the resistance?" Anandur asked.

"They are." Aru looked directly at Andrew. "But since it's always possible that someone could be a spy for the Eternal King, we don't talk freely among ourselves. Everything is compartmentalized and on a need-to-know basis."

Dagor snorted. "Yeah. But somehow, you know more than anyone else, including the commander. I wonder why that is?"

Aru gritted his teeth not to reprimand Dagor for saying stuff like that in front of others. He would have to talk to him later.

"It just seems like that to you because I know more than you do. I'm sure other team leaders know as much, if not more, than what I was entrusted with."

"Truth," Andrew said, but he did so with less conviction than the other times.

Was he trying to be helpful? And if so, why?

Dagor let out a breath. "I should not have said that. Apologies, sir."

The guy never called him 'sir' unless they were in the presence of higher-ranked commanders.

"Accepted." Aru nodded.

"Do you really know more than others?" Kian asked.

"I can't answer what I don't know. I'm not privy to what everyone on the patrol ship is entrusted with."

Andrew shrugged. "That was an Igor-style answer. Evasive. Neither truth nor lie."

Kian cast Aru a calculating look, and there was understanding in his eyes. Perhaps he had finally realized that there were things Aru couldn't reveal in front of his teammates.

He pushed to his feet. "Join me in my old office for a few minutes." He glanced at Gabi, who looked worried. "I won't keep him long."

"It's okay. I'll stay to chat with Edna." She gave him a dazzling smile. "She can examine my soul. I have nothing to hide."

Edna cleared her throat. "Perhaps some other time. Today, I need to reserve my energy for the gods. I don't expect it will be easy to probe them."

"That's a shame." Gabi pouted.

The judge turned to Negal. "We can do this in your room if you're comfortable inviting me in."

"I will be delighted to host you in my room, judge." Negal pushed to his feet and offered Edna his hand. "I have not entertained any ladies there yet. You will be the first."

She gave him a polite smile. "Just so there is no misunderstanding, I'm happily mated."

Negal's eyes widened. "My apologies, judge. I did not mean it like that. I know that you are mated. I can smell him on you."

"Gross," Gabi muttered. "That's the one thing I don't like about gods and immortals. Talk about lack of privacy."

12

KIAN

As Kian led Aru and Andrew to his old office, unease churned in his gut.

There was a reason Aru had refused to be probed by Edna, and it might have nothing to do with ill intent toward the clan, but it left a void in the security blanket Kian was trying to form around his stubborn mother.

It wasn't even that he disagreed with her. She was right about refusing to live in fear, but she was a hypocrite. It was much easier to gamble with her own life than with the lives of her loved ones, which was why she insisted that Kian never leave the village without taking two bodyguards with him.

In his bachelor days, Kian had been much the same as her, and hadn't hesitated before walking into danger. Since he'd mated Syssi and they had Allegra, he was mindful of the pain and suffering his death would inflict on his mate and daughter.

There was also the memory of being helpless under Igor's control. That experience had shaved off a significant portion of Kian's bravado.

"Please, take a seat." He motioned for Aru and Andrew to sit on the couch while he pulled out one of the chairs and turned it around to face them.

Letting out a sigh, he pinned Aru with a hard stare. "You are making it difficult for me."

"It can't be helped. All I can say is that the information I'm protecting has nothing to do with nefarious intentions toward you or any of your people, including the gods living among you."

"Truth," Andrew said.

"I assume you haven't told your teammates about the gods yet."

Aru nodded. "I have not."

"Why not?"

"Because you asked me not to. What is this all about, Kian? Why the sudden paranoia attack? Have you learned something new that bothers you?"

"It's nothing new." Kian groaned. "It's the same as always. My mother is making my life difficult."

Aru arched a brow. "Your mother?"

"She wants to meet you and your friends, which means the cat will be out of the bag very soon."

Light shone in Aru's eyes as he realized what Kian was implying.

"Your mother is a goddess. I should have known. You look more like a god than an immortal because you are a demigod."

Kian grimaced. "I don't think of myself that way. It sounds so bombastic. My mother wanted to meet you and your teammates as soon as possible, but I convinced her to wait a little longer."

The light in Aru's eyes dimmed a little. "In that case, I need to tell Negal and Dagor about the gods living among you."

Kian lifted his hand. "I want to test them before you do that. I need Edna and Andrew to question them and give me the green light or tell me that they are not to be trusted. If that's the case, I'll tell my mother she can meet you but not the others."

"I can vouch for Negal and Dagor's trustworthiness."

Kian chuckled. "Then why are you keeping secrets from them?"

"I told you. We keep each other safe by compartmentalizing. Every member of the resistance only knows what she or he has to. That way, if any of us are discovered, we don't take down the entire organization with us."

It sounded logical, and Kian agreed that it was good practice given who they were dealing with, but it could also mean that Aru himself was not trustworthy.

"Even if Edna and Andrew clear them, don't tell them yet. Wait until I give you the green light."

"When is the meeting going to take place?"

"Two and a half weeks."

Aru frowned. "Is there a reason for this timeline? Does it have anything to do with Gabi's recovery and our stay in this penthouse?"

"No, but it's a happy coincidence. You, Gabi, and your teammates are going on a vacation with me and my family."

He didn't want to tell Aru about the cruise yet or that most of the clan would be there. As the god himself had said, compartmentalizing information was a prudent safety precaution.

Aru seemed taken aback, but he was a skilled politician who plastered an amiable smile on his too-handsome face. "Thank you for inviting us. I'm sure it will be a wonderful opportunity to get to know each other and perhaps develop more mutual trust, but may I inquire about the destination and duration of the trip?"

"Mexico," Kian said. "Ten days round trip."

"I've never been to Mexico. I'm looking forward to it. Will formal attire be required for any part of the trip?"

That was an incredibly good guess. Had Anandur blurted something about the cruise weddings even though Kian had warned him not to?

The rest of the clan hadn't been given the exact sail date yet, and Amanda was still working on the itinerary, but it had to be done soon. People had work obligations they needed to rearrange. Come to think of it, new clothing for the trip and evening wear for the celebrations would need to be purchased. After all, they would be attending several weddings, and the ladies would no doubt want a different gown for each night.

It would be difficult to keep the cruise a secret from Gabi.

Kian nodded and leaned back in his chair. "I wanted to keep the details a secret for a little longer, but your question about formal attire made me realize that it wasn't the best idea. We are going on a cruise, and each night is reserved for a different couple's wedding. So yeah, you will need a tux or two, and Gabi might want to get several evening dresses."

The light in Aru's eyes intensified. "Gabi will be thrilled. She'll probably want to get married on the ship, too. Are there any nights still available?"

"Not as far as I know, but you can have a lunchtime or morning wedding."

The light dimmed. "I don't think Gabi will want that. I'd rather wait and give her the wedding of her dreams."

Aru seemed entirely enchanted with the idea of a wedding cruise, and unless he was a superb actor, he wasn't thinking about it as an opportunity to do harm.

Since Andrew was already there, Kian might as well ask a question or two to make sure.

13

FRANKIE

Frankie waved at the waiter. "Another round of margaritas, please."

Mia regarded her with concerned eyes. "It's your third one. You're gonna puke."

"I'm going for passed out." Frankie glanced at Tom, who was pretending not to have heard the puke remark.

It was embarrassing to get plastered with her besties around, but it was doubly embarrassing with a hot guy at the table, even if he belonged to Mia.

Tom had offered to leave and come back later to collect his girl, but Frankie had invited him to stay in the hopes that the Perfect Match job would come up, but so far, he pretended that he hadn't connected the dots.

Men. Even the smart ones were stupid.

Frankie had invited her besties to a night of drinking to lament the job she'd lost. Couldn't he have figured out that she desperately needed a new one?

She'd filled out a bunch of applications, but so far, she hadn't gotten an answer from any of them. There was no reason to panic yet, and she had only been unemployed for a total of four days so far, but given that no one had bothered to even acknowledge her application, her prospects weren't looking good.

There wasn't much she could do with her worthless college degree in English other than teach or go to grad school and become a lawyer. Her minor in performing arts was good for nothing, as well. She'd taken it for fun and had enjoyed every moment. Still, she wasn't a great actress or singer despite what her family kept saying.

After she'd told her parents about getting fired, her mom suggested grad school, but Frankie didn't want to accumulate even more student debt, or at least that was what she had told her parents. She didn't want to go back to school and put her life on hold again.

As the waiter arrived with their drinks, Margo removed the paper umbrella and added it to the other two she'd collected. "It's not the end of the world, Frankie, and getting fired from that dead-end job is no reason to drink until you pass out."

"Words of wisdom, as always, but it's not just about the job, and you know it."

Margo grimaced. "I'm not having any more luck than you in that department. There are no good men to be found these days." She cast Tom an apologetic glance. "Except for you, of course."

"What about the gentlemen Mia's grandparents introduced you to?"

"What about them?" Margo asked. "None of them asked either of us on a date." She looked at Mia. "Your grandma is awesome, but she's a bit of an airhead. The guys she found for us were all gorgeous but talk about awkward. Frankie and I felt like we'd stepped back in time."

Mia grimaced. "Yeah, that wasn't the best idea. I'm sure they wouldn't have been as awkward if my grandparents weren't there."

Possibly. Or maybe the guys hadn't found her and Margo attractive, interesting, or smart enough, or whatever they had been looking for in a girl.

Talk about a blow to the ego.

"So, Tom." Margo leaned back with her margarita in hand. "What about those Perfect Match jobs you and Mia were talking about? It would be great if at least one was available for our Frankie."

Thank you, Margo. Frankie could have kissed her on both cheeks.

"There have been some delays." Tom gave Frankie an apologetic look. "The tech department was busy with another project that took precedence, but now the parts are in, and they are working on it. The machines should be ready in a couple of weeks, so if you can hold off until then, I can see what I can do about a job for you."

Mia cleared her throat. "You are forgetting about the cruise. No one will be there to train Frankie."

"Right." He smoothed a hand over his enviably silky dark hair. "I forgot about that."

Margo looked at him with incredulous eyes. "Are you taking everyone in the company on a cruise?"

"Not everyone," Tom said evasively.

His answer could have meant he was taking only a few or almost everyone.

Mia uttered a little gasp, which usually meant that she'd thought of something that could be amazing. "Maybe Margo and Frankie can join us on the cruise? We could bring the machines onboard for everyone's entertainment."

"That's not feasible." Tom gave her a stern look.

"Why not? It's only ten days, and the memories created in a short time are easily... you know, forgettable."

What the hell was Mia talking about?

Frankie lifted two fingers up to check how drunk she was, but they still looked like two and not three or four, so she wasn't drunk enough to misunderstand Mia's strange comment.

"When is the cruise leaving?" Margo asked.

"Two and a half weeks. We are going to cruise down to Mexico and back to Long Beach. It's not so much about the excursions as it is about the ship and spending time with family and friends. Several couples are getting married on the cruise, so it will be fun."

"I don't know if we have room," Tom said. "I need to ask."

Mia waved a dismissive hand. "There is plenty of room. I bet not everyone who was invited will come."

"Thanks for the invitation, but I can't go." Margo made a miserable face. "Lynda is having a bachelorette party in Cabo. I have to be there even though I would rather have consecutive dentist's appointments. She will make my brother suffer if I bail for any reason."

"Oh, right." Mia's face fell. "Their wedding is in a month." She looked down at her legs. "I'm still not going to be able to walk on my own. It's taking so long."

Frankie leaned over and patted her friend's shoulder. "It's a miracle that you are regrowing your legs at all. It doesn't matter how long it takes, as long as it happens, right?"

14

TOVEN

Mia's legs were progressing beautifully. Her body had just started regenerating her feet, but since those were the most complicated parts of the reconstruction process, they would take a while.

That was one of the reasons why the two of them were not getting married on the cruise. Mia wanted to dance at her wedding, and she also wanted her best friends to be there. If the two proved to be Dormants, moved into the village, and transitioned, the wedding would occur either in the village square or on another cruise. However, if Margo and Frankie were fully human, Mia had suggested a small wedding in Zurich.

Toven liked the idea of a smaller wedding with just the close family attending, but at the end of the day, he knew that he would do precisely what Mia wanted and how she wanted it.

"I know," Mia sighed. "I'm so grateful." She turned to Toven with so much love on her beautiful face that he would have given her the moon if she had asked for it. "Can Frankie come?"

Or at least tried.

He had a feeling that convincing Kian to let Frankie join the cruise might be more difficult than getting her the moon.

"You know it's not up to me, love."

"Aren't you the boss?" Margo asked.

"I have partners, and they are very reclusive."

"Oh." Frankie's face fell. "So, they are the ones organizing the cruise." She turned to Margo. "There is no chance in hell they will invite us. Remember how secretive they were when Mia and Tom first met them?"

Margo nodded. "I can't come anyway, but I'm sorry you can't."

"We can pick you up at Cabo," Mia said, as if her friends joining her on the cruise was a done deal.

Margo winced. "It's a week-long thing, and Lynda is not the compromising type. I have to be nice to her because she's about to become family, and I will be stuck with her for as long as she and David are married."

"Excuse me, ladies." Toven pushed to his feet and put his hand on Mia's shoulder. "I'll be back in a few minutes."

A secretive smile blooming on her face, she nodded and lifted a hand with crossed fingers but only as high as her thighs so her friends couldn't see it.

Of course, she'd guessed that he was going to call Kian.

It was after working hours, but he knew Kian would take a call from him. Lifting Frankie's mood might not be high on Kian's list of concerns, but she was a potential Dormant, or at least Toven hoped she was, and it was time to put the suspicion to the test.

It was a shame that the girl had no paranormal talent to strengthen her case, but who knew? Perhaps they would discover that she had a hidden ability like Mia's.

His mate had thought she had no talent but had ended up with one of the best. Enhancing the powers of others was invaluable, as had been proven during the Kra-ell rescue mission.

He couldn't have done what he had without her help.

Stepping outside into the cool night, Toven walked a few feet up the block before calling Kian.

"Toven," he answered right away. "Is everything okay?"

Obviously, he knew that Toven and Mia were not in the village and immediately assumed something had happened to them.

"Mia and I are fine. We are at a bar with Mia's friends, drinking margaritas."

"Ah." Kian sounded relieved. "That's my sister's favorite drink. Amanda and Syssi started their bonding over margaritas that Onidu made for them." He sighed. "It was a long time ago, when we were still living at the keep, and Amanda's penthouse was across from mine."

"Do you miss those days?"

"Only the incredible excitement of falling in love with Syssi, but then I fall in love with her every day anew."

It was odd to hear Kian express such romantic feelings. He must be in a good mood, which could be helpful now. He might not say no right away.

"I know how you feel. I look at Mia every morning when I wake up and thank the Fates for bringing her into my life. There isn't anything I wouldn't do for her, which brings me to the reason for my call. Mia's friend Frankie got fired from her job. Do you remember who I am talking about?"

"Yes, of course. Frankie and Margo are Mia's best friends, and you wanted to hire them as beta testers for the Perfect Match adventures."

"I'm impressed with your ability to hold information in your head. As you know, the machines in the village are almost ready, but by the time they are, we will be sailing to Mexico. To cut a long story short, Mia wants to invite her friends on the cruise."

"That's—"

"Hold on before you shoot the idea down. The cruise is only ten days long, so I can erase their memories at the end of it without causing them damage. Frankie getting fired two weeks before the cruise might be the Fates' doing. Perhaps they are trying to tell us something."

It was a feeble attempt, and Toven felt ridiculous for invoking the Fates for such a frivolous cause, but he wanted Mia to have her friends on the cruise, and Kian was a believer.

Kian laughed. "That's a stretch, but I get it. You want to do this for your mate."

"Very much so. I know that the case for Margo and Frankie being Dormants is weak, but they are nice girls, and it's worth a try."

Kian sighed. "Yeah, I hear you, and I also owe you and Mia for your help with the Kra-ell."

"Is it a yes, then?"

"Yes, conditional on you taking full responsibility for them, erasing their memories from the cruise, and creating new ones so they won't wonder why they can't remember anything."

"I've done that before." Toven chuckled. "Perhaps that was what got me writing in the first place. I was creating elaborate stories for my lovers to fill the missing time from the memories I had to erase."

"Good, then you know what to do. I don't expect either of them to find a truelove mate and start transitioning during the cruise, so this is not hypothetical. You will have to do it."

"I know." Toven started walking back to the bar. "There is one more complication. Margo is attending a bachelorette party in Cabo, and we might need to collect her from there. Is a stop at Cabo part of the itinerary?"

15

FRANKIE

"Did you start looking for a new job?" Mia asked Frankie after Tom left.

Frankie pushed the half-empty margarita glass away. "I've sent out resumes, but no one's gotten back to me yet."

"It has only been four days," Margo said. "Give it time."

"I don't have time. I have no savings to speak of, and my parents are barely making it as it is. They can't help me."

"You can move in with me," Margo offered.

"You live in a studio."

"So? Beggars and choosers and all that. You can sleep on the couch. You've slept on it before."

Crashing on her friend's sofa occasionally wasn't the same as giving up on having her own place. "I could also move back in with my parents and sleep in my old room. I'm twenty-seven, Margo. I should be independent by now."

"You are, honey." Margo reached for her hand. "You moved out of your parents' house when you went to college and never moved back. Many people our age can't do that these days. People are renting by the room or staying home long past the age they should."

Frankie let out a long-suffering sigh. "My apartment is crappy, but it's mine, and it's affordable. If I give it up, I'll never find anything I can afford and will have to room with other people."

Her place was in an iffy part of town and an old apartment building that desperately needed renovations. She'd furnished it with second-hand stuff and decorated it with pillows, throws, and other bargains from discount stores. It wasn't much, but it was cozy, it was hers, and it pained her to give it up.

Mia shook her head. "When Tom comes back, I will ask him to find you a job in one of the Perfect Match studios. You could be an adventure coordinator or a receptionist until something better opens up."

"Don't. That's probably what happened to my job at Hoffesommer and Partners. His niece or lover needed a job, so I got the boot. I don't want anyone fired to make room for me."

"No, of course not." Mia slumped in her wheelchair. "But maybe they are hiring, you know? A position might open that's right up your alley."

"Yeah, and pigs might fly. Sorry, Mia, but even when I'm drunk, I can't think magically."

"That's a shame." Mia slurped her margarita through a straw while looking at Frankie from under lowered lashes. "Magic happens. Just look at Tom and me. I couldn't have dreamt him up. A fairy godmother must have sprinkled me with magic dust."

As the subject of their conversation suddenly appeared behind Mia, Frankie blinked a couple of times. One moment, there was no one there, and then he just appeared as if out of thin air. Was she really that inebriated?

"Hello, ladies. Anything interesting happen in my absence?"

Mia looked up at him with adoring eyes. "Frankie is freaking out about losing her apartment because she has no savings. Can't you find her a job in one of the studios? It could be something temporary until we return from the cruise, and she can start on her beta tester's job."

Would strangling Mia make Frankie a terrible person?

How could she embarrass her like that? It was one thing for her besties to know how desperate her situation was and another thing entirely for a rich dude like Tom to know, someone who had never known what struggling to pay rent felt like.

She didn't want him to pity her and look down his nose at her like he did with most people. For some reason, Tom liked her and Margo and treated them as if they were special. It was probably because they were Mia's friends, and the dude would do anything to make his fiancée happy.

It was so damn enviable.

Tom frowned at her. "Why do you want to keep your apartment? Once the machines are up and running, you and Margo will move into the compound and live rent-free."

It would be rude to tell him she didn't trust his promises because he and Mia had been dangling that elusive job in front of her for months, but there was no way around it.

"I don't know if I can rely on that. Until now, I had a job, so I could wait patiently for your offer to materialize. But I can't afford to do that now. I need a new job yesterday."

"I understand." Tom smiled. "Here is what I suggest you do. Give your landlord notice that you are vacating the premises in two weeks. Pack up your things, and I will arrange for them to be stored until your new place in the compound is ready. In the meantime, you will get to know your future coworkers while enjoying a luxury cruise courtesy of your future employers."

Uttering a small gasp, Mia put a hand over her heart. "Did you speak with Kian?"

Tom nodded. "It took some convincing, but he agreed to host both of your friends." He turned to Margo. "I need the exact dates of the bachelorette party, so we will know when to pick you up from Cabo."

Margo's eyes turned as wide as saucers. "Are you serious? You will really have the ship dock at Cabo just so I can come along?"

He smiled. "The ships dock outside of Cabo, and passengers use water taxis to get on and off them. The cruise itinerary is flexible to some extent, but not much. If the dates don't work, I'll fly you to one of our other shore excursions."

As Margo jumped out of her chair, wrapped her arms around Tom, and kissed his cheek, Mia's expression turned almost feral.

Frankie hadn't known that her best friend had such a possessive streak. Tom was a catch, and Mia was right to guard her turf, but she had nothing to fear from Margo, and she knew that.

"Thank you," Margo squealed. "You are the best."

"That's enough," Mia hissed, and Frankie could have sworn that her friend's eyes started glowing.

"Sorry." Margo let go of Tom and smiled sheepishly. "It's just that no one has ever gone to so much trouble for me."

Frankie lifted her margarita and examined the remaining liquid for residual sediment.

Who could have drugged her while she was with her friends, and why?

She shook her head after briefly scanning the room and not seeing anyone shady. "I need to find out what kind of tequila they use in these margaritas. It must have been exceptionally potent."

16

KIAN

After ending the call with Toven, Kian returned to the living room and sat next to Syssi on the couch.

Across from them, Amanda looked like she'd run her fingers through her hair too many times. The short strands stood up like little antennae, making her look like an anime character.

Still, despite her disheveled appearance, Kian knew that she was having the time of her life planning the ten cruise ceremonies. If their mother's favorite thing was presiding over weddings, Amanda's was planning them.

The truth was that Kian had gotten caught up in the excitement as well. It was a pleasant distraction from worrying about the Eternal King, the future of everyone Kian loved, and the fate of Earth and its entire population.

He still wasn't sure whether he wanted to warn Navuh as Annani had suggested. He very much doubted that their archenemy would decide to join them just because they had a mutual enemy much more powerful than either faction could defend against, and they needed to combine forces.

Perhaps once Aru got concrete instructions on how to proceed, there would be something to tell the clan's archenemy.

"Can we make the cruise a day longer?" Amanda asked.

"Why?"

"I'm trying to convince Sari and David to have their wedding ceremony on this cruise, too. It would be perfect if all three of us got married in the same week, but we don't have any dates left, and none of us want a shared ceremony. Unless I can convince one of the other couples to give up their date, I can't even nag Sari about it."

Kian cast her an apologetic look. "I hired the crew for those specific dates, and I know for a fact that they can't stay for another day. I was lucky to secure the dates on such short notice."

"I'm pretty sure that Kri and Michael will not mind waiting," Syssi said. "They are still so young, and the only reason Kri jumped on the idea was because all the other head Guardians are getting married on the cruise, and she didn't want to be the only one left out."

Amanda grimaced. "She's shopping for a wedding dress, so I know she's committed. She will give up her spot for Sari, but it wouldn't be fair. "

"Carol and Lokan would probably have liked to get married too." Syssi leaned her head on his shoulder. "They have so few opportunities to celebrate with the family."

Kian rubbed his hand over her exposed arm. "Perhaps some of the couples wouldn't mind a double wedding."

"Mey and Jin are close." Amanda tapped a finger on her lower lip. "Maybe they wouldn't mind a shared ceremony."

Syssi chuckled. "I think you will have more luck with Wonder and Callie."

"You might be right." Amanda sighed. "I'll make the calls tomorrow. The thing is, Sari is not at all eager to join Alena and me in seafaring nuptials. She wants to have her wedding in the castle with all her people. I told her it's silly since most of them are coming and will be there anyway, but I think it's a matter of pride with her. She is the all-important European regent, and it's beneath her to get married at the same time as her sisters."

Kian shook his head. "It's not about pride. I think her people would not like her to have her wedding on my turf so to speak. If she doesn't want to get married on the cruise, don't pressure her to do it. We have enough drama going on as it is."

He still hadn't told them about Mia's friends.

Amanda frowned. "You mean the three gods?"

He nodded. "I'm apprehensive about them meeting Mother."

Syssi turned to him. "Why? You had Edna probe them and Andrew verify their answers. Luckily, they weren't immune to our best methods of interrogation."

"True, and it gave me some peace of mind, but Aru refused to let Edna probe him, which worries me. He said that the secrets he keeps have nothing to do with us, but still. He might have told only a partial truth. Andrew's lie detection ability is not infallible."

Syssi seemed offended on her brother's behalf. "Andrew is never wrong. When he's not sure whether someone is telling the truth, he admits it."

"Yeah, well, he wasn't sure with all of Aru's answers. Some were evasive." Kian reached for one of the scones Okidu had made for dessert. "That's not all the drama either. I just got a call from Toven, and he implored me to allow Mia's friends to join us on the cruise. I agreed since they are potential Dormants and the cruise is short."

Amanda clapped her hands. "That's fabulous. There is no better way to spark romance than a cruise vacation. A couple of clan males will be very thankful."

"That was why I agreed. I also told Toven that he was in charge of erasing their memories after the cruise."

Syssi tilted her head. "But what if they find their truelove mates by then? What's the point of erasing their memories? You can just bring them straight to the village. Anyway, the plan was for them to start working as beta testers for the Perfect Match scenarios. Since Toven will be paying their salaries, that's a win-win all around." She smiled at him. "Isn't that your preferred way of doing business?"

"It is." He wrapped his arm around her shoulders and kissed her head. "And speaking of business, I should get back to it. I have a pile of work waiting on my desk."

17

ARU

Aru tried to slip out of bed without waking Gabi up, but she opened her eyes as soon as he pulled his arm off her.

"Where are you going?"

"I need to do something. I'll be back before you are ready to wake up."

She frowned. "What is it about?"

He leaned closer so his mouth was on her ear. "I need to contact my commander, and I don't want to do it from here."

Despite Kian's assurances that there was no surveillance equipment in the penthouse and despite the fact that Kian and his people most likely were not familiar with the language of the gods, Aru wanted to make the call outside, where he was sure no one was listening in on it.

"What happened? Did he contact you?"

Aru nodded. "I got pinged, and I have to respond within twenty-four hours, or they will assume that something has happened to us."

Nodding, she lifted her head and kissed his cheek. "Come back soon. And if you want to be my hero, bring me some pastries from the café downstairs. I'm craving sweet things."

"No problem." He kissed her forehead. "I'll get us coffee too."

Her smile was dazzling. "You are the best. I love you."

He chuckled. "You are easy to please, my love."

It had been almost a week since she'd completed the first stage of her transition, and during that time, Gabi's appetite had been ravenous in more ways than one. She couldn't get enough of him and his venom bites, for which he was thanking the Fates daily and often more than once. She was also eating quantities that exceeded what Negal and Dagor combined consumed in a day.

She'd been worried about gaining weight, but Julian had reassured her that a ravenous appetite was common for newly transitioned Dormants. Since Gabi had grown a little over an inch, she needed to replenish what her body had used to make her grow taller.

When dressed, Aru walked into the living room and was relieved that Negal and Dagor weren't up yet.

Their relationship had been strained lately, probably because the males resented him for their being stuck in Los Angeles instead of searching for the missing Kra-ell pods.

He should remind them how much they had complained on the trek through Tibet.

Down in the lobby, he waved at the guards. "Getting coffee and sweet things for the lady," he said, knowing they were reporting to someone who was reporting to Kian.

Without meaning to, Gabi had given him the perfect excuse for his early morning outing.

As he stepped outside and walked around the corner of the building, Aru glanced over his shoulder to ensure no one was following him and then lifted his gaze to the sky, searching for a drone.

The irony of what he was doing wasn't lost on him.

He'd been peeved at Kian for bringing Edna and Andrew to test them because he didn't trust them, but he wasn't trusting Kian either.

Leaning against the wall, he pulled a cigarette box out of his pocket, took one of the cylinders, and put it in his mouth. He wasn't a smoker, but it was an excellent cover for spending several minutes outside, presumably doing nothing other than puffing on the stick.

His communicator was in his ear, which was covered by his chin-length hair. As he gave the verbal command for the connection to be made, he lit the cigarette and puffed out a plume of smoke.

The commander came online a few puffs later.

"Greetings, team leader Aru. Is everything well with you and your teammates?"

"It is, commander. Thank you for asking. Is everything well on board?"

"It is. Do you have anything to report?"

"Unfortunately, not yet." Aru hated lying to the male. It was one thing to omit information and another to lie outright. "We are still searching for the Kra-ell from the compound."

"Are you sure that they were not thrown overboard? The Kra-ell are not good swimmers, and you said the water was freezing in that area. They would have died, and their transmitters would have stopped broadcasting."

The scenario the commander suggested was plausible, and Aru should use it, but he just couldn't bring himself to do that.

"It occurred to me that someone might have used the threat of throwing the Kra-ell overboard to get them to talk, but I don't know what they hoped to learn. Humans would want to examine the aliens and wouldn't have disposed of them so quickly. They would have taken them to a research facility, and that's the lead we are following. Even if the abductors were Kra-ell, I can't believe they would have killed everyone unless they had a vendetta against them. It also occurred to me that they might have killed the original settlers and taken those born on Earth with them. In short, I feel compelled to continue the investigation."

He'd listed all the things he'd suspected before discovering that none of those scenarios was what had really happened. He had told the commander some of them before. Eventually, he would have to settle on one and ensure he had some supporting evidence he could show the commander.

"The high command seems to share your opinion because I have just gotten instructions to leave you and your team on Earth and not pick you up on our way back unless all the pods are found and all the Kra-ell are accounted for." The commander sounded apologetic. "Was there something you or one of your teammates did before this tour of duty to earn a punishment?"

Aru did his best to contain his joy and keep it from seeping into his voice. "Not that I know of, but you never know, right? Perhaps I said something offensive to someone."

The Supreme worked faster than Aru had expected.

"That is possible, and it is also a shame. I do not like losing you, Dagor, and Negal." There was a short silence, and Aru imagined the commander stifling a sigh. "We can drop more supplies for you when we pass by, but once we cross the barrier, you will lose communication with Anumati. The human satellite technology is in its infancy. You can't use it to communicate with home."

The commander was downplaying what humans had achieved in the last six hundred years on purpose, but it wouldn't work long-term.

"I know. I'm comforted by the knowledge that I will still have the ability to communicate with home for the next three hundred Earth years or so.

Perhaps by then, we will be forgiven and allowed to return. Would you come back for us?"

"Of course, provided that the high command allows it and wakes me up from stasis."

"Naturally."

18

DAGOR

Dagor had heard Aru leaving the penthouse, and he'd also known why. The commander had pinged all three of them last night, but Aru was responsible for responding. Dagor or Negal were to respond only if Aru was compromised.

Dagor had woken up, put the coffeemaker to work, and prepared a simple breakfast of eggs and toast for him, Negal, and Gabriella if she chose to join them.

Food on Earth tasted better than it did back home, probably because the ingredients were still mostly natural, but it wasn't reason enough to want to stay. He wasn't enthused about going home to Anumati either. Still, there were several colonies he was planning to check out after his tour of duty was over.

He'd heard that Peronia was beautiful and peaceful. It was an old and well-established colony with advanced technology and most of the comforts of Anumati, but it wasn't as stifling, and the class divide was less sharp. Nenillia was another good choice. It wasn't as well developed, and it had several species of dangerous predators, but it was also rumored to be a hub of burgeoning technology, where commoners like him could get the kind of education that only nobility could afford on Anumati.

When the door opened, and Aru walked in with a tray of coffees and a bag of pastries, Dagor lifted his coffee mug in salute. "You shouldn't have. I've also made eggs and toast for breakfast."

"We can have both." Aru smiled, but his expression was tense, and Dagor wondered what news he'd heard from the commander. "Is Gabi up?"

"Not as far as I can tell. She hasn't emerged from your room yet."

The newly transitioned immortal required longer sleep than the three of them, and she usually wasn't up before eight in the morning.

"Good." Aru put the tray and the paper bag on the counter. "I need to talk to you and Negal."

Dagor's gut twisted. "Is everything okay back home?"

Negal put his fork down and wiped his mouth with a paper towel.

"Nothing bad happened to anyone we love, or at least nothing that the commander was aware of. This has to do with the three of us."

Negal let out a breath and went back to shoveling scrambled eggs into his mouth as if their fate was of no consequence to him.

"What about us?" Dagor prompted.

Aru winced. "We are not going home. Unless we find all the pods and all the Kra-ell are accounted for, they are not picking us up on the way back, but they will drop off more supplies."

For Dagor, this was worse than a death sentence or just as bad. There was no way to find all the pods and account for the Kra-ell. Some pods were undoubtedly submerged in deep water, and some might have been destroyed.

They were being abandoned on a forbidden planet. In three hundred years, they would no longer be able to communicate with home. They would be as good as dead to their families.

"Why?" Dagor stared at Aru. "What did you do?"

"Nothing, as far as I know."

That was a lie. The guilty look in Aru's eyes betrayed the truth he was trying to hide.

"Out with it. If I am to be buried on this godforsaken rock, I at least want to know why. It must have been something terrible to merit such extreme punishment."

"I don't think it's a punishment, and I don't think it's forever either. We are tasked with investigating what happened to the Kra-ell and searching for the survivors. Someone higher up must have realized that a hundred and fifteen years is not long enough to achieve these objectives. We might get picked up by the next patrol ship deployed for the sector." He smiled. "Or we can go home on a human-made ship. At the rate they are going, they might develop interstellar travel ability during the next seven hundred years."

Aru didn't seem upset, which was understandable since he'd found his truelove mate on Earth and couldn't take her home with him.

Dagor was happy for him and liked to think of himself as a progressive god, but he hoped that the mate the Fates chose for him was a goddess and not a hybrid. He really didn't want to get stuck on Earth for eternity.

He wasn't overly fond of humans, and their primitive technology left much to be desired. As little as he knew, he could teach the best of them a lot about programming and building hardware. He would have been an exceptional engineer if his family could have afforded the tuition. He could probably also learn a lot from them.

"I don't think they will." Dagor let out a sigh. "The best we can hope for are satellites that will allow us to communicate with home."

Aru turned to Negal, who had snatched the paper bag and was pulling out all the pastries and organizing them on a plate. "You don't seem to be upset."

"I'm not." Negal chose one of the pastries and put it next to what was left of his eggs. "I like the food here."

"What about your family?" Dagor asked. "Aren't you upset about not seeing your parents?"

Negal shrugged. "I'm not very close to them."

"A mate then? Aren't you disappointed that you will have to wait for another thousand years to have a chance to find her?"

The trooper shrugged again. "I'm not a young god like you two, and I've been all over the galaxy, but I haven't found my one and only yet. I don't think the Fates have one for me." He tore off a piece of the pastry, stuffed it in his mouth, and chewed quickly. "Maybe I'm not deserving enough to merit such a boon from the Fates."

19

ARU

The good news was that Negal didn't seem to mind their extended, or maybe even permanent, stay on Earth. The bad news was that Dagor seemed more upset about it than Aru had expected.

"You have suffered," Dagor said to Negal. "You were oppressed, and yet you remained a good person. Therefore, you deserve a boon from the Fates. Do not give up hope on ever finding your truelove mate."

Negal smiled. "That is true of most people, and yet only a few ever find their one and only. I think more is required to qualify, but no instruction manual details the feats of bravery or sacrifice needed."

"I think that's a myth," Aru said. "I found my truelove mate, and I haven't sacrificed more than the two of you or performed heroic acts."

Dagor groaned. "Maybe you've gotten Gabi as a reward for the suffering you will endure in your future."

Aru wasn't sure whether Dagor was being his usual sarcastic self or if he really believed in that. In either case, the words didn't sit well with him and brought a sense of foreboding.

Nevertheless, he was the leader of this team, and it was his job to inspire the others.

"We can do great things here." He touched Dagor's shoulder and gave it a light squeeze. "The news was a shock, and when you have had more time to think about it, you will realize it's not that bad." He let go of Dagor's shoulder and pulled one of the coffee cups from the tray. "Besides, if what you said is true, and I got Gabi as a reward for future suffering, and by that you meant being stuck on Earth, then you and Negal should get rewarded as well."

Dagor arched a brow. "Do you see any goddesses milling around here? Because I don't, and I do not wish to be tied to a hybrid female whom I can never bring home to my parents."

It was the perfect opening for revealing the secret Aru had been hiding from his men. Still, while he was thinking of a good way to broach the subject, Negal said, "I agree with Dagor. But since I'm not looking for a truelove mate or any kind of mate, I'm good." He let out a sigh. "Human females are so fragile, though. I hope we will get to meet sexy immortal ladies who will want to try out a god in bed." He waggled his brows. "How does the saying go? Once they sample a god, they'll never look back?"

Dagor chuckled. "That doesn't sound right, but I'm all for trying out those immortal females. It would be nice not to have to be so careful, for a change." He turned to Aru. "You said something about going on a vacation with some of the immortals?"

"They invited us to their clan's cruise, and many immortals will be on board." Aru leveled his eyes at his teammates. "I need your vow that you will never reveal what I will tell you next. Especially not to anyone on the patrol ship, because our communication channel with the commander is not secure. We must assume that everything said over that line is reported to the Eternal King's secret agents."

The men nodded, and Dagor put his hand over his heart. "A vow shouldn't have been needed. A promise would have been enough, but here it is. I vow not to reveal what you will tell us to anyone outside of Earth or on it. It will stay between the three of us."

As Negal repeated the same vow, Aru let out a breath. "Gods are living among the immortals. Turns out that Kian's mother is a goddess and wants to meet the three of us."

Aru had expected surprise, maybe some questions for which he would have no answers, but he hadn't anticipated that Negal and Dagor would exchange knowing looks.

"You knew?"

Dagor nodded. "We've seen the recording you deleted of Gilbert telling Gabi about the gods." When Aru opened his mouth to berate them, Dagor lifted his hand. "I only checked because I was afraid that you might have mistakenly deleted something important. I never expected you to hide things from us. We are a team, and you should have known you could trust us."

Son of a gun.

They had known for days and had kept it to themselves, waiting for him to tell them.

"Kian asked me to keep the information about the gods to myself, and I did. He didn't tell me that he was protecting his mother, but I should have guessed. He looks like a god."

"Why does she want to meet us?" Negal said. "And why didn't we find any clues about her when we searched?"

"I don't know." Aru put his hands in his pockets. "Kian didn't say. His mother must be curious to learn about people from her home world. I assume that she was born on Earth, and therefore had no tracker, so we didn't know she was alive. As to hints, the ancient texts we read were full of stories about gods, but then they disappeared, and the logical assumption was that they had perished, because we knew they couldn't have gone home."

"How many gods are there living with those immortals?" Negal asked.

"I don't know that either. But since Gilbert could have only been induced by a male god, there must be at least one male. Maybe Kian's mother and the male god are a couple."

Negal looked like he wanted to ask something else when the door of the master bedroom opened, and the sound of Gabi's light footsteps sounded in the hallway.

Aru had wanted to deliver the good news to her in private, but it was too late for that. Negal or Dagor might blurt out something and steal his thunder.

As soon as she walked into the living room he rushed to her, wrapped his arms around her, and lifted her to look into her blue eyes.

"I have something to tell you." He grinned at her sleepy face. "I'm staying on Earth. The commander informed me that we are not getting picked up when the patrol ship completes its rounds in this corner of the galaxy."

Gabi squealed, wrapped her legs around him, and kissed him hard. He started walking toward the bedroom with her when a throat clearing reminded him that his friends were there, and they were not done talking.

Turning around, he walked Gabi to the kitchen counter and sat her on a stool. "Dagor and Negal are staying too, and Dagor is unhappy about it. Negal doesn't care one way or the other."

Instead of joyously showering him with kisses, Gabi frowned. "I don't understand. Did you ask your commander to let you stay and stipulate that if you do, your teammates must also stay?"

"I didn't ask. I couldn't tell him about you, remember?"

"So, how come he's abandoning the three of you on Earth?"

"That's what I want to know," Dagor murmured.

"It's probably punishment," Negal said. "One of us must have said something offensive about the Eternal King and was overheard. It doesn't take much to get booted out into a hostile colony, or in this case, the forbidden planet."

20

KIAN

As Kian escorted Annani onto the cruise ship, his eyes darted in every direction even though the Guardians were securing the area and Yamanu was shrouding it.

He'd instructed the team to return from China, not only because Yamanu and Mey were one of the couples who wished to be married on the cruise, but also because he could utilize Yamanu's unique talent to safeguard the excursion.

The truth was that there had been no reason for them to stay longer, and the only objective that they could claim to have achieved, if he could call it that, was improved relations between the Kra-ell and the clan members.

Peter and Kagra had become an item, but according to Syssi, who had heard it from Amanda, who had heard it from Mey, who had heard it from Yamanu, they were adamant about not making a big deal out of it. They claimed not to be fated to each other, and their fling was about having a good time and nothing more.

"Relax, my son." Annani adjusted the wide-brimmed hat that obscured most of her face and probably made it difficult for her to see. "You are overthinking it again. You will not have any fun if you let your paranoia flare."

"I'm aware of that, Mother. I will be less concerned once we are out on the water, but we have about eight more hours before we can set sail."

As soon as they were inside, she removed her protective sunglasses. "We could have waited until everyone was here, and then you would have had less to worry about, but you wanted me to be the first to board the ship so no one would witness my arrival. You cannot have it both ways, you know."

"You are not the first one to board. The Guardians, crew, and serving staff boarded yesterday, and Syssi's parents arrived early this morning. Besides, most of the immediate family is boarding along with you."

Annani looked over her shoulder at his sisters and smiled. "Indeed. Let us all go to my cabin and have a drink to celebrate." She turned to Syssi. "You probably want to say hello to your parents first."

"I spoke with my mother when they got here, and she said that they were going to sleep. I won't bother them until she calls me, and I know they are awake."

"Awesome." Amanda threaded her arm through Syssi's. "We can have margaritas. I just hope that the cabins are stocked with all the necessities."

"They are stocked," Kian said. "I put Wonder and Callie in charge of ordering supplies. As you know, Callie used to work in Brundar's club, so she knows a lot about cocktails." He also had an expert bartender, but that was a surprise they would discover later.

Pretending not to hear the remark about Brundar's club, his mother hid a smirk.

Only certain people in the clan knew about the Guardian's side hustle, and especially not what type of clientele the club catered to. Kian was absolutely sure that his mother knew all the details. She knew everything that was going on in her clan.

As they entered the elevator, Dalhu stood next to Kian with his hands resting on the handle of Evie's stroller. "Amanda told me that you hired the humans who came with the Kra-ell to be the serving staff."

"I did. Originally, I thought to hire an experienced serving crew and just thrall their memories after the cruise. Still, Eleanor convinced me to take the Kra-ell's former...employees." Kian didn't want to use the word slaves, but the truth was that they hadn't had much choice in what they did for a living and where they lived, so slaves was apt. "She said that they would be thrilled to visit Mexico, and since we managed to get proper paperwork for all of them, they can take turns with shore excursions. They are also very happy about the extra income."

Dalhu listened patiently to Kian's semi-apologetic explanation for his choice. When he was done, he clapped him on the back. "Yamanu said they have a great cook who runs an efficient kitchen. That's good enough for me."

Their group spilled out as the elevator doors opened, and Kian led them to Annani's presidential suite.

"This is beautiful," Alena said. "Is our cabin as nice as this one?"

"It's a little smaller but just as luxurious." Kian walked over to the bar and opened the cabinet. "I think Onidu has everything he needs to make margaritas."

The Odus were coming on a separate elevator with everyone's luggage, and given that Amanda didn't know the meaning of traveling light, it would take Onidu a couple of trips to bring up all of her suitcases.

When the ladies continued to check out the two bedrooms, Orion walked up to Kian. "Did you bring your cigars?" He looked longingly at the balcony doors. "I wouldn't mind a smoke, some good whiskey, and even better company."

"I don't have them on me, but I can pour us drinks." He glanced at Dalhu. "Can I tempt you with a shot?"

It was not even noon, but they were on vacation, and a shot of whiskey was an excellent way to start it off on the right foot.

Dalhu cast a look at his sleeping daughter and nodded. "As long as no one is smoking, I can take her out on the balcony."

A few moments later, the three were seated on lounge chairs outside.

"When is Kalugal arriving?" Dalhu asked.

"Soon. He and Jacki were supposed to leave with us, but he needed a little more time with his men. Some were unhappy about the village being locked down in our absence."

The Kra-ell weren't allowed to leave the village without supervision yet, so they didn't mind. Still, Kalugal's men were free to come and go as they pleased, and they didn't respond well to the news of being locked down for ten days.

"What is he going to do about it?" Orion asked.

"The usual." Kian took another sip of the whiskey. "Give them bonus pay to compensate them for the inconvenience. He already doubled their salaries for staying to guard the village and tripled it for the lockdown."

Dalhu shook his head. "I was surprised to hear that you were willing to leave the village to the Kra-ell and Kalugal's men to protect. I was sure you would leave at least half of the Guardians behind."

"It wouldn't have been fair." Kian wished he had his cigars with him because Dalhu's comment made him nervous. It hadn't been an easy decision, but he had taken all possible precautions. "William has every inch of the village under surveillance, and the lockdown ensures no one can enter. Besides, I invited the three gods to join us on the cruise so I can keep an eye on them here and not have to worry about them being a threat to the village."

Orion frowned. "Are you worried that they are a threat?"

"Not really, but you know me. I always prefer to err on the side of caution."

The balcony doors were flung open, and Amanda stepped out with a margarita glass in hand. "Here you are, darlings. The Odus brought up our luggage, so we should head to our cabins and unpack. Mother wants to see what ours look like, so you'd better get moving."

21

FRANKIE

"Thank you so much." Frankie watched the taxi driver unload her suitcase, carry-on, and makeup bag, ensuring he didn't forget anything inside the trunk.

Mia had told her that Tom had paid for the taxi, but she wanted to at least tip the driver. When he was done, she pulled out her wallet, but he lifted his hand to stop her.

"It's all been paid for, miss. Enjoy your vacation."

"Thank you."

Her suitcase was enormous and weighed a ton, but thankfully it had wheels. Not great ones, so Frankie still had trouble dragging it behind her, but at least she didn't need to lift it.

Hopefully there would be no stairs, or she would have to ask for help.

It was only ten days, but the thing was stuffed to bursting, and to close it, Aunt Rachel had to sit on it, contributing all of her two hundred and something pounds to the packing effort.

Most of it wasn't even Frankie's.

Her cousins Angelica and Bianca had collected evening dresses from her other female cousins, ensuring she had a new outfit for each of the ten weddings.

Some of the dresses were too big, others were too small, and most were too long on her petite frame, but several were nice, and only worn once or twice before. Still, Frankie didn't want to offend any of her cousins, so she packed all of them.

Then there were the shoes, a matching pair of heels for every dress, and those were all her own.

Frankie had a weakness for high-heeled, fancy-looking shoes, but since she'd gotten them all on sale, she had zero guilt about splurging on her one obsession.

Thankfully, the bikinis took up only a little space. She had two of her own and three more on loan from Angelica.

Frankie hadn't taken Tom up on his offer to store her things and had brought everything she wanted to keep to her parents' house.

Surprisingly, it was very little.

Moving was an excellent opportunity to get rid of old stuff, and she had donated at least half of her wardrobe and all the furniture, keeping only a few pictures, pillows, and throws.

Taking a deep breath, Frankie squared her shoulders and trudged toward the dock number indicated on her invitation, pulling the suitcase behind her.

It was easy to find a ship named the Silver Swan, and as she got closer, the two men standing at the entrance looked at her as if she was a lost tourist and there was no way she was getting onboard.

Did she look so out of place that they immediately knew that she was an outsider?

Nah, that was a stupid thought. The two probably worked for Perfect Match and knew all the employees. They simply didn't know who she was and that she would soon join their ranks.

Or so she hoped.

"Hi, I'm Frankie Canal." She pulled out her phone with the invitation. "Tom and Mia invited me."

One of the men said something very quietly into his earpiece while the other checked her invitation.

They were both very handsome and tall, making her feel tiny by comparison.

She was petite, only five feet two inches tall, but she was wearing four-inch shoes, and five feet six inches was a decent height for a woman.

"Welcome aboard, Ms. Canal. Can I see your passport?"

"Yes, of course." She fumbled in her purse until she found it. "Mia told me I would need one since we are going to Mexico." She handed him the document.

He flipped through it before handing it back to her. "Hold on to it. You will need it to go on shore excursions."

"Yes. I know." She looked at the darkened entrance. "Can I go in now?"

"Ms. Mia is on her way. She wants to welcome you on board and take you to your suite."

Her eyes widened. "A suite? Why am I getting a suite? Am I sharing it with someone?"

"I don't know." The guard said. "You will have to ask Mia."

"Sure." She put a hand on her hip and struck a pose. "Do you guys work for Perfect Match?"

The one on the left frowned. "No. Do you?"

"Frankie!" Mia drove her wheelchair at breakneck speed. "I told you to call me when you got here. I would have waited for you."

"I forgot." Frankie embraced her friend. "I guess I was too excited." She looked up. "Where is Tom?"

Usually he didn't leave Mia's side, which was sweet but, in Frankie's opinion, a little stifling. She didn't like her boyfriends to be so clingy.

"On his way." Mia turned her wheelchair around. "Come on, he'll meet us upstairs."

Frankie trotted behind her friend while pulling the suitcase behind her and wondering why Mia was in such a rush. She was also wondering why there was no one else around. "Where are all the guests?"

Mia turned to look at her over her shoulder. "The cruise organizers didn't want the usual mess of everyone boarding at once, so people were given different windows of arrival time. They are slowly trickling in and getting settled in their suites."

"About that." Frankie followed Mia into the elevator. "Who am I rooming with?"

"You have a suite of your own until Margo gets on board, and then you will share it with her."

"That's so fancy. I've never even been in a hotel suite or on a cruise. Now I'm getting both at the same time. I feel like a princess."

When the elevator door opened, Mia drove the wheelchair out into the wide corridor and kept going. "You are in suite number 217." She stopped before the double door, leaned over, and typed on the glass keyboard. "The code is your suite number, but you can change it if you want." She turned to look at Frankie. "Open the door."

"I'm almost afraid to." Frankie pushed the door open. "Wow, Mia. I even have a balcony."

Mia laughed. "What did you think, that we would put you below decks with the sheep and goats?"

Frankie frowned. "Are there animals on board?"

Mia waved a dismissive hand. "It was just an expression."

It wasn't one that Frankie had heard before.

"It's just that I'm not anyone important in the company." She walked in and parked the suitcase by the door. "I didn't expect to be treated like royalty. There is a kitchenette and a bar and everything." She turned around to look at Mia. "Can I live here? Because it's much nicer than any apartment I've ever rented."

"The village homes are just as nice if not nicer. I mean the compound. Some call it the village."

"It sounds better." Frankie sat on the super-comfy couch and didn't even try to stifle her delighted moan. "When you said compound, I imagined a dreary place with a big wall around it. Village makes it sound like a place full of greenery."

"It is." Mia smiled.

As a knock sounded on the door, Mia beat Frankie to it and opened up for Tom.

"Hi, sweetheart." He leaned down and kissed her on the lips.

Frankie rose to her feet and looked the other way, admiring the view from her balcony.

When the couple was done with their amorous greeting, she walked over to Tom and kissed his cheek.

"Thank you for inviting me and for everything else."

22

DAGOR

"What kind of a name is the Silver Swan?" Dagor grumbled as he, his teammates, and Gabi walked up to the cruise ship, dragging their luggage behind them.

The ship was small compared to the others docked next to it, looking almost like a yacht next to the giant floating hotels that could accommodate thousands of guests.

"What's wrong with Silver Swan?" Gabi gave him a reproaching look. "I think it's a very nice name."

He shrugged. "I'm not a fan of ships."

"You're not a fan of anything," Negal said. "I don't think I've ever heard you get excited about anything other than a piece of tech to disassemble and reassemble."

"I find it interesting to take things apart and see how they work because I didn't get to do that on Anumati. Besides, you are one to preach. What do you get excited about besides a nice pair of legs?"

Negal shrugged. "To each his own. I have my hobbies, and you have yours."

The dock appeared nearly deserted, with Kian's redheaded guard waiting for them at the bottom of the gangway, while other Guardians were trying to blend in and look inconspicuous.

"Welcome to the Silver Swan." Anandur offered Gabi his hand. "It's her maiden voyage under the new name."

"Hi." Gabi put her small hand inside the guy's huge paw. "What was her name before?"

"It's a secret." Anandur winked. "Let's get you people inside. We are operating on a tight schedule."

Dagor looked behind him to see if there were any other passengers, but the four of them were the only ones. "Is Gabi's family already on board?"

"Yes, they are, and you can go see them later, but first, I need you to get settled in your suite."

Great, so they were sharing a suite again.

Hopefully, there was a lounge chair on the top deck and a bar, so he and Negal would have a place to escape and leave Aru and Gabi to their honeymooning.

When they entered the spacious elevator, Anandur pressed the button for deck number six.

"We figured that you would want to be together, so we put you in one suite, but if that's not convenient, we might be able to find accommodations for the bachelors on the lower decks."

"How good is the soundproofing on this ship?" Negal asked.

"Excellent. It belongs to the clan, and it's built for immortals."

As the door opened, Anandur walked out, and the four of them followed.

"Is everyone on board immortal?" Gabi asked.

"Not everyone." Anandur stopped next to a suite marked with the number 608. "The crew is human, including the captain and his officers, the servers, the cooks, and the maids. A few guests are human too, but there's only one who does not know about us." He typed in a code and opened the door. "We are going to thrall everyone who is not supposed to know about gods and immortals at the end of the cruise to forget any peculiarities they might notice, so you should feel free to be yourselves, but if you can limit using the terms gods and immortals to when you are in the company of people you know, that would be helpful. The fewer memories we need to suppress, the better."

Dagor looked around the suite and had to admit that he was impressed. It wasn't big, but it was very nicely decorated and had all the amenities, including a small kitchen and a bar stocked full of various liquor bottles.

"Do you want me to give you the tour?" Anandur asked.

"I think we can figure it out." Aru rubbed the back of his neck. "So, what's next? Is Kian going to come over and say hello? Are we meeting with everyone for dinner? We weren't given an itinerary."

"The welcome dinner is at seven-thirty in the evening, and it includes everyone. You can look up the itinerary on the cruise channel." He pointed at the large screen. "Right now, we are getting everyone on board and settled. If you are hungry, there is food in the refrigerator, or you can call room service." He pointed to the phone on the coffee table. "If you want to call Kian, you can use the clan phone you were given, but he's a little busy right now, so perhaps a text message would be better."

"Of course." Aru nodded.

"Okay then." Anandur flashed them a bright smile. "Get comfortable, nap, or sit on the balcony, and I'll see you all later."

After Anandur left, Gabi opened the door to one of the bedrooms and walked inside. "That's the master. We are taking this one."

Dagor looked at the other door and groaned. "We are sharing a room again."

"Let's just hope that there are two beds." Negal clapped him on the back and kept walking toward the other door.

"I'm not sharing a bed with you. I'd rather take Anandur up on his offer to find me a place below decks."

As nice as the suite was, privacy was priceless.

"We have two beds," Negal said from inside the room. "Come take a look."

"I'll take your word for it." Dagor had no intention of staying in the suite until dinner. "I'm going to explore."

23

FRANKIE

After Mia and Tom left, Frankie unpacked, hung her dresses in the closet, and watched television on the living room's big screen.

Sometime during the show, an announcement came on about a welcome dinner at seven-thirty that evening, but that was more than three hours from now, and although there were snacks in the fridge and plenty of drinks to tide her over until then, she was bored and a little hungry.

If Margo were with her, they would have been having drinks on the balcony, munching on the snacks, or better yet, looking for hot dudes to flirt with at the bar.

What was stopping her from doing it on her own?

"Absolutely nothing."

Well, flirting with strangers on her own without her bestie's backup wasn't something Frankie was comfortable with. Still, she could explore and mark potentials for when Margo joined them in Cabo.

She stopped to check her makeup at the entry mirror, smoothed a few flyaway strands, and dotted her wrists with fresh drops of perfume.

After closing the door, she used the camera on her phone to take a picture of the suite number so she wouldn't forget it and trotted down the corridor toward the elevators.

No noises were coming through the doors she was passing by. It would have been completely quiet if not for the soft ambient instrumental music playing on the loudspeakers.

Was everyone taking an afternoon nap, or had no one on her deck arrived yet?

Shaking her head, she called for the elevator. When it arrived and the doors started to open, Frankie plastered a smile on her face, expecting to see people inside, but it was just as empty as the corridor.

Had she stepped into *The Twilight Zone*?

Where was everybody?

Perhaps she should call Mia and ask her to come up to the upper deck and join her for a drink. Hopefully, the bar was open for business, and Frankie wasn't the only one seeking the company of other human beings.

Nah, Mia and Tom were probably resting, and if Mia came, Tom would too, and as much as Frankie liked the guy's generosity and what he was doing for Mia, she found him too stiff and standoffish even when he was trying to be friendly.

He was also too gorgeous to be human, and it was unnerving to look at him.

Who would have thought looking at an unnaturally beautiful guy would be disturbing? But it was.

Frankie's type was the guy next door, someone with a friendly smile who was good with his hands, mowed his lawn, and could build a swing set or a new deck.

In short, she wanted a man like her father, just a little better looking. Not that her dad hadn't been handsome when he was young, but he was on the shorter side, and she had a thing for tall guys. It was nature's way to ensure balance. A tall guy would counterbalance her short genes, so their kids would be average height.

Did it work that way, though?

She remembered learning about dominant and recessive genes in high school, but that had been long ago, and she had forgotten most of what she'd been taught.

Heck, where had the time gone?

It seemed like only yesterday she was starting college and had her whole life ahead of her. She'd blinked and was twenty-seven, still single, still struggling financially, and her family considered her an old spinster because all of her cousins had been married by the age of twenty-four.

She really needed a drink now.

Exiting the elevator on the top deck, Frankie walked over to the sliding glass doors that led to the outdoors, and as they swished open, she let out a relieved sigh.

She'd feared that, with her luck, the doors would be locked.

The ship was still docked, but most passengers had yet to arrive or were holed up in their cabins because no one was there.

Not ready to give up yet, Frankie headed to what looked like a bar, given the barstools and tables. It wasn't closed, but it didn't seem like anyone was tending it.

Still, she walked until she was at the counter and almost fainted when a robotic metal head popped up and smiled at her. "Good afternoon, mistress. It is my pleasure to serve you. What would you like?"

Her hand resting on her racing heart, she let out a breath. "You scared me. You shouldn't pop up like that and startle people."

She'd seen a robot serving cappuccinos in a coffee shop in Seattle, but there had been a big sign outside warning customers before they got inside that their barista would be a robot.

Also, the robot in the coffee shop looked like it had been modeled after something other than C-3PO from *Star Wars*, just with more arms.

The robot frowned, which looked very odd on his metallic face. "My apologies, mistress. I will do better in the future. What can I serve you?"

"A mojito, please."

"With pleasure. Would you like the passion fruit mojito, the mango, or the classic?"

"Classic, please."

"Coming right up."

The robot swiveled on its axis, and its long robotic arms reached for the required ingredients. All four of them.

Watching him prepare the drink with all the flair she would have expected from an experienced bartender was fascinating.

Was it a *him*, though?

The voice was male, and the face its creators had given it was male, too, but it had four arms, so 'they' might be more appropriate.

"Here you go, mistress." One of his four hands placed a napkin on the bar counter while another put the drink on top. "Would you like something to snack on with your drink?"

"Sure. What do you have?"

"We have peanuts, pretzels, and assorted nuts."

"Can I have all three? I'm a little hungry."

"Of course, mistress." He swiveled his robotic torso again, and three of his four arms filled small containers from the dispensers.

"Do you have a name?" Frankie blurted out.

The robot grinned. "I do. It's Bob."

She stifled the giggles that were about to escape her mouth.

Was that a joke?

"Nice to meet you, Bob. I'm Frankie. Can I ask you something?"

"You can ask me anything, mistress, but my ability to answer is limited by my programming."

"I understand. I'm curious if Bob is short for Robert or whether it has another meaning."

"I do not know, mistress. That is the name I was given by my creators."

24

DAGOR

Sprawled on a lounger with his back to the bar, Dagor stifled a chuckle. The exchange between the woman named Frankie and the robot named Bob was most amusing, but he didn't wish to startle her.

The poor woman had enough of a scare when Bob popped up from behind the bar, and her heartbeat was only now returning to normal.

She hadn't noticed him, which was how he preferred things to remain.

He hadn't come up here to socialize. He'd wanted to drink alone and ponder his uninspiring future. However, discovering Bob had perked him up a little, giving him food for thought.

The robot was much more advanced than anything he'd seen humans produce, and he suspected that it had been built by the immortals. Their technological know-how in cybertronics seemed superior, and although it was primitive compared to Anumati's, it was still more than he knew. He was very much interested in learning from them.

Since it looked like Dagor's dreams of saving up enough credits to attend one of Anumati's engineering schools were not going to materialize for the next millennium, or maybe ever, he should learn what he could from the immortals and perhaps even work with them to further develop their technology.

Besides, if he was honest with himself, his chances of passing the entry exams were slim, even if he could return as planned and have enough to pay for the tuition. The elite ensured commoners did not have access to the schools that prepared the best for higher education.

Supposedly, Anumati was a democracy, and no god was barred from achieving the highest station regardless of who their parents were. Still, in reality, the elite was an impenetrable clique of those with royal blood and old riches.

The best a commoner could hope for was one of the lower-tier schools that prepared workers for lower-tier positions.

"Oh, I didn't see you there." The woman startled him. "Do you mind if I sit here?"

The voice belonged to Bob's only customer, Frankie, but with the blazing sun behind her blinding Dagor, all he could see was a dark silhouette. Shielding his eyes with his hand and squinting, he tried to see more than the outline of her petite body, but the sun's glare made it nearly impossible.

Not that he cared what she looked like. He hadn't come up here to flirt, and she was encroaching on his private time.

"You can sit anywhere you want. This is not my ship."

There were at least thirty other loungers, and she could have chosen to sit anywhere else on the deck.

Why the hell did she have to sit next to him and disturb his peace?

Well, that was obvious.

Human females found his godly features appealing and weren't bashful about approaching him, Negal, and Aru. He could usually deter them with a scowl, but a squint was not a scowl, and it was hard to do anything else with the damn sunshine blinding him.

He should have brought his sunglasses, but he'd forgotten.

"Someone is grumpy," she murmured as she walked away.

Dagor felt like an ass, and when she sat down on the last lounger in the row, he sighed. "I'm sorry if I offended you. It wasn't my intention."

"I get it. You just want to be left alone." She lifted her drink in a salute, took a sip, and reclined while crossing her legs.

Maybe he'd been mistaken, and she hadn't planned on flirting with him after all. Even squinting, he still couldn't see her clearly, but he could tell that she had shapely legs and wore shoes with enormous square heels.

How could she even walk in those things?

Was she really that tiny?

Curiosity getting the better of him, he pushed to his feet and walked over to her.

Now that he had his back to the sun, he finally got to see the little pixie, and she was lovelier than he'd expected. She had a pert little nose, pouty lips painted with bright lipstick, and a compact figure that still had all the required feminine curves.

A discreet sniff confirmed what he'd suspected, though. She wasn't an immortal. She was human, and Anandur's instructions had been to avoid mentioning gods and immortals unless necessary.

"Hi," he said. "May I sit next to you?"

She pursed her lips. "I don't own this deck, so you can sit anywhere."

He chuckled. "Touché. I'm Doug." He crouched next to her and offered her his hand. "Doug Farkash." He introduced himself with the name on his fake identity, which was what he usually did with humans.

"Frankie." She looked at his hand as if it was going to bite her. "My hands are wet from the condensation on the glass, so I'll skip the handshaking."

"As you wish." He dropped his hand on his thigh.

He didn't mind that her hand was damp, but she seemed reluctant, and he wasn't going to insist. Instead, he pushed up and sat on the lounger next to her, cradling his drink and trying to come up with something clever to say.

"Is Farkash a Yugoslavian name?" she asked, saving him the trouble. "I've never heard that name before, but it sounds Eastern European."

"It's Hungarian."

"You don't sound Hungarian." She chuckled. "Not that I know what Hungarian sounds like. What I meant to say was that you sound American."

Dagor was thankful for the gods' ability to absorb languages effortlessly. Having a universal translator helped make the process even faster. Still, their innate ability allowed them to master the nuances of accents so they could sound like natives wherever they were.

"My grandparents were from Hungary." That was another lie that worked well. If she asked him about them, he would say they were dead.

As a long silence stretched between them, he tried to come up with another topic of conversation that did not involve his fake Hungarian roots.

Anandur had said something about the staff being comprised of humans, so maybe she was one of them and on a break. However, given her shoes, she probably worked in accounting or something else that did not require extensive standing or walking.

She also wasn't wearing a uniform, but since Dagor had yet to see any staff or guests, he didn't know whether the service crew even had uniforms. After all, it was a private cruise for clan members, so things might be more casual and relaxed, and no identifying attire was needed for the humans.

"Are you a staff member?" he asked.

25

FRANKIE

Doug's question cut through Frankie like a knife.

Was it that obvious that she didn't belong as a guest on this fancy cruise? Was everyone working for Perfect Match so loaded that their outfits were from Nordstrom, Saks, or some other fancy place?

That wasn't likely.

The most logical explanation was that Doug knew everyone who worked there, and since he didn't recognize her, he assumed she was a crew member.

With how gorgeous he was, his job was probably modeling for the creators of the male avatars. She wouldn't mind beta-testing an adventure with an avatar modeled on him, but in real life she would never go for a guy who was so much prettier than her.

"I don't work here." She waved a hand over the deck. "Tom promised me a job at the new Perfect Match testing lab as soon as the machines are ready, but there have been so many delays that I almost despaired of ever working there." She smiled. "I've been waiting for that position to open up for months, and I can't wait to start. It's so exciting."

Doug stared at her as if he had no clue what she was talking about.

Had she been mistaken about his part in the company? Everyone probably brought their significant others on the cruise, and Doug could be the trophy husband of one of the silent partners Tom had talked about. But hadn't he said that they were a married couple?

Not that it excluded him being a third partner.

Who knew?

A wealthy married couple could have a live-in lover boy to play with.

"Who is Tom?" Doug asked.

The guy must be as dumb as he was gorgeous. Even if he didn't work for Perfect Match, he should at least know who was hosting the cruise.

"He's one of the owners of the company. How come you don't know him?"

He still looked perplexed. "What company? Are you still talking about those virtual matchmaking studios?"

"Well, duh." She waved a hand. "This is a company cruise. All the guests are involved with the company in one way or another." As it occurred to her that he might not belong, she narrowed her eyes at him. "Are you a stowaway?"

That was not likely, given the tight security. Still, given his question, maybe he'd asked her if she was a staff member because he was a stowaway?

"I'm not a stowaway. I was invited."

"By whom?"

"Kian."

"Oh." Tom and Mia had mentioned asking someone named Kian if it was okay to invite her and Margo on the cruise. The guy must be Tom's silent partner or perhaps his assistant or manager. "How do you know Kian?"

Doug grimaced. "We are very remote cousins, and we have just discovered that we are related. We hope to get better acquainted during this cruise."

That explained why he knew nothing about Perfect Match, but she wondered why mentioning his distant cousin had made him grimace.

"That sounds lovely, and it was very nice of Kian to invite you. Why the face, though?"

He arched one dark brow. "What face?"

"The grumpy face." She waved a tiny hand with perfectly manicured nails over him. "Going on a cruise with newly discovered family should be exciting."

He shrugged. "I'm not the cheerful sort. In fact, my friends accuse me of always being a grouch."

Frankie didn't buy it. "Is there bad blood between you and your distant family?"

He shook his head. "I don't mind getting to know my relatives, but I'm unhappy about the cruise. I'm not a fan of deep water, and I also don't like sharing a cabin with my other two cousins, especially since one of them is newly engaged. He and his fiancée are in the honeymooning stage if you know what I mean."

Frankie laughed. "I do, and I envy you. It's awesome to be around people who are in love. Their happiness is infectious, and it brings good luck." She leaned over and pretended to whisper. "You might soon fall in love yourself."

"Fates, I hope not."

She frowned. "Why not? Being in love is the best thing in the world. We all live for the moment we find that one special person."

"I don't." He lifted his legs onto the lounger and reclined. "Love complicates things."

It wasn't a big surprise that a guy like him was not interested in a meaningful relationship. He could have anyone he wanted, so why choose to be stuck with just one person?

Frankie closed her lips around the straw and slurped the dregs of her mojito. "I wonder if Bob can serve drinks poolside." She turned to Doug. "Do you know if he is stationary or mobile?"

"I don't, but I can find out." He sat back up and extended his hand, reaching for her empty glass. "Do you want the same drink or something else?"

"Another mojito would be lovely, thank you."

"It's my pleasure." He dipped his head before pushing to his feet.

Frankie watched Doug walk over to the bar, admiring his tight backside.

The guy was a dream, but only looks-wise. He was emotionally stunted and vacillated between being borderline rude and overly polite.

Heck, she wasn't even sure that he liked girls.

Still, when she fantasized about Doug later tonight, she would pretend that he was into her and that they were having a fabulous time between the sheets in a Perfect Match adventure environment of her choosing. Better yet, she could create a new one just for the two of them.

26

DAGOR

As Dagor walked over to the bar, there was a lightness to his step that he hadn't felt for the longest time.

Frankie was entertaining, and she was beautiful in a very human way.

He liked that she took great care with her appearance, and everything about her was polished to perfection, from her hair to her nails and everything she wore.

But what he liked most was that her blue eyes were full of life.

Yes, that was it. That was what he found most charming about her. She looked like someone who was upbeat by nature and didn't take things too seriously. She could be a perfect fling companion for this cruise and an antidote to boredom.

"What can I serve you, master?" Bob asked with a smile on his shiny metallic face.

"The lady you served earlier is wondering whether you can serve drinks poolside or are you confined to the bar."

"I am free to move around, master. Shall I bring you both new drinks?"

"Yes, please. Frankie wants another mojito, and I wouldn't mind another serving of the superb Japanese whiskey you suggested. Can I snatch a photo of the bottle? I would like to order some for myself."

"Of course, master." The robot reached for the bottle with his long arm and put it on the counter before Dagor.

"Tell me something, Bob," Dagor said while snapping a picture. "Do you have a record of everyone on board?"

"Naturally, master. I have the roster but don't have pictures attached to the names." He smiled again. "I am learning, though. Eventually, everyone will stop for a drink, and I will put their face next to their name on the roster."

"Who is your creator?"

The robot did an excellent job of mimicking a frown. "I have many creators. It takes more than one person to build a Bob."

"Are there more of you?"

"Not at the moment. I am a prototype. If I prove successful, more of me will be built." The robot froze momentarily as if listening to instructions and then smiled again. "I shall bring the drinks to you and Mistress Frankie." He turned around.

Someone must be monitoring Bob's interactions with people, and whoever that was had realized that they should have better safeguarded what he could say and to whom.

When Dagor returned to Frankie's side, he was greeted with such a strong scent of female arousal that he was nearly knocked off his feet.

Had she been talking to a paramour while he was ordering drinks for them?

It was her right to do so, but it annoyed him for some reason. The reason was that he'd had plans for her, and if she was involved with someone, she wouldn't be open to spending the night with him.

"Bob will bring us the drinks." He sat back on the lounger.

Frankie uttered a throaty chuckle. "Since you walked over there, you could have brought the drinks already."

He arched a brow. "I thought that you were curious to see Bob serving drinks away from the bar, and the truth is that I'm curious, too."

As a whizzing sound announced Bob's approach, they both turned to look over their shoulders at the robot.

His torso was attached to a trapezoid base that moved on wheels, not legs. He held their drinks in two of his hands and bowls of snacks in the other two.

The body was crude for such a sophisticated artificial intelligence, and Dagor wondered whether it had been done on purpose. Humans were still wary of robots that looked and acted too much like them, and he couldn't blame them.

Even the gods realized that machines shouldn't be given humanoid features.

"Your drink, Mistress Frankie." Bob offered her the mojito. "And the whiskey for the master." He handed Dagor his. "I also brought more snacks." He smiled at Frankie. "In case the mistress is still peckish."

"Thank you." Frankie gave Bob a dazzling smile that went straight to Dagor's groin.

He'd been in trouble from the moment he had scented her arousal and tried not to respond because it hadn't been for him, but that smile was like throwing gasoline on a raging fire.

"Thank you, Bob. That will be all," Dagor said.

The robot bobbed his head in a way that was too similar to Kian's Odu, and then whizzed away.

"You were rude," Frankie said. "Bob was being nice."

"Bob is a machine, and he does what he is programmed to do. He's not a person, and he doesn't have feelings."

"Still, no reason to be rude." Frankie closed her lips around the straw, and Dagor felt his fangs starting to elongate.

"Excuse me for a moment." He put his drink down, pushed to his feet, and walked to the men's room.

Usually, he had better control over his reactions.

Back home, flashing fangs was considered bad manners, and on Earth, it was dangerous and required thralling whoever happened to see them. Being in control of such a reaction was second nature to Dagor, but Frankie had an odd effect on him, and he couldn't understand why.

She was pretty, but he had met prettier, and her compact body was curvy in all the right ways. Still, he had come from the planet of the gods, where every goddess was perfect in every way.

He was immune to physical beauty.

Frankie was entertaining in her directness, but again, that was no reason for him to react like a boy who had just discovered the wonders of sex.

After several long breaths and a splash of cold water on his face, Dagor felt composed enough to return to Frankie and discover what made her different from all the other females he had ever encountered.

27

FRANKIE

Something wasn't right about Doug. Why had he bolted like that? Because she'd told him that he was being rude?

Eh, whatever.

There was no reason to agonize over his peculiar reaction.

Frankie had already relegated the guy to the realm of dreams, where everything was possible. She could make him into Prince Charming or a bad boy mafioso with a heart of gold, depending on her mood.

It was a shame that real men couldn't be programmed to act according to her whims.

Closing her eyes, Frankie imagined a Bob who didn't look like the bartender aboard the Silver Swan, but like a real flesh and blood handsome guy, who could be whoever she wanted him to be and get out of her hair when she didn't want him around. No girl would ever want the real thing if there was a robot like that.

Well, except for procreation, but that could be managed with artificial insemination from donors.

Yeah, but children needed fathers, and she doubted a robot could be a good substitute. She couldn't imagine growing up without her dad's bear hugs, silly jokes, and the one-liners from movies that she and her brothers pretended to be sick of but secretly loved.

Frankie had a great family, and she would miss them when she moved into the secret compound of the eccentric owners of Perfect Match.

She would probably meet them on this cruise, and how exciting was that?

She had a strong feeling that her life would finally get on track, and if it meant that she couldn't see her family so often, she could deal with that.

As the saying went, nothing ventured, nothing gained. In other words, good things require giving up other good things or suffering through bad ones.

The universe demanded a balanced ledger.

"I'm back." The lounger next to her groaned as Doug lowered his big body onto it. "Sorry about earlier. I must have eaten something that didn't agree with me."

Oh, so that was why he'd been so grumpy. No one was in a good mood when they needed to pass gas, especially when trying to impress a girl.

Had he been trying to impress her, though?

If he had, he had a strange way of going about it.

"Do you feel better now?" she asked.

"Yes, much. Thank you for asking."

She chuckled. "I wondered why you were Mr. Grumpy one minute and Mr. Polite the next. Your tummy has been bothering you on and off."

Nodding, he leaned over to the side table and picked up his drink. "Now that I feel better, I remember you thought this cruise was for Perfect Match employees. What made you think that?"

She tilted her head. "It isn't?"

"Not as far as I know."

"So, who is it for?"

"I think it's mostly Kian's family and friends."

So, Kian was the name of the secret partner. He was the guy whom Tom had called to ask if he could bring her and Margo along, so it made sense.

"Yeah, well, he and his wife own half of Perfect Match Virtual Fantasy Studios, so it might be a combined event."

"I didn't know that." Doug finished his drink and put it on the side table. "I've seen the ads on television. Is the experience as good as they claim?"

"I've never done it myself, but I hear it's amazing." Frankie took a long slurp of her mojito and dove into telling Doug about Tom and Mia falling in love in a Perfect Match adventure. She omitted the part about Mia regrowing her legs because she wasn't supposed to tell anyone about it, but she told him about the Swiss heart clinic Tom had taken Mia to and the miracle treatment she'd received there. "That's why Tom bought half of Perfect Match. He wanted them to have access to it whenever they wanted."

"That sounds very romantic. I might have to try one of those adventures and see for myself."

"They are very costly." Frankie sighed. "That's why I wanted to become a beta tester for the adventures and help Mia develop new ones. There was no way I could afford them on what I was making as a glorified secretary."

He frowned. "I was not aware of a position titled glorified secretary. How is it different from a regular secretary?"

Was he teasing her?

He seemed perfectly serious, though. How was it possible that he had never heard that expression?

"An executive assistant is a glorified title for a secretary, and that was my job until two weeks ago. I'm supposed to start working for Perfect Match after the cruise. I assumed that all the employees were here, so I couldn't start right away, but that was silly of me. There is no way that all the studios worldwide are closed for ten days so every employee can be here. It must be just the company's top executives with a few key employees, and they are the only ones who can handle hiring new people."

28

DAGOR

Interesting. So, the clan of immortals was involved with the Perfect Match Studios. Given the amount of advertising on network television and cable, it was a successful enterprise, and the clan was making a lot of money. The question was whether they used Anumatian technology to create the interface.

When Dagor had seen the ads, he'd dismissed Perfect Match as an over-hyped multiplayer video game that was also trying to be a matchmaking service. But if the clan contributed advanced programming to the enterprise, it could be all that it promised to be.

On Anumati, entertainment of this kind was trendy, but no one expected to find their perfect match there. It was pure escapism and didn't require being hooked up to the contraptions he'd seen in those ads. It was as simple as crossing a threshold and stepping into the virtual world. Every patrol ship had several rooms that provided entertainment during the long intervals of travel between planets.

Stasis was practical for the extended period of time required for travel from Anumati to the sector the patrol ship was about to cover and for the return trip. However, it wasn't practical while they were actually performing the duty of checking on the different planets the gods had seeded in that sector.

"Doug? Is your stomach bothering you again?" Frankie looked at him with genuine worry in her expressive blue eyes.

"I'm sorry. I didn't realize that I had zoned out." He smiled to reassure her that he didn't have stomach issues. "I'm fine."

"What were you thinking about?" she asked.

"About Perfect Match and wanting to try out an adventure. Would you like to go on one with me?"

If she said no, he would know that there was someone else, but if she said maybe, a committed relationship was not a factor. He could initiate a hookup for tonight.

"I don't know." Her heartbeat accelerated. "We've just met, and as you know, those adventures are romantic. Also, I can't afford it unless we can beta test for the company. The sessions cost nearly four thousand dollars."

That was so expensive that most people couldn't afford it.

"Does it cost that much per person or per couple?"

"Per person. They might offer a discount to a couple wanting to join an adventure, but I'm not sure they do."

He could ask Aru for the funds. They'd come to Earth with a stash of pure diamonds that was worth enough to cover several centuries of living expenses for the three of them, and then Aru had also found a side hustle they could do while looking for the Kra-ell pods, and they'd made money on that. Still, they couldn't throw it around like they had an endless supply of it.

"It's probably too rich for my wallet too." He turned on his side and smiled at her. "If they let us beta test, what kind of adventure would you like to experience?"

"Space pirates," she answered without having to think about it. "Then the mer underwater adventure."

"Mer? Like mermaids?"

"Like mer people. I could go for a merman prince."

He frowned. "Aren't they supposed to have fish tails?"

"Yeah, so?"

"You said that the adventures are romantic in nature. How are they supposed to, you know...?"

She arched a brow. "Have sex?"

"Yeah."

"How do dolphins have sex? They are mammals, and all mammals have sex more or less the same way."

"I know that. But it's weird. Count me out for the mer adventure."

"How about the space pirates?" Frankie's breath hitched, and the scent of her arousal flared.

"I would love that one." He reached for her hand, and he smiled when she didn't pull it away. "Perhaps we could start planning it tonight. From what I understand, a lot of customization goes into those adventures."

She swallowed. "That's true. Mia spent hours filling out the questionnaire and drawing her avatar. She was very beautiful in her adventure. She's also beautiful in real life, but she had those cute pointy ears in the virtual world, and she jokes that they were the reason Tom fell in love with her."

"I'm sure her physical beauty was just a small part of the attraction." He leaned over and kissed the back of her hand softly. "It's what's inside that matters the most."

She chuckled throatily. "Says the guy who looks like a god."

Did Frankie know about gods and immortals?

That would make his life so much easier.

"I am a god, and all gods and goddesses are beautiful. That is why I can say with authority that physical beauty is not reason enough to fall in love with someone."

Frankie laughed. "You certainly have an ego, but I don't blame you. If I looked like you, I would have an enormous ego as well."

It seemed he'd been wrong, and Frankie didn't know about gods. Luckily, she'd thought that he'd been boasting or teasing.

He'd also failed to reassure her that he found her attractive, which could give her reason to refuse his invitation.

"I was just joking about the god thing, but I was serious about beauty not being reason enough for falling in love. I don't mind that you are gorgeous, though, and I'm still very interested, so how about it? Do we have a date for tonight?"

Frankie looked at him as if she was trying to gaze into his soul, and after a long moment, she nodded. "It's a cruise, and I'm supposed to have fun, so why not." She pulled out her phone. "Give me your number. I'll call you if I'm not too tired after dinner tonight. I don't know what they offer regarding entertainment, but maybe we can go dancing or something."

Was she being coy?

"I'm sure we can come up with ways to entertain ourselves with just the two of us for company." He gave her a pointed look.

Frankie chuckled. "Usually, I would ask your place or mine, but since you have roommates and I don't, I guess it will have to be my place." She looked at him from under lowered lashes. "We can listen to music, watch a movie, or talk."

Was she teasing him?

He could peek into her mind and get his answer, but what would be the fun in that? It would also be an invasion of privacy that he found abhorrent.

"How come you have a suite to yourself?"

"It's only until my bestie joins the cruise in Cabo."

"Your bestie? You mean your best friend?"

"Yeah. Margo, Mia, and I have been best friends since childhood. Margo is also going to be a beta tester for Perfect Match."

"I see." He leaned closer and tried to inhale her intoxicating scent as inconspicuously as possible. "Tell me more about the space pirates' adventure. What is it all about?"

29

ANNANI

"I'm nervous." Alena lowered herself onto the couch.

Her pregnant belly was quite evident by now, making sitting down and standing up a little more difficult.

"Why are you nervous?" Sari asked. "Are you worried about Carol and Lokan getting here tonight?"

Alena chuckled. "I completely forgot about that, and I'm not worried about them. I think they are being extra cautious, and that's a good thing. I'm nervous about the wedding."

"It's just a ceremony." Sari waved a dismissive hand. "It doesn't change anything between you and Orion. You are fated mates."

Annani gazed lovingly at her four daughters—the three she had birthed and the one she had acquired through her son's marriage. As soon as Sari arrived and settled in her suite, Annani invited all four for an afternoon tea. It was not often that she got to enjoy all of them at once.

While the ladies were having tea, Kian treated their mates to cigars on his and Syssi's balcony. Syssi's parents had Allegra, and Evie was in the hands of the clan's two young babysitters, Lisa and Cheryl, with Onidu on standby in case the girls needed help.

Alena rubbed her belly. "Orion and I are going first, which means our wedding will have the most blunders. It doesn't matter to me, but it does to Orion. I don't want him to be disappointed."

"He won't be." Syssi leaned over and patted her shoulder. "I'm more worried about whether you'll still fit into your wedding dress. Have you tried it on lately?"

Alena's wedding cruise had been postponed many times. In the meantime, the baby in her belly kept growing, so there was a good chance that the dress she had commissioned two months ago might not fit.

"It fits." Alena smiled. "I tried it this morning before packing it. It's so loose that I could get married the day my water breaks. I wasn't taking any chances."

"That's good to know." Amanda crossed her legs and put her hands on her knees. "I'm not nervous about my wedding, but poor Dalhu is. You know how he hates being the center of attention."

"He won't be." Syssi shifted her eyes to Annani. "All eyes will be on the Clan Mother, which brings the issue of tonight's welcome dinner to mind. How are you going to handle it?"

Annani frowned. "What do you mean?"

"You will need to shroud yourself from the human crew and staff."

"Kian has not said anything to that effect, and I do not see a reason to hide who I am while celebrating with my family. The crew and staff will get their memories altered at the end of the cruise."

Syssi nodded. "That's true, but perhaps we should let them gradually get accustomed to your presence. Otherwise, we will have broken dishes and spilled food everywhere."

Amanda snorted. "These humans lived with the Kra-ell, and in my opinion, the purebloods look much stranger than a glowing goddess. It won't be as shocking to them as you expect it to be."

Annani lifted her hand. "I am willing to suppress my glow when I enter the dining hall, and I can keep it down until the food is served. Once that is done, the doors can be closed, and the staff will be told not to come in. I will only release my glow when they are no longer present."

"The glow is not the only thing giving you away," Syssi said. "Your beauty and the way you dress are also pretty conspicuous."

"What do you suggest, Syssi, that I eat alone in my suite?"

"Of course not." Syssi recoiled. "But maybe we can dress you in something more contemporary and braid your hair. That will somewhat diminish the impact."

"I will do no such thing. This is my family, my clan, and I will present myself to them how they are accustomed. I will not make compromises to accommodate the humans."

"Eating in your suite this first evening is not a bad idea," Amanda said. "Did you forget about the three gods you want to meet? If they see you at dinner, you will lose the element of surprise. Your options are to meet them before dinner, which leaves you little time, or eat in your suite tonight and schedule the meeting for tomorrow.

Annani did not want to stay in her suite while her family gathered in the dining hall. It was a shame she would have to cut short her tea time with her daughters, though.

"I will call Kian immediately and tell him to get the gods here as soon as possible. You are welcome to stay and witness the meeting."

Sari and Amanda exchanged glances with Alena and Syssi, and then all four nodded.

"We will stay," Amanda said. "Although it might get crowded here with our mates and all the Guardians Kian will bring to protect you."

"We will manage." Annani pulled out her phone.

30

KIAN

"Everyone who is supposed to be on board is here already." Anandur looked up from his tablet. "We can set sail."

"Inform the captain," Kian said.

"Will do, boss."

As Anandur walked back inside, Orion leaned against the railing and tapped the ash from his cigar into the water. "This is your first time on the ship, right?"

Kian nodded. "I was supposed to be on her maiden voyage, but then the Kra-ell needed rescuing, and her first passengers included a flock of sheep and goats." He grimaced. "I was afraid they would never be able to get rid of the smell, but thankfully, the restoration contractor brought her back to her pristine condition. We changed her name, though, so you can say that it's her maiden voyage as the Silver Swan."

"It was the Aurora before." Anandur closed the balcony door behind him to prevent the smoke from entering the cabin. "I liked that name—the goddess of the dawn. The Silver Swan has a negative connotation."

Kian wasn't aware of it. The only comment he'd gotten so far about the name was that it was also the name of a soy sauce. "What's the connotation?"

Anandur lifted one bushy red brow. "Don't you ever read comics? The Silver Swan is Wonder Woman's adversary. Wonder got upset when she saw the name, but I told her that you probably didn't know when you renamed the ship."

"Of course, I didn't. I also didn't know that the two of you read comics."

The only thing that bothered him was that Wonder had gotten upset for no reason. When the new name for the ship had popped into his mind, Kian hadn't questioned it.

Anandur opened his mouth to say something, and closed it as Kian's phone chimed with the ringtone he'd assigned to his mother.

Pulling the device from his pocket, he answered, "Hello, Mother. How is the tea going?"

"We are enjoying a very pleasant afternoon, but your very clever mate made a most relevant suggestion about my meeting with the three gods. I cannot wait until tomorrow to meet them because they will see me tonight at dinner, and I will lose the element of surprise. If I want to see their response, it must happen today."

"That's less than two hours from now."

"I am well aware of the time constraints, but since you did not want me to meet them before the cruise, it will have to happen right now. You can invite them to my suite. Your mate and sisters want to witness the gods' reactions to me, and they asked me to let them stay. I suggest that you and my sons-in-law join us as well." She chuckled, and as always, the sound made the skin on his arms rise with goosebumps. "I will hold court in my suite, and you all can be my courtiers. The Guardians will be my royal guard."

"I see that you have given it a lot of thought."

His mother laughed. "Two minutes were enough to imagine a grand setting. It comes naturally to me."

"Yes, I know."

"We should also invite Toven. Aru and his teammates will immediately recognize him for who he is, so it would be better for him to attend the meeting as well."

"If Toven suppresses his glow, he could be mistaken for an immortal. He and Orion look practically the same."

Next to him, Orion made a face. "I'm not as perfectly made as my father. The differences are subtle, but they are there, and they are noticeable."

He had a point, but Kian needed to find out if Aru would notice. He'd said that Kian looked more like a god than an immortal, and combined with everything else he'd said, it was clear that not all gods were as perfect as Annani or even Toven.

"You are right. Toven should be there, and therefore Mia. Where are we going to fit everyone in?"

"Amanda and Sari are shoving furniture into the other rooms, or rather directing my Odus where to take what. Their idea is to leave only one armchair in the living room and for everyone else to stand."

"Or kneel!" Amanda yelled. "I don't want anyone looming over our mother."

"We can put the armchair on top of the coffee table and drape it with the bed cover," Syssi suggested. "It will make it look like a real throne."

Kian shook his head. "I will leave the decorating details to you and your army. I need to call Aru."

"Yes, please do. I will await them at six o'clock sharp."

"Yes, Mother."

"Thank you." As she ended the call, Kian put the phone in his pocket and turned to his future brothers-in-law and the Guardians. "Well, you heard the Clan Mother. You will all meet the new gods sooner than you expected."

"I can't wait." David looked at his half-smoked cigar. "I should have saved this for after the meeting."

"I'm glad that we are heading out of the harbor." Anandur rubbed the back of his neck. "We have one more guest who doesn't know about gods and immortals yet, and when she finds out during dinner tonight, she won't be able to escape the ship."

"Who are you talking about?" Dalhu asked.

"Ms. Francesca Canal. Mia's best friend and a potential Dormant."

31

DAGOR

"You look happy." Gabi regarded Dagor with a critical appraisal. "What did you find out on your exploration of the ship?"

Dagor couldn't wipe the smile off his face, but he didn't want to share Frankie with Gabi or with his friends. It was nice to have someone who was just his, even if it was for one night. He had gone on way too many double and triple dates with his teammates.

"I discovered a bar on the top deck, got a drink, and lounged in the sun."

Gabi looked skeptical. "That must have been a very good drink."

"It was. I even took a picture of the bottle to order it for us later, but the bartender was the most interesting part about the top deck bar. It's a very sophisticated robot—a far cry from an Odu, but superior to the simple robots they have on other cruise liners."

The truth was that he had yet to learn about robots serving drinks on other ships. He'd found out about them by searching the internet on his way back to the cabin.

Over on the couch, Negal chuckled. "Some males get excited over meeting an interesting female. Dagor gets excited about meeting an interesting piece of machinery."

"Bob is very exciting." Dagor sat next to Negal on the couch.

"Bob?" Gabi chuckled. "They named him Bob?"

Frankie had reacted similarly to the name, and Dagor wondered what was so funny about it. He'd met many humans named Bob.

"Why do you find the name amusing?" he asked.

Gabi laughed, and her cheeks reddened. "Bob, as a guy's name, is not funny. It's only amusing when it's given to a machine."

"You still didn't explain why."

Letting out a breath, Gabi lifted her eyes to the ceiling. "BOB is also an acronym for a battery-operated boyfriend."

Dagor's eyes widened. "I was not aware that humans had invented such sophisticated lifelike pleasure robots. Where can I get my hands on one?"

Gabi's shoulders started shaking, and a moment later, she was laughing so hard that Dagor and Negal couldn't help but join her even though they didn't understand what was so funny about the question.

When Aru entered the living room and saw the three of them laughing, he arched a brow. "What did I miss?"

It took Gabi several steadying breaths before she was able to talk. "I explained to Dagor what BOB stood for, and he asked me where he could get his hands on one."

Both of Aru's brows shot up. "Why are you interested in a female self-pleasuring device?"

"Gabi said that BOB means a battery-operated boyfriend. If humans have developed advanced robots like that, I would like to reverse engineer one."

"I see." Aru ran a hand over his mouth, and a moment later, his shoulders also started shaking. "Perhaps you should show him," he told Gabi between one snort and the next.

"No way. He can find a picture on the internet."

That was a good suggestion, and Dagor implemented it right away, pulling out his phone and typing his query into the search engine.

"Oh." He frowned as he read the description. "It's a very crude device. I'm surprised that it's so popular among Earth ladies."

Gabi shrugged. "You are welcome to develop a fully functional Bob like your bartender, who could do more than serve drinks."

"Why bother with a BOB? You already have a neural link virtual reality service that can give you a fully immersive experience inside your mind—no robots required."

"Yeah, but who can afford that, and who has time to spend three hours in a studio whenever they get the itch? BOBs are inexpensive toys that are available whenever they are needed." By the end of her explanation, Gabi was as red as a beetroot. "I can't believe that you made me say that." She cast an accusing look at Aru, turned around, walked into their bedroom, and closed the door behind her.

"You've embarrassed your mate," Negal said. "You should apologize."

"It wasn't me." Aru lifted his hands in the air. "It was Dagor."

"What did I say?" Dagor crossed his arms over his chest. "I just wanted to know why she was laughing. How was I supposed to know that it was a sensitive subject?"

Women, whether human or formerly human, were touchy about anything that had to do with sex, yet they pursued it with quite the determination.

Aru's clan phone rang, thankfully ending the Bob episode.

He pulled it out of his pocket. "Hello, Kian. I've noticed that we set sail. I think the customary thing to say is *bon voyage,* right?"

"Yes," the immortals' leader said in his gruff voice. "But I'm not calling to wish you safe travels. My mother informed me that she wants to meet you today at six o'clock sharp. You and your teammates need to be ready five minutes earlier. I'll send someone to escort you to her suite."

Aru swallowed audibly. "How should I dress for the meeting?"

"You are going to a formal dinner straight from there, so dress formally. I hope you and your men have gotten tuxedoes. We are celebrating ten weddings on this cruise."

"We did. Should we bring Gabi with us?"

"Of course. The Clan Mother would love to meet her."

32

FRANKIE

"You lucky girl," Margo squealed in Frankie's ear. "You've been on that cruise ship for what, three hours? And you scored a gorgeous guy already? How did you do it?"

"Luck, I guess. But I feel kind of iffy about it." Frankie thought about opening the doors to her balcony and stepping outside, but she didn't want anyone to overhear her talking about Doug. Instead, she sat on the couch, kicked off her shoes, and tucked her feet under her. "You know about my minimum of three dates rule. I don't do first-date hookups. But this is a cruise, and he's out-of-this-world gorgeous, so I decided to break my own rule, and now I feel guilty and a little scared. I don't know anything about him besides that he is a guest of Tom's partners. Aside from what he'd seen on television, he didn't know anything about Perfect Match. How could he be a good friend of the owners and not know more details about their business?"

"Frankie," Margo interrupted her tirade. "Take a deep breath and think. You are on a ship full of people. If this guy is not to your liking, throw him out, and if he refuses to leave, holler, and someone will help you to get rid of him."

Frankie snorted. "That's what you think. So far, I've seen the guards who checked my paperwork, Mia, Tom, and Doug. I haven't seen anyone else, and unless this place has the best soundproofing ever, I'm the only one on this deck. I feel like I am in *The Twilight Zone*, with elevator music playing in the hallways to entertain the ghosts."

There was a moment of silence before Margo let out a breath. "That is odd. Maybe the ship has great soundproofing. With how reclusive and paranoid Tom's partners are, I wouldn't be surprised if they'd ordered a custom-made interior built to the highest privacy standards."

"That could be." Frankie looked around the beautifully decorated living room of her suite. "The ship is really luxurious. I can't wait for you to join me so I won't be alone in this suite. It has two bedrooms, a living room with a kitchenette and a bar, and it's bigger than my apartment."

"That's lovely, but I'm worried now," Margo said. "If Doug is an ax murderer, no one will even hear you scream."

Frankie grimaced. "Thanks for that visual. Now I'm never calling him to come over." She chuckled. "I'll stay loyal to Bob."

She proceeded to tell Margo about the robotic bartender. As the two of them were having a good laugh about it, the doorbell rang.

"Hold on. Someone rang my doorbell." Frankie pushed her feet into her platform shoes and trotted to the door.

After what Margo had said about no one hearing her scream, Frankie wouldn't open up without checking who was on the other side. Thankfully there was a peephole, only it wasn't installed with short people in mind, and even in her four-inch platform heels, she had to stretch up on her toes. "I swear. This country discriminates against shorties. We need to start an equal rights movement. And unless the person on the other side is as short as I am, a ghost just rang my bell."

"Maybe it's Mia," Margo said.

"Could be, but after you scared me with talk about ax murderers, I'm afraid to open the door."

As a buzzer sounded, Frankie's heart leaped into her throat before she realized it was an intercom and pressed the button. "Yes?"

"It's Mia, and I'm getting old waiting for you to open the door."

The relief made Frankie weak at the knees.

"Sorry. Hold on." She unlocked the door and opened the way for Mia. "Blame Margo. After I told her about how quiet it is here, we figured that the ship had good soundproofing, and if I invited a guy to my suite and he turned out to be a creep, no one would hear me scream."

"Hi, Margo," Mia said loudly as she drove her wheelchair into the room. "How is Cabo?"

"Terrible," Margo said in Frankie's ear.

"Let me activate the speaker so Mia can hear you." She pressed the icon and propped the phone on the table. "Go ahead. Tell us why Cabo is terrible."

"It's not Cabo. It's Lynda and all her weirdo friends. They are all like her. It's amazing how many Karens there are."

Frankie chuckled. "I assume you don't mean they are all actually named Karen."

"Three of her nine friends are called Karen, and the rest just act as if they are, and they are not even middle-aged."

"You know how the saying goes," Mia said. "Show me your friends, and I will tell you who you are, and since I have awesome friends, I must be awesome, too."

"You are." Frankie hugged her. "Margo, you are missing a group hug."

"I know. I can't wait for your ship to get here. I plan to make up a story about a fabulous guy I met who invited me to join him on a cruise. Even Lynda could not be mad about me leaving a day early."

"Speaking of great guys." Mia pinned Frankie with a mock hard stare. "Who's the guy you want to invite to your suite?"

Pretending innocence, Frankie arched a brow. "Who said anything about a guy? It could have been a hypothetical."

"Could have been but wasn't. So, who is he?"

"His name is Doug, and he's Kian's guest."

"Oh." Mia frowned. "I don't know anyone by that name. I wonder who he is."

"Of course, you don't know him. He doesn't work for Perfect Match, and he's a guest. I met him on the top deck when I went for a drink. Oh, did I tell you about the robotic bartender?"

Mia lifted her hand. "Hold that thought. My phone is buzzing." She pulled it out, read the message, and frowned. "I'll have to hear the rest of the story later. I need to accompany Tom to a meeting." She reached for Frankie and gave her a hug. "I'll see you at dinner. You can show me the guy you want to invite later tonight, and I'll tell you if it's a good idea."

33

ANNANI

"I truly feel like a queen now." Annani took Kian's hand even though she did not need his help to climb her makeshift throne.

He chuckled. "Only now? I thought you always felt like a queen or an empress."

Annani laughed. "After all, royalty runs in my blood." She made herself comfortable on the armchair that was standing on top of a coffee table and covered with a brocade bedspread. "You knew that even before the Kra-ell and these gods shed more light on Anumati's politics. I am Ahn's daughter, destined to rule over the gods, and was groomed accordingly." She smiled sadly. "I expected to rule fairly and benevolently, with Khiann by my side to balance my impulsiveness with his rational and calculating mind, but Fate had other plans for us. Our happily-ever-after was cut painfully short."

As she realized that her words had made everyone in the room uncomfortable, Annani squared her shoulders and gave them a bright smile. "Thank you all for preparing this room and building me a makeshift throne."

It was unnecessary, and Annani had agreed only because her daughters had insisted and seemed to have great fun preparing the room for the gods' visit. Annani would have preferred to leave the room as it was and accept the gods sitting on the couch, as she usually did when meeting with her clan members.

Her grandeur came from the inside—the power, the radiance, the regal bearing. She did not need external symbols of power.

Kian waited until she was done arranging the folds of her gown to her liking. "I would appreciate it if you did not mention your royal blood to your guests. They already know that you glow, so they know that you have some royal blood in you, but I don't want them to know that you are the Eternal King's heir. Not yet, anyway." He turned to the assembled company, which mainly consisted of his family and Guardians. "The same goes for you."

Annani regarded her son with a smile. "How am I supposed to become the heart of the resistance if they do not know I exist?"

"Did you change your mind about getting involved?" Kian put his foot on the coffee table and leaned his elbow on his knee. "I was very happy with your prior reluctance to become the resistance's alternative to the Eternal King. I think it was a wise decision. I want to keep your identity a secret for as long as possible. You know what will happen the moment your grandfather learns of your existence. It's not just your life on the line. It's the life of everyone on the planet."

"I know, my darling son." She leaned and cupped his cheek. "I have not decided anything yet. Let us play it by ear, shall we?"

Kian was about to respond when the doorbell rang twice, the signal he'd agreed on with Anandur, announcing that he had the guest gods with him.

Annani waved her hand, and Ogidu walked over to the door. Oshidu and Sari's and Alena's butlers stayed by her side. As a precaution, they had temporarily returned command of their Odus to Annani.

Ogidu opened the door and bowed. "Good evening, masters and mistress. The Clan Mother is awaiting your arrival. Please, come in." He moved aside and bowed again with his arm extended toward her.

"Thank you," she heard one of the gods say, and liked that he was polite toward the Odu.

As the three gods entered the room with a lovely young lady who she assumed was Gabriella, there was an intake of breath, and all four sets of eyes widened in unison. The gods dropped to their knees a split second later and lowered their foreheads to the floor. Following their example, Gabriella did the same, which was quite a feat with her tight evening dress.

"Your Majesty," the gods said in chorus.

Evidently the charade had worked, and her guests were impressed with her makeshift throne. A bit too impressed for the gods, though. Annani had expected the former human to react with awe to a glowing figure of otherworldly beauty. Still, gods should have been more reserved in their show of deference.

A simple bow would have sufficed.

"Please rise. It is permitted to gaze upon my face."

Their leader lifted his head but stayed on his knees, and a few heartbeats later, his companions did the same.

"Your Highness is a miracle," he whispered. "I had no idea." He dropped his forehead to the floor again, and his companions followed his example.

"Oh, enough of that." Annani rose to her feet and took Kian's offered hand to climb down from the coffee table. "Please, get up. I will not smite you with a blast of my power or any other means you fear."

"We do not bow out of fear." Aru lifted his head but kept his eyes downcast. "We revere the legitimate heir to the Eternal King's throne."

34

KIAN

Kian's breath caught in his throat. How did they guess it so quickly? According to his mother, she had inherited much of her father's personality but not his looks. She claimed she looked a lot like her mother.

Motioning for him to stay where he was, Annani approached Aru and put a hand on his shoulder. "How did you know?"

Damn. Kian closed his eyes. She should have laughed it off, denied it, put doubt in their minds. Confirming their suspicions was the last thing she should have done.

The god tilted his head to look at her face and forced a polite smile. "Your Highness is the spitting image of her grandmother, the Eternal King's mate, and the only one whose descendants are considered legitimate heirs."

How could they know whether Annani was Ahn's daughter from his official wife or a concubine?

They were making assumptions, which happened to be accurate. Still, Kian hoped his mother realized she could lie about it if she decided not to get involved and use this as her exit card.

The only one who could attest to Annani's legitimacy was Toven.

Casting a quick look at the god, Kian offered a slight shake of his head. Toven nodded just as inconspicuously, indicating that he understood the wordless communication.

Annani smiled at Aru. "I might be the spitting image of my fraternal grandmother, but that does not necessarily make me a legitimate heir. I could be the daughter of a concubine or a paramour and not my father's official wife."

Annani was so petite that she was at eye level with Aru even though he was on his knees. The Odus and the Guardians were ready to jump in if needed, and so was Kian, but he had a feeling that his mother had things under control, and he was glad she had put doubt in the gods' minds.

Aru's face fell, and his two companions looked even more despondent.

The god took a deep breath. "No one needs to know that. I assume that there are no witnesses left to attest to Your Highness's legitimacy. No one can prove that Your Highness's parents were not officially married when Your Highness was conceived."

Annani laughed. "Please stop referring to me as Your Highness. The cumbersome third-person address is a tongue-twister. You can call me Annani, or Clan Mother if you prefer a formal address."

Aru swallowed. "As you wish, Clan Mother."

Annani motioned for Kian to stand by her side. "Let us put an end to this charade. I want to sit down and do not wish for everyone else to remain standing. Please tell the Odus to bring chairs for everyone and then serve refreshments."

"Yes, Mother." He helped her get back to her chair.

Not wanting the Odus to leave his mother's side even for a moment, he motioned for the Guardians to bring the chairs. As soon as Annani realized what he was doing, she leaned over toward her Odu. "Can you please lift this armchair off the coffee table and put it on the floor?"

As two Odus grabbed the chair on both sides and lowered it to the floor, Annani turned to look at Aru and his companions, who were still on their knees. She took her place again on the chair. "My daughters thought it would look grand to make me a makeshift throne, but I do not need one to feel important." She moved her knees to the side and leaned forward. "To tell you the truth, I have never owned a throne."

A muffled chuckle from behind the gods reminded everyone that they had forgotten Annani's fourth guest.

"Gabriella." Annani waved her hand. "Please rise and approach me."

"Yes, Clan Mother." Gabi pushed to her feet and walked over to Annani's armchair. "I don't know what I'm supposed to say, so I'll go with what I know. It's an honor to meet the mother of this clan of immortals who have done so many wonderful things for humanity."

Annani smiled brightly. "Who told you about that?"

"My brothers and their mates. They visited me and Aru several times, full of stories about how your clan lifted humans from the Dark Ages and taught them what they should strive for as a society. But I don't think they know who you really are, or maybe they do and are not allowed to tell me because I'm with Aru." She cast him a sidelong glance. "Why are you still kneeling?"

"It's improper for me to tower over her Highness."

That got another laugh out of Annani. "That is a really silly custom. Given my height, everyone around me would have to walk on their knees not to tower over me. Please rise and take a seat."

"You are most gracious, Clan Mother." Instead of rising, Aru lowered his head nearly to the floor again.

Watching these gods acting so deferential to his mother eased the knot of stress in Kian's stomach. He hadn't expected any trouble from them, and his precautions were out of an abundance of caution. Still, it was difficult for him to relax when his mother put herself out there.

Regardless, it seemed that the only threat these gods represented was showing Annani too much deference and reverence and inflating her ego to dangerous proportions.

"Don't worry about towering over my mother." Kian chuckled. "If she can look down her nose at me even though I'm nearly a foot and a half taller than her, she can do the same to you."

The Guardians were still bringing chairs, but there were already enough seats for the gods and Gabi to take, and all the ladies were seated.

Looking as if he was chewing on lemons, Aru nodded and pushed up, but he didn't straighten to his full height. Instead, he backed into a chair so he wouldn't have to stand or turn his back on Annani.

35

DAGOR

Dagor pushed to his feet with trembling knees. Discovering that an heir survived was a shock he was still reeling from, but it wasn't the only one he'd experienced upon entering her Highness's chambers.

Four Odus guarded the goddess, two on each side, and none of them was Kian's butler.

How many Odus did the clan have, and did they know how incredibly valuable these cyborgs were?

These Odus had been built before the manufacturing process moved to the solid-state model that was impervious to reverse engineering. The Odus had been only one of the reasons for the change. The big conglomerates did not want their technology stolen by small operators in the colonies, where it was more difficult to ensure compliance with Anumati's laws.

The Odus guarding the heir were relics, but some of their components were no doubt solid state as well. Still, the rest might lend itself to reverse engineering.

Dagor would have loved to take a look, but the truth was that without formal qualifications in engineering, he didn't know enough to do so safely.

Once everyone was seated and the Odus had served drinks and other refreshments, the heir reclined in her armchair and regarded Aru with a kind look. "Tell me about my grandmother and in what way I resemble her."

"With pleasure." Aru put his water bottle on the floor beside his chair. "I wish I had a picture to show you. You have her face, down to the most minute details, but her hair isn't red, and she's much taller."

Kian's wife lifted a hand to her chest. "Is her hair silvery?" she asked.

"It is." Aru darted his gaze around until it landed on the tall brunette Dagor had taken notice of before. She also bore some resemblance to the heir. "The Eternal Queen is about your height, and you also have some of her features. You must be her Highness's daughter."

Turning her head toward the brunette, the goddess smiled fondly. "This is my daughter, Amanda. The charming blond lady is my daughter Alena, and the auburn-haired one is my daughter Sari. She is the regent of the clan's European branch."

As the heir continued introducing her family, her son's eyes shot daggers at her, and Dagor could not blame him. The goddess was too friendly and too trusting. If she ever set foot on Anumati, she would be eaten alive by its political sharks, which would save the king the trouble of having her murdered.

It would take many years of training before she was a suitable candidate for the throne who could swim with the sharks on Anumati, but then the resistance was in no rush.

The problem would be getting someone knowledgeable in Anumati's complicated web of politics to Earth to train the inexperienced heir.

There was an heir to the throne, though, and that was the best news the resistance could have hoped for.

Aru would have to relay it somehow to the resistance's leaders without arousing the suspicion of those listening to the patrol ship's communications.

"Dagor." The heir turned to him. "Tell me about yourself and why you joined the resistance."

He'd zoned out momentarily and must have missed part of what had been said. Darting a look at Aru, he got a nod from his leader.

"I was unhappy with the way the elite perpetuated its status. We are supposed to be a democracy, and every citizen of Anumati is supposed to have equal opportunity. Still, nothing could be further from the truth. The elite families, those with royal blood in them, are the only ones who can afford the lucrative learning institutions that prepare students for the entry exams to higher education in certain fields. I wanted to study engineering, but even if I could pass the exams, which is practically impossible without having access to prior tests, I could not have afforded the tuition. This is a broken system, and it has to go, but the king will not do anything about it because he needs the support of those elite families to stay in power."

The heir regarded him with compassion and understanding in her eyes. "My uncle Ekin was a great engineer, but without the proper tools and materials, he could not build the mechanical wonders he must have known about and was forbidden to share. I did not know about Anumati until we rescued the Kra-ell, and Jade told us where we came from. The exiled gods did not tell their children they came from somewhere else in the universe. Growing up, I believed that gods had always existed on Earth, just like humans had. When I got older and met my beloved betrothed, he told me what his father had told him in secret, but even my Khiann did not know much." She smiled sadly. "I hope the three of you know your history well and can educate me about my home planet."

36

ARU

Aru couldn't stop staring at the miracle before him. An heir to the Eternal King. The resemblance to her grandmother was uncanny, with the most significant difference being their hair color.

It suddenly dawned on him that Kian's wife knew somehow that the Eternal Queen had silver hair, and the only way she could have known that was via a vision. It wasn't the loss of color that humans experienced as they aged, but instead was her family's trademark. Some even called them the silver-haired nobles.

But since there was no way Syssi could have seen a picture of the queen, she must have seen her in a vision, and that worried him, although a lot less than it had before. The secret of his telepathic communication with his sister would not stay a secret for long. Soon, he would have to tell her Highness Princess Annani that he could communicate with Anumati, and relay messages between her and her grandmother through his sister and the Supreme.

"There is one more thing that I forgot to mention." The princess looked at her son. "I don't see any reason to hide it." She smiled at the one called Toven and motioned for him to come forward. "My cousin, Toven, is the son of my favorite and only uncle, and he's a full-blooded god, not the immortal he was pretending to be."

As the god started glowing, Aru and his companions bowed their heads to the noble.

"Did I fool you?" Toven asked with a smile.

"Yes," Aru admitted. "I suspected Kian of being a god, but he is only a demigod, so I assumed that Your Highness was also a descendant."

Aru was trying to decide whether he should call Toven 'Your Highness.' Toven's father had also been the Eternal King's son, but not from the Queen. He was the son of a concubine, and therefore not in line to the throne, and the same was true of Toven.

"Please, call me Toven. I cringe at being addressed as Your Highness."

"Very well." Aru inclined his head. "It is a pleasure to meet you, Toven, son of Ekin."

Next to Princess Annani, Kian groaned. "Kalugal will never forgive us for not including him in this meeting."

"I've heard that name before," Aru said. "How is he related to you?"

The princess looked as if she wanted to say something, but a glare from her son stopped her.

"Kalugal is the grandson of my brother," Toven said. "Who is no longer with us. Thankfully."

"Oh, that's right." Aru nodded. "Now I remember. He's Navuh's son who crossed over to join forces with the clan."

"That's right," Kian said. "Except for the fact that Kalugal fled his father's control many decades before he joined us. He did so to escape tyranny and potentially a threat to his life."

"Why did he fear for his life from his own father?" Aru asked. "Was he also an heir with aspirations to the throne?"

"Kalugal was never interested in taking over from his father, but he wasn't as easy to control as some of his other brothers, and therefore Navuh considered him a threat."

Aru sensed that Kian was telling him a slightly altered version of the real story, mainly because the princess averted her gaze and pretended to be preoccupied with the folds of her silk gown.

She was not a good liar and would need extensive coaching to overcome that shortcoming. It was also possible that she was uncomfortable hiding things from him and was doing so only because of her son.

Aru could use that to his advantage to determine what Kian was adamant about keeping from him. The princess wanted to learn about Anumati, which could provide an excellent excuse for him to spend time with her without Kian hovering over her and censoring what she could and couldn't say.

It wasn't right for the son to censor his mother even if he was her most trusted advisor. Still, these immortals needed to learn the proper etiquette for royalty.

For now, though, Aru should focus on other issues, and the one that concerned him the most was Syssi's visions.

"Forgive me for changing the topic of conversation, but I have to ask." He looked at Syssi. "Did you see the queen in a vision? Is that how you knew that she had silver hair?"

Syssi nodded. "I had a vision of a goddess so luminous that I couldn't discern her features. I could only tell that she was tall and slim and had long, silver hair. She also wore a silver gown, if that's helpful."

"That sounds like our Queen. I've never had the privilege of meeting her in person or even seeing her from afar, but we've all seen her portrait as well as her televised addresses to the citizens of Anumati, and footage of her attending charity events."

"Is she a nice person?" Syssi asked.

He chuckled. "No one can survive Anumati's politics for as long as our Queen has done and be nice. Behind her gentle façade, she is as dangerous as the king."

Luckily, she was on the rebellion's side, or they would have no chance of ever succeeding, but that was a secret he couldn't reveal yet. In fact, he'd thought he would never have to reveal it. One day, when the resistance won, the queen would admit her part in toppling her husband's rule.

Or not.

Aru wasn't privy to her plans. He was just one more pawn in her very long game.

37

FRANKIE

The evening dress Frankie had gotten from her cousin Claudia was sapphire blue. The bodice clung tightly to her form, emphasizing her curves. Claudia was a little skinnier and a little taller, so it was a bit too tight and a bit too long, but other than that, it was great.

The neckline was a delicate scoop, showing her collarbone but covering her breasts and drawing attention to her exposed shoulders, which were one of her better features. The ballet lessons she had taken as a kid in the community center had yet to make her a great ballerina. Still, they had done wonders for her posture and deportment.

From the hips down, the skirt flared and was longer in the back than in the front. The dress made a statement and was not demure despite the conservative neckline and modest hemline.

The matching necklace and earrings were also Claudia's, and she'd boasted of getting both items for under thirty bucks in a discount store that Frankie had been planning to check out after the cruise. Since she didn't need to pay rent and had even gotten her deposit back, she had cash to buy a few new pieces of fake jewelry.

Would anyone notice that it wasn't real?

Eh, who cared. She looked good. Frankie smiled at her reflection in the mirror. "Doug is going to like."

As her doorbell rang, she walked over to the intercom. She pressed the button to activate the camera mounted above her door, which she'd discovered after Mia's previous visit.

It was her bestie again, but this time, she had her fiancé with her, and they both looked like a million bucks even when looking at them on the small screen.

Frankie opened the door. "You two look fancy."

"So do you." Mia smiled. "This dress is gorgeous. Where did you get it?"

"From one of my many cousins." She glanced at the time displayed on the screen. "It's still a bit early to head to the dining hall. Do you want to come in for a drink?"

"Sure." Tom rubbed the back of his neck. "We need to tell you a few things before we head out."

Tom looked uncomfortable, and Mia looked excited.

Was she pregnant? Was that what they needed to tell her?

"Then come in." Frankie walked over to the bar. "What will it be?"

"Water for me," Mia said. "I'm only allowing myself one drink daily, and I'm saving that for the welcome dinner."

The pregnancy hypothesis was growing stronger.

"I'll have some of that whiskey." Tom pointed at one of the bottles. "We don't have much time, so I'll try to make it short, which makes it very difficult."

Maybe Mia wasn't pregnant after all.

"I've got this." Her friend drove her chair to the bar. "Do you remember the Perfect Match adventure Tom and I shared?"

"Yeah. What about it?"

"What if some of it was real?"

Frankie snorted. "Of course, some of it was real. You two fell in love."

"I'm not talking about that. Can you believe that gods and immortals and people with all kinds of paranormal talents exist in the real world—our world?"

Frankie handed Mia a glass of water and Tom his whiskey. "I believe that aliens are real, and I also believe that they visit from time to time. As for people with paranormal talents, not so much." She grimaced. "My aunt Susanna claims to get messages from beyond, but so far she hasn't learned anything useful, so I doubt she does. She doesn't charge for it, so she's not a crook, but most of the others you see on television are fakes who do party tricks for money. What are you trying to say?"

Her friend took a deep breath. "I'm immortal. I wasn't before, but I always had the genes in me. They just needed someone to activate them, and Tom did that. That's how my heart was miraculously healed, and I started re-growing my amputated legs. It wasn't thanks to the fancy Swiss clinic or the experimental treatments I told you about." She smiled sheepishly. "I'm sorry about lying to you, but I'm sure you can understand why I couldn't tell you the truth."

Frankie gaped at her friend, waiting for Mia to tell her that it was an idea for a story she was writing. She'd wanted to see Frankie's reaction so she could describe it better. Or it was a stupid prank someone had put her up to.

Mia was too nice to pull something like that.

A long moment passed, and no one laughed or shouted 'Smile, you're on candid camera' or something to that effect. Frankie shifted her eyes to Tom. "Are you immortal?"

He made a face that was a mix between a grimace and a wince. "Yes, but I'm more than that." He flicked his fingers, and his skin started glowing. "I'm a member of a species of people who call themselves gods, and the reason I'm telling you all this now is to prepare you for what and who you are about to see during the welcome dinner. I don't want you to get alarmed when you see a beautiful, glowing goddess give the welcome speech."

Frankie looked down at the gin and tonic she'd made for herself. It couldn't be drugged because she hadn't drunk from it yet. She looked up, but Tom's skin was still luminous. Every part that wasn't covered by clothing was emitting a soft glow.

"It gets better," Mia said. "We think that you are also a dormant carrier of godly genes and can be turned immortal, and the same goes for Margo." She grinned. "We can be besties forever, for real."

Frankie felt dizzy. "I knew that I was in *The Twilight Zone*."

38

TOVEN

As Frankie started to fall, Toven zipped around the counter and caught her before she could hit the floor. "Is your friend prone to fainting?"

"Not that I know of. Maybe she's wearing a compression garment under that dress. It looks awfully tight."

He frowned. "I didn't know ladies still wore corsets. That silly fashion used to be a major reason for fainting." Carrying Frankie to the couch, he laid her down gently.

"Compression garments are not as bad as the corsets of yesteryear, and they shouldn't restrict breathing, but Frankie is not used to them. She probably put one on only because of the dress."

"What do we do now?" Toven looked at the woman and listened to her breathing and heartbeat. Both sounded fine, but he wasn't a doctor. "Do we call Bridget?"

"Let's give Frankie a moment." Mia parked her chair parallel to the couch and leaned over to brush her fingers over her friend's cheek. "Frankie, sweetheart. Can you look at me?"

The girl's false lashes fluttered, and then she opened her eyes. "What happened?" She lifted a hand to her forehead.

"You fainted. Is something wrong with you that you are not telling me about?"

Frankie pursed her lips. "I've never fainted before. But then I've never had my friend tell me crazy stories about gods and immortals and scare the bejesus out of me."

"Why were you scared?" Mia frowned. "Do you find me or Tom frightening?"

Frankie glanced at him and promptly closed her eyes. "Can I go back to sleep and wake up again, and you'll tell me that none of this is true?"

He'd forgotten to suppress his glow, and his skin was still luminous.

Mia sighed. "You don't have to fall asleep for Tom to make you forget this conversation ever happened. But there is a reason we dumped all of this on you now instead of doing it gradually."

Frankie opened her eyes and turned her head toward Mia. "And the reason is?"

Mia took Toven's hand. "Tom is not the only glowing god attending the welcome dinner tonight, and we didn't want you to freak out when you saw the Clan Mother enter the dining hall in all of her luminous glory. Besides, most people on this cruise are immortal and are here to celebrate several weddings. They don't want to have to be mindful of the one human who doesn't know about them and hide who they are."

"They don't all glow, though, right? Otherwise, you would be glowing too."

That was an astute observation, which Toven hoped meant that Frankie was over her initial shock.

As the girl licked her lips, Mia turned to him. "Can you bring a bottle of water for Frankie?"

Toven was glad to have something to do instead of standing beside the couch with his hands in his pockets.

"So, your boyfriend is a god?" Frankie whispered, unaware of his exceptional hearing.

"He is, and he can hear you, no matter how quietly you whisper. That's one of the perks of being a god or an immortal. Enhanced hearing, eyesight, physical strength, speed, stamina, and most importantly, the ability to heal almost anything, including re-growing amputated limbs."

Toven uncapped one of the bottles of water he'd brought and handed it to Frankie. He gave the other to Mia. "By the way, most people on board call me Toven. I go by Tom and Toven, so you can keep calling me Tom."

"Okay." Frankie lowered her feet to the floor and sat up. "I must have drunk a bit too much today."

"How much did you have?" Mia asked.

"Actually, not that much. Earlier, I had two mojitos at the bar, and I made myself one gin and tonic before you came and another one after, but I didn't even take a sip from it yet."

Mia leaned closer to her friend. "Are you wearing Spanx?"

"No." Frankie glowered at Mia. "That's not why I fainted, and if Tom, aka Toven, can hear your whispers, why do you bother?"

"Habit, I guess." Mia smoothed her hand over her short hair. "I was human most of my life and an immortal for about half a year. It takes time to get used to all the peculiarities of that world."

Mia hadn't complained to him about it. Still, he could imagine that the transition was about more than the physical changes and was more challenging than Mia made it seem.

"You will have to save the rest of your questions for later," he said. "We should get moving if we don't want to be late for dinner."

Frankie looked panicked. "Will I be the only human there?"

"No." Mia smiled. "All the serving staff are human, and several clan members are either too young to transition or can't for other reasons." When Frankie still looked like a deer caught in the headlights, Mia put a hand on her knee. "Gods, immortals, and humans are all people. The same things make them happy or sad, make them laugh or cry. As long as you remember that, you'll be fine."

As Frankie shifted her gaze to Toven, he nodded. "I put my pants on one leg at a time like everyone else. You've known me a long time yet never noticed that I was different."

A snort escaped Frankie's mouth. "Oh, I noticed, but it never occurred to me that you didn't just look like a god and talk like a king, but that you were indeed a god, and probably at some point in the past also a king."

39

KIAN

After the gods left with Gabi, Toven departed with Mia, and the Guardians returned to their stations; the Odus restored Annani's living room to its previous condition.

Before dinner, there wasn't much time left to reflect on the meeting, but Kian wanted to hear her impression of the three gods.

Usually, his mother was a better judge of character than he was.

"So, what do you think?" He sat on the armchair facing the couch where his mother sat down with Amanda on one side and Sari on the other.

Syssi joined him in the large armchair, sitting in his lap and leaning against his chest.

"To see them drop to their knees and hear them call me Your Highness was startling." Annani's lips lifted in a sly smile. "It was quite refreshing to garner such reverence. Perhaps you all should start calling me Your Majesty."

"I'm serious, Mother. You wanted to see their unguarded response, which was a success. They couldn't have faked their reaction."

Syssi adjusted her position in his lap to accommodate the floor-length gown she was wearing. "We should get Tim to draw a portrait of the queen from their descriptions. I'm curious to see her face without the glow masking her features."

"That's not a bad idea," Amanda said. "We should have a portrait of the Eternal King as well." She smiled at Kian. "We can hang it in the room dedicated to Navuh and his adopted sons. One more evildoer to add to the wall of adversaries bent on our destruction."

"I agree." Kian smoothed his hand over Syssi's bare arm, feeling the goosebumps rise at his touch. "Tim should definitely draw their portraits so we know what they look like." He smiled. "Given the guy's uncanny talent, there is a slight chance that Tim is a Dormant, but given the antipathy most feel toward him, there's certainly no affinity."

"You should give him a chance," his mother said. "I remember him as an entertaining individual. Perhaps he has a personality disorder, and Vanessa can help him become friendlier."

"His friendliness or lack thereof is not the problem." Kian kept running his hand up and down Syssi's arm. "But I don't want to waste time talking about him. I want your impression of the gods before it can fade."

His mother nodded. "I did not sense deceit from any of them. Aru is more than he claims to be, though. Once he was over the initial shock of seeing me and recognizing me for who I was, I caught a calculating look in his eyes. He was planning something."

"Of course, he was," Alena said. "He realized that he found the one person in the galaxy pivotal to the resistance's success, and he needed to find a way to communicate that to the leaders without the information of your existence falling into the wrong hands."

Aru claimed to have a way to communicate secretly with someone in the resistance, and after he and his teammates had been released from the obligation to return to the patrol ship when it passed over Earth on its way to Anumati, Kian no longer doubted that.

The god must have contacted someone and told them about wishing to stay on Earth to be with his fated mate. Given that his request had been granted almost immediately, Aru must be very well connected.

"Aru is scared of me," Syssi said. "It was the second time that mentioning my visions elicited a fearful reaction from him. He is afraid I'll see something that he's hiding."

Amanda waved a hand. "Then find out what it is."

Syssi shifted to look at her. "You know that's not how it works. I ask for one thing and get another that may or may not be related to what I asked for."

Amanda didn't look impressed with Syssi's self-deprecating comment. "So, sometimes it works, and other times it doesn't. You wanted to find David's missing parents, and you did." Amanda lifted one finger. "You wanted to find out whether the new signals were coming from a friend or foe, and you saw the gods." Amanda lifted two fingers. "And when you asked about the gods again, you saw the queen. We still don't know what your last vision was about, but we will find out soon, just as we discovered the identity of the first goddess you saw."

Syssi let out a breath. "So, what are you saying, that I should court more visions?"

His mother and sisters all nodded.

"Oh wow, talk about pressure." Syssi chuckled nervously. "I can't do that every day. It takes too much out of me."

"Do only what you are comfortable with," Alena said. "But do it as often as you can without letting yourself get exhausted. Aside from being incredibly fertile for an immortal, I don't have any paranormal talents. However, I believe the more you practice inducing visions, the easier they will come, and they will also be clearer."

Then, there was Allegra's contribution that Kian didn't know how to feel about. Their daughter was asleep in her crib and had still managed to enhance Syssi's vision. What would happen when she was older and could do more?

40

DAGOR

Dagor ran a comb through his hair, put it in his tuxedo breast pocket, and straightened the lapels.

It was his first time wearing a formal outfit. It was very different from the latest fashion in formal wear on Anumati and much more stifling.

"You look dashing." Negal walked past him, opened the door, and exited their cabin. "Coming?"

"Aren't we waiting for Aru and Gabi?"

Negal cast a glance at the closed door to their room. "Nah. Let's go."

They had stopped by their cabin at Gabi's request to freshen up, and she knew they didn't have much time.

Now that Dagor knew who would deliver the welcoming speech, he was adamant about being there on time. One didn't offend nobility and get away with it without repercussions. The princess might seem kind, but he didn't want to put it to the test.

"I'll remind them to hurry up." Dagor walked over and knocked.

The soundproofing was excellent, so he couldn't hear what was happening inside the room, but his knock would be heard.

The door opened a crack. "Gabi needs another minute. You and Negal go ahead, and we will catch up."

"Don't be late. We don't want to offend the princess."

"We will be there on time." Aru closed the door.

"They are going to be late," Dagor murmured as he walked out the front door of their cabin. "You know what the consequences of such blatant disrespect would be on Anumati. I just hope that Princess Annani is more merciful."

Negal shrugged. "The heir seems much less strict than her grandmother."

Dagor nodded. "Do you think that Aru knew and didn't tell us?"

"Aru was just as stunned as we were. Kian does not look like his mother, so none of us could have known. The son must have taken after his father."

Dagor lifted a brow. "His human father? I doubt he was that handsome."

"He might not have been as good-looking as his son, but the godly genetics improved what was there." Negal pressed the button for the elevator.

The heir's children were nearly as beautiful as gods and goddesses, but not entirely, and the other immortals in the room were even less so. The more human blood they had, the less perfect they were.

The princess was incredibly fertile for a goddess, but perhaps the humanity of her partners had something to do with that. One thing was for sure, though. Her grandmother would not be happy when she found out about her hybrid great-grandchildren.

As the elevator doors opened, the cabin wasn't empty, and Dagor smiled at the group of immortals who were regarding him and Negal with puzzled expressions.

"Hi," he said with a smile. "I'm Dagor, and this is Negal."

"You are the new gods," one of the females said. "Nice to meet you. My name is Evelin, and this is Leah."

The introductions continued until the elevator doors opened on the dining hall's deck. Still, Dagor doubted he would remember any of their names.

He'd been too busy examining their faces and comparing their imperfections to the flawless faces of gods.

Why was he bothering, though?

Everyone on Anumati was physically perfect, but some were just more stunning than others, especially those with royal blood who were luminescent. Still, beauty and physical perfection weren't important to him. He was more interested in character and brains, another reason he was part of the resistance.

As they entered the dining hall, Dagor scanned the place for the human girl he had met earlier on the top deck, but she wasn't there, and he wondered whether she had lied about being a guest and not a staff member. Why would the immortals invite a human girl to their clan's celebrations?

Ten weddings were planned for the upcoming ten days, with the first two being of the heir's daughters. Alena, the oldest, was pregnant and marrying her mate, a demigod like her. Amanda, the Clan Mother's youngest child, was getting married the following day to a hulking immortal who wasn't nearly as good-looking as the others in the room had been, but he looked formidable.

"Welcome." A young human smiled at them. "What are your names?"

"I'm Negal, and this is Dagor."

"Excellent." She tapped on her tablet. "You are seated at table three."

"Thank you, miss." Negal dipped his head.

"The girl was human," Dagor said. "You don't need to bow to her."

"It's a habit." Negal scanned the tables. "I always dip my head to a lady."

Dagor chuckled. "You forget that I've been spending every moment of the day with you while we were mingling with humans. You didn't bow to any of them."

"It was easy to remember not to do that when humans were the only people we interacted with. Here, it's more challenging and better to err on the side of politeness. Don't you think?"

"The immortal females don't expect you to bow to them either. You only need to bow to the heir and the god named Toven."

Dagor spotted table number three and was glad no one else was sitting there. But given that there were six chairs and only four in their party, they would be sharing the table with two other immortals.

"Who do you think is going to sit with us?" Negal asked.

"If we are lucky, no one." Dagor turned to look at the entrance to the dining hall, where the human girl was still standing with her tablet and welcoming the guests.

People were trickling in slowly, but Aru and Gabi were still a no-show, and there were only a few minutes left before the doors closed, provided that these immortals were punctual.

Given how no one was in a rush, though, it didn't seem like they expected the head of their clan to start the festivities right on time.

Glancing at the doorway, Dagor's eyes nearly popped out of their sockets.

Toven, his wheelchair-bound immortal mate, and Frankie arrived together. They were waiting for the girl to tell them their table number.

What was Frankie doing with the royal?

Perhaps she was a personal servant to the mate?

That wasn't likely, given how she was dressed. The blue dress was a show-stopper, especially the way it accentuated Frankie's every curve.

She looked stunning. *For a human,* Dagor reminded himself.

He planned on spending an enjoyable night or two with her, but he wasn't stupid enough to get attached to a human.

41

FRANKIE

Frankie walked in a daze, keeping her hand on Mia's wheelchair for balance.

Her best friend was mated to a god. Mated, not married, which was supposedly stronger than marriage, but some of these immortals were getting officially married on this cruise for the fun of it.

Mia had told her a few more things on the way to the dining hall. Still, Frankie's ability to process the bizarre was apparently limited, and she didn't want to faint again.

Her life so far clearly hadn't been eventful enough because she'd never heard anything that had caused her to faint before.

Well, that wasn't entirely true. When Mia's heart had given out, and the doctors had to amputate her legs, Frankie had felt like shattering into pieces, but somehow, she hadn't.

The helplessness had been overwhelming, but at least she could be there for her friend and try to support her as best she could.

She could have been more resilient back then. Perhaps her ability to absorb things had been better.

"You are seated at table seven," the girl with the tablet said. "Enjoy your evening."

Mia lifted her eyes to her. "Are you okay?"

"Yeah, I'm fine. I'll just hang on to your chair if you don't mind."

Mia nodded. "I'll go slow."

It was funny that the one with the healthy legs was relying on the one in the wheelchair to lead her. The good news was that Mia wouldn't need the chair for much longer. Her feet would take another month or two to form, and she would start walking again.

Talk about miracles.

As they made their way to the table, Frankie felt as if everyone was watching her and wondering what the lone human was doing in their midst.

Wait, was Doug an immortal?

Of course, he was. He probably was one of the immortals from Scotland, which was why Mia didn't know him. He'd told her he was from Hungary, but that might have been a lie.

Why Hungary, though?

It was such a random country to choose.

"Good evening." A beautiful brunette she remembered meeting at Mia's old house smiled at her. "Do you remember me? I'm Geraldine. My daughter Cassandra and I met with you several months ago." She smiled sheepishly. "But we are not Toven's cousins. I'm Toven's daughter, and Cassandra is his granddaughter." She turned to the handsome man sitting next to her. "This is my mate, Shai."

"Nice to meet you again." Frankie sat in the chair Toven had pulled out for her.

She wanted to shake her head but stifled the impulse, plastering an amiable smile on her face instead.

A god had pulled out a chair for her. His daughter looked like his sister or cousin, and her daughter looked older than her mother.

It would take time to get used to the idea of immortals and gods. She had to remind herself of what Mia and Toven had told her. They were just people; the same things made them happy or sad.

Well, they weren't really gods, right? They were just aliens who lived forever and did what?

Mia hadn't had enough time to tell her. Still, she and Toven had promised to continue their introduction to the alternative world after the welcome dinner.

"Cassandra is sitting over there with my other daughter, Darlene," Geraldine continued with the introductions. "Darlene is mated to Eric, who is Gilbert and Gabi's brother, and they are sitting at the next table over. It's difficult to plan seating arrangements when everyone is related in one way or another." She continued prattling until a hush fell over the rest of the crowd, and everyone turned toward the entrance.

A procession entered, with a tiny glowing figure in the center and four couples escorting her.

The goddess was just as magnificent as Toven and Mia had described, with her luminescence and ethereal beauty clearly otherworldly. The Clan Mother was supposedly ancient, but she looked so deceptively young that it was freaky.

Frankie's eyes were still glued to the goddess when six butlers entered behind the procession. They were dressed in full butler regalia, and two of them were pushing strollers with babies inside of them.

The curious thing was that the butlers looked like sextuplets, nearly identical, but upon closer inspection, she could see the slight differences between them.

The goddess continued to a small podium erected toward the far end of the room, but in the center so everyone could see her, and no one had to stare at her back.

For a moment, Frankie wondered whether the goddess was hiding wings, but unless they were the magical type that disappeared when not in use, neither Tom nor the Clan Mother could fly.

Toven, she reminded herself. He used Tom when dealing with humans.

"Good evening." The goddess lifted her luminous bare arms. "I am overjoyed to have you all here with me. The last time we were all gathered was for Kian and Syssi's wedding, but not everyone was present. We also had a big show of people for Nathalie and Andrew's wedding in the castle, but this time, we will celebrate ten weddings in ten days with nearly all of the clan. The first wedding will be Alena and Orion's, followed by Amanda and Dalhu's." She turned to look at the table where the couples who had escorted her to the dining hall were seated. "We have all been waiting for these two to get married, and they are finally ready."

As everyone clapped and cheered, the goddess smiled fondly at her people. "You've all been given the itinerary of the ten weddings and other events we've organized for this first-ever clan cruise. The itinerary can also be found on the clan's bulletin board, which you can find on your cabin's television or your phones and other devices."

Frankie glanced at the fancy folded page beside her plate, which she'd assumed was the menu. She would look at it later. Right now, she didn't dare to look away from the goddess.

"While we are all gathered here tonight," the Clan Mother continued, "I would like to take this opportunity to introduce to you our distinguished guests." She turned toward one of the tables. "Please come forward and introduce yourselves."

As three guests rose to their feet and approached the podium, they bowed low to the goddess.

"It is my pleasure to introduce three gods from our home planet to you." She motioned for them to turn around and face the crowd.

Frankie's heart flipped in her chest. Was that Doug?

He looked so different in a tux, and he didn't glow like the Clan Mother or Toven, but the goddess had introduced him as a god.

"He said he was a god," she murmured. "I thought he was teasing." As the same dizzy feeling from before washed over her again, she tried to fight it, but it was no use, and as darkness consumed her, she felt herself falling.

42

DAGOR

Something was wrong with Frankie. Dagor saw her sliding from her chair, and Toven catching her before she could hit the floor.

Turning around, Dagor hastily bowed to the goddess. "My apologies, Your Highness, but I need to check on that human."

"Go." She dismissed him with a nod toward Frankie.

He sprinted to the god holding Frankie in his arms.

"What happened to her?"

"You," Toven's mate accused. "You call yourself Doug, am I right?"

He nodded.

"She has just discovered that you are a god."

Dagor extended his arms. "I'll take her back to her suite and explain."

Toven shook his head. "What is your connection to Frankie?"

"None," his mate said. "He met her earlier at the bar, and they shared a few drinks. We should take her back to her cabin."

Toven looked conflicted. "You need to eat, Mia. Bridget was very clear about the importance of you getting enough nutrition."

"You didn't eat either," Mia said. "And neither did Frankie, which is probably why she keeps fainting. We can ask for food to be sent to her suite."

Dagor was ready to pry Frankie out of Toven's arms, but as he became aware of the power radiating behind him, he turned around and quickly bowed. "I apologize, Clan Mother. I offered to take Frankie to her cabin, but Toven doesn't trust me with her."

The heir looked at Frankie with concern in her eyes. "What is wrong with the girl?"

"Let me take a look at her." A redheaded female with an authoritative voice approached them.

"Thank you, Bridget," Toven said.

He hadn't addressed her as 'doctor,' and she wasn't wearing a doctor's coat, but it was evident that she was a physician.

Bridget checked Frankie's pulse and lifted her eyelids one at a time. "She might be hypoglycemic."

"What does that mean?" Dagor asked.

"Low blood sugar." The doctor turned to Toven's mate. "Do you know if she suffers from the condition?"

Dagor still did not know what low blood sugar meant. His knowledge of human physiology was less than elementary.

"Not as far as I know," Mia said.

"What's happening?" Frankie murmured.

Dagor released a relieved breath. She was talking, so she wasn't dying.

"You fainted again." Toven smiled at her reassuringly. "We are taking you back to your cabin, and we will have food delivered. The doctor thinks you have low blood sugar."

"I said that I suspect it," the doctor said. "Further tests are needed. Tomorrow morning, I want to see her at the clinic." She turned back to Frankie. "Please call me when you are ready."

"I will."

"Can I at least come with you?" Dagor pleaded.

Toven's mate looked at him with compassion in her eyes. "Of course. I'll have food delivered for you as well."

"Thank you." He bowed to her.

She might be just an immortal, but she was mated to a royal, so perhaps she deserved the same courtesy as the other royals.

When the four of them reached Frankie's cabin, Dagor noted the number. Once Toven and Mia left for the night, he would return to ensure that Frankie was okay.

Humans were so fragile, and she was alone in the suite. She needed someone to take care of her.

As Toven laid Frankie down on the couch, his mate parked her wheelchair, blocking her from Dagor's view.

"Frankie, sweetheart, you should take off this dress. It might be the culprit behind your fainting spells."

"Yeah, that's a good idea. But it's such a damn shame. I wanted Doug to see me in it. I mean Dagor."

"I did." He walked over and crouched next to the wheelchair. "You look spectacular, but then you looked just as good this morning."

A bright smile illuminated her unnaturally pale face. "You weren't kidding when you said you were a god."

"I'm afraid not." He smiled apologetically. "Once you get to know me better, you'll realize I don't have much of a sense of humor."

"That's okay. I have enough for the both of us."

Frankie's eyelids fluttered closed, but given that her lips were still curved in a small smile, he assumed she hadn't fainted again.

As Toven's mate moved her chair, giving Dagor more room next to the couch, he scooted closer to Frankie and took her hand. "Have you eaten anything other than the bar snacks today?"

She shook her head. "I was too nervous."

"That's understandable. You were about to dine with gods and immortals. I don't know why Toven invited you into their world. Still, it must be overwhelming for you to suddenly discover that humans are not the only intelligent species on this planet." He cast an accusing look at Toven. "Why did you invite her to the cruise without preparing her?"

"We planned to do it as soon as the ship sailed, but we got delayed, and we had to rush it."

"I didn't know," Frankie murmured. "I mean, I didn't know about any of it when I talked to you earlier. Mia and Toven came to my cabin just before dinner and told me the highlights so I wouldn't freak out when I saw a glowing goddess, but I freaked out anyway. I fainted when they told me and then again when I saw you."

So, Mia was right, and he had been the reason Frankie had fainted.

"I'm so sorry. I didn't mean to scare you."

43

FRANKIE

"You didn't scare me." Frankie lifted her hand and cupped Dagor's cheek.

He was warm to the touch, and other than the perfect symmetry of his face, the bright blue shade of his eyes, and the absolute smoothness of his skin, he didn't look alien.

He could have been a human with excellent genetics or some corrective plastic surgery, colored contact lenses, and an excellent skin routine.

But what moved her most of all was the concern in his eyes.

They had spent no more than an hour chatting at the Lido bar, and the attraction was there in force, but there was a difference between wanting to bed a woman and caring about her, and for some reason, Dagor seemed to care.

"You fainted." He leaned into her hand for a moment.

"It was just too much to process, and this dress is too tight."

"Do you need me to help you get to the bedroom so you can change?"

She chuckled. "Are you that desperate to see me naked?"

"Yes, but I promise not to look."

"People," Mia said, "did you forget that you are not alone?"

Frankie smiled. "Yes, I did, but can you blame me? Did you see Dagor's eyes? They are hypnotic."

Frankie had a reputation for being overly direct, though she usually wasn't as open with men she'd just met. But Dagor was a god, and he could most likely read her mind, so what was the point of trying to play coy?

"He does have beautiful eyes," Mia agreed.

"Thank you." Dagor's lips turned up in a satisfied smirk. "I must find your eyes just as hypnotic because I, too, forgot that we are not alone." He put one arm behind her back and the other under her knees and lifted her. "I'm just taking you to the bedroom and bringing you a change of clothes. Then I will leave, and Mia can take my place."

"I'm fine," she protested weakly.

The truth was that being held in his arms and pressed against his chest was a treat. It was also a tiny taste of what she could expect later, provided that she didn't faint again and that Mia and Toven would trust Dagor with her.

"You are not." He glanced between the two doors. "Which one is your room?"

"The one on the left." She wrapped her arms around his neck.

As he carried her to her room, she was glad she had made her bed and hung up all the dresses she had tried on before choosing the blue one.

Perhaps she had done it subconsciously to match the color of his eyes?

When Dagor deposited her on the bed, Frankie immediately missed the warmth of his embrace and chided herself for getting carried away in her infatuation with the guy.

He was a god, and she was a human who might or might not have some godly genes. The most she could hope for was a shipboard romance, and she needed to be careful and guard her heart while giving in to the attraction. She also needed to remember what Mia and Toven had said about gods and immortals not being all that different from humans. They felt the same emotions and responded to the same stimuli.

She would treat Dagor the same way she would any hunky guy she wanted to hook up with.

Dagor opened the closet and peered at the selection of clothes. "I see mostly evening dresses. Where are your comfortable clothes?"

"Open the second drawer. I have some casual things there. You can pull out any combination you like."

It was cruel to give a guy loose instructions like that, but she was curious to see what Dagor would choose. Would he bring the entire drawer contents to her, or would he pick something?

She was betting on the second option.

Surprising her, he spent a few minutes lifting items and putting them back before deciding on an outfit. When he turned around, holding a pair of biker shorts and a breezy T-shirt with a colorful print on the front, she approved of his selection.

"Not bad." She smiled at him when he handed her the items. "Do you have a sister?"

Dagor shook his head. "I'm an only child. Most gods are lucky to have one, and very few get two. The Clan Mother was blessed by the Fates to have four children. Or maybe her human partners contributed to her fertility."

The Clan Mother was the glowing goddess, and her children were probably among the couples who had escorted her into the dining hall, but that was the extent of Frankie's knowledge.

She was dying to grill him for more details about his world and what it meant to be a god, but right now, she needed to get out of the too-tight dress so she could breathe normally.

"I have many more questions, but I should change clothes before I faint again. It happens every time I learn something new that gets my pulse racing.

The look in his eyes changed, becoming predatory. "I still intend to see you naked tonight. I might as well help you with your dress."

"Nope." She smiled. "You'll have to wait. Besides, I haven't made up my mind about inviting you tonight, so don't get cocky assuming that being a god means you've got it in the bag."

"I never assume anything, Frankie. You are the boss, and what you say goes." He smiled to reassure her. "I'll tell Mia that you are ready for her."

"Thank you."

44

GILBERT

As Gilbert and Karen entered the elevator, it was already packed and they were the last ones to fit in, or so he thought, until Ingrid and Atzil squeezed in just as the doors closed.

"We made it." Ingrid laughed and high-fived Atzil.

"Barely," Gilbert grumbled. "I hope we don't exceed the weight limit."

As the elevator lurched, he let out a relieved breath and prayed that they wouldn't get stuck.

"Come join us for drinks in our suite," Karen said to Ingrid. "The little ones are sleeping over at Kaia's tonight, so we have the suite all to ourselves."

"We would love to." Ingrid looked up at Atzil. "You're not tired, are you?"

"Nope." He unbuttoned his tuxedo jacket and let out a breath. "But first, I must get out of this monkey suit." He shrugged his massive shoulders. "I can barely move in this thing."

"Of course." Karen nodded. "I would like to put on something more comfortable as well." She cast Gilbert a sidelong glance. "Although I have to admit that you look very dashing in your tux, and I will be sorry to see you take it off."

Usually, Gilbert would have loved the suggestive undertones in her voice and demeanor, but knowing what she was plotting, he was seething.

It was true that they had talked about it, deciding that it was the only way to go, but Gilbert wasn't ready. He needed more time to get used to the idea, even if it only involved Ingrid and Atzil getting it on in the other bedroom and Atzil rushing over to bite Karen when his fangs and venom were ready for action.

When they got to their cabin, Gilbert glared at Karen. "You shouldn't have invited them without checking with me first. I'm not ready to proceed with the plan yet."

"We don't have to do anything tonight." She stepped out of her high heels and bent down to retrieve them. "I invited them for drinks, and that's all we are obliged to do." She continued to their bedroom.

Gilbert followed. "Eric said that I would need to be chained to the bed to prevent me from attacking Atzil."

Unzipping her dress, she cast him an amused glance. "Even in your new immortal body, you are no match for the cook. Did you see the muscles on the guy?" She stepped out of the dress and draped it over the bed.

For a moment, he just looked at her, desire stealing the words out of his mouth. Even after all the years they had been together, he still had difficulty keeping his hands off her.

Now was not the time, though. "That's not the point. I know he can beat me up, but neither of us should get hurt in the process, and for that to happen, I should be restrained. Besides, what if you start transitioning immediately? I don't think the clinic on board the ship has the equipment to monitor you. Also, do you really want to miss all those weddings?"

Knowing Karen, the last part was the one that would convince her.

"As I said, I only invited them for drinks." She reached for a loose summer dress and pulled it out of the closet. "It's not easy for me either, but I think the more time we spend with Ingrid and Atzil, the more comfortable we will become with them, and it will get easier." She pulled the dress on.

Letting out a breath, Gilbert shrugged off the tux jacket. "Yeah, you're right." He took out a hanger and draped the jacket over it. "I just don't know if Atzil is the right guy. It would have been nice if you could be induced by a god."

She cast him an incredulous look. "We are not asking Toven. There is no way he will agree, and even if he did, I would die of mortification."

"I wasn't thinking of asking Toven."

"Then who?"

"Aru."

Karen laughed. "You are kidding, right? He is mated to your sister."

Gilbert ran a hand through his hair, which was becoming thicker by the day. "I know it's a little weird to make love to you in our room while Gabi and

Aru are doing the same in another, but I wouldn't feel as weirded out by Aru biting you because I know he has absolutely no interest in you."

Karen grimaced. "Thanks for making me feel like an old hag."

Reaching for her, he pulled her into his arms. "You are the most desirable woman in the world to me, but Aru only has eyes for Gabi. Atzil and Ingrid are not bonded mates, so he can feel lust toward you, and I know that he does."

Her eyes widened. "Did you smell it? He could have been having lustful thoughts about Ingrid."

"Perhaps. But I know how a man looks at a desirable woman, and that was how he looked at you."

"Well, that's good, right? Otherwise, he might not want to bite me. Which Aru might have a problem with, since he's bonded to Gabi, or at least we assume that he is. He might be repulsed by me."

That hadn't occurred to Gilbert. What if Aru wasn't able to do it? Or just plain wouldn't want to?

What if Gabi couldn't tolerate the idea of her mate biting another woman, even if it was Karen?

"We can ask, or rather I can ask. I know that it would be too embarrassing for you."

Karen shook her head. "Don't. You'll just get Gabi upset, and Aru will think that you are weird. In fact, both of them will think that you are creepy, but Gabi knows you and loves you, and she will forgive you, while Aru might not want to have anything to do with you."

"My request won't be received well, but if they agree, there are two significant advantages to Aru doing the deed. He's a god, so his venom is more potent than any immortal's, especially a diluted immortal like Atzil. He could also thrall us both to think that he is not there and that I am the one biting you. That would make all the difference."

Karen pursed her lips. "You make a good argument, but I won't jeopardize our relationship with Gabi and Aru just to make things easier for us."

"I agree. The best way to test the waters is to tell them our plan with Atzil and Ingrid and wait for them to volunteer."

She sighed. "If you have your heart set on a god inducing me, you can talk to the other two gods who are not mated. Just try to be tactful and broach the subject delicately."

Gilbert pretended to scowl. "When am I not tactful and delicate?"

Karen laughed. "You're funny."

45

DAGOR

When Dagor returned to the living room, a couple of humans were busy setting up the dining table. They had brought a cart loaded with fragrant dishes and were transferring trays to the table.

"I think Frankie can manage on her own, but just in case she faints again… "

He didn't get to finish the sentence when Mia swiveled her chair and drove into the room he'd just left, leaving him alone with the royal and the humans.

Surprisingly, the servers smiled at Toven as if they knew him, and he smiled back and addressed them by name.

When the humans had removed the last trays from the cart and put them on the table, Toven thanked them, and then they were truly alone.

"Take a seat." Toven motioned at the table. "The ladies will join us as soon as they are ready."

"Are the humans working on this ship from the immortals' village?"

"No. Save for a few exceptions, Kian doesn't allow humans in there." Toven filled his glass with water and offered the pitcher to Dagor. "I'm surprised that you don't recognize them. They are from the Kra-ell compound, which you spied on for five years. When we liberated the Kra-ell, we also freed the humans, and they chose where they wanted to settle from several options that we gave them."

"Yes, I'm aware of that. I just didn't make the connection. The truth is that we should have paid more attention to the humans in the compound. Our job was to monitor the Kra-ell and find the rest of the pods, meaning we were gone for months at a time. The monitoring we did was sporadic."

"Did you find any more pods?" Toven asked.

Shaking his head, Dagor sighed. "To borrow a human expression, it's like searching for a needle in a haystack. We followed rumors of strange materials and places that emitted unexplained radiation. Aru came up with a great cover story for us that made it less suspicious for us to ask strange questions and also supplemented our funds. We searched for flea-market finds and hunted for artifacts. We made good money on the things we found and sold, but we had no luck with the pods." He took a sip from his glass of water. "By the way, we were told that the humans from the compound were settled in a resort that belongs to the clan and that they were given housekeeping jobs."

"That's right. The resort is actually owned by one of Jade's former tribe members, but the clan got a share of it in exchange for investing in the property. I'm told that it was in dire need of renovations."

Dagor cast him a stern look. "So basically, the clan still treats the humans as serfs, just as the Kra-ell did."

"Not at all." Toven didn't seem perturbed by Dagor's accusation. "They were more than happy to return to the ship that brought them to freedom and repay their rescuers with the best service they could muster. Obviously, they were also offered bonus pay." He smiled. "Kian is a great believer in win-win solutions. This is just one example of his philosophy."

The puzzle pieces started to fall into place in Dagor's mind. Toven's familiarity with the human occupants of the compound meant that he had been there, helping to free them. The only reason the immortals would have dragged a god along for such a dangerous mission was because he could do what they couldn't—override Gor's compulsion.

"You must be a powerful compeller." He looked at the god. "You were there when the Kra-ell were liberated, and you helped free these humans."

Toven acknowledged his statement with a nod. "I am a pretty strong compeller, but it wasn't an easy task to free the Kra-ell, especially the purebloods. The humans were a piece of cake."

"The Kra-ell are impervious to thralling and shrouding, and compulsion is the only mental power that affects them. Usually, the strongest female of the tribe has power over her subjects. Gor was a perversion."

"So, his original name was Gor? He wasn't very creative picking his fake name."

Dagor chuckled. "It's easier to remember when the sound is familiar. I chose Doug, Aru chose Uriel, and Negal chose Ned."

"And I chose Tom."

As the door to the bedroom opened and the ladies came out, Dagor rose to his feet and pulled out a chair for Frankie while Toven removed one of the chairs to make room for Mia's wheelchair.

"How are you feeling?" Dagor asked as she smiled up at him.

"I feel great." She sat down. "I'm sure the fainting spells won't come back."

"I hope not." He lifted her chair and pushed it closer to the table.

Frankie laughed. "My dad used to do that to me all the time. He would pick up my chair with me in it and push it closer to the table."

"Is he still around?" Dagor asked with trepidation.

"Oh, yes. He's very much around."

Dagor let out a breath. "Human lives are so fleeting."

Frankie's smile melted away. "They are."

Mia cleared her throat and smiled brightly. "We should eat before everything gets cold."

46

FRANKIE

All throughout dinner, Frankie kept stealing glances at Dagor, and each time, he looked even more gorgeous to her. Especially when he smiled. He was also brilliant, asking Toven about the technology behind Perfect Match and whether it had been developed by humans or by the immortals.

Thankfully, Toven wasn't much of a tech guy, so his answers were easy to understand.

"I would love to try out an adventure, but I don't think Aru will authorize the expense. We need to be frugal with our resources."

"Can Dagor be a beta tester like me?" Frankie asked. "That way, he can get to experience it for free."

Toven shook his head. "Regrettably, our three distinguished guests cannot enter the secret compound."

Frankie arched a brow. "And I can?"

"You can be thralled or compelled to forget where you've been," Toven explained. "They cannot. The mind tricks that work on humans don't work on them."

"I see." Frankie cut off a piece of cake and put it in her mouth.

It wasn't a big deal that Dagor couldn't come with her to the compound. She'd already decided that their fling would be confined to the cruise. Once that was over, they would part ways.

"Don't look so crestfallen," Mia said. "I'm sure you will be allowed to leave the compound to visit your family, and you could meet Dagor in the city."

Toven shook his head. "Dagor and his companions are searching for the missing Kra-ell pods. They will probably return to the search right after the cruise."

Dagor nodded. "We were waiting for Gabi to get strong enough to travel. She is no longer under the doctor's supervision, so nothing is holding us back now."

Why did his words hurt?

Hadn't she already concluded that she would have fun with Dagor during the cruise and no more?

"What was wrong with Gabi?" Frankie asked.

Maybe the gods emitted some sort of radiation that was harmful to humans?

"She transitioned into immortality," Mia said. "Aru induced her transition the same way Toven induced mine."

"Not exactly the same way," Toven said. "Aru didn't even know what a Dormant was and that they could be induced. I knew, but I didn't realize that Dormants were still to be found so many generations later. It had never occurred to me."

Frankie shot Dagor a glance before returning her gaze to Mia. "You said before that I might be a Dormant. What makes you think that?"

Mia looked uncomfortable. "The affinity. The theory is that immortals and Dormants feel affinity toward one another. It's like recognizing like." She smiled at Toven. "Apparently, gods feel it too, and it transcends physical proximity. Toven and I fell in love inside a Perfect Match simulation."

"Is it really that good?" Dagor asked Toven.

The god nodded. "It's uncanny. I forgot who I was for those three hours or three days inside the virtual world. In there, I wasn't a god; I was just an enhanced human like many others, and I served a god." He shook his head. "This was before I owned half of Perfect Match, and I feared my identity would be discovered inside the simulation. So, I designed the adventure to include gods in case I said or did something while in the virtual world to reveal my identity. The end result, though, was more than I had expected. The story had an almost prophetic feel to it. I tried to hunt down the programmer that helped me create it, but he turned out to be a phantom."

"What do you mean?" Frankie said. "As the company's owner, you can access all its employees. How hard could it be to find out who it was?"

"He called himself Brian, and there were several Brians working at Perfect

Match headquarters at the time. I spoke to each one, and they all sounded different from the Brian I spoke to. I had a phone number and an email for him, but those belonged to a lady named Gina, who had no idea who had been using her email and phone extension."

"Those were the Fates," Mia said. "There is no other explanation. One of them pretended to be a programmer named Brian."

Frankie was lost. "What do you mean the Fates? Who are they? And how did we end up talking about a guy named Brian? I want to know what makes me a Dormant aside from some elusive thing like affinity. I'm an easygoing, likable girl. Many people feel affinity toward me."

"There was also Lisa. Remember her?"

"Yeah, Geraldine's niece."

"Lisa is not really her niece. Anyway, she claims to be able to sniff out Dormants. So once Toven mentioned how much he liked you and Margo, we thought it might be affinity, and we brought Lisa to do her thing. She thought that both you and Margo were Dormants. That's why Toven offered you the jobs as beta testers. The idea was that you would come to the village, I mean the compound, and find nice immortal males to bond with who would induce your transition."

Frankie felt dizziness assail her again and lifted her hand to stop Mia from saying anything more. "I need a moment."

47

DAGOR

Dagor didn't like the comment about other immortal males inducing Frankie, and it annoyed him that he was bothered by it. Even if Frankie was a Dormant who could turn immortal like Aru's mate, Dagor didn't want to be saddled with a hybrid he could never take home with him. He had no intention of spending his immortal life on Earth.

"I need a moment." Frankie's quivering voice got his attention.

"What's wrong?" He leaned to look at her ashen face.

"It's all too much. I can't process it all at once. I need time to think."

"Do you want us to leave and let you rest?" Mia asked.

Yes, please leave. Dagor wanted to be left alone with Frankie.

"Not yet. So, let's say that I am a Dormant. How do I become immortal, and what does it take?"

Mia frowned. "You just said it was too much, and you couldn't take it all in at once. Perhaps we should continue with the Immortals 101 course tomorrow after you've had a good night's sleep."

Frankie nodded and then turned to Dagor. "Can you stay a little longer? I'm afraid I will faint and no one will be here to revive me, and I don't want Mia and Toven to lose sleep because of me."

"We can stay," Mia said.

"No, I'll stay." Dagor took Frankie's hand. "I can spend the night on the couch in the living room. Just leave the bedroom door open so I can hear your breathing."

She gave him a dazzling smile. "We can both be on the couch or in bed and watch television until we fall asleep."

The faint scent of her arousal indicated that watching television was not what she had in mind.

"Sounds like a plan to me." He lifted her hand to his lips and kissed her knuckles.

Toven rose to his feet and pinned Dagor with a hard look. "Can I have a moment with you outside?"

Long years of deferring to royals had Dagor incline his head. "Of course."

Cursing his automatic response internally, he pushed to his feet and followed Toven outside the suite.

Frankie rolled her eyes. "Are you going to give him the big brother speech of treating your little sister with respect?"

"Something like that." Toven's smile looked strained.

"I'll wait for you here," Mia said. "I'll help Frankie clear the table."

"Don't touch anything. I'll do it when I return," Dagor shot behind him as he followed Toven.

"Bossy, bossy," Frankie murmured as she got to her feet. "Clearing dishes will not make me faint. It's your outlandish stories that make me dizzy."

Dagor was about to reply, but Toven's hand on his shoulder sent a clear message that the god had no patience for waiting.

Once they were out in the hallway, Toven let go of his shoulder. "So here is a crash course about Dormants. The transition gets triggered by venom and semen, meaning sex. We don't know what exactly happens, but it seems that the chemicals in our venom and semen are the catalysts. If you have sex with Frankie tonight, use a condom to prevent inducing her transition. She's just learned about our world, and she's not ready, neither mentally nor physically. The doctor can tell us more about the physical aspects tomorrow after she runs some tests. Is everything clear so far?"

"I think so, except for where to get condoms. I never use them." He wanted to add that the god probably didn't use them either, but it was none of his business.

Toven smiled. "They have them in the clinic. You can dash there, and I'll tell Frankie that you need to get something from your room. We will not leave her side until your return."

"Thank you." Dagor bowed his head.

"No need to do that." Toven clapped him on the back. "We are not big on protocol here, and until you came along, we were convinced that all gods were luminous. We didn't know that the glow signified nobility. I would like to keep things informal if you don't mind."

"As you wish." Dagor fought his instinct to dip his head again. "I'll be quick about it."

As it turned out, finding the clinic was more challenging than he'd thought. There were no signs indicating its location, and there was no one to ask since everyone was still in the dining hall.

When Dagor finally found it, he was surprised that the clinic wasn't deserted.

"How can I help you, Dagor?" a white-haired immortal asked with a curious gleam in his pale blue eyes.

"Who are you?"

"Forgive me." The guy inclined his head. "My name is Merlin, and I'm one of the clan's three physicians."

Oh well, at least the guy would know why Dagor needed what he came for. Since he couldn't contract or transmit sexually transmitted diseases, and he couldn't get anyone pregnant either because chances of that were so low that they were negligible, a god had no use for condoms unless he needed to avoid inducing a Dormant's transition.

"I was told that I could find condoms in the clinic."

The doctor frowned. "What for?"

Apparently, he didn't know. Perhaps Frankie, being a potential Dormant, was only known to some.

"I was told that using a physical barrier was the only way to prevent a Dormant from transitioning before she was ready."

"Ah." Merlin's eyes widened. "Now, that makes perfect sense." He opened a drawer and pulled out two boxes of condoms. "Have you ever used them before?"

Dagor shook his head.

"Perhaps you need to practice first on a banana." Seeing Dagor's mortified expression, Merlin chuckled. "Just kidding. There are instructions inside. Read them before you attempt it or let the lady do it. She might have more experience than you in rolling one on."

Dagor preferred to think about something other than how Frankie might have acquired that skill.

The thought was odd, and her having other partners shouldn't bother him. She wasn't his, and he didn't plan on her ever becoming his, so why the human-style possessiveness?

"Thank you." He tried to flatten the boxes to fit in his tuxedo pockets.

"Hold on." The doctor pushed to his feet, walked over to one of the cabinets, and opened it. "I have a little gift for you and your lady." He pulled out a gift bag and handed it to him. "The boxes should fit in there."

Peering into the bag, Dagor saw a small box of a famous chocolate brand. "Does chocolate have a therapeutic effect on immortals?"

"In a way, it does." Merlin chuckled. "I'm the clan's fertility specialist. The elixirs I produce don't taste good, so I give them out along with the chocolates to help the medicine go down." He ended with a wink. "One of the biggest problems with patient care is ensuring compliance. If the couples I treat don't drink the potions because they taste bad, then how will they conceive?"

"Do your potions really work?" Dagor pulled out the chocolate box, stuffed the two condom boxes inside the bag, and then put the chocolates on top.

The doctor shrugged. "So far, I've had only one success, and time will tell if that was a fluke. I hope it wasn't."

48

FRANKIE

"Where is Doug? I mean, Dagor?" Frankie asked as Toven returned without him.

What had the god told Dagor to scare him off?

"Don't worry," Toven said. "He's coming back. He just needed to get something from his cabin."

"Like what?"

Toven shrugged. "He didn't say. Maybe he wanted to change out of his evening attire and get a toothbrush."

That made sense, and Frankie's momentary panic eased. "Yeah, that makes sense. Although there are new toothbrushes in the bathroom. Heck, there are even face lotions and makeup remover towelettes. Whoever equipped these cabins thought of everything."

Mia nodded. "No expense has been spared." She turned to Toven. "You probably want to take off the tux as well. I'll stay with Frankie until Dagor returns."

The god frowned. "I'm perfectly comfortable in the tuxedo. I'll wait with you."

Of course, he was.

The guy looked like a tux model and seemed perfectly at ease in it, most likely because it had been custom-tailored for him.

Mia rolled her eyes. "Whether gods, immortals, or humans, males have a problem getting hints. I want to talk to Frankie alone."

"About what?" Frankie chuckled. "I don't need the birds and the bees talk."

"Oh, you definitely need the immortals and gods style birds and bees talk."

Toven nodded in agreement. "I doubt that Dagor knows how to explain it properly. I'll leave you ladies alone to have the talk." He smiled. "Good night, Frankie. And good luck. I hope you feel better."

As the god closed the door behind him, Frankie frowned. "What did he mean by good luck? Are gods difficult to seduce or do they have trouble getting or keeping it up?"

Mia laughed. "If anything, they have the opposite problem. Not that it's an issue. Multiple orgasms are the norm and no morning-after soreness. You are in for the best sex of your life, but there are a few things you need to know, and I suggest that you lie down on the couch first."

"Why?"

"You fainted twice today already after getting too worked up in your head, and what I'm going to tell you might have a similar effect."

"I'm fine. It's not going to happen again."

"If it does, and you fall, I can't catch you." Mia glanced at the door. "You'd better hurry up and lie down before Dagor returns, or you will have to learn about the birds and the bees from him."

With a sigh, Frankie stretched out on the couch. "Would that be such a bad idea? Letting him teach me would be like being a virgin all over again, just without the pain. Could be fun."

Mia shrugged. "It's up to you. If you are more comfortable with Dagor explaining things to you, I have no problem. Still, I just think that hearing it from me would be less traumatic and therefore less likely to induce panic and fainting."

She had a point, and since the word traumatic had been included, Frankie was starting to panic already. Did these aliens have different anatomy than human males?

Mia had mentioned multiple orgasms and no soreness in the morning, so whatever it was couldn't be too bad.

"Okay, tell me." She crossed her arms over her chest with her hands resting on her throat.

"What are you doing?" Mia tilted her head. "You're freaking me out with this coffin pose."

"Sorry." Frankie lowered her hands to rest on her tummy. "Please enlighten me, oh goddess of love and lust."

Mia snorted. "I wish. Anyway, let's start with the anatomy."

Frankie winced. "I was afraid of that."

"Male gods and immortals have elongating fangs and venom glands. Their fangs respond to two triggers: one is aggression, and the other is arousal, and the two do not mix. They get aggressive only when they have the urge to fight, and it's always toward other males."

"What if they are sexually interested in other males? The signals could get mixed."

"I don't think so, but I don't know that for sure. I'll have to ask Toven." Mia narrowed her eyes at her. "So far, you are taking it surprisingly well. What's the deal with that?"

"You know how much I like reading vampire romances. The thought of losing copious quantities of blood scares me, but the fangs on their own do not."

Mia's suspicious expression morphed into a smile. "That's what you think. Wait until you see Dagor's fully elongated fangs. They are really scary, but the good news is that gods and immortals don't use them to drink blood. They are for injecting venom, which does wondrous things. It's a euphoric, an aphrodisiac, and a healing tonic all in one. You're going to orgasm like you never have before, then you're going to soar over the clouds and see strange and wonderful things, and when you wake up, you'll feel like a new woman, energized, vibrant, and ready for another round."

Frankie turned to look at her friend and grinned. "Why did you think telling me that would make me faint again? That sounds amazing."

"It is out of this world, literally, but after you reacted so strongly to what we told you before and to seeing the goddess and discovering that your new friend was a god, I was sure the mention of fangs would induce another fainting spell."

"Yeah, well. I fell down the rabbit hole, and it was scary, but now that I'm already in Wonderland, I'm ready to explore all it has to offer."

49

DAGOR

Dagor stopped by his room to grab a quick shower, brush his teeth, and put on a pair of jeans and a T-shirt.

When he emerged from his room with the gift bag Merlin had given him, he found his companions sitting in the living room, Aru and Negal still in their tuxedos and Gabi in her evening gown.

"Is the girl okay?" Gabi asked.

"For now, she is. I will spend the night in her cabin to keep an eye on her, and tomorrow, the doctor will see her."

"How do you know her?" Aru asked.

He didn't have time to explain. "I met her on the Lido deck; we shared a drink and got friendly. Now, if you'll excuse me, a royal is waiting for me to show up and release him from his post of keeping an eye on his mate's best friend."

Dagor didn't wait for a response as he walked to the door and opened it. "Have a good night. I'll see you tomorrow at breakfast."

"Have fun," Gabi called after him.

He intended to, but he needed to figure out what fun he would pursue.

Something was wrong with Frankie, so perhaps watching television in bed would be all they could do. It was a shame because she looked so sexy in the comfy outfit he'd chosen for her.

There was also the issue of his fangs. Did she even know about that?

Surely her best friend had shared the details with her, but if not, he would have to do it, and he wasn't sure how. He had thralled all the other human females he'd been with to not notice his fangs or glowing eyes. After they had woken up from their stupor, he'd reinforced the thralling with fake memories.

There was no need to do that with Frankie, and since he planned on enjoying her company more than once, he shouldn't thrall her.

On the other hand, he might save her a fright, which was an essential consideration given her propensity to faint when overwhelmed.

When he got to her cabin, Dagor rang the doorbell and waited for the door to open while wondering if she'd discovered that she could open it with the remote. Until he'd told Gabi about it, she hadn't known that she could see who was on the other side of the door on the television screen and not just on the small one next to the door.

As the buzzing sound ensued, signaling that the lock was disengaged, but no one opened the door, he figured Frankie had found out about the first but not the second.

He pushed the door open and walked inside. "Hello." He smiled at both ladies. "My apologies for taking so long. I stopped by my room to shower and change."

"Toven told us." Frankie eyed the little bag with curiosity. "What did you get?"

"A surprise." He turned to Mia. "Did your mate leave already?"

"He did." She reached with her hand and put it on his arm. "Goodnight, Dagor. Take good care of my friend."

"I will."

After Mia left, there was a long silence, with him and Frankie appraising each other. She was spread out on the couch, and he didn't know whether to sit next to her or on the armchair.

"Come sit with me." She scooted back and patted the spot she'd vacated. "And show me what's in the bag. I love surprises."

Dagor pulled out the box of chocolates. "I hope you like them."

"I love them." She took the small box from his hands. "Thank you." Instead of opening it, she glanced at the paper bag that still looked full. "What else is in there?"

"Hope." He smiled sheepishly. "Maybe not for tonight, though."

When her eyes widened, and he sniffed a faint scent of arousal, he knew that she'd guessed the contents of the bag.

"Where did you get them and why? You're a god. Mia said that you can't catch or transmit diseases, and I'm on the pill."

It appeared as if Mia hadn't told her friend everything yet. "Did Mia tell you how Dormants are activated?"

She shook her head. "I asked, but I didn't get an answer. Mia said that we should leave it for tomorrow, and after you and Toven left, we talked about other stuff, and I forgot to ask her about it again."

Damn.

It was up to him to tell her. "Do you at least know about us having fangs?"

"Yes. Mia told me about that. But I wanted to ask whether the females had fangs too and never got to."

"They do, but they are minimal and don't elongate."

She frowned. "Mia's teeth are still the same as before she met Toven."

Dagor smiled apologetically. "I really can't comment on it because I know next to nothing about what happens during transition. Gabi gained half an inch in height, but she didn't grow fangs."

Frankie's eyes sparkled with interest. "I would love to gain some inches. I'm not saying I want to transition, but if I do, it would be nice to get a little taller."

He took her hand and brought it to his lap. "You are perfect the way you are."

"And you are a flatterer," she said with a chiding tone, but her eyes shone with satisfaction at his compliment. "Now tell me about your fangs."

"I've always thought of my fangs as a defensive weapon or as a way to bring pleasure to my paramours, but I've never thought they could be used in the way the clan does. I've only learned recently about the existence of immortals and dormant carriers of godly genes that can be activated with venom." He felt uncomfortable bringing up the second part of the equation.

He would ease into that.

50

FRANKIE

That was a lot of new information, but Frankie wasn't getting dizzy, and her mind was focused and sharp.

Perhaps because she was lying down this time?

Dagor was so cute when he used old-fashioned terms like paramour instead of lover or sex partner. It was a nice change from the guys she dated, who cussed left and right.

The truth was that she used the f-bomb quite often, but mostly quietly, so her boss wouldn't hear her.

Her ex-boss.

Her new boss, or who she hoped would be her new boss, was such a perfect gentleman that she was sure the f-bomb wouldn't pass her lips even once while working for him.

It was all about the company one kept, as her mom kept saying. Luckily, she approved of Margo and Mia, or Frankie wouldn't have heard the end of it.

"What are you thinking about?" Dagor's thumb drew circles on the back of her hand.

She smiled at his gorgeous face. "That I'm doing okay and not fainting from brain overload. So, from what I understand, to induce a Dormant, an immortal or a god needs to bite her or him and inject them with his venom?"

"That's what I was led to understand. But there is more." With a sigh, he pulled a box of condoms from the gift bag. "It has to happen during unprotected sex, so if we get intimate, but you don't want to transition just yet, we need to use these."

The face he made was like they were the vilest things in the world.

But they were a necessity.

Still, it was kind of awkward to talk about sex when they hadn't even kissed yet. Well, Dagor had kissed her knuckles, but that didn't count.

"They are not so bad." She closed her eyes for a moment. "But perhaps it's a little premature to talk about condoms when you haven't kissed me yet. Besides, I have a three-date rule. I don't have sex with a guy until at least our third date."

Dagor's smile was predatory. "But it is our third date."

She laughed. "By what count?"

"The first one was this morning on the Lido deck."

"That doesn't count as a date."

"I beg to differ. We shared a drink, talked, and made plans for another date."

"What about the second one?"

"We've met in the dining hall, and when you fainted, I followed you here. Then I left and came back with a gift, and that counts as a third date."

"That's a very convoluted count, but I'll accept it because this is a cruise vacation, so regular rules don't apply."

If he would only stop talking and kiss her already, things would progress smoothly from there, but Dagor seemed hesitant to start anything. Should she take the initiative and kiss him?

He was obviously interested.

But maybe he wasn't sure?

He was a god, and she was a human, and maybe he was still undecided about wanting to slum it.

Nah. She could see the desire in his eyes but also the conflict.

She had two options. She could lift to her knees and straddle him, or she could pull him on top of her. Given her fainting spells, the second option seemed better.

Tugging on his hand, she signaled her intent and hoped he would follow because she doubted that she could actually pull him on top of her if he didn't cooperate.

He leaned over but remained seated, and as his eyes began glowing, Frankie tensed.

"Are your fangs elongating?"

He nodded.

"Would you be able to kiss me without hurting me?"

When he nodded again, she realized he didn't want to open his mouth.

"Show me. I want to see."

He shook his head.

"I promise that I will not freak out. I watched all five *Twilight* movies five times, and I had a big crush on Edward."

"Who's Edward?"

"Got you." She pointed at his mouth. "I saw your fangs, and I didn't panic."

Shaking his head, Dagor smiled, showing her his fully extended fangs, which were indeed monstrous.

How was he even able to close his mouth?

"Is that as big as they get?" She reached with a finger.

He caught it so fast that she didn't see him move. "Careful, they are sharp, and no, this is not their full length."

He sounded a little slurred, but it was sexy.

Heck, everything about the guy was sexy.

"You move as fast as Edward."

"You still haven't told me who this Edward fellow is."

It was easy to forget that Dagor wasn't really from Hungary, or from Earth for that matter, and that he hadn't seen *Twilight* or read the books.

She liked that he was jealous, though.

"Edward is a fictional character who is a vampire, but not an evil one. He is one of the good guys, and he protects humans."

When Dagor stared at her with confusion in his incredibly blue eyes, she frowned. "You know what a vampire is, right? As in a bloodsucker?"

His eyes brightened. "Like the Kra-ell."

"Who and what are the Kra-ell?"

51

DAGOR

"Never mind." Dagor waved a dismissive hand. "There are none on this ship. They don't like deep water."

Frankie gaped at him. "I still don't get it. Are they people who suck blood from other people and animals like vampires do, or are they some bat-like animal that lives on blood?"

"They are people from my home planet, and they mostly drink from animals. They are a different species."

"You mean different from the gods."

"Yes."

"Why do you call yourselves gods?"

He smiled. "Because we are the creators of all intelligent life in the galaxy, including Earth."

Her eyes widened. "Get out of here."

"Did I offend you? Is that why you want me to go?"

Frankie's lips twitched with a suppressed smile. "It's just an expression. I don't want you to leave."

He let out a breath. "That's a relief. I'm sorry about not getting some of your cultural references. I'm not much of a television or movie watcher, and I don't read fiction. My interests are more technical in nature."

She lifted her hand and cupped his cheek. "You would have been perfect for my other bestie, Margo. She loves smart nerds. But I call dibs, meaning you are mine because I saw you first."

"I'm good with that." He dipped his head and pressed a soft, experimental kiss to her lips.

Her eyelashes fluttered. "Really? You are okay with being mine?"

Not forever. For the length of the cruise, he was willing to be exclusive with Frankie, but she might not like his answer.

Still, he didn't want to mislead her.

"I'm yours until the end of the cruise. After that, my team is heading out to Tibet, and you are starting a new job at Perfect Match, so the best we will be able to do is talk on the phone or send each other messages." He smiled. "Long-distance relationships are difficult to maintain."

Frankie wrapped her arms around his neck. "We've just met, and I don't have any grand expectations from you. I just want to have some fun with a god." She frowned. "Damn, I won't be allowed to brag about it, right?"

"No."

"Oh well. I can still talk about you with Mia and Margo." She lifted her head so their lips were nearly touching. "And I'll cherish my memories privately."

There was a good chance that she wouldn't be allowed to keep even that, but he wasn't going to spoil the mood by mentioning it now. It could wait for later.

Much later.

"I am going to pick you up and carry you to your bed. Is that okay?"

Frankie nodded enthusiastically and then looked at the condoms. "Don't forget these. I don't want you to induce my transition."

He lifted her into his arms. "Ever?"

"I don't know." A shadow passed over her eyes. "To gain something, something else needs to be sacrificed. I'm unsure if I want to trade my family for immortality."

He carried her to the bedroom and put her down on the bed. "Your family is that important to you? You would give up immortality so as not to outlive them?"

"Yes. Perhaps I could have my cake and eat it too, which means that I will get to keep both, but I don't know the rules of the game yet, and I don't want to make any rush decisions, so for now, a condom is a must."

Dagor chuckled. "Condoms, as in plural. Didn't Mia tell you about the gods' stamina? Once is not enough for us." He dipped his head and nuzzled her breast through her shirt and bra. "We can go on and on, but since you are human, I will have to go easy on you."

It was so liberating to talk freely about who he was with a woman and not fear her reaction.

She arched into the touch. "Can you dim the light? I'm not bashful, but this much light is not romantic."

"Sure." He got off the bed.

"I thought you could do that with your mind. Isn't that what gods do?"

"No." He smiled as he did what she asked. "What we do is make you think that we dimmed the light. We have power over human and immortal minds. We don't have telekinetic abilities."

"Bummer." Frankie gripped the bottom of her shirt and pulled it over her head. "I thought that you could also teleport, but I guess the answer to that is 'no' as well?"

Dagor removed his shirt and tossed it over the back of a chair. "Sorry to disappoint you with my lack of talent in those areas, but I'm sure you won't be disappointed with my other talents." He prowled over her.

"You are such a show-off." Her eyes roved appreciatively over his muscled torso. "But hey, if you have it, flaunt it, right?" She wrapped her arms around his neck and pulled him down for a kiss.

52

FRANKIE

Frankie's bravado melted when Dagor lowered his body over hers and took over the kiss.

How did he manage to knead her lips so perfectly with those huge fangs in his mouth?

It was hard to concentrate and figure out anything while his hard body was pressed to hers, his powerful arms holding her to him and her skin tingling from the contact.

He was only kissing her, and it still felt like the most intense sex she'd ever had. Maybe it was the feel of the rigid rod still hidden inside his pants pressing against her thigh or the raw energy he was emitting, making her skin erupt in goosebumps.

Could he be dangerous to her?

What if that tingling electricity that made her so moist and needy was some radioactivity that could harm her?

The worry was like a distant humming in her mind, all too easy to ignore. Right now, she wanted to reach between their bodies and wrap her hand over that bulge, but without the barrier of his jeans in the way. She wanted them both to be naked, skin to skin.

As his lips moved to her neck and his hands smoothed over her sides, her hands roved over the rugged ridges of his back, and when he let her come up for air, she murmured against his lips, "Take off the rest of your clothes."

The smile he gave her somehow looked like a sexy smirk despite the fangs.

The man was so gorgeous that even those sharp and scary things did not distract from his allure.

Not a man, she reminded herself, *a god*.

Sliding back, Dagor got to his feet and reached for the button of his jeans. "Are you curious, Frankie?" He popped the button.

"Very."

By now, she knew he could move with such incredible speed that she could barely see it. It was almost like teleporting. Now, he was going slowly so she could enjoy the show. Maybe he wanted to watch her reaction when he took his pants off, and she hoped he wasn't hiding anything weird behind the denim. Although, as hungry as she was for him, she was willing to forgive a lot of alienness as long as it wasn't something that would cause her pain.

She'd once dated a guy who had piercings on his shaft. Frankie had taken one look at that and shown him the door.

Who in their right mind did that?

Taunting her, Dagor turned around and gave her a spectacular view of his ass as he pushed the jeans down his thighs and then let them drop the rest of the way.

He either hadn't worn any underwear, or he'd pushed them down along with the pants.

Frankie held her breath as he stepped out of the pile on the floor and turned around.

A gasp escaped her throat as she saw his erection. There was nothing alien or strange about it, but it was massive.

"Wow. You're really big."

A frown creased his brow. "Is that a good thing or bad?"

She chuckled. "It's not about the size. It's about how you use it." It was a little about the size too, but there was no reason to make the god even more cocky.

His eyes blazing with inner light, he put one knee on the bed, then the other, and crawled toward her.

"You're overdressed, my darling."

Hooking his thumbs in the elastic of her biker shorts, he tugged them down her legs and tossed them on the floor.

Her panties got more gentle treatment, and when they were off, Dagor inhaled and closed his glowing eyes for a moment as if savoring a fragrant bouquet.

Mia had said that gods and immortals had enhanced senses, and he was probably smelling her arousal. It would have been embarrassing if not for the blissed-out expression on his face.

Putting his hands on her knees, he looked into her eyes and applied light pressure, indicating that he wanted her to spread her legs for him.

Frankie liked that he was asking permission and not assuming he had the right to pry her knees apart. Nevertheless, this level of intimacy with a guy whom she'd kissed for the first time only moments ago felt awkward.

Still, it was only fair. After all, he'd shown her his, so she needed to show him hers.

Not applying any counter-pressure, she allowed him to spread her legs, and the expression on his face turned from lustful to reverent.

A god was looking at her as if she was something special and didn't that make her feel like a goddess. A very aroused goddess who needed him to touch her before she went up in flames.

Just having him look at her like that brought her to the edge.

When he reached with his hand and gently brushed a finger over her wet folds, she bit on her lower lip to keep from pleading with him to put it inside of her, but when he brought that same finger to her entrance and just circled it, she couldn't hold it in any longer.

"Please," she half begged, half hissed.

A smirk lifting one side of his lips, he slid the finger inside of her. "You are so wet for me." He finally pressed his thumb where she needed it most.

The tension that had been building, first slowly and then speeding up exponentially, reached critical velocity, and Frankie had no choice but to let go.

When a breath whooshed out of her, she expected Dagor to get between her legs and feed her that enormous erection of his. Still, the guy had the self-control of a god, and instead of his shaft, she was treated to his tongue.

"Oh, my God, Dagor." She threaded her fingers in his hair.

"Yes, sweetheart?"

"Just keep doing what you're doing."

53

DAGOR

After Dagor had wrung out every last drop of pleasure from Frankie, and she pushed on his head to make him stop, he crawled up on top of her and took her mouth in a kiss.

She was dazed, her arms wrapping weakly around him, but she hadn't fainted and hadn't freaked out. He'd given her plenty of opportunities to see his fangs and feel how sharp they were when he nicked her inner thighs and then licked the little hurts away.

Every time he had done that, her arousal had spiked higher.

"Mmm." She licked her lips once he let go of them. "I taste good on you. I wonder how you will taste on me."

He was already harder than an iron rod, and the image she painted in his mind made him harden even more. But having those luscious lips of hers wrapped around his shaft would have to wait. Right now, he needed to be inside of her more than anything. Even if the patrol ship had swooped by and offered to take him home, he wasn't sure he would have been able to stop.

"I need to be inside of you." He gripped his shaft and positioned it at her entrance.

"Wait." She put a hand on his chest. "Condom first."

He'd forgotten all about it.

With a groan, he rolled off her, reached for the box, tore it open, and pulled out a packet. "You'll have to put it on me. I've never done it before." He handed it to her.

"Oh, wow. How exciting." Frankie sat up, threw a knee over his thighs, and straddled them.

Tearing the packet open with her teeth, she took the small latex ring, which didn't look like it could encompass his girth, and placed it over the tip. "I hope it fits."

"So do I." He watched as she expertly pinched the top with the fingers of one hand while rolling it down with her other.

Surprisingly, it fit.

When she finished with a kiss to the tip, he nearly climaxed just from that. And when she lifted her bottom and positioned herself above him, he nicked his lower lip with his fangs.

"Is that okay?" She gripped his length and positioned it so the tip was at her entrance.

"It's perfect."

Holding up his sheathed erection, Frankie rubbed it in her juices but didn't push herself on it yet. "Some men don't like to be under a woman."

He smiled, which should have terrified her, but the sight of his fangs seemed to excite her. "You can be over me, under me, to one side or another, and upside down. I'll take you any way I can get you."

"Sexy devil." She leaned forward and brushed her lips over his.

"Don't you mean god?"

"Sometimes it's hard to tell the difference." She lowered herself, taking in just the tip.

Dagor saw stars. "Take me deeper."

"Patience, lover god. You're large, and I'm small. I need to do this slowly."

He nodded. "Take as long as you want, but just know that you are torturing me."

She smiled. "Your self-control is impressive. Any other guy would have surged up already."

Hope shone in his eyes. "Do you want me to?"

Frankie shook her head. "I'll let you know when you can take over." Her smile turned evil. "Let's see how long you can manage to hold back."

Silly woman. She didn't know that he would do anything to win a challenge.

Fisting the sheet to avoid gripping her thighs, he returned her evil smile with one of his own. "I won't move a muscle, but I can't guarantee that there will be no spontaneous eruption."

"You'd better not." Her hold on the base of his erection tightened. "You will wait until I tell you that you can come."

Dagor suppressed a laugh.

The tiny sprout was a closet dominatrix. Or maybe she was openly dominant?

He could definitely see her in the role, wearing a leather corset, thigh-high boots with enormous platform heels, and wielding a crop.

Dagor had never thought he would enjoy being dominated by a female during sex, but as long as it was just fun and games, he could play along.

"You're on, darling." He released the sheet and lifted his arms over his head. "Take me. I'm yours."

54

FRANKIE

Frankie had a god sprawled under her, and he was putting himself at her mercy.

Talk about a heady feeling.

She had no intention of tormenting him for long because it would be torturous for her as well. Still, she had no doubt that the moment things got more intense, he would flip them over, and the little game she was playing would be over.

Just watching him sprawled out under her was a treat.

Dagor was a self-proclaimed nerd, yet he had an impressive eight-pack and a drool-worthy chest.

In fact, Frankie was drooling already.

With his sizable shaft firmly lodged inside of her, she could let go of it and brace both hands on those defined pectorals for purchase.

Lifting a fraction of an inch, she came down, taking a little more in and feeling the stretch.

The guy, correction, the god, was bigger than any man she'd ever been with, and she also hadn't had anything bigger than BOB inside of her for nearly six months.

Compared to Dagor, though, BOB was a toy in more ways than one.

"You're evil," Dagor hissed.

"Says the guy with the razor-sharp fangs." She wiggled her bottom, getting him a little deeper, but not by much.

Realizing that she wasn't doing this just to torture him, Dagor lifted one of his arms and reached with his finger to gently massage her clit.

"Take as long as you need. Worst case scenario, I'll provide extra lubrication to ease in."

She lifted up almost to the very end and then pushed down, this time getting nearly half of him in.

"You have a condom on, so your lubrication won't help." Panting, she held herself still. "I don't think I've ever been with a guy who talked so casually about premature ejaculation."

As he laughed, his abdominal muscles rippled. "That's because it won't slow me down. I will be up and ready again immediately." The glow in his eyes got so intense that it was difficult to look at him. "Again and again for as many times as you want me."

"It must be nice to be a god." She lifted up and, gritting her teeth, pushed down, intending to get him all the way in but not quite managing it. "Damn. This is like being a virgin again."

This was supposed to be a sexy game. Still, her arms were trembling from the effort of keeping herself suspended above him. The stretched-out, slightly burning feeling of having him inside of her was just on the right side of painful.

His finger kept drawing lazy circles around her clit. "Do you want me to take over?"

"Only if you can be patient."

"I have all the time in the world." He wrapped his arms around her middle and rolled her under him. "This angle will be better for you."

He dipped his head and kissed her neck while pushing a hand under her bottom. Squeezing her butt cheeks together, he lifted her bottom a little. It should have made things more difficult, but to her surprise, the new angle was enough to allow for a smoother glide.

When he was fully seated inside of her, they both groaned, and then he kissed her again while gently rocking in and out of her.

The god was the most considerate lover she'd ever had, and the thought brought tears to her eyes because he wasn't hers to keep.

"Frankie," he breathed her name as if it was precious to him.

The gentle rocking continued for a while longer until he was gliding in and out of her with ease, and she wanted him to start going faster.

He must have sensed the change in her, and everything about him changed between one blink of an eye and the next.

Gone was the gentle lover, replaced by a lustful beast who grunted as he pulled nearly all the way out and slammed all the way in, hitting the end of her channel.

All she could do was wrap her arms and legs around him and hold on for dear life.

The sensation of him inside of her, on top of her, all around her, was incredible. Soon, she was coiling up, readying for another explosion. When it slammed into her, she heard herself saying things she had never spoken to any other guy out loud, the f-bomb combined with harder and faster.

Dagor hissed and clamped a hand over her head, tilting it sideways. As his erection kicked inside of her, announcing his release, he licked the tender spot between her neck and shoulder and struck.

She felt his fangs slicing into her flesh, but the pain she'd expected never came. It was more like pressure with a little sting, and then something cool entered her bloodstream, and she came again.

The string of orgasms that followed rocked through her and exhausted her to the point of blacking out. Then she was soaring above the clouds and looking at the most beautiful surreal alien landscapes. Only they weren't totally alien because she remembered someone describing them to her.

It was nearly impossible to string together two coherent thoughts while soaring, and she promised herself to think about that later after she floated back to Earth.

55

ARU

Aru waited for Gabi to be deeply asleep before contacting his sister. It wasn't that he feared his mate could see or sense what he was doing, but she was a distraction. He needed to concentrate to open the channel and deliver the news about the heir.

It was good that Aria had developed excellent memorization skills since becoming the Supreme's scribe, so she would be able to recount everything he would tell her word for word.

The problem was the oracle's relay to the queen.

The oracle was only sometimes entirely in this world, and often she confused reality with what she saw from all over the universe and sometimes from other universes.

Most oracles as powerful as she had gone mad at a young age, but Sofringhati, the most powerful oracle ever born, had outlasted the best by many thousands of years.

Perhaps it was her sense of humor that kept her sane or her long friendship with the queen. Still, it was a miracle that she was lucid enough to keep the best-guarded secret on Anumati and beyond. Without her, the resistance wouldn't have been possible.

The queen couldn't have done it all on her own.

When he sensed Gabi was deeply asleep, Aru opened the channel to his sister. *Are you available to talk?*

Yes, brother of mine. It is night-time over here, and I am in bed. What news do you bring?

How did you know that I have news?

She laughed. *We are twins, Aru. I can sense your excitement even when you try to appear calm.*

He needed to tell her about the heir, and a long preamble wouldn't do. Finding the princess was such an unexpected miracle that no amount of hinting could make Aria guess what news he was bringing. He had to take the risk and assume that no one could eavesdrop on their mental conversation and speak plainly.

I have incredible news. The queen's son had a daughter, and she lives. The only legitimate heir to Anumati's throne was born on Earth and lived on after the bombing, and she seems to be just the type of ruler we need.

How do you know she is the daughter of Ahn?

Annani is the spitting image of our queen. They have the same face, but Annani's hair is red, and she is about a foot shorter than her grandmother. She must have inherited her diminutive size and hair color from her mother.

The Eternal King was not a large male either. In fact, he was quite short, but no one dared to say that out loud or make fun of the fact that the king and queen never addressed the public together because she was half a head taller than he was.

Did she inherit any traits from her grandfather? Aria asked.

I do not know. I have only spent about an hour with her, and she did not disclose her abilities. Her power is palpable, though, so I do not doubt she inherited at least some of his strength. But that is where the resemblance ends. Annani is benevolent, leading her clan of immortals with wisdom and care. They call her Clan Mother, and they all love and respect her.

When Aria did not respond for a long moment, Aru asked, *are you there?*

Yes. Forgive me, brother. A thousand thoughts are going through my mind while I try to memorize what you have told me word for word. Did you find out how big the clan is?

He had expected that question and knew that his sister, the oracle, and the queen would all think that leading a small clan did not equate to leading the galaxy. *The clan is only several hundred people strong, but they have done a lot of good for humans throughout the millennia since the other gods were eliminated, and they did it while fighting their archenemy, who has a stronger army of immortals and whose goals are opposite to theirs. Where Annani and her people want humans to become an enlightened global society that promotes equal opportunity for all and meets all the basic needs of Earth's citizens, their enemy wants humans to remain dumb, backward, and in-fighting so he can easily subjugate it.*

Over the past two weeks, Aru had conducted many conversations with Kian about the clan's history, what it had achieved, and its plans for the future. He had only recently learned that Kian was not the head of the clan but only the regent for his mother, leading the American arm of it. His sister Sari fulfilled a similar role in Europe.

I will do my best to relay everything you've told me to the Supreme. I hope she will understand the details when she sees the queen and tells her the good news.

Can't you go with her? Aru asked. *You are her scribe. It will not look suspicious.*

It will. Aria sighed. *The queen and the Supreme have been meeting for thousands of years in seclusion. It is always just the two of them with no witnesses. We cannot change the tradition without arousing suspicion.*

56

DAGOR

Dagor had stayed awake most of the night, listening to Frankie breathe, monitoring her heartbeat, and thinking about his future.

She had exceeded his expectations in every way. Even though he'd been more careful and reserved with her than with most of the human females he'd been with, it had been one of the best nights of his life, and it hadn't been only about the sex.

He'd had fun with Frankie, and he'd felt something for her that he hadn't felt in a very long time.

He wanted more with her.

When Dagor was a young god, barely of the age of consent, he'd fallen in love with a young goddess who'd lived nearby. They had been together for nearly a full Anumati year, and then she had left to serve on one of the colonies, and he'd been drafted to the service. For a while, they had kept in touch, but slowly they had drifted apart. There was no point in keeping the flame going when there was no chance for them to be together.

In time, the love he'd felt for her had dimmed until it faded completely. He'd been lucky that Lilat hadn't been his fated mate or the separation would have devastated them both.

Being fated mates could have added gravitas to their request to be stationed together. Still, it was difficult to prove the claim, and commoners like them were rarely accommodated, even in extreme cases.

Turning onto his side, Dagor gazed at Frankie's sleeping face.

She was a lighthearted girl, easy to smile and laugh, and generous with her body and her feelings. It was a shame that they wouldn't see each other after the cruise.

He was going to Tibet, and she was going to the immortals' village to start her dream job as a beta tester for the Perfect Match adventures.

Perhaps he could convince Aru not to leave immediately, so he could try out one of those adventures with Frankie. He was curious about the technology and how much of the gods' know-how had gone into it.

He would love to spend time in their headquarters and work with their programmers. He had never received an official education in the subject. Still, he'd taught himself much about Earth's tech from watching instructional videos.

Frankie's eyes suddenly popped open, and a smile spread over her face. "You stayed."

"Of course. I told you I would. I was watching over you."

"The entire night?"

He nodded. "Gods don't need as much sleep as humans. I can catch up on some shuteye later. How do you feel?"

"I feel great." She scooted closer and tucked herself into him. "I have my own guardian angel." She kissed the underside of his jaw. "So, what's the plan for today?"

"Breakfast." He put his hand on her stomach. "Your belly started rumbling about an hour ago. I was sure it would wake you up."

"I had wonderful dreams. I didn't want to wake up." She closed her eyes. "I'm having a hard time deciding between staying awake to be with you and going back to sleep so I can dream some more."

Smoothing a hand over her naked back, he reached her buttock and gave it a gentle squeeze. "We can get up, have a cup of coffee, grab something to eat, and get back in bed." He was already hardening, and since she was pressed against him, she was feeling it.

"Right." She chuckled. "I fell asleep after your first climax and deprived you of the chance to show me your impressive recuperating time."

"You didn't fall asleep. You blacked out."

Frankie paled. "Did I faint again?"

"No, that wasn't it. It's normal for the female to black out after a venom bite. The euphoric element of the venom sends you on a fun trip that you are not in a rush to end. Do you remember any of it?"

"I do." Her eyes lost focus as she looked inward. "It was out of this world, literally. I saw translucent beings that were made of energy. They smiled and waved at me while I was passing over them." Her eyes refocused on him. "Do you know who they are?"

He shook his head. "Everyone reports more or less the same experience, but I don't know whether they are common hallucinations induced by chemicals contained in the venom, or something more."

"What about your spiritual leaders? Don't they have something to say about it?"

She could only imagine what humans would have made out of that. Some would have blamed the devil and called it a grave sin, while others would have made it into a religious experience.

He smiled. "If I could get an audience with an oracle, and if one was willing to grant me an answer, I could ask that question, but oracles are rare, and getting an audience is nearly impossible. People wait many years until their name is drawn in the lottery."

57

FRANKIE

Dagor's home world sounded fascinating, and Frankie wondered how much he would be willing to tell her about it. Still, right now, she was most interested in those translucent beings made of energy.

If the oracles had the answers, how come no one had asked them about it yet?

That didn't seem likely. Dagor was probably just avoiding answering her question to keep up the mystery.

Still, it was possible that the goddesses on Dagor's planet didn't see the same things human females saw when tripping on venom. They might not be as susceptible to the venom's effect.

It was difficult to think with Dagor's hands roving over her back in a very suggestive way, but Frankie commanded her libido to stand down. Her body had already been sated last night, and it could give her mind a chance to satisfy its curiosity.

"I have a few questions."

Dagor smiled. "Usually, human females are much more loopy when they wake up from a venom trip. You seem perfectly lucid and ready to fire away."

"What can I say?" She batted her eyelashes. "I'm special. Do goddesses react the same way to the venom?"

"Not as strongly, but yes. They do."

"Do they see the translucent energy people?"

He nodded. "Everyone sees them when they are tripping. Even males sometimes see them, but since they usually have short trips, they don't remember much from them."

"How do males get to trip? I mean the heterosexual ones." She looked at him from under lowered lashes. "Do you have bisexual and gay gods?"

He laughed. "People who live forever eventually try everything, but there are those who are predominantly one or the other."

"That makes sense. So, what about those who never engage with other males? How do they get to trip on venom and see people made of energy?"

"In fights, gods bite other gods, and that's how they experience a venom bite, but in a very different way than females do. The venom is more concentrated, and its effect is stronger and shorter, but since we are very civilized now and no longer try to kill each other, the fighting is limited to sports, which are not very popular."

"That's good. I wish it was the same for humans." As his finger brushed over the seam between her butt cheeks, Frankie squirmed. "Are you doing this to make me stop asking you questions?"

He smirked. "No, you can keep asking for as long as you can hold back. This is payback for keeping me on the edge last night."

That was fair, and it was also a game Frankie knew that she would win. He had no idea how stubborn she could be.

"Did you ever get to experience a venom trip?"

Dagor nodded. "Troopers train in hand-to-hand combat. To my great shame, I often lost and got bitten."

"Why shame?"

He shrugged. "You know how males are. Gods, immortals, and humans are all the same in that regard. We are prideful, and we want to best our opponents."

Since the gods created people in their image using their own genetic material, it made sense that there were many similarities.

She cupped his cheek. "It's not the strongest who wins, but the smartest and those who persevere. I'm sure that you won in all the mind and strategy games."

"I won many of those, but there were better gods than me. It's hard to be exceptional in a society of trillions."

She couldn't imagine so many people. Earth's population was about eight billion. One trillion was a hundred and twenty-five times that.

"How many trillions?"

"There are about three trillion gods on Anumati and one trillion Kra-ell."

Frankie let out a whistle. "That's five hundred times Earth's population."

"That's only Anumati. Together with the colonies and settlements around the universe, it's close to double that."

"Incredible. Now I understand why it takes so long to get answers from the oracles, especially if there aren't many of them."

"I think that only the Supreme can answer questions of that magnitude," Dagor said. "Still, even if she could, it doesn't mean she would. She might decide that this is not the kind of information mere gods should possess."

As Dagor's fingers dipped into her moist center, Frankie's eyes rolled back in her head. "You win. The rest of my questions can wait for later."

He chuckled. "You are supposed to call the doctor and tell her when you are ready to see her. Can that wait, too?"

"Definitely."

58

ARU

"Good morning," Gabi greeted Dagor with a knowing smile. "How is Frankie doing?"

Given that the two had entered the dining hall holding hands and smiling at each other like a couple in love, Gabi's assumption wasn't surprising. Dagor seemed to have no problem with everyone knowing that Frankie was his. He'd even kissed the girl's cheek, and as she tried to pull her hand out of his to go to her friend's table, he'd held on for a couple of seconds too long before letting go.

"I wasn't allowed inside the patient room, but Frankie told me that the doctor wasn't too concerned. For now, she should be more mindful of her eating habits, and if the symptoms persist, she should see her regular doctor and have some tests done."

"I'm glad the human is fine," Negal said. "You seem taken with her." There was a gleam in the troper's eyes.

The guy would never admit it, but he was a romantic.

"Frankie is fun to be with, but it's just a vacation fling, so you can wipe those smug expressions from your faces. I'm not in love with her, and I won't be. Once this cruise is over, we go our separate ways."

Aru put down his fork. "Frankie is rumored to be a Dormant, just like Gabi was. If you feel a connection to her, she might be the one for you, and if she turns immortal, you can have a future together."

The stubborn expression Dagor often displayed slammed over his features. "I'm happy for you and Gabi, but this is not a path I can follow. I don't want to spend the rest of my immortal life on this godforsaken planet. I want to go home one day, even if it's in a millennium, and I can't bring a hybrid mate."

It was a valid point, and trying to figure out a way around it was keeping Aru awake at night. Like Dagor, he also wanted to go home one day and introduce his mate to his parents and sister. Still, as long as hybrids were considered abominations on Anumati and its colonies, that wasn't an option.

"I don't know if that's a wise approach," Gabi said. "A thousand years is a long time to be alone."

"Who said anything about being alone? I can enjoy myself with various females like I have been doing for five years. It hasn't been a hardship."

Aru didn't respond because it was futile to argue with Dagor. Sooner or later, he would realize that his reaction to Frankie was different and that there was more to their meeting than a casual sea-voyage trip.

"I'm always fascinated by matters of the heart," Negal said. "The heart takes over from the mind and commandeers the driver's seat."

"Not in my case." Dagor snatched a piece of toast from the tray and started spreading butter over it, but he was pressing too hard, and the toast was crumbling. "Damn. Why don't they use tougher bread?" He dropped the pieces on his plate and took another slice.

Negal chuckled. "As I said, matters of the heart take priority. I'm so glad no female has ever gotten her hooks into my soul."

"That's a rude thing to say," Gabi admonished. "You make it sound like I did something bad to Aru."

Aru took her hand and brought it to his lips for a kiss. "You illuminated my life, my love. Before you, I lived under a cloud and didn't even realize that not enough sunshine was coming through."

"Oh, Aru." Gabi brought their conjoined hands to her lips and kissed his knuckles. "My heart overflows with love for you."

Dagor chuckled. "And that's why I will never allow it to happen to me. Love turns perfectly normal people into sappy puddles of sweetness."

"I don't know what that girl sees in you," Negal said in their native language. "You have the tact of a monkey. Perhaps I should offer her a better alternative." Negal started to rise.

"Sit." Dagor clamped his hand on the trooper's shoulder. "For the duration of this cruise, Frankie is mine. So, back off."

People sitting at the neighboring tables were glancing their way. Aru wasn't sure how much of their language they understood. But even if they didn't understand a word of the gods' language, it wasn't difficult to interpret Dagor's response to Negal's suggestion to take Frankie off his hands. First of all, he'd said her name, and secondly, the barely contained rage in his tone had been impossible to miss.

"Relax." Negal clapped Dagor on the shoulder. "I was just trying to prove a point, and I did."

59

FRANKIE

"What did Bridget say?" Mia asked as soon as Frankie got to her table.

She had expected her friend to ask about the night she'd spent with Dagor, which was much more eventful than the short visit to the clan doctor. But maybe she didn't want to do that in front of Toven and the others sharing their table and was waiting to have that kind of talk with her in private or with Margo on the line.

It was only fair that Mia would demand the details. After all, Frankie and Margo had done the same to her. Still, now that the shoe was on the other foot, Frankie regretted hassling Mia to reveal intimate details.

It was okay to talk about dates and hookups, but it was different when the person was someone she'd grown to care about. She'd known Dagor for less than twenty-four hours, but the connection had been pretty immediate. Perhaps her mother hadn't been a silly romantic when she'd said that when the right person showed up, Frankie would know.

Was Dagor the one for her, though?

He didn't seem interested in a long-term relationship, and she'd told him that a cruise fling was all she was interested in, too. It wasn't fair to him to change her mind and start talking about forever.

Besides, they were basing their assumptions about possible dormancy on her likability, which was the least scientific method she could think of.

Chances were that she was just a human. If so, a future with Dagor was impossible regardless of his aversion to long-term relationships.

Sitting on the chair Toven had gallantly pulled out for her, Frankie shrugged. "She said that it was probably because of excessive alcohol consumption without eating. It can prevent the liver from releasing glucose from its glycogen stores to the bloodstream, leading to hypoglycemia." She chuckled. "At least I've learned something thanks to my fainting spells. I didn't even know that the liver stores glycogen. Did we learn that in school?"

Mia shook her head. "I don't remember. You told me that you had bar snacks with your drinks, and before going to the bar, you also snacked in your room. Those weren't the healthiest choices, but you had something in your stomach. You shouldn't have fainted."

Frankie had forgotten entirely about the snacks and had told Bridget that she hadn't eaten. Well, according to her mother, a few pretzels and a small bag of mixed nuts didn't count as a meal, but Mia was right about her stomach not having been empty.

"Maybe it wasn't enough. Anyway, the doctor told me to eat regular meals and see if the problem returns. If it does, I'm to march myself into my regular doctor's office and ask for a fasting glucose blood test to start with and a bunch of other tests to determine the underlying cause."

"You should do that regardless of whether the fainting returns." Mia handed Frankie the tray with the assorted cold cuts. "Now eat and tell me about your night with Dagor. Did the two of you end up watching television?"

"Yes." Frankie batted her eyelashes. "Until the wee hours of the morning and then again before seeing the doctor."

Mia stifled a laugh. "The movies must have been exciting."

"Yes, the best."

Toven's lips twitched as he pretended to be absorbed in his oatmeal. Still, the other couple sitting at their table were grinning and not trying to hide their amusement.

"What are your plans for the rest of the day?" Mia asked. "I mean until the wedding or a little before to get ready." She narrowed her eyes on Frankie. "Just don't wear the dress you wore yesterday, and make sure to eat throughout the day and not wait to stuff yourself at the reception."

That was precisely what Frankie had intended to do. To keep her weight under control and still enjoy her social life, she often skipped meals before a dinner date or an event.

"I know, I know. I've learned my lesson. I told Dagor that I intend to laze by the pool and enjoy Bob the robot's drinks. It would be great if you and Toven could join us."

Mia grimaced. "It's going to be hot up there, and the sun glare will make it miserable for Toven. Your boyfriend will probably not enjoy it either."

"He's not my boyfriend." Frankie cast a sidelong glance to where Dagor was sitting with his teammates and Aru's mate. He didn't look happy, and it seemed like he was arguing with Negal.

Was it about her?

"You are right." Mia chuckled. "Dagor is not a boy. He's not even human. Maybe we can call him your god-friend?"

"Just a friend." Frankie cut a piece out of the omelet and put it in her mouth.

She wasn't a breakfast person, and the eggs made her nauseous. A piece of toast would have been better, with a little jam.

Except, she had a feeling that it wasn't the eggs that were making her stomach roil. It was the aggravated expression on Dagor's face. She much preferred to see him relaxed and flirty.

Did it have anything to do with her?

She swallowed with difficulty. What did she care about what made him angry? As long as he was nice while with her, she shouldn't worry about arguments he had with his friends, right?

God, she was such a damn people pleaser.

Well, her former bosses would strongly disagree with that statement. A contrary brat would be their more likely description of her.

That was because she was only eager to please those she cared about, and for some reason, she had added Dagor to that list. Given her enormous family, there were many people she cared about, but other than that she didn't have a lot of friends.

In fact, her only real friends were Margo and Mia, and they were more like sisters to her. The rest of the people she knew were acquaintances.

There were a couple of boyfriends that she'd cared about in the past, but getting into her bed didn't automatically mean getting into her heart, especially not in one day.

60

KIAN

There was no assigned seating for breakfast, and as Kian scanned the dining hall, Kalugal waved him over, pointing to the two chairs at the table where he sat with Jacki, Amanda, and Dalhu. The rest of the family wasn't there, and he wondered whether they were late or had already eaten.

His mother was probably having breakfast in her cabin, and perhaps Alena and Orion had joined her. Although if that was the case, why hadn't she also invited him and Syssi?

"Good morning," Syssi greeted the two couples.

Kian repeated the greeting and pulled out a chair for Syssi. "Are Lokan and Carol still asleep?"

"I guess so," Kalugal said. "We waited for them until four in the morning. The speedboat they chartered to the ship was not as fast as its owner had claimed. Lokan was ready to go back and strangle the guy for lying to him."

The speedboat had been supposed to catch up to the Silver Swan two hours earlier, so Lokan had a good reason to be pissed.

"I don't know why they bothered in the first place." Amanda poured coffee into her mug. "Yamanu was shrouding the entire dock, and the Guardians took care of the port's surveillance cameras. Carol and Lokan could have just gotten on board without any trouble."

"I'm always in favor of more caution." Kian sat Allegra down in the highchair. "If they had a tail, it couldn't have followed them on the water without them seeing it."

Kalugal nodded. "I agree. If we didn't need Lokan to be our ears and eyes in the Brotherhood, I would have advised him to fake his own death a long time ago and cross over."

Lokan wasn't interested in joining the clan, though. He still dreamt about liberating the island from his father's yoke and rehabilitating its inhabitants.

The guy was a dreamer, and in this respect, he reminded Kian of Annani. His mother also believed in rehabilitating the monsters.

Kian was not as forgiving, perhaps because he'd been exposed to their evildoing and hadn't shared the details with his mother to save her the heartache.

His philosophy was simple. Anyone who had raped and murdered didn't deserve to live and was beyond redemption. Then again, Dalhu had ordered Mark's murder, a defenseless civilian, and here he was, mated to Amanda, father to Evie, sitting at the table with the family.

Dalhu had been following orders, but sometimes Kian wondered how far his obedience would have gone. If Navuh had ordered him to rape and murder children, would he have done it?

Compulsion was a powerful force, but Kian had a feeling that Dalhu would have slit his own throat before obeying such orders.

Besides, even Navuh wasn't that evil.

"Kian." Kalugal waved a hand in front of his face. "Whatever you are thinking about right now, think about something else. The waves of aggression you're emitting are unhealthy for our children."

"You are right." Kian took a deep, centering breath and glanced at Allegra's worried little face. "It's okay, sweetie. Daddy is not angry."

Fates, one day the responsibility for all this crap would fall on her shoulders, and he wanted better for her. He wanted the utopian world his mother imagined, but he knew that it would never come.

Wishing it wouldn't make it so, nor would all the effort his mother and his clan had put into changing things for the better.

The best he could do was keep his people safe and hope his efforts would do.

"I'm not going to warn the Brotherhood about the Eternal King's threat." He reached for a piece of toast. "Navuh would not help us. If anything, he and his minions would try to sabotage our efforts."

Kalugal took Darius from Jacki and cradled the baby to his chest. "Regrettably, I have to agree. I just want to save my mother."

"People," Amanda said in an exasperated tone. "We are here to celebrate, and you are depressing everyone."

"Sorry about that." Kian cast her an apologetic look.

Kalugal, being Kalugal, plastered a smile on his face. "I haven't been introduced to the new gods yet, and I'm offended that Jacki and I weren't invited to the meeting with them yesterday."

"I can introduce you right now." Kian pushed away from the table.

The disturbing thoughts had ruined his appetite.

Kalugal handed the baby back to Jacki. "Do you want to come with me to meet them?"

His tone indicated he wasn't in favor, and Jacki must have picked up on it.

She shook her head. "Perhaps later."

As he and Kalugal headed toward the gods' table, Kian wondered whether Aru had contacted his leaders on Anumati. If what he suspected was accurate and the god could communicate telepathically with someone on his home planet, he could do that from anywhere and could have done it already.

Aru and his teammates had met Annani and figured out who she was. Now, the question was what he would do with the information. Kian needed to get Aru alone and ask him point blank how he communicated with his leaders.

Stressed couldn't begin to describe how Kian felt.

Perhaps that was why he had been inundated by thoughts of the past that he thought he had suppressed. The past never stayed in the past, and the cycle of horrors was always repeated. People just never learned.

As they got to the gods' table, Kalugal offered his hand to Gabi first.

"I'm Kalugal, Kian's much better-looking and more charming cousin. I'm also a council member."

"Hi." She gave him her hand and rose to her feet. "I'm Gabi. It's nice to meet you."

After hearing that Kalugal was a council member, the three gods rose to their feet as well.

"No need to stand." He smiled. "I just came to introduce myself."

He shook hands with the three gods, who remained standing, exchanging names and pleasantries.

"Please, join us." Aru brought over a chair from the next table for Kian, and Negal did the same for Kalugal.

"By the way, congratulations." Kalugal turned to Gabi. "On your transition as well as on finding your mate. You must have done a lot of good in your short life to deserve such a boon."

She shook her head. "I have no idea what I have done to deserve a god for a mate, but I'm thankful to the universe and the Fates for blessing me so."

"Indeed." Kalugal nodded.

"By the way," Kian said. "We are having an impromptu bachelor party for my future brother-in-law in my suite. Would you like to join us for whiskey and cigars?"

He might get an opportunity to take Aru aside and talk to him privately, away from the ears of his companions.

The god inclined his head. "We would be honored to attend."

61

ALENA

"Carol!" Alena squealed as the tiny blonde sauntered into the cabin. "You are a sight for sore eyes." She opened her arms to welcome the clan's hero.

The petite blonde walked into the embrace with a grin on her face. "Why are your eyes sore? This is your wedding day. You should be merry."

"Your being here makes my day even merrier." Alena kissed her on both cheeks.

After extracting herself from Alena's arms, Carol turned to Annani and dipped her head. "Hello, Clan Mother. How have you been?"

As the question seemed to take Annani by surprise, Alena realized that people rarely asked her mother how she was feeling, which was a testament to how well she played her role.

"I am overjoyed to be here, helping Alena get ready for her wedding." Annani smiled at Carol.

Carol nodded and moved to hug Jacki and caress Darius's cheek. "Hello, little guy. I've missed you all so much." She walked over to the couch and sat next to Syssi. "And where is your little darling?"

"Allegra is with my parents. I won't get her back until the wedding tonight. She and my mother are bonding."

Carol smiled. "It may persuade your parents to finally retire and move into the village."

"I doubt it." Syssi sighed. "My mother is one stubborn lady."

Carol patted her knee before changing the subject. "I heard that I missed a big event last night."

"Yeah, well." Syssi put her half-empty margarita glass on the coffee table. "Everyone already knew about the gods, but only a few had seen them before last night. Then we had a bit of excitement when Mia's human friend fainted."

Carol frowned. "Since when is Kian allowing human friends to visit clan territory, which this ship technically is?"

"Frankie is a potential Dormant," Amanda said. "Toven likes her and Mia's other best friend a lot, and given that he's a recluse who doesn't like many people, we suspect that it's affinity at work. We also had Lisa sniff them both, and she thinks they are both Dormants."

"Lisa, David's little sister?" Carol looked doubtful. "She's still human, so even if she can identify Dormants, I find it hard to believe it's developed enough to work."

"True." Syssi sighed. "But Toven insisted on inviting Frankie and Margo on the cruise, and at the end of it, he will thrall away their memories of immortals and gods or compel them to silence, depending on whether they come to work for him in the village."

Carol shook her head. "I find all of the latest developments strange. We have a new group of aliens living among us, and Kian's entrusted the village's protection to them, and now humans are coming to work in the village. What happened to him?"

Alena sighed. "That's just the tip of the iceberg. I'm glad that we have the Kra-ell to reinforce our ranks, although, given the danger we are facing, they will not be all that helpful."

"Can you stop that?" Amanda got to her feet. "Stop talking about depressing things. You are getting married tonight, and we are here to help you get ready, not only with makeup and hair but also with mood."

"It's hard." Alena caressed her belly. "I can't help worrying."

Amanda grimaced. "And I can't even get you drunk because you're pregnant. That would have helped get you in a festive mood."

"Maybe Carol can entertain us with stories about China," Annani suggested.

"Lokan and I are enjoying China more than we expected. Lokan is in his element, talking to government officials and meddling, and I practically run the fashion business, which is very exciting."

As Carol kept telling them about the clothing industry and the difficulties of working with and around the Chinese regime, Alena leaned back against the couch cushions and closed her eyes.

"You look tired," her mother said. "Perhaps you should rest a little before the party."

"I can't." Alena opened her eyes. "I'm too excited to rest."

"Do you want me to sing you to sleep like I did when you were a little girl?"

Alena laughed. "I'm over two thousand years old. I don't remember ever being a young girl."

"I am much older, and I remember." Annani smoothed the folds of her gown. "I remember every lesson my mother taught me even though I did not want to follow her instructions. It took me long years to realize the wisdom of her lessons." She sighed. "I still miss her, and I miss my father. That never goes away." Her eyes misted with tears. "But most of all, I miss Khiann. Not a day goes by that I do not think of him."

Following her mother's words, a sad hush fell over the room, but it didn't last long.

"This is a time to celebrate." Amanda glared at their mother. "I don't know what has gotten into all of you. No negative thoughts are allowed in here." She waved at Onidu. "I need another margarita."

"Yes, mistress. Another margarita is coming right up."

"Where is Evie?" Annani asked.

"Napping in her stroller. I put her in the bedroom with a baby monitor." Amanda tapped her ear. "If she wakes up, I'll hear her."

"I hope she wakes up soon," Carol said. "I want to see her."

"Careful," Syssi said. "Babies are known to be contagious."

Carol laughed. "I'm immune. There are no babies for me as long as Lokan is playing the double agent role. It's too dangerous."

As everyone nodded and another hush fell over the room, Amanda shook her head. "What did I say about bringing up depressing topics? Only happy thoughts are allowed in here."

62

ANNANI

The truth was that Annani was trying to appear cheerful for Alena's sake, but at times like this, she missed Khiann more than ever.

He should have been there with her, celebrating the weddings of his children, but the Fates had been cruel to her and robbed her of a life with him.

The children born to her had been fathered by humans, good, intelligent, courageous men whom she had picked carefully. They all resembled her Khiann in one way or another, so she could pretend that he had been their real father, and maybe in spirit he was.

The prophecy she had been given had said so, and it had promised her two more children.

Except, that would be a tough act to pull off, given how rarely she got intimate with humans lately. It was not like her to abstain, and it worried her that, as of late, she had no desire for the pleasures of the flesh.

Was she getting to the age when some gods were starting to lose their minds?

Was she depressed?

Having Vanessa assess her mental state was out of the question because Annani had an image to uphold. Her clan looked up to her, and she needed to appear strong at all times. Her only option was to seek out a human psychologist in the city and shroud herself while going to sessions.

It could be fun to get out of the village a couple times a week and spend an hour talking to someone who did not know who and what she was.

Annani chuckled to herself. The therapist would probably think that she suffered from delusions of grandeur and had a god complex.

The other problem was that she would have to tell Kian, and he would get worried. Oh well, she could always blame her melancholy on loneliness. Since losing Alena as her companion, Annani had been lonelier than ever.

"I have been thinking about the Fates lately," Syssi said, pulling Annani out of her somber thoughts. "Are there only three for the entire universe, or does each planet get its own trio? Maybe even each continent?"

Jacki chuckled. "I think there should be a trio of Fates for each zip code. Just think how much work they have to do."

"That's an interesting concept." Amanda tapped her margarita glass with the tip of her fingernail. "They may be known as the three Fates because they always work in teams of three. Kind of like the gods. Perhaps it's not a coincidence that Aru's team has three members."

Alena put her teacup down. "One thing is for sure. The Fates did not take over the bodies of these three gods to send us a message. Those three are just too male to house the energy of female entities."

The same thought had occurred to Annani, and checking her hunch that the Fates had guided the gods to the clan had been one of the reasons she had wanted to meet them in person. Regrettably, she had dismissed the idea for the same reason Alena had. There was nothing even remotely feminine in the way those gods conducted themselves. If the Fates had been involved, they had done it through other means. They had not taken over the gods' bodies.

"I think I met the Fates," Syssi said quietly. "My grandmother, may her soul rest in peace, had three dear friends in the retirement home she lived in until she died. I used to visit her and read to them, and after she had passed, I continued to do so. They were always pushing my buttons for the fun of it, making me read racy stories to them just to see me blush. Still, when I met Kian and brought him with me to my reading session, they really went overboard, pushing me to overcome my shyness and show Kian that I was interested. Then, after Kian and I became a couple, the three of them suddenly decided to move to Florida, and I lost track of them. I think that's very suspicious."

With a groan, Alena pushed to her feet. "As fascinating as the subject of the Fates is, I should start getting ready. I will run a bath and soak in it until I feel relaxed." She turned to Amanda. "After that, I'm all yours to do with as you please."

"Can I cut your hair?" The dangerous gleam in Amanda's eyes did not bode well for Alena's hair.

She lifted the heavy rope of her long blond hair and pursed her lips. "I loved this hairdo I got when I was pretending to be a Slovakian supermodel, but it wasn't me. It also doesn't fit my simple wedding dress."

Carol lifted a finger. "A fairy princess style. That's what you should go for."

Alena smiled brightly. "That's what I'm aiming for."

63

FRANKIE

"I want to see Bob." Mia swiveled her chair around in an expert maneuver that had Frankie shaking her head. "Toven is with Orion and the rest of the guys, smoking cigars and drinking whiskey, but I was not invited to Alena's pre-wedding get-together."

Frankie arched a brow. "Were you hoping to be invited?"

Mia shrugged. "I think it's only her mother and sisters. Anyway, put on your bikini and let's go. Dagor is with Toven and the others, and based on past events, cigar smoking takes a long time. We have at least two hours."

That answered whether she should wait for him or go alone.

"My bikini is already on." She opened her robe to show Mia. "What do you think?"

Mia grinned. "That purple color looks amazing on you. When Dagor is done smoking and comes looking for you, he will have a hard time keeping his fangs from elongating once he sees you."

The reminder had Frankie's nipples pebble, and as she pulled the robe closed, she hoped that Mia hadn't noticed. "Thanks." She tied the belt around her waist. "What about you? Still too self-conscious about being seen in a swimming suit?"

They'd argued about this before, with Frankie trying to convince Mia that she looked hot despite her condition and should put a swimming suit on and enjoy the beach.

"I'm not going into the pool, so there is no point. I'm comfortable as I am."

It was on the tip of Frankie's tongue to point out that Mia's legs were nearly fully regenerated and that no one on the ship cared about her having no feet, but she swallowed the retort and nodded. "You're the boss."

As they left the cabin, Frankie was glad to discover that the hallway wasn't deserted, and other occupants were emerging from their cabins or returning to them. Several had their bathrobes on, so she assumed that they were on their way to the pool as well.

"I have a feeling that we are not going to be alone on the Lido deck today."

Mia nodded. "It's going to be crowded, but that never bothered you before, so why should it now?"

Frankie chuckled. "Yeah, but that was with normal people and not gods and immortals."

"You are dating a god." Mia drove her chair into the elevator. "So that shouldn't faze you."

As people made room for her, Frankie squeezed by and didn't respond.

Mia had made her comment before entering, so no one had heard her, but Frankie wondered how many knew about her and Dagor.

According to Mia, he had rushed to her side when she'd fainted and everyone had seen it, so there must be rumors, but she wasn't going to confirm it for them.

When the elevator stopped on the top deck, she waited until they were outside before leaning over to whisper in Mia's ear. "I don't want to make our relationship public. I don't know how many people know about it and if Dagor is okay with it."

Mia laughed. "After your entrance to the dining hall this morning, I doubt that there is anyone who doesn't know. He held your hand, looked at you lovingly, and kissed your cheek. Given that public display of affection, I don't think Dagor minds everyone knowing you are together. In fact, I think he was making a statement to deter others from approaching you."

Frankie swallowed. "I forgot about that."

After the night and morning they had spent together, holding hands and kissing had been natural, and it hadn't registered as anything unusual.

Maybe she'd still been loopy from his bite.

There was a lightness, a floaty feeling that she'd ascribed to the fabulous sex, but maybe there was more to it. She should have remembered to let go of his hand before entering the dining hall.

Who needed all the rumors?

Frankie lifted her head and scanned the people sitting around the pool.

Several looked at her, some with smiles, some with frowns, and some with interest.

They probably wondered what a god saw in her, a mere human.

"Maybe it wasn't a good idea to come up here." She tied the belt tighter around her waist.

Mia regarded her with a raised brow. "Who are you and what have you done with the Frankie who is unafraid of anything?"

"I'm not afraid. It just feels weird to have everyone looking at me."

"Let's get a drink." Mia steered her chair toward the bar. "I want to see Bob."

There was a long line in front of the bar, and when people offered to let Mia go ahead of them, she refused.

As their turn finally came, Bob greeted her with a big smile on his shiny chrome face. "Mistress Frankie. It is so good to see you again. Would you like a mojito?"

"Yes, please." She turned to Mia. "What would you like?"

"A lemonade, please."

When Bob started on the drinks, Frankie leaned down to whisper in Mia's ear. "He remembered the drink I ordered yesterday. Isn't that fabulous? He must remember every drink he ever made and who ordered it. Bob is the perfect barman."

"Not quite," the guy standing behind them said. "Earlier, I tried to share my woes with him, and he just looked at me with round, unblinking eyes. A real barman would have offered advice." He smiled and extended his hand. "I'm Max."

"I'm Frankie." She shook what he offered. "I'm Mia's friend."

"I know." He waved his other hand around. "Everyone here does."

Given his tone, Max hadn't meant that everyone knew she was Mia's friend. He was referring to her relationship with Dagor.

Well, calling it a relationship was an exaggeration. It was a prolonged hookup.

Ten days, with only nine remaining.

"Oh, God." Frankie rubbed a hand over her face.

He chuckled. "Yeah, that too. Gossip is a big problem in a small community. You'll get used to that."

"Here are your drinks, mistresses," Bob announced cheerfully, handing a beverage to each of them with his long robotic arms.

"Thank you." Frankie brought the glass to her lips and took a small sip. "Just as perfect as the one you made me yesterday."

"I'm glad that you find my service satisfactory." Bob turned to Max. "What can I make for you, master?"

"Same as before," he said.

"Coming up." Bob swiveled his torso and reached for one of the bottles hanging from the bar's ceiling.

Max turned to Frankie. "Save a dance for me tonight?"

She felt her cheeks warm. "Normally, I'd say I would be delighted, but I don't know whether Dagor will be okay with me dancing with someone else."

Max's expression turned predatory. "Perhaps you can save me a dance for when you arrive at the village. The god is not welcome to follow you there, and when he leaves to search for the missing pods, I will be waiting for you."

Talk about direct.

This guy didn't mince words or beat around the bush, and usually she liked that, but right now, it just made her uncomfortable.

Which was stupid.

Max was handsome, charming, and confident, and if she weren't with Dagor, she would have flirted with him right back. But Dagor was leaving soon, and Max was a perfectly suitable replacement. Yet, she couldn't bring herself to even think about him in romantic terms, let alone show interest.

64

KIAN

"Orion, buddy." Kalugal wrapped his arm around Orion's shoulders. "Let me give you the prescription for married bliss."

Kian felt that his cousin was inebriated, although he hadn't seen Kalugal drinking to excess. Four of the ten bottles of whiskey he'd brought for the occasion were empty. Still, given the number of partakers, that wasn't enough to get anyone drunk.

Anandur had brought two cases of Snake Venom, though, so perhaps Kalugal had gotten some of that before moving on to the superb whiskey.

"I'm all ears." Orion's smile was a tad too bright.

Maybe they had started drinking before coming to the bachelor party. That was the only way they could already be drunk.

"Never disagree with your wife," Kalugal lectured with a raised finger. "Say yes first, and then present counterarguments if you have any. It'd be better if you didn't, though. Most of the time, it's not worth the effort because she will get her way no matter what you say, and arguing about it will only rattle your nest."

Orion pretended to consider his words for a long moment. "I don't see how this is any different from what I'm doing now. Given that my mate is much older and wiser, it only makes sense for me to defer to her."

Toven lifted his glass. "My son is a smart male."

"What about you?" Dagor asked. "Your mate is a very young female. Do you defer to her judgment?"

Toven's expression turned serious. "On some subjects, yes. I'm ancient, but I still have a hard time understanding humans. Mia is better at this than I am."

Kian hoped others would join in the discussion so he could take Aru aside and ask him whether he had communicated his findings about Annani to his supervisors on Anumati, or wherever the resistance leadership was located.

"Relationships are complicated," David said, "but if there is mutual respect and open communication, even couples who don't see eye to eye on some things can have a successful relationship."

Catching Aru's eyes, Kian lifted his drink and motioned for the god to follow him to a corner of the balcony that wasn't occupied.

Aru said something to Negal and then followed Kian. "Don't you find the discussion interesting?" He leaned against the railing, cigar in one hand and a glass of whiskey in the other.

"I do, but since my cousin summarized married life so succinctly, I have nothing to add."

Aru's lips quirked on one corner. "I sincerely doubt that."

Kian leaned on the railing next to him and puffed on his cigar. "In many ways, females are smarter than us. The things males do better are not the qualities I'm proud of."

Aru nodded. "I know what you mean. I have been fortunate not to fight in real battles, only simulations, but even those consumed a piece of my soul. I don't like killing, even if it's computer-generated evildoers."

The answer made Kian's heart constrict with sympathy and foreboding. Aru was still young, but he was eternal, which meant that one day he would have to fight and kill to protect those he loved. The cycles of peace and war might be longer on Anumati, but from what Kian had learned from Jade, the gods had yet to evolve out of warfare.

It was an ugly world, and it was kill or be killed, or rather, kill or see your loved ones murdered.

Shaking his head, Kian took another puff of his cigar and then one more until he felt the tension abate. "Have you communicated to your leaders what you learned yesterday?"

Aru affected a frown, but it looked fake. "How? I haven't left the ship."

It was an evasive answer, but it wasn't an outright lie, which meant that Aru didn't enjoy lying or that lies didn't come easily to him. In either case, his response earned him merit points with Kian.

"Let's cut to the chase," Kian said. "I suspect that you can communicate telepathically with someone on Anumati, and that person has access to the resistance leadership. You don't need to leave the ship to do that."

Aru didn't confirm it, but the fear that passed through his eyes was as good as an admission. "What makes you think that?"

"Logic and conjecture. Two members of my clan, a mother and her daughter, can communicate telepathically as if they were conducting a phone conversation. They can do that regardless of distance, no matter how vast. It's a rare ability, and they are the only two I know of who possess it, but if mere immortals have it, then I'm sure some gods can do it as well."

"It's a rare ability among gods, too," Aru said. "Those who are found out are either eliminated by the Eternal King or made to work for him."

"I see." Kian took another puff. "You are afraid of admitting your ability because you are protecting the person on the other end, who I assume is a family member. I don't need to know who they are, only that they can access the resistance leadership." He pinned Aru with a hard look. "You've learned my most guarded secret. It's only fair that you share yours with me."

Swallowing, Aru nodded. "It has to stay between the two of us. No one else can find out."

Kian lifted a brow. "Not even the heir to the throne if she decides to join your cause?"

"For now, I need your word that it stays between us. If further down the line we need to include the princess, we will."

65

ARU

Aru had as much as admitted that Kian had guessed correctly, but he couldn't go the final step and tell him more.

"Let's assume that I can communicate with someone. I'm not saying I do, but if I could, what would you like to say to them?"

Kian let out a breath. "I don't know. I don't want my mother anywhere near the resistance, but it's not my call to make. She's still the head of the clan, and I answer to her. What I want to know is what their response was to the revelation that a legitimate heir to the throne lives on Earth."

Tension radiated from the immortal, and Aru could understand why. Kian was protecting his loved ones as best he could.

"I didn't get a response yet, but I assume it would be greeted with jubilation. The person that this information will be delivered to will protect it with their lives. You have nothing to fear from them."

"Is it the queen? Ahn's mother?"

Kian's guesses were too accurate for Aru's comfort.

"I can't confirm or deny because I'm not privy to that information."

Kian chuckled. "Should I call Andrew over and verify that statement?"

Damn. Aru had forgotten about the truth-reader.

He shook his head. "The same way you are protecting yours, I am protecting mine. I will not say more. I cannot."

"I understand." Kian took a puff of his cigar. "I'm anxious to hear their response, and I'm even more anxious about my mother's reaction to it. She's reckless, especially when she believes in a cause, and she believes in yours."

"And you don't?"

Kian shrugged. "I don't know enough to pass judgment. The Eternal King has kept the gods in line for hundreds of thousands of years. Who knows what would have happened with someone else at the helm? I've seen enough examples of rulers who were too decent for the good of their people, and in the end, the people suffered. I've also seen rulers who weren't good and restricted their people's freedoms. Still, once they were removed from power, the so-called liberators became much worse monsters. I don't think my mother can be ruthless enough for people to fear her, and therefore keep the peace. The most important thing for a ruler to realize is what kind of enemies they have and in what way those enemies will respond to them. As human history indicates, enemies raise their heads when they perceive weakness."

"The gods don't have enemies."

Kian smiled. "Right now, they don't because the Eternal King rules mercilessly over them. With a weaker ruler at the helm, factions might break away from the collective and form their own countries or planets or whatever. Wars could start over resources, over colonies, over ideologies, and the Fates know what else. Take us and the Brotherhood. We are the same people, and we both need to hide from the humans, but Navuh and his mercenary army want to annihilate us, and there is nothing we can do to change their minds about it. We can either hide, fight, or die. Those are our only three options. And since we can't fight a force so much larger than us, we must choose the first option."

"What about technology?" Aru asked. "Can't you get a leg up with that? From what I have observed, brute force is no longer the determining factor. Whoever controls the technology wins."

"Only to a certain degree." Kian finished the last dregs of the whiskey. "Besides, Navuh realized the same thing, and now his focus is to bring his forces to the twenty-first century, and soon we won't have even that advantage."

Aru didn't envy Kian his position. It seemed hopeless.

"Why does he want to eliminate your clan?"

"Different ideology. We want peace and prosperity for all; he wants to dominate and subjugate. It also serves his agenda to have a handy scapegoat to rally his troops." He gave Aru a sad smile. "That's actually the one speck of light in the dark. He might not want to do away with us completely because he would lose his scapegoat. Humans are not a good substitute for a hated enemy."

"The Kra-ell are," Aru said.

"He doesn't know about them. Not yet, anyway. I hope it stays that way."

Aru finished his drink and took another puff of his cigar. "You need the resistance to establish its headquarters here and to be on your side. That's why you are willing to help us."

Kian nodded. "It's one of the reasons. I'm much more afraid of the Eternal King than of Navuh's Brotherhood. Given what you've told me, though, it might take thousands of years before the resistance makes a move, and it might be too late for us."

"Then we need to impress upon the resistance leaders the urgency of the situation on Earth. The heir's survival could be at stake if they don't act more swiftly."

66

DAGOR

Dagor watched Aru depart with Kian and huddle in the farthest corner of the balcony, wondering what it was all about.

He knew Aru was hiding something, but he no longer cared. What he wanted was to leave and go to Frankie.

What was she doing right now?

Should he call her or text her?

Nah, he'd better not. He was getting attached to a girl he'd met a little over twenty-four hours ago, and if he wasn't careful, he would end up like Aru or worse.

At least Gabi was an immortal who could live as long as Aru did. Frankie might be a Dormant, but she also might not, and if he fell in love with her, he would be setting himself up for a lot of heartache.

"To the groom!" Anandur raised his glass for the umpteenth time.

"To Orion!" All the guys cheered and emptied their glasses. Again.

The redhead grabbed another bottle of whiskey, uncapped it, and poured everyone a new shot. "One more time! To Orion!"

Was he trying to get everyone drunk before the wedding?

Orion seemed unsteady on his feet, and Dagor wasn't the only one who had noticed.

The god wrapped his arm around his son's shoulders and led him to a lounge chair. "I think you've had enough. You don't want to be drunk for your own wedding."

"*Pfft.*" Orion waved a dismissive hand. "I'll burn through it in minutes. I'll be fine."

Toven smiled indulgently at his son. "Can I get you a cup of coffee?"

Orion nodded. "That would be nice. Thank you, Father."

The god's expression changed, surprise flickering through his eyes for a moment, and a smile bloomed. "My pleasure." Toven opened the balcony doors and stepped inside the cabin.

Was the reaction about Orion thanking him or about him calling the god Father?

Dagor sat down on the lounger next to Orion. "How are you feeling?"

"Excellent." The immortal beamed. "How about you? Do you like being on Earth?"

"Not really."

Orion's smile turned into a frown. "Why not?"

"It's not home, and it's far from civilized. People are still killing each other because of religion and other nonsensical reasons, kidnapping and selling young defenseless women for sexual slavery, and the list goes on. Anumati has problems, but it's light years better than here."

"I can't argue with that, but I would like to point out that the Kra-ell we rescued don't have such a favorable opinion of your home planet."

Apparently, the immortal wasn't as drunk as he appeared.

"I don't have a good opinion of it either. I hate the politics, the class differences, the lack of privacy, and many other issues. Still, I'll take it over Earth's crap any day."

Orion sighed. "I guess utopia doesn't exist anywhere."

"Maybe it does." Dagor thought about the energy beings that Frankie had described. "Maybe there are other universes where all beings coexist in harmony. Perhaps it's the next step in evolution."

Orion nodded sagely. "Perhaps that's what's waiting for us beyond the veil."

"I wouldn't go that far." Dagor leaned over to find the ashtray someone had left at the foot of the lounger and tapped his cigar to dislodge a pillar of ash.

"Why not?"

"Because we don't know if anything exists beyond the veil. It might be just stories we tell ourselves to diminish the fear of death."

"Right," Orion agreed. "I believe in the Fates, though. They are innocuous enough. At least no one kills anyone in their name."

"True." Dagor puffed on his cigar. "That's one more reason why Anumati is superior to Earth."

"The Kra-ell believe in the Mother of All Life," Anandur said as he sat down on Orion's other side. "What are we talking about?"

"He doesn't like Earth." Orion pointed an accusing finger at Dagor. "Tell him why he's wrong."

"Everyone is entitled to their opinion." Anandur smiled at Dagor. "But since you are stuck here for the foreseeable future, you should learn to like it more."

"Wise words." Orion lifted his empty glass. "Mind refilling this for me?"

Anandur shook his head. "Your father is getting you coffee. Once you sober up, I will be happy to get you drunk again."

"That doesn't make any sense." Orion held the glass up. "Just one more."

As Dagor's phone pinged with an incoming message, he put his half-smoked cigar on the edge of the ashtray and pulled the device out of his pocket.

His heart skipped a beat when he saw it was from Frankie.

You didn't ask, so I'm asking instead. Will you be my date for the wedding tonight?

Smiling, Dagor typed his answer. *I will be honored to be your date. It's going to be our fourth. Is there anything special I should know about the fourth date?*

Frankie had told him about the three-dates rule, so maybe there was also a four-dates rule?

Hmm. Maybe. You will have to find out.

He chuckled. *Can I find out before the wedding? Where are you now?*

When his phone rang a moment later, he excused himself, pushed to his feet, and walked in the opposite direction of where Aru and Kian were. Thankfully, the balcony wrapped around the bow of the ship and offered plenty of space for the guests to spread out.

"Hi," he answered.

"Hi, yourself. How is the bachelor party going?"

Given the noise in the background, Frankie was up on the Lido deck, and the itch to go to her got even more urgent.

"The cigars are fine, the whiskey even finer, and the groom is drunk and demanding more booze."

"That's all? No strippers?"

He laughed. "Just a bunch of guys smoking cigars and drinking whiskey and beer. It's actually nice. I'm getting to know some of the immortals. How about you? From the sound of it, you are on the upper deck."

"Yeah, I'm here with Mia. She wanted to meet Bob."

Dagor relaxed. "Did she like him?"

"Of course. What's not to like? He remembered who I was and the drink I ordered yesterday, which was awesome, but then the guy who stood in line behind us said that Bob couldn't replace a real bartender because he couldn't offer life advice."

Dagor's good mood turned into irritation. Someone had flirted with Frankie, and perhaps he was still around.

"It depends on the programming. Who's the guy?"

"An immortal named Max. Why?"

"Tell him that you're taken."

Frankie chuckled. "He knows. You made quite the statement this morning at breakfast when you kissed my cheek in front of everyone. Was it intentional?"

"No. I just felt like kissing you, but now I'm glad I did. For the duration of this cruise, you are mine, and I want everyone to know that."

67

FRANKIE

Frankie stood before the mirror and examined the intricate coif Mia had arranged. "This is amazing. And to think that you did it by following YouTube instructions."

Behind her, Mia grinned. "Necessity is the mother of invention. As fabulous as this cruise is, there is no hair salon or spa. Perhaps I should drop a note about it in the suggestion box."

Frankie didn't know if there was a suggestion box or if Mia was talking hypothetically. "Who is doing the bride's hair?"

"Her sisters, I guess. They were holed up in her cabin the entire afternoon." Mia brushed a hand over her short hairdo. "I'm so glad you and Margo convinced me to cut my hair. I don't need to do anything to make it look great."

"True." Frankie turned to her friend. "But you still need to get dressed."

She'd done Mia's makeup and had offered to do something with her hair, but Mia was happy with it the way it was.

"Are you okay by yourself here?" Mia asked.

"I'm ready." Frankie turned in a circle. "Cinderella is awaiting her prince." Dagor was coming to her cabin and would escort her to the wedding.

Mia mock-frowned at her. "Don't let him convince you to have a quickie before the wedding. I will never forgive you if you ruin this updo."

"Yes, ma'am," Frankie saluted.

"You've been warned." Mia pointed a finger at her before turning her chair around. "See you at the wedding, Cindy, and please, don't lose your glass slipper."

"Not a chance."

The prince might not come looking for her with the glass slipper in hand. Besides, her lilac chunky heels were strapped to her ankles, and they were not coming off unless she unstrapped them.

They matched the lilac chiffon evening dress she'd gotten from one of her cousins. It had a deep V-neckline that showcased her collarbone, and just the very tops of her breasts, and the dainty straps allowed her shoulders to be on display. The bodice was adorned with intricate embroidery that attracted the light, adding a hint of shimmer to the subdued color. From the cinched waist, the chiffon cascaded in gentle layers, creating a floor-length skirt that swayed with every move she made.

If not for the five-inch platform heels, the dress would have been too long, but with the heels, it just barely cleared the floor.

"Not bad, Frankie," she told her reflection. "You clean up nicely."

When her phone rang, she rushed to retrieve it from the nightstand and almost tripped but managed to reach it without incident.

Expecting it to be Dagor, she was surprised to see Margo's face on the display.

When she accepted the call, there was a slight delay, reminding her of the security rerouting Mia had warned her about.

"Hi, Margo." She sat on the bed and cradled the phone to her ear. "How are you surviving Cabo?"

"Barely. I can't wait for your ship to get here so I can get out of this place. Not that there is anything wrong with Cabo, it's a lovely vacation spot. It's the company that I can't stand."

"You'd better learn to. Lynda is going to be your sister-in-law."

"I know. I can tolerate her in small doses. But let's talk about you. What happened with that guy you were planning on hooking up with?"

Frankie smiled. "He's picking me up to escort me to the wedding."

"That's not the answer I wanted. Details, Frankie. I want them now."

Even if there was no surveillance, Frankie wouldn't have been able to tell Margo anything about Dagor being a god, or that he had fangs, or that he had bitten her, or about the venom trip. Toven had made sure of that with his compulsion.

"The only thing I can say is that it was out of this world and that I want more."

"Oh my God, Frankie. Don't tell me that you are falling in love with him."

"I'm not. What makes you think that I am?"

"Your refusal to tell me details. It means that you care about him and want to keep seeing him."

"Well, yeah, but it's still just a shipboard romance. After that, he's going to Tibet."

"Why Tibet?"

"I don't know. Something about treasure hunting, flea market finds hunting, or something like that. Doug and his friends deal in antiques that they find all over the world."

"That's a damn shame. How long is he going to be gone?"

"I don't know." Frankie put a hand over her chest. "I don't plan on waiting around for him. I met another guy today." She wasn't interested in Max, but she could introduce him to Margo. "You'll like him. He has that boy-next-door charm with a little bad boy mixed in."

"Ooh, tell me more. Is he tall?"

"Yep." She was about to continue when her doorbell rang. "I'll tell you about him tomorrow. Doug is here to pick me up."

"Have fun tonight."

"Thank you. You too."

"I'll try." Margo sighed. "Snap a picture of him and send it to me."

"Whose? Doug's or Max's?"

"Both."

Laughing, Frankie ended the call, put her phone in her evening bag, and walked to open the door.

"Hello, handsome." She gave Dagor a thorough once-over.

Standing with his hand in his pocket and one eyebrow lifted, he made a great James Bond impression, only she didn't think that he'd seen any of the movies.

Dagor always had an air of quiet confidence about him, but draped in a finely tailored tuxedo, he exuded sophistication. The jacket hugged his broad shoulders while the trousers accentuated his lean physique. Polished black shoes completed the ensemble. Every detail, from his cufflinks to the subtle pocket square, spoke of a man who had put a lot of thought into his appearance, and she wondered whether he had done it for her.

He'd never looked more like a god than he did now.

The dark hair that was impeccably styled, the piercing blue eyes, the chiseled jawline with a hint of stubble added a touch of ruggedness to his otherwise polished appearance—it was enough to make a girl get dizzy and suffer another fainting spell.

However, it never came because Dagor reached for her waist and pulled her to him. "Wow, Frankie. You look stunning."

With the spell broken, Frankie lifted a hand to his chest. "Don't mess up my hair, or Mia will kill us both. She spent over an hour on this updo."

Dagor laughed. "I wouldn't dare." He let go of her waist and took her hand. "Come on, princess. Let's do this wedding."

68

ORION

As Orion stood at the foot of the podium with his groomsmen and his father by his side and his newfound family seated around the tables, his eyes were glued to the dining hall's closed doors.

Soon, his bride would be coming through there, and they would pledge their lives to each other. It wasn't as if they needed the ceremony for that, but it felt right to tell Alena how he felt about her in front of her entire family.

They were all there, looking at him with acceptance and fondness that made him feel like he belonged.

The feeling was priceless.

Letting out a breath, Orion tore his eyes away from the doors to appreciate the work that had gone into transforming the ship's dining room into a grand banquet hall for the wedding.

The tables were draped in white tablecloths, and a golden fabric runner bisected each. The chairs were also draped in white and adorned with golden sashes tied in the back in large bows. Tall golden candelabras with dozens of candles were placed on each table, and between them were arrangements of flowers, their fragrance wafting through the air and creating a pleasant blend of fresh scents.

Through the tall windows, the vast expanse of the ocean stretched in every direction, the gentle waves casting shimmering reflections of the moon in a cloudless sky.

It reminded Orion of the centuries he'd spent alone, thinking that he was the only immortal on Earth, a freak of nature who couldn't age or die from injuries that killed other men.

He'd been adrift in the ocean of life.

The Fates had guided him to the clan and to Alena, his one and only, the light of his life, the mother of his unborn child, his everything.

As a soft melody started playing, signaling the start of the ceremony, a hush fell over the gathering, and all eyes turned to the double doors of the hall.

Two Guardians dressed in fine tuxedos opened the doors, and in walked Alena's bridesmaids. Their dresses were different yet somehow coordinated, but Orion didn't pay them any attention.

His heart thundered in his chest as he waited for his bride to appear. There she was—his Alena, effortlessly striking in her simple loose gown and her pale blond hair flowing freely down her back in soft waves.

Orion smiled, his heart swelling with love and gratitude to the Fates for granting him this incredible boon.

His stunning bride hadn't let her sisters paint her face or style her hair in an elaborate coif. Other than the shimmering fabric of her dress and the jewelry she had donned, all gifted to her by him, she hadn't done anything special for her wedding. She looked the same as she did every day, and she was perfect.

Alena smiled back, but then her gaze shifted to the guests she was passing by. She smiled and nodded at her children and grandchildren and great-grandchildren, reminding him that she was the de facto Mother of the Clan.

And yet, she had chosen him, a young immortal only five centuries old. How had he gotten so lucky?

Why had the Fates chosen him for Alena?

Was he worthy of her?

His father's hand on his shoulder fortified Orion's confidence. He was, after all, a demigod, and so was she. Perhaps they were better matched than his momentary panic had him believe.

As she turned her eyes back to him, so full of love and adoration, the last vestiges of his doubt evaporated, and Orion squared his shoulders.

He might not be worthy of Alena now, but they had eternity before them, and he would dedicate his life to her. They might not have another dozen children together, and the clan she had created would always outnumber their new family, but that was okay. His goal was not to father a new clan.

All he wanted was to make her happy and raise the child she was carrying together. If the Fates granted them more children, he would be overjoyed. Still, he was perfectly satisfied with what he already had.

69

ALENA

The rhythmic pulse of the ship was a backdrop to the anticipation that filled the air, or maybe just Alena's lungs. She hadn't expected to be so excited, so breathless.

The wedding had been postponed many times, and she would have been delighted with leaving things the way they were or just having a small ceremony in the village square.

After all, a clan wedding had no official significance. It was merely a celebration of her union with Orion. In her mind, weddings were needed only for arranged marriages because they provided a binding legal agreement between the parties. But she and Orion were truelove mates, which was as binding as it got.

Still, butterflies fluttered their wings in her stomach, or maybe it was the life growing in her womb.

"Breathe," Amanda whispered in Alena's left ear.

On her right, Syssi reached for her hand and gave it a gentle squeeze. "Just look straight at Orion when you enter the dining hall."

Nodding, she forced a breath into her lungs.

Why was she so anxious?

The excitement hadn't hit her until two days ago when it had become clear that it was happening and there would be no more delays.

It would have been less unnerving if she had followed Syssi's example and entered the room holding hands with her groom instead of doing it the more traditional way and having him wait for her.

It had been Amanda's suggestion to do it that way. Since Alena trusted her sister to plan the perfect ceremony for her, she hadn't argued. But maybe she should have been more involved with the plan instead of leaving everything to Amanda.

It might have made her less anxious.

As the first notes of the age-old melody she'd chosen for the occasion began to play, Alena took another deep breath, and her fingers feathered over the soft curve of her belly.

Once her bridesmaids took their stations next to the podium, Alena entered, fixing her gaze on her striking groom as Syssi had suggested.

Orion stood tall and regal, his dark hair smoothed back and his piercing blue eyes glowing with love for her. But it was his sensual smile, the one that had won her heart, that sent a wave of calm washing over her.

Whatever happened, he was there for her, and she would never be alone again.

With each step Alena took, memories of her long life flashed before her eyes — moments of joy, sorrow, love, and loss. Shifting her gaze to her guests, she searched for the faces of her children, and when she found them, it was a relief to see the approval and support in their eyes.

It meant a lot to her that they had all accepted Orion as her mate.

To the side, a lavish dessert table caught her eye. Towering wedding cakes, delicate pastries, and an array of sweets were displayed on ornate platters, and she wondered whether her grandson had made them.

No one else was such a talented chef, and it warmed her heart that Gerard had done that for her.

But the biggest thanks she owed to Amanda.

Her sister had truly outdone herself with this celebration. Between transforming the dining hall into an elegant event venue and coming up with a menu the human staff could pull off with the help of the Odus, she'd crafted a perfect celebration.

Turning back to the podium, Alena looked up at her mother and smiled.

The mischievous gleam in her mother's eyes was softened by the love that radiated from her almost as powerfully as her glow. Yet, Alena was suddenly worried about Annani's plans for the ceremony.

Her mother's unique and unpredictable style promised a unique and exciting experience. Still, since she never prepared and always made up her speeches on the spot, it was somewhat unnerving for Alena, who loved structure and didn't like surprises.

As she reached the podium, Alena took her place beside Orion. When he took her hand, the warmth radiating from it and the love shining in his eyes soothed the remainder of her frayed nerves.

She was ready, and together they turned to face Annani.

70

ANNANI

Annani regarded her eldest daughter with a mix of motherly pride, love, and a little bit of sadness.

Alena had been her companion for the first two thousand years of her life, but now that she had found her one true love, she needed to spend her days by his side.

That was how things should be, and every mother should wish that her daughter found love and safety in the arms of a worthy partner.

Orion was that and more, but he was taking Alena away, and as much as Annani tried not to resent him for it, a little bit of it still lingered. She might be a goddess, but that didn't make her a selfless angel.

Stifling a chuckle, Annani smiled benevolently at the couple and lifted her arms to signal that she was about to begin.

"Usually, I open the ceremony by addressing my children, grandchildren, great-grandchildren, and so on, but my community has grown to include my nephews, mates who are the descendants of other gods, three new gods, Kra-ell, who are not here for various reasons, and even a few humans. So, from now on, I will address you as ladies, gentlemen, gods, immortals, and young souls."

A few chuckles sounded among the guests, and Annani waited patiently for them to end.

"We gather here aboard the Silver Swan to witness a love that transcends time. I have presided over several ceremonies, each unique and a testament to the power of love, but today, I once again stand not just as the officiant but as a mother. The first wedding I ever officiated over was my son's and his lovely bride Syssi, and today, I'm marrying my daughter Alena and Orion, the son of my cousin Toven."

She paused, looked fondly at the couple before her, and then back at the hall filled to bursting with her people.

"In the vast tapestry that the Fates weave, every soul has a string—a path. For a few lucky ones, these paths intersect, creating unbreakable bonds that last an eternity. Intertwined, they continue their journey to write a shared destiny.

"Orion, with your youthful spirit and unwavering determination, you have brought light into my daughter's life. Your love brings her joy and hope for the future.

"Alena, my dear child, you have journeyed by my side through millennia, gathering wisdom and experience, but it is time for you to spread your wings and soar through the clouds with your chosen companion. In Orion, you have found your perfect match, a mate who complements your strengths and a shield against life's inevitable hardships.

"Love, in its truest form, is not just an emotion. It is a force, a power that binds, heals, and elevates. As you both stand here, ready to embark on this new chapter in your lives, remember that love is your anchor. In moments of doubt, let it guide you. In moments of joy, let it amplify your happiness.

"To the union of two souls, two legacies, and two eternities, I bestow my blessings. May your love be as boundless as the ocean on which we sail, as enduring as Earth herself, and as radiant as the stars lighting up the night's sky.

"I now pronounce you bound by love, united in soul, and partners in eternity. Let your journey together be filled with adventures, laughter, and endless joy."

As Annani ended her blessing, the ambient glow of the lights of the dining hall shimmered a bit brighter, casting a golden hue over the couple standing before her.

Turning to Orion, Alena took his hands in hers. "From the first moment we met, I felt a pull that drew me to you. I tried to resist it because I was afraid of losing myself to you, but you showed me that my fears were groundless and that together, we were much more than the sum of our parts. Today, as I stand before you, with eternity stretching out ahead of us, I vow to cherish the light you've brought into my life and to be the beacon for you in times of darkness, just as you have been for me. I vow to be your partner in every adventure and to celebrate every joyous moment together. I vow to respect and honor the differences between us, for it is in our differences that our strengths lie. I vow to stand by you, to uplift you when you're down, to laugh with you, and to offer my strength when yours needs bolstering. And above all, I vow to love you unconditionally and eternally with every beat of my heart."

She took the ring Annani handed her and slipped it over his finger. "Orion, son of Toven, you are mine forever, and I am yours."

As Orion gazed at Alena, his eyes shone enough light to illuminate the entire ship.

"Alena, from the very first moment I heard you sing, I knew you were destined to be mine, and when I first gazed into your eyes, I knew I would do everything I could to win you over. Today, I stand before you humbled and honored to be your chosen one. I vow to protect and cherish the love we've built, to be your anchor in the stormiest of seas and your compass if you ever feel lost. I vow to be your partner, your confidant, and your best friend, to share in every high and low and to walk beside you every step of the way. I vow to honor and celebrate the history you carry, the family you have raised, and to build a future that pays homage to both of our pasts. And most importantly, I vow to love you, deeply and truly, for all the days of our eternal lives and beyond."

He took the ring from Annani and slipped it on Alena's finger. "Alena, daughter of Annani, you are mine, and I am yours."

Her gaze locked onto her mate's, Alena's eyes glistened with tears, and he, usually so composed, seemed overcome with emotion. His hand trembled slightly as he lifted Alena's, pressing a gentle kiss to the back of her hand.

As the dining hall erupted in applause, cheers, and whistles, the couple turned to face their guests. Annani took the opportunity to step down from the podium.

Her heart was heavy with a mixture of happiness and sorrow. Watching her eldest daughter basking in the love of her mate and her clan was bittersweet. Somehow, Annani had never expected Alena to leave her side, and letting go of her was more difficult than it had been with her younger siblings.

Syssi placed a reassuring hand on her shoulder. "It's hard, isn't it?" she whispered. "Seeing your children grow, change, and choose their own paths no matter their age."

Annani nodded, her gaze still fixed on the joyous couple. "Every parent's dream is to see their child happy. But parting, even for the best of reasons, is never easy."

Syssi smiled gently, "Alena is not going far, and soon she will have another child for you to dote over. These are happy times, Clan Mother."

"Indeed." Annani patted her daughter-in-law's hand. "You are wise beyond your years, my child from another mother."

Syssi laughed. "Don't let my mother hear you say that. She'll get jealous."

Annani patted Syssi's hand again. "Perhaps it will inspire her to retire and move into the village to be near you."

"Not a chance." Syssi smiled sadly. "I learned to let go of that hope a long time ago."

71

DAGOR

"That was so beautiful." Frankie dabbed at her eyes with the napkin.

Dagor didn't know whether she was referring to the goddess's speech or the vows the couple had exchanged. The truth was that he was a little moved himself.

The ceremony was very different from the ones he'd witnessed on Anumati. Over there, an oracle always presided over the wedding, giving the couple her vision of their future. They were also done with much more pomp and ceremony. Gods invested heavily in the wedding parties for their children. After all, most were lucky to have one offspring, so one wedding celebration was all they would ever get to have. There was also the issue of good luck, which many believed was tied to how grand the party was and for how long guests talked about it—a silly superstition that was probably propagated by the owners of wedding venues.

"Indeed." Gabi lifted her champagne goblet. "It puts pressure on us to come up with even lovelier vows."

Aru arched a brow. "No need because we are not getting married."

"Why not?"

"Because I'm not getting mated without my family, and since they can't come to our celebration, we can't have one. We will just need to stay unmarried."

Gabi gaped at him. "Where did that come from? I thought you were happy staying on Earth so we could be together."

"I am. But do you really need a ceremony to make our love official?"

Gabi deflated. "I guess not." She rose to her feet. "I should spend some time with my family." She gave him a tight smile before walking away.

Even Dagor knew that Aru had messed up, and he wasn't an authority on females, not by a long shot.

Negal shook his head. "You shouldn't have said that. Some things are better left unsaid."

Dagor couldn't agree more. Turning to Frankie, he extended his hand. "Would you like to dance?"

"I thought you would never ask." She took his offered hand and let him pull her up. "Do you even know how to dance?" she whispered in his ear. "Or did you just want to escape the argument between Aru and Negal?"

"I can dance," he dodged the answer. "I am a god."

She laughed. "That doesn't mean that you can move. Do they have dances on Anumati?"

"Of course." He pulled her into his arms and started swaying in place. "You see? This is not difficult."

"That's a slow dance," she murmured as she melted into his embrace. "What are you going to do when they change the beat?"

He hoped they wouldn't do that anytime soon. Holding Frankie felt incredibly good, and he was reluctant to let go of her. "I've been to clubs. I can emulate what I've seen."

Resting her cheek on his chest, she put her hand right over his heart as if guarding it so it wouldn't jump out. "I like being with you, Dagor. And it has nothing to do with you being a god. I would have liked you even if you were human."

Dagor froze as her words resonated through him, causing an earthquake and cracking his armor. The truth was that he liked being with Frankie as well, and he would have liked her whether she was human, immortal, or a goddess.

But he couldn't allow himself to feel that way. He wouldn't change his eternal life trajectory just because he'd met a female he liked.

It didn't matter that he felt more comfortable with her than with any of the goddesses he'd dated and that being with her was as easy as breathing. It didn't matter that she made him smile and eased the tightness in his chest.

"I like you a lot, too." He gently rubbed her back through the bodice of her dress. "Especially when you are naked and under me."

It wasn't a lie, but it wasn't the entire truth either.

He liked her in bed and outside of it.

Frankie stiffened for a moment, and Dagor wondered if he'd offended her by his comment about liking her in bed. It hadn't been one of his finest moments, and he regretted resorting to such an immature statement to guard himself against his own feelings for her.

But as the music continued to play, and he held her close, she relaxed against him again. The steady rhythm of her heartbeat was like his but not as strong, and it made him think of her humanity, her fragility, and the transient nature of her existence. There was a vast chasm between their worlds, unbridgeable, and the differences in their lifespans weren't even the most critical part of it.

When the melody changed, becoming more upbeat, Dagor felt a moment of panic. He hadn't lied about being able to dance, but he wasn't in some random club where no one knew him, and he didn't want to make a fool of himself by moving too much or too little.

Frankie looked up at him with amusement dancing in her eyes. "Don't worry. Give me your hand and follow my lead."

As soon as he did as she'd instructed, she spun them around and faced Dagor. Placing one hand on her hip, she extended the other, beckoning him to follow. With a playful twirl, she moved to the beat, her feet tracing intricate patterns on the floor, which was truly an acrobatic achievement given the size of her heels.

Dagor followed her lead effortlessly, mimicking her moves. After all, he might not be a good dancer when pitted against other gods, but he could hold his own against immortals and humans.

Frankie moved closer and took his hand, guiding it to her waist, and with her other, she directed his movements, teaching him without words. Her steps were fluid and confident, and soon Dagor was dancing as if he had known those movements since he was in the cradle. Frankie transitioned into more complex moves, spinning under Dagor's outstretched arm and pulling him into a series of gyrations that had their bodies popping and locking in sync with the beat.

The laughter and chatter around them faded as they lost themselves in the dance, their movements becoming more synchronized with each step. She was a great teacher, telegraphing her next steps so he had no problem adjusting his accordingly.

Dancing with her felt natural, instinctive.

When the song ended, Frankie was breathless, her face flushed with the exhilaration of the dance. Dagor looked down into her eyes and was about to lean in for a kiss when Negal's voice interrupted them.

"That was quite the performance, Dagor."

"You should compliment Frankie. Without her, I wouldn't have known which foot went where."

She laughed. "Not true. You are a natural. All you needed was just a little guidance."

Dagor smiled. "Don't be modest, Francesca. You are an inspired dancer. Did you take lessons?"

"Yes, I did." She looked proud as she squared her shoulders. "I owe my fabulous posture to the ballet classes I took throughout elementary and middle school."

"What happened to make you stop?"

She laughed. "Boys. There were none in my ballet classes."

72

FRANKIE

As the music took on a mellow tone, signaling the winding down of the night, the dancers began to exit the floor. Some made their way to the bar for a final drink, while others lingered by the dessert table.

Frankie took Dagor's hand and led him off the dance floor.

"Where are we going?" he asked when she stopped by their table to snatch her purse.

"The Lido deck."

"Why? They are still serving drinks at the bar."

She rolled her eyes. "I want some fresh air."

"Oh." He let her drag him along.

Dagor's romantic intelligence needed some nurturing. It was funny that a god interested in engineering had the same emotional issues as a human interested in the same topics.

Evidently, Toven was right, and there was little difference between humans, immortals, and gods. It made sense since the gods had used their genetic material to create humans.

As they reached the Lido deck, it became apparent that they weren't the only people who had thought about strolling in the fresh air after the party started winding down. Still, thankfully, the place was far from crowded.

"It's beautiful," Frankie said, leaning on the railing and gazing at the vast expanse of the ocean stretching out before her.

The moonlight bathed the gentle waves in a soft glow, making it look magical.

"Yes, you are."

She turned to him and smiled. "You are such a flatterer."

"I mean it." He cupped her cheek and dipped his head to take her lips in a gentle kiss. "I've had more fun today with you than I can remember ever having."

That was such a sweet lie. He was probably ancient, and spending time with a mere human was meh compared to the gorgeous goddesses on his home planet.

Arching a brow, Frankie looked at Dagor from under lowered lashes and asked the question she'd been too chicken to ask until now. "How old are you?"

He frowned. "There is no straightforward answer. It depends on your frame of reference. I'm very young for a god."

"What's considered young? Two hundred years, three hundred?"

"I'm sixty-nine, not counting the time I spent in stasis. That adds several hundred years to my lifespan."

"Sixty-nine," she repeated. "You lived for sixty-nine years, and you call yourself very young."

"That's right."

She shook her head. "The way you regard the passage of time will take some adjusting to."

As worry crossed his eyes, he tightened his arm around her waist. "Are you feeling faint?"

"I'm fine." She put her hand on his chest. "I'm no longer shocked by what I learn, so I don't get dizzy. I'm twenty-seven, but since in human years, I've depleted about one-third of my lifespan, I'm much older than you. It's like we count dogs' age differently than human age. For every human year, we count seven dog years."

Smiling, he put a finger on her lips. "Please, stop. It's irrelevant how old we are compared to each other. What matters is that we enjoy each other's company. Right?"

"Right." She looked into his piercing blue eyes. "For the duration of the cruise."

He nodded. "That's all we can have."

Frankie wasn't sure of that, but Dagor wasn't ready to hear that perhaps they could have more.

Cupping his cheek, she forced a smile. "Whatever happens, I want you to know that what we have is real, even if it can only last nine more days. For me, it's not just about the physical attraction or the novelty of being with a god. I feel a connection to you. We are good together."

Dagor took a deep breath, "Frankie, I..."

She placed a finger on his lips, silencing him. "It's okay," she whispered, "you don't need to say anything."

Sometimes, it was better to leave things unsaid and let Fate or circumstances pave the road ahead.

Frankie turned her gaze back to the ocean, the rhythmic lapping of waves against the ship's hull providing a comforting backdrop to the words they had just exchanged.

The moon's silvery glow made the waters shimmer, and it occurred to her that the beauty of the night seemed to encapsulate the fleeting nature of their relationship.

Dagor's hand found hers, their fingers intertwining. "In my world, time has a different meaning. Decades and centuries pass differently for us. But these moments with you are real."

She smiled wistfully. "For humans, every moment is precious. We learn to treasure the time we have because it's limited."

"It might not be for you. You can become immortal."

"Maybe I can, and maybe I cannot." She turned around and leaned her back against the railing. "I don't even know if I want to be immortal."

The truth was that she didn't believe she was indeed a Dormant, and convincing herself that she wasn't sure that she wanted to become immortal was easier than discovering that she could not.

Dagor looked at her, a hint of sadness in his eyes. "Do you regret it?"

"Regret what?"

"Meeting me, knowing that our time has an expiration date."

Frankie sighed. "Life is full of chance encounters and fleeting moments that can change the course of our lives. I don't regret meeting you even if the ten days of this cruise are all we will have. I'll cherish this time with you forever, but I won't lie by saying that it doesn't make me a little sad that something so wonderful has to end. I would have liked to see where it could lead."

Dagor pulled her close, dipped his head, and rested his forehead against hers. "The future is uncertain, and the present is all that matters. We will make each minute of each day count."

She wrapped her arms around him, pulling him into a tight embrace. "I just wish we had more time."

Dagor kissed the top of her head. "Time is a construct, Frankie. What matters is how we spend it. And I intend to spend every moment I have with you, making memories that will last me an eternity."

She pulled back slightly. "Promise me something?"

"Anything."

"When this cruise ends, and we go our separate ways, you won't forget me."

Dagor cupped her face, his thumb gently wiping away a tear that had escaped the corner of her eye. "I could never forget you, Frankie. You've left a permanent impression on my heart."

She chuckled. "A good one, I hope."

"The best."

73

ANI

As the giant red sun of Anumati cast its dimming radiance upon the city, Queen Ani's hovercraft glided smoothly toward the Temple of the Supreme Oracle. The sprawling capital, constantly buzzing with life and energy, seemed to quieten as people raised their heads to follow the royal craft on its unscheduled journey.

It was not her usual once-a-month visit to the temple. People must be wondering why she was making the journey today. Still, Ani had made unexpected visits to the Supreme before, so it was not entirely out of character.

Looking out through the shimmering dome of her craft, Ani wondered about the cryptic message from her friend, inviting her for a fortune reading.

Had Sofringhati seen something without being asked to part the veil of destiny?

That was different from how an oracle's visions usually worked, but sometimes she gleaned information while fulfilling petitioners' requests, and perhaps she had something of value to impart.

As the hovercraft descended, Ani watched the temple attendants assemble on its steps to welcome her. Their ceremonial robes seemed to shimmer in the dying light, and the long semi-sheer veils covering their faces fluttered in the ever-present wind.

As the craft touched down gently on the temple's landing platform, the queen's guard disembarked first, forming two formidable rows to shield her even though there had never been an attempt on her life. But then, perhaps no one had ever dared because of the diligence of her personal guard and the rumors of their ferocity.

Once the guards were in place, half of her attendants disembarked ahead of her, and as she descended the steps, the other half trailed behind her. The pomp and ceremony were one of the many costs of queenly life, one that Ani was so used to that she hardly noticed it anymore.

The vast doors of the temple opened silently, revealing the antechamber to the inner sanctum where the Supreme awaited and where Ani could enjoy an hour or two of privacy with her old friend without anyone watching every move and every expression she made.

As she traversed the courtyard, the weight of countless decisions, hopes and fears pressed in on her, but in the presence of the Supreme, she would not only find insight into the tapestry of fate, but also the respite of friendship with no strings attached.

The temple of the Supreme Oracle was an architectural marvel, a testament to the grandeur of Anumati's ancient civilization. As Ani stepped inside, she lifted her eyes to the grand vaulted ceiling soaring above. It seemed to touch the heavens, with the intricate carvings of stars and planets symbolizing the Supreme's connection to the universe.

Each colossal column had been carved from a single block of luminescent alludium and etched with spiral scripts running their lengths. The scripts represented pivotal prophecies given by one Supreme Oracle or another, and thousands of them had been collected since the temple had been erected.

The torchlight cast shifting shadows on the columns, making the spirals seem alive, moving, writhing, their words changing with the passing epochs, but it was an illusion.

The scripts never changed; only their interpretations did.

Lowering her gaze to the mosaic floor of azure and gold tiles that were arranged in patterns mirroring constellations in Anumati's night sky, Ani took a moment to appreciate the workmanship before lifting her eyes toward the back of the chamber where the Oracle sat on her throne-like chair.

Elevated by three steps, the podium was made of delludim, the dark light-absorbing stone contrasting starkly with the alludium columns. Upon it sat the Oracle, and behind her hung an enormous tapestry depicting the Tree of Life, its branches and roots intertwined with symbols of past, present, and future.

On either side of the podium, large bronze braziers burned, filled with fragrant herbs. The scent permeated the chamber, a mix of aromatic herbs inducing a sense of calm and reverence and a bit of something else that most petitioners were not aware of.

The Supreme possessed an incredible power—the ability to peer into past and future and even pierce the veil between worlds, but she had some tricks up her sleeve to make the experience even more epic for the petitioners and increase the level of their contributions.

Her other trick was the complete privacy of the grand chamber.

No modern technology was allowed, not even electricity, and the walls, made of smooth gray stone, absorbed sound.

Ani's entourage, a mix of guards, advisors, and ladies-in-waiting, followed in precise formation, their movements practiced and synchronized.

The Oracle, draped in deep indigo robes, met Ani's gaze with an inscrutable expression. Until they were alone in the chamber, they had to follow protocol and ceremonial formalities.

It was a dance the Oracle and the queen had performed countless times.

Respectful words of greeting were exchanged while the attendants watched with bated breath, always vigilant, always trying to catch hidden meanings.

Ani knew that her husband had spies among them, and she knew precisely who they were, but she pretended that she did not.

Then, as the last formalities and rituals were concluded, a silent signal from Ani sent the attendants retreating to the edges of the chamber and out its doors.

Once the vast doors closed with a soft thud, leaving the two most powerful women on Anumati alone in the heart of the temple, the air between them grew charged.

The Oracle's stern demeanor softened, and Ani's shoulders relaxed ever so slightly.

They approached each other, not as monarch and seer, but as old friends.

"Ani," Sofri whispered as she pulled her into her arms. "Oh, Ani."

"What is it?" Ani leaned away and looked astonished at her friend's tear-stricken face.

"I have good news."

As they pulled apart, Sofringhati's eyes communicated layers of emotions without words.

"Why are you crying?" Ani asked.

Sofri took her hand and led her to a stack of cushions. "My heart is overflowing with emotion," she said, her eyes glistening as she brushed away a tear with the edge of her robe. "There are revelations that change the course of destinies. Brace yourself, Ani, for what I am about to tell you is this. Your son had a daughter, and she is alive and well on Earth."

MATTERS OF THE MIND

1

ANI

Tears shone in Sofringhati's eyes. "There are revelations that change the course of destinies. Brace yourself, Ani, for what I am about to tell you is thus." The Supreme Oracle took Ani's hands. "Your son had a daughter, and she is alive and well on Earth. This is not a vision or a prediction, my dearest friend. This is reported by Aru, who met her in person."

The news struck Ani like a bolt of lightning. It was as if time had come to a halt, and for a few heartbeats the world around her blurred, with only Sofri's voice and the fire in the braziers anchoring her to reality. But then logic and doubts burned away the haze.

"That is impossible. She must be an imposter."

Sofri smiled. "She is not. Aru told Aria that Annani's resemblance to you is striking. The moment he saw her, he knew right away that she was your descendant because your faces are identical. Unlike you, though, she is petite, has red hair, and is quick to laugh. According to Aru, she also exudes immense power. Does that remind you of someone? It is also obvious that your son paid homage to you by naming his daughter Annani."

Could it be? Had some part of Ahn survived?

He hadn't had red hair, and he had been a tall male, but he'd exuded power, and his glow had been legendary—a glow that had been snuffed out by his own father.

A torrent of suppressed emotions came flooding back. The pain of Ahn's death resurfacing, the wound that Ani had dressed in duty and resolve bled anew.

She had never allowed herself to truly feel the depth of sorrow and despair that had threatened to swallow her whole, always putting the needs of her people first. But now, with the news Sofri had brought, those old scars were torn open, revealing her raw, unhealed grief.

Memories of Ahn danced before her eyes, the serious young boy who had grown into a remarkable male. He had given her and the people of Anumati hope, but he had acted too soon, and the price of his haste had been his life.

Ani had suspected that the exile was only the first step in the Eternal King's plot to get rid of his one legitimate heir and the other gods who had conspired against him, including Ekin and Athor, two of the many children he'd sired with his scores of concubines. But there had been so little Ani could do without being accused of treason and sent to join Ahn on that accursed planet at the far reaches of the galaxy.

Had it been only her life on the line, she would have done that in a heart-beat, but with Ahn gone, she was the only one left to continue her son's work and lead the resistance. She had been the only one who could save Ahn and the other exiled gods from the king's assassins.

Except, everything she had done had been for naught.

She had arranged for the arrival of the Kra-ell settler ship to be delayed by thousands of years, and in the meantime, she had sent seven Odus to Earth, hoping Ekin would know what to do to restore their memories and build an army of Odus to defend against the Eternal King's emissaries of death.

But Ekin must not have understood the significance of the gift, or perhaps he had lacked the means to manufacture more of them with the limited resources he had on Earth.

Ultimately, the king's assassins succeeded in their mission despite her efforts.

In a rare unsolicited vision, Sofringhati had seen what the king had done, but even the greatest oracle of all time had not dared to make her vision public.

How had Ahn's daughter survived the bombing?

Tears stung the back of Ani's eyes, but she refused to let them fall, even if only in the presence of her best friend and confidant.

"Why have you not seen my granddaughter before?" she asked.

Sofri lifted her hands. "You know that I do not see everything, my queen, and even what I see is not always easy to interpret. The universe chooses what it wants to show me."

It was not Sofri's fault. It was hers.

She should have asked whether Ahn had any children born to him on Earth. Her spies in the king's court had told her that the king suspected their son had fathered the Kra-ell queen's twins, and his suspicion had been reinforced when it became known that they had been smuggled among the settlers aboard the Kra-ell ship.

Except, Ahn had never told Ani about his relationship with the Kra-ell queen, or rather the princess she had been before ascending to the Kra-ell throne, not even a hint, and Ani very much doubted that there was truth to her husband's paranoid suspicions.

It had been just one more excuse to despise his own son and justify his murder.

Gods did not easily produce offspring, and they did not rush into official matehood unless they were fortunate enough to find their fated true love. Ahn had still been a young god at the time of his exile. Given the selection of goddesses accompanying him to his new home, Ani could not see him officially mating any of them.

None had shone as brightly as her son.

Ahn might have chosen a mate after the communications with Earth were severed, but he also could have fathered Annani with a concubine.

"Do you know if she is legitimate?" she asked.

"Aru did not say anything that would lead me to think that she is not. Besides, do we care if Ahn had her with his official wife or a consort? Who would be able to deny our claim that Annani is the daughter of his official wife?"

"It will be demanded of her to prove that she is legitimate. Her word alone will not suffice. To be an heir to the throne, Annani has to be the child of Ahn's official wife and be able to prove it. But for now, we should not worry about that. First, I need to ascertain whether she has what it takes to be the next leader of Anumati. Tell me everything Aru told Aria about her."

The cloudy look in Sofri's eyes was troubling. Hopefully, she was still lucid enough to relay the information factually and not embellish or mix it up with visions and fantasies.

Being the most powerful oracle on Anumati came with a price.

Sofri squinted as if she was trying to see in the dark, and perhaps that was precisely what she was doing—looking into the vast fabric of the universe instead of trying to remember what she had been told.

"I took great care to memorize what Aria told me." Sofri lifted a hand to clutch the Supreme Oracle's amulet as if it could ground her in reality and prevent her mind from wandering. "Annani is benevolent, and she leads her clan of immortals with wisdom and care. They call her the Clan Mother, and they all love and respect her. The clan is only several hundred people strong, but even though their numbers are small, they have done a lot of good for the humans throughout the millennia since Ahn and the gods were lost. Not only that, they have done so while fighting their archenemy, who has a stronger army of immortals and whose goals are opposite to theirs. Annani and her people want humans to become an enlightened global society that promotes equal opportunity for all and meets all the basic needs of every person on Earth. Their enemy encourages infighting and wants humans to remain dumb and ignorant so he can easily subjugate them."

That sounded a lot like what Ahn would have done if he had been allowed to live. It seemed that his daughter was continuing his legacy.

But what was that about immortals?

Had Sofri gotten confused?

"You said immortals. Did you mean gods?"

Her friend shook her head. "There is more I need to tell you—things that Aru told Aria before, and I did not share with you."

"Why didn't you?"

Sofri tilted her head. "Until Aru found out about Annani, I did not want to upset you by telling you what Ahn had allowed."

Ani had a feeling that she already knew the answer to that.

"He allowed the gods to procreate with humans."

Ani knew that such unions would not result in abominations like most believed thanks to the propaganda, but despite her sympathy toward the created species, she was not in favor of gods procreating with them. Why dilute the genetics they had perfected over countless years and numerous generations?

Sofri nodded. "He had no choice, Ani. The few gods on Earth did not have enough genetic variety for viability. Once the contact with the colony was severed, Ahn knew that no more gods would be coming to fortify their genetic pool and that their only chance of survival was creating a new hybrid species. Part god and part human."

The irony was not lost on Ani. "Humans were created with the genetic material taken from the gods. Ahn just took it one step further by ignoring the taboo and allowing the creation of immortals."

2

DAGOR

As Dagor slowly stirred to wakefulness, he was greeted by the warm morning sunlight filtering through the gaps in the curtains and casting a soft glow on the room. He'd dreamt about home, about being with his family, his neighbors, his friends, and for a moment he thought that he was still on Anumati, but the illusion didn't last long.

Anumati's sun cast a red glow, not yellow.

Blinking rapidly to dislodge the cobwebs of dreams, he became aware of the woman sleeping beside him.

Frankie.

He was in her cabin, in her bed, and it was morning. It was also the second time he'd spent an entire night with a human female and had woken up beside her.

It was against the rules that he and his teammates had adhered to throughout the five years they had been on Earth, but if Aru could break them for Gabi, Dagor could do the same for Frankie.

It was nice to spend the night with her and not sneak out to go back to the cabin he shared with Negal. There was something special about waking up next to someone he cared about—a sense of belonging, a sense of connection, which Dagor had not felt with any female before, not even with the one goddess that he'd thought he loved.

What was it about Frankie that made him feel that way?

They weren't even from the same species.

Shifting to his side, Dagor propped his elbow on the mattress and supported his chin on his fist. As he watched her sleeping, he wondered why her forehead was scrunched in a frown.

Was she having a bad dream?

That shouldn't happen after a venom bite. She should be calm and blissed out.

As he smoothed his finger over the creases, her facial muscles relaxed, but she didn't wake up, which didn't really surprise him. Frankie was human, and she needed much more sleep than he did.

What was it about this human girl that made his heart swell with emotion in a way that none of the perfect beauties back home ever had?

Dagor was starting to understand Aru's infatuation with Gabi. Had Gabi also made Aru feel more alive than he had ever been?

Tracing the curve of Frankie's cheek with his finger, Dagor wanted to kiss her, but he stifled the impulse and just watched the gentle rise and fall of her chest as she breathed.

So vulnerable. So human.

A pang speared through his heart as a new realization hit him. Frankie's charm, the thing that attracted him the most to her, was deeply rooted in her humanity and her approach to life. She wasn't living in a holding pattern like most gods were. She strived to enjoy each moment, and she'd somehow managed to infect him with her exuberance.

Given that he was a humorless, logic-driven guy who did not find most things worth getting excited about, that was no small accomplishment. Nevertheless, in his logical mind, he was well aware that falling for a human was not good for him in the long term, no matter how good it made him feel in his heart in the short term.

Dagor had always been a guarded person, and people thought of him as dry and flat, and they weren't wrong. Before meeting Frankie, the only thing that excited him was finding a piece of tech that he could take apart and reconstruct. He wasn't impressed by stories someone had dreamt up, so fiction was a pass, whether in books or in movies. Music did not move him, and art left him indifferent.

But with Frankie, he felt like more. He felt alive.

Damn, he had to get a grip on himself and stop this foolishness. He needed to distance himself from the girl, perhaps not physically but definitely emotionally. It might be difficult at first, but it would spare them both heartbreak when the cruise ended in seven days, and they went their separate ways.

He'd given her his promise that they would be together for the duration of the cruise, and Dagor wasn't the type who went back on his word, but he didn't need to spend every moment of every day with her to fulfill his promise.

If Frankie was a Dormant, the more time he spent with her, the more he risked bonding with her, and then it would be game over for him like it was for Aru. He could kiss his life plans goodbye and accept that he was going to stay on this godforsaken planet for the rest of his never-ending life.

In the back of his mind, a small voice whispered that Aru was happy with his immortal mate, but a louder voice countered that Dagor wasn't like Aru and that he could never give up on going back home someday.

He had to cling to that hope.

He could spend his days away from Frankie, claiming he had things to do. They could meet for dinner and continue to bed, but once she was asleep, he would leave and go back to his cabin.

Once they picked up Frankie's best friend on their way back from Acapulco, she would have someone to spend her days with, but until then Frankie had nothing to do, which meant that she would want to spend time with him.

Avoiding her would be difficult.

With a sigh, he gently brushed a stray strand of hair from her face and feathered his fingers over her cheek one more time before gathering the resolve to get out of bed.

Searching for something that could distract him from obsessing about Frankie, Dagor thought about the only fascinating piece of equipment on board the ship—the robotic bartender on the Lido deck. Hopefully, examining him and learning all he could about him would do the trick.

Regrettably, Dagor couldn't take Bob apart, so he would have to be satisfied with just talking to him and perhaps getting him to reveal the name of his creators. If they were on board, Dagor would love to have a chat with them.

3

AMANDA

The aroma of freshly brewed coffee filled the air, enticing Amanda to get out of bed. She stretched her arms over her head, reached for her silk robe, and draped it around her nude body.

Now that she and Dalhu were parents, Amanda no longer indulged in parading naked through the master suite as she used to do. Their daughter was only six months old and didn't mind her mother's state of dress or undress, but Dalhu didn't approve. He was a by-the-book kind of parent, which was annoying.

Those archaic modesty rules existed for humans and did not apply to immortals, but it wasn't important enough to make a fuss about. The secret to a good relationship was not to sweat the small stuff.

At least in Amanda's book.

Dalhu also didn't like her parading naked around Onidu, which was absolutely ridiculous. So yeah, her Odu was sentient now, but he didn't have sexual urges because he was sexless. Besides, he had seen her naked plenty of times before. Dalhu had even insisted on Onidu staying in a cabin on the lower decks so they would have their privacy. It was utterly uncalled for, but she humored her old-fashioned mate because she wanted him to be comfortable and enjoy the cruise.

As it was, their upcoming wedding was stressing Dalhu, so she was trying to be as accommodating as possible.

And to think that people called her difficult, high maintenance, or spoiled. She was none of those things. She was a paragon of compromise.

Entering the living room, Amanda smiled at her mate and sauntered toward him. "You know how to get me out of bed in the morning."

He chuckled. "Ever since I kidnapped you, I've learned how to take care of you."

"That you have." She nodded as memories of their stay in the remote mountain cabin filled her mind.

Was she weird for thinking fondly of when she'd been Dalhu's prisoner?

Not at all.

They were fated mates, and she'd known that from the very start.

Well, maybe not at first glance, but shortly thereafter. At first, Dalhu had terrified her.

Amanda leaned to kiss Evie's drool-covered cheek. "Good morning, sweetie."

"Ma-ma." Evie offered Amanda her teething toy.

"Thank you, sweetie." She kissed her again. "Mommy is going to drink her coffee now, so you can keep chewing on your toy."

Whenever their daughter called her Ma or Ma-ma, Amanda's heart swelled with love. Dalhu was Ta or Ta-ta instead of Da or Da-da, but he didn't mind. The guy was putty in their daughter's little hands.

He placed a bowl of instant oatmeal with blueberries on the table. "That's the best I could do with what I had to work with."

"It's perfect." Amanda wrapped her arms around his neck and kissed him on the lips. "Do you know why?"

He smiled. "Why?"

"Because you made it for me with love."

His smile widened. "Does it taste better when sprinkled with affection?"

"Of course." She let go of his neck and sat down.

Dalhu took out two cups of coffee from under the coffeemaker, put them next to the oatmeal bowls, and then added a container of creamer and another one with sugar cubes.

Sitting on Evie's other side, he glanced at their daughter's half-eaten cereal. "Do you want to feed her?" He lifted his gaze to Amanda. "She might be inclined to eat a little more if you are the one holding the spoon."

"If she doesn't want to eat any more, I won't force it. She'll eat when she's hungry."

It was one of the things that they did not agree on. Dalhu wanted to do everything by the book, while Amanda believed in being flexible and taking her daughter's wishes into account even though she was just a baby.

She wanted their daughter to grow up to be independent and resourceful.

Dalhu grimaced. "Evie doesn't eat enough because she's teething and it hurts her gums, not because she's not hungry."

Rolling her eyes, Amanda lifted the baby spoon, dipped it into the cereal, and offered it to their daughter.

Surprisingly, Evie opened her mouth.

"Look at you," Amanda grinned. "Such a good girl."

"You shouldn't say that," Dalhu murmured. "It's in the book. If you praise her for eating, she might associate that with pleasing you and overeat."

"Make up your mind." Amanda put the baby spoon down. "Do you want her to eat more or not?"

Running his hand over his hair, he sighed. "I'm sorry. I'm irritable today."

Amanda had a good idea why, and it was sad. They were getting married tonight, and this day was supposed to be idyllic, but the closer it got to the ceremony, the more stressed Dalhu became.

She put the cream and sugar in her coffee, gave it a stir, lifted the cup to her lips, took a sip, and sighed. "This is perfect. Thank you."

Perhaps the compliment would help Dalhu relax. He'd been tense since the day they packed their things for the cruise, and he got a glimpse of her wedding dress.

Her big guy believed in silly superstitions—like seeing the bride in her wedding gown before the wedding was bad luck—and even though he'd only seen the train peeking out from the garment bag, he still thought it was a bad omen.

Of course, the real reason for his nervousness was his aversion to being the center of attention, and everything else was like sprinkling more pepper on an already uncomfortably spicy dish.

Dalhu offered her a half-smile, his gaze drifting to the window. "You are most welcome."

He always got overly polite when he was anticipating a difficult task.

It may have been ingrained in him during his service in the Brotherhood. Meeting his commanders and getting his despicable orders had been painful, and he had been forced to do that while bowing graciously and acting as if they were all that.

Reaching across the table, she placed a comforting hand over his. "This is our day, Dalhu, and there is no reason to dread the ceremony just because you don't like having all eyes on you."

He winced. "You know why I dread it. Not everyone is okay with me joining the clan and mating their princess."

Squeezing his hand, she leaned closer to him. "They have all accepted you, and no one is going to give you the stink eye. If anyone dares, they will have to deal with me, and no one wants that. We're celebrating our love, and everyone here is happy for us."

Dalhu nodded. "Perhaps, but I intend to look only at your mother and you and ignore the crowd."

Amanda chuckled. "You also have to look at your groomsmen."

"Right."

"And the bridesmaids."

"Fine. But that's it."

Amanda's gaze softened. "Don't forget to smile during the ceremony, my love. When our daughter sees the recording when she's older, I don't want her to think that you were not happy about marrying her mommy."

He turned to look at Evie, who lifted her eyes to him with a toothless smile with the toy still stuffed in her mouth. "Speaking of Evie," he said as he shifted his gaze back to Amanda. "Are we bringing her to the ceremony? I worry it might be too much for her and also about the practicality. You will be in your wedding dress, and I will be in my tux, and we don't want her drooling over either of us. But having her in the stroller during the ceremony would be weird."

"What if Onidu holds her?" Amanda suggested.

"That could work. He can stand behind us."

"Or even better, I can ask one of the bridesmaids to hold Evie." Amanda grinned. "That's actually perfect. Evie can be one of my bridesmaids, and I even ordered a dress for her from the same fabric and in the same style as theirs." She leaned and pressed a kiss to the top of her daughter's head. "If you were older, you could have been our ring girl, but I think being a bridesmaid in your mom and dad's wedding is special enough."

4

ANI

Ani did not condone Ahn's decision to allow gods to take human partners and produce offspring with them. She had supported almost everything he had wanted to change about Anumati and about the way the lesser species were treated by the gods, but there was a big difference between allowing them the same privileges that were available to the commoner gods and actually producing hybrid offspring with them.

"Are those immortals abominations?" She pinned Sofri with a stern look.

"They are not. They are precisely what you would expect a child of a god and a human to be. They heal fast but not as fast as gods, and they are immune to diseases. They can thrall and shroud in varying degrees of ability, and they possess an array of other mind talents like we do. But since there are so few of them, their talents do not run the full gamut as ours do. Aru met a seer who has occasional visions, but she is not nearly as powerful as even our weakest oracles."

"That is a relief." Ani let her shoulders relax a fraction. "El always feared that hybrids might be more powerful than us, and naturally, he could not allow that."

"It is possible that a child born to a Kra-ell and a god parent will have superior powers."

Ani let out a breath. "You never should have told the Eternal King that prophecy. He was already paranoid, but after hearing that a descendant of his would be more powerful than him and would usher in a new era of revival and prosperity to Anumati, he became much worse."

Most fathers would have loved to receive a prophecy like that, but all the king had heard was that he would be replaced and outshone by a descendant.

Tears leaked from the corners of her friend's eyes. "He asked, I have seen the future, and the prophecy just left my mouth. I am not always in control, and you know that."

"I do."

The weight of her own isolation, of the sacrifices she had made, and of the love she had lost pressed down on Ani, but she had not let them bring her down before, and she would not do so now that Sofri's prophecy might finally come true.

There was a glimmer of hope, a new purpose. Her bloodline had not ended with Ahn. There was still a part of him, a part of her, alive and breathing on Earth.

Could it be that Annani was more powerful than her grandfather?

The truth was that only fools relied on visions and prophecies. El had thousands of offspring, and any one of them could one day produce a descendant who was more powerful than the Eternal King.

For all she knew, the rumors were true about Ahn having fathered the Kra-ell queen's twin children, and one or both of them could be more powerful than El.

They were not legitimate, but did it really matter? If it was true, they were the descendants of two royal houses, and the female twin could ascend to the Kra-ell throne with ease.

But what if it was Annani, after all?

It was both comforting and terrifying to hope for. But whether Annani was more powerful than the Eternal King or not, Ani needed to protect her granddaughter, no matter the cost.

"There is more," Sofri said.

Ani arched a brow. "Does Annani have siblings?"

Sofri snorted in a very undignified way. "Not that I know of. But Aru is concerned about the king finding out that humans are no longer a bunch of primitives fighting each other on horseback. They have developed technology, and their population has exploded. There are eight billion of them. Your mate might decide to cull the numbers and destroy their progress, or he might decide to do away with them altogether."

Ani hated it when people referred to the Eternal King as her mate. It had been a political marriage, and she had not loved him for even one minute of it.

She had endured him until she had produced an heir, and if she had known what he would do to his own son, she would have refused the king in her bedchamber from the very start. She had enough political sway of her own to prevent him from punishing her for that.

"He will not do away with all humans, but he might send a pathogen to cull their numbers. What is the state of their medical progress?"

"I do not know," Sofri admitted. "Aru might have told Aria, but she did not tell me."

"I need much more information." Ani adjusted the folds of her gown. "Instruct Aria to collect as much as she can. I will come to see you every day from now on."

The Oracle paled. "You cannot. It will be suspicious."

"I can easily excuse it. I can say that you are in one of your states of fugue, and I cannot get you to counsel me on the important issues I rely on you for. That is why I need to be here every day. Or I might come up with something better. I need to think about it some more."

Sofri shook her head. "I have petitioners who have been waiting for centuries to have an audience with me. I cannot just turn them away, not even for the queen."

Ani waved a dismissive hand. "From now on, shorten every visit by a few minutes. Review the protocol with your attendants and see where you can cut corners. By the end of the day, you should have saved enough time to dedicate an hour to me."

Sofri bowed her head. "As you wish, my queen."

"Oh, stop that." Ani slapped her friend's thigh. "I am Ani to you, never the queen."

Sofri lifted both brows. "You sounded so imperious just now that I was compelled to call you 'my queen'."

Ani winced. "Ingrained habits. Can you pull it off?"

"I will do my best."

5

FRANKIE

"He left before I woke up this morning," Frankie complained to Margo.

"Did he leave a note?"

"Nope." Frankie sighed. "But enough about me. How are you doing?"

"I'm good. Lynda and her friends are much nicer when drunk, which is most of the time now. They finally let loose and stopped their silly posturing."

"Good." Frankie chewed on her thumbnail. "I'm glad that you are enjoying yourself."

She could really use Margo right now. They could go to the Lido deck, flirt with all the hunky immortals, and make Dagor jealous.

He might have left early for a good reason like his boss needing him or a meeting with the goddess or with Kian, but he could have left a note or a message on her phone. So yeah, he was an alien who had only been on Earth for five years, and most of them had not been spent in the States, so he might not know that he was supposed to do that, but it still rankled.

If he cared for her, he would have bothered to let her know why he'd left and when she could expect him back.

"By the way, don't go ashore in Acapulco," Margo said. "I heard really bad things from the girls."

The ship had docked in the port early in the morning, and Frankie had planned on exploring the city with Dagor or without him.

"Like what?"

"The cartels have turned it into a war zone. They are kidnapping people and killing them. Very few cruise liners go there these days."

"What are the Mexican police doing about it?"

Margo snorted. "Most are on the cartels' payroll. Anyway, if I were you, I would skip it. Stay on the ship and enjoy margaritas by the pool."

"I wouldn't be going alone. Some of the guys here look fierce enough to scare off a horde of potential rapists and murderers."

Cartel thugs were nothing to the immortal security force, but Frankie didn't know whether they would be escorting the people getting off. The port area was probably safe, but she would feel better if some of them were around.

Dagor alone could most likely take care of any human with nefarious intentions, but she didn't know for sure what powers the gods possessed. Besides, he might have other plans.

Perhaps she could check with Max and ask him if he was going ashore with some of his buddies. If he was, she had a feeling he wouldn't mind if she wanted to tag along.

Toven and Mia might plan on going sightseeing, too, so she could opt to go with them. Toven wouldn't risk taking Mia to see the city if he didn't believe that he could protect her, and if he thought he needed more protection, he would take a large security detail with him.

"You're just saying that to ease my mind," Margo said. "You know that I love computer geeks, but I wouldn't describe them as formidable with anything other than a game controller. Well, maybe they can also shoot well after all the shooting games they play, but I wouldn't bet my life on that, even if they were armed."

Right. Margo still thought that this was a company cruise for the Perfect Match employees.

"Not everyone here is a programmer. Tom's partners employ a large security force, and I plan to join a group that has at least several of them accompanying it."

It was a little white lie, or rather, a half-truth. Members of the security force were not on board in any official capacity. They were part of the community and had come to celebrate their friends' and family's weddings.

That they could also defend their clan while enjoying the celebrations was an added bonus for everyone involved, and it was good to know that she was safe because the people around her knew how to defend her and the other guests on the ship.

Once Margo got on board, she would not only learn the real story but also get to meet some of those guys, and she could find someone to have a vacation fling with, too.

Frankie winced.

Dagor was supposed to be just that, but he was turning into more, and it was evidently one-sided.

"Are the security people armed?" Margo asked.

"I don't know, but I assume that they are."

"Make sure. Muscles won't be much use against machine guns."

"I'll check, and if they are not armed, I'm not going."

"Promise me, or I won't be able to enjoy myself until you are back safe and sound on board the ship."

"Who said I'm safe here?" she said to tease Margo. "What if those gangs decide to attack the ship? To them, a luxury cruiser like this would be an irresistible target, what with all the rich people on board who they can kidnap for ransom."

Margo groaned. "I know that you are not serious, but it could happen. Now I won't be able to relax for sure."

"Forget I said anything and stop worrying for nothing. You know how the news is. They only report the bad stuff, so it seems like the world is ending."

"Yeah, you're right." Margo let out a breath. "I'm going to join the ladies in the bar, get drunk, and spend the rest of the day by the pool."

Frankie frowned. "By the way, is Cabo safe? You seem better informed about the cartel problem than I am."

"It is safer than Acapulco, and I have no plans to leave the resort to explore, so I don't feel threatened."

"It's sad." Frankie sighed. "What is the world coming to?"

Margo snorted. "Says the girl who only a moment ago blamed the news for making everything seem more dire than it is."

"It does, but it's always done that, and yet it seems like it's much worse now than it was only a few years ago."

"It's anarchy," Margo said. "Today it's Mexico, tomorrow it's the States. Soon, there will be nowhere safe to hide." She chuckled. "Maybe Tom's eccentric partners are not so eccentric after all. Perhaps they are better prepared for the bleak future than the rest of us plebs. They have their own security force and a secret compound. We are lucky to get invited there."

"Yes, we are."

Margo didn't know how right she was. The immortals were hiding from all humans, not just the bad players from Mexico and other evildoers from around the world, and that made their village a real sanctuary.

Was there a chance they would let her bring her entire family if things got really bad in California?

Probably not.

What was she going to do?

Frankie was not about to abandon her family while she had a nice cozy place to hide.

"Tom and his partners are rich and well connected," Margo murmured. "They might know things that the general public is not privy to. The elite is in the know, while the rest of us are fumbling in the dark while trying to survive."

"Right. But Tom and his partners are the good guys. It will be beneficial for us to be around them because when they hear about the danger that the rest of us aren't aware of, they will sound a warning."

"Or so you hope. Should I remind you what happened on the Titanic? The rich got in the rescue boats while the crew barred the poor from leaving, condemning them to drown."

"Don't believe everything you see in the movies."

"I don't." Margo huffed out a breath. "Usually, they try to sugarcoat things, not the other way around. Face it, Frankie, we are part of the faceless, voiceless masses, and the elites don't care what happens to us. They only care about power and money."

Frankie rolled her eyes. "You read too many conspiracy theory books and get upset over things that you cannot change regardless of them being true or false. Switch to romance novels, and you will be much happier. Ignorance is bliss, right?"

"Yeah, but it's also irresponsible. I refuse to be a sheep, ignorantly and blissfully led to slaughter."

6

DAGOR

When Dagor got to the Lido deck it was still early in the morning, and there was hardly anyone there. One guy was swimming in the pool, two sat on the edge with their feet dangling in the water, and several females were sunbathing on the lounge chairs with their eyes covered with dark sunglasses.

No one was at the bar, which was a great opportunity for an uninterrupted chat with Bob.

As Dagor sat on one of the barstools, the robot turned around to face him with a silly grin on his shiny metallic face.

"Hello, Master Doug. What can I serve you?"

"How about a glass of sparkling water?"

"Certainly, master." One of his long arms reached for a glass and put it under a spout while the other one pressed the lever to release the stream.

"Do you know what my real name is?" Dagor asked as Bob handed him the glass.

"Of course, master. I thought that you preferred to be called Master Doug, but if you wish, I can call you Master Dagor."

"Why do you use the honorific 'master'? Most humans use Mister or none at all."

Bob blinked, which looked oddly human on his metallic face. Not that he'd been designed to approximate a human. His head was much too small for the size of his body, he didn't have a nose, and his eyes were round, but they had a shutter that looked like an eyelid.

"This is how I was programmed to address my clients. Master for a gentleman and mistress for a lady."

Dagor chuckled. "They should have expanded your gender vocabulary, but I guess your creators are old-fashioned."

The robot blinked again, which seemed to be his way of expressing confusion or astonishment. "I do not know what you mean, master."

"That's okay." Dagor took a sip from his sparkling water. "So, tell me, Bob. What can you do besides serving drinks?"

"I can clean the glasses and the countertop, order new bottles when needed, and I can schedule my own maintenance."

"Is that all?" Dagor asked.

"What else would you have me do, master?" Bob smiled in what was a pretty good imitation of a real smile.

"You also know the names of all of your customers and what they look like. Have you been equipped with facial recognition software?"

"Of course, master. Otherwise, how would I know who I am looking at?"

"Good point." Dagor emptied the rest of his glass and handed it to Bob. "I'm a little hungry. What do you have as far as food?"

"I have snacks, master." Bob waved one of his arms at the selection of chips, nuts, and pretzels. "What would you like, master?"

"Can I have one of each?"

"Of course." Bob pulled down several bags and put them in front of Dagor. "Master must have skipped breakfast."

"That's a very good observation."

The robot nodded. "I am constantly learning, master. I have noticed that people eat more snacks when they do not have a proper meal. I also learn more facial expressions every day." The robot tilted his head in a very human manner. "Right now, master looks tense. Perhaps a cocktail is in order? Bloody Mary is a good morning drink."

"That's a great suggestion, thank you."

Unless Bob had been trained before in the immortals' village, he was learning fast, given that he had been working only two days.

"Here you go, master." The robot put a napkin on the counter and a red drink on top of it.

"Thank you." Dagor took a sip. "This is very good."

"My pleasure, master."

"I have another question. Are your creators here on board the ship?"

"Yes, master."

"Can you tell me their names?"

"Many were involved in my creation, but Master William was the head of the lab."

That was easier than Dagor had expected. Bob volunteered the name without having to be tricked into it. "I would love to have a chat with Master William. Are you capable of projecting his image so I would know who to look for?"

"I do not possess projection abilities, but I can point him out to you." Bob moved a foot to the side. "He is the gentleman wearing a Hawaiian shirt."

Dagor turned around in the direction that Bob was looking. A couple that he hadn't seen before were sitting on two loungers by the pool, and the male had a blue Hawaiian shirt on. He was wearing dark sunglasses like everyone else on the deck, but his mate wasn't.

"Thank you, Bob." He finished his drink and put the empty glass on the bar. "I'm going to ask William a few questions. I hope he won't mind."

"He will not," Bob said. "From what I observed while in the lab, Master William enjoys talking about his work."

"Excellent." Dagor smiled. "A guy after my own heart."

7

KIAN

"I've never been to Acapulco before." Jacki spread jam over her toast. "I'm excited." She glanced at Kalugal. "And I'm even more excited about visiting the Tehuacalco site."

Kian turned to Kalugal with a raised brow. "What's in Tehuacalco, and why do you want to take your wife into dangerous territory? After reading about the cartels ruling the entire area, I didn't even want to stop at this port, but my sisters twisted my arm." He cast Sari an accusing look. "With you being the most vocal one."

She shrugged. "David and I were planning to just tour the area near the port, which is safe. I wanted to do some shopping, but now that Kalugal's mentioned the archeological site, I'm intrigued."

Kian groaned. "Don't. Do you have any idea how bad it is in this area? Not too long ago, four dismembered bodies washed up on a popular beach."

"That's terrible." Alena put a hand over her pregnant belly. "I'm not leaving the ship."

Sari leaned over and put her hand on Alena's. "You and Orion are welcome to join David and me. I think we are going to stick to our original plan for the day."

Kian was relieved. "Smart."

Kalugal waved a dismissive hand. "Tehuacalco is a popular tourist attraction, and it's only an hour's drive away. I don't expect any trouble. I hired a reputable local guide with a converted truck that can take seven passengers, so we can easily accommodate one more couple and three Guardians. If more want to join the expedition, I can arrange for drivers with more vehicles. The more of us go, the safer we will be, right?" He smiled at Kian. "Not that I really need much help. With my compulsion and shrouding ability, I can handle any human threat. But I don't want you to worry, so I will ask several Guardians to join us."

Kian had forgotten about Kalugal's compulsion ability. However, for it to work Kalugal needed to be heard, and if thugs ambushed him and started shooting, would they hear him above the gunfire?

"Can we come?" Negal asked from the table next to theirs. "Aru and I are fighters, and we can easily handle a gang of human criminals."

"Speak for yourself," Aru said. "I'm not risking Gabi. She's a newly turned immortal, and her transition is not complete yet."

Negal shrugged. "Then I'll go alone or with Dagor if he wants to join." He pulled out his phone. "I'll ask him."

"Excellent," Kalugal said. "The more the merrier."

Kian wasn't sure about that, but he couldn't forbid them from going. Thankfully, Syssi didn't seem interested at all.

After a quick exchange of texts, Negal leaned toward Kalugal. "Dagor asks what's so interesting in Tehuacalco?"

"Aha." Kalugal leaned back in his chair with a satisfied smile. "A while back, I bought an ancient treasure map. Supposedly, a powerful amulet is hidden under the ruins of Tehuacalco. The source and authenticity are questionable, but since I'm already here, I want to take a look." He lifted Jacki's hand and kissed the back of it. "The amulet is supposed to magnify a seer's ability to see the future. It will be the perfect gift for my lovely wife."

She smiled. "Provided that we find it, which we most likely will not. But it's a good excuse to have a little adventure. I also want to try the Xtasea. It's supposed to be the world's longest zip line. I haven't done anything daring since turning immortal, and this seems like a great opportunity to confront my former fears."

Kian shook his head. "You don't have the time to explore the ruins beyond a brief tour. Amanda and Dalhu's wedding is tonight. You need to get back in time to shower and get ready."

"The reception starts at eight in the evening," Sari said. "That's thirteen hours from now. We have plenty of time to enjoy both attractions and get back by six to get ready for the wedding."

"Dagor says that he would love to come." Negal looked up from his phone. "He also wants to bring Frankie along."

"Not happening." Kian crossed his arms over his chest. "She's human. Too vulnerable."

"Dagor and I can protect her." Negal's smile never left his mouth, as if he were mocking Kian's concerns.

"Let me give you some more information about what's going on in the lovely city of Acapulco and its surrounding area. It is experiencing one of the highest levels of violence in Mexico as gangs fight over control of the port with the support of much larger cartels that operate on a national level. At least sixteen crime syndicates are active in the Guerrero state. They engage in drug and human trafficking, kidnapping, and extortion, and they have such control over the local communities that when two drug lords were arrested, thousands of residents showed up in the state's capital, demanding their release."

"Why?" Syssi asked. "Don't they want to get rid of the cartels?"

"They do." Kian uncrossed his arms and put his hands on the table. "But they were told to do that, and if they hadn't, the repercussions would have been horrific. The cartels are so powerful that the police and even the Mexican army are afraid to engage them."

Kalugal didn't look impressed or frightened in the slightest. "That's the reality of this region, and there is nothing they can do about it, but we don't need to worry."

Kian took a deep breath. "I can't stop you, but I hope that you have enough sense to leave your son on the ship."

That wiped the smug smile off Kalugal's face. "What do you take me for? An irresponsible fool? Darius is still human. He will stay on the ship with Shamash."

"Forgive me." Kian dipped his head in mock apology. "But you seemed so certain there was no danger that it worried me."

"To immortals and gods, there is no danger, and we can probably keep one or two adult humans safe, but that's as far as my risk tolerance goes."

8

DAGOR

Dagor walked over to where William and his mate were lounging. "Good morning." He produced his best smile. "I hope I'm not interrupting. I'm Dagor." He dipped his head.

"Hi." The blond shaded her eyes with her hand and squinted at him. "We know who you are, and you are not interrupting. You and your friends are celebrities." She sat up and offered him her hand. "I'm Kaia."

"A pleasure to meet you, Kaia." He gently took her slender fingers in his and gave them the slightest of shakes.

"I'm William." Her mate offered him his hand. "Please, join us."

"Thank you." Dagor sat down. "I was chatting with Bob and was impressed with how quickly he was learning to anticipate and respond to conversations. He told me that you headed the team that created him. I'm fascinated by the technology, and I would love to learn more about Bob's capabilities. He's definitely not like any of the other robots serving drinks on cruise ships."

Not that Dagor had been on any other cruise ship or encountered any other server robots, but after meeting Bob, he had read about them and watched a few YouTube videos.

William smiled, but his shoulders tensed, and his mate regarded Dagor with suspicion in her eyes.

"There is nothing unique about Bob," she said, lifting her drink from the side table. "We used widely available technology to build him. Usually, ships' robotic bartenders have limited capabilities because there is no reason to invest in a more sophisticated model, and Bob is by far too advanced for the simple task we gave him, but it was a good opportunity to test the prototype. We intend to test his performance and learning capabilities in a wide array of tasks, not just bartending."

As Kaia launched into her explanation, Dagor noticed William's shoulders losing their rigidity, but he still didn't take part in the conversation. Bob had said that his creator loved talking about his work, so his lack of response wasn't because he was shy and preferred his mate speaking for him.

Dagor had a feeling that Kaia was simply better at evasive answers, and there was more to Bob than she had admitted.

"I'm surprised that you find Bob so fascinating," William finally said. "Coming from Anumati, the planet that created the Odus, you must have encountered much more sophisticated artificial intelligence?"

"I have, but I was not privy to the technology."

"The creation of Odus was outlawed, right?" Kaia asked. "That's what the Kra-ell told us, but things might have changed after the settlers left."

"A less humanoid-like version was created to replace the Odus. Also, everything manufactured on Anumati is now tamper-proof. This means that after a product leaves the factory, neither programming nor any other component can be altered. If something malfunctions, it's decommissioned and disposed of."

Kaia put her glass down. "Isn't that wasteful? They can't even reuse the parts?"

Dagor shrugged. "Building new is less resource demanding than ensuring that the technology isn't stolen or altered to be used in nefarious ways."

William nodded in what Dagor interpreted as agreement. "That actually makes sense to me. Companies invest heavily in research and development only to have their products reverse engineered by unscrupulous competitors and sold for less. I wouldn't be surprised if human tech goes a similar route. If the product is destroyed when tampered with, no one can reverse engineer it." He smiled at Dagor. "I encountered that problem when I tried to take apart the trackers that we removed from the Kra-ell. How did you manage to alter the trackers you found in China?"

"Older technology," Dagor said. "They were made before the shift to solid state."

"Did you alter the trackers?" Kaia asked.

Dagor shook his head. "I'm mostly self-taught, and my knowledge is limited, so I couldn't do it alone, but I helped, and after it was done, we erased the memories of the techs we hired for the task."

"I'm mostly self-taught as well," William said. "I've attended classes in various engineering schools, and I've also engaged experts in one-on-one lessons, but my official degree is fake."

Dagor regarded the guy with even more respect. "I would appreciate your guidance in self-education. I had dreams of returning home and applying to one of Anumati's engineering schools, but since I'm not going home anytime soon, I'd better utilize the time to learn what I can on Earth."

He didn't add that his chances of getting accepted to one of those schools were nearly nonexistent. As a commoner, he needed to be truly gifted and exceptional to have a chance, and he wasn't. He was smart and somewhat talented, but that was not enough to get him in.

"What fields are you interested in?" Kaia asked. "There is so much to learn even on our backward little planet."

He rubbed his chin to hide his smile at her comment. "Anything that has to do with robotics interests me, but I'm also interested in communications and spyware. The problem is that much of Anumati's technology is based on our genetic expertise, and that field is just in its infancy on Earth."

Kaia's eyes sparkled with interest. "That's where my expertise comes into play. I'm a bioinformatician. William and I are collaborating and merging our knowledge to—"A sharp look from her mate had her clamping her mouth shut for a moment. "To research the possibilities." She smiled sweetly at Dagor. "Perhaps your limited knowledge from Anumati can help point us in the right direction."

"I would gladly share with you everything I know."

As Dagor's phone buzzed with an incoming message, he pulled it out of his pocket and read it.

"It seems like a group of your friends is going ashore and heading to a nearby archaeological site."

"Not interested." Kaia lifted her drink and leaned back in her lounger. "Sweating on a dusty dig site is not my idea of fun."

9

FRANKIE

Frankie sat with Mia and Toven at the breakfast table while keeping an eye on Dagor's teammates, who were seated several tables over.

She'd thought she would find him in the dining hall, but evidently, he was somewhere else, and it wasn't in a meeting with Aru and Negal or with Kian. He also wasn't having tea with the Clan Mother because Kian would have been there as well.

Where the hell was he?

"You are not eating," Mia said. "What got your panties in a twist?"

Mia knew very well why Frankie was upset. They had been friends forever, and it shouldn't be too difficult to guess that dining alone after spending the night with a guy was disappointing, to say the least.

"Nothing." She reached for a piece of toast and added it to the heap of scrambled egg she'd put on her plate before.

"Did you have a disagreement with Dagor?" Toven asked.

"We had a lovely time last night at the wedding and later in my cabin. I don't know what chased him out of my bed early in the morning or why he didn't bother to at least leave a note."

Toven's eyes shone with understanding. "He probably didn't mean anything by it. He just doesn't know what is expected of him in a relationship."

Frankie tried very hard not to glare at the god. "I'm sure things are not much different where he came from, and the ladies there expect the same courtesy that we lowly humans do."

Toven opened his mouth to say something but closed it and shook his head. "I don't know what the customs are on Anumati. I was born on Earth."

Mia and Toven had told her about what had happened to the other gods. They hadn't elaborated, and what she knew could barely fill one page of the series of books that would be needed to contain all there was to know about the gods and the immortals, but she knew that a small group of gods had arrived on Earth a long time ago and some of them had taken human partners, which was how the first immortals had been born.

"Just think about how your father treated your mother." Mia put her coffee cup down. "And if your parents were born on Earth too, how your grandparents interacted with each other, and you will have your answer."

Toven smiled sadly. "My father was a great god who wasn't born on Earth, but he was a philanderer. My mother was one of many goddesses he bedded, and his relationship with her was cordial at best. They preferred not to be in the same room at the same time."

Without giving it a second thought, Frankie reached over the table and patted Toven's hand. "I'm sorry. That must have been difficult for you growing up."

"Not really. Whenever I felt too stifled in my mother's house, I would go to visit my father and have a grand time building all kinds of contraptions with him. He realized early on that I didn't have a knack for science and engineering like he had, so the projects he pretended to be working on when I visited were simple, and I had fun making things with him and trying to solve problems. I learned a lot, and I got to spend time with my father, whose household was the exact opposite of my mother's."

Mia put down her fork and dabbed her mouth with a napkin. "And yet you married a goddess who was precisely like your mother."

Frankie's eyes widened. "You were married before?"

He nodded. "My wife perished with the rest of the gods while I was away. I've never forgiven myself for not being there for her."

"You would have died too." Mia took his hand and gave it a squeeze. "I'm so happy that the Fates prompted you to get away in the nick of time."

Mia and Toven were so adorable together that it brought tears to Frankie's eyes. She averted her gaze to spare them the emotional display, and as she looked at the table where Aru and Negal were sitting with Kian and several other immortals, her phone buzzed with an incoming message.

Pulling the device from her pocket, she looked at the screen, and if not for Toven sitting right next to her, she would have stuck out her tongue at it.

Dagor's text didn't contain an apology or an explanation for his stealthy morning departure. Instead, he was inviting her on an outing to some archeological site that Kalugal was arranging. It was only an hour away from Acapulco, and there was a treasure hunt for a lost amulet. He also mentioned that it might be dangerous because of the cartels operating in the area but promised to keep her safe, which was the only thing that stopped her from ignoring the text and not bothering to answer him.

"What is it?" Mia asked.

"Kian's cousin is organizing an outing to Tehuacalco, and Dagor's invited me to join them. Do you want to come?"

"It's too dangerous." Toven put his hand on Mia's thigh. "You shouldn't go either."

"Dagor thinks that it's fine. He promises to protect me." She leveled her gaze on Toven. "Aside from being stronger and faster, what can a god do that a human cannot?"

"It depends on the god." Toven shifted in his chair. "I can compel the gangsters to drop their weapons or turn on each other, but as far as I know, Dagor doesn't have compulsion ability."

"But Kalugal does," Mia said. "His compulsion even works on other immortals, which is a big deal, but he is not as powerful as Toven."

10

ANI

"Will there be anything else, Your Majesty?" Lileth asked after turning Ani's bed down.

"No, thank you. You may leave."

"Good night, my queen." Her maid bowed and retreated from the room, walking backward as was customary for servants when leaving the presence of a royal.

It occurred to Ani that the nobles should do the same. Although most of the backstabbing was political in nature, assassinations usually happened off the planet, on one of the colonies where locals could be blamed. It was never prudent to turn one's back on the vipers in court.

That was the main reason Ani never left Anumati to visit the colonies, even though it was one of her queenly duties. Getting rid of her was not politically beneficial to her husband, but even though he kept her in the dark about most of his machinations, she still knew too much for his comfort.

With a sigh, Ani walked to the window and peered outside at the city below.

The beauty of it never ceased to move her despite the many thousands of years she'd been gazing at it from her palace quarters.

Bioluminescent flora cast a serene glow over the subterranean city, mimicking a starry sky, and the buildings that were carved from the very bedrock were aglow with the soft light of embedded crystals. Bridges arched over chasms, connecting districts that, during designated daylight hours, burst with activity.

In the center of the palace's plaza, terraced pools cascaded in a series of concentric circles, each level pouring into the next. The water, which was infused with minerals, gleamed like flowing silver, reflecting the luminescent glow from above and around.

The lush gardens surrounding the terraced pools had been cultivated to flourish in the bioluminescent light, their leaves and petals shimmering in hues of emerald, sapphire, and amethyst.

Stone pathways meandered through the gardens, dotted with benches positioned to afford the best views of the pools and the flora, and along the edges, luminous orbs hung from the sculpted archways, providing soft light to complement the natural bioluminescence.

If not for the many sculptures depicting the Eternal King that dotted the gardens, it would have been Ani's favorite place to stroll through, but it was impossible to walk more than twenty paces without bumping into her husband's likeness.

For the sake of appearances, several statues were dedicated to pivotal figures in Anumati's history, and there were even three of her, but the one of Ahn had been demolished after his exile and replaced by one more of the king.

From her window high up, though, Ani could only see the tops and could still enjoy the beauty of the plaza.

The gardens extended beyond the palace, and a river surrounded the gardens, with bridges connecting it to the rest of the city. It was wide enough to make jumping over impossible even for a Kra-ell, and any attempt to swim through or fly over would have been dealt with by the patrol drones.

Only those with legitimate business in the palace were allowed through the checkpoints, and the scanners verified that no contraband or uninvited guests got smuggled in.

Still, it didn't mean that assassinating the king was impossible. If Ani put her mind to it, she could probably pull it off, but that was premature. His hold over Anumati was such that his elimination would plunge it into chaos, and as a historian, Ani knew the horrors that could and would ensue.

The resistance needed to replace the king with an equally competent ruler and to make the transition smooth, the new queen or king had to be a descendant of the king. Ani's royal bloodline was ancient, but it would be much more difficult for her to take the throne than it would be for El's granddaughter.

Ani was popular and capable, but at least half of Anumatians would not accept her as the Eternal Queen. She might be able to hold things together for a short time, but she lacked El's charisma and political genius to cement her rule for eternity.

Did her granddaughter have what was needed?

Even if Annani had all of her grandfather's attributes, she would still need massive training in Anumati's complicated politics, and the only one who could provide it was Ani.

Could she do that from afar?

Communicating through the telepathic twins was an incredible advantage that Ani wished had been available to her when Ahn was still alive, but it was cumbersome. To teach Annani what she needed to know, Ani would have to teach Sofri, who would need to teach Aria, who would have to teach Aru, who would need to teach Annani.

There was no way it would work.

Could Annani learn what she needed just from watching pivotal moments in Anumati's past and reading Ani's records?

The team of historians working for her did a great job recording events, but she doubted reading about them would be enough for Annani to understand her grandfather's special gifts.

Most of the Eternal King's opponents assumed that his incredible compulsion ability was the main ingredient in his success, and possibly it was, but it wasn't the only one. El had something extra that was beyond charisma and charm. It was that nameless extra quality that had blinded Ani to his real nature when she had agreed to the arranged mating, but the truth was that she would have mated El even if she had known his true nature.

The union between them solidified Anumati and allowed it to prosper. Ani represented the noble families controlling the manufacturing conglomerates, and the king needed them on his side, which was why she did not fear assassination.

The only way her husband could get rid of her without losing the support of the leading families was if he found out her role in the resistance and could prove it.

Her mistake had been giving El an heir, which she would not have done if she had known what was hiding beneath the façade her husband projected. Then again, if Ahn had never been born, his daughter would have never existed either, and Annani might be the only hope for the future of a free Anumati.

Ani sighed.

For a short period of time in Anumati's history, things were good, or as good as they could get with a vast population like theirs, and people practically worshiped her husband for bringing peace and prosperity to all while respecting personal freedoms and being mindful of the people's needs.

Not everything had been perfect, though, and the Kra-ell problem had been festering without most of the gods being aware of it, but things had started to deteriorate long before the Kra-ell rebellion, and they had continued getting worse long after it had been quelled.

11

DAGOR

As Dagor watched Frankie walk across the deck, he couldn't help the smile that spread over his face.

Her excitement was evident in the quickness of her steps, the sparkle in her eyes, and the smile on her face. He wondered whether she was excited about seeing him or about the excursion to Tehuacalco that he was starting to have second thoughts about.

She wore khaki cargo pants and a black T-shirt, but that was where her safari look ended. Her feet were clad in a pair of flip-flops, and he suspected the reason for the inappropriate footwear was that she hadn't packed anything more suitable.

After all, visiting Tehuacalco hadn't been on the itinerary, and for a good reason.

Dagor hadn't been aware of how volatile the area was. Lawlessness ruled, and the criminals were armed to the teeth and cruel in the extreme. The vile barbarian acts served to cow the local population and prevent opposition in any form.

He was confident in his ability to protect Frankie, and the large group of Guardians accompanying them could handle any human threat, but she was so fragile, and her life could be snuffed out too easily.

Regrettably, Aru had not allowed him to bring the disruptor or any of their other weapons, and the only ones who were armed were the Guardians.

He'd watched them gather around their leader and listened to the instructions they had been given. They seemed to know what they were doing and were capable of protecting the civilians in the group.

"Hi." Frankie smiled up at him. "I didn't know what to bring. Were we supposed to pack lunch?"

It hadn't occurred to him because he could go without a meal until dinner tonight, but Frankie needed to eat at regular intervals.

"No one said anything about it." He pulled her in for a quick kiss on her lush lips just because he couldn't help himself. "I'll ask."

"That's okay." She patted his arm. "I know Max over there. I'll ask him." She left his side and sauntered over to the leader of the Guardians.

Wasn't Max the guy who had flirted with her by the Lido bar?

Jealousy surging in his chest, Dagor followed Frankie to the guy and stood behind her as she inquired about lunch arrangements.

"We didn't pack anything." Max turned to Kalugal, who was the organizer of the trip. "Do we need to bring food?"

Kalugal smiled. "No need. Luis is bringing water and snacks for us."

"Who is Luis?" Dagor asked.

"Our tour guide." Kalugal wrapped his arm around his mate's waist. "He's such a find. Originally, it was supposed to be just Jacki and me, my second-in-command with his mate, and a couple of Guardians, but when the group grew to twenty-two people, I called him, and he said that he would arrange three more vehicles. There is room for eight in each, including the driver. The front truck will have mostly Guardians, the next one will be ours, with three couples and one armed Guardian next to the driver. If you and Frankie want to ride with us, we can chat on the way."

"Can I get a weapon? I'm not comfortable having just one armed guard in our vehicle."

Grinning, Kalugal lifted his vest to reveal two handguns strapped to his chest. "I'm pretty good with these, and my second is even better." He turned around and waved over a formidable-looking dude with a machine gun strapped over his shoulder and his arm wrapped around Edna, the judge who had probed their team.

"This is Rufsur, and this is his mate, Edna."

"We have met." Dagor dipped his head to the judge.

"But we haven't." Rufsur extended his hand to Frankie first. "I know who you are. You are Mia's friend."

She nodded. "I'm Frankie. Nice to meet you both." She shook his hand and then offered hers to the judge.

"Hello." Edna regarded her with a smile. "You're a brave soul for coming with us."

"Why, because I'm human?"

"Why else?" Edna tilted her head as if that was a silly question. "Until you transition, you are vulnerable. By the way, do you have any paranormal talents?"

"I can sniff a sale a mile away. Does that count?"

Edna laughed. "It might. Depends on how accurate your predictions are."

"I'm rarely wrong."

"Then perhaps that's your paranormal talent."

"I think everyone is here." Kalugal scanned the group. "Is anyone missing?"

"Negal," Dagor said. "Where did he go? He was here a few moments ago."

"He went to get guns for the two of you," Max said. "Do you know how to use it? I don't want you to accidentally shoot yourself or, worse, your mate."

"We know how to operate firearms, and Frankie is not my mate."

The grin that spread over Max's face demanded a punch to wipe it off, but Dagor stifled the urge. "Don't get any ideas." He wrapped his arm around her waist and pulled her closer. "For the duration of the cruise, she's mine."

Max arched a brow at Frankie. "Is that true?"

She shrugged. "It depends."

Dagor glared at her. "On what?"

"On how well you behave." She smiled sweetly at him. "I can give you the list of acceptable and unacceptable behaviors right now or later. Your choice."

"Have I offended you in any way?"

"As I said. Now or later. Choose."

With Max being an ass and listening in eagerly, the answer was obvious. "Later."

Grinning, Frankie stretched up on her toes and kissed Dagor on the lips. "That's what I thought."

12

FRANKIE

Usually, Frankie didn't like jealous, possessive guys. They were bad news. But in Dagor's case, she welcomed his jealousy.

He'd been so smug with his assertions that their romance would only last until the end of the cruise, but given his reaction to Max's barely-there flirting, he was falling for her, and it felt effing awesome.

A god was falling in love with her.

Talk about bragging rights. Except, she was under compulsion to keep her mouth shut about gods and immortals, and that was a damn shame.

As their group walked down the gangway, Frankie eyed the four converted trucks lined up just beyond the inspection point. They had canvas canopies for shade and four rows of two seats in each.

Having no air conditioning was going to be miserable, but it was too late to back out now. Besides, it was an opportunity to spend more time with Dagor, and Frankie wasn't going to give it up just because she was a spoiled city girl who didn't like to sweat.

Thankfully, she'd had the foresight to smear bug repellent over every area of exposed skin, including her feet.

She showed her passport, Dagor flashed his, and they walked through.

"What nationality do you claim?" she whispered.

"We all got Portuguese passports. They are one of the best in the world. It gives us the right to settle and work in any of the EU countries, and it also provides us with visa-free access to nearly two hundred countries and territories."

"Who do you mean by all? Everyone in the clan or just you and your god friends?"

"I don't know what the clan does for passports. I was referring to Aru, Negal, and myself."

At that, Frankie looked over her shoulder to glance at Negal and found him chatting with a couple of Guardians. "Is he okay back there? I don't mind him hanging out with us. I don't want him to feel as if he has to keep his distance."

Dagor waved a dismissive hand. "Negal is loving this. He's missed having the camaraderie of fellow troopers."

"Good. I'm not the kind of girl who hogs her guy's time and wants him all to herself."

He arched a brow. "You still didn't tell me your rules of engagement."

"Later." She followed Kalugal to the second vehicle in the row. "I'll tell you when we are back in my cabin. Alone."

"I don't think I can last that long," Dagor murmured as he climbed into the vehicle behind her. "Something is bothering you, and I want to know what it is, so I don't repeat the mistake."

She waited until he'd sat next to her before leaning her head on his shoulder and whispering, "Next time you wake up before me and decide to leave, you should scribble a note or send me a message. Otherwise, I might think that you were disappointed about our night together and that you don't want to see me again."

His arm tightened around her. "I'm sorry that I made you feel that way. It wasn't my intention."

She looked up at him. "Then what was it?"

He let out a breath. "Let's talk about it later."

The two other couples in the jeep were pretending not to hear their exchange, but she knew that they had heard every word, and she didn't want to give them any more gossip fodder. Besides, she hadn't actually made a list other than what she'd already told him.

How was she going to explain relationships to an alien? Especially since she didn't know whether he was really clueless, overwhelmed by how fast their relationship was moving, or just emotionally stunted.

But maybe he was being smarter than her about it. She could already feel the pain of separation, and they had a full week left to enjoy each other.

As the vehicle in front of them started moving, Frankie watched Negal talking with a couple she wasn't familiar with. The guy was tall and lanky, and the girl was short and pretty.

"That's Vlad and Wendy." Edna turned to look at her as if she had been reading her mind. "They are one of the couples who are getting married on this cruise." She turned back.

"Good to know," Dagor said.

"Are they both..." Frankie stopped as the word immortal refused to leave her mouth, "...you know, different?"

Frankie had forgotten that she couldn't talk about the forbidden subjects because the driver was human. She was pretty sure that Kalugal had taken care of thralling Luis or compelling him so it was safe to talk around him, but that didn't change the nature of Toven's compulsion. Unless the god altered the phrasing, she couldn't say anything about gods or immortals.

"They are." The judge's mate turned to look at them. "You can talk freely around Luis. Kalugal told him about the movie script we are working on." He winked and added in a lower voice, "Later he's going to thrall his memories of this excursion away. As to your question, Wendy is a newly turned immortal." He shifted his gaze to Frankie. "You can talk to her about transitioning."

"Mia can tell me all I need to know."

The movie script idea could be a convenient work-around of Toven's compulsion. If Frankie pretended that she was talking about a script, she could say anything she wanted.

"True, but it's always good to get another perspective," the guy said. "Especially on something as pivotal and irreversible as turning immortal or remaining human."

The vehicle cruised along the smooth pavement, but the comfortable ride didn't last long. As soon as they left the city limits, cutting a swath through the foliage on either side of the road, things became bumpy even though it was still paved. There were potholes everywhere, and fallen vegetation necessitated maneuvering around them.

The seats were old and stiff, and bumping over them was sure to leave her sore by the end of the trip.

"This is going to be tough on my butt," she murmured.

"That's unacceptable," Dagor said, and the next moment she found herself sitting in his lap. "Better?"

"I'm not sure." She smiled and leaned against his chest. "There is still something hard under my butt."

Edna's mate snickered, but the judge remained focused on the road, her shoulders tense and her eyes vigilant.

Dagor must have noticed that as well because he asked, "Forgive me, Edna, but seeing how you are scanning the jungle, I wonder if you can sense the intentions of potential attackers?"

"Unfortunately, no. I need to be close and preferably touch the person. But two of the passengers in the vehicle behind us have intuitive powers. Yamanu and Arwel can sense if anyone has nefarious intentions toward us and sound the alarm."

"What about the others?" Frankie asked.

Edna smiled. "Mey and Jin's talents are incredible as well, and I have no doubt that Kalugal invited them to join our expedition so they could help him locate the artifact."

13

KALUGAL

Kalugal turned around and looked back at the two rows of elevated seats. Rufsur and Edna were about six inches above him, and the last row where Dagor and Frankie sat was higher by a foot.

It was a good configuration for sightseeing, but it forced him to crane his neck.

"I'm particularly interested in Mey's talent. She can listen to conversations embedded in the walls. So, if this map is for real, which I very much doubt, then perhaps she can hear long-ago conversations that can lead us to where the amulet is."

Edna lifted a brow. "If you are doubtful about the authenticity of the map, why are you taking us into the jungle?"

The female had no sense of adventure. "The search for the artifact is as exciting as finding it, my dear Edna, and while we are at it, we can appreciate this unique site." He assumed his Professor Gunter voice, just without the German accent. "Tehuacalco was the cradle of ancient mystique, dedicated to the worship of mountains, which the Yope people and many other indigenous cultures revered as gods. The mountains were thought to be pillars of the world and the source of divine power."

Rufsur snorted. "That's a nice spin to put on the selection of a strategically advantageous location."

"True," Kalugal agreed. "In the past, everything was attributed to the gods." He smiled at Dagor. "The site's architecture aligns with the solstices and equinoxes, which is their nod to the gods. As for defending their city, the Yope fortified the natural barrier of the terrain, making it a natural stronghold against invaders."

"What happened to the Yope?" Jacki asked with a smile lifting the corners of her lips. "And it would be fun if you could deliver your lecture in Professor Gunter's accent."

He arched a brow. "Really? You like that?"

"I love that. It always makes me laugh."

"Well, in that case, I'm happy to oblige you, my love." He leaned over and planted a chaste kiss on her lips that promised more passionate kisses later, provided that Darius slept as soundly as he had the previous night.

Their son seemed to love the gentle rocking of the ship.

"Thank you." Jacki's eyes gleamed with the same promise his kiss had made.

Shifting to make himself more comfortable and hide the evidence of his desire for his wife, Kalugal pointed at the village they were passing by. "The Yope were eventually absorbed into these communities," he continued as Professor Gunter. "The Yope didn't leave many written records, so there is very little known about them, and their language and customs are lost to us. What we know about them comes from the stones of Tehuacalco and the legends passed down through generations."

As the paved road ended and the truck thundered over the gravel, Kalugal had to raise his voice to be heard. "It's said that the Yope were fierce warriors, but they also had seers who could commune with the divine. Some believe that their seers helped guide the construction of Tehuacalco, to make it not just a place of worship, but a conduit for celestial power."

Once again, Rufsur snorted. "Is that factual, or are you embellishing it to make our excursion more interesting?"

Kalugal mock-glared at his second-in-command. "I was extrapolating as a preamble to the amulet quest. Way to steal my thunder."

"I'm sorry." Rufsur lifted his hands in the peace sign. "Please, continue."

Kalugal regretted not having the round spectacles he wore as Professor Gunter or the rumpled brown suit. Hopefully, the accent was enough to embellish the story and please his mate. "Legends speak of an artifact of great power capable of bridging the mortal realm with that of the gods. The map I obtained claims that it is hidden in Tehuacalco to safeguard it from those who would use its power to harm others."

"Isn't that what an amulet is supposed to do?" Edna asked. "Protect those who wield it against their enemies and therefore harm them?"

"Well, yes, but then it is used in a righteous way—in self-defense. Those who are not righteous would use it to harm others, subjugate them, and do other terrible deeds." He sighed dramatically. "Perhaps the amulet's discovery will unveil the fate of the Yope—whether they merely faded into history or ascended beyond it as some stories suggest."

"Star people?" Frankie asked. "Is that what ascending beyond means?"

Kalugal shrugged. "Maybe. The truth is that I'm not an expert on Mesoamerican cultures."

"You sound like an expert to me," Dagor said.

"Thank you." Kalugal dipped his head. "I'm well-read, so I know a little, but there is much more to learn, and I wish I had the time, but I'm a father to an infant son who still doesn't sleep well most nights, and my free time is extremely limited." He turned around and wrapped his arm around Jacki's shoulders. "This is the most fun we've had as a couple in a long time."

She settled against him. "We should do this more often. You still haven't taken me to Egypt as you promised."

He winced. "Things were a little iffy in the area, and I kept waiting for them to get better before I took you there, but they just seem to be getting worse."

Jacki frowned. "In what way?"

"I don't want to bore you with the details, love. Let's just enjoy this trip without worrying about things we cannot control."

"I thought that you controlled everything."

"I wish I did, but I'm not there yet, and perhaps I never will be. Have you heard about the law of unintended consequences?"

"Of course."

"It's a bitch, and it has teeth."

14

DAGOR

What had Kalugal's mate meant by her comment about him controlling everything?

It might have been a joke or a tease, but usually it referred to something real.

Dagor hadn't gotten the impression that Kalugal was a pivotal figure in the clan, let alone someone who controlled everything, but he had an arrogant aura about him that reminded Dagor of the royals and other high nobility on Anumati. He mitigated it with charm and humor, and his impersonation of an old German professor had provided comic relief that had eased some of Dagor's anxious energy, but he still didn't like the guy.

"Trouble with InstaTock?" the judge asked.

What the hell was InstaTock?

Kalugal sighed. "The young people of today are too easily impressed by the wrong kind of players, and my platform is being hijacked by promoters of evil ideology. I hate censoring free speech, but I can't condone what's going on, especially since it is so grossly misguided. This generation is figuratively digging its own mass grave and has no clue what is going on. Their ignorance is appalling."

That was a far cry from the levity the immortal had displayed only moments ago.

"What do you mean?" Dagor asked.

Kalugal waved a dismissive hand. "It's not something I want to discuss while we are on our way to a pleasurable treasure hunt. I want to show my wife a well-deserved good time."

Given the tightening of the judge's lips, she didn't like Kalugal's answer. "Is it something we should put on the agenda of our next council meeting?"

Kalugal nodded. "I don't think the clan can do much about it, but I suspect that most of the council members are not aware of what's going on with the human youth of today. If not for my involvement with InstaTock, I wouldn't have been aware of the severity of the problem either and would have continued operating in mindless bliss. I feel that it is my obligation to share what I know with the council."

Jacki rested her head on his shoulder. "You are so wise, my love."

Dagor turned to look at Frankie. "Do you know what he's talking about?"

She shrugged. "I'm not a fan of social media in general, and InstaTock in particular. Those platforms are a mindless time suck. I prefer to spend my time more productively."

"Oh yeah?" He arched a brow. "What do you like to do in your spare time?"

"Visit with family and friends." She grinned at him. "That's what's important in life. Spending time with the people you love and care about is so much better than staring at your phone's screen for hours and reading bullshit that someone or some bots posted. Haven't you noticed how all the articles recycle the same information without even trying to rephrase it? I don't know how they are not sued for plagiarism."

He chuckled. "I did it when we were trying to find hints about surviving gods and Kra-ell. It's frustrating, but how else are we going to find clues that will lead us to the missing Kra-ell pods?"

The smile slid off Frankie's face. "Yeah. How else?" She leaned back and returned to watching the vegetation on her side of the vehicle.

It took him a moment to figure out why she'd gotten upset. Talking about his mission was a reminder of the limited time they had left together, and it didn't make Dagor happy either. He didn't like to think about leaving Frankie behind, and he liked even less the idea of her finding an immortal male to induce her transition. But he had a mission to complete, and as impossible as it was, he had to do it if he wanted to ever get back home.

As the vehicle bumped along the dirt path, the vegetation on both sides was so overgrown that they had to occasionally duck to avoid being hit by branches. He pulled Frankie closer to shield her, and she let him, for which he was grateful.

At the moment, he wasn't sure whether she was even willing to continue their romance, tryst, hookup, or whatever it was that what they had could be described as. It could only work as long as both of them kept their hearts out of it, but he was struggling with that, and she seemed to be as well.

He would have to ponder the situation later, though. Right now, he needed to keep his senses alert to defend the little sprite who was depending on him to protect her.

His eyes flickering constantly to the dense foliage flanking the road, Dagor searched for hidden signs of danger. The green façade could hide any number of threats, and regrettably, he wasn't gifted with telepathy. Still, he was a god, and he was equipped with a primal alarm system that had served him well in the past.

It wasn't easy given the cacophony of sounds, which might have seemed calming to mortal ears. Birds called to one another in a chorus of high-pitched melodies, and the rustle of leaves and branches moving in the wind could mask the approach of assailants. The air was thick with the scent of damp earth, its musky aroma mingling with the sweet fragrance of flowering vines and the sharp tang of ripening fruit. It was sensory overload, yet beneath it all, Dagor searched for the distinct rankness of ill intentions, the kind of scent that would taint the air with the stench of malevolence.

He could not shake off the feeling of foreboding, and he didn't know whether it was rooted in what Kian had said, the few articles he had read earlier, or his instincts that were fueling his unease the deeper they drove into the heart of the territory.

Over the roar of the old engine, Dagor cataloged every snapped twig, bird call, insect buzz, and distant rustle.

He had to remain vigilant. Reaching out with his senses beyond their immediate surroundings, he scanned for malevolence. If he got even a whiff of danger, he would sound the alarm and shield Frankie or do that in reverse order.

His first priority should be protecting her.

15

FRANKIE

It felt as if they had left civilization behind and entered a wild world untouched by humans, but that was just an illusion created by the dense vegetation and the sounds of nature surrounding them.

Frankie had never traveled far away from home. Heck, the farthest she'd gone had been Vegas, and she hated to admit it, but it was nicer than this expedition into the jungle or rain forest or whatever it was called. She'd imagined a jungle being even more dense than what they were passing through.

She didn't like the oppressive heat and humidity, and she didn't like the bugs, but she very much liked having Dagor next to her even though clinging to him was making her sweaty.

He, on the other hand, seemed unperturbed by the heat or by her body being pressed closely to his, but his eyes kept darting around as if he expected someone to jump at them out of the foliage.

She wasn't worried, though. Luis, their driver, appeared unconcerned, and he knew the area and its dangers well. After Kalugal's little lecture, he took it upon himself to explain the history of the region, the various plants that grew there, and the local customs. His English was surprisingly good, and she wondered whether Luis had spent time in the States or was just talented with languages.

He pointed out the towering ceiba trees considered sacred by many Mesoamerican cultures, including the Yope people, explaining that the colossal trees were believed to connect the underworld to the terrestrial realm and the skies above.

"The ceiba trees were also used to make medicine," Luis said. "The bark is boiled, and the water is used as a diuretic, an aphrodisiac, to relieve headaches, and even to treat diabetes." He turned around and grinned at them. "Have you heard of Ayahuasca?"

"Of course," Kalugal said. "It's a psychedelic drink with some nasty side effects."

"The ceiba tree bark is also used to make different versions of it. Many of the flowers that grow here were used for medicine making." Luis pointed to the orchids clinging to the tree trunks. "Like these ones."

While Frankie found the tour guide's prattle relaxing, it was obvious that Dagor didn't. His posture was stiff, and his eyes were constantly scanning, but he wasn't looking at what Luis was pointing out.

"Hey," she said quietly. "Relax. If there was any danger, do you think Luis would have been talking about trees and flowers? He would have been scanning the area the same way you're doing."

"What if he is in cahoots with the criminals?"

She chuckled. "Kalugal hired him, and I don't think that guy would have taken chances with someone un-vetted. I'm sure he came highly recommended."

Dagor didn't look convinced. "I don't know Kalugal well, and neither do you. I prefer to keep my eyes open, especially since you are here. I need to protect you."

Her heart warmed at his words. "That's sweet." She lifted her head to kiss his cheek. "I feel safe with you."

"Look at this *cotorro*." Luis pointed at a parrot with vibrant colors perching on a limb above their heads. "The Yope people have a legend about a god who could communicate with the people through parrots."

Frankie chuckled. "Can you talk with them?"

"Only if they speak a language I understand."

As the vehicle skirted the edge of a deep ravine, Luis looked back, and Frankie's heart lurched into her throat. "Please look ahead, or you'll get us killed."

He grinned at her as if she was being foolish. "I've driven this road so many times that I can do it blindfolded."

"Please do not," Kalugal said in a stern voice.

Shrugging, Luis turned to look at the road ahead. "I just wanted to say that the Yope utilized the topography created by volcano activity to build their settlements in defendable fortresses. In a moment, we will start seeing the ruins."

The vegetation suddenly cleared, and stone structures appeared.

"This is the ball court," Luis said. "The games were ceremonial, and the losing team was sacrificed to the gods."

Frankie shivered. "I hate that part of history. People used to be so bloodthirsty."

Edna turned around and gave her a sad smile. "They still are, Frankie."

16

DAGOR

As the vehicles rolled to a stop, Dagor stepped out of the truck and took a moment to cast his senses far and wide to scan the area.

Nothing suspicious registered, but he couldn't shake the unease in the pit of his stomach.

"Stay close to me," he said, offering his hand to Frankie.

"That's not a problem." She took it and let him pull her against his body as soon as her feet were on the ground.

He wondered whether she'd acquiesced so quickly because she wanted to be close to him or because she also had a gut feeling that not everything was as tranquil as it seemed.

The air was thick with the scent of earth and growth, the sound of the surrounding forest a steady buzz against the quiet of the weathered stones of the ruins, but aside from the sounds of nature and the noise their group was making, he couldn't discern any other human activity.

Casting a sidelong glance at Kalugal and their tour guide, Dagor noted that neither looked concerned, which should have been reassuring but wasn't. He'd learned long ago not to put his trust in the ability of others to keep him safe.

As Negal sidled up to him, Dagor leaned toward his teammate. "Is it just me, or does something smell off about this place?"

Negal shrugged. "I don't smell anything that is not supposed to be here, but I'm not letting my guard down." He patted the weapons he had strapped under his vest. "I wouldn't mind giving these a try, but I doubt any animals would dare attack us. We are at the top of the food chain predators, and they know that."

Frankie chuckled. "Is that what gods are? Top of the food chain predators?"

"You betcha." Negal's eyes scanned the area.

"Doesn't it bother you that we are the only tourists here?" Dagor whispered. "This is supposed to be a major tourist attraction, so where are all the visitors? Were they all scared away by rumors of cartels operating in the area?"

"Perhaps it's for the best," Negal said. "If we get ambushed, which we won't be, because we will hear them coming from miles away, the Guardians won't need to worry about protecting random humans in addition to the members of our group."

"I know." Dagor let out a breath. "I don't know why I'm so antsy. We are gods. What can a bunch of humans do to us?"

"Precisely." Negal clapped him on the back before walking over to where Kalugal stood.

"Please gather around." Kalugal lifted his hand, and when they'd formed a small circle around him, he produced a stack of folded pages from his pocket. "I made copies of the map for everyone and included translations wherever possible. We can either proceed as a group or split into teams to search for the amulet."

Looking at the piece of paper, Dagor had his doubts about the original's authenticity, and not just because the map looked like something a kid had scribbled.

Noting his expression, Kalugal smiled. "Given the source of this map, I don't really expect us to find anything, but a treasure hunt is a fun way to explore the ruins." He motioned for one of the Guardians to come forward. "If any of you want to get your hands dirty, I also brought some tools for you to use."

As the guy opened the large duffle bag, several people approached, including the two females with the special talents that Kalugal had mentioned before.

"The ancient Yope carved their lives into these rocks, leaving behind a legacy beneath these roots and vines for us to uncover." Kalugal's gaze swept over the crumbling pyramids and fallen columns.

The tall immortal who could shroud a city block walked up to the Guardian and took an ax pick. "I prefer for us to stay together if you don't mind." He glanced at the human drivers and then back at Kalugal. "Do you want me to employ my special skill on them?"

"What does he mean?" Frankie whispered in Dagor's ear.

"He can shroud our entire group, including the trucks, so no one will see us. It will be as if we are not even here."

"Nifty trick," she murmured.

Kalugal frowned. "That's not a bad idea, Yamanu, but I don't want you to miss out on the fun. Save it for now, and if needed, employ it later. Sounds good?"

The Guardian nodded. "You are right. I'd rather keep an eye on Mey."

His mate scoffed. "I can take care of myself."

"I know you can." He wrapped his arm around her. "But we came here to have fun together." He flashed her a bright smile. "Who knows? Maybe we will find the amulet after all?"

She laughed. "If we find anything, it will be a fake that Kalugal planted in the ruins beforehand."

"Hey!" Kalugal affected an offended tone. "When would I have done that? We arrived here together."

With a hand on her hip, she struck a pose. "You could have sent Luis or someone else to bury it somewhere, and you could have done it days in advance."

The immortal smirked. "Perhaps I did, and perhaps I did not." He scanned the faces of everyone gathered around him. "We have two hours to find the treasure. Let the hunt begin."

17

KALUGAL

"Once we find the entrance to the underground, I will need volunteers to stay behind and guard it." Max looked at Yamanu and Arwel. "I assume the two of you want to escort your mates on the hunt."

"Correct." Arwel nodded. "I don't sense anything threatening in the vicinity, but things can change in a heartbeat, so it's a good idea to leave a couple of Guardians on watch duty."

"I'll stay," Sheldon said. "Unlike most immortals, I don't like being underground."

"I'll stay too," Eric volunteered. "I came along for the zip line, not the ruins and a fake treasure hunt."

After two more Guardians joined the sentinels, Kalugal was happy with those who were left. Nine Guardians, including Yamanu and Arwel, two gods with unknown abilities, one three-quarters god with formidable compulsion power, and Rufsur were more than enough to safeguard the ladies in the underground portion of the hunt. Then there was Vlad, who was half Kra-ell and rumored to be incredibly strong. He didn't have any training, but sometimes brute force was more important than skill. Kalugal still remembered quite vividly what had happened at the excavation site in China. The underground passage had been booby trapped, and if not for the Odus, they would have had a much more difficult time with the rescue.

Then again, they might not need any of that if they didn't find the entrance to the underground, or if it didn't exist at all.

The crook who had sold him the thing had been convinced that the map was an authentic artifact, and the parchment was the right age to support his claim, but Kalugal had gone on enough treasure hunts to know not to expect anything other than some excitement and entertainment.

It was also possible the amulet had been a legend of the Yope, and someone a long time ago had decided to draw a treasure map either to preserve the story or to sell to some long-dead patsy.

The original map was in a safe back in his home, and Kalugal unfolded the copy to remind himself of the directions.

"Follow me, people." He walked over to a section that was in disrepair and marked with a 'do not enter' sign.

He threw a leg over the rope and then offered his hand to Jacki to help her do the same, even though she didn't need his help.

"Please, be careful." He turned to the group following him. "We don't want anyone to break anything."

Negal looked up from his copy of the map and frowned. "That doesn't look anything like what's on the paper. Are you sure you know where you're going?"

"I'm sure." Kalugal smiled indulgently. "Don't forget that the map was drawn when these buildings still stood in all of their glory. It takes the eye of an archeologist to imagine what was from what is."

Negal nodded. "You're the expert."

"That's right." Kalugal held on to Jacki's hand as he led her and the rest of their group toward a section of the wall that had caught his eye. "Do you see how precisely the stones are aligned?"

She nodded. "Maybe it's a more contemporary section of the structure. The stones look less worn, and the carvings are clearer."

"That they are." He grinned as he ran his hand over several of the symbols. "What we are looking at is an ancient locking mechanism." He moved aside so the others could see. "If you look at your maps, you will notice a sequence of symbols next to what is marked as a doorway. Compare it to what's on this wall."

"I see it," Jin said. "What do they say?"

"I don't know," Kalugal admitted. "I don't think it matters. What matters is pressing them in the right sequence."

He looked at the symbols on the map before finding their equivalent on the wall and pressing them in the order indicated. When he pressed the last one, and nothing happened, his heart sank with disappointment, but then a low rumble started, a cloud of dust flew into his eyes, and as he blinked it away, a section of the wall receded and shifted to reveal a passageway.

"I'll be damned," Rufsur murmured. "Frankly, I did not expect that."

Kalugal chuckled. "Neither did I."

The entrance was small, barely large enough for one person to squeeze through, and the darkness beyond was so complete that even his immortal eyesight couldn't penetrate it.

Reaching into one of the many pockets of his vest, he pulled out a flashlight and pointed the beam into the opening.

The walls of the passage were lined with the same stones that the exterior of the structure had been built from, and it sloped down.

"I'll go first," one of the Guardians volunteered.

If Jacki weren't with him, Kalugal would have scoffed at the suggestion and gone first, but he wouldn't risk his mate, and there was no way she would let him go ahead of her.

"Thank you." He stepped aside and let the Guardian through.

A moment passed before the guy called out the all-clear, and the rest of them followed inside.

"At least it's cool here." Jacki pushed a strand of hair out of her face. "It's a relief to be out of the sun."

"I'm surprised at the technology," Edna said. "This guarded the secret of the site from the uninitiated for centuries. I assume that only the priests knew the right combination to enter the underground complex."

"Correct." Kalugal turned his flashlight on the walls, searching for writing or drawings, but they were devoid of decoration. "Given the unadorned walls, I suspect that we are heading to some kind of storage facility. It doesn't seem like this passage was used for ritual purposes."

18

DAGOR

Dagor made sure that he and Frankie were walking in the center of the group, which was the safest spot in case they encountered booby traps. He also held her tucked close to his side, almost carrying her, because he was worried about her inappropriate footwear that left her toes vulnerable.

He was starting to realize that keeping a human safe was a full-time job. It wasn't that he minded being Frankie's protector. In fact, it filled a void in his soul that he hadn't been aware of having, but he was very much aware of how impossible their relationship would be if he wanted it to continue past the cruise.

His decision to keep it casual had been sound, and he needed to stick to it even if it was getting harder and harder to do.

As his arm around Frankie tightened further, she chuckled. "Do you want me to just hop on your back?"

"That's a fantastic idea."

She was so tiny that holding an arm around her and propping her up wasn't comfortable. It would be much easier for him to just carry her.

He was about to swing her onto his back when she stopped him with a vigorous shake of her head. "Don't even think about it. I was just teasing. Trust me. I'm not as fragile as you think I am."

She was, but arguing with her about it was futile. He admired her spunk and her fearlessness, and he didn't want her to lose her confidence, but she was much more fragile than she thought.

At the front, Kalugal stopped. "Houston, we have a problem."

As far as Dagor knew, none of the people in their group were named Houston.

He leaned to whisper in Frankie's ear. "Who is Houston?"

She smiled up at him. "It's a quote from a movie. People say that when they encounter an obstacle that is difficult to overcome."

When those ahead of them split down the middle to allow everyone to see what had caused the halt in their progress, Frankie gasped. A deep chasm split the passage ahead of them, its depth hard to measure since its walls plunged into the darkness.

Dagor craned his neck as Kalugal shone his flashlight into the void and then on the walls around it. The gap was too wide to jump even with his superior abilities. He might have been able to use the small crevices in the rock walls to climb across, but it was too dangerous for Frankie and probably the other ladies as well.

A treasure hunt wasn't worth anyone getting injured.

"Can we make a bridge?" Kalugal's mate asked.

He shook his head. "The gap is too wide, and the edges are crumbling. Even if we had the materials and tools to build it, I wouldn't trust it to carry us over safely."

"So, what now?" She put her hands on her hips. "Do we go back?"

"Not necessarily." Kalugal shone his flashlight first on one wall and then the other.

"The symbols carved into the stone on both sides are similar to the ones at the entrance to the subterranean tunnel. I bet that they are another Yope puzzle." He walked closer to the wall on the left and started pressing symbols in a sequence that made no sense to Dagor.

When nothing happened, Kalugal shone his flashlight on the other wall. "Someone needs to press the corresponding symbols on the other side." He took out a folded piece of paper and traced the outlines of the symbols in the same sequence he had pressed them before and handed the page to his mate. "I numbered them. When I say one, press the first symbol, and so on. We need to do that simultaneously."

"Got it." Jacki walked over to the other wall. "I'm ready."

As Kalugal called out the numbers and he and his mate pressed the symbols, Dagor wondered about Kalugal's confidence that he had figured out the sequence correctly. What if they pushed them in the wrong sequence and, instead of creating a bridge, collapsed the entire tunnel?

It was good that some of the Guardians had stayed outside so someone would know to come to rescue them. The problem was Frankie and whether he could shield her when the stones came crashing down on them.

Preparing to cover her with his body, he leaned over her so her head was protected.

Except, Kalugal had been right, and as he and Jacki pressed the last symbol, a grinding rumble began, and a few minutes later a platform rose from the depths of the chasm. It kept inching up until it was flush with the floor of the tunnel.

"Don't step on it yet," Rufsur said. "Let's test it first." He took off his heavy backpack and tossed it as far as he could onto the platform.

When it didn't even shake, he nodded. "Seems stable, but I suggest that we cross with extreme caution, one person at a time."

"I agree." Kalugal started walking without further preamble.

When he was on the other side, he motioned for his mate to proceed.

Rufsur lifted his arm to stop her. "Your mate is too rash sometimes. I'm more careful. Allow me please to tie a rope around you. Once you make it to the other side, release it so we can tie it around the next person."

Jacki nodded. "Good thinking." She looked at Kalugal. "You shouldn't have crossed without a rope."

Rufsur grinned. "Keeping your hubby safe is a full-time and thankless job. He never appreciates what I do for him, and he hardly ever listens."

"That's not true," Kalugal said from the other side of the platform. "I appreciate everything you do, but that doesn't mean I have to follow your suggestions to the letter."

Holding the length of rope over his arm, Rufsur arched a brow. "Do you want me to tie it around Jacki or not?"

There was a moment of hesitation before Kalugal nodded. "I'm almost certain that there is no need for it, but now that you've planted the seed of doubt in my mind, I can't ignore it."

19

FRANKIE

Once they were all safely on the other side of the platform, Frankie smiled up at Dagor. "I feel like I'm in an Indiana Jones movie. I hate to think these wonderful memories will be erased at the end of the cruise. It would be such a shame to lose them."

Dagor's eyes seemed haunted as he looked at her. "Since you're going to their village right after the cruise, there's no need to erase your memories."

Frankie didn't want to point out in front of everyone that she had only a limited time to find an immortal to bond with and then transition. If she didn't, she couldn't stay in the village, and her memories would be erased.

"It might be necessary," said the Guardian mated to Jin.

She couldn't remember his name. Was it Ariel? No, that didn't sound right.

"Why?" Dagor asked.

"Two weeks' worth of memories is more or less the limit of what can be safely erased with a thrall. Compulsion to stay silent about us lasts longer, but it needs to be periodically reinforced, which means that we would have to keep tabs on Frankie throughout her life. The best thing for her is to attempt transition as soon as she can, so if she's not a Dormant, and we need to make her forget about us, the damage will be minimal."

Dagor swallowed. "I understand, but Frankie is not ready to decide whether she wants to turn immortal, and it's too big of a decision to rush into."

Arwel, now she remembered the name, cast Dagor a knowing smile. "The decision is much easier when the Dormant bonds with an immortal." He paused for a moment. "Or a god."

"We are not—" Dagor halted mid-sentence as Kalugal lifted his hand to signal for everyone to stop.

Nevertheless, Frankie had no trouble guessing what he had intended to say, and the rejection pierced her heart. It shouldn't have, not after all the self-talk of convincing herself that she was just having a shipboard fling.

Swallowing, she affected a nonchalant tone. "What is it? Why did we stop?"

"Take a look." Dagor tapped the shoulder of the Guardian blocking her view.

As the guy moved aside, Frankie gasped.

Ahead, the tunnel turned into a wide corridor that was lined with statues of fierce warriors, each gripping a weapon and poised for battle. The detail was extraordinary, making the statues look eerily lifelike. Each held a different battle pose as if they had been frozen mid-movement.

Kalugal pulled out his phone and started snapping pictures, but he didn't move from his spot, and soon everyone else was following his example and taking photos, including Frankie.

If she didn't transition, would they erase the pictures she'd taken on the trip as well?

Probably. But maybe she could convince them to just alter her memories so she wouldn't remember anything about them being immortals or gods but could retain everything else.

"These are the guardians of the treasure," Kalugal murmured while snapping away. "I bet that this corridor is booby trapped."

His matter-of-fact voice echoed through the gallery, breaking the oppressive silence that emanated from the frozen statues. He was right about suspecting the significance of their battle-ready poses. They were a warning as much as a threat.

"The floor tiles have a pattern," Jacki said. "Some are a little elevated compared to the others. The question is whether we should step on the elevated ones or avoid them."

"Most likely, we should avoid them." Kalugal crouched to observe the floor. "The elevated stones probably house pressure-sensitive triggers."

"Let's test it." Negal moved forward with his pickax. Crouching, he reached with his tool for the nearest elevated stone and tapped it.

Nothing happened.

"Apply more force," Kalugal said. "It's supposed to respond to a person's weight."

"Right." Negal lifted the pickax, turned it to its blunt side, and brought it down on the stone with enough force that dust rose from it in a billowing cloud that blocked Frankie's view.

At the same time, a swishing sound was followed by a thump, and when the dust settled, she saw an arrow embedded in the head of the statue nearest the stone.

"As I said." Kalugal rose to his feet. "The elevated stones have triggers. But I think some of the others do, too." He lifted his flashlight to the face of the warrior whose bow had released the arrow. "His eyes are trained on the stone Negal activated, and so was his arrow before he fired it. I bet that's true for the other statues as well."

He turned to Rufsur. "I need some chalk."

When his second-in-command handed it to him, Kalugal extended his hand to Negal. "I also need that pickax."

"What are you going to do?" Negal asked as he handed it to him.

"I'm going to tap the stones that I think are safe, step on them, and mark them so the rest of our group can cross safely."

"I can do that," Negal offered.

Kalugal hesitated for a moment before nodding. "You need to avoid the ones that are in the statues' direct line of sight and where their weapons are pointed. Those are the rigged ones."

"Got it." Negal took the chalk from Kalugal and proceeded to tap the stone next to the one he'd activated a moment ago.

Frankie held her breath as Negal tested one stone after the other, marking a zigzagging pattern for the rest of them to follow. It took him a long time to mark a path across the corridor, or maybe it just seemed like that to her.

"Breathe," Dagor murmured. "Negal is a god. Even if he gets hit with one of these arrows or javelins, it's not going to kill him."

"I know. But I don't want him to get hurt." She looked up at Dagor's gorgeous face. "You feel pain the same way as humans do, right?"

He nodded. "Yes, we do."

20

DAGOR

Frankie had meant physical pain, and she was right. Gods felt pain the same way as humans, but right now, the pain Dagor was thinking about was the one in his heart.

Why the hell had he gotten attached to the little sprite so fast?

Without her high heels she was tiny, barely reaching his chest, and they probably looked ridiculous together, but that was the least of his concerns. Princess Annani was just as tiny, and she was a magnificent goddess, powerful beyond compare and just as lovely.

Still, Frankie had managed to burrow into his heart and sink her little claws into him.

It had been a mistake to invite her on this adventure. The danger was more perceived than real, but it still triggered every protective instinct in him, and that exacerbated the complicated feelings he already had for her.

When everyone had finally made it over the stone warriors' gallery, Kalugal continued at a snail's pace, examining every etching on the walls and every paving stone under their feet.

Sloping down and turning in large circles, the tunnel continued for about five hundred feet until it opened into a cavernous chamber.

Once again, Negal tested the archway and the area right in front of it before allowing the rest of them to follow.

Dagor had a feeling that they had been going in circles around this chamber, and since the path was sloping down, they had gone about seventy feet below, which seemed to be the height of the ceiling. The Yope had carved this chamber out of the bedrock, along with a tunnel spiraling around it.

What these primitive people had managed to achieve was quite impressive.

It occurred to Dagor that Kalugal might have planned this trip months in advance and that he had created the entire experience as some sort of future amusement attraction that tourists would pay handsomely to visit, and their group was the test run.

Dagor hadn't had many opportunities to talk to the guy, but he'd gotten the impression that the immortal was very smart and motivated by financial gain. He might have seen an opportunity to exploit the ruins to make money.

Then again, given that tourism to Acapulco had dried up because of the cartels, that wouldn't have been a smart business decision.

Shifting his eyes back to the chamber, Dagor waited for Kalugal to make his next move.

The large circular platform in the center of the room was surrounded by a moat-like gap that was about thirty feet wide. He and Negal could probably jump over it, but he doubted even the immortal Guardians could do that.

The ladies, for sure, had to use the stepping stones, and those were probably just as tricky as in the two previous obstacles.

Kalugal took a couple of steps forward and examined the symbols etched into the platform. "These are ancient astrological signs," he said. "Each of them corresponds to a celestial body known to the Yope. The sequence of the stepping stones might be determined by the correct chronological sequence of the astrological areas as they understood them during the time they built this place."

"No offense, but that sounds convoluted," Dagor said. "I would trust more the pattern of wear and tear on the stones. Those that were used often will show more signs of erosion and have smoother edges."

"Let's draw a map." Kalugal reached into his pocket and produced another folded piece of paper. "I will chart the path based on the sequence of the astrological signs, and we will see whether those stones have more wear and tear."

Once he had the map, Kalugal took the chalk out of his pocket and proceeded to the edge of the moat.

"Wait," Negal said. "I can probably jump across. Do we all need to get to the platform? There is nowhere to go from there, and if the amulet is on it, I can just retrieve it, and we will be done with this adventure."

"What would be the fun in that?" Kalugal murmured while reaching into his pocket. "Let's consult the map." He pulled out one of his folded pages, unfurled it, and examined the drawings. "According to this, there is a staircase leading from the center of the platform down into another chamber and from there to a smaller one where the amulet is supposed to be. So, it seems that we all need to cross." He lifted his eyes to Negal and smiled. "Besides, I wouldn't want you to risk making the jump and missing. I would much rather employ the scientific approach and deliver you uninjured and in one piece back to the ship."

Negal shrugged. "You're the boss."

The tall Guardian who could shroud a village chuckled. "I could jump across and check whether there is a staircase leading down or not, but I know better than to suggest it." He smirked. "Kalugal would never forgive me if I take away an opportunity for him to prove how smart and knowledgeable he is."

Kalugal scoffed, "I can also jump thirty feet with ease, but why take the risk? To save a few minutes? It doesn't make sense. Using smarts is always better than relying on brawn."

"Boys." His mate lifted a hand. "You can compete to find out who can jump farther when we get back on the ship. We have a wedding to attend, and this has already taken almost two hours. We need to finish this treasure hunt and head back."

21

FRANKIE

As Frankie had expected, Kalugal had been right about the sequence following astrological signs, and they had all crossed safely across the moat, stepping on the stones he had marked for them.

He waited until everyone was over before pointing to the opening in the floor. "The staircase is right here, just as it was marked on the map, but it's narrow, and there is no guard rail. Please, watch your step."

He was probably talking to the only human because the others would have no problem navigating the narrow staircase.

When their turn arrived, and Frankie looked down, she turned to Dagor. "You need to let go. We can't fit side by side on the stairs."

He grimaced and reluctantly removed his arm from around her waist. "Give me your hand. I'll go first, and you follow, so if you fall, I'll catch you."

Smiling, she stretched on her tiptoes and kissed his cheek. "I like your protector act. It's kind of cute."

"It's not an act."

"I know." She gave him her hand. "Let's go. We are holding up the line."

The truth was that the narrow staircase scared her. It was a spiral, so she couldn't assess how deep down it went, and that bothered her.

Holding on to her with one hand and the flashlight in the other, Dagor started the descent, going one step at a time and annoying everyone behind them who didn't need to be as careful.

"We can go a little faster." Frankie put her other hand on the wall for balance more than anything else. There was nothing to hold onto, and she was grateful for Dagor's hand.

He kept the same pace despite her comment, and it was a good thing because the staircase kept spiraling down without any landings to break it up, and she was getting dizzy. Not only that, but her leg muscles were starting to hurt something fierce, and she cursed herself for not keeping up with ballet practice or at least hitting the StairMaster in the gym.

When they finally reached the bottom, she leaned her forehead against Dagor's side. "My head is spinning. I need a moment."

"Take your time." Dagor rubbed soft circles on her back.

She was still sweaty and warm from going down the stairs, but the chamber was so cold that soon she was shivering.

Wrapping an arm around her, Dagor brought her tighter against his side. "My offer to carry you on my back still stands. You'll be warmer."

"Not a chance." She wasn't going to embarrass herself in front of all the immortals.

The only illumination in the chamber was coming from the flashlights that they were all holding, but it seemed like it was empty. Perhaps at one time it had served as a storage area for the temples, but now all that remained were some etchings on the walls that seemed much cruder than the ones they had encountered before.

"Should I do it here?" Mey asked Kalugal.

"Do you feel like you should?"

She nodded. "This place gives me the creeps, so I'm not sure that I want to. I have a feeling that the echoes in these walls are not going to be pleasant."

Kalugal regarded her for a moment. "Can you even do that with everyone here?"

She let out a breath. "Usually, I would have said no, but this place reeks of tragedy."

"It's up to you," Kalugal said. "If you don't want to do it, don't. After all, we are here to have fun, right?"

Frankie was disappointed but also relieved. She would have liked to see Mey's talent at work, but she didn't want to hear about ancient tragedies. She wasn't much of a history buff, but the ancient Mesoamericans were known for their bloodthirsty religions and rituals. What if this was a ritual chamber where they had sacrificed people to their gods?

"I'll do a quick listen." Mey motioned for everyone to give her space. "If you can all be quiet for a few minutes, that would be helpful."

Her mate looked worried, and as the two exchanged silent communication, Frankie was sure that he was trying to convince Mey not to do it.

Yeah, good luck with that.

If Frankie had Mey's talent, she wouldn't have been able to resist either. How often did Mey have a chance to be in an ancient chamber that seemed like it hadn't been visited in centuries?

Well, perhaps this was her job, so it might be quite often.

Frankie didn't envy Mey. She wouldn't have wanted to have her talent and listen to sad stories lingering in ancient walls, no matter how well it paid.

22

MEY

Why am I doing this?

It was morbid curiosity, and Mey knew she would pay for it with nightmares, but she couldn't shake the urge to listen to those tragic echoes.

Was it Kalugal's doing?

Was he compelling her somehow without actually saying the words?

As far as she knew, that wasn't possible. Compulsion didn't work like thralling. He couldn't reach into her mind and command her to do something she didn't want to do. He had to verbalize his command, and he hadn't.

He had left the choice to her.

The thing was, no one else could bear witness to the lives lost in this dark place, and Mey felt like it was her obligation to do so because she was the only one who could.

As her companions moved aside to clear space for her and the chamber fell silent, she sat on the floor in the lotus pose and closed her eyes.

She didn't even need to meditate to hear the echoes. The walls vibrated with the intense emotions embedded deep within the rock. At first, the whispers were indistinct, a cacophony of highs and lows, but as she attuned herself, the emotional pitches became clear—sharp cries of fear, the authoritative shouts of orders, the low murmurs of desperate pleas.

The language was foreign, and Mey couldn't make out the words, but emotions transcended the barriers of language. The terror was palpable, the suffering deep, and the finality of the cries indicated a tragic end. The vibrations spoke of a massacre, of lives violently and abruptly extinguished within these very walls.

The intensity of the emotional imprints was overwhelming, and with a gasp, Mey opened her eyes and severed the connection. Her heart was racing, her breath shallow, and with a hand on her chest, she shook her head.

"I shouldn't have done this. It was a slaughter. So much fear and pain..." She trailed off, unable to continue.

Yamanu knelt next to her and wrapped her in his arms. "It was a very long time ago, love."

"I know." She lifted her eyes to him. "But tragedies like this still happen today. We think that humanity has evolved since those dark days, but it hasn't. Not really." She turned to look at the two gods. "When I was still human, I believed in God, the creator, the divinity, and I held on to that belief even after turning immortal, only adding the Fates to my arsenal of entities to pray to. But after witnessing things like this, it's difficult to believe in a benevolent force."

Negal looked lost for words, and Dagor regarded her with sympathy in his eyes. "We don't have any answers, either. Perhaps the Kra-ell have it right, and their Mother of All Life is a merciless deity that rewards the brave and punishes the cowardly. Who knows, right?"

Mey offered Dagor a sad smile. "Apparently, no one. We are just specks of nothing on the enormous tapestry of the universe."

"I prefer to think that we are everything," Kalugal said. "We are the creators of reality, and therefore, we are all divinities. Each one of us." He grinned. "Well, the good who create are divinities. The bad who destroy are monsters and demons, and it's a never-ending battle in which the good eventually wins."

Mey didn't know whether to laugh at Kalugal's bombastic statement or to actually ponder it, but in either case, it made her feel a little better.

Rising to her feet, she dusted off her jeans and leaned on Yamanu for comfort. "I don't know if that's true, but it's definitely a more positive outlook. Thank you."

"You're welcome." Kalugal tilted his head. "Now, the question is whether you learned something useful from these walls."

"Only that this chamber was used for sacrifices. If the amulet is nearby, perhaps we shouldn't touch it. What if it induces a killing spree?"

"Or turns people insane," Jacki said. "Did anyone think to bring gloves?"

"I did." Jin produced a pair of latex gloves from her back pocket. "I thought that Kalugal would make us dig for the treasure, and I didn't want to get my fingernails dirty. They are a bitch to clean."

"Good thinking." Mey clapped her sister on her back. "If we find the amulet, we will use the gloves to pick it up."

"Where to now?" Jacki asked Kalugal.

He consulted his map again, turned in a circle, and pointed toward a length of the wall that didn't seem any different than the rest except for the symbols carved on it.

"I guess we need to decipher the riddle of the symbols again."

Jacki peered over his shoulder at the map. "It doesn't provide the sequence for this entrance."

"It doesn't, but I think I can figure it out. If not, we can always blow a hole in the wall to get in."

Rufsur patted his huge duffle bag. "I have all we need for that in here."

23

FRANKIE

When a section of the wall started to retract, Frankie wasn't surprised that Kalugal had figured out the sequence. He had repeatedly proven that he knew what he was doing.

When the wall stopped moving, a narrow entrance less than five feet tall was revealed. Even Frankie would have to duck to get through, and Yamanu would probably need to bend in two.

"Wait." Negal stopped Kalugal with a hand on his shoulder. "Let me go in first."

Turning, Kalugal blocked the entrance with his body. "I am grateful for your assistance, Negal, and for putting yourself in harm's way to protect me, but I am three-quarters god, and I really don't need protecting."

Negal frowned. "How can you be three-quarters god?"

Frankie wondered the same thing. As far as she knew, Annani and Toven were the only two gods other than Dagor and his teammates, and they were cousins who had never been romantically or otherwise involved. Also, neither of them was Kalugal's parent.

"That's not important," Kalugal said. "I'm going in first, and if you are so concerned about my well-being, you can follow right behind me."

Negal waved a dismissive hand. "You are the boss."

"Thank you." Kalugal smiled before ducking through the narrow entrance.

Negal followed and, a few moments later, reappeared to tell the rest of them that they could come through.

Frankie and Dagor entered behind Mey and Yamanu, with Jin and Arwel entering right behind them.

Frankie was surprised to see torches flicker, casting the stark chamber in soft illumination.

Kalugal hadn't brought them with him, so they must have been left behind in the chamber, surviving for centuries. Was there magic involved?

The hewn-out room was simple and unassuming compared to the elaborate decorations and contraptions they had encountered on the way.

Humidity clung to the air, making Frankie's breathing laborious. It indicated that there was a source of water somewhere in the underground because she doubted that the moist air had come from the outside. But then, she was no expert on caves and underground structures, and maybe the moisture from above was seeping through the earth and stone.

After all of Kalugal's hype, she'd expected the inner chamber that housed the amulet to be grand, and after Mey's revelations, she'd expected to find skeletons lining the walls, but the only two interesting elements about the place were the cleverly disguised entrance and the pedestal that stood at its center.

From where Frankie stood, it just looked like a column of rough stone with some symbols etched on its surface. Unless the amulet was housed inside a hidden compartment, it wasn't there.

"What does it say?" Jacki asked as Kalugal carefully approached the column. The subdued lighting from the flickering torches was not optimal.

"No clue." He reached out and tapped the top of the stone with the pickax. "The only thing I can tell you is that they are different than the ones that opened the way. My guess is that they are warnings."

"The map doesn't say anything either," Rufsur's mate said.

Frankie pulled out the copy Kalugal had given her and unfolded it to confirm, even though it made little sense to doubt Edna's assessment.

"I have a bad feeling about this." Jacki rubbed her hands over her arms. "Maybe we should just leave it be."

Kalugal turned to look at her with a frown. "How bad is the feeling?"

She shrugged. "I'm not sure. I need to touch the column."

"Not happening until I determine that it's safe." Kalugal moved closer and tapped the column with the pickax again, more forcefully this time.

Leaning against Dagor's solid body, Frankie felt safe enough, but she shared Jacki's premonition of dread. It wasn't overwhelming, but it was there.

The question was whether it was just a reaction to what Mey had said, the buildup of anticipation, or something that she should actually heed.

Kalugal repeated the tapping a couple more times, and when nothing happened, he put his hand on the pedestal and shone his flashlight on its top.

"I think I've found what we came here looking for." He turned to Jin. "Can I have the gloves, please?"

She shook her head. "They won't fit your hands."

"They will fit mine," Jacki said. "I only need one."

"Be careful." Jin handed the glove to her. "There might be snakes, scorpions, or poisonous spiders in there, or worse, a booby trap that will chop off your hand when you reach for the amulet."

Jacki grimaced. "Thanks for the images. I hate spiders."

Frankie hated all creepy-crawlies, but she was more worried about a possible booby trap. From everything they had encountered so far, that was the most likely danger.

"There's an item right at the top of what appears to be a carved-out bowl," Kalugal said. "I can't see what's under it, and I'm worried that once the weight is removed, the entire chamber will collapse around us."

Rufsur chuckled. "This isn't an Indiana Jones movie."

"It sure feels like one," Jacki murmured. "Does anyone have anything that can fit in here that weighs around a pound and is disposable? We need to make a quick swap."

"You can take this." Edna removed her chunky necklace and handed it to Kalugal. "I knew there was a reason for choosing to wear this particular accessory today."

"Thank you." Kalugal walked around the pedestal and held the necklace. "Are you sure you don't mind losing it?"

"I'm sure," Edna said. "It's a relief to get it off."

Snapping the glove onto her hand, Jacki looked at Kalugal. "On the count of three."

He nodded.

Frankie held her breath, and at her back, Dagor wrapped himself around her, shielding her with his body.

If the situation wasn't so tense, she would have turned around and kissed him.

"One," Jacki started the count, "two, three!"

As she snatched the thing up, Kalugal replaced it with Edna's necklace so fast that Frankie didn't see him move.

For a moment, everyone held their breath, waiting for the ceiling to start crumbling on top of them or the walls to start moving in to crush them, but when several moments passed and nothing happened, a collective sigh of relief sounded.

"Now I know for sure that Kalugal planted the trinket." Dagor pointed at the package in Jacki's hands. "No paper or twine would have survived this long without falling apart."

Kalugal smiled and put a hand over his chest. "I don't know whether I should be flattered or offended. To plan such an elaborate setup would have been the work of a genius." He winked at Dagor.

24

JACKI

Jin approached Jacki with the other latex glove in hand. "You can't unwrap the package with just one gloved hand without it touching your skin. You will need both."

Looking at the small package she was holding, Jacki didn't reach for the glove. "I need to touch it to know what it does." She lifted her eyes to Kalugal. "How else will we know?"

He seemed conflicted, but then his mouth narrowed. "Let me touch it first. If it doesn't bite, I'll hand it over to you."

His gallantry was appreciated, but Jacki wasn't some wallflower who needed to be swathed in bubble wrap and protected. Why should her mate put himself in harm's way for her sake?

"What can you do that I can't?"

He smiled indulgently. "I don't like to point it out, but my lineage makes me much more resilient. If this thing is dangerous and unleashes hell, I have a better chance of surviving whatever it does."

That was a fair point. Jacki was a weak immortal who'd taken forever to transition, and her mate was three-quarters god, as he liked to boast.

"Fine." She handed it to him.

"Thank you." He took the package without hesitation, tore the twine apart with ease, and then carefully unwrapped the material that wasn't paper like Dagor had thought but some kind of fabric that was soaked in faintly fragrant oils.

"Do you feel anything?" Jacki asked.

Kalugal shook his head. "It's old, it is made from gold, and it houses a large fire opal." Kalugal lifted the amulet by its chain to let everyone see.

The opal was magnificent in size and in color. The kaleidoscope of fiery hues started with a fierce orange core that looked as if it was alight with an inner flame. It was bordered by flashes of red, green, and yellow that shifted as the amulet gently swung from Kalugal's fingers on its chain. The gold edges of the housing were etched with symbols or glyphs, and Jacki assumed that they were either incantations that were supposed to be uttered at ceremonies or represented power, protection, or maybe even a blessing.

It didn't radiate evil, but it didn't project anything good either. In fact, it seemed like a pretty trinket that looked impressive but held no power.

"It's beautiful," Frankie said. "But it's also terrifying."

Jacki frowned. "Why do you say that? Do you feel anything?"

She shook her head. "I'm not talented that way, but those red splotches look like blood. It's possible that I'm still being influenced by what Mey said about the other room."

Frankie might have the simple gift of human intuition, and Jacki wasn't going to dismiss it. Turning to Kalugal, she extended her hand. "Can I hold it now?"

"Not yet." He dropped the amulet into his other hand and closed his fingers around the stone. "I need to make sure that it's not poisonous."

Jin snorted. "If you are worried about poisons, you should have worn the gloves when you unwrapped the amulet. The fabric was soaked in some sort of oil."

"I'm well aware of that, and I did it on purpose. If there was anything in it, I wanted to feel its effect before I handed the amulet to Jacki." He opened his fingers and extended his hand to her. "You can take it now."

Finally.

Under her mate's watchful gaze, Jacki took the chain and lowered the stone into her other hand. She didn't even need to close her eyes for the vision to surge into her mind with perfect clarity.

But unlike most of her visions that were of an object's distant past, the amulet sent Jacki's mind to a recent scene.

As she watched the horrific events unfolding, Jacki was dimly aware that there was no way that the amulet was being worn or held by any of the victims or the monsters attacking them. The power of the amulet enhanced her psychic ability, showing her an event that was unrelated to her or anyone she knew.

Jacki had never witnessed such brutality, and wanting the vision to stop, she dropped the amulet, but the images continued, and she was forced to watch as the cartel monsters slaughtered adults, children, and babies, as they violated young girls and old women alike, and after corralling the young girls and women, they set the village on fire to eliminate the evidence of the slaughter.

One by one, the faces of the kidnapped girls flashed before her mind's eye —their red-rimmed eyes brimming with tears of pain and grief, their broken souls calling out to her.

The amulet was no longer in her hands, but it still funneled the horror of their reality into her mind with a visceral force, each sob and plea another bleeding slash to her heart.

"Jacki!" She heard Kalugal's panicked voice. "Open your eyes, sweetheart. You are safe. I've got you."

His voice chased the last of the horrors away, and she collapsed into his arms, sobbing. "We have to save them. They are not far from here. There is still time. We have to get them before they are moved, and we lose them forever."

"Who, sweetheart? Who do we need to get?"

"The girls. We need to save the girls."

They also had to destroy the accursed amulet, but that wasn't urgent. They would do it after rescuing the victims.

25

DAGOR

As Kalugal's mate recounted the atrocities she'd seen in her vision, tears streamed down her face, and her voice trembled. Her words painted a harrowing picture of the suffering inflicted on the innocent, but Dagor had a feeling she was censoring some of the most horrific parts to spare Frankie and the other ladies the worst of it.

Males were better equipped to deal with such things than females, the pain turning into rage and igniting a fire that prompted them to action.

Dagor would tear off the heads of those monsters one by one with his bare hands.

It wouldn't help the dead and the tortured, but justice would be served, and the innocents would be avenged. To let evil triumph by allowing it to get away was almost as bad as standing by and not doing anything to stop it.

He didn't care that it wasn't his fight and that he and his teammates were specifically forbidden to intervene. He was stuck on this rock anyway, so he'd better clean up his new home as best he could.

First, though, he had to get Frankie to safety.

Turning to her and seeing her tear-stricken face only hardened his resolve to get her as far away as possible from this blasted place and back to the ship.

"Don't worry, sweetheart. I won't let anything happen to you." He leaned to kiss the top of her head.

"I know." She turned to bury her face in his shirt and continued crying.

If only he could lend her some of his rage, maybe it could burn away her tears, but he couldn't.

Frankie was strong, and Dagor had no doubt that she would find her own coping mechanism.

"Can you guide us to where they are being held?" Kalugal asked his mate.

Nodding, she took the amulet from him. "I will use this thing to find the girls, and once they are safe, we will drop it in the middle of the ocean." Her face twisted with disgust as she lifted the chain and let it dangle from her fingers. "It derived its power from all the people who were sacrificed in the other chamber. I will use it to save the lives of these girls but for nothing else."

For a moment, Kalugal looked like he wanted to argue with her, but then he nodded. "Let's move out. There is no time to lose."

Dagor ran soothing circles over Frankie's back as she continued sobbing quietly against his shirt. "Negal and I will fight by your side, but we need to get Frankie and the other ladies to safety first. We can give them one of the vehicles, and they can return to the ship."

"I'm not going anywhere," Jin hissed. "I will tear those monsters' throats out with my fangs, and before I do that, I will gouge their eyes out with my claws."

Her ferocity was a song to his ears, but it was also shocking to see her elongated fangs. Had the immortals mutated over time? Or was she a descendant of the Kra-ell?

"I'm not going back either," Mey said. "I can fight humans. Besides, those girls will need to see women coming to their rescue. After what was done to them, they will be terrified of men." She glanced at Frankie. "I'm sorry, but we can't give you one of our three vehicles so you can return to the ship. You'll have to come with us."

Frankie nodded. "I want to help in any way I can."

Mey smiled. "The best way for you to help is to stay in the truck and hide while we take care of business."

Kalugal nodded. "I agree." He turned to Dagor. "Your job is to keep Frankie safe. The rest of us can handle the cartel and the rescue operation."

"I'm a god," he protested. "I can freeze them in place with one mind command."

"So can I," Kalugal said. "I know that you have military training, but we are not going to fight an army, and the Guardians are well trained for precisely these kinds of operations. Your abilities will be best utilized protecting Frankie."

Dagor's jaw clenched. The need to avenge the lives lost and destroyed was burning in his soul, but he also needed to protect Frankie, and Kalugal was right.

Besides, Negal could fight on the immortals' side, and he was a more experienced trooper than Dagor.

"I'll shroud our convoy," Yamanu said. "They won't know what hit them, and it will be over before it started."

Max bared his elongated fangs. "That sounds like a letdown. I want them terrified and peeing in their pants; I want them to experience what these innocent villagers did when they attacked them out of the blue, and I want to tear their throats out and watch them bleed."

"Gross," Frankie murmured against Dagor's shirt. "But I totally approve."

If Dagor wasn't already in love with her, he would have fallen for her right then and there.

Wait, what?

He loved her?

Right now wasn't the time or place to panic because he had feelings for the girl, but he would revisit that disturbing revelation after the mission was executed, the cartel monsters were dead, and the girls were on their way to safety.

26

FRANKIE

As they retraced their steps through the labyrinthine passages of the caverns, Frankie's heart pounded with a mix of fear and resolve. Thankfully, Kalugal's chalk marks had not been erased by the many footsteps that had passed over them, and they carefully navigated the traps without triggering them on their way out.

She kept close to Dagor, his solid body and protective presence a comfort against the sheer magnitude of what Jacki had seen and what they were about to do.

The most dangerous thing Frankie had ever done was fighting off a horde of shoppers at the semi-annual Nordstrom sale, and even though they had been vicious, none of them had carried machine guns.

Emerging into the sunlight, she squinted and pulled out her sunglasses. Next to her, Dagor did the same.

Some of the other immortals and Negal also donned protective eye gear, but Mey and Jin didn't. By now, Frankie knew that harsh sunlight was a problem for the immortals, and she speculated whether the sisters were transitioned Dormants, and that was why they were less sensitive to the sun.

After Kalugal explained the situation to the Guardians who had stayed behind, he also told Luis and the other drivers about what Jacki had seen. They reacted in alarm and wanted to rush off to check on relatives who lived in the small villages in the area.

There was no cellular reception, but the clan's phones operated via satellite, and the Guardians allowed the drivers to each place a couple of calls to check with loved ones.

The curious thing was that none of them doubted Kalugal's assertion that his wife had seen the massacre in a vision.

When they were reassured that their relatives were fine, an argument started when they tried to guess which village had been attacked, but Kalugal put a stop to it with one voice command.

Kalugal's Spanish was flawless, but Frankie's was barely enough to understand what they were saying.

As their group quickly settled in the trucks, the engines roared to life, but this time Frankie and Dagor were not riding together with Kalugal and Jacki.

They were once again in the middle vehicle, but the other couple took the lead so Jacki could point the way.

Dagor's arm was tight around Frankie's shoulders, and she was grateful for him being there for her. Knowing that a god who was practically indestructible was protecting her kept the panic at bay.

She reminded herself that all of them were formidable immortals and that the cartel monsters stood no chance against this force of tourists turned rescuers—defenders of the innocent against the encroaching shadow of evil.

A sense of stupid pride filled her for being associated with this group of extraordinary people. Upon hearing Jacki's account of what was at stake, none of them hesitated even for a moment before rushing to help the victims.

In the back of her mind, Frankie cataloged that feeling in the pro-transition arguments. Her family was a heavy weight in the against-transition pan, but this impromptu rescue tilted the scales so the two pans were almost balanced now.

Frankie wanted to be part of the force for good.

Except, Dagor wasn't part of the clan and never would be. If a miracle happened and he changed his mind about leaving right after the cruise, he still couldn't come with her to the immortals' hidden village.

This reminded her that Yamanu was supposed to be shrouding their convoy, but since she could still see everyone, he wasn't.

"When is Yamanu going to start shrouding us? These trucks make so much noise that they can probably be heard all the way to the ship."

"He's already doing it," one of the Guardians sitting behind them said. "You are not affected by it because he's excluding you and the human drivers from the shrouding."

"Ha," Dagor exclaimed. "I didn't know that it was possible. He needs to teach me his trick."

The Guardian smiled. "It took him a long time to learn to do it, and his shrouding ability is legendary. I don't think he can teach you to do it overnight."

"How do you know the shroud is on?" Frankie asked. "I don't see or hear anything different. Is it like a bubble around us?"

"That's how he does it," Dagor said. "He's not excluding the humans from the shroud. Instead, he creates a bubble around the convoy. The drivers can see and hear what's going on outside of it, but no one can see or hear inside."

"I guess so." The Guardian rubbed a hand over his light stubble. "I'm not much of a shrouder myself, and I can't sense Yamanu's shroud, so I'm not sure what technique he uses."

"Let me get this straight," Frankie said. "To someone looking at the convoy from the outside, we are invisible and soundless, right?"

Both Dagor and the Guardian nodded.

"What about the tracks the wheels make in the mud?"

Dagor regarded her with appreciation in his eyes. "The bubble moves with the convoy, so once it passes over a spot, anyone can see the tracks it leaves behind. But to notice that, someone would have to be watching the ground right as we drive by and see that the tracks are new. I don't think it's much of a problem."

27

ANI

In her private dining room, Ani sat at the head of a gleaming white table and listened with half an ear to the idle chatter of her ladies-in-waiting.

It was not that they were dull or insipid. Her four companions were shrewd manipulators and spies, each installed by one or more of the leading families to follow her every move and listen to her every word so they could report back what they had learned.

There was nothing wrong with that, and it was not personal. They were not her friends, nor were they her enemies. They were just doing their job.

Ani's only real friend was Sofri, and she cherished that friendship dearly.

Ani had no siblings and no cousins, and many thousands of years ago her parents had chosen the long slumber to escape the ennui of their never-ending life.

One day, she would awaken them, but not before the resistance triumphed and her husband was king no more. Perhaps they would find the new world order interesting enough to stay awake for a while.

In the background, tucked into a corner of the room, a quartet of string instruments filled the space with a pleasant melody by a new composer who had won many accolades.

There was really nothing that could compare to live music, no matter how advanced the recording and reproduction technologies were. Naturally, not everyone could afford live entertainment during a nothing-special midday meal, but being queen had its perks.

The first course was served with the practiced dance performed with perfect precision and choreography born of countless meals just like this one, and Ani smiled at her attendants to show her approval.

The delicate consommé was served in fine crystal bowls that were as much a work of art as the soup itself, and the rich aroma was appetizing enough.

The chef was a true master of the craft, coming up with new flavor combinations she would have never expected, and given how many meals she had consumed throughout her long life, that was impressive.

As Ani savored the chef's latest masterpiece, her ladies-in-waiting kept chattering about new gowns for the upcoming ball and casting her occasional glances to see if they could pull her into their conversation.

Ani couldn't care less.

Dressing her was a job for her designers, and they did it well. She had no reason to waste her time on picking out fabrics, going over styles, or getting fitted by seamstresses.

A perfect replica of her had been made for them to work with.

If only she could animate the copy and use it to attend the various functions for her, that would have been such a relief, but actual cloning was prohibited, and for good reason.

Ani shivered at the thought.

It was an abomination.

"I've commissioned a gown with layers of silk and gossamer," Avinshti said between one spoonful and the next. "Silver is the color of the season." She glanced at Ani. "It is your favorite color, Your Majesty."

"It is favored by my designers." Ani's tone communicated her lack of interest in the subject, and her ladies were intelligent enough to pick up on it.

Having lunch in her quarters with just the four of them was a rare occurrence. Most days, Ani's lunches were political or industrial meetings with the movers and shakers of Anumati. Thankfully, there had been nothing scheduled for today, so she had time to come up with a plan for communicating with her granddaughter, but it was not easy to think and plot against the backdrop of chatter and the servers milling around.

The second course was a selection of fresh salads garnished with edible flowers and an array of dressings that were as much a feast for the eye as for the palate. It was a parade of vibrant colors and exquisite flavors, another masterpiece of the talented chef.

Hopefully, he would never plot to poison her, or she would have to send him away to one of the more violent colonies to meet a certain death.

"The new university will be an architectural marvel," Vanashaia said. "I have seen the holographic model, and it is so exquisite that I am tempted to go back to school."

"I just hope we raise the necessary funds during the ball." Avinshti put her fork down and reached for the wine. "The project is ambitious even for Anumati's building mastery. It is going to cost a fortune."

"The guest list is impressive," Yashanoda said. "When they auction the university's name, the bidding will be rabid. All the major families want it to be named after their houses."

As the main course arrived, the attendants unveiled platters of roasted pivoats from the Palmoara colony and vegetables from Santica. The rare delicacies were served only in the royal palace and perhaps a couple of the richest houses. The cost of transportation was prohibitive.

If only Earth was not a forbidden planet, Ani could have found a way to smuggle records of Anumati's history to Annani. She could potentially smuggle them on the next patrol ship that left for the sector, but that would take too long, and Ani was impatient, which was a novel sensation for her.

She was the queen of long-term plans, never in a rush, and always looking for the safest way to go about them. But discovering that she had a granddaughter was a game changer. She wanted to talk to Annani, to get to know her, and that would not happen if she used the method that she had devised the day before.

Ani wanted to communicate with Annani in real time, which meant that Aria needed to be there when she visited Sofri. It also meant that Aru would have to be with Annani at the same time she was with his sister. That way, she could have a direct conversation with her granddaughter, or as direct as it could be when communicated through the twins.

The problem would be to come up with a convincing reason for Aria to be present during Ani's visits to the Supreme Oracle, and that was a major obstacle.

The rulers of Anumati always met with the Supreme in private to safeguard her prophecies regarding them. Her predictions about matters of state were not made public unless the queen or king made them so, and no one had ever questioned the need for secrecy during those meetings.

But no one had expected the queen and the Oracle to become best friends and co-conspirators.

The progression of their relationship had been long. It had started off formal, then became more friendly, and at some point, Sofri had started looking through the fabric of the universe for rare new talents at Ani's behest.

Finding them before the king's secret service did so was crucial. With the help of the resistance, they were given passage to one of the safer colonies, avoiding detection. Had the king's agents found them first, they would have been forced to work for him or sent to one of the more volatile colonies that had low survival rates.

That was how Sofri had discovered the twins' existence. It had taken some manipulation to get the two of them to the capital and give them jobs that allowed them access to Sofri and, through the Oracle, to Ani.

The Supreme had much more leeway than the queen, and her activities were less scrutinized, but that did not mean that she could be anything less than super careful. Every move was shrouded in layers upon layers of relays, so nothing could be traced back to her.

As the quartet shifted to a livelier melody, Ani allowed herself to get distracted and enjoy the music and the spectacular array of sweets that were served for dessert.

When tea and coffee were served along with the sweets, she sipped on her tea and pretended to look at the musicians as a new plan started forming in her head.

28

KALUGAL

When Jacki put the amulet around her neck, Kalugal grimaced, but he knew that arguing with her about it was futile right now.

His mate was a stubborn woman.

Still, he couldn't just say nothing. "You said that this amulet was evil. I know that you need to touch it, but you don't have to wear it."

"I didn't say that it was evil. It's just an object."

"Semantics. You said that what was done to imbue it with power was evil, and that makes it evil."

Jacki let out a breath. "Maybe it is, and maybe it isn't, but it doesn't matter. I need its help to navigate toward the captives."

He couldn't argue with that. "As soon as we find the girls, take it off. I don't want this thing to contaminate you."

Jacki let out an exasperated sigh. "The amulet is neither good nor bad, and that's despite it having been imbued with power by human sacrifices. It's like a container of blood. The way the blood is collected doesn't affect the container. That being said, I still intend to toss it into the ocean as soon as we are done with this mission, not because it is evil, but because I don't want it to fall into the hands of someone who would exploit it for any other reason than saving lives."

Kalugal hoped she wasn't thinking of him as that someone, yet at the same time, he also didn't want to get rid of the amulet. He just didn't want her to wear it. "Think of it from another angle. If we can keep using the amulet to save lives, we honor those who died to give it power."

When she arched a brow, he put a hand over his heart. "You wound me, mate. I would never use the amulet for gain. But if you don't trust me, we can give it to my goodie-two-shoes cousin. You trust Kian to use it only for good, right?"

Jacki deflated. "I trust you. I know that you will never go back on your promise to me."

"Good. I wasn't sure for a moment there." He gave her a bright smile. "So, we are keeping it?"

"I don't know. Let's see how this mission turns out. I'll decide when we get to the ship."

Kalugal was smart enough not to point out that the decision wasn't exclusively up to her. Technically, the amulet belonged to him because he had paid for the map and had organized the treasure hunt. He was also willing to share it with the clan and let Syssi use it whenever she needed a boost to her prophetic powers. It wasn't fair for Jacki to decide the fate of the amulet for everyone involved.

Still, he was a married man, and he knew what was good for him. He was also a patient guy who knew that sometimes it was better to keep his mouth shut until it was the right time to start an argument.

Right now wasn't the right time.

Clutching the damn amulet and holding it to her chest, Jacki pointed at a thicket of trees about five hundred meters ahead. "That's where the girls are being held. Do you want to stop here and continue on foot?"

"They can't hear or see us, so there is no need for us to trudge on foot. We could drive right over the scum, and they wouldn't even know what hit them until they were under the wheels of the trucks. The only problem with that plan is that it's not satisfying enough. I want to get up close and personal with their throats." He flashed her a smile with his fully elongated fangs.

Jacki grinned at him. "You say the nicest things, my mate."

He leaned over and kissed her. "I love you, my bloodthirsty wife."

"When should I stop, boss?" Luis asked without turning back to look at him.

Kalugal had thralled him to ignore the fangs and glowing eyes that many of the immortal males were already sporting, and he had compelled him to follow his instructions to the letter.

"Drive up to that truck over there."

"Where?" Luis asked. "I don't see anything."

The camouflage the cartel thugs had done to hide their vehicles was pretty shoddy, but it seemed to be enough to fool Luis.

"Just drive. I'll tell you when to stop."

The drivers had been instructed to stay in the trucks and hide under the dashboard while the Guardians took care of business. Kalugal had used compulsion to ensure that none of the human men decided to be heroic and join the fight.

As their convoy came to a halt near the grim enclosure where the girls were being kept, the barbed wire gleaming in the harsh sunlight made Kalugal's blood boil in his veins.

The girls were huddled together, some rocking back and forth, while others were slumped on the ground, either asleep or catatonic from the trauma they had suffered.

His fangs itched, and his venom glands pulsated, but he suppressed his murderous urges in order to clear his mind and think. He wouldn't be doing the girls any favors by attacking without taking into account the situation and formulating an appropriate plan.

Jacki's vision had focused on the girls, and she couldn't tell him how many cartel thugs they would be facing or what weapons they had.

From what he could see, they were all armed with machine guns, and their vehicles were probably armed with rapid-fire equipment, too.

Most of the monsters were gathered around a fire pit, laughing while roasting some animal, and there weren't even that many of them. He counted fifteen around the fire and six more guarding the enclosure.

He needed the Guardians to split up, with some taking out one group while the others took out the second.

Casting his senses wide, he scanned for more of the scum and found two more inside the vehicles and three deeper into the wooded area, taking a piss or a shit.

Even with their superior fire power, the scum had no chance against a bunch of angry immortals, but the trick was to take them out before they had a chance to fire and just as importantly, without letting the girls see them getting torn to pieces by what would look to them like a bunch of demons.

They were traumatized enough already, and Kalugal didn't want to add to it by tearing out the throats of their captors in front of them.

Yamanu was still concentrating on keeping the shrouding bubble around them, and Kalugal wasn't sure if he could just incorporate all the cartel thugs into the bubble so the fight would be invisible and soundless to the girls.

Kalugal could shroud the small enclosure area separately, but his fangs were itching for some monster blood, and he couldn't do that and shroud at the same time.

Leaning over, he put his hand on the Guardian's shoulder to get his attention. "Can you create another bubble around the girls? I don't want them to see the bloodbath. "

"I can't do more than one. I can only include them in our bubble, but that is not going to help them."

"Right. Can you include the perpetrators instead?"

"I'm not sure. They are spread out."

So, he sensed it as well.

"Perhaps Dagor can help. He's not joining the fight anyway. I'll go talk to him." He jumped out of the truck and walked to the middle one where Dagor and Negal were seated with Frankie, Jin, Arwel, and two Guardians.

The god was holding Frankie against his chest and not letting her see the girls, but his own eyes were trained on the enclosure, and his fangs were on full display.

He looked up at the god. "Can you create a shroud around the girls so they won't see us tearing their captors to pieces?"

Dagor frowned. "Can't Yamanu extend the shroud to cover the battlefield so the girls won't see or hear anything?"

"The thugs are too spread out, and Yamanu can't cover all of them. I could shroud the women, but I'm itching for some scum blood, and I can't do both at the same time. You are not joining the fight because you are staying to guard Frankie, so you are the only other option, provided that you can create a large enough shroud bubble."

29

DAGOR

The truth was that Dagor wasn't sure he could cast a bubble large enough to encompass the enclosure. It wasn't that the place was big, and there were only about twenty women in there, but he had never created a shroud bubble that size before.

He had done simulations during training, but that had been a long time ago, and the only shrouding he had done since arriving on Earth had been limited to covering himself and his companions.

"I'll give it my best shot," he said. "But it's not going to be nearly as good as Yamanu's."

Kalugal smiled. "I don't expect it to be. Just do your best, starting now."

"Yes, boss." Dagor gave him a mock salute.

"Much appreciated." Kalugal repaid him with a dip of his head.

"Here goes nothing," Dagor murmured as he cast his shroud over the enclosure.

The women should have noticed that they were suddenly encased in silence and couldn't see their captors, but none of them reacted, which was a sad testament to the state they were in.

He still hadn't let Frankie get a good look at them, and thankfully she was happy to have her face buried in his shirt.

As Kalugal motioned for those of their group who wished to get their fangs dirty to disembark, one of the thugs guarding the enclosure turned to look their way and frowned.

Obviously, he couldn't see them, or he would have sounded the alarm, but there was no doubt in Dagor's mind that the thug was sensing something.

He was about to tell Negal to take care of that when the thug lifted his machine gun and fired blindly in their general direction.

Chaos erupted as the rest of the gang followed, their gunfire slicing through the still air. Inside the truck, Dagor's reflexes kicked in, and he grabbed Frankie, pulling her down to the truck's floor and shielding her with his body. A rain of bullets pelted the truck, and he winced as several hit his back and his left arm, but he wasn't worried about them doing any lasting damage. His body was already expelling the foreign objects and healing the damage.

Beneath him, Frankie shivered and whimpered, probably feeling every impact as his body vibrated when hit with bullets, but he couldn't offer her words of solace while ignoring the pain and still trying to maintain the shroud around the barb-wired enclosure.

The snarling sounds of his companions were music to his ears, and as the screams began, he grinned like a savage despite the excruciating pain in his back and his left arm.

When the scent of blood reached his nostrils, it confused him. It wasn't his, and the thugs who were being torn to pieces were too far from him for the smell to be so strong.

Besides, the blood smelled too good to be theirs...

Lifting a few inches off the woman he was shielding, he saw where the smell was coming from. Frankie's side blossomed with vivid crimson, the blood that was seeping out too quickly painting a terrifying picture.

"Frankie!" He dropped the shroud and gently turned her face to look at him, but her eyes rolled back in her head, and she passed out.

With his own pain only a distant thunder against the lightning strike of Frankie's injury, Dagor knew he had to act fast, but he was momentarily paralyzed with the kind of fear he had never experienced before.

Around them, the battleground was still a whirlwind of noise—full of the Guardians' snarls, the crack of gunfire, the screams of the thugs, and the terrorized girls who could now see and hear the horrors he had been shielding them from.

"Luis is wounded," Jin said from somewhere behind him. "We need to get him to a doctor."

He heard the sound of tearing fabric and then Luis groaning.

"Frankie was also hit," he finally managed to say.

"Oh, crap," Jin cursed. "I'm taking them both to the ship."

"I'm coming with you," Negal said, and then the truck dipped as he jumped in. "Pedal to the metal, Jin. I'll call Aru to send the doctor to meet us halfway."

Thank the merciful Fates for the clan's satellite phones, but would the doctor make it in time to save Frankie?

"Don't let her bleed!" Jin yelled from the driver's seat. "Take off your shirt and hold it against her wound!"

As she turned the truck around and raced towards salvation, Dagor followed her instructions, tearing off his shirt and pressing it against Frankie's side.

The roar of panic in Dagor's mind was pierced by the whine of the engine as Jin navigated the rough terrain like a bat out of hell. The jostling and bumping were not doing Frankie any favors, but slowing down to make the ride a little smoother was not an option either.

With the truck careening through the landscape, time became the enemy, and each second stretched out with excruciating sluggishness.

While Negal made the call to Aru, explaining the emergency, Dagor cradled Frankie in his arms, trying to absorb as much of the bumps as possible.

With panic clawing at Dagor's insides, the tremor of his own heart mirrored the stuttering beat of hers, and he pressed the shirt down on her wound harder, trying to stem the tide of her life's blood seeping out.

30

KIAN

Kian scrubbed a hand over his face. "This is not happening. Can I have one effing day of peace?"

"Is there anything I can do to help?" Aru asked.

"I'm calling the doctor. Give Negal my phone number and have him call me in a couple of minutes to give me a full update."

The phone Negal had been given didn't have Kian's number programmed into it, and the only one of the newly arrived gods who had it was Aru.

What Negal had told his leader was that Frankie and the human guide had been shot during an altercation with cartel thugs and the girl needed urgent medical assistance. They were driving toward the ship but asked that the doctor drive toward them because they weren't sure Frankie would make it.

Given the urgency of getting the girl medical help, he hadn't given Aru any other details. Nevertheless, Kian could guess what had happened. They had been attacked by cartel thugs just as he had warned them they would, and on top of that, they had disregarded his advice and taken the human with them.

He really hated being the prophet of doom. For once, it would have been nice to be wrong.

Shaking his head, he called Bridget. "We have a medical emergency," he said without preamble. "Frankie and one of the drivers were shot. Jin is driving them back here, but Frankie is losing a lot of blood, and they might not make it in time. You need to head out to intercept them. Collect what you need, and Anandur will take you on his motorcycle."

Anandur arched a brow. "I will?"

"I'm on my way." Bridget ended the call.

After Julian had gotten a new bike, Anandur bought his old one and brought it to the ship. Perhaps he had been prompted to do so by the Fates so he could now save the injured human.

Kian turned to him. "Do we have any other vehicle available to us immediately?"

"Not that I'm aware of." Anandur pushed to his feet. "I'll take it to the dock and meet Bridget there."

"Thank you."

As Anandur left the cabin, Brundar frowned, which was almost as uncharacteristic for him as smiling. Usually, his face was expressionless. "Isn't it dangerous to send Bridget and Anandur out alone? What if they get ambushed?"

"It will take too long to arrange for another vehicle, and the motorcycle is the only thing we have on board aside from the jet skis. I don't think they can be used on dry ground."

"I'll take care of getting us more vehicles." Brundar pulled out his phone. "If Jin took one of the three trucks, they will be short on seats."

"Wait." Kian stopped him. "I need to hear from the guys what's going on and what exactly they need. I can't believe none of them have called me yet."

As his phone rang, though, it was Negal and not one of his people.

"The doctor is on her way. Please tell me what's going on in as few words as you can."

"Yes, sir," Negal said. "Kalugal found an amulet, Jacki touched it and had a vision about abducted women, and we decided to rescue them before they got moved and we lost track of them. Yamanu shrouded our convoy, but one of the thugs must have sensed us and started shooting, and then all his buddies did the same, and bullets were flying everywhere. I think the one that got Frankie went straight through Dagor because he was shielding her with his body and taking the hits. The driver was also shot. Jin took the wheel and is driving us back like she's being chased by demons. The driver is holding on, but Frankie is losing a lot of blood. Dagor is pressing his shirt to the wound, but with all the jostling, I don't know how effectively he is staunching the blood flow."

"What about the abducted women?" Kian asked.

"They are in pretty bad shape. There are about twenty of them, and they are traumatized. That's all I know. As soon as I realized that Frankie was hit, I left your people to finish the job of tearing the monsters apart and jumped back into the truck to escort Dagor and Frankie back. They needed someone to cover them in case they encountered more thugs."

That had been good thinking, probably born from Negal's military training.

"Given what my people are probably doing to those thugs, I can't even contact the local authorities."

"Yes, that has occurred to me," Negal said. "We will need to torch the evidence, and we also need a few more trucks or a bus to get the women out of there."

"I will arrange it."

"When is the doctor going to get here?"

"I don't know. I have no idea where you are."

"So how will she find us? I assume that there aren't many roads out here, but there must be more than one."

"Her driver will hone in on Jin's signal."

"She has a tracker?" Negal's tone lost its warmth.

Kian chuckled. "She has a clan phone. That's just as good as a tracker."

"I see." Negal's tone returned to its normal amiability.

"How is Frankie doing?" Kian asked.

There was a short pause before Negal answered, and Kian imagined him checking with Dagor. "Not so good, but she's still breathing."

That didn't sound encouraging, but it was what it was.

"If anything changes, let me know."

"I will."

As Kian ended the call, he turned to look at Brundar, and the Guardian lifted his head from his phone. "Anandur and Bridget are on the move."

That was fast. "We need to get four trucks or a bus to the scene."

Brundar nodded. "I'm on it."

When Kian's phone rang again, he was glad that the caller was Yamanu, but he was also mad as hell that no one had thought to update him before rushing to rescue the humans without a solid plan or asking for backup. He was going to chew the heads off everyone who should have known better, including Yamanu's, but not right now.

"I assume that the thugs were dealt with, and the kidnapped women are safe?"

"You assume correctly," Yamanu said. "The thugs are in pieces, and I don't mean that figuratively. Even if we hadn't known what they did from Jacki's vision, it was enough to see the state the women were in to get all of us into a killing rage. I don't think any of us fired a single shot. It was all done with fangs." He sighed. "And now we have twenty-three severely traumatized women and girls on our hands, not only because they were violated repeatedly after seeing their families slaughtered by the cartel, but also because they saw a bunch of demons tearing apart the monsters who did it."

"You should thrall them to forget what they saw."

"I tried to calm them down, but it wasn't enough. Kalugal put them to sleep first to stop the hysterics and is thralling them to forget what they saw while out."

"Good. That's the first step. Brundar is trying to arrange vehicles to transport them so we can return them to their people."

There was a pause before Yamanu responded. "They no longer have a home. Their entire village was destroyed, and all their relatives murdered."

Cursing under his breath, Kian shook his head. "Can we take them to some of the other villages? They should have relatives there who would be willing to take them in."

"I don't know about that," Yamanu said. "I'll try to speak to them after Kalugal is done manipulating their memories."

It didn't sound like Yamanu thought that finding the women new homes in the surrounding villages was a viable solution, but Kian had no intention of bringing them on board. This wasn't the same as the rescue missions they ran back home, where they brought the victims to the sanctuary for rehabilitation. This was a cartel war, and the rules were different. Taking these women away from everything they knew was not a good solution to the problem, but scattering them among the other villages might not be a good one either.

Kian couldn't think of any other options, but he had learned a long time ago to accept that not every problem could be satisfactorily solved. Sometimes, slapping on a temporary patch was all that could be done.

31

ARU

Aru had asked Negal to call him right after he was done talking to Kian, but more than five minutes had passed, and he hadn't called yet.

Given Frankie's condition, time was of the essence, and Aru needed to tell his teammate about the lifesaving transfusion that could be given to her.

Kian had asked him to keep secret the information about what a god's blood could do, but this was an emergency. Frankie was important to Dagor whether he wanted to admit it or not, and if she died, he would be devastated.

Besides, her life was more important than the promise Aru had given Kian.

In this case, it would be best to provide the information to his teammates first and ask for Kian's forgiveness second.

He could lie and say that his friends knew about their blood-healing properties and that he hadn't told them a thing, but Aru preferred not to.

When several more minutes had passed, Aru refused to wait any longer and placed the call to Negal, and when he didn't answer immediately, Aru's gut twisted with worry.

Were they under attack?

Had their truck crashed? The female driving the truck was probably not being too careful in her rush to bring the injured humans to someone who could help them.

"Nothing new here," Negal finally answered. "The doctor is on her way."

Negal's tone, along with the cacophony of sounds streaming in from the other end, painted a vivid picture of urgency. The rumble of the truck's engine as the vehicle pushed across rugged terrain was punctuated by sharp jolts and thuds, and Aru could hear the clatter and rattle of items in the vehicle as they rolled about.

If Aru closed his eyes, he could see the vehicle hurtling through the landscape, with the female in the driver's seat battling against nature's resistance and time itself.

"How is Frankie doing?" he asked.

"Not good. I hope the doctor gets to her soon."

"Damn." Aru rubbed a hand over his face. "Do you know about the healing properties of a god's blood?"

"What are you talking about?" Another bump had Negal's voice hitched on the last word.

"A small transfusion of your or Dagor's blood can save Frankie. It will give her system a boost that will help her heal, but you need a syringe to perform it. Is there a medical kit in the truck?"

"There isn't. We searched because we could have used some bandages and tape to staunch the blood flow."

"Damn. You will have to wait until the doctor arrives and take one from her. After you are done, you will have to thrall the immortals and the human driver to forget that they saw you doing it. No one is supposed to know what our blood can do. I promised Kian that I would not reveal the secret because if humans learned about it, it would put the heir, Toven, and us at great risk. But we have to save the girl, so I will just have to apologize later and tell him that we've mitigated the risk."

"How much blood does she need?" Negal asked.

Not beating around the bush and getting straight to the point was one of the things Aru appreciated about the pragmatic trooper.

"Very little. About the size of the very tip of your pinkie. I think it's better that you do it because Dagor is most likely not thinking straight, and he might give her too much, which for all we know could kill her."

"How do you know about it in the first place? We were never told that our blood could heal humans."

"Since only a few of us would ever have contact with humans, there was no reason for us to be told. But it works the same on most of the created species. My sister had told me about it. She studied to be a healer, and they were taught to use their blood if there was no other choice and it was important to save the person."

"Well, that's good to know. So, let me repeat. When the doctor gets here, I ask her to give me a syringe, take some of my blood, inject it into Frankie, and then thrall everyone to forget what I did."

"That's right."

"Does it matter where I take the blood from and where I inject it?"

Aru couldn't tell him that Aria had given him instructions on how to help Gabi, but if asked, he could say that he'd learned it from YouTube and wouldn't be lying.

"You can take the blood from the crook of your elbow and inject it into any visible vein. Whatever healing properties our blood has will help heal Frankie no matter where it is injected."

"Good deal. I'll keep you posted, boss."

32

DAGOR

The world narrowed to the pale, unresponsive girl in Dagor's arms. Her bleeding had lessened, but the pallor of her skin and the erratic, faint rhythm of her heartbeat sent waves of fear through him.

As the truck raced over the rough terrain, each bump and jolt fueled his anger and added to the sense of helplessness that he detested.

He was a god, for Fates' sake.

Why couldn't he do something to help her?

The rough ride couldn't be avoided, but each vibration and harsh jerk worsened Frankie's fragile state. Unyielding and relentless, the rugged dirt road was the enemy, but it was leading them to the doctor who could save Frankie's life.

Dagor prayed to the Fates that they would make it in time.

Now that he was experiencing what Aru had when Gabi had texted him from the hospital, he could empathize with Aru so much better.

No wonder Aru had been going insane.

The difference was that Gabi hadn't been bleeding or unresponsive, not while she'd texted Aru anyway. Later, when her transition had kicked in full force, she had been going in and out of a coma, and he'd seen how difficult it had been on his commander.

Squashed between the two front rows of seats, Dagor was absorbing all the bumps and shielding Frankie as best he could, ignoring the cramping in his legs and the ache in his back that had nothing to do with the bullets it had expelled. With his rapid healing, he could barely remember where he'd been hit, but the back of the seat in front of him was digging into his skin, and there was nothing he could do about it without moving Frankie.

Any attempt to adjust her position might worsen her condition, and the fear of causing further harm kept him frozen in place despite the discomfort.

The helplessness was suffocating, debilitating.

Dagor's body was one big knot of tension. His chest felt like it was being squeezed in a vise, his arms and hands tingled, and not just because he hadn't moved or because his blood circulation was impaired. It was the anxiety that made it hard for him to breathe and boiled his blood, so it was running hot in his veins and making his hands tingle.

Underneath it all was the gnawing fear of loss.

Frankie's unresponsiveness was a deafening silence in the chaotic drive, a void that he was terrified would become permanent.

The thought of losing her was unbearable. He tried to push the thought away, but it refused to go, lurking in the background and submerging him in despair.

Dagor's world had been reduced to a maelstrom of fear, anger, and desperate hope, all centered on the fragile human in his arms.

Behind him, he could hear Negal talking on the phone, but the engine roar combined with the howling wind and the turmoil in his mind made it impossible for him to hear what was being said.

"Dagor." Negal leaned forward, poking his head between the seats so his mouth was as close as it could get to Dagor's ear. "Aru just called," he said quietly. "There is something we can do to help Frankie heal faster, but it requires secrecy and careful handling."

Hope warring with skepticism, Dagor nodded. "Whatever it is, I'll do it."

Pushing his shoulder through the gap between the seats, Negal got even closer to him. "Did you know that a god's blood could heal a human?"

Dagor frowned. "I've never heard of such a thing. Did Aru tell you that?"

Negal nodded. "A small amount no bigger than the tip of your pinkie can make all the difference. The problem is that we need a syringe, and there is no medical kit in the truck. We have to wait for the doctor. The other problem is that it's a closely guarded secret. Kian doesn't want anyone to know, not even his own people, because it could put the heir, Toven, and us at risk. If word ever reached the humans, they would do everything to get to us and use our blood to heal those who would pay the most for it."

"Yeah. He's right about that. But how do we do it without the doctor knowing? Do we thrall her?"

Thankfully, immortals were almost as susceptible to gods' thralling as humans, but Dagor didn't feel right about deceiving their new allies.

Negal glanced at Jin's back, but nothing in her posture indicated that she'd heard anything. "That's precisely what Aru told me to do if we can't swipe a syringe from the doctor and administer the transfusion while she is tending to Luis. You can draw your blood yourself and administer it to Frankie, or I can do that if you don't have the stomach for it, with either my blood or yours."

"Mine," Dagor said. "Your hands are probably steadier than mine right now, so you will have to do it, but you will use my blood."

Negal smirked. "I knew you would say that."

Dagor ignored what Negal was trying to imply. "What are the risks?"

"To Frankie?"

Dagor nodded.

"None that Aru mentioned. He just said not to get overzealous and give her too much. That might be dangerous to her."

"But there is a chance it can save her?"

"That's what he said."

Aru had thrown him a lifeline to pull him out of the turbulent waters of despair, but to implement Aru's suggestion, they needed the doctor to get there in time.

"I just thought of something," Negal said. "It's not only our blood that has healing abilities. Our venom and our saliva do, too. I don't think the saliva would be effective for this, and the doctor still needs to get the bullet out anyway, but you don't need to wait for the doctor to bite Frankie. It might just give her enough of a boost until the doctor arrives."

Negal's idea of using venom to help Frankie was absurd. The notion that he could bite her while she was unconscious and barely clinging to life was utterly ludicrous.

"Do you think I can get my fangs and venom glands going while Frankie is unconscious?"

Negal shrugged. "You can think about the monsters back there and get your venom going with aggression."

Dagor shook his head. "It doesn't work like that, and you know it."

"Desperate times call for desperate measures, right? I was trying to think outside the box. Maybe you can think back to when you and Frankie were intimate, and the memory will be enough to activate your fangs and venom."

"I can't think sexy thoughts while my mate is dying in my arms."

Mate?

Why had the word slipped from his lips?

With Frankie's life hanging by a thread, the realization that she might be his mate hit Dagor with the force of a freight train.

The term mate had always been a distant concept for him, something that was not relevant to his carefully-laid-out future plans. But the fear for Frankie's life was like a jolt of clarity amidst the fog of urgency and desperation.

This recognition brought about a surge of protectiveness and a profound sense of connection. Could Frankie, the human girl who had unexpectedly entered his life, who had challenged him, fascinated him, and now lay dying in his arms, be his mate?

33

ARU

Aru had planned on waiting to confess to Kian what he had done after the transfusion was administered and Kian couldn't stop it, but his conscience wouldn't allow that, and he found himself walking over to Kian's cabin and ringing the doorbell.

Since his calls were no doubt monitored, it wasn't the kind of conversation he could have over the phone, but even if no one was listening it still needed to be done face to face, no matter how awkward it was.

As the door swung open and he stepped in, Kian regarded him with a raised brow. "How can I help you, Aru?"

Aru glanced at the blond Guardian, who was sitting on the couch with the phone glued to his ear. He was talking with someone in rapid Spanish, arranging rental vehicles to be delivered to the dock.

At the dining table, Kian's assistant was busy typing on his laptop, and he only acknowledged Aru with a slight nod.

Aru nodded back before answering Kian. "I need a word alone with you if you don't mind."

A knowing look in his eyes, Kian rose to his feet. "We can talk out on the balcony while I smoke my cigarillo. Can I interest you in one?"

Aru only smoked when he needed to conduct a private conversation and used smoking as an excuse to step outside, but in a way, this situation fell into the same category, so he nodded. "Thank you. I would love to try one."

Kian smiled. "What about a shot of fine whiskey? Can I interest you in that as well?"

"Sure. Why not."

Kian walked over to the bar, poured two shots, and handed one to Aru.

"Thank you." He sniffed the whiskey the same way Kian did and followed the immortal out the doors to the expansive balcony of the luxurious cabin suite.

Kian closed the doors behind them and motioned for Aru to take a seat on one of the loungers.

A pack of cigarillos was on the side table, along with an ashtray and a lighter.

Kian sat on the other lounger, took the box, and opened it to offer Aru one of the brown sticks. "Every time I try to quit, another disaster pops up, and I turn to my one vice."

"You have only one?" Aru pulled out one of the cigarillos. "That's not so bad."

"Why? Do you have more?"

Aru laughed. "Apart from being in the resistance, not really."

"I wouldn't call fighting for your rights a vice." Kian flicked the lighter on and lit Aru's cigarillo.

"It's not good for my health, that's for sure." Aru took a puff of the surprisingly tasty and aromatic tobacco.

Smiling, Kian lit his own stick. "Yeah. I know what you mean."

For a moment, they sat in silence, puffing smoke and enjoying the mild ocean breeze.

"So," Kian broke the silence. "What is it that you need to talk to me privately about?"

"You've probably guessed it already. I told Negal about the healing properties of a god's blood so he could tell Dagor. I know that I promised you I wouldn't tell anyone, but given the situation, it was necessary. The problem is that they need to wait for the doctor because they need a syringe. I instructed Negal to take precautions so the doctor and Jin wouldn't find out, and if they do, to thrall their memories away."

"I see." Kian didn't look like he approved. "You should have checked with me first."

"Frankie is not doing well, and if she dies, it will devastate Dagor. He's stubborn and not willing to admit how much she means to him, but it's evident in every look he casts her way. Besides, she's Toven's mate's best friend, and Toven would never forgive us if we didn't do everything we could to save her."

That was his trump card, and given Kian's sigh, it had worked.

"Right." Kian leaned back. "Toven doesn't know what's going on yet, and neither does Mia. It's not that I'm trying to hide it from them, but I'm using the lack of time as an excuse to postpone it."

Aru took another puff of his cigarillo. "Do you want me to inform them? I'm at your disposal for any task you need to be done."

"Thank you." Kian took a sip of his whiskey. "But I'd prefer to wait until Bridget sees Frankie, and I can tell Mia that her friend is not going to die." He put the glass down on the side table. "If Frankie holds on until Bridget gets there, and Dagor gives her his blood, I can tell Mia that her friend is going to make it, and I'd rather do that than worry her needlessly."

"Makes sense. Thank you for understanding."

"I still don't like it," Kian said. "The more people know about the healing properties of a god's blood, the bigger the chance the secret will be exposed. Make sure that your teammates keep the information contained. We can't afford a breach."

"You have my word that I'll do everything I can to keep it contained. I know that Negal and Dagor will follow my orders, but I will restate the need to keep this in the strictest confidence, and if need be, I'll thrall the doctor and Jin myself to forget they ever saw Dagor or Negal with a syringe."

"Be careful. Bridget's mind is too precious to mess with."

"Don't worry. I know what I'm doing."

Kian tapped his cigarillo to dislodge the ash. "The transfusion might not be necessary. Bridget is a very capable physician, and Frankie is a young woman. The doctor's intervention might suffice."

Aru nodded. "I'll call Negal and tell him to hold off on the transfusion and only administer it if it's absolutely necessary." He rubbed a hand over the back of his neck. "The problem is that neither Negal nor Dagor can judge that accurately, and they can't ask the doctor without showing their hand."

"They shouldn't wait until the last moment. After Bridget patches Frankie up, she will give them an assessment of her condition, and she's not the type to sugarcoat anything. She tells things like they are."

"Good." Aru took another small sip from the whiskey. "We will play it by ear. I appreciate your pragmatic approach, Kian. I was afraid you would forbid it."

"I'm not happy about it, but I don't want to lose the girl either. That being said, there is more at stake than just keeping the secret contained. Do you know what the blood transfusion will do to Frankie besides saving her life?"

"What?"

Kian tilted his head. "I thought that I told you that. If Frankie is a dormant carrier of godly genes, the transfusion might induce her transition. But since she is unconscious, she can't give Dagor her consent, which is problematic. This is not the kind of thing that should be decided for her."

"You are right, but what choice do we have? We can't let her die without doing all we can to save her."

"I know, and I agree." Kian sighed. "Decisions are never as simple as black and white, yes or no, this or the other. Most involve an array of conflicting factors and are about making a choice between different shades of gray."

Aru's mind raced with the implications. "How soon after the transfusion would we know if she's transitioning?"

"It varies," Kian said. "Each Dormant responds differently. Some might start showing signs the next day while others might take longer."

"Is that a sure thing? I mean, will one small transfusion guarantee her transition, provided that she's a Dormant?"

Kian frowned. "Not necessarily. Come to think of it, one of our Dormants was very sick before attempting his transition, and we gave him a transfusion to heal him first and then another one to help him transition. Since Frankie is injured, it might work the same way for her."

Aru let out a breath. "I hope that's what happens. I don't know her well, but she seems like the kind of woman who will hate having the decision made for her."

"You should inform Negal and Dagor about the possible unintended consequences."

"Of course." Aru extinguished his cigarillo and pushed to his feet. "I need to call Negal right away. I hope I'm not too late."

"You are not. Anandur would have called me if he had found them already."

Aru didn't know whether he should be glad or concerned that the physician wasn't with Frankie yet.

"Let me know if there is anything I can do to help."

Kian waved a hand. "Call Negal. I have enough people helping me with this situation. I just hope it's resolved before the wedding tonight."

34

DAGOR

As Negal's phone rang, Dagor's anxiety spiked. Had the doctor encountered a problem on the way?

She could have been ambushed by the cartel, or her vehicle could have crashed.

With how Jin was driving, it was a wonder that they hadn't. The dirt road was not meant for fast driving, and Jin was flooring it.

Cradling Frankie's limp body in his arms as the truck jostled them mercilessly over the rough terrain, Dagor dreaded each bump. He could feel Frankie's heartbeat, but it was weak and erratic under his touch.

"What's going on?" he asked Negal after the call ended. "Where is the doctor?"

"She's on her way." Negal poked his head between the seats. "The redhead is bringing her on his motorcycle, which should make their journey even faster." He glanced at Jin over Dagor's head and continued in a hushed voice, "Aru says to wait on the transfusion. Kian wants the doc to assess Frankie first, and if she says that Frankie is going to make it, we don't need to do it."

"Why not? It can only help."

Negal winced. "There's more to it. If Frankie is a Dormant, a god's blood could trigger her transition. It shouldn't be done without her consent unless it's the only way to save her life."

Dagor's heart sank even further. The idea of Frankie undergoing such a monumental change without consenting to it was disturbing, but the alternative was unthinkable. He glanced down at her pale face and the way her chest was barely moving with the shallow breaths she was taking. He didn't know much about human bodies, but it was obvious that her condition was severe.

"She can hate me for it later," Dagor muttered, more to himself than to Negal. "If it comes to that, I'll beg for her forgiveness. But I can't let her die."

"It might not come to that," Negal said. "The clan's best doctor is going to treat her, and that might be all she needs."

"I hope so."

A surge of anger filled Dagor's chest. He was angry at the circumstances that had forced them into the impossible situation, angry at the unpaved road that was impeding their journey and causing more damage to Frankie, angry at himself for not doing a better job of protecting her. But beneath that anger was an overwhelming fear.

Fear of losing Frankie or having to force her to transition without her consent.

"I don't know why it's taking the doctor so long to intercept us," Negal said, giving voice to Dagor's frustration. "I thought that the motorcycle could navigate the terrain better, and they would get to us faster."

The truth was that it hadn't been even half an hour since Jin had taken the wheel, and if his estimate was correct, they had been more than an hour away from the ship at the start of the mad rush back.

Dagor adjusted his hold on Frankie, trying to make her as comfortable as possible in the cramped space between the seats. She probably couldn't feel a thing, though, which was a small blessing.

As the roar of a motorcycle cut through the tense air, announcing the arrival of the doctor, Dagor released a relieved breath.

Jin slowed the truck to a stop, and as the redhead pulled up alongside it, the doctor dismounted and retrieved a cooler from the bike's storage compartment.

Bridget's swift, purposeful movements offered him a measure of reassurance.

"Get her on the floor and give me space," the clan's physician instructed as she climbed into the truck.

Dagor laid Frankie down on the floor with the utmost care, his eyes lingering on her for a moment longer before he climbed up to sit beside Negal in the back. From there, he could observe everything without being in the doctor's way.

Jin, who had jumped out of the truck the moment she'd pulled to a full stop, watched the doctor from the side with a concerned expression on her face. Even the injured driver propped himself up so he could watch what Bridget was doing.

There were too many eyes on the doctor and Frankie, and Dagor worried that the onlookers might distract the physician, but she seemed unfazed, and her focus remained laser sharp as she worked.

"I'm giving Frankie a morphine shot first to make sure that she doesn't wake up from the pain." She administered the shot with a practiced hand. "I'm going to take out the bullet now, so if anyone is squeamish, I suggest that you look away."

Dagor usually wouldn't have been fazed, but this was his mate's body that the doctor was about to poke into, and his stomach roiled. Still, it was his duty to watch over Frankie, and hopefully, he wouldn't puke.

As the doctor started cutting off Frankie's shirt, Dagor glared at Luis, who was watching from the front. "Turn around," he commanded.

Negal didn't need to be told and shifted his gaze to the side.

As the doctor ignored the exchange and removed the bullet with steady hands, Dagor swallowed the bile that had risen in his throat, and when she stitched up the wound, he had to look away for a moment to settle his stomach.

The physician's confidence and singular focus calmed him, dulling the sharp edges of his fear, but evidently the effect didn't extend to his stomach.

"Now I'm going to give her blood to replenish what she's lost." The doctor opened the cooler, revealing its contents. "These are units of packed red blood cells and plasma, and both are universal, so don't worry. We were lucky to have them on board. I ordered several units of them because of the human crew."

As Dagor watched the doctor begin the blood transfusion, he felt a strange sense of detachment, as if it wasn't Frankie lying there and receiving a stranger's blood to save her life. It was as if he was watching a scene from a movie.

Throughout the procedure, Dagor remained by Negal's side, his eyes never leaving Frankie. The doctor worked efficiently, her hands steady and sure.

She looked up at Dagor. "I need you to come back here and hold the IV bag up so it doesn't fall."

It was hanging from a portable stand that the doctor had assembled, and it looked flimsy, but he could see the blood begin to flow into Frankie's veins, and that was a relief.

"This will help stabilize her," the doctor said with a comforting note of confidence.

"Tell me the truth," he said. "Is she going to make it?"

The doctor smiled. "Frankie won't die from this injury. But we need to get her to the clinic."

As Bridget turned her attention to Luis's injuries and took her equipment with her, Dagor and Negal exchanged loaded glances as they both realized that they had missed the opportunity to secure the syringe without alerting the physician.

It seemed like it wasn't needed at the moment, but they still had to get Frankie back to the ship, and things might take a turn for the worse.

"I need to take a piss," Negal said with a wink as he jumped down from the truck.

Was he planning on swiping the syringe from the doctor without thralling her, Jin, Anandur, and the driver?

They had too many witnesses to pull it off without employing mind tricks.

Anandur, who had sidled up to Jin and had been observing from the sidelines, stepped closer and offered Dagor a reassuring smile.

"Trust the doc. Bridget wouldn't have told you that Frankie was going to be okay if she didn't believe it a hundred percent. You can take her word to the bank." He chuckled. "Though in her case, it would be the blood bank."

Jin snorted as if the redhead had just told her a joke, but Dagor failed to see what was so funny about it.

"All done," Bridget said. "Let's get these two to the ship where we can properly clean them up."

She closed her bag and looked back to where Negal had been sitting. "Where did he go?"

"He needed to relieve himself," Dagor said. "He should be back in a moment." Hopefully, before the doctor took her bag back to the motorcycle.

It seemed like Negal had really needed to take a piss, and it hadn't been an excuse to steal a syringe.

"I'm riding back with you." She offered Dagor a small smile. "In case my patients need further assistance."

Anandur laughed. "Liar. You just don't want to ride back with me."

She huffed. "That's a given. I'm not a fan of motorcycles on a paved road, let alone off-road."

35

KALUGAL

It had taken Kalugal a long time to thrall away the memories of the most recent horrors the abducted women had witnessed. While he was at it, he had been tempted to also erase the worst of what they had been subjected to before their rescuers arrived, but doing so without their consent was unethical.

They were entitled to remember and mourn their families and friends, and what had happened to them after they had been taken was also their choice to remember or forget. The problem was that to do that, he would have to wake them up, and the cleanup of the area hadn't been completed yet.

The one thing he couldn't allow them to remember was how the monsters were dealt with. Upon waking up, they would remember that the cartel barbarians had run away when their rescuers arrived.

Yamanu waited for him outside the enclosure. "I spoke to Kian about what to do with the women. He wants us to take them to the neighboring villages."

Kalugal shook his head. "We can't. These people are barely scraping by and are terrorized by the cartel. They will be afraid to take them in. Besides, they need therapy and rehabilitation, and they will get none of that here."

Jacki joined him and Yamanu even though he'd told her to stay in the truck and not look at the carnage. "I agree. There is no future for them here, and I don't need to spell out the reasons for it. We need to take them to the sanctuary."

"They don't speak English," Yamanu pointed out.

Living in Southern California, where a large percentage of the population spoke Spanish, meant that most of the immortals residing in the village were fluent. The Scottish and Alaskan members of the clan less so.

The question was whether the therapists working in the sanctuary spoke the language.

"Is there any room left?" Jacki asked.

"I can check with Vanessa," Yamanu offered. "She didn't join the cruise because Mo-red couldn't come."

With so many clan members on board, Kalugal hadn't noticed Vanessa's absence, which should have clued him in that he was getting complacent. Usually, he wouldn't let a detail like that escape his notice.

"We need to enlarge the sanctuary," Jacki said. "Is it okay with you if I double the donations so the clan can add another building or two?"

Kalugal smiled. "Of course, it is. But the problem is not only where to house them. Vanessa is constantly understaffed. Therapists just don't last long there. For many, dealing with what victims of trafficking suffered is too much."

She nodded. "I get it. I'm not squeamish, but I don't know if I could do that day in and day out."

"Vanessa will make room for them," Yamanu said. "Also, most of her therapists speak Spanish because many of the girls we rescue are native Spanish speakers who were trafficked to the US."

"Good." Kalugal expelled a relieved breath. "Now, all we have to do is convince Kian to let them onto the ship." He looked at Yamanu. "You will have to shroud our arrival."

"That's not a problem." The Guardian flashed him a smile. "Convincing Kian is. I think you should call him."

"Why me? You are his trusted head Guardian. He will listen to you."

"And you are a council member." Yamanu turned to scan the two remaining trucks. "Where is Edna? We need her to help us make a case."

"She's over there," Jacki pointed. "Helping bury the evidence." She shook her head. "Edna is one gutsy lady."

"She is," Kalugal agreed. "She's lived through much bloodier epochs than you, my dear. This is nothing new to her."

Jacki's eyes softened. "It's sad. No one should get used to things like that."

He put his arm around his mate's shoulders. "Death is part of being human. One way or another, they all die. Regrettably, not all from old age."

Mey joined their group, rubbing her hands to clean them as best she could. "I pray for the day when no humans die from disease, acts of violence, or natural disasters, but I know that day will never come. Living peacefully is not in human nature."

Yamanu pulled her against his chest and kissed her forehead. "Why did you go digging? We have enough males to do that and not enough shovels."

"I wasn't digging. I was decorating the graves so they would not stand out. Besides, I want to be done with it sooner rather than later so we can get out of here. The trucks Kian sent our way should be arriving shortly, and unless you want to thrall the new drivers as well to forget what they find, we need the place to be free of body parts by the time they arrive. We also still have a wedding to attend tonight, and I want to at least shower first."

"Are we going to make it on time?" Jacki asked.

Kalugal glanced at his watch. "Not unless they set it back a couple of hours. I'd better call Kian."

36

KIAN

When his phone rang with Kalugal's ringtone, the anger Kian had managed to stifle resurged. "Hello, cousin. I've been waiting for you to call me."

"You must be psychic because up until a minute ago, I was arguing with Yamanu about who was going to call you."

"I plan on having a word with my Guardians later, but the fact that neither you nor any of them bothered to call me before rushing to rescue the women from the cartel monsters is so irresponsible that I still can't wrap my mind around it. What were you thinking?"

"Would you have tried to stop us?" Kalugal sounded incredulous.

"I would have asked you what the plan was, arranged for transportation, and sent reinforcements. If you had made a better plan, perhaps no one would have been injured."

Kalugal sighed. "You are right. I should have called you. What Jacki saw in her vision stirred such a killing rage in us that we didn't stop to think. We wanted to obliterate the monsters as much as we wanted to save the women, and we were afraid that they would be moved from where Jacki had seen them, and the opportunity to do both would be lost."

Kian's eyes widened in surprise, and the rage inside of him subsided. "That's as close to an apology as I have ever gotten from you."

"I never had a reason to apologize before."

"Really? What about kidnapping my head Guardian and Jacki and holding them hostage?"

"If you expect me to apologize for that, then you need to apologize for sending Jin to tether me. I've never made a move against you, so you had no justification for that."

"It was a preemptive measure to ensure that you had no malevolent intentions toward my people. I'm not going to apologize for it."

Kalugal let out a sigh. "Fine. Let's agree that neither of us needs to apologize to the other. The important thing is that we have overcome our initial rough introduction and found common ground. Who would have thought that we would be living together in peace and harmony?"

"Indeed. We've achieved something truly rare, and I'm proud of it. I'm also glad to have your devious mind on my council. You offer a perspective that my other council members don't have."

Kalugal chuckled. "You just can't help yourself, can you? You can't give me a compliment without caveats."

"That wasn't my intention. Everything I've said was meant as a compliment. You are incredibly smart, and you think outside the box. You are one of the most interesting people I have ever had the pleasure to converse with."

"Oh, wow, cousin! You make my heart fill with fuzzies. I enjoy bantering with you and don't mind the occasional barbs. They are actually quite fun. But this unqualified praise is new, and it's welcome."

"It's also overdue. I just wanted you to know I really like you despite our banter sometimes getting out of hand."

"Thank you. The same is true for me. I greatly enjoy our talks, especially when they are over your fine whiskey and cigars."

"You are invited any time."

"Much appreciated, cousin."

Kalugal was being more amiable than usual, which meant that he wanted something, and Kian had a feeling that he knew what it was. "Did the transport Brundar arranged for arrive?"

"Not yet, which is a good thing. We are just finishing the cleanup, and the girls are still asleep. I thralled away their memories of our attack, but I didn't feel it was my right to thrall away the rest of their trauma. They need to agree to it first."

"Indeed, but if you want to thrall those who want it, you should wake them up before the transport's arrival. There won't be much time to do that when they get there."

"Yes, about that." Kalugal paused. "I didn't thrall those memories away, but I've seen them, and there is no way the other villagers are going to take the women in. They are terrified of the cartel that controls this area. We've only taken out one team of many, and we can't stay and clean up all of them. The women also require a lot of rehabilitation after what they have been through, and there will be none of that available in these poor villages. Yamanu contacted Vanessa, and she said that she had room for them in the sanctuary. Also, most of her therapists speak Spanish, so the language barrier is not going to be a problem either."

Closing his eyes, Kian let out a breath. "Let me guess. You are suggesting that we bring them on board."

"I would have sent my jet to collect them, but there isn't enough room. Your big jet could have sufficed, but both of your pilots are here. We have plenty of room on the lower decks, and I'm sure some of the ladies will volunteer to take care of the women and provide solace until they can get professional help. Vanessa can provide them with a crash video call how-to session."

"I see that you have it all figured out."

"Yes, well, it's not like it requires a genius to arrive at the conclusion that this is the right thing to do. I also think that you should ask Amanda to organize a shopping trip in Acapulco to get new clothing and other necessities for the ladies. Jacki says that they need everything, and that Amanda will know what she means by that."

"Amanda is getting ready for her wedding tonight, but I'll ask Syssi and Alena."

"Yes, about that." Kalugal sounded apologetic. "We should push the celebration back by at least a couple of hours. Otherwise, there is no way we will get it all sorted out in time for the wedding."

"Good idea. I'll let Amanda and the kitchen staff know."

37

AMANDA

Amanda held up her empty margarita glass. "Onidu, another round, please."

Sari chuckled. "You should go easy on the alcohol, or you're going to show up drunk for your own wedding. *No bueno.*"

She was overdoing it a little, and if her mother was there she would not approve, but she wasn't, and until she came, Amanda was going to keep drinking.

"Look at you." Amanda grinned at Sari. "You are learning Spanish for our Mexico trip."

For some reason, Sari had never spent more than a day or two in Spain, and her visits to California had also been too brief to learn the language.

Her sister laughed. "That's the only phrase I know, and I've been using it for years. It has nothing to do with the cruise."

Syssi raised her glass, which was still mostly full. "*Hasta la vista,* baby." She snorted. "Turning immortal didn't make me any better at learning languages. That's about all I know in Spanish."

"I'm fluent," Amanda boasted.

"Of course, you are." Syssi affected a grimace. "You are good at everything."

Amanda snorted. "Except singing. The Fates decreed that this would be the one thing I suck at, which really rankles since my mother and sisters all have wonderful singing voices."

She was slightly tipsy but in a good way. It was still many hours until the wedding reception, and her fast immortal metabolism would ensure that she was completely sober by then.

The only thing casting a shadow on her jubilant mood was Dalhu's reluctance to have his own bachelor party with the guys. Knowing her brother though, Kian would not take no for an answer, but he hadn't called Dalhu yet, so maybe they were not ready, or maybe they were preparing something special.

Naturally, there would be no strippers or any other kind of debauchery that was common in human bachelor parties, but perhaps Anandur was planning on pulling a prank on Dalhu like he had done for Kian, and dressing as a stripper, complete with fishnet stockings and lipstick.

"What are you smiling about?" Syssi asked.

"Anandur dressing up as a stripper for Kian's bachelor party. I was thinking that maybe he was going to do that for Dalhu. My guy needs a good laugh to loosen up before the ceremony."

"A bottle of whiskey and a couple of cigars should do it," Sari said. "He'll be fine."

Amanda sighed dramatically. "Dalhu would prefer to stay with Evie in the other room and watch baby shows with her. It's sweet that he loves spending time with his daughter, but I just wish he'd show more enthusiasm about our wedding tonight instead of dreading everything about it."

"Not everything." Syssi smiled. "He doesn't like the idea of pledging his life to you in front of the entire clan, but I bet he would love it if it was just your mother and the two of you."

Alena nodded in agreement. "I have no doubt."

Amanda took the fresh margarita from Onidu. "Thank you, darling." She took a sip as she considered how to respond. "I know that, but I can't accommodate his wishes, and not just because I love big parties. I'm a public figure whether I like it or not, and my wedding celebration needs to be grand and shared with my entire clan. He knew that when he mated me."

"It's not like he had a choice," Sari pointed out. "The Fates chose to bring the two of you together."

Amanda grimaced. "That sounds as romantic as doing laundry." She snorted. "The only time I've actually laundered my own clothes was when Dalhu kidnapped me. We were in the cabin, and he bought me horrendous outfits that I wouldn't wear even to bed, so I tried to wash what I had on." She laughed. "That didn't end well."

"I bet," Sari scoffed over her margarita.

As the doorbell rang, Amanda lifted her tablet to see who was on the other side and was delighted to see that it was Kian.

It was so nice of him to come to collect Dalhu in person. That way, her mate could not decline the invitation.

Onidu opened the door and bowed. "Good afternoon, Master Kian. Please, come in."

"Thank you." Kian strode into the cabin's living room. "Hello, ladies."

Amanda rose to her feet. "If you've come to get Dalhu, you should have called first because he's not dressed yet." She kissed his cheek. "I'll let him know that you are here."

The look of regret in his eyes gave her pause. "What's going on, Kian?"

"Let's sit down." He walked over to where Syssi was sitting in an armchair and joined her. "I didn't come to take Dalhu to his bachelor party, which regrettably is not likely to happen. The group that went to visit the ruins at Tehuacalco decided to turn the tour into a rescue operation."

When Amanda took her seat again, Kian continued to explain what had happened, and the cheerful atmosphere they had been enjoying turned somber.

"Those women have been through hell," Kian said. "And they have nowhere to go. Kalugal convinced me to take them to the sanctuary, which means that they are coming here. I need help organizing cabins for them on one of the lower decks, getting them clothes and other necessities, and helping them get settled. Tonight's celebration has to be moved back by at least two hours."

"That's not a problem," Amanda rushed to say. "I don't mind waiting until almost midnight. I just need the ceremony to be done before that so Dalhu and I can welcome the new day as a married couple."

"I can do the shopping," Syssi offered.

Alena lifted her hand. "I'll help."

"So will I," Sari said. "We will bring our Odus with us to help carry everything back to the ship. How many women are there?"

"Twenty-three," Kian said. "Aged fourteen to twenty-two."

"Damn," Amanda cursed under her breath. "Fourteen?"

He nodded. "The monsters have been dealt with."

"Good. I'm glad. I hope our guys didn't show them mercy."

"They didn't." He smiled at her with a pair of elongated fangs. "They got up close and personal if you know what I mean."

"Oh, I do. Good for them."

Kian had been careful in his description of what had been done to the women's relatives and to them, but only as far as his choice of words. He hadn't omitted any of the atrocities they had committed, and if Amanda had fangs, she would have helped tear those monsters apart.

"Are they bringing the amulet on board?" Syssi asked.

Kian's eyes blazed with light as he turned to look at her. "Don't even think about touching that thing. It's evil."

"Is it?" She arched a brow. "Did Jacki or Kalugal say that?"

"They didn't need to. It was powered with the life force of countless victims."

Syssi shivered. "Yeah, you have a point. But it has just helped us save these women, so at least those lives weren't lost for nothing. It's not that I want to touch it, but maybe we should save it in case an emergency comes up, and we need a glimpse of the future."

"There is always one emergency or another, so using that logic, we would be using the damned thing all the time. Luckily, it belongs to Kalugal, so the only one who will be using it is Jacki."

Syssi frowned. "I'm sure he would let me borrow it if I asked."

"He probably would, but I don't want you to ask."

Syssi's expression turned stubborn. "We will see about that." She pushed out of the chair. "If we want to get stuff for the girls, we should get moving."

"I'm coming with you." Amanda started rising to her feet.

"No, you don't." Syssi put a hand on her arm and pushed her back down. "You need to rest and take it easy. Your sisters and I can handle a simple shopping trip."

38

DALHU

As the door to the bedroom opened, Dalhu looked up at his gorgeous mate. "Evie fell asleep."

"I can see that." Amanda smiled at the sight of their daughter curled on her side next to him on the bed. "Did she get bored with her shows?"

"Not really, but she got tired and couldn't keep her eyes open. It was funny to watch her trying to fight it."

Amanda sat on the bed next to Evie and caressed her small back. "We shouldn't let her watch that much television. It's not good for her."

"I know, but I ran out of ideas for keeping her entertained." He tilted his head and glanced at the door that she had left ajar. "What happened to your bachelorette party? I can't hear anyone in the living room."

"It's over." Amanda cast him a sad smile. "They all went shopping."

He gaped at her. "Without you? How dare they?"

"I know, right?" She sighed. "Something came up, and we have to move the wedding reception back by two hours."

"What happened?"

When she was done telling him, Dalhu shook his head. "Maybe this is an omen that we shouldn't get married. We're perfectly fine as we are. We don't need a ceremony to prove our commitment to each other."

She chuckled softly. "I love it that you are superstitious like some old grandma, but this is not a bad omen. The way I see it, it's a sign that what we are doing is right."

His mate was an expert on manipulating things to her advantage, but she rarely used that talent on him.

"I can't wait to hear how this is a sign of something good."

Amanda kicked off her shoes and lay on her side next to Evie. "We get to help others on our wedding day, which implies that our future together will be filled with good deeds, compassion, and love."

Dalhu looked into her warm eyes. "You actually believe that?"

"I'm convinced of it."

Her ability to find the upside in nearly every situation was just one of the many things he loved about her. "Then you must be right."

She arched a brow. "What? Not arguing with me and trying to convince me that our nuptials will bring the end of the world?"

"I've never said that." He reached for her cheek over their daughter's sleeping form. "I'm only uncomfortable about the ceremony and having to pledge myself to you in front of all these people who still judge me. If I survive that part, I know that everything else will be wonderful because you will make it so."

"That's so sweet." She leaned over their daughter and kissed his cheek. "Speaking of vows, are you done with them?"

He'd been struggling for weeks to come up with the right words, and he still wasn't sure that what he had ended up with would convey the enormity of what he felt for her.

"I am, but don't expect much. I'm not as eloquent as Orion."

"You don't have to be." She propped her elbow on the mattress and her chin on her fist. "All you need to say is that you will love me forever and stand by my side no matter what. I don't need any fancy words."

"Says the professor who has probably written the most beautiful and elaborate pledge ever made."

Her sheepish smile confirmed his suspicions. "I can tone it down if you want."

"No way. I want to hear every word of it and have it etched on my soul forever."

Amanda beamed at him, her eyes sparkling with emotion. She got off the bed, came to his side, and kissed his lips.

Wrapping his arms around her, he pulled her down on top of him. "I love you, and I will always stand by your side and have your back no matter what."

He smiled. "I just wanted to say that in case something else comes up and our wedding gets postponed again."

"I love you too, but it's not going to work." Touching her nose to his, she rubbed it Eskimo style, or rather what she had told him was Eskimo style.

Dalhu had no idea how northern people kissed and if it involved rubbing noses.

"What's not going to work?"

"You are not going to trick me into pledging myself to you right here, in our bedroom. If you want to hear my pledge, you will have to stand by my side at the altar and let my mother join us."

"Worth it." He wrapped his hand around the back of her neck and pulled her in for a kiss.

39

DAGOR

During the mad rush up to the meeting point, dust had been flying everywhere as Jin navigated the rough dirt roads, but after Bridget had patched Frankie and Luis up, she drove the rest of the way at a much slower pace.

When they reached the dock, two Guardians waited for them at the gangway with a gurney for Frankie, but since there was no room to maneuver in the truck, Dagor lifted her in his arms while Negal held up the IV bag to keep the transfusion going.

As he laid her down on the gurney, one of the Guardians started pushing it, but Dagor stopped him. "Thank you, but I'll take her."

"No, you won't." Bridget gave him a stern look. "Go to your cabin, wash the dirt off, and then come to the clinic."

"I'm not leaving her side."

"She's not in critical condition, but she is human, and I don't want any bacteria that might be clinging to your clothing or body to infect her. Scrub yourself clean, and then come to see her."

Dagor was shirtless because he had used his shirt to stem the blood flow, but the doctor was right about him being covered in dirt and blood.

He looked at Frankie, who was just as dirty as he was. The doctor had cut off her T-shirt, so the only thing covering her was Negal's shirt, leaving him bare chested as well, and his shirt was just as dirty as everything else they had on.

"What about Frankie? She's dirty too."

"The nurse is waiting for her, and she will clean her up."

He didn't know that they had a nurse on board, but he wasn't going to stand there asking questions and delay Frankie's arrival at the clinic.

"I'll be there in five minutes," he told the doctor and started sprinting for the elevator to the upper floors.

From his previous visit to the clinic, Dagor knew that the doctor would take Frankie in the service elevator to the lower deck where it was located. Otherwise, he would have taken the stairs to the top deck even though it would have taken him longer.

When he burst through the door, he was glad that Aru and Gabi weren't in the cabin and thanked the Fates for the small mercy.

He didn't have time to explain.

After a rushed but thorough shower, he threw on clean clothes and ran out of the place.

People jumped out of his way as he sprinted toward the elevator with his god-like speed, and as he stepped in, no one followed him inside.

Thankfully there was no one in the elevator, and as he pressed the button for the clinic level, he prayed that no one called it on the way.

Of course, the Fates couldn't be that merciful, and when the elevator stopped on the second deck, he lifted his hand to stop the people who wanted to come in and pressed the button to close the doors.

He should have taken the stairs.

Running ten floors down would have taken longer than the elevator ride, but not if the damn thing stopped on the way. Besides, it would have saved him the aggravation of having to deal with people when his nerves were frayed, and his patience was stretched to its limit.

When he burst through the clinic door, he was greeted by a female who appeared to be the nurse, even though she wasn't wearing the right apparel.

"Hi, Dagor." She smiled at him. "I'm Hildegard, and I was just about to wash Frankie. You can wait here if you wish."

"Can I be there while you do it? We are a couple, and I know she wouldn't mind me seeing her nude."

Hildegard hesitated momentarily, but the frazzled look in his eyes must have touched her heart because she nodded. "Bridget will have my head for this, but I'm sympathetic to what bonded mates go through when their partners are hurting."

"We are not bonded. I'm a god, and Frankie is human, but I care deeply for her regardless."

Smiling, Hildegard gave him a knowing look. "Right." She opened the door.

Frankie looked so pale and so small as she lay on the hospital bed. The wires connected to her body served to monitor her vitals, and there were tubes delivering essential fluids that were keeping her alive.

Dagor was grateful to Hildegard for letting him come in, for volunteering to work while on vacation, and for caring for Frankie with the tenderness of a mother.

Did Hildegard have children?

Was that why she was so gentle?

He watched the nurse cut off the rest of Frankie's clothing, clean her up with wash cloths, and remove all the dirt and grime accumulated during the mad rush to get her to the ship.

Frankie didn't look good despite the doctor's reassurances, and he had second thoughts about not giving her some of his blood. Aru's instructions were to not do it unless Frankie's life was in danger, but Dagor contemplated disregarding his commander.

Right now, his blood was the only thing that could help her heal faster, and the need to keep it a secret from everyone was not a good enough reason to deny her. He was a god, and these immortals were as susceptible to his thrall as humans.

He could give her the transfusion and keep the secret from getting out.

40

KIAN

Kian met Aru at the elevators. "Are you going to see Frankie?"

Aru nodded. "Are you?"

"Yes." Kian looked around to make sure that they were alone. "Do you know if Dagor did what you advised him to do?"

"He didn't. Negal said that the doctor stabilized the girl and assured them that she was going to make it." He looked over his shoulder at the group of immortals heading their way. "He also admitted that they were so busy watching the doctor and helping her that they forgot to take the thing that they needed for the mission."

Acknowledging that he understood with a slight nod, Kian turned to exchange a few pleasantries with his clan members.

With Syssi's coaching, he was getting better at that, but then, anything was an improvement over ignoring them or acknowledging them with a grunt. Thankfully, his people appreciated what he was doing for them and had been forgiving of his lack of social skills. But if he had been a human running for office, he would never have been elected.

"Does Frankie's friend know?" Aru asked.

"I asked Toven to hold off on her visiting Frankie until I spoke with Bridget and got an update about the girl's condition."

Aru arched a brow. "The doctor said that Frankie's condition was stable."

"That's doctor speak for she's not going to die right now."

"I see." The god pushed his hands into his pockets. "That's not very reassuring."

"No, it's not." Kian smiled as the last of their elevator companions departed on the main deck.

When the doors opened again on the clinic level, the two of them stepped out and strode side by side toward the clinic.

Bridget met them at the reception room, which was less than one-fourth of the waiting room in the village clinic, and that room wasn't big. Perhaps he should make some modifications and enlarge the size of it. After all, not everyone on board was immortal, and humans were prone to getting sick and injured.

Given that Bridget's hair was still wet, and she had no makeup on, the doctor had been in a rush to return to her patient, which again told him that Frankie wasn't in great condition.

"Hello, Bridget," Kian said. "How is the girl?"

She cast a quick look at Aru as if she wasn't sure he should be there, listening to her providing information that usually was reserved for the patient's family members, but she must have decided that he was okay.

"The bullet entered from the side, but since it was slowed down by going through Dagor first, it didn't do as much damage as it would have otherwise done. Still, Frankie's lost a lot of blood and experienced what we call hemorrhagic shock. I've given her IV fluids to help stabilize her blood pressure and replace the lost blood volume. The goal is to ensure adequate blood flow to her organs and prevent further complications. She's stable now, and we're monitoring her closely. The next twenty-four hours are critical, but I'm optimistic about her recovery."

Kian wondered whether the minuscule amount of godly blood that the bullet collected while passing through Dagor had any effect on Frankie's recovery. Perhaps that was why she had not been on death's doorstep when Bridget got to her. Her body might have already started fixing the damage.

"So, is she out of the woods or not?" he asked.

"As I said, I think she will recover, but I can't guarantee it. Frankie might have other underlying issues that she will have to address later, and they might interfere with her recovery."

"Well, it is what it is, right?" Kian darted a look at Aru. "It's a waiting game. What is certain is that Frankie won't be dancing at Amanda's wedding tonight, and I bet she will be upset about it when she wakes up."

His attempt at lightening the mood worked, with the doctor and Aru smiling.

"Can we see Frankie?" Aru asked.

"Dagor is with her, but I guess you can come in for a few minutes to offer your support. The guy looks like he was hit by a freight train. I would have offered him some anti-anxiety medication, but I don't know if it would work on a god." She looked at Aru.

"I can't give you an answer because I've never tried any. I know that people back home use all sorts of recreational drugs to entertain themselves and alleviate boredom, but I've never tried them, and neither have my teammates." He smiled. "It's not about the three of us being goodie-two-shoes, like humans like to say. It's that those drugs are very expensive, and none of us come from rich families."

Bridget chuckled. "It's similar here, but people still find ways to finance their bad habits."

Kian grimaced. "That's what feeds the cartels and other monsters around the world. They get rich by ruining people's lives or just snuffing them out to spread terror so no one dares to oppose them."

Aru put a hand on his shoulder. "There is no point in getting upset about things that you can't change. You are already doing everything you can to save as many victims as possible."

"That's rich coming from you—a member of the resistance. Would you have joined if your attitude was like that?"

Aru smiled, but there was no mirth in it. "I joined to do everything I can to change things for the better, and I'm doing my best. I try not to get upset about the slow pace, and I accept that things will probably get worse before they get better. It's not easy, but it's better than spending my life in a state of rage."

"Mizaru, Kikazaru, and Iwazaru," Bridget said. "These are the Japanese names for the three wise monkeys: see not, hear not, and speak not. The monkeys advise us not to dwell on evil thoughts because they are corrosive to our minds and bodies. In the West, the monkeys symbolize a lack of moral responsibility by people who refuse to acknowledge wrongdoing, look the other way, or feign ignorance, but that's not the original meaning of the proverb."

Kian shrugged. "I wish I could compartmentalize like that, and I applaud those who can, but I can't, especially not when I'm about to receive a group of traumatized women who have seen their families murdered in front of their eyes and then were violated by the monsters who did it."

41

DAGOR

As the doctor opened the door, Dagor was surprised to see Kian and Aru standing behind her.

"They would like to come in," Bridget said. "Is it okay?"

"If it's okay with you, it's okay with me."

She smiled. "Usually, I'm not so accommodating, but Frankie is not the only one who needs help."

He cast a worried glance at Kian. "Did anyone else get hurt?"

"Bridget meant you." Kian pushed a rolling stool into the room and sat down on it. "She's concerned about you."

Except for worrying for Frankie, Dagor was perfectly fine. Why would the doctor be concerned about him?

Aru walked in, holding another stool. "It must have been difficult for you. Negal told me that you shielded the girl with your body and were hit multiple times."

Dagor waved a hand in dismissal. "I've already forgotten about it. My body expelled the bullets and healed almost immediately."

"I'll leave you guys to talk in private." The doctor closed the door.

Aru put a hand on his shoulder. "It must have been terrifying to see the woman you care for bleeding and not knowing if she would make it."

Dagor wouldn't have admitted the fear voluntarily, but he wasn't about to deny it either. "It was difficult, and I'm still worried." He looked at Frankie's pale face. "She should have woken up by now."

"Maybe Bridget put a sedative in the IV," Kian said. "It might be better for Frankie to sleep for a few hours."

The doctor had admitted that the next twenty-four hours were critical, and Dagor had reconsidered using his blood to help Frankie recover, but the ramifications were not just a faster healing, and he didn't want to induce her transition without getting her consent first. He wanted to ask Aru and Kian to tell him more about it, but he wasn't sure that it was safe to do so in the clinic.

Kian was adamant about keeping the information about the healing properties of a god's blood a secret.

Glancing around the room, Dagor looked for hidden cameras or listening devices, but he knew better than to trust his eyes. The spy drones his team used were so small that even someone with his superior eyesight could miss them.

Supposedly, the ship had been commissioned by the clan, so Kian should know every security measure that was installed in every room.

"Is it safe to talk in here?" he asked.

The guy nodded. "There are no listening devices in here. The monitoring equipment is sending information to Bridget, but she can't hear what's being said in here."

Dagor released a relieved breath. "I didn't give Frankie the transfusion, but I think I should. I don't want to risk her taking a turn for the worse."

Kian shook his head. "It's no longer an emergency, and now that Bridget knows the precise extent of Frankie's injuries, she would know that some thing was up when Frankie healed too fast. I can't justify the exposure."

Dagor wanted to point out that it wasn't Kian's decision and that he had no say in what Dagor did with his blood, but he was well aware of the delicate diplomatic position they were in.

Antagonizing their host was a bad move.

He needed to convince him.

"I don't want to take any chances with Frankie's life. Aru or I can handle the doctor. We can thrall her and make her believe the wound wasn't as severe as she thought."

Kian shook his head. "Bridget is not stupid. Frankie's wound might mend completely, and that kind of miraculous healing of a human can't be explained away, which means it can't be thralled away either. The only way to do that would be to erase the entire incident from her mind and from the minds of everyone who was there and saw Frankie get shot."

Was it possible to perform such a massive mind wipe? Perhaps if Aru and

Negal joined the effort, the three of them could do that. Hell, they could even thrall Kian to forget that it was ever an issue.

But again, subterfuge wouldn't help them in the long run and might undermine all the work they had done so far.

As Dagor's gaze shifted back to Frankie, he was torn between his desperate need to ensure her safety and the potential consequences of his actions.

"Maybe we should look at this as an opportunity," Aru said. "Maybe we should tell the doctor the truth. Bridget is a trusted member of the council, and one of your top advisors. Is it really necessary to keep this secret from her?"

"It is." Kian's brows furrowed. "It's for her own protection. If she doesn't know, she can't be forced to reveal the information under torture." He shifted his gaze to Frankie, and his expression softened. "It's not that I don't empathize with you, Dagor. I do, and I wish my answer could be different, but revealing this secret to anyone is too risky."

"There are pros and cons," Aru said. "And personally, I believe that the pros outweigh the cons. I'm not advocating making this common knowledge, but in my opinion, your council members should know."

Kian shook his head again. "Once they know about it, they might tell their mates even if I have them vow to keep it to themselves. It's very difficult to keep secrets between bonded mates. I would have to have all of them compelled to silence."

"Then do it," Aru said. "Your mother is a powerful compeller, and so is Toven. Either of them could ensure that none of the council members would reveal the secret even under torture."

"You are forgetting the elephant in the room." Kian leveled his gaze at Dagor. "The transfusion might trigger Frankie's transition. I've spoken with Toven, and apparently, he gave Mia small transfusions for weeks before she started her transition, so perhaps her body needs to be fully healed first, and perhaps the venom is still a necessary component, but if I were you, I would still get her consent first."

Dagor arched a brow. "Even if she was dying?"

"Except that. But Frankie is stable, and she should be waking up soon. When she does, ask her."

Dagor nodded. "I will. What about the doctor?"

Kian sighed. "We will cross that bridge when we get to it. I need to discuss sharing the information with the council members with my mother and Toven."

42

FRANKIE

The smell was the first thing that clued Frankie in to where she was, and the second was the soft hum of equipment in the background with the occasional beep.

She still remembered those smells and sounds all too vividly from when Mia's heart had given out. She and Margo had spent too many days to count in the hospital, anxious and distraught as their best friend had fought for her life.

Frankie wished never to see the inside of a hospital again, but that was where she was now, and she'd better open her eyes and take a look.

Easier said than done.

Her eyelids fluttered open for a moment and then closed again, refusing her command. With a herculean effort she forced them to obey, and at first, everything seemed like one big blur to her until her vision managed to focus and piece together her surroundings. She was either in a private hospital room or back in the clinic aboard the Silver Swan.

"You're awake." Dagor's face filled her field of vision. "Thank the merciful Fates."

He looked haggard, his usual cocky confidence nowhere to be seen, his expressive blue eyes full of worry, even fear.

Frankie's throat felt dry as she tried to speak. "What's wrong? You look like someone has died."

"You almost did." Dagor clutched her hand. "You lost so much blood, and I was afraid the doctor wouldn't reach us in time."

She remembered the shooting and Dagor covering her with his body, and then there was pain and then nothing.

"I got shot."

"Yes."

"How? How did it manage to get to me?"

He swallowed. "The bullet went through my arm and into your side. Thankfully, it slowed it down enough so it didn't kill you, but it could have." He swallowed again. "I'm sorry. I did a shitty job of protecting you."

As the implications of what he had told her finally sank in, Frankie's eyes widened in horror. "Are you okay? I mean, your arm? Were you hit anywhere else?"

He'd been shielding her with his body, and if one stray bullet found its way to her, she could only imagine how many more he had stopped from hitting her.

He let out a short, humorless laugh. "I'm a god, remember? My body heals incredibly fast. It expelled the bullets and mended the flesh and skin. But you... you're human. I never want to go through that with you again for as long as I live, which is forever."

Forever.

What had he meant by that? Did he want her by his side for as long as he lived? Or was she reading him wrong, and all he meant was that he didn't want to experience seeing a human he cared about getting hurt?

The way he looked at her, his haunted expression, the slight tremor in his voice, it was so unlike him that it was jarring. The only thing that could explain his reaction was that he loved her, but he hadn't said so explicitly or implicitly.

She wanted to ask him if he did, but she was afraid he would give her an evasive answer and shatter her hope. The question lingered in her mind, but even though the answer shone in his eyes, she couldn't bring herself to voice it.

He would tell her when he was ready.

Perhaps if she closed her eyes and opened them again, the emotion in his gaze would be gone, but she was afraid to put it to the test, because first, she wasn't sure she would be able to open her eyes again, and second, she didn't want to lose what she saw in his expression.

Frankie's eyelids were so heavy, though, and keeping them from dropping down was as much of an effort as it had been lifting them in the first place.

She felt woozy, and there was a dull ache where she'd been shot, but she wasn't in any real pain, which meant that the doctor had pumped her full of painkillers, and she was thankful for that.

The downside was that staying awake was a struggle.

Dagor leaned closer to her, and his hold tightened on her hand. "I'm going to tell you something that's a big secret, and I need you not to freak out. Can you do that for me?"

He was so serious that she couldn't help but let her sass come out to play despite the shitty state she was in. Feebly squeezing his hand back, she mimicked his serious expression. "That's okay, Dagor. If you are pregnant, I will marry you and make an honest man out of you. We will raise the child together."

He frowned. "Are you delirious? Should I call the doctor?"

She rolled her eyes. "It was a joke. You looked so solemn, and usually when a girl tells a guy that she has big news and asks him not to freak out, the news is that she's pregnant."

He still looked like he didn't understand. "That's not what I was about to say. The big secret is not me being pregnant, although that could have been huge, but it's something that I can do to make you heal much faster."

"Oh, right. Your venom bite." She looked at all the wires and tubes connected to her body and grimaced. "I bet that I look as sexy as I feel, but if you can close your eyes and imagine how I am when not recovering from a gunshot, maybe you can get your fangs and venom going."

He let out an exasperated breath. "I wasn't referring to the venom. My blood can do for you even more than the venom can, and all it will take is a tiny transfusion."

"Really? What will it do?"

The way he looked at her made her heart race. "You'll heal faster, much faster than normal. Instead of weeks, you might be healed in hours, and there will be no scars left."

That got her attention. "Then what are you waiting for? Is it dangerous? Are there side effects?"

He winced. "Yeah, there might be. It might induce your transition. Kian thinks that it might not, because you need to be healthy to transition, but there is a chance that it will, and I didn't want to do it without your consent. I know that you haven't yet decided whether you want to become immortal, and there is also the issue of choosing someone to bond with after I leave."

His words were like a punch to her gut, and if she had the strength, she would have punched him in his too-perfect face for hurting her like that.

Instead, she did the next best thing and closed her eyes so she wouldn't have to look at him.

"I need you to be safe, Frankie," Dagor continued, his voice breaking slightly. "I can't lose you. I can't stand the thought of you being hurt or worse."

The anger that burst out of her burned through the wooziness and made her eyes fly open effortlessly. "You are so full of shit, Dagor."

43

DAGOR

That was the last thing Dagor expected Frankie to say.

He tilted his head. "Excuse me?"

"You heard me." Her eyes shot daggers at him. "How can you say that you can't lose me or see me hurt right after saying that you are leaving and that I might have to find an immortal to bond with? How can you be so disconnected from your feelings?"

Every word she said radiated hurt and frustration, and her voice, so full of anger and pain, cut through him.

There was a tightness in his chest that he struggled to understand.

Was it fear for her life and well-being? Or perhaps it was fear of losing Frankie, not because she died, Fates forbid, but because she didn't want anything to do with him.

Did he love her?

He'd called her his mate after she'd been shot, and he'd felt the rightness of the word when he said it, but he'd been under a lot of stress, and that might have sharpened his feelings for her. Now that the worst of it was behind them, he was no longer sure of that.

Frankie couldn't be his mate.

As lovely as she was, she was human, and gods couldn't bond with the lesser species. As the rebel gods had proven, they could love them, be with them, even have children with them, but not bond with them.

If Frankie was an immortal, there might have been a slight chance that they had bonded, but he was certain that it wasn't possible before she transitioned.

"Frankie, I..." he started, his voice trailing off. How could he explain the conflict raging within him? "It's not that I feel nothing. You know that I care for you. It's just that things are complicated, and we can't be together no matter what we want. That doesn't mean that I don't have feelings for you, I do, and I would be devastated if you died."

Frankie's eyes softened slightly, but her expression remained guarded. "Because of your duties? Because you are a god, and I'm a lowly human?"

Dagor sighed. "Yes, but there is nothing lowly about you." He would never tell her that the gods referred to humans as a lesser species. The polite term was created species, but everyone knew what it meant. "After this cruise, I'm bound for Tibet with Aru, and you have your own path to follow. You've been invited to join the immortal village, which is a big deal. You told me how much you were looking forward to working as a beta tester for the virtual reality studios."

"Where there is a will, there is a way," she whispered. "You just need to figure out your priorities."

Dagor felt a pang of pain at her words. He wanted to reach for her and pull her into his arms to comfort her, but she was hooked up to all those things that beeped, buzzed, and dripped.

"I'm not free to prioritize, Frankie. I follow orders, I do my duty, and—"

He couldn't finish his sentence, the words catching in his throat. It sounded cold even to his own ears, but Dagor had never allowed himself to feel this deeply for anyone, and he used his duty as armor to block anyone from getting inside his heart and to protect himself from reaching out to anyone as well. And yet, here he was, bleeding from the cuts Frankie had inflicted on his stupid heart with just a few words.

He cared for her, yes, but to admit to love, to a bond he had vowed never to form—that was a step he couldn't take. Not when their worlds were so vastly different, not when he knew there was no future for them together.

Frankie sighed and closed her eyes. "I'm too tired to try to pierce through your armor. I need to go back to sleep."

There was resignation in her voice that slashed another cut across his heart, and yet he couldn't bring himself to say the words that would chase away that sadness from her face.

"You didn't answer me about the transfusion. I need to know that you are okay with that in case your situation worsens, and I need to do it to save your life."

"If it looks like I'm dying, you have my permission to give me the transfusion." She didn't even bother to open her eyes.

"Can I also do it just to make you heal faster? You're not feeling pain now because the doctor put something in the IV bag to numb it, but without my intervention, the wound you suffered might bother you for the rest of your life."

"Not if I turn immortal." She cracked one eye open. "When I get to the village, the first thing I'm going to do is find a nice immortal male to bond with, and once I transition, all my blemishes will disappear. So, you see, you have nothing to worry about. You can leave for Tibet with a clear conscience."

44

FRANKIE

Frankie had never resorted to the underhanded tactic of making a guy jealous to get him interested.

She was awesome enough not to need silly tricks like that, but she was at her wits' end with Dagor. He was so stubbornly clinging to his rigid convictions and ignoring what was obvious to everyone else that she needed to shake him out of the mental cage he'd locked himself in. He needed to internalize what it would feel like when she chose someone else because he had left for Tibet.

When he said nothing, Frankie opened her eyes to look at him, and seeing the glow in his eyes and his elongated fangs, she felt a sense of profound satisfaction, but when he still remained silent, her temporary giddiness evaporated.

"What, nothing to say?" she taunted. "You can start with wishing me the best of luck on finding my perfect mate, or with just having a great life after you leave, or maybe even asking me to send you a picture of my firstborn. That's what a friend would do. Someone who cared about me."

The angrier Dagor became, the more alive Frankie felt. Maybe she didn't need his blood to heal faster after all. Maybe all she needed was to continue poking the dragon and to enjoy his squirming as he tried to deny his feelings for her.

Dagor pushed to his feet. "I'm going to look for a syringe in case you decide to accept my offer."

"Coward," she murmured under her breath. "Running away when things get uncomfortable."

He scowled at her. "I'm not a coward. I'm just pragmatic."

"Whatever you say." She let out a breath and turned her head away from him.

She would have loved to turn on her side, but with all the tubes and wires connected to her, it was too much of an effort.

As Dagor huffed out a breath and turned around, a part of Frankie felt guilty for pushing him, for making him confront his emotions and push the boundaries of his comfort zone. But the other part of her, the part that had gotten her in trouble countless times, felt exhilarated. She had managed to make a crack in his resolve, and that was satisfying, even if it amounted to nothing.

At least she had fought for them.

The little human had more guts than the god. Figure that one out.

As the door closed behind Dagor, Frankie let out a sigh, her gaze drifting to the cream-colored ceiling of the clinic. She was tired of the games, tired of the unspoken words and buried feelings. She had always been direct, always spoken her mind, and sometimes it had gotten her in trouble, but it never felt wrong. She was living authentically, truthfully, unswayed by the convictions and expectations of others.

She was a rebel and proud of it.

As a dull ache in her chest made breathing difficult, she closed her eyes and concentrated on drawing enough air into her lungs.

Perhaps it was the wound's fault or whatever was dripping into her veins from the IV line, but most likely it was her silly heart that was aching for Dagor and wishing he would wake up and tell her he loved her.

If he would just admit it, she would wait for him to be done with his expedition to Tibet, maybe even meet up with him from time to time if her new job allowed it and if she made enough money to afford the plane tickets.

Frankie had never had to chase after a guy before or manipulate him into chasing after her, and she wasn't going to do it now. She didn't regret showing him the consequences of his stubborn refusal to admit his feelings, but this was as far as she was willing to go.

If Dagor didn't get it, so be it.

She would get over him and find someone else.

Yeah, keep saying that to yourself until you actually believe it.

She would be no better than Dagor if she pretended that was an option.

Perhaps she was approaching the whole thing from the wrong angle?

Dagor doubted that she was a Dormant, which to be honest she doubted herself, and as long as he thought of her as a human, he couldn't envision a future with her.

It wasn't even a remote possibility.

But if she turned immortal, that would change everything. He could no longer hide behind the excuse of her short lifespan causing him tremendous heartache if he let himself love her.

Glancing at the medical equipment around her, Frankie felt oddly reassured by the steady hum and the beeping of the heart monitor. The dull pain in her side and the lethargy she felt was a reminder of her brush with death and her fragile state, but the machinery was a reassurance that she was in good hands and that she wasn't going to die from her injury.

So yeah, not having an ugly scar was a bonus that she would gladly accept, but that wouldn't be the main reason she would agree to Dagor's blood transfusion.

It wasn't just about healing faster or more completely. It was also about finding out if she belonged in the magical world of gods and immortals she'd been invited to by Mia and Toven.

The truth was that she was afraid to find out, and that made her as much of a coward as Dagor.

There was also the issue of her family, but just as she demanded of him that he make an effort to work things out for them, she should do no less. She had a couple of decades until her lack of aging became noticeable, and then she could use makeup and maybe even wear a padded suit to make herself look the age she was supposed to be. The extra effort was a small sacrifice to make in the name of love.

Did she love Dagor, though?

Or was it the classic response of a damsel in distress to her savior?

So yeah, he was gorgeous and a real god in bed, and he was fun to be with despite his dry humor and his obsessive interest in technology. But was it love?

As her thoughts were interrupted by the sound of the door opening, she turned her head, half expecting, half hoping it would be Dagor returning not just with the syringe but also with some newfound clarity or confession.

Instead, it was a woman she vaguely remembered seeing at Alena and Orion's wedding.

"Hi, Frankie." She smiled. "I'm Hildegard, your nurse. How are you feeling?"

She didn't look like a Hildegard. First of all, she wasn't blond, and secondly, she was way too young for an old name like that. But then, she might be centuries old.

"Nice to meet you, Nurse Hildegard. I feel as well as can be expected. What's my prognosis?"

"It's very good." The nurse went about checking her vitals. "You are young, strong, and you are healing. It will take time, and you will probably feel that wound for years to come, but you will live, and that's what's important."

"I won't feel the wound if I transition, right?"

The nurse lifted her eyes to her. "That's right. You will also have no scars left. The downside is that you can never get a tattoo or a piercing." She glanced at Frankie's ears. "The ones you have will close up, so you will have to switch to clip-ons."

"That's a small price to pay for immortality."

"Indeed."

"Do you think I will, though? I don't have any paranormal talents, and I'm as average as they come." She chuckled. "I just compensate for that with a lot of attitude."

The nurse looked at her with fond eyes. "I think that the Fates brought you here for a reason. They wouldn't have bothered if you had no chance of making some lonely immortal or god happy."

45

DAGOR

After leaving Frankie's room, Dagor scanned the small reception area for the medical supplies closet. When he couldn't find it, he stepped out of the clinic and strode down the hallway, searching for a door that was identified as a supply room. But with his attention turned inward and his mind churning with the accusations Frankie had hurled at him, he might have missed the place because he reached the end of the corridor and had to turn around.

Her words still echoed in his head. She'd called him a coward, and although he'd scoffed at the notion, her accusation stung.

He was many things, but he wasn't a coward.

Would a coward have joined the resistance?

Would a coward conspire against the might of the Eternal King?

Of course not. Only the brave or the foolish dared to do so.

Striding fast, he almost bumped into the nurse as she stepped out of one of the rooms. "Excuse me," he apologized. "I didn't see the door opening."

"That's okay." She smiled at him. "Were you looking for the restrooms?"

"Yes, I was," he lied easily. "None of these doors have signs on them."

She tilted her head. "You must have been preoccupied. The bathrooms are clearly marked, and you've just passed them."

Embarrassed, Dagor rubbed the back of his neck. "My head was somewhere else. Frankie is awake, by the way."

"I know. I'm going to see her now."

She patted his arm before heading down the hallway and opening the door to the clinic.

He waited a few seconds to make sure she wasn't coming back and ducked into the room she'd just left. Hopefully, there were no surveillance cameras inside.

The light turned on automatically, and Dagor found himself inside a supply room that held much more than just stuff for the clinic.

Shelves with janitorial supplies lined one wall, and towels and other housekeeping items lined the other. The medical supply cabinet was straight ahead at the back of the room.

The good news was that he could claim to have needed a new bottle of shampoo or soap, and that would provide him with plausible deniability. The bad news was that the cabinet was locked, and his burglary skills were lacking.

He could easily break it open, but that would defeat the objective of keeping the operation a secret.

The lock seemed simple, though, like the ones people put on their mailboxes that anyone with a thin blade could open, but he didn't have any tools on him and needed to improvise.

A quick scan of the room revealed a section of the shelving that was dedicated to cutlery, and he found what he needed there.

Fortunately, the lock was as simple as he had imagined, and as he gently turned the blade inside it, the door swung open.

Finding what he needed, he swiftly pocketed a package containing a syringe. The needle portion looked too big for the task, but it seemed to be the only kind they stocked. All the other packages looked exactly the same as the one he took.

On his way out, he stopped by the toiletries section and put two little shampoo containers in his other pocket and two small soap bars on top of the syringe packet.

Even if someone had seen him going in and came to investigate, he doubted they would frisk him or search his pockets. He would just show them the toiletries, and if they insisted on doing more, he would thrall them to forget about it.

After all, he was a god.

Stepping out into the hallway, Dagor glanced both ways to ensure no one had seen him and closed the door quietly behind him.

As he made his way back to Frankie's room, Dagor once again reflected on what she'd said to him. Was she right? Was he refusing to acknowledge his feelings and hiding behind his duty and his determination not to tie himself to a female who wasn't a goddess?

Shaking his head, Dagor tried to streamline his thoughts.

The problem with love was that it was impossible to quantify or measure it, or to determine its validity. Everything else about the big decisions he had taken throughout his life had been rational and straightforward, and he didn't have the necessary tools to deal with abstract notions and feelings that contradicted his own.

46

FRANKIE

The Fates wouldn't have bothered putting Frankie in Dagor's path if she had no chance of making him happy. That was what the nurse had implied, and her words had been playing on repeat in Frankie's head.

She was the only human onboard the ship who wasn't a confirmed Dormant, and from what she'd been told, Kian had made an exception for her and Margo only because Lisa, Geraldine's fake niece, had said that she felt they were Dormants.

The girl's ability wasn't confirmed, but her endorsement was better than its absence.

In either case, Frankie decided to let Dagor give her the infusion. At the very least, it would get her back on her feet faster and maybe eliminate the scar that she would otherwise have.

Not that it was such a big deal. A small scar under her ribs could be easily hidden with clothing, and even if she wore a bikini, she could just keep her arm over it. Still, if there was such a simple way to get rid of it, why not?

As the door opened and Dagor walked in, she welcomed him with a smile. "Success?"

"Yes." He patted his pocket as he walked over to her bed and leaned to kiss her forehead. "You seem to be feeling better." He brushed a lock of hair off her cheek.

"I am. Hildegard said I'm doing well; the wound is healing nicely, and my blood pressure is more than okay given how much blood I lost." She smiled. "I'm a healthy girl despite the fainting spells my first day here."

"Thank the merciful Fates." He sat on the stool next to her bed. "Have you given the transfusion some more thought?"

She nodded. "I want it."

"Do you accept the possible consequences?"

What was he doing? Was he trying to convince her not to do it now?

"I'm well aware of them. Are you having second thoughts?"

"Your life is no longer in danger, so it's not necessary, and the truth is that Kian wouldn't approve of me giving it to you under these conditions. He was only willing to allow it to save your life. Also, I will have to thrall you to forget that it ever happened. In fact, I should have done that before the nurse came to see you."

"I didn't tell her anything. You said it was a secret."

"She could have plucked it right out of your head. Luckily, the clan has rules about thralling humans for frivolous reasons, so she wouldn't have done that unless she was forced to do it to save someone's life or to keep the existence of immortals a secret."

Despite the gentle kiss he'd given her, Dagor sounded so cold and detached that Frankie was starting to have second thoughts about her decision.

Perhaps she'd been wrong, and what she'd interpreted as love was a worry for her life or guilt for failing to protect her as he had promised.

If he didn't love her, she didn't want him to be her inducer. She would do what everyone was expecting her to do and choose a nice immortal male who would be delighted to have her as his mate.

She deserved to be wanted, goddammit, to be desired and cherished, and she wouldn't settle for less.

"You know what? Forget it. I don't want to antagonize Kian. Although I don't understand what the difference is between this and being later induced in the village by an immortal who would fall head over heels in love with me." She batted her eyelashes at him. "I deserve nothing less."

"You are absolutely right." He took her hand and lifted it to his lips for a kiss. "You deserve to be cherished and adored. But the difference between giving you a transfusion of my blood and doing this the traditional way is that the blood is a big-time secret while the venom bite is not. If you miraculously heal, Bridget will know that something is up because you are in no state to get randy with me right now."

"So? You can just thrall her like you were planning to do to the nurse."

"What about everyone else on the ship? The rumor about your injury has spread all over by now."

"It has? Then where is Mia? Why hasn't she come to see me yet?"

"Toven is waiting to hear from Aru that it's okay. He didn't want her to see you while you were unconscious, and since I needed to discuss the transfusion with you, I didn't inform anyone other than the nurse that you were awake."

"Right." She let out a breath. "Well, since it's not really necessary and it will anger Kian and create a huge headache for you, I'd better not do it now."

In a way, it was a relief.

People thought that she was impulsive, but the only impulsive thing about her was her big mouth, which she didn't know when to shut. Other than that, Frankie was levelheaded and she didn't like to rush into things.

She'd known Dagor for such a short time. Even if he had been all for it, she shouldn't tie her life to his based on the little time they had spent together.

If she hadn't promised Dagor to be his for the duration of the cruise, she could've started scoping out the available immortal males as soon as she was up to it. But she'd promised, so it would have to wait until she got to the village, which was better anyway because she wouldn't have to rush.

She would have plenty of time to choose a mate and make sure that he was someone she could see herself spending her immortal life with.

47

DAGOR

Dagor's relief was mixed with a profound sense of loss that didn't make any sense. Frankie was right about refusing his offer, and he should feel relieved instead of disappointed.

"You're making a wise decision." He tried to sound unaffected and hide the turmoil he felt. "It doesn't make sense to rush into life-altering choices in the absence of a compelling reason."

He could feel a wall building between them, a barrier made of unspoken words and unacknowledged feelings, but he couldn't see a way around it.

Despite Frankie's naive belief that where there is a will, there is a way, not every challenge in life has a workaround. Sometimes, the price is either too high or too difficult to determine to justify moving in one way or another.

"There are plenty of compelling reasons," Frankie murmured. "I don't want to spend the rest of the cruise stuck in the clinic or in my cabin. I have nine more fancy dresses to wear to nine more weddings, and I want to have fun with you. None of that will be an option if I have to heal at a normal rate."

His heart skipped a beat.

Frankie still wanted to do it with him, not some immortal in the clan's village, and the only reason she had told him that she'd changed her mind was what he'd said about Kian disapproving of the procedure and how difficult it would be to hide her rapid recovery from everyone on the ship.

But what if they found a way to do that so no one would know?

The hope in Frankie's eyes as she looked at him added fuel to his determination to find a solution. It wasn't about turning her immortal because it probably wouldn't, but rather about making her whole again.

"I have an idea." He took her hand. "How good are your acting skills?"

She frowned. "What do you mean?"

"Once you no longer need to be hooked up to the IV, I can thrall Bridget into releasing you from the clinic into my care. I can convince her that I was trained as a medic and release her from the need to take care of you. She will have enough work with the women who are on their way here as we speak. I will give you the transfusion, which will most likely heal you in a matter of hours, but you will have to pretend to still be injured. You can't dance at the weddings, and you will need to affect a wince here and there, but at least you'll get to attend and wear your fancy dresses."

The smile that bloomed on Frankie's face was bright enough to melt his heart. "I can do that. I will also hold my side and limp a little." Her smile turned sultry. "But when we are alone, I won't have to pretend, and we can dance as much as we want."

Dagor chuckled. "Are you sure that we are talking about dancing?"

"Among other things. After all, if the transfusion is not enough to induce my transition, we will need to do it the old-fashioned way."

The room seemed to spin as he processed her words. "I thought that you wanted to wait until you got to the village?"

"I changed my mind again. I want you to do it."

"Why? Don't you want to find a mate among the immortals?" The words tasted like dirt in his mouth, but he needed to say them.

Frankie needed to enter this with a clear head.

It suddenly occurred to him that her indecision, which was not typical of her, might be the result of drugs that the doctor had put into the drip bag. He didn't know much about that, but he'd read that opioids used for numbing pain could have undesirable side effects and even become addictive.

How could Frankie give him her informed consent when she was in a compromised state?

And why hadn't Kian thought of that when he suggested Dagor should wait for her to wake up and then ask her?

Pulling her hand out of his, Frankie sighed. "You are even worse than me. One moment, you are trying to persuade me to accept your transfusion, and the next, you are trying to dissuade me. Make up your mind."

He groaned. "I'm sorry, but it has just occurred to me that you might be under the influence of drugs and that you are not in the proper state of mind to give your consent."

"Don't be ridiculous. My mind is perfectly clear, and I know precisely what I want."

"It doesn't look like that from where I'm sitting."

She glared at him. "So maybe you should change seats."

"Or maybe you need to convince me that you are not compromised."

48

FRANKIE

Frankie had never been so close to slapping someone across the face as she was now.

Good thing that she didn't have the energy to lift her hand to do so or Dagor would have been the first person she'd ever assaulted.

He was so infuriating. Not only was he obtuse and disconnected from his feelings, he couldn't make up his mind about a single thing.

Instead of harming him physically, not that a slap from her would have hurt anything other than his overinflated ego, she just glared at him. "You want me to convince you that my mind is clear?"

"Yes, please."

"How very polite and considerate of you."

"Is that sarcasm?"

"Brilliant observation, my dear Watson."

He frowned. "That's not my name. Are you sure you are thinking clearly?"

"Ugh, you are insufferable. Watson is a fictional character from a famous detective series. The detective is the very astute Sherlock Holmes, and Dr. Watson is his assistant."

"Oh, okay. I get it now. I've heard of that detective. British, right?"

As if that had anything to do with anything. "Yes. He is. Or was. I don't remember the name of the author, but he was British."

Dagor nodded. "I'm still waiting for you to convince me that you are not affected by drugs and that your judgment is sound."

Frankie huffed out a breath. "My judgment is probably not sound, but it has nothing to do with me being under the influence of drugs or not. For some unexplainable reason, I want you despite how annoying and hard-headed you are, and it has nothing to do with you being a damn god, so don't you dare say that." She pointed a finger at him.

"I'm not saying anything."

"Good. So here is what I've been thinking. It made sense only minutes ago, but I'm no longer sure. So, I know that you don't want to get attached to me because I'm human, and I'm not going to live long even if I die from old age. But if I was immortal, that objection would be out, and the only one that would remain would be me not being a god like you, but that's just snobbish on your part, and I figured it wouldn't be too difficult to beat it out of you."

He shook his head. "It's not about snobbishness. I don't care whether you are a pureblooded goddess or a hybrid half-human, or even ninety-nine percent human and one percent goddess, as long as it makes you immortal. What I care about is that if I bond with you, I would never be able to go home. Hybrids are considered an abomination on Anumati, which means that I can't take you with me, and I can never introduce you to my family or live near them. My parents' greatest wish is to see their son bring home a mate and perhaps one day bless them with a grandchild. It's the greatest wish of any parent in my home world, and it's my duty as a son to do my best to give them that."

Frankie swallowed.

As much as she would have loved to poke holes in his reasoning, she couldn't because she knew precisely what he was talking about. One of her biggest objections to becoming immortal was her family and how she could manage to be with them while keeping her immortality a secret. She hadn't even thought about the complications of bringing her mate to meet her parents, her brothers, her cousins, and aunts and uncles. Would she be willing to give all of that up for a guy?

For Dagor?

She'd only known him for such a short time. There was no way she would give up her entire world for him.

Or was there?

Her gut was whispering quite loudly that she would because he was the one for her, and he was worth it, but her mind didn't agree.

Given that her heart always spoke louder than her mind, she might have followed her heart's advice, but Dagor was much too cerebral for that.

His mind was in the driver's seat, and he was putting up a ferocious fight with his heart, which she had a strong feeling was whispering the same things to him as her gut was whispering to her.

With a sigh, she reached for his hand and clasped it. "It seems to me that the one who needs more time to decide is you, not me. I love my family, too. They are very important to me, so I understand why this is difficult for you and why you cannot commit to me yet. But you will. It's only a matter of time."

49

DAGOR

Frankie's certainty that he would commit to her in the end was both unsettling and comforting. The notion that she believed so firmly in a future for them was both a balm to his conflicted heart and a challenge to the barriers he had meticulously constructed around it.

She wasn't wrong.

He knew in his gut that she was right, but his mind was still refusing to cooperate. He had too much to lose. But he also had so much to gain.

To have someone else grapple with the enormity of the choices he had been wrestling with in the silence of his own mind was a novelty.

Aru and Negal knew his preference for a traditional mating that would meet with his parents' approval, but they had no idea how close he'd come to giving it all up to be with Frankie.

Hell, he hadn't even admitted that to himself.

"Are you okay?" She smiled. The warmth from her hand clasping his was spreading through his body and bridging the chasm of differences and uncertainties between them. "You look a little shell-shocked."

"I am." He smiled back. "You are very confident. I like that."

"Do you still think that I'm under the influence of drugs and not thinking clearly?"

He shook his head. "You have more clarity than I do."

He was still acutely aware of the complexities of their situation and the expectations and responsibilities placed on him. Choosing Frankie would entail a price he wasn't sure he would be allowed to pay, but he was starting to believe that if the choice was left to him, he would choose to pay it because it was worth it.

Gazing into her warm eyes, he saw something he had never dreamt of having—the love of a mate. But the hope filling his chest was thwarted by fear.

"I'm glad that you understand. It means a lot to me, and it also lessens the guilt I feel. But it's not just about me and my decisions. You and I are pulled in different directions, and I don't see a solution for that."

Dagor refrained from saying that choosing her might mean losing everything he had ever known to be true about himself for a woman he had just met. He needed space, he needed to think, and he felt like he had his back up against the wall.

It was suffocating.

Frankie's grip on his hand tightened slightly. "The only thing you need to decide on right now is allowing yourself to feel. All I'm asking is for you to open your heart to me and let me in. What happens next happens. You don't need to feel obligated to me just because I want you to induce my transition. This is my way of giving us a chance. We still might say goodbye to each other at the end of the cruise, but at least we will get to enjoy what's left of our time together. And if what we have does deepen, we will figure out how to proceed from there." She smiled hesitantly. "I don't have to become a beta tester for Perfect Match. I can accompany you on your quest to Tibet."

He snorted. "I can't imagine you camping out in the wild and wearing the same clothes for days on end."

Frankie pouted. "What kind of woman would I be if I demanded you make all the sacrifices? I'm willing to suffer some discomfort to give us more time together. After all, great things require great sacrifices. Besides, you and I sleeping in a small tent doesn't seem so bad. We will keep each other warm."

He arched a brow. "With Aru and Gabi in the tent right next to ours and Negal on the other side?"

"Aru and Gabi will be busy with each other, and Negal will have to put on earphones and blast loud music."

"You have it all figured out, don't you?"

She laughed and immediately winced. "Don't make me laugh. It hurts."

"I don't understand what's funny."

"I don't have anything figured out. I'm making it up as I go along."

"You're very good at it."

"I know." She smirked.

Her logic was hard to argue with, and it had done a better job of crashing against the shores of his rational mind and eroding the barriers he had so carefully built than her previous appeal to his emotions. She had given him a glimmer of something that had been absent in his life for a long time—a thrill of the unknown and the allure of a path less traveled.

"So, what's our next step, lady strategist? Do I administer the transfusion now, or do I get Bridget to release you to my care first?"

"Do it now, and then call her and convince her to release me before the women arrive so she will have room in the clinic. I will not heal as fast as you do, but if I'm a little better when Bridget comes to check on me, you might not even need to thrall her to convince her. After that, she will be so busy with those poor women that she will forget all about me."

"How did you get to be so smart?"

She rolled her eyes playfully. "I was born that way. Now get that syringe out and do it before Hildegard decides to check up on me again."

"Yes, ma'am." Dagor's hand trembled as he reached into his pocket.

He had no idea what he was doing.

"Can you do it?" he asked. "I've never held a syringe in my hand, and I don't want to hurt you."

"I know what to do. Give it to me," she commanded.

"All you need is this much." He showed her the tip of his little finger.

Frankie nodded. "Got it."

50

KIAN

Kian stood to the side of the gangway and scanned the group of women being carefully guided inside.

They were in a semi-thrall, their expressions calm and unquestioning while they were gently herded along. Walking beside them, Yamanu shrouded their arrival from the Mexican authorities guarding the port.

Kian regretted that Syssi wasn't there. She hadn't returned from the shopping mission that she, Alena, Sari, and several of the other females had embarked on to supply the victims with fresh clothing and other items.

Kri was there, though, spreading her calming influence and aiding the thrall that Kalugal had cast over the women.

With plenty of experience dealing with similar situations, Kri navigated the role she'd taken upon herself with practiced ease. She'd talked with the human staff serving on the ship and assembled a group of older females to help the women once Kalugal released them from his thrall.

There was a limit to how long it was safe to keep their minds floating on whatever fantasy he was feeding them, and Kian didn't want to be there when they woke up.

First of all, after what had been done to them, they would be terrified of any male in their vicinity, and secondly, he didn't have what it took to handle their pain.

He knew how to lead and how to kill, and if the monsters who had done that to these poor women weren't dead already, he would have killed them, but he was not good at offering comfort, and the rage bubbling inside of him had no outlet.

Hell, he doubted that even Syssi could have handled the enormity of what these women had been through. She was too soft, too empathic, and seeing them would have slain her.

If he could keep her away from them, he would.

The human ladies were doing great, though. With their kind faces and soft murmurs, they were a soothing presence. They didn't speak Spanish, but their gentle demeanor transcended language barriers.

As they took the elevators to the lower level where they were to be housed, he took the stairs and got there just as they exited.

He watched as Kri and the older ladies escorted them to the cabins, putting two in each, not because they lacked available rooms but because they needed each other's company for support.

Kalugal walked up to him with an uncharacteristically somber expression on his face. "You didn't have to come."

"I did."

"Your eyes are glowing, and your fangs are elongated. Luckily, none of them saw you because of my thrall."

"When are you going to release them?" Kian asked.

"I'm waiting until the last of them is in her cabin, and then I'm going to ease them into reality."

It was an impressive ability to keep up the thrall while conducting a conversation. "How are you doing that and talking to me at the same time?"

"I'm using a very simple thrall and running it on repeat. A placid lake surrounded by green meadows with chirping birds and beautiful butterflies. I can do this in my sleep."

"In that case, what did you do about the drivers?"

"Well, I had them under compulsion to stay in the vehicles and ignore what was going on as we took care of the cartel thugs. Once we got everyone to the dockside, I looked inside their minds to make sure that there was nothing there that shouldn't be and thralled away whatever memories they managed to retain despite the compulsion to ignore what we were doing."

"Good. Now, tell me more about the amulet."

Kalugal grimaced. "I've never believed in dark magic, but that thing proved me wrong. There is true evil in this world, and it has nothing to do with our esteemed parents, the gods."

"There must be some other explanation."

Kalugal quirked a brow. "You believe in Mey's ability to hear echoes of past events in the walls, and you believe in Jin's ability to attach a tether of her consciousness to people. Why is it such a stretch for you to believe that an object could be powered by the life force of human sacrifices?"

"Good point. Can I see it?"

"You'll have to ask Jacki because it belongs to her. At first, the plan was to toss it into the ocean once the mission was completed, but Jacki changed her mind. She wants to keep it for emergencies."

"What kind of emergencies?"

"When we need answers we can't get any other way, and we need to either induce a vision or make it clearer. It seems that the amulet magnifies prophetic visions. It's possible that its power was depleted to fuel the one vision that Jacki had, but it's also possible that it can fuel more until it runs out of juice."

"We don't need the damn amulet for that. We have Mia."

He wondered how it hadn't occurred to him before to suggest that. Syssi could ask Mia to be next to her when she courted a vision, and Mia's enhancing power could provide her with the same boost that the amulet had given Jacki, but without the evil taint.

"Right." Kalugal nodded. "Why haven't we used her in that capacity before?"

"I don't want Syssi to chase visions, so naturally, I didn't think of ways to make it easier for her. But she found her own methods. Evidently, our daughter's presence has a similar effect on her as Mia's presence has on other talents."

"Allegra must be a seer," Kalugal said.

That was a given, but it didn't make Kian happy. He wanted his daughter to have a good life and not to struggle with visions of doom like her mother. "I hope Allegra chooses to be a musician or a painter and lets her natural paranormal ability remain dormant. I want her to be passionate about something that doesn't involve darkness and pain."

51

FRANKIE

"How are you feeling?' Dagor asked for the umpteenth time.

He'd given Frankie the transfusion about half an hour ago, but he had also snuck in a cup of coffee for her, so she wasn't sure whether her improved vitality was the result of his godly blood or the elixir of the gods, which coffee must be.

"I feel just as well as I did when you asked me five minutes ago."

He looked disappointed. "Perhaps try to move a little and see whether it hurts?"

She could do that, but it would have been better if Dagor had just peeled back the bandage and taken a look. She'd suggested that, but when he turned a shade of green, it was obvious that he didn't have the stomach for it.

And to think that the guy was a soldier, or a trooper as he called himself. Was there a difference? She planned to look it up when she had a chance...

"Oh, damn. Do you know what happened to my phone?"

He frowned. "I don't know. Bridget cut off your clothes, and I covered you with Negal's shirt because mine was saturated with blood. I don't know what she did with them."

"Ugh." Frankie slapped a hand over her face. "Margo might have called and gotten frantic when she couldn't get me. Or my mom or my cousins. I need that phone."

"I can ask the nurse." He pushed to his feet.

"If Bridget was the one who cut off my clothes, she's the one you should ask."

"She's busy with the women we rescued from the cartel. I don't think she will be available anytime soon."

"Can you at least call Mia for me? If Margo couldn't get ahold of me, she would have called Mia, and the same goes for my family."

"I can do that." He sat back down. "Do you also want me to tell her that she can come visit you?"

"Yes, please." Frankie smiled. "Do I really need to pretend that I'm half dead when she comes?"

The green hue returned to his pale face. "Please don't say things like that. Just dial back on your energy level."

Everyone who knew her was accustomed to her exuberance. If she pretended to be subdued, they would assume that she must be half dead.

"I'll try." Frankie let out a breath. "Or I can blame the contraband coffee."

"Please, don't. If Bridget finds out, she might kick me out. By the way, do you happen to remember Mia's number? It's not in my contacts."

"I don't. Who remembers numbers these days?"

"Right." He smiled. "I'll text Aru and ask him to get it for me."

"Good thinking."

As Dagor typed a message to his boss, the door opened and Hildegard walked in. "How is my favorite patient doing?"

"I'm your only patient, and I'm feeling fine, thank you."

"That's good to hear." The nurse walked over to her bed and checked the readouts. "Your blood pressure is back to normal all of a sudden. It might be a malfunction of the automatic monitor."

The thing started on its own in half-hour intervals, and every time it did, Frankie felt as if it was cutting off her circulation and her arm was going numb.

The nurse pulled out an old-fashioned blood pressure cuff from her coat pocket and wrapped it around Frankie's other arm.

Thankfully, she was much gentler with it than the automatic cuff had been, and after measuring Frankie's blood pressure twice, she shook her head. "It must be your youth." She put the cuff away. "I'm going to replace the blood transfusion with just liquids."

"Can you take everything out?" Frankie asked. "I can drink now on my own, so I don't need an infusion of liquids, and if you take out the thing down below, I can probably get to the bathroom with Dagor's help."

Hildegard looked conflicted. "That's something for the doctor to decide."

"I know. But she's busy, right?" Frankie cast the nurse her most charming smile. "The sooner I can get out of here, the sooner she can treat other patients that might need this bed."

"True. I'll stop the transfusion and call her." As the nurse went about removing the needle from Frankie's hand, she cast a glance at Dagor. "Can you give us a few moments, please? You can wait in the front room until I call you."

He didn't look happy about it, but Hildegard's tone didn't leave room for argument.

Nodding, he pushed to his feet and walked to the door. "I'm right here. I'm not going anywhere."

Frankie smiled at him. "While you are there, can you get me more of that wonderful elixir?"

"I'll see what I can do about a cup of water for you."

When the door closed behind him, Hildegard chuckled. "Don't think that I don't know about the coffee."

Frankie feigned innocence. "I don't know what you're talking about."

"Right." The nurse put away her equipment. "The most common reaction to transfusion is mild itching or hives. That's an allergic reaction and can be treated with antihistamine." She folded the sheet up to expose Frankie's lower half and gently removed the catheter. "The other potential side effects might be a fever in the first twenty-four hours following the transfusion. You might also experience some dizziness, a bit of nausea, headache, chills, or a general feeling of discomfort. These are normal reactions, and you can take Tylenol to ease the symptoms. But if you are experiencing anything more serious than that, you need to let us know."

"Got it." Frankie let out a breath when Hildegard covered her with the sheet.

The nurse put the blanket over the sheet. "Are you warm enough? Do you want me to get you another blanket?"

"That would be nice, thank you."

When the door opened, Frankie expected it to be Dagor and wondered why he hadn't waited for the nurse to tell him that it was okay. It wasn't like he hadn't seen everything Frankie had to offer up close and personal, but that wasn't the point.

Except, instead of Dagor, a woman entered. "Hi, Frankie. Sorry to interrupt, but I'm here to replace Hildegard. I'm your new nurse, Gertrude."

"Hi." Frankie forced a smile.

She liked Hildegard, and she wasn't happy about having a new nurse.

"What's going on?" Hildegard asked. "No one told me anything."

Gertrude winced. "The women are here, and Bridget needs your help with them."

"I see."

"I've already packed the supplies she requested. They are on the desk in the reception area."

"Thanks." Hildegard cast a smile at Frankie. "I'll ask Bridget if it's okay to release you when I see her."

Frankie nodded. "Thank you. You were very kind to me."

"It was my pleasure. Gertrude will take care of you now. You're in good hands."

"I have no doubt. Can Dagor come back in now?"

Hildegard nodded. "If he's done hunting for the elixir." She winked before going out the door.

Gertrude arched a brow. "What elixir is she talking about?"

"Just water." Frankie smiled sweetly. "The elixir of life."

52

DAGOR

"You can go in now," Hildegard told Dagor while lifting the package the other nurse had prepared for her.

"Thank you. Is there anything I should be aware of? Anything to look out for?" He cradled the coffee cup he'd gotten for Frankie, pretending it was his.

"I told Frankie what the possible side effects are, and they are mostly mild. But she's not going anywhere yet. Gertrude will keep an eye on her, and if Bridget approves her release, which I doubt, Gertrude or I will come to check on her from time to time, so you don't have to worry about it."

He didn't want them coming to check on Frankie. "I'm sure the two of you will have your hands full with those poor women. I can keep an eye on Frankie, and if I think that she needs to be looked at, I'll either bring her here or ask you to come see her at her cabin."

The nurse regarded him with a critical eye. "Are you going to be with her twenty-four-seven?"

"Absolutely. I will not leave her side."

She tilted her head. "What if your boss calls a meeting?"

"I'll either bring Frankie with me or tell him that he has to hold the meeting in her cabin."

That seemed to meet with Hildegard's approval, and she nodded. "Good. I'll let Bridget know."

After she left, he let out a breath and knocked on the door before opening it and walking in.

"I was just leaving." The new nurse straightened the blanket over Frankie. "If you need me, I will be in the front room."

"Can I ask you a question, Nurse Gertrude?" Dagor put the coffee cup on the side table.

"Just Gertrude, and sure. What do you want to know?"

"Why did Hildegard leave to help the doctor, and you took her place here instead of just going down to assist Bridget?"

She grimaced. "Hildi is better suited for that kind of work, while I'm better at monitoring patients."

There was a story there, but he felt like the nurse didn't want to talk about it, and he didn't want to press. "Frankie's friend Mia is on her way. I hope that's okay."

"Of course." The smile returned to Gertrude's face. "I'll let her in as soon as she arrives. Will Toven accompany her?"

"I don't know," Dagor said. "Can he come in as well?"

"If it's okay with Frankie, it's okay with me."

"It is," Frankie said.

After the door closed behind the nurse, Dagor handed her the coffee cup. "Here is your elixir, my lady."

"Thank you, my brave knight. Did you have to fight a dragon for it?"

He laughed. "If Hildegard was a dragon, then yes. I pretended that it was mine, but she saw right through me."

Frankie took a sip and rolled her eyes. "I can't believe that crappy instant coffee tastes so good when there is nothing else."

"All the sugar and creamer I put in it masks the taste." He sat on the uncomfortable little stool and rolled it closer to the bed. "Mia said that Margo didn't call her, and neither did your parents or any of your cousins."

She frowned. "That's disappointing. It's good because they're not worried about me, but why the hell not? Shouldn't they check on me?"

He put his hand on her thigh. "It feels like a lot of time has passed since you spoke to them last, but it was only yesterday. They have no reason to worry about you."

"Right." She sipped her coffee. "I really feel better now. Like a lot better. It's amazing what a difference a tiny amount of your blood can do. What's in it? Do you have nano-healing or something?"

"It's part of my genetics. I'm not a geneticist, so I can't tell you what exactly it does and how. The truth is that I didn't even know my blood could heal you.

Aru told me, and the reason that he knew was that his sister studied to be a healer for the lesser species."

Frankie's forehead creased in a deep frown. "Lesser species? Is that what they call us?"

Oh damn. He shouldn't have said that. "Created species is a better term, but many still use lesser. I'm sorry. I shouldn't have said that, and I don't even believe it. I'm a member of the resistance."

"What kind of a resistance?"

He'd forgotten that Frankie wasn't privy to all that the clan had learned about him and his teammates, and he hadn't told her much about himself other than the basics. They really needed to have a long talk about who he was and what his goals and aspirations had been before he'd been told that Earth was it for him for the next thousand years or so, or maybe even forever.

53

ARU

"You look stunning." Aru rubbed a hand over his face, commanding his fangs to behave. "That dress is even more beautiful than the one you wore for Alena and Orion's wedding."

Gabi beamed at him. "Thank you. What do you think of the sandals?" She lifted one foot to clear the full-length skirt of the gown.

"Very pretty. But will you be able to walk in them?"

She chuckled. "Walk, yes. Dance, I'm not sure. You might have to hold me tight."

His fangs vibrated in his mouth. "I can do that."

Sauntering up to him, she cupped his cheeks and planted a soft kiss on his lips. "Hold that thought, lover god. Karen is waiting for me to come over so she can do my hair. Cheryl is in charge of makeup, which is a little scary, but if I don't like what she does to my face, I will just wash it off and do it myself."

He frowned. "Isn't she too young to wear makeup?"

"She's sixteen, and Karen allows her to put on only a little, but she watches lots of tutorials about it on InstaTock and is supposedly an expert."

"I need to check that platform out."

"Don't." She waved a dismissive hand. "It's mostly nonsense posted by misguided teenagers and influencers pushing products that they are paid to advertise. The makeup tutorials are probably the only ones worth watching."

Are you alone? Aria's voice sounded in Aru's head.

Give me five minutes, he sent over their telepathic connection.

"Aru?" Gabi waved a hand in front of his eyes. "Where did you go just now?"

He shook his head. "I was just thinking that Dalhu is probably not going to get the bachelor party that was planned for him, which is a shame. I was looking forward to one of Kian's superb cigars and a few shots of equally excellent whiskey."

It wasn't a lie per se because everything he'd said was true, except for what had really been the cause of his momentary distraction.

Gabi pursed her lips. "There is still plenty of time, and Dalhu doesn't seem like the sort of guy who will fuss about his appearance."

"It's not so much about the lack of time as it is about the lack of motivation. Everyone is in a bad mood, and it seems wrong to celebrate when we have the victims of a horrific tragedy on board."

Visibly deflated, Gabi nodded. "I know. I'm trying not to think about it." She sighed. "On the one hand, I'm thinking that by allowing it to crush my spirits I'm letting the monsters win, but on the other hand I feel like a weakling who can't handle that much suffering and shuts her mind to it."

Walking up to Gabi, Aru pulled her into his arms. "Cling to the first part because it's the right approach. We can't let evil win by demoralizing us, but we cannot turn a blind eye to it either. We all need to do our part to eradicate evil, even if it's just by pushing against the darkness to celebrate a joyful occasion."

"You are right." Gabi took a fortifying breath, squared her shoulders, and plastered a smile on her face. "I'm going to have fun with my sisters-in-law and my nieces even if I need to drink myself silly to enjoy my time with them."

"That's the spirit." He kissed her forehead. "Just don't drink too much."

Smirking, she pushed out of his arms. "I'm immortal now, and it takes a lot of alcohol to get me drunk. I also burn through it in no time." She patted his shoulder. "Call the guys and try to organize a bachelor party for Dalhu. It's not fair to deprive him of the one time in his life that's all about him."

"I'm not a close friend of his, and it's not my place to organize anything, but I can send Kian a text and ask him if it's still happening. It will serve as a nudge in the right direction."

"You're such a diplomat, my love. I don't know why you were relegated to a simple reconnaissance mission on Earth instead of getting promoted to something more, but their loss is my gain."

It pained him that he couldn't tell her how important his mission really was and who he was reporting to. The search for the Kra-ell settlers and the missing pods was just a cover for his real mission on Earth.

So far, he hadn't had great success with the former, but his success with the latter exceeded everyone's wildest expectations.

54

FRANKIE

"Frankie!" Mia rolled into her room with such speed that Frankie feared she would crash into the hospital bed, but she stopped by pivoting the wheelchair at the last moment and aligning it with the bed.

Dagor had jumped out of the way just in time, but he shouldn't have been worried. Mia's chair hadn't even touched him.

Frankie chuckled. "You can be the first getaway wheelchair driver."

"How are you doing?" Mia reached for her hand. "And don't you dare say fine."

"But I do feel fine. Bridget's taken great care of me. She patched me up and gave me some blood to replenish what I'd lost, and I'm on the mend. You have nothing to worry about, at least not about me."

Frankie wasn't doing a great job of pretending to be worse than she was, but what choice did she have? Mia was accusing her of doing the exact opposite.

"But I do worry." Mia gave her hand a gentle squeeze. "I worry about all the dresses that you are not going to wear for all those weddings that you were hoping to dance at."

That was indeed a pity. If not for Dagor's blood, she definitely wouldn't have been able to dance at those weddings, so there was no way she could do that without arousing suspicion. She would have to dance with him in the privacy of her cabin suite, and when Margo joined them, she would be even more restricted.

Eh, who cared.

She was alive, and she owed her life to Dagor who had taken the barrage of bullets for her. And now she was getting back on her feet much faster thanks to his blood transfusion. She should be grateful, and she was.

"It's okay." Frankie squeezed Mia's hand back. "Thanks to Dagor, I will get to dance at many more weddings, just not on this cruise."

Mia turned to him. "Thank you for saving my bestie. I heard that you took bullets for her."

"Of course, I did. I'm practically indestructible."

When Mia pressed her lips together in that stubborn way of hers, Frankie braced for a lecture.

"You should have let Dagor induce you instead of waiting until you got to the village."

"It wouldn't have happened that fast even if we went for it. From what you told me, I understand that it can take days, and sometimes weeks. Dagor and I haven't been together long enough."

"True." Mia brushed a hand over her short hair. "It just seems like so much longer. It's funny how time moves differently depending on the situation, and the paradox is that it's counterintuitive. When a lot happens in a short period of time, it seems like it stretches on forever. But when nothing happens, it sometimes feels as if days passed instead of years."

"Profound," Frankie said. "You should put that in one of your books."

Mia chuckled. "My books are for children between the ages of two and four. I don't think they are even aware of the concept of time."

"I was joking. Maybe you can put it in one of your Perfect Match scenarios."

"That's a better idea." Mia sighed. "It's such a shame that you are going to miss Amanda's wedding."

A pang of regret hit Frankie. She had been looking forward to that one in particular. Amanda would no doubt wear the most magnificent wedding gown, and she really wanted to see it. "Yeah, I'm bummed about it. You'll have to take lots of pictures for me. I want you to snap a photo of Amanda in her wedding gown from every angle."

"She's going to look spectacular." Mia snorted. "Not that she doesn't look like a million bucks first thing in the morning when the rest of us mere mortals are a mess."

"Reminder. You are no longer mortal, mere or otherwise." Frankie glanced at Dagor, who was standing very quietly next to the equipment and looking at them with a small smile lifting the corners of his lips.

He was so motionless that she'd forgotten he was there for a moment.

Mia sighed. "The truth is that I feel weird celebrating and having a good time while those poor women are grieving in their little cabins on the lower deck."

"Life goes on," Dagor said. "What happened to them was tragic, but it wasn't our fault. We saved them, and Kian is taking them to a place where they will get help."

"I know." Mia turned to look at him. "I'm really proud of how our community came together to help these strangers. Syssi, Alena, Sari, and several others went shopping so the women would have fresh clothing to change into after they showered and got patched up by Bridget, and several ladies from the service staff volunteered to take care of them. "

"They've been through so much," Frankie said quietly, her gaze drifting. "It's going to be a long road to recovery."

Mia nodded. "They are getting the best help possible. The clan has been rescuing trafficking victims for years, and they operate a charity that rehabilitates them. The lady who runs it has plenty of experience dealing with traumatized victims."

"I'm glad." Frankie glanced at Dagor. "We were at the right place at the right time to save them. Perhaps your Fates had something to do with it?"

"I'm sure they did," Dagor said. "But we won't know their plans until they are ready to reveal them."

"How true." Mia let go of Frankie's hand. "I should let you rest. Is there anything you need? Do you want me to get you a nightgown from your cabin? A brush?"

Until Mia's offer, it hadn't occurred to Frankie that she probably looked like roadkill. And to think that she'd been talking with Dagor about commitment and feelings while looking terrible was so damn embarrassing that she felt like pulling the sheet over her head.

"Yes, please. I need a brush and a mirror, my facial creams, deodorant, perfume... in short, the works."

Mia patted her arm. "I've got you, girl. I'll pack a bag for you and come right back."

"Thank you. You are a lifesaver."

"I thought that was me," Dagor murmured.

"You too, darling. You are both my life savers."

55

ARU

In his bedroom, Aru lay on his back, closed his eyes, and opened the channel to his sister.

I am alone now, he sent.

It took a couple of moments for her to answer. *This will take some time. Are you going to be alone for a while?*

Aria's mental voice was devoid of its usual warmth, which probably meant that she wasn't alone, and that someone was telling her what to say. It didn't matter that only he could hear her. Her demeanor influenced her inner voice.

I have about an hour.

That is sufficient. The Oracle assures me that while I am in the temple, we can communicate without fear of anyone eavesdropping on our telepathic communication. This is important in the context of what I need to tell you next. The queen wants to speak to her granddaughter through us. Meaning that I will be present when she comes to visit the Supreme, and you will need to be with the heir at the same time.

Aru frowned. *That is too dangerous. For thousands of years, the two of them have met in complete seclusion. Is there a way for you to sneak into the reception hall without the queen's attendants noticing? Some secret passage that only the Supreme knows about?*

There is not. But the queen came up with a good cover story for why she suddenly needs to visit the Supreme Oracle daily and why I need to be there.

No cover story will be good enough, Aria. Any deviation from tradition will be met with suspicion.

As Aria chuckled inwardly, the inner sound of her amusement traveled over their communication channel in the form of bubbles that were a little tickling. *You are talking about the queen of Anumati, Aru. The most seasoned politician after the Eternal King. She is going to announce her latest project at the gala for the new university that is in three days, and it cannot be suspicious if she makes it public.*

What kind of a project?

The only one that could involve the Supreme Oracle and her scribe. Making a written record of all the greatest prophecies. She will ask the Oracle to look back into the distant past and report what her predecessors have predicted. The queen will decide which prophecies should be included in the official canon and which should be kept in the royal archives for the king's and queen's eyes only. That not only gives a legitimate reason for her daily visits, but it is also something that the king will covet and encourage.

Aru was impressed. Their queen was as devious as she was brilliant.

Naturally, she will need a scribe to write them down.

Aria chuckled again. *Naturally.*

That sounds patriotic enough, but how are the three of you going to pull it off while facilitating conversation between the queen and her granddaughter? Are you going to make the prophecies up?

Some are already engraved on the columns, so I only need to copy them. Nothing says that everything the Oracle sees needs to be new. Great prophecies have been engraved on the columns from time immemorial, but since the king does not trust their accuracy, he would be very happy about the Oracle verifying that they were recorded properly and also that they came to pass according to the prophecy. That will require the Oracle and me to spend some time courting those visions, but we do not need to rush. The queen will warn that the project might take many years because the Oracle's visions are often unclear and the requests need to be repeated.

Aru could see the queen's plan working. The more she talked publicly about her project, the more believable it would be. That would cover her side, but he still needed to figure out obstacles on his.

I see one more problem that the queen might not have taken into account. If I need to stay near Annani and be available daily to her, I can't continue searching for the missing pods, which is the official reason for my presence here.

Well, to call it official was a misstatement. The public wasn't aware of the galactic patrol ship stopping by the forbidden planet and dropping off scouts to search for the Kra-ell. It was a secret mission authorized by the king.

How am I going to explain that?

Give me a moment, Aria said. *I need to consult with the two most important ladies on Anumati.*

As he waited for Aria to return to him with a solution, he wracked his mind for ideas as well. Even if the queen or the Oracle managed to change his mission on Earth to something that would require him to stay put, how was he going to explain it to his teammates? Also, how was he going to excuse his daily visits to Annani?

More than a moment had passed until Aru sensed Aria's presence again.

I have some questions, Aria began. *The communication device you use to get in touch with the clan, does it come with global connectivity?*

It does. Kian gave me one of the clan phones, and they are connected to the clan's satellites. They work from anywhere in the world.

Excellent. The queen says that there is no need for you to be in the heir's presence while they converse through us. You can talk with her via the device.

That is not going to be easy to explain either. Kian knows, and obviously, the princess would have to know as well, but we cannot let anyone else know about our telepathic connection.

Give me a moment, Aria said.

This time around, it really did take only a moment for Aria to return to him. *Here is what you need to do: you will explain to the heir that she must publicly demand that you call her daily and educate her about Anumati, its politics, and the Eternal King. The princess should repeat the request in front of your teammates, so they won't question it. Even if they overhear you talking about those things, they will have no reason to suspect that you are being fed the information. They will assume that you are talking from personal knowledge.*

Our queen is brilliant.

Aria chuckled. *Thank you. That was my idea.*

You were always the smart one, sister.

56

DAGOR

"I have good news for you, Frankie." Gertrude entered the room, pushing a cart with various medical equipment. "Hildegard has convinced Dr. Bridget that you can be discharged on two conditions. One is that Dagor watches you for the next twenty-four hours, and the other is that I check in on you from time to time."

Dagor rose to his feet and pushed his stool against the wall to give the nurse room to maneuver.

"That's awesome." Frankie pushed up on the hospital's elevated bed, forgetting that she needed to pretend to be in pain.

When Dagor lifted his brows as a reminder, she affected a wince and slid back down a little. "I feel so much better that I keep forgetting that I should limit my movements."

"On the contrary," Gertrude said. "As long as you don't do anything to pop the stitches, which is difficult to do even if you try, you should move as much as you can to encourage circulation."

Dagor hadn't known that, and given Frankie's surprised expression, neither had she.

"That's good to know. In fact, I should have known that. My cousin Monica was encouraged to walk within hours after her C-section."

"That's right. Back in the day, it was believed that bed rest sped up healing. But today, patients are encouraged to walk as soon as they can." The nurse smiled. "Not while receiving blood, though."

Frankie lifted her arms, which were free of tubes and wires. "That's done."

Slanting a glance at Dagor, Gertrude lifted a brow. "Are you squeamish?"

"I don't think so. Why?" He was when it came to Frankie's injury, but he wasn't going to admit it.

Besides, it should be mostly healed by now.

"I'm going to change Frankie's dressing and check on her wound."

"I held a shirt to that wound to slow the blood loss for over half an hour until the doctor arrived." He crossed his arms over his chest. "I'll be fine."

He needed to be there to thrall her in case she questioned Frankie's rapid healing, which she would.

With a nod, the nurse went to work.

Dagor watched intently as Gertrude gently peeled the bandaging away and exposed Frankie's wound, and as the last layer was removed, the nurse's expression shifted from professional focus to surprise.

"That's remarkable," Gertrude murmured as she examined the wound, or rather the thin scar, bruising, and discoloration that remained. "I've never seen a human heal this quickly." She looked up at Frankie and Dagor and lifted her brows. "Did you two start on the transition process? Because if Frankie is transitioning, that could explain the rapid healing.

Winking at Dagor while the nurse's attention was on him, Frankie chuckled. "We did, but I didn't expect it to happen so fast."

The lie wouldn't work once Gertrude did the math and realized that there was no way Frankie could have been induced and transitioned so quickly.

He would need to thrall the nurse once she'd re-bandaged Frankie.

Gertrude shrugged. "I guess every Dormant transitions differently, but I'm surprised your injury hasn't halted the process. From the limited experience we've gathered, it appears that the body needs to be healthy to be able to sustain the transition."

Employing a subtle thrall, Dagor changed the narrative in the nurse's mind. "You'd better be done quickly. I'm sure the doctor needs this room for her new patients."

Gertrude blinked, her expression clouding for a moment. "Yes, she needs this bed. I'd better remove the stitches."

Frankie winced a little as the nurse clipped the stitches and pulled them out one at a time using tweezers, but Dagor didn't feel any distress coming from her.

When the nurse was done, she looked at the wound again and shook her head. "I don't even need to bandage it."

"Yes, you do," Dagor said while pushing an image of a much angrier-looking wound into her mind.

He could remove the bandage after the nurse was gone, and when she came to check on Frankie again, he would employ another thrall to convince her that she'd seen it and it was fine.

It wasn't a good idea to use thralling that often, but he was using so very little that it wouldn't have a significant impact on Gertrude's brain.

"On second thought, I'd better re-bandage it." The nurse reached for the supplies she had brought with her.

"Thank you," Dagor said.

It took mere minutes for Gertrude to be done, and when she rose to her feet, she gave both of them a fond smile. "If you don't mind people seeing you in a hospital gown, you can leave now. I don't have a wheelchair for you, but your mate can carry you."

They both stiffened at the nurse's casual use of the word.

"I'm waiting for Mia to bring me a change of clothes," Frankie said. "She should be here any minute now, but if you need the bed urgently, I can wait in the front office."

"No rush." Gertrude smiled. "I don't expect new patients just yet."

As the nurse left, Frankie let out a breath. "Is she going to be okay? I mean, you thralled her twice, right? Mia told me that thralling should be used sparingly."

"Gertrude will be fine. I barely touched her mind."

57

FRANKIE

Mia drove into Frankie's patient room at a much slower speed than during her previous visit. "I'm sorry it took me so long." She lifted a small bag from her lap. "I couldn't find anything in your cabin that you could wear comfortably with that injury. All your clothes are form-fitting, even your pajamas."

Frankie grinned. "As I have always told you, if you've got it, flaunt it, and I have it." She mimicked, smoothing her hands over her sides.

Thanks to Dagor, she would be back in her clothes much sooner. It was a shame she had to pretend to be hurting for a while.

Mia chuckled. "Indeed, you do, but right now, the only thing you will be flaunting is a Mumu."

"What's a Mumu?" Dagor asked.

Frankie affected a horrified expression. "I'll show you in a moment, but the better question is how a Mumu found its way into Mia's wardrobe." She shifted her gaze to her friend. "Even your grandmother doesn't wear them."

Mia shrugged. "It's long and roomy and hides my legs, so I don't need to drape a blanket over them when I hang out by the pool. It's way too hot outside for that." She pulled the floral monstrosity out of the bag. "It's actually a pretty print. And the fabric is so soft that it's like wearing a nightgown." She pinned Frankie with a hard look. "This is not the time to think about fashion and looking good. It's about healing and not having anything rub against your wound."

Frankie was dying to tell Mia that she was almost healed and could probably wear her yoga pants and a T-shirt, but she had to maintain the charade even in front of her best friend. It felt wrong, but then Mia had hidden plenty of stuff from her and Margo as well, and for a good reason.

"Fine. I'll wear your Mumu. Now, hand me the mirror and the brush." She grimaced. "I'm scared to look at myself."

"You look fine." Mia brought the chair closer to the bed and handed Frankie the bag. "Considering that you were injured, that is."

"Was that supposed to cheer me up?"

It had done the opposite, and as she pulled the compact mirror out of the bag and flipped it open, she braced herself for what she was about to see. It wasn't as bad as she'd imagined.

She looked like roadkill, but not one that had been rotting for days.

Pulling out the brush, she started working on the tangles in her hair. The nurse had washed it with a special moist towel that was made just for the purpose of cleaning the hair of a patient who couldn't shower, so it wasn't gross, but it was all tangled up and sticking in all directions.

If she needed proof that Dagor loved her for who she was and not because he just lusted after her, she'd gotten it and then some. He hadn't left her side unless it was absolutely necessary and had fussed over her like a good boyfriend should.

He hadn't declared his love for her yet, but he would soon. She'd get it out of the stubborn god.

"Much better." Frankie put the brush back in the bag

"Did you call Margo?" Mia asked.

"Not yet, why?"

"I need to know what to tell her if she calls me."

"Don't tell her anything. If she asks about me, tell her that I will call her and tell her myself."

Mia grimaced. "We are talking about Margo. She will be on me like a dog on a bone."

Frankie waved a dismissive hand. "I'm much worse than she is. Just pretend like you don't know anything, and if need be, I'll back you up."

Mia's eyes narrowed slightly, not in a squint but enough to sharpen her gaze, giving the impression that she disapproved, but she knew better than to argue with Frankie. "I should get back." She put her chair in reverse. "I need to start getting ready for the wedding."

"When is the ceremony?" Dagor asked.

"Eleven at night. It got postponed because of everything that has happened, but it's all good. Immortals like to celebrate late at night for some reason."

"Maybe it's because they don't need to sleep as much," Frankie said.

"I guess." Mia cast her a smile. "Maybe you will feel up to it by then. I have a portable wheelchair I can loan you, and Dagor can push you."

Frankie lifted the tent-like dress. "I'm not showing up to the wedding wearing this."

"Of course not." Mia rolled her eyes. "I have a very nice evening dress that is not clingy and will look incredible on you. It's pearl pink, shimmery, ties at the neck and cascades down to the floor, or the footrests in our case."

Frankie turned to Dagor. "I would like to at least witness the ceremony. I heard that the goddess makes up a new one for each wedding, and I'm curious what she will do for her youngest daughter."

"Call me," Mia said. "Or better yet, I'll just ask Toven to bring the chair to the clinic, and I'll drop the dress at your cabin. If you decide to come, you'll have everything you need."

"Thank you." Frankie blew her friend an air kiss. "You are the best."

"Right back at ya, bestie."

58

SYSSI

"I hate shopping." Syssi removed her shoes as soon as they crossed the gangways and put them in her tote. "I thought it would get better now that I'm immortal and have the stamina for it, but the heat and the humidity were too much."

Alena, who looked as calm and collected as ever, cast her a soft smile. "I don't enjoy going from store to store either, but it was for a good cause. I'm sure the things we bought will be appreciated."

Behind them the four Odus were barely visible under the pile of boxes they were carrying, and the two Guardians who had accompanied them were holding multiple shopping bags in each hand.

They'd probably gone a little overboard with the number of things they had gotten, but Syssi's reasoning had been that they weren't equipping the women just for a few days. They had nothing, and they needed everything. Gifting each one with a duffle bag that she could stuff with things that fit her would bring a tiny measure of normality to their shattered lives.

It was a naive thought. Syssi was aware of that. New clothing couldn't heal the deep wounds that would require years of therapy just to scab over, let alone heal. But there wasn't much else she could do, so she'd poured her heart into buying everything she could think of.

Kri met them at the lower deck that had been designated for the women. No one who wasn't there to help them would step foot on that deck.

The Guardian cocked a brow. "You know that there are only twenty-three of them, right? It looks like you bought stuff for a hundred."

Alena shrugged. "We figured that the women would feel better about arriving at the sanctuary with a duffle bag full of their belongings. No one wants to go to a new place feeling like a beggar."

"True." Kri let out a sigh. "I wish we could take them straight there instead of keeping them down here until we are done with all the weddings. They need Vanessa and her helpers now."

Syssi frowned. "You are right, and there is no reason we can't do precisely that." She handed Kri the two bags she was carrying. "I'll speak with Kian." She turned to her shopping companions. "Do you need me here, or can you manage without me?"

"Go." Sari waved her off. "We can manage from here."

"Thank you." Syssi shifted her eyes to Alena and the three other clan ladies who had joined them on the shopping expedition. "Are you sure it's okay with you?"

When they all nodded, Kri motioned for them to follow her. "We can sort the supplies in the laundry room."

Syssi had forgotten that the laundry was located on that level, and she was very happy to have an excuse not to enter another space that was hot and humid.

Pulling out her phone, she dialed Kian.

"Hello, my love. Did you ladies leave anything in the shops in Acapulco?"

It didn't surprise her that he knew she was back. He probably had the Guardians reporting their location and progress to him every fifteen minutes.

"Not much. Where are you?"

"Our cabin. Are you coming up?"

"Yes. I need to talk to you about something."

He chuckled. "That one sentence still fills me with dread even though I know you love me with every fiber of your being."

"I don't believe it." She entered the elevator and waited for the doors to close behind her. "But just not to keep you in suspense, I'll tell you what I want to talk about."

"I'm all ears."

"I'll get straight to the point. Kri says that the women shouldn't have to wait to get help until we are done with our celebrations. It's not fair to them or to us. Everyone feels guilty about partying when there are brutalized women on board who are grieving the loss of their families and trying to deal with what was done to them."

"What do you suggest? That we cancel the weddings and go home?"

He sounded way too eager to do that.

"No." Syssi exited the elevator on the top deck and headed to their cabin. "We can turn around, sail back to Long Beach, where a bus will wait for the women to take them to the sanctuary, and then continue cruising."

Kian waited for her with the door open and pulled her in for a quick kiss. "It's not as simple as that. Vanessa is in the village, and the place is on lock-down until our return. She can't leave."

The clan's therapist had decided to stay in the village with her mate. Syssi had tried to convince Kian to allow Mo-red on board, but he'd been adamant about the Kra-ell remaining behind. His excuse had been that according to his sentence, Mo-red was performing community service, and going on vacation wasn't one of the conditions of his sentencing.

"Then unlock the village so Vanessa can get out. You can even let her take Mo-red with her. He can continue his community service in the sanctuary."

59

KIAN

"Mo-red would scare the crap out of the residents. He looks too alien." Kian looked down at Syssi's bare feet and smiled. "What happened to your shoes?"

"They are in my bag." She walked over to the couch. "It's nothing that dark sunglasses and a baggy shirt can't fix. You know that Vanessa will be miserable there without him, especially if she has to stay for a few days, which I suspect is unavoidable. These women are even more traumatized than the trafficking victims we normally rescue."

She dropped her large purse on the coffee table and waved at Shai, who was working on his laptop. "Hi, Shai. Enjoying your vacation?"

He snorted. "What can I say? Your husband is a slave driver."

"You enjoy it, so stop complaining." Kian walked over to the bar and poured himself a shot of whiskey. "Can I get you a drink, my love?"

"Yes, please. I need one."

"Margarita?"

She shrugged. "Why not? When in Mexico and all that. What are you working on?"

"The impossible." He ran a lime wedge around the rim of the margarita glass. "What I've been striving my entire life to do." He poured salt over a paper towel and dipped the glass in it. "Eradicating evil."

She grimaced. "Good luck with that. You know what they say, though. In the same way as cancer needs nutrients to grow, evil needs money. Cut the money supply, and you might be able to at least shrink it. But as long as there are big profits from selling drugs and sex slaves, that's not feasible."

Kian opened the bottle of tequila and poured a shot into the glass. "That's precisely what Shai and I are trying to figure out—how to stop the money flow to the cartels, but I'm afraid that we are too small of a fry in the big monsters' game. They all seem to be connected."

"Like attracts like." Syssi let out a breath. "Only it seems that evil is better organized."

"Of course." He squeezed fresh limes into the glass. "There is a fortune to be made in perpetrating evil, while doing good costs money."

Closing her eyes, Syssi slumped against the couch cushions. "It's hopeless."

Guilt assailed Kian for bringing her mood down even more than it was when she walked in.

"Hey, you're supposed to say that I'm your invincible knight and that I can do anything I put my mind to."

She cast him a smile. "If anyone can do it, it's you, my love."

"That's better." He smiled back and added ice to her margarita.

"Did you check on Allegra?" Syssi asked. "Should I go get her?"

"My mother doesn't want to hear about giving her back. They are enjoying each other's company."

Syssi's eyes sparkled with excitement. "I'm glad that Allegra is spending so much time with the Clan Mother. I want her to turn immortal as soon as possible. I want our baby to be indestructible."

Kian nearly choked on the sip of whiskey he'd taken a second ago. Syssi still didn't know how his mother turned the little girls immortal and believed in the story that just being around the goddess triggered their transition.

"You know that she won't really be indestructible, just more resilient."

"Of course. But I'll take it over her remaining human."

"Yeah. I know what you mean." He handed her the margarita. "So, what do we do about the weddings, cancel them?"

"We keep them going," Syssi said. "Those couples have waited long enough. We can head out to sea tonight and go straight for Long Beach instead of stopping at Cabo and the other two ports on the itinerary. After we drop off the girls, we go back to Cabo to collect Mia's friend and continue the cruise as scheduled. This will add two to two and a half days to the trip, so maybe I'll manage to convince Sari to celebrate her union with David on board as well."

"Even if it was possible to add days to the trip, there is no chance Sari will agree." He sat next to her on the couch. "She didn't get a wedding dress. Besides, she wants to get married in her castle. It's a matter of pride for her."

Syssi lifted a hand. "Hold on. Why can't we add days to the cruise?"

"Because the crew can't stay longer."

"What if you offer them a bonus? That always works."

He smiled. "They have prior obligations, so adding days to the cruise is a no-go. We also can't make it back in two days. We were going full speed to get to Acapulco first and then planned to go slow on the way back. It will take us about twice as long to get back to Long Beach, so you need to figure on three and a half to four days. We can still do it and just idle at sea for the remainder of the cruise, but we won't be able to pick up Margo, which is not a big deal. If she wants to join the cruise so badly, she can fly to Long Beach and meet us there. "

Syssi sighed. "That just adds complexity and doesn't solve the problem."

Cupping her cheek, he leaned and took her lips in a soft kiss. "Let me suggest a better plan. We will stop at Cabo like we planned, spend half a day there so people can get ashore and enjoy a taste of the place, and collect Margo. Then, instead of continuing to Mazatlán and Topolobampo, we continue to Long Beach, drop the women off, and head out to sea again just so we can finish celebrating the rest of the weddings."

"That doesn't shorten the time the women have to spend on board by much." Syssi worried her lower lip. "Do you think Vanessa can help them via tele-meetings?"

"That's the best idea you've had so far, my love." He took her hand and brought it to his lips for a kiss. "That way, I don't have to lift the lockdown, and Vanessa doesn't need to leave Mo-red behind. She can choose to do group therapy or have individual sessions with the women."

This latest idea seemed to cheer Syssi up. "We need to clone Vanessa. Do you know if there are any therapists in the other clan locations? Maybe we can bribe them to join the village."

"We can ask my mother. She would know."

Oddly, the study of psychology didn't seem to attract more immortals, even though issues of the mind afflicted immortals as much as humans. Then again, one therapist had been enough to take care of the clan population, but that equation changed when Vanessa took upon herself the management of the sanctuary.

Perhaps now that she was mated to Mo-red, who couldn't join her there, she would be open to transferring the job to an administrator. After all, the humans they rescued were served by human therapists, and the only reason an immortal needed to be in charge of the operation was to make sure that no one figured out who the rescuers were.

60

DAGOR

Toven had arrived with Mia's spare wheelchair before Frankie had a chance to get dressed, but he hadn't entered the room, and wished Frankie a speedy recovery without looking in.

After he left, Frankie sat up in bed and put the garment her friend had brought for her in her lap.

"I can't believe that I'm being allowed to leave here so soon." She fumbled with the ties on her hospital gown.

"Can I help you with that?" Dagor offered.

"I am fine." She opened them one at a time and let the gown drop back.

He loved that she was comfortable enough around him to get naked without asking him to turn around.

From his experience, women got bashful about their nudity when not actively engaging in sex, but his Frankie was a confident female, and rightfully so.

Her breasts were perfection, and he had a hard time telling his fangs to stand down and stop elongating. Despite her rapid recovery, she was still not well enough for rigorous activities.

"I'm not going to bother with a bra." She pulled the shapeless garment over her head, hiding her perky breasts from him. "No one will notice it with this tent on, and I'm going to hit the shower as soon as I get to my cabin, so there is no point." She offered him a hesitant smile that was not like her usual ones.

He frowned. "Is something wrong? Are you feeling any discomfort?"

"No, I don't feel any pain at all, which is freaking me out a little."

Maybe that was why she wasn't smiling at him as radiantly as usual. Hopefully, it wasn't anything he had done or said or something that he had failed to do or say. Females had a tendency to expect their partners to know what they wanted and to get upset when they didn't.

Dagor was in a unique position of being able to peek into Frankie's mind and see what she wanted, but that was an invasion of privacy, and the only time it was justified was when lives were on the line. That left him guessing, and he wondered whether other males had such a difficult time figuring out what the proper thing to say or do was.

As with everything else, there was a spectrum, and he was probably closer to the lower end of the spectrum when it came to the ability to decipher subtle cues.

As Frankie swung her legs over the side of the bed, he caught her before her feet touched the floor. "Small steps." He held her to him for a little longer than necessary before helping her into the wheelchair.

It had just felt so good to hold her like that, but now he was paying the price with an uncomfortable erection straining his jeans.

Frankie lifted her face to smile at him with the full radiance he had gotten used to seeing before her injury. "That was nice. I was afraid that seeing me like this had cooled your attraction to me. I'm glad to be proven wrong." She lowered her gaze to his zipper, which was right at her eye level.

Crouching next to her, he put his hands on her knees. "You are always beautiful to me, Frankie. Even when you are covered in dirt, and your hair is sticking out in all directions."

She cupped his cheek. "That's sweet of you to say, but I know that you like seeing me nicely put together."

"I do," he admitted. "But I also love seeing you unravel when I pleasure you and you don't have a stitch of clothing on you. I see the real you underneath the makeup, the form-fitting clothes, and the high heels, and I love what I see. I appreciate the care you put into your appearance because it reflects your personality and not because it makes you look better for me."

Her expression turned soft. "I would kiss you, but I haven't brushed my teeth, and my mouth stinks."

He leaned forward and gave her a soft kiss on her lips. "Never." He straightened up, grabbed the bag Mia had brought, and handed it to Frankie. "Let's get out of here."

"Wait." She lifted a hand to stop him. "I need to find my phone."

"We can ask Gertrude where it is." He opened the door and pushed the chair into the front office of the clinic.

"Leaving so soon?" Gertrude asked.

"The sooner the better," Frankie said. "Do you happen to know where my phone is?"

"If you didn't lose it in the commotion, it should be here." Gertrude opened one of the desk drawers and pulled out a zip-lock bag with a phone and some spare change. "Is that yours?"

"Yes, thank you." Frankie took the bag, pulled out her phone, and opened the case. "I'm glad to see that none of my credit cards were lost." She chuckled. "Not that I need them. They are for decoration only at this point because I can't charge anything until I start earning an income again."

Dagor frowned. Frankie didn't seem to be poor. He didn't know much about female fashion and how much it cost, but she had a lot of clothes and shoes.

The nurse gave her a knowing smile. "I've heard that you are going to work in the new Perfect Match studio as a beta tester. I bet that pays well."

"Yeah," Frankie answered without much enthusiasm in her voice. "I can't wait to start."

61

FRANKIE

As Dagor pushed Frankie's chair toward the elevator, she thought about what he had said to her before they'd left the clinic.

The word love had passed his lips several times but not once in reference to his feelings for her. He just loved how she looked in various states of dress or undress.

The question was what to do about it.

Should she just tell him that she knew he loved her and dare him to deny it?

If she weren't a coward, she would have done that, but on the remote chance that he would refute her claim and break her heart, she preferred to take a less bold approach.

She hadn't told him that she'd fallen in love with him either, so what did she expect from an emotionally stunted god?

Perhaps she should be the one who went first.

Except, that was just as scary as informing Dagor that she knew he loved her and chancing that he would deny it.

The fact was that under normal circumstances, neither of them should have been talking about love yet, but these were anything but.

Dagor had taken a barrage of bullets for her, had stayed by her side like a husband or a boyfriend would throughout her stay in the clinic, and had given her his blood, which could potentially activate her transition.

If it didn't, she had every intention of letting him induce her the traditional way.

No more condoms for them.

Then, there was the impending end of the cruise and the fork in the road awaiting them.

Dagor was going to Tibet while she was heading to the village, where he was not invited for whatever reason. He still hadn't given her the details about his team's relationship with the clan and why they were prohibited from visiting the village, but it was strange that he and his friends had been invited to the cruise but not to where the clan lived.

The village was supposedly a hidden compound, but if she and Margo were invited, why not let the gods visit?

The thing was, there wasn't much Dagor could do about that or about changing the path he had to follow, but Frankie could.

If she gave up on the job offer to beta test for Perfect Match, she could go with Dagor. Gabi was joining their team, so there was no reason Frankie couldn't. Well, except for the pitiful state of her bank balance, the amount she still owed on her student loans, and her credit card debt.

She couldn't just globe-trot with Dagor and not work for a living.

He might have the resources to cover both of them, but she never wanted to be dependent on anyone for her every need. Not even someone she loved and who loved her back.

"Are you okay?" Dagor asked as he opened the door to her cabin. "You've been uncharacteristically quiet."

"I'm tired. That's all."

It wasn't a lie. Perhaps the effect of Dagor's blood was subsiding, and she was finally feeling the exhaustion her ordeal entailed.

Heck, even if she hadn't been injured, the events of the day would have been enough to sap her energy.

Dagor patted her shoulder. "I'll help you shower and then tuck you in bed. A few hours of sleep will do you good."

"Sounds like a plan." She waited until he stopped pushing the wheelchair to get up and immediately swayed on her feet.

Dagor caught her elbow. "Easy, tigress. You've been through a lot and shouldn't push yourself."

"Getting up and walking is not pushing myself, and Gertrude said I should move as much as possible."

"Carefully." He led her to the bathroom and sat her down on the bench in the shower. "Is it okay if I undress you? Or do you want to do it yourself?"

Suddenly, she felt a little more energetic. "You can help. But if you want to be in the shower with me, you need to get naked too."

At the moment, it was more bluster than any real intent to engage in fun and games, but seeing the god naked was a treat she could enjoy even in her weakened state.

He pretended to scowl at her. "Don't get any ideas. You need to rest."

"Me?" Frankie batted her eyelashes at him. "I don't have any ideas." She smirked. "For now, I will be happy to just watch. After I rest, though, I do have a few ideas that pertain to both of us being naked."

"Ugh, you are wicked." He cupped his erection over his jeans. "Look what you have done."

Frankie laughed. "Get naked, and I promise to be good and not to tease you."

"Too late for that." He whipped his shirt over his head.

His jeans hit the floor a moment later, and then he was standing in front of her in all his naked glory with his erection pointing at her face.

She was tempted to reach for it, but she'd promised to be good, and Frankie always kept her promises.

Closing her eyes, she let out a groan. "I'd better not look, or I might get naughty."

"We wouldn't want that." His voice sounded pained, but she still kept her eyes tightly shut.

In the next moment, he removed her dress and started on the bandages Gertrude had so carefully wrapped around her wound.

"You should take a look at this," Dagor murmured. "Even the bruising is fading."

She opened one eye and glanced down her side. "Unbelievable."

"Indeed."

Dagor got the water running, checked that it was the right temperature, and proceeded to wash her hair with a tenderness that brought tears to her eyes.

Luckily, he couldn't see them with the water running down her face or smell them over the strong scent of her shampoo.

When Dagor was done washing her, he wrapped her in a big towel, carried her to the bed, and gently laid her down. "Rest." He pressed a kiss to her cheek.

"Thank you." She sighed in contentment as he covered her with the blanket and tucked the edges in. "Please wake me up in a couple of hours," she murmured. "I don't want to miss Amanda's wedding."

62

ANNANI

As the doorbell rang, Oridu opened the door and bowed. "Good evening, Master Kian. The Clan Mother is expecting you."

"Thank you." Kian walked in. "Good evening, Mother." He leaned and kissed her cheek. "How are you? Did my daughter tire you?"

"Not at all, my son." She patted the spot next to her on the couch. "I had a wonderful time with Allegra today, and I was sorry to see her go, but Syssi insisted that she needed a nap so she could attend Amanda's wedding tonight."

Kian smiled. "You must have exhausted her because she fell asleep on the way to our cabin. Syssi is napping with her, which is adorable."

Annani frowned. "You should have stayed with them and napped as well. You look tired and troubled."

He let out a breath. "I am much less troubled now than I was earlier when the women arrived."

"I can imagine." Annani sighed. "I wish I could assist in some way."

He shook his head. "The less they interact with us, the better. Kalugal has already thralled them to ease some of the emotional pain, and I don't want to have to thrall them more than necessary."

"I understand. What can we do for them before delivering them to the sanctuary?"

"Syssi and I came up with a solid plan to help, and I came to give you an update."

"Thank you. I appreciate you coming to deliver it in person. You've had a busy day, and it is not over yet."

"Ain't that the truth." He raked his fingers through his hair. "Kri, Bridget, and several human volunteers helped the women settle in their cabins. Bridget has administered medical care to those who needed it, and we even found a local pharmacy that carries the morning-after pill."

Her son did not need to explain why the pill was needed, and Annani applauded Bridget's foresight.

"Physically, they're stable," Kian continued. "But emotionally, it's a long road to recovery, which brings me to the plan Syssi and I hatched. Vanessa is going to help them via video calls, and once she deems it safe for them to talk to humans, she will organize a group of human therapists who will start working with them one-on-one via the same method. Syssi wanted us to head straight back to Long Beach so we can deliver the women to the sanctuary as soon as possible, but it wasn't practical for several reasons, so we are going to continue with our itinerary as planned and arrive at Long Beach when the trip is over."

Annani was relieved. The couples about to get married on this trip had waited long enough for their special day. It was not fair to them to postpone it again. If the women's situation was critical, it would have naturally superseded that, but if they were physically stable and were getting emotional support on the way, there was no reason to shortchange everyone's enjoyment of the trip.

It was not every day that nearly the entire clan spent time together and celebrated joyous occasions.

"I am glad you found a way to continue the trip while helping these poor women." She patted his arm. "You and Syssi are a good team."

That got a genuine smile out of Kian. "We are. By the way, do you know if any of our younger members have studied or are studying psychology? Vanessa has too much on her plate, and we need more than one therapist for the clan."

"Sheila is about to graduate college this year, but she still has a long road ahead of her until she becomes a doctor, and you need people now."

He chuckled. "I need to beseech the Fates to send us Dormants who are already licensed therapists."

"Indeed." Annani motioned toward the coffee table. "Oridu made tea. Can I offer you some?"

"Sure. I've had too much coffee today, and tea sounds lovely right now."

As Oridu rushed over to pour each of them a cup, Annani leaned closer to her son. "In all of today's turmoil, you must have forgotten about Dalhu's bachelor party."

"I didn't forget. There wasn't time."

"A shorter party is better than none. Please make an effort for him. The poor male is so anxious about facing the entire clan, and he would benefit from a relaxing hour with friends, whiskey, and a good cigar. Your sister will be grateful."

"I'll see what I can do." As Kian's phone buzzed with an incoming message, he pulled it out of his pocket. "May I?"

"Of course." Annani nodded. "It might be an emergency."

As Kian read the message, his forehead furrowed. "Aru requests an audience with both of us. He says he has something urgent that he needs to discuss with you."

"Then invite him over. I just hope it will not take too long and prevent you from spending time with Dalhu."

63

KIAN

Kian suspected the reason Aru wanted an audience with Annani was that he had gotten instructions from his counterpart on Anumati or he had a message for her from the leaders of the resistance.

What Kian didn't know was whether he should be excited about that or anxious.

First, though, Aru would have to tell Annani about his ability to communicate telepathically with someone on Anumati and reveal who the message or instructions were from.

"Do you know what Aru wants to talk to me about?" Annani asked. "He promised to tell me more about Anumati, but I doubt he will insist on doing so now while we are dealing with a crisis and getting ready for Amanda's wedding."

"I have an idea what this is about," Kian admitted. "But I don't want to presume. We will hear what he has to say in a few moments."

When the doorbell rang less than a minute later, Oridu opened the way and bowed. "Good evening, Master Aru. Please come in."

"Thank you." Aru walked in with an expression that radiated excitement tinged with trepidation.

That was enough to confirm Kian's suspicion.

"Good evening, Your Highness." Aru bowed to Annani.

"Good evening, Aru. Please, take a seat." She motioned to the armchair across from the couch.

"Thank you, Your Highness." Aru sat on the very edge of the chair.

"Would you like some tea?" Annani asked.

"Thank you. That would be lovely."

The god was definitely nervous, and it was affecting Kian. After seeing the battered and haggard women arrive, Kian had already been in an agitated state, and Aru's energy was just fueling it.

Oridu rushed over with another teacup and saucer for the god, poured him tea from the teapot, and handed him the cup.

"Thank you." Aru leaned back and looked at Kian. "I communicated with my source, and I have a response."

Kian nodded. "You should start by explaining to my mother the method of your communications with the resistance and also why you demanded secrecy from me."

"Of course." Aru turned to Annani. "My apologies, Your Highness, for not telling you sooner, but I had to get approval. Kian guessed how I communicated with the resistance, but I asked him not to reveal it until I was ready. That's why he kept it from you."

Annani tilted her head. "I assume that you are ready to tell me now?"

The god glanced at the Odu, who was hovering nearby. "This requires absolute secrecy."

Annani lifted her chin and looked at the god haughtily. "My Odus would never reveal anything that is said in my presence, and their loyalty is unquestionable. They have been with me for five thousand years and have not betrayed my trust even once. I guess that is their advantage over a fully biological being. Their programming is infallible."

"I believe you, Your Highness, but I would appreciate it if you sent your Odu away and asked him not to listen to our conversation."

"As you wish." Annani turned to Oridu. "Please go to your room, close the door behind you, and do not listen to anything that is said here."

Oridu bowed. "Of course, Clan Mother."

When the Odu closed the bedroom door behind him, Aru's pinched expression visibly relaxed. "I understand that you have a mother and daughter in the clan who can speak mind to mind regardless of the distance between them. I can communicate this way with someone on Anumati. To safeguard my counterpart, I guard this secret with my life, and I beg that you do not tell a single person about what I am about to reveal. Kian knows because he guessed, but it must stay between the three of us. Not even my teammates know about my special connection."

Annani regarded him for a long moment. "First of all, you can drop the

'Your Highness' honorific. I prefer Clan Mother or simply Annani. Secondly, should I assume that you were sent to Earth on a different mission than the one your teammates were tasked with?"

"Not different, Your Highn...Clan Mother, but additional. My team's job was to find out whether the Kra-ell settler ship had arrived on Earth, and we did. My secret mission was to find out whether there were any rebel survivors, and I did that and much more." He grinned. "Your grandmother was overjoyed to discover that she has a granddaughter on Earth. She wishes to talk to you."

64

ANNANI

Annani's heart skipped a beat, then another, and then started hammering with such vigor that she lifted her hand and put it over her chest. "You can communicate with my grandmother?"

"Not directly," Aru said. "I communicate with someone who works for someone she trusts."

Next to her, Kian groaned. "I understand your need to protect your sister, but it is obvious that she is the one you are communicating with telepathically. Your secret is safe with us, and it will save us a lot of roundabout talking if you just call your contacts by name."

Aru looked as if Kian had punched him, and it took a long moment for him to finally nod. "I guess you are right. It's just difficult to find the balance between safety and moving forward. Perhaps that's the resistance's biggest problem. We don't want to repeat the mistakes of the past and lose so much again, so we progress at a glacial pace."

Kian nodded in agreement. "Luckily for us, we live among humans, and their short lifespans add urgency to our lives that we might not otherwise feel."

"Makes sense." Aru lifted his teacup to his lips, gulped down the liquid, and put the empty cup back on the coffee table. "My sister works for the Supreme Oracle of Anumati, who is Queen Ani's oldest and dearest friend. For thousands of years, the queen and the Oracle met once a month in private in the Supreme's temple. The reception hall in the temple is probably the only place on Anumati that is entirely devoid of technology and, therefore, free from spyware. It has no windows, the walls are at least a meter thick and made from Anumati's equivalent of granite, and the illumination comes from torches and the fire pit. The Supreme learned about my sister and me in a vision, searched for us, and brought us to the temple. At the time, my sister was studying to be a healer, and I was training to become a trooper. She recruited us both."

"To do what?" Kian asked.

"At first, nothing unusual. Aria became the Oracle's scribe, and I was introduced to the captain of the galactic patrol ship that was leaving for this sector. At the time, we didn't know what our mission would be or that we would actually be working for the queen. The Oracle and the queen have been searching for telepaths like Aria and me for many years. It's an extremely rare ability and one that the Eternal King considers a threat and tries to eliminate. People like us are demonized in Anumati's society. Aria and I were lucky not to manifest our ability until we were old enough to understand that we needed to keep it a secret. Not even our parents know. But we couldn't hide from the Oracle."

Annani lifted her hand to stop him. "You call the queen's friend the Supreme Oracle. Does it mean that there are many others less powerful than her?"

He nodded. "There are many oracles. Along with the Fates, they constitute Anumati's religion. The oracles are said to transcend space and time and connect to the energy source of all the known universes. The Supreme can even get glimpses from the other universes that co-exist alongside ours but resonate at different frequencies."

The concepts Aru was talking about were too esoteric for Annani to wrap her mind around, but she felt no need to understand them fully at this time. What she wanted to know was how Aru and his sister were hidden from all the other oracles.

"If the Supreme saw you and Aria in a vision, what would prevent other oracles from seeing you too?"

Wincing, Aru rubbed the back of his neck. "I do not know, but the Supreme assured us that no one else could find us. I don't know whether she did something to hide us from the other oracles or if searching for individuals with special talents is beyond the scope of the other oracles' abilities, but I trust her word."

"Did my grandmother relay a message to me?" Annani asked.

"Her Majesty wants to talk to Your Highness directly, or as directly as possible, with Aria and me acting as your mouthpieces. The queen will talk to Aria as if she is talking directly to you. Aria will repeat it through my telepathic connection, and I will repeat it. It's not ideal, but since it will be happening in real time, there is less chance of things getting lost in the retelling; the same thing will be done in reverse. Your Highness will talk to me. I will repeat it for Aria through our channel, and she will relay it to the queen."

65

ARU

"Thank you." Tears shining in her eyes, the princess did the last thing Aru had expected.

Pushing to her feet, she walked up to him and embraced him. "I am grateful for the incredible gift you are giving me at such great risk to you and your sister. I will forever be in your debt."

Frozen in place, Aru could not string two words together in response even after the heir let go of him, smiled, and returned to her spot on the couch.

The heir to the throne of Anumati had touched him, embraced him, and told him that she was grateful for the service he was providing her. None of the nobles back home would have done so, let alone any of the royals.

It was unheard of.

Kian chuckled. "I think you stunned Aru, Mother."

She laughed, the sound sending goosebumps up Aru's arms. All goddesses had beautiful voices, and the sound of their laughter was melodic and beguiling, but it was obvious that Annani was not like other goddesses. Even if she weren't the spitting image of the queen, he would have suspected that she was a high-ranking royal, most likely one of the Eternal King's many children.

They were all-powerful, but they did not have that something extra that the queen brought to the mix. Ani was extremely powerful in her own right, and it was not due to any hidden supernatural talent. She was smart, calculating, and a seasoned politician. There were very few Anumatians, if any, who did not like the queen, and what was more important, the king knew how popular she was and that getting rid of her was not an option.

"I apologize for stunning you into silence," the princess said with amusement lacing her voice. "But I need you to snap out of it and tell me when my first conversation with my grandmother will take place. Since I will be presiding over weddings every evening until the end of the cruise, I do not want this all-important conversation to happen during the celebrations."

He shook his head to dispel the shock and comply with her very pragmatic demand. "Of course, Clan Mother. The queen will need to be in the temple to conduct those conversations in private, and those visits are usually arranged ahead of time, so I can ask for a schedule."

Kian leaned forward and refilled his teacup. "I'm sure that Anumati's days do not align with Earth's. Scheduling will be problematic."

"What is Anumati's orbital speed?" Annani asked.

"It's actually not that different from Earth's even though it is a much larger planet. I think there is only a few minutes' difference. We also measure it in twenty-four intervals, but those are not precisely the same length as Earth's. On the other hand, it takes Anumati thirty times longer to complete one orbit around our sun."

"So essentially, we can schedule a specific time," Annani said. "How often does the queen intend to speak with me?"

"Once a day."

The princess and her son were both taken aback.

"Why so often?" Kian asked.

Aru shrugged. "I was not told. But we will find out soon enough. The queen came up with a fictional project of collecting ancient prophecies that required daily meetings with the Oracle in her temple. The project will take many months or even years to complete, so I assume that the queen has a lot to say to you."

Annani smoothed a hand over the skirt of her gown. "I prefer midday meetings, but I will try to accommodate any time that is convenient for the queen except for the nine evenings of the upcoming weddings." She smiled. "I am not used to working around someone else's schedule, but I cannot make demands on the queen of the gods."

Aru dipped his head. "I will communicate your wishes, Clan Mother."

Kian's forehead furrowed. "How will you be able to attend those daily meetings when you are supposed to be searching for the pods? Can the queen arrange your release?"

Aru shook his head. "It would look too suspicious, especially to my teammates. I need to keep up the charade, but there is a solution to that. I do not need to be in the same room with the Clan Mother for it to work. I will call using the clan phone that I am told has reception everywhere. If you wish, we can even do a video call."

"How will you explain those daily calls to your teammates?" Kian asked.

"Easy." Aru smiled at the princess. "You will publicly demand that I call you every day and tell you about Anumati's history, economy, politics, demographics, etc. When I make the calls, I will use earpieces and distance myself from my teammates, but if they overhear me talking, they will assume that I'm answering the heir's questions from my own knowledge. They will have no way of knowing that I'm being fed the information."

66

AMANDA

Syssi regarded Amanda's reflection in the mirror with a smile. "Do I want to know how much that wedding dress cost?"

As celebrity wedding gowns went, it wasn't nearly as expensive as the one Rena McGregor had worn for her wedding or Talia Smith's, but it probably cost half of an average yearly salary. Amanda had commissioned it from an unknown designer, who she had no doubt would someday be dressing leading ladies for the red carpet, but since the designer was only starting out, her price had been reasonable, and the dress turned out spectacular.

Crafted from beautiful cream-colored silk and sheer, strategically placed inlays, it had a high neckline that looked modest from the front but plunged so low at the back that it was almost indecent. Tight through the bodice and hips, it flared toward her feet and ended in a long train. The sleeves were long but sheer, and the entire thing was adorned with tiny pearls that would sparkle beautifully in the reception hall's lighting.

Not much had gone into styling Amanda's short hair because there wasn't much that could be done with it, and her makeup was as flawless as usual but a little more dramatic for the occasion.

She smiled at her sister-in-law in the mirror. "It didn't cost nearly as much as it should. I'm selfish and vain, but I'm not an egomaniac."

"You are vain," Sari said. "I'll give you that, but you are not selfish, and I don't want to hear you deprecating yourself on your wedding day."

Turning around, Amanda lifted the skirt of her dress so the long train wouldn't drag on the floor. "I can't help but feel guilty for celebrating while those poor women on the lower deck are grieving. Dalhu wanted to cancel the whole thing, and I gave him a pep talk about how our celebration was an affirmation of the important work we are doing for the victims of trafficking, but I still feel guilty about being happy today."

Alena rose to her feet, walked up to her, and took both of Amanda's hands in hers. "What happened to them is not your fault. You could not have prevented it, and you should not feel guilty for being happy. Letting evil depress us is letting it win."

Amanda shook her head. "I know, but witnessing evil is depressing. It is incomprehensible to me that humans are still capable of such atrocities after all we have done for them, and I can't stop thinking about it." She lowered her voice. "Maybe the gods are right in calling humans and other created species lesser."

"Stop that." Alena squeezed her hands gently. "The gods are not so great themselves. They had millions of years of a head start, and genetic science so advanced that they could have bred evil out of their citizens, but they didn't. Mortdh is proof of that."

"Do not say that name on this joyous occasion." Their mother floated into the bedroom, wearing her ceremonial gown. "You look absolutely spectacular, Mindi." A radiant smile spread over their mother's face. "I am so excited about marrying you and your darling Dalhu. You should have celebrated your union a long time ago."

Something was off about her mother, but Amanda couldn't put her finger on it. She was too excited, too bouncy, and Amanda doubted it was joy over marrying her daughter. She hadn't been that giddy before Alena's wedding.

Leaning forward, she sniffed, expecting to smell alcohol even though her mother rarely indulged, but all she could smell was a faint aroma of Annani's favorite tea and her innate scent that was no doubt the product of the gods' genetic engineering. No one smelled that good without putting on cologne or perfume.

"We almost canceled getting married tonight." Amanda waved Onidu over. "Can you please pour me a gin and tonic?"

"Of course, mistress."

"Since when do you drink that?" Syssi asked.

"Since I don't want any stains on my beautiful wedding gown, so I'm drinking only non-staining liquids as long as I'm wearing it."

"Makes sense." Syssi glanced at where Evie was playing with a mobile on the floor. "Although it's inevitable."

"As long as I walk down the aisle with a clean dress, I'm good. Whatever happens after the ceremony is less of a concern for me."

Her mother's joyous expression faded a little as she tilted her head to regard Amanda from under her lowered eyelashes. "Why did you consider canceling your wedding? Did something happen?"

Amanda huffed out a breath. "Of course, something happened. We saved a bunch of women from monsters, tore those monsters to pieces as they deserved, and brought the victims to the ship to deliver them to the sanctuary. My darling Dalhu is superstitious, and he took it to be a bad omen. I had to convince him to go ahead with the wedding. But the truth is that I should have offered my help instead of spending the afternoon and evening pampering in preparation for the party."

"We have enough volunteers to care for the women," Syssi said. "Your particular talents lend themselves to many tasks but not to dealing with traumatized females."

Amanda lifted her glass. "To my lack of nurturing instincts." She emptied half the glass in one go.

"We each have our own unique talents," Alena said. "You don't have to be the best at everything."

"I'll drink to that." Sari lifted her margarita glass and waited for Amanda to clink it with hers. "May we all recognize our limitations along with our strengths and learn how to best utilize them for our own satisfaction and for the greater good."

67

DALHU

On the sprawling balcony of Kian's cabin, Dalhu gazed out at the gentle waves. The ship had left the harbor hours ago and was sailing toward Cabo, but his heart was no longer on the trip.

He and his groomsmen, all dressed impeccably for his wedding, were talking loudly and gesturing with their hands, trying to affect the same boisterous atmosphere that Orion's bachelor party had enjoyed, but he could tell that their hearts were not in it.

They were doing it for him, though, and he appreciated the effort. The least he could do was to pretend along with them.

"Fake it until you make it," he murmured under his breath.

The weight of the day pressed down on his shoulders, as it did on the shoulders of his groomsmen, and the nervous energy pulsating between them was explosive. If they were a less civilized bunch, it could have easily turned into a brawl.

He wished he could have been there when the Guardians had torn the monsters apart. Perhaps revenge would have eased the tension squeezing his chest and making his breathing laborious.

Opening his by-now-famous cigar box, Kian got their attention. "Gentlemen, pick your cigars. We don't have much time, so I suggest you choose the smaller ones this time."

As the groomsmen approached Kian, Dalhu hung back, waiting his turn.

"Nathalie is going to grumble about the stink," Andrew said as he drew out one of the big cigars. "We should have done this earlier so we could shower and change clothes before the reception."

"There was no time," Kian said. "We needed to get the women settled in their cabins, get them medical assistance, and arrange for Vanessa and her volunteers to speak to them via video chats. Most of that was done by the ladies, but I figured it wasn't fair for us to be drinking whiskey and smoking cigars while they were still busy performing all those tasks."

Andrew nodded. "You're right." He accepted a glass of whiskey from Anandur, who was working in tandem with Okidu, distributing the glasses.

The scene was so normal, one that Dalhu had taken part in many times, and he still wondered how he had gotten so lucky.

How these males had accepted him as one of their own.

Not everyone did, and some clan members still looked at him with resentment in their eyes or avoided looking at him altogether, but those were people he didn't know. Those who knew him appreciated him for who he had become and had forgiven who and what he had been.

Dalhu hadn't.

He still felt guilty over his past deeds. Perhaps if he had joined the rescue missions, he would have felt as if he was more deserving of the life he had with Amanda, but he needed to stay away from combat as much as he could.

From time to time, the itch to go on a killing rampage became almost unbearable, especially on days like today when evil had been so close that he could still smell it in the air, but the problem was that succumbing to that itch was dangerous.

He didn't want to be the male he had been before. Violence was tainting, even if it was morally justified and directed at evildoers to make it safer for the decent and the innocent who were the monsters' victims of choice, the filthy cowards who would piss their pants rather than engage someone like him in battle.

"Easy, my man." Anandur handed him a glass of whiskey. "You look like you are getting ready for a battle, not the wedding altar."

"Thank you. I need it."

"No shit. I could feel the waves of aggression wafting from you." Anandur regarded him with a knowing look. "I'm sorry to have missed the fight too. It would have helped with the riot going on inside me. I didn't know how bad it was until I heard reports from the Guardians."

Dalhu didn't even try to pace himself with the alcohol and emptied his glass. "Yeah. I didn't hear all the details, and I don't want to. Not today."

"Right." Anandur lifted the whiskey bottle and refilled Dalhu's glass. "One detail I heard will interest you, though." He leaned closer to whisper in Dalhu's ear. "Dagor stayed in the truck to protect Frankie, but Negal joined the fight, and in the scant moments before Frankie got injured, he dispatched six monsters with his own hands and fangs. Max said that he moved with the speed and strength of the Kra-ell, at least. Not that of a god. Then, when Frankie got injured, he jumped back into the truck to protect his teammate as Jin drove them to meet me and Bridget."

"Negal doesn't look anything like a Kra-ell. Besides, don't the gods frown on hybrids?"

"He is not a hybrid, but he's definitely enhanced, and I bet that the other two are enhanced as well."

Dalhu shrugged. "Since they are on our side, I'm not worried."

He took another sip, the warmth of the whiskey easing the pressure in his chest, or maybe it was Anandur's gossip about Negal's impressive fighting skills.

In either case, it was welcomed, if not sufficient to dispel the dark shadow of rage lurking just beneath the surface and threatening to boil over.

Kian lifted his glass high in the air to get everyone's attention. "It is difficult to set aside the anger each of us feels clawing at our souls. But despite this day's events, this night is all about love and hope. It's about the happy home that Dalhu and Amanda have built and the celebration of their union." He turned to Dalhu. "Don't let the pain and anger overshadow the love you feel for my sister. The celebration tonight symbolizes everything that's good about this world, and it shows us that even in the darkest of times, there's light, there's joy, and those are worth fighting for."

Kian's words resonated with Dalhu, peeling away another layer of darkness and letting warmth spread in his chest.

Raising his glass, he met the eyes of the males standing around him. "To love, to hope, and to the brighter future we're all fighting for."

68

FRANKIE

A soft brush against Frankie's lips pulled her back to consciousness.

Blinking her eyes open, she smiled at Dagor. "That's a nice way to wake up. How long was I asleep?"

"Several hours." He sat on the bed next to her. "The wedding is in an hour. Do you still want to go, or do you want to stay in bed and sleep until tomorrow?"

"I want to go." She stretched her arms over her head and yawned. "Oh, wow. I totally forgot about the wound. It didn't even hurt." Curiosity piqued, she lifted the blanket and looked at her side.

The wound looked almost healed, the skin knitting together in a way that would have been impossible in such a short amount of time if not for Dagor's miracle blood. She prodded at the area gently, expecting to feel at least some tenderness, but there was none.

"Can I keep you around me always? Does your blood also cure headaches and menstrual pains?" Seeing the panicked look in his eyes, Frankie laughed. "I'm just joking. But seriously. Can I keep some of it in my freezer for emergencies?"

"Is that another joke?"

"It is." She reached for his neck and pulled him down for a proper kiss.

When she had to let go to draw a breath, Dagor groaned. "That wasn't fair."

She smirked. "I told you that after I rested, I would have a few ideas that pertain to both of us being naked." She flung the blanket off. "I'm already not wearing anything, and I know how fast you can get naked."

"If you want to attend the wedding, that's not happening."

"Why?" She pouted. "We have plenty of time. I don't need a full hour to get ready."

He cocked a brow. "Did you forget what happens to you after my bite?"

"Oh, right. I pass out. Can you maybe not bite me this time?"

He shook his head. "I'd better not test my restraint." He leaned closer and cupped one of her breasts, tweaking the nipple. "But since you can't dance at the wedding, we can leave early, and then you are mine. I intend to make love to you all night long."

"That's not fair." She arched her back, pushing more of her breast into his hand. "You can't start things and just leave me hanging. I have needs."

His smile was wicked when he moved his hand to her other breast and repeated the gentle teasing. "Delayed gratification enhances pleasure. You'll be thinking about me doing all those deliciously naughty things to you throughout the wedding, and you won't argue when I say it's time to go."

She glared at him. "I'm going to get you back for this."

"I'm counting on it."

Frankie was about to describe in detail how she was going to torment him when the doorbell rang in the living room.

"Hold that thought." Dagor threw the blanket over her and pushed to his feet.

When he left the room, she got out of bed and pulled the Mumu over her head.

She had to admit that Mia was right about how comfortable and airy it was. The colors and pattern were pretty, reminiscent of Hawaii, but it was like wearing a tent.

When she heard Dagor welcome Mia into their cabin, she jumped back into the bed, pulled the blanket up, and affected a pained expression.

Dagor entered the room first. "Mia is here. She brought you a dress to wear for the wedding."

"Oh, that's so nice of her." She winked at him. "Tell her to come in. I don't have the energy to get out of bed."

Mia didn't wait for Dagor to issue the invitation and drove her wheelchair into the room. "How are you feeling?"

"Much better, thank you." Frankie offered her a small smile. "It still hurts, but not as badly. I showered and slept, and that helped a lot."

Mia aligned her chair with the bed and lifted a garment bag off her lap.

"You can't wear any of the evening dresses hanging in your closet, and the Mumu is good as a poolside coverup but not as a party dress. I brought you something that you might like."

Despite how Mia had described the dress in the clinic, Frankie doubted that it looked as good as it had sounded. It was probably another tent-like dress that she would have to draw in.

"Let's see." She pushed up on the pillows, took the garment bag, and pulled down the zipper. "What is this?" She pulled out a shimmery piece of fabric that felt like liquid on her skin.

"It's shaped like a toga but nicer. It's not form-fitting, but it's not huge, either. You will look great wearing it."

The thing probably cost a fortune because Toven, aka Tom, only bought designer clothes for Mia. Frankie had never worn something that felt so luxurious, so even if the fit wasn't perfect, she would still feel like a princess in it.

"It's beautiful." She shifted her eyes to her friend. "But what about you? Didn't you plan on wearing this to one of the weddings?"

Mia shrugged. "It's not long enough to cover my feet or lack thereof. I wasn't going to wear it anyway."

Frankie didn't ask why Mia had brought it with her if she hadn't planned on wearing it. Her bestie would just make up another excuse for why Frankie should have it.

"Thank you." She reached for Mia's hand. "You're the best."

"Back at ya, bestie."

69

AMANDA

Amanda took a deep breath, steadying the fluttering in her stomach as she stepped into the grand reception hall. The room was elegantly decorated, every detail precisely as she had planned it, but all she could focus on was the male waiting for her at the dais.

Dalhu, her love, her life, stood there with his groomsmen, his eyes glowing with excitement and love for her.

She was flanked by her bridesmaids, three on each side, a support system of family and close friends. Her sisters, Sari and Alena, stood proudly by her side, beaming. Syssi, her sister-in-law, radiated happiness. Jacki, Kalugal's wife, Carol, Lokan's mate, and Nathalie, Andrew's wife, completed the line of strong, amazing women accompanying her to her mate.

So yeah, none of them was a maiden, but Sari and Carol had not had a wedding ceremony yet, so they could count as such.

Not that it mattered.

Every clan mating celebration was different and tailored to each couple.

The song she and Dalhu had chosen, "You are the Only One for Me," by Jalina, filled the hall with its upbeat melody and lyrics that encapsulated her and Dalhu's unique love story.

Onidu walked in behind her, holding Evie, their precious daughter, who was growing to be a miniature vision of Amanda and was dressed for the occasion in a gown similar to those of the bridesmaids.

In the end, Amanda had decided that her butler would hold Evie throughout the ceremony instead of handing her over to one of her bridesmaids. Her precious butler had been by her side since the day she was born, and Amanda wanted him to be part of the wedding ceremony. He couldn't be a groomsman or a bridesmaid, so holding Evie was the best way to include him.

As Amanda walked towards the dais, her heart swelled with love for her incredible mate. They had been each other's one and only since the day Dalhu had unexpectedly entered her life, kidnapping her from a store after obsessing about her for weeks.

She'd had one moment of fear but had realized pretty quickly that the hulking Doomer was much more than he seemed. That had been the beginning of their extraordinary journey together.

As she walked toward Dalhu, their eyes never veered from each other, and as a smile bloomed on his handsome face, she felt a wave of gratitude wash over her. Their journey hadn't been easy, and they'd had to fight for each other, but neither of them had given up, and it had all been worth it.

Taking the final steps towards Dalhu, Amanda reached out to him, her hand slipping into his, their fingers intertwining in a familiar, comforting grip.

Together they turned to face her mother, who beamed happily at them.

Slowly, the hall hushed, and every eye fixed on them and the luminous goddess presiding over the ceremony.

Annani's eyes shimmered as she smiled at them. "Tonight, we gather not just to celebrate the union of two souls but to acknowledge the power of love, resilience, and compassion. Amanda and Dalhu, your journey together has been unconventional in many ways. You proved that former enemies could become not only lovers, but also life-long mates and that no difficulty was too great for true love to overcome." She paused, her gaze sweeping over the crowd before settling back on Amanda and Dalhu. "The beginning of your love story is the stuff of legends, and it will be told for many generations to come. It is therefore not a surprise that the day of your joining is also marked by extraordinary events. A magical amulet, the rescue of those twenty-three women from a terrible and short-lived future is, on the one hand, a reminder of the darkness that still fills this world, but it is also a reminder of the opposite. Our clan is a beacon of light piercing the darkness, even if no one knows its source. We are the champions of light, love, and compassion."

As tears prickled the backs of Amanda's eyes, she commanded them to retreat. It wouldn't do if she started crying and ruined her makeup.

Her mother continued, "Amanda and Dalhu, my youngest daughter and her formidable mate, your extraordinary love story is one of courage and transformation." She turned to Dalhu. "You came into our lives unexpectedly, to say it mildly, and your welcome was challenging, but you have done everything in your power to prove your love and dedication to my daughter, redeeming yourself and, in the process, gaining our respect. You have become a cherished part of our family."

Dalhu dipped his head. "Thank you, Clan Mother."

As another surge of emotion rocked Amanda, it became more difficult to hold the tears back, and then her mother turned to her, and Amanda prayed she wouldn't say anything that would cause the dam to burst.

"Amanda, my beautiful daughter. You have the heart of a lioness. Full of love, courage, and dedication both to your family and your life goals. Your journey with Dalhu is a reflection of your strength and your unequaled ability to see the good in others. Together, you've faced challenges with grace and emerged victorious."

Annani reached out, placing a hand on each of their arms. "Let your union be a symbol of hope and resilience. May your love continue to grow, to inspire, and to bring light into our lives."

Her mother turned to the guests. "Tonight, we celebrate the power of love to overcome any obstacle, to heal the deepest wounds, and to bring forth the brightest light. Amanda and Dalhu, may your marriage be blessed with endless love, joy, and the courage to face whatever lies ahead." She smiled. "Is there anything you want to say to each other before I place the rings on your fingers and tell Dalhu to kiss the bride?"

Dalhu dipped his head. "We do, Clan Mother."

70

DALHU

Dalhu turned to Amanda and took her hands. Feeling the weight of every gaze in the room on him, some approving and some not, he couldn't remember the words he'd written and memorized.

"Look into my eyes," she whispered so low only he and her mother could hear. "Ignore everyone else."

Obeying her words, Dalhu locked his gaze with hers. In that moment, the room seemed to melt away, the murmur of the crowd fading into a distant hum. All that remained was Amanda, his gorgeous, courageous, smart mate, whose eyes were brimming with love, acceptance, and trust. She was his anchor, his calm in the storm.

"My love," he began, his voice strong despite his momentary freeze. "From the first moment I saw your picture, I was enthralled and obsessed by you, and that was before I knew who you were. Then, when I first saw you in person, walking down Rodeo Drive, you were so much more than a picture could ever convey, and I knew that I would move mountains to be with you." He smiled. "And as it turned out, that wasn't an exaggeration. You captivated, challenged, and changed me in ways I never imagined possible. You've shown me the true meaning of love, compassion, and partnership. I vow to cherish and honor you and to stand by your side through stormy seas and sunny days. I vow to support each of your dreams and goals, respect our differences, and nurture our love. I will be your confidant, your partner, and your best friend. I commit to being there for you in your moments of joy and your times of sorrow, to always listen with an open heart and mind. I promise to love you unconditionally, to protect you, and to be the best father to our daughter and, Fates willing, her brothers and sisters. You are my one and only, my truelove mate." He took the ring from Annani and slipped it on Amanda's finger.

Amanda's eyes shimmered with tears of joy. She looked radiant as she smiled at him, and he felt profound gratitude for the love she had for him, love he always felt like he didn't deserve.

And yet, this female who had become the center of his universe loved him without reservation.

"Dalhu, my love, my one and only, my mate." Amanda's voice rang clear and strong. "From the day you entered my life, you turned my world upside down and changed me in ways I couldn't have imagined. Fighting for you taught me courage, and keeping you taught me forgiveness. Both made me a better person, a better mate, and a better mother. Your unwavering love and dedication to me have become my anchor. I vow to stand by you through thick and thin, through good times and bad, with laughter and tears, and always with love and understanding. I vow to support your dreams, encourage you, push your boundaries, and catch you if you fall. I will be your anchor, your rock, and together we will overcome any challenge the Fates throw our way. You are my one true love, my destiny, and tonight, in front of everyone we love and who loves us back, I reaffirm our commitment to each other, our daughter, and her future siblings, Fates willing."

Amanda took the ring from her mother's hand and slipped it on his finger. The moment felt surreal, and the ring felt right, a tangible reminder of the commitment they had just made to each other.

"Mine." Amanda wound her arms around his neck and kissed him.

The room erupted in cheers and applause, but Dalhu was only dimly aware of the other people around them.

It felt as if he and Amanda were the only two people in the world.

He kissed her back, his arms winding around her back and his hands landing on the incredibly smooth skin of her exposed back.

She hadn't allowed him to see the dress before the wedding, and he had only seen the front, so it was a surprise to discover that her back was fully exposed.

Too exposed.

As a surge of jealousy coursed through him, he had to remind himself that most of the males present were her family, but even if they weren't, her commitment to him was so complete that he shouldn't begrudge others getting an eyeful of the perfection that was his mate.

As they pulled away, the cheers and applause suddenly became thunderous, as if the moment their lips parted, his singular focus on Amanda was broken.

The sound reverberated through Dalhu's body, and as he looked around and saw the sea of faces, all smiling and cheering for them, for him, he was stunned by the level of acceptance. He hadn't expected so many to approve of their princess's chosen mate.

Taking Amanda's hand, he turned toward their guests, lifted their conjoined hands, and smiled, really smiled, at the people who had welcomed him into their fold, grudgingly at first, and then wholeheartedly.

They were his family, his clan, and he was theirs—his commitment to them was as strong as his commitment to their princess.

71

DAGOR

As the ceremony ended with the couple holding up their conjoined hands, the impact of the vows they'd exchanged stayed with Dagor. Clapping and cheering with everyone else, he wondered why he felt tightness in his chest.

Typically, he was not the type to get emotional, but he'd found himself unexpectedly moved by the heartfelt exchange between Amanda and Dalhu.

Their vows resonated with something inside of him.

It wasn't only the words, though. People often exaggerated their feelings or their statements for a greater impact on their audience. But the looks Dalhu and Amanda had exchanged, the expression of devotion on their faces, those were much more difficult to fake or seem more remarkable than they were.

Their love was authentic, deep, and evoked a yearning in Dagor that he was tired of fighting against.

He wanted what Amanda and Dalhu had, and he wanted it with Frankie, a human who might or might not be a Dormant who he might or might not turn immortal.

How could he allow himself to fall for her, given so much uncertainty?

Perhaps the nurse was right, and the Fates had brought him and Frankie together for a reason, and hopefully, it wasn't to torment them.

Dagor had done things that he wasn't proud of, but none had been serious enough to justify retribution from the Fates. A few pranks that hadn't been as funny as he had hoped and a few arguments that had gotten heated and resulted in hurt feelings or long-held grudges did not make him a bad guy who needed to be taught a lesson.

Everyone had some of that in their past.

Had Frankie? Perhaps the Fates wished to teach her a lesson?

Casting a glance at her, he chuckled. She was clapping much too enthusiastically for a human recovering from a gunshot, but when he saw the sheen of tears in her eyes, he didn't have the heart to tell her to stop.

Evidently, she'd been moved by the ceremony as much as he had been.

Were the same thoughts coursing through her mind?

Of course, they were.

Then again, even though she had been very clear about her expectations of him, she hadn't really verbalized her feelings for him.

Did she love him?

Feeling ridiculous, he shook his head. He was a god, young but not a boy, and he had always been pragmatic and goal oriented. Loving Frankie was illogical and impractical, and therefore, he should stop with the nonsense of thinking about her as his mate.

When Frankie had gotten hurt, Dagor had been overwhelmed with guilt and shame for failing to protect her as he had promised, and those feelings had clouded his thinking.

"It was so beautiful." Gabi wiped tears from her eyes with the napkin. "I need to start working on my vows for when we get married because the competition is stiff. Amanda and Dalhu's vows were even more impressive than Alena and Orion's."

Aru shook his head. "It's not a competition. All I want you to say is that you are mine forever, but since that doesn't need saying, a smile and a kiss will suffice."

"I need food." Frankie glanced at the doors leading to the kitchen. "When are they going to serve dinner? It's nearly midnight."

"I'm hungry too," Negal said. "All I've had since we came back were peanuts and pretzels."

As dinner was finally served, Frankie attacked the roasted chicken, mashed potatoes and asparagus with gusto, and at the rate she was going, Dagor would need to ask the servers to bring her another helping.

Was it a sign that she was entering transition?

Had Gabi been more ravenous than usual when hers had started?

Regrettably, Dagor couldn't ask Aru without revealing what he had done.

Aru had been the one who had suggested the transfusion, but only if it was necessary to save Frankie's life.

She hadn't been in danger when they had decided to do it anyway for their own very selfish reasons. They wanted to enjoy each other for the remainder of the cruise, which wouldn't have been possible if Frankie had spent the entire time convalescing.

Besides, Dagor didn't want any scars to mark her perfect skin. He felt guilty enough for failing to protect her as it was. Since it wasn't certain that she would transition, the only way to eliminate scarring was with the help of his blood.

From the corner of his eye, Dagor noticed Bridget looking at Frankie with a frown and probably wondering why her patient had such an appetite while recovering from a gunshot wound and taking strong painkillers.

He leaned over to Frankie and whispered, "Slow down. The doctor is watching."

"I can't," she said between one forkful and the next. "I'm starving,"

"Perhaps we should get food delivered to the cabin." He waited for Bridget to look away before swapping Frankie's plate with his.

"What did you do that for?"

"So it won't be so obvious that you gobbled down everything on your plate in two minutes."

Frankie turned to him. "You'll be hungry."

"I'll go to the kitchen and ask for a box to go." He leaned closer to her. "We can leave right after you finish what's on the plate."

They had plans that he was getting impatient to get to.

"I want to stay a little longer." She smiled. "I want to see the bride and groom's first dance. After that, we can leave."

72

FRANKIE

After enjoying two hearty plates of delicious roasted chicken, Frankie finally felt sated. Dagor's blood was the catalyst in her fast healing, but it seemed that her body needed more fuel than usual to facilitate it.

"Full?" Dagor asked. "Or should I request another plate and pretend to eat it?"

He had done so with the two previous ones, so it looked like he had eaten those enormous quantities of food.

Leaning toward him, Frankie smiled. "My knight in shining armor, always ready to come to my rescue."

He winced. "I didn't do such a great job of it today."

She lifted her head and mock glared at him. "You saved my life, so stop blaming yourself."

He opened his mouth, ready to argue, when the background music changed to a love song, and the newly married couple took the dance floor.

"They are so beautiful together," Gabi said across the table. "Amanda is stunning, and Dalhu is sex on a stick."

"Hey!" Aru leaned away from her and whispered, "You are not allowed to talk like that about anyone other than me."

"Shhh!" an immortal from the next table over hissed.

Watching Amanda and Dalhu take to the dance floor, a wave of longing washed over Frankie. Their love was radiant, evident in every movement as they swayed in perfect harmony to the music and in every look and smile they exchanged. It was as if the rest of the world ceased to exist for them.

Reaching for Dagor's hand, she gave it a light squeeze, which he returned.

Frankie wanted to get up, tug Dagor to his feet, and join the newlyweds as other couples started drifting toward the dance floor.

She hated being a silent observer of the festivities. She longed to feel the rhythm of the music, to move freely and celebrate the occasion. Instead, she had to maintain the pretense of being injured.

At least she wasn't sitting in the wheelchair but on a normal dining chair, which had been a small victory. At first, Dagor had argued against it and had made room at the table by moving one of the chairs out. But when she'd insisted, he had lifted her from the wheelchair and placed her gently in the regular chair, and she'd played along, pretending that she couldn't have done it without his help.

They were an awesome team.

Her heart ached for Mia, who had been stuck in a wheelchair for over six months.

Mia must have sensed Frankie thinking about her and drove over to their table. "How is the dress?" she asked.

Frankie had forgotten about it. Suddenly concerned that she'd stained it in her rush to gobble down an entire chicken, she looked down at the shimmery, flowing fabric. "It's perfect. I'll have it dry-cleaned before returning it to you."

"No need." Her friend waved a dismissive hand. "Keep it for the other weddings. I know that you had your heart set on wearing a different gown for each of them, but you can't. They will make you miserable."

"It's okay." Frankie smiled. "I'm more peeved at having to sit while everyone is dancing. You can dance, you know. Toven can easily hold you."

Mia shook her head. "I will dance when my feet are fully regrown. By the way, Margo called me, and as I expected, she's mad at you for not calling her."

Frankie gasped. "I hope you didn't tell her about the injury? I didn't call my family either, and I don't want them to find out from Margo."

Mia gave her a look that spelled 'are you serious.' "Of course, I didn't. I told her that you had a scary run-in with cartel thugs, but our security force scared them off. You were so shaken by it, though, that you had to take a nap to recuperate, and that's why you haven't called her yet."

Frankie let out a breath. "Good save. I'll call her tomorrow. It's too late to call now anyway."

"I don't know how late Lynda's friends stay up and party, but Margo might still be awake."

"I'd rather do it tomorrow. The nap helped, but I am still really tired. I think I should call it a night and get in bed."

"Of course." Mia gave her an understanding look and gently squeezed her hand. "I hope you will wake up feeling much better tomorrow."

73

DAGOR

"Ready to call it a night?" Dagor pushed to his feet.

"I really wanted to dance." Frankie's gaze followed the couples on the dance floor with an expression that conveyed wistfulness thinly veiled in a mask of feigned resignation. She was still playing the part of a convalescing patient, probably for the doctor's benefit.

Bridget was watching her once again, but Dagor couldn't tell whether she was motivated by suspicion or just concern for her patient.

"Before you go, Frankie." The doctor rose to her feet. "I want to remind you that I expect you to be in the clinic tomorrow morning."

Frankie frowned. "Gertrude didn't tell me that I need to come in for a checkup. She said that she would come to my cabin."

The doctor looked surprised. "She must have misunderstood my instructions." Bridget lifted her hand to look at her wristwatch. "Given that it's nearly two in the morning, let's make it ten?"

That wasn't good. Dagor had a feeling that the doctor would be much more resistant to his thrall than the nurse. Her personality type usually was.

Frankie cast him a worried sidelong glance. "I'm so tired that I might oversleep. Dagor will most likely have to reschedule for me." She turned to him. "Do you have Bridget's number?"

"I do. Gertrude programmed it into my phone along with her number and Hildegard's."

He would have to make the doctor see a wound that was no longer there or, even better, thrall her to think that she'd already seen Frankie.

Bridget gave him a stern look. "Call me if Frankie develops a fever, a rash, or any other sign of trouble."

"Of course. I want to thank you again for the exceptional care you've given Frankie. You saved her life."

Bridget's expression softened. "I feel bad about discharging a patient without seeing her first, but sometimes shortcuts are necessary."

"That's okay," Frankie said. "I'm fine, and those poor women needed you more than I did."

The doctor nodded. "I'm glad that you are healing so well. Have a good night." She cast a sidelong glance at Dagor. "Frankie needs a lot of rest. I advise against any strenuous activity."

Dagor bit the inside of his cheek to stop the chuckle that her warning evoked.

"I promise to take good care of Frankie."

With one last nod, Bridget turned on her heel and walked over to the family table where Amanda and Dalhu were taking a break from the dancing.

Frankie's gaze followed the doctor. "Should we go to congratulate them too?"

He was eager to take her to the cabin and engage in all those strenuous things that the doctor advised against, but good manners demanded that they do.

"Let's do it quickly." He gently lifted her from the chair, pretending to be mindful of her injury.

She wound her arms around his neck and rested her cheek on his chest. "I love how strong you are."

He chuckled. "You are practically weightless." He carried her to the wheelchair that he'd parked next to the dining hall entry.

"You're such a flatterer."

He wasn't, and he wouldn't have known how to be even if he tried. Frankie was tiny, and her weight was insignificant even though the way her body molded to his was very much the opposite.

"It's the honest truth. Given that I can carry a car, you really weigh nothing to me."

She pouted. "You shouldn't have said that."

He frowned. "Why?"

Smiling, she cupped his cheek. "I'll explain some other time. You need to put me down now."

Dagor hadn't even noticed that he was standing next to the wheelchair. "What if I don't want to? Can I carry you back to your cabin? I can come for the chair tomorrow morning."

"We still need to congratulate Amanda and Dalhu, and I'm not doing it while you are holding me in your arms."

"Right." Reluctantly, he lowered her to the chair and started pushing it back into the center of the dining hall.

"What about Aru, Gabi, and Negal? Shouldn't we tell them that we are leaving?"

They were all on the dance floor, and Dagor had no wish to wiggle his way between the dancers with Frankie in her chair just to state the obvious that they were leaving.

"They'll figure it out." He navigated the chair toward the family table.

"Congratulations," Frankie said as they got within Amanda and Dalhu's earshot.

As Frankie gushed over the moving ceremony and Amanda's beautiful wedding dress, Dagor's eyes shifted to their little girl, who was in Alena's arms. The baby was a miniature of her mother, but there was a fierceness in her that was all her father's. Kian's daughter was sitting in a highchair and watching him with eyes that seemed too old and too knowing for such a young child. Physically, she was the perfect combination of her parents, but he had no doubt whose character she'd gotten. She was all Kian's fierce determination. But then she smiled at him, and as his heart melted a little, longing molded that softened tissue.

He would love to have an adorable little girl or boy like those two, a child who looked like Frankie and had her lively personality. The wistful thought brought a smile to his face, but it wilted with the realization that if Frankie was the mother of his children, his mother would never get to see them.

If he chose the selfish path and remained on Earth forever to be with Frankie, he would live with endless guilt.

His only hope would be the resistance, finally toppling the Eternal King and ending the prejudice against hybrids. With Annani at the helm, those would be gone in no time. She would never allow anyone to think less of her children, who were all hybrids.

When Frankie was done, Dagor leaned over and offered Amanda his hand. "Congratulations. The ceremony was beautiful."

The bride smiled brightly. "Thank you. I thought it was lovely, too." She shifted her gaze to Frankie. "I wish for the two of you to be as happy as Dalhu and I. As you have probably figured out, the beginning of our story was not easy, and there were many obstacles to overcome, but love persevered."

This time, Dagor was smart enough not to say anything other than thanking Amanda.

After shaking hands with Dalhu and congratulating him, Dagor and Frankie exchanged a few pleasantries with their family members who were sitting with them and then said their goodbyes and headed out.

Frankie sighed. "Can we make up an excuse for the next wedding so I can dance?"

A smile curled the corners of his lips, and he leaned over the back of the chair to whisper in her ear. "We can have a private dance in your cabin, provided that you are not tired, that is."

Frankie's eyes sparkled with mischief. "I'm not."

Exiting the reception hall, Dagor made sure that no one could see them and jogged toward the elevators, pushing the wheelchair in front of him.

Frankie laughed, lifting her legs and her arms as if she was on a roller-coaster.

"That was fun," she said as he came to a halt and pressed the button to summon the elevator.

Leaning over her, he nuzzled her neck. "I can't wait to peel this dress off you. Those perky nipples of yours tormented me the entire evening, and I could barely manage to keep my eyes from straying away from your beautiful face, not to mention keeping my fangs from elongating."

Her cheeks pinkening, Frankie giggled. "I didn't have the right type of bra to wear with a one-shouldered dress, so I didn't wear one. I thought that no one would notice."

"Oh, I noticed, and I wasn't the only one. I wanted to pluck all those males' eyes out, figuratively, of course."

74

FRANKIE

Frankie shouldn't have enjoyed the jealous note in Dagor's tone so much. Possessive guys were bad news—they were jerks with confidence issues.

Right.

Not Dagor, though. Who would a god be jealous of?

Other gods, of course, but Toven and Aru were taken, and the cool thing about immortals and gods was that once they bonded with their truelove mate, they couldn't even have sexy thoughts about anyone else.

Fidelity for life was guaranteed, and there was no room for jealousy.

As soon as Dagor closed the door behind them, Frankie started to rise, but her feet never got the chance to touch the floor. Grabbing her, he pulled her into his arms, and the room blurred as he carried her into the bedroom.

She half expected him to throw her on the bed, but she should have known that he wouldn't risk hurting her.

After gently laying her on top of the covers, Dagor pulled back to look at her with a pair of glowing blue eyes.

"Dagor," she whispered. "Your eyes are so incredible."

"You are incredible." He leaned over and kissed her softly and then pulled back and looked at her again as if he was trying to memorize every little detail about her.

There was need in his eyes and lust, but there was also more, and the urge to tell him that she was in love with him got so overwhelming that Frankie had to bite her lip to stop herself from uttering the words and scaring him away.

Slowly, with a gentle touch that belied his incredible strength, he pulled the dress down her body until it was down around her hips.

She should have known that he would want to check her wound, but it had already been mostly healed before they had left for the wedding, and now all that remained was a hairline scar and a yellow bruise.

Dagor feathered his fingers over it. "Does it hurt?"

She chuckled. "I can't even feel you touching it."

When he applied a little pressure, she smiled. "Stop fretting. I'm more than fine to engage in the most rigorous activities you can dream up."

"Oh yeah?" Smirking, he ran his hand up her side until it reached her breast and cupped it in his large hand. "I might not be the most imaginative guy, but I can think of a few things that even you couldn't dream up."

"Like what?"

"Like this."

Dagor hadn't moved, but suddenly, she felt a phantom hand fondling her other breast.

"How are you doing that?" she breathed.

His grin widened. "It's called a thrall. Your mind doesn't know the difference between what's real and what I put in there."

It was hard to think with what he was doing with his hands, the physical one and its phantom twin. "So, it's all in my mind?"

"It feels real, though, doesn't it?"

"Yes."

When he pulled the dress all the way down, it was with a real, physical hand. Mind tricks could only affect what she felt, they couldn't remove garments any more than they could turn the lights off remotely.

Her panties were next, leaving her nude, and as Dagor leaned back to admire what he'd revealed, two phantom hands kept stroking her body.

"Can you feel it?" Frankie murmured. "Does it feel as if you are touching me?"

He shook his head. "When I'm in your head, I feel what you feel. It's a different experience. It's fascinating."

His tone was just as full of wonder as his expression, and Frankie was jealous. "When I transition, will I be able to get into your head and feel what you feel?"

"I don't think so." He whipped his shirt over his head and tossed it on the nightstand.

"Bummer."

"Yeah." He got rid of his pants. "Are you ready for more mind tricks?"

"Yes." She wasn't sure.

What if he did something she wasn't comfortable with?

Dagor smiled. "I'm in your mind. If something isn't pleasurable to you, I will stop."

If he was any other guy, that wouldn't have reassured her, but she trusted him.

"Okay."

As the glow in his eyes intensified, she felt four phantom hands grip each of her limbs, and then he was on her, licking and sucking on her nipples as his hands slipped down her sides, her hips, and then dipped between her thighs.

A moan escaping her throat, Frankie arched, willing him to touch her where she needed him most, but his fingers only skimmed over the edges of her moist lips, teasing her.

"Touch me," she pleaded.

"I'm touching you," he murmured around her nipple.

"You know what I mean."

"I do, but I'm not ready yet."

Insufferable god.

Dagor pretended that he was in no rush and that he had all the time in the world, but the hard length pressing against her thigh was evidence to the contrary.

Frustrated, Frankie tried to tug her wrists free, but the phantom hands were just as strong as his real ones. Still, their touch was soft, warm, and reassuring.

Finally, when Dagor was done feasting on her nipples, he slid down her body and positioned himself between her spread thighs, and when his tongue slid along her slit, she nearly orgasmed just from that.

If only he would touch her clit, she would detonate like a firecracker, but he was adamant about keeping her on the edge and not letting her climax yet.

Damn, the god was wicked. What was he trying to do?

"Dagor, if you don't stop teasing me right now, I'm going to start calling you names."

Lifting his head, he smiled at her with his fangs on full display. "That's not much of a threat."

The crazed look she was sure he saw in her eyes must have been more effective than her silly threat because he shifted up her body and positioned himself at her entrance.

"Tell me what you want, Frankie."

"I want you inside me. No more teasing and no condom."

"Are you sure?"

"Positive."

His wicked grin was the only warning she got before he slammed into her. She'd been more than ready for him. "You feel so good."

"It's just the beginning, my precious."

His precious, not his love.

Would she have to pry the words out of his mouth?

Frankie made a feeble attempt to tug her wrists free from the hold of his phantom hands, but as he started moving inside of her and a phantom tongue started circling the most sensitive spot on her body, the fight left her, and she surrendered to the coil winding tightly inside of her.

"Dagor," she mewled as the stimulation became too much.

The overload prevented the coil from springing free, winding it impossibly tighter instead.

Suddenly, the hold on her ankles was gone, and as she lifted her legs and wrapped them around his torso, the angle changed, and as his thrusts became more frenzied, the hold on her wrists was gone along with the tongue.

Likely, he was unable to keep his concentration and had been forced to let go of the phantom extensions of himself, which was good because Frankie couldn't have survived another minute of the overstimulation.

Digging her fingers into his nape, she was dimly aware that her nails were probably drawing blood, but as his shaft swelled impossibly large inside of her, all coherent thought fled her mind.

When he surged into her one last time, and the tightly wound coil inside of her was sprung, his hand clamped on the back of her head and he tilted it sideways.

Erupting, Dagor hissed, and the next moment, his fangs sliced into the soft skin of her neck. The pain registered almost as an out-of-body sensation, and then it was gone, and a venom-induced climax rocked her body.

The aftershocks continued until the euphoria stole her bodily sensations and she soared to the clouds, but not before she heard him say those most important three words.

"I love you."

75

KIAN

Kian watched his people swaying on the dance floor, enjoying the happy expressions on the dancers' faces. This late, most of the couples had retired to the tables, and the ones left were predominantly the clan ladies. They were dancing with each other, some trying to talk over the music, others singing along. Occasionally, a peal of laughter could be heard over the noise.

He wondered why females seemed to enjoy dancing more than males. Were they less reserved because of differences in upbringing?

Or maybe it was innate? Perhaps their perception of rhythm and their ability to move in sync with music was better?

"What are you frowning about now?" Amanda asked. "Be joyful, brother of mine. You finally got to marry me off."

He smiled at her. "I am joyful. I was just wondering why the dance floor is full of single ladies but markedly less single gentlemen."

Amanda snorted. "That's obvious. Females dance for the joy of it, but males dance only to impress females, and since all of these ladies are their cousins, they have no incentive to get out there and perform for them."

His sister was beyond merely tipsy, but that didn't invalidate her observation.

"That's more or less what I was thinking. Females are naturally happier than males provided that they are safe, and I hate that so many are not."

Dalhu nodded. "I'm glad that our daughters will be immortal and able to deal with human male scum. I just wish that they could do the same with our own kind."

Dalhu's comment was a chilling reminder that the Brotherhood was still out there and that most of those Doomers would do incomprehensibly evil things to their daughters if given the chance.

The relative quiet the clan had enjoyed in recent months could have been intentional, a tactic to lull them into a false sense of security.

"Oh, please." Amanda huffed out a breath. "Enough of that. Tonight is all about joy. You can be all gloomy tomorrow. "

"It is tomorrow," Kian pointed out. "But you are right."

The party was gradually winding down, and the energy in the room was slowly shifting from lively celebration to a comfortable, tired hum, but people seemed reluctant to leave, maybe because they wanted to remain in the happy bubble of celebration for a little longer. The moment they set foot outside the reception hall, reality would rush back, and the events of the day before would remind them of all the ugliness out there.

Syssi kissed the top of their daughter's head before laying her down in the stroller. "We really should go and put Allegra to bed." She turned to Jacki. "Is there a chance you can show me the amulet before we retire for the night?"

Kian frowned at her. "What's the rush? It's still going to be there tomorrow." He turned to Jacki. "You are not still planning on throwing it overboard, right?"

"I'm not." She grimaced. "But I'm not planning on touching it either. I have it wrapped in a cloth and tucked into one of Kalugal's shoes."

The horrified expression on Kalugal's face was comical. "Why did you use my shoe for that? Now, I can never wear it again."

She smiled sweetly at him. "That's why I didn't put it in mine. There is no safe in the cabin, and I need every pair I brought, while you have three pairs of black dress shoes that are almost identical. Besides, my shoes are not big enough to house it."

Kian stifled a chuckle. "I'm sure we could have found a proper container for the amulet so no shoe would have to be sacrificed on its altar."

Kalugal groaned. "Bad choice of words, cousin."

"It was deliberate." Kian lifted his whiskey glass. "I thought it was quite clever, but I see your point."

"I really want to see the amulet," Syssi said. "I've been thinking about it the entire evening."

"Why?" Kian put his glass down. "I hope you are not entertaining any ideas about touching it."

Given the guilty expression on Syssi's face, that was precisely what she'd been planning. "I just want to see it. I'll get some gloves from the kitchen so I don't touch it by accident."

Annani, who until now had been happy to hold the sleeping Evie to her chest and leave them to their conversation, shifted her granddaughter so her head was resting on her shoulder. "I am curious about the amulet, too. I suggest that we all meet for breakfast in my cabin tomorrow morning and take a look at it together."

The idea of a shared breakfast was appealing. They could observe the artifact all at once and be done with it. Kian could wake up early and find a proper container for it so it could be locked away. A portable safe would be a good choice.

When they got back, he would have William put it in one of his impenetrable lead containers, the kind he'd used to store the alien trackers in. If Jacki agreed, he would also store the artifact in one of their warehouses downtown instead of keeping it in the village.

But all that could wait until tomorrow.

Right now, all he wanted was to enjoy the rest of his night and think as little as possible about future threats from humans, Doomers, and Anumatian gods.

76

DAGOR

The bedroom was dimly lit, the muted light coming from the moon casting a gentle glow through the slightly parted curtains of the balcony doors. If Dagor could tear his eyes away from the slip of a girl lying next to him in bed, the barely perceptible sway on the ship as it glided over the waves would have lulled him to sleep, but even though he was tired, he couldn't stop looking at her.

Propped on one arm, he lay on his side and watched Frankie sleep. Her chest rose and fell with steady, peaceful breaths; her expression was relaxed, even blissful, and her pouty lips were swollen from their kisses.

His heart swelled with emotion that could only be described as love.

The one time he had thought he'd been in love couldn't compare to what he felt for the tiny human, and it was ludicrous given that he had known her for mere days compared to the many years he had known his first and only love until now.

It was time to stop deceiving himself and acknowledge that he was in love with her.

He'd said the words in the height of passion, but that didn't make them any less true.

He was keenly aware of all the downsides of loving Frankie, of all the reasons why a relationship with her was asking for heartache and devastation, but all the cons seemed suddenly inconsequential compared to the alternative of not having her in his life.

As the deep, resonating truth of that settled over his heart, he replayed in his mind all the moments they had shared that had somehow coalesced into something meaningful. Something deep.

She was only human, at least for now, and yet she was more perfect for him than any goddess he had ever met.

The mischief and lightness in her eyes, the innate humor, and the unfailing assertiveness were refreshing. She was gutsy without being reckless, and she was unapologetically herself. He thought of her laugh, the way her eyes sparkled when she was excited, the way she spoke her mind.

Being with her was fun, and to him, it was all the more precious because he rarely experienced levity.

As he watched her in the moonlight, a realization dawned on him. Love wasn't just the sensation of tightness in the chest, the pangs of desire, or the burning of lust. Love was a choice, an acceptance, a completeness of being.

It settled over him like a warm blanket.

As the first light of dawn filtered through the curtains, Frankie's eyes fluttered open, and as she saw him, her face lit up with a radiant smile. "You're awake."

He chuckled. "And so are you."

"I had the most incredible trip. It was so vivid that I felt like I was coming home, except I had a tether tied to my pointer finger with a bow, and I knew that I had to follow it back to you."

"I'm glad that you remembered me. It's scary to hear you say that you felt like the alien place was your real home."

Her eyes softening, she lifted her hand and cupped his cheek. "You are my home, Dagor. The alien place was just somewhere I felt welcomed and accepted, but even while experiencing it, I knew it was a dream." She scrunched her nose. "It's hard to explain. It's like that moment you are drifting off to sleep and feel the calm wash over you. That's the feeling I had there."

Resting his elbow on the mattress and his chin on his fist, he leaned toward her as he listened to her tale of alien landscapes and of soaring over otherworldly terrains that were bathed in ethereal lights. Her descriptions were so vivid that the images they painted played like a movie in his mind, but as incredible as they were, he was more focused on watching her talk with a sparkle in her eyes and excitement in her voice.

Frankie's energy, her spirit, her unrestrained joy as she shared the experience with him, brought about a warmth that spread through him, and the words just slipped from his lips again, "I love you."

She fell silent for a heartbeat, the weight of his confession hanging between them, but then her smile widened, and she threw her arms around his neck. "I thought that I dreamt you saying that before I blacked out. I love you too, Dagor. So much that my heart is full to bursting."

77

FRANKIE

The love words they had exchanged hung in the air, feeling almost surreal.

But as the initial rush of finally hearing those words and saying them back subsided, reality crept in, and Frankie's mind raced with thoughts, most of them worries.

What if her transition didn't happen?

What future could they possibly have?

She looked into Dagor's eyes, searching for answers to questions she was afraid to ask. "It feels like I've been waiting forever for you to say that you love me, and I'm so happy that you finally did, but now I'm thinking that maybe we shouldn't have said that to each other."

The smile melted off Dagor's face. "It's too soon, isn't it?"

"No, it's not that at all. What if I don't transition?"

Shifting over her so his body blanketed hers, Dagor braced his forearms on the mattress on both sides of her head and looked into her eyes. "I don't have all the answers, and it doesn't sit well with me either. I like having everything planned out and organized. I can't have it with you, but I can't not have you either. All we can do is take one day at a time and try to make the most of it. Whatever happens, happens."

It was hard to argue with him when his hard length was pressing against her inner thigh and distracting her.

Was he doing it on purpose?

Did she care if he was?

Mustering her resolve, Frankie pushed on his chest, and he let her roll him off her and then straddle him. "I know so little about you." She braced her hands on his chest. "We really should spend more time talking to each other."

He grinned at her. "Talking is overrated. I'd rather be doing." He lifted his hips, grinding his erection against her needy center.

"I don't even know why you're here on Earth, aside from looking for the pods everyone talks about. What's in those pods that's so important?"

"People." He cupped her bottom and squeezed. "The Kra-ell settlers. But that's a long story that I'm not in a mood for right now." He moved her back and forth over his length, coating it with the moisture that gathered at her lower lips.

Frankie opened her mouth to argue, but seeing the look in his eyes, she closed it.

It wasn't just lust, or need, although both were there.

In that moment, with his gaze locked onto hers, his eyes were full of love, and Frankie felt a surge of warmth that was only partially because of the delicious friction he was creating below.

Talking could wait.

So, yeah, there were uncertainties, fears, and a thousand unanswered questions, but there would be plenty of time to address them later. Right now, all of that seemed to fade into the background.

"Don't think you are off the hook." She leaned and took his lips. "But I have my priorities straight. Making love to you comes first."

MATTERS OF THE SOUL

1

SYSSI

Ever since Syssi had heard Jacki recount the vision that revealed the atrocities the cartel monsters had committed, she couldn't shake off the rage and frustration that clung to her like radioactive sludge.

The monsters had slaughtered those poor villagers just because they could. There had been no one to defend the defenseless. The atrocious act was probably perpetrated to serve as a warning to others to keep their heads down and comply with every demand the cartel thugs made, even if they asked that virgins and babies be delivered to them to be violated or sacrificed to whatever demon they served.

If the Eternal King learned what level of evil the gods' creations were still capable of despite all the progress that had been made, he would order that the entire planet be destroyed. It wouldn't be because he cared about the pain of innocents, but because he would be disgusted and ashamed of what his people had created. Humans had been enhanced with the help of the gods' superior genetic material, and the king wouldn't want creations like these to exist and mar the gods' reputation.

Syssi reached for her daughter. "Ready to see Nana, sweetie?"

As she lifted Allegra, her daughter's soft breaths whispered against her neck, easing some of the tension, and the baby's sweet scent soothed the turmoil in her head. Slowly, the tight coil of anger and frustration unraveled, and the warmth from her daughter's little body seeped into her own, relaxing

Syssi's stiff shoulders and releasing some of the vise-like discomfort that had settled over her heart.

Glancing up at her with eyes that appeared to know more than they should, Allegra grabbed her favorite rag doll, hugged it to her chest with one hand, and waved with the other at Kian. "Go, bye-bye."

It seemed like her vocabulary was growing by the day, but it wasn't surprising that she was learning to speak earlier than other babies her age. Allegra had started communicating clearly with only minor changes in pitch and sound almost from day one.

"Daddy is coming too." Syssi smiled, hoping that Allegra's excitement over seeing her grandmother would distract her from sensing the turmoil raging inside her mother.

"Are you okay?" Kian's forehead furrowed with concern.

Damn, Syssi had been doing her best to hide the storm raging inside her from him, and so far, it had worked. Her mate wasn't the most empathetic fellow, but he knew her well, and the only reason he hadn't seen past her composed façade before was that he had too much on his plate. The last thing he needed was to deal with her emotional meltdown on top of everything else.

Her only option was to fake it and deflect his attention to another subject.

Syssi plastered a bright smile on her face. "I'm excited about tonight's wedding. I have no doubt that Anandur is planning some goofing around. I just can't imagine what he will come up with."

Kian grimaced. "Neither can I, which worries me. Hopefully, he will think of his bride and not embarrass Wonder in front of the entire clan with something too outlandish."

"Maybe you should have a word with him when you guys meet for whiskey and cigars later?"

Kian chuckled. "I'm afraid of bringing it up in case he hasn't thought of it, and he gets the idea from me."

"Good point." Syssi kissed their daughter's cheek.

"Na-ni," Allegra said with a commanding tone and pointed toward the door.

"Are you excited about having breakfast with Nana, sweetie?" Syssi asked.

"Na-na." Allegra nodded.

Syssi was excited, too, but for reasons of her own. Finally, she was going to see the amulet that had enhanced Jacki's prophetic ability and enabled the rescue of the surviving victims.

It scared the hell out of her, but she was going to touch that thing anyway.

Hiding her anxiety and fear from Kian hadn't been easy. If she were still human, he would have smelled her emotions and realized what her calm façade was hiding and what she was planning, but she was immortal now, and the emotional scents she emitted were not as strong as they were when she was a human.

Kian didn't want her to touch the amulet, and she wasn't too eager to do so either. She wasn't sure she could stomach what Jacki had seen, but if there was a chance that she could discover the identities of the masterminds behind the atrocities, she was willing to suffer through the horror so she could provide the information to Kian, and then he could mobilize the clan to wipe them off the face of the Earth.

Kian made it to the door first and held it open for her. "I wonder if my mother has told Allegra to call her Annani or if she picked it up from others."

"She repeats what she hears." Syssi managed to keep her tone casual as she entered the wide hallway. "That's why I call your mother Nana or Grandma when Allegra is around."

"Yeah, I do too. But she still says Na-ni more than Na-na."

"It's confusing." Syssi stroked Allegra's soft hair. "The two sound so similar."

The small talk was helping, but her heart was still racing as fear mixed with excitement.

"Mama?" Allegra put her tiny hand on Syssi's chest, her big eyes scanning her face with worry.

It was much more difficult to fool Allegra than to fool her father.

"Yes, sweetie." Syssi kissed the top of her head. "Mama, Dada, and Allegra are going to Nana's cabin, and your aunts and uncles will be there too."

She knew that hadn't been what her daughter had tried to convey in her one-word question, but she had to keep Kian in the dark about it for a little longer. If he guessed her plan, he would give her another lecture about why she shouldn't touch the amulet, saying all the things she knew to be true and couldn't dispute. The visions would upset her, she wouldn't be able to sleep for weeks or even months, and it would affect Allegra.

It already had.

There was very little that escaped their daughter's notice. She might not understand much of it, but she sensed and internalized her mother's emotions.

"Nana." Allegra pointed at the door on the other side of the corridor.

The Clan Mother's cabin was the most luxurious on the ship, but Syssi couldn't tell the difference between theirs and the goddess's, and it didn't really matter to her. What mattered was that she had her family with her, the one by birth and the one by marriage, and she felt incredibly blessed and guilty.

She was experiencing many of the classic symptoms of survivor's guilt even though she hadn't lived through what had happened to those villagers.

The poor women on the lower deck had lost everyone they loved in terrible and gruesome ways, and then they had been violated by the monsters who had done it.

Thinking of them and their immeasurable suffering made Syssi's skin prickle with heat, and the tips of her fingers tingle. It was an odd and disturbing reaction, given that she was immortal now, and her blood pressure wasn't supposed to spike when she was upset or angry.

Perhaps it was the rage she was trying to stifle for the sake of her husband and daughter.

The monsters were dead, torn to pieces by the Guardians, and that gave her a small measure of satisfaction, but vengeance wasn't enough. It couldn't bring back all the innocent people they had barbarically and sadistically slaughtered, the children, the mothers and fathers, grandmothers and grandfathers that they had maimed and violated before killing.

There was no erasing the images Jacki's words had etched on her psyche, and they were going to haunt her for the rest of her immortal life.

That was why touching the amulet and taking the risk of summoning a terrible vision no longer terrified her as much as it should.

Syssi was already traumatized just by what her mind was reconstructing on repeat from Jacki's account, and her sleep was disturbed because the images haunted her in her dreams, so if she could gain more information by exposing herself to the amulet's power, things shouldn't get markedly worse.

As Kian rang the doorbell, Syssi hugged Allegra tighter, plastered a bright smile on her face, and summoned courage she didn't feel.

All the females in the cabin she was about to enter were so much more resilient than she was. Annani and her daughters were strong and brave, Jacki had nerves of steel and seemed almost unaffected by what she'd seen in the vision, and Syssi refused to be the only weakling who couldn't face suffering and horror without falling apart.

The door opened, and Oridu bowed deeply. "Good morning, Mistress Syssi, Mistress Allegra, and Master Kian. The Clan Mother awaits you at the breakfast table."

2

FRANKIE

Frankie opened the balcony doors, stepped outside, and inhaled the fresh ocean air. "It's such a beautiful day." She leaned her hands on the railing, lifted her face to the warm sunlight, and closed her eyes to shield them from the glare.

Dagor's footsteps sounded behind her, and a moment later he leaned over her back, placed his hands on the railing next to hers, and enveloped her body with his.

"You are beautiful." He nuzzled her neck.

She laughed. "You're such a flatterer."

"It's true." He peppered her neck with tiny kisses that were tickling and sweet at the same time.

"I love your lips on me." She giggled when he touched a ticklish spot under her ear. "I love your hands on me, too."

"Oh, yeah?" He moved his hands from the railing to her waist and started a slow trek over her ribcage. "Like this?"

The effect was instantaneous, and she considered getting back in bed and continuing what they had been doing through most of the night.

They had hardly slept, in part because Amanda and Dalhu's wedding had ended so late and in part because of the strenuous activities they had engaged in after returning to her cabin, but thanks to the effect of Dagor's venom, she'd woken up quite early and was feeling great.

She pushed her bottom against his groin and gave it a little wiggle. "Do you think I can get away with not using the wheelchair today?"

Groaning, he pressed against her from behind. "I don't know. If you were healing on your own, would you be ready to walk around less than twenty-four hours after getting shot?"

"Maybe." She leaned her head against his chest. "But since everyone knows that we are together and that you are pumping me full of your venom, they will attribute my rapid recovery to its healing properties."

"Good point." He scraped his fangs over her neck, eliciting a shiver of delight. "Just remember to say nothing about the thing that Kian insists on being kept a secret," he whispered.

"I don't blame him."

The tiny quantity of Dagor's godly blood had been a miracle cure, healing her gunshot wound in hours instead of weeks, but it was also a big secret for a very good reason. If people discovered what Dagor's blood could do, even his godly powers wouldn't keep him safe. He would be hunted down, and his pursuers wouldn't quit the chase until he was caught, no matter how many casualties they sustained in the process.

He was a god with mind control powers and superior physiology, but he was not invincible. Even a god had limits, although she didn't know what those limits were.

Not yet, anyway.

They still had so much to talk about, so much she needed to find out about her alien lover, and there were only seven days left on the cruise.

After it was done, they were supposed to go their separate ways, but she was working on a plan that would allow them to be together without either of them having to sacrifice their objectives.

Well, saying that she had a plan was a little presumptuous. She was still trying to come up with ideas on how she could be a Perfect Match beta tester remotely, but that qualified as working on it, right?

Turning in Dagor's arms, Frankie leaned against the railing and looked into his mesmerizing blue eyes. "Why don't you just thrall me to forget that you gave me your blood?"

He winced. "I don't want to thrall you. I love that you know who and what I am and that I don't need to pretend to be someone I'm not."

That was so sweet it deserved a kiss.

Lifting on her toes, she wound her arms around his neck and planted a soft kiss on his lips. "I love it that you can be yourself with me, but erasing the knowledge about the blood transfusion from my mind is not going to change that. I will still know that you are a god, and that you love me and that I love you back."

He smiled, but it looked a little forced. "I don't want to keep secrets from you that I don't have to. Fates know I have enough of those."

She frowned. "What do you mean? What secrets?"

Also, why had his smile looked forced when she'd said he loved her? Had he had a change of heart?

No, that wasn't likely. Dagor wasn't the kind of man who said things he didn't mean.

Not a man, she corrected herself. A god.

Well, a more accurate term was an immortal alien with super-mind powers, but saying that she had a god for a boyfriend was cool, even if she could tell practically no one, so god it was.

If only she could tell Margo about him.

Perhaps she could call him a god jokingly?

Toven had compelled her to refrain from saying anything about gods or immortals to anyone outside the ship, but she might say that Dagor was a god in bed or that he was as gorgeous as a god and get away with it.

Dagor shrugged. "I'm a trooper. A lot of what I know is classified information that I'm not allowed to share with you or anyone else."

He'd told her about his mission to find some missing pods that were supposed to have some Kra-ell settlers in them, whatever that meant. Was the identity of those people the big secret, or did he have more clandestine missions that he couldn't talk about?

Tilting her head, she looked into his eyes. "Who would I tell? Even if I could talk about you and the immortals, people would think that I was tripping on drugs. Your secrets are safe with me."

3

DAGOR

"I know." Dagor dipped his head and kissed the top of Frankie's nose. "But that doesn't change the fact that I was sworn to secrecy about the things I've learned, and I can't break my vow just because the woman I love is curious. I trust my parents implicitly, but I won't reveal any of that to them either."

Smiling, Frankie lifted her hand and cupped his cheek. "That's okay. There are plenty of things I don't know about you that you are allowed to tell me. Once we exhaust those, I'll start nagging you about the other stuff, but it will probably take years for us to get to that point."

Dagor's mouth suddenly went dry.

They didn't have years, not unless Frankie transitioned, and even if she did, the only way they could be together was if she gave up her dream of working for Perfect Match Virtual Studios and joined him on his pod recovery mission.

It wasn't fair of him to ask her to give up everything that was important to her to be with him, especially since it was not going to be fun for her. Frankie wasn't the outdoorsy type, and she would quickly grow tired of sleeping in a tent on frozen ground.

On second thought, though, it could be fun keeping her warm.

She tapped a finger on his temple. "What's going on in that head of yours?"

"Breakfast," he lied.

"I don't want to go to the dining hall." She made a pouty face that was so cute he wanted to kiss her again. "I want to be in the sun and breathe fresh air. Can we go to the Lido deck instead?"

"Sure. We can have Bloody Marys and pretzels for breakfast."

She narrowed her eyes at him. "Are you being sarcastic, or do you really mean that? It's hard to tell with you."

"I mean it, even though I should probably insist that you eat something nutritious. Do you remember what happened the last time you had drinks and snacks on an empty stomach?"

"I fainted." She smiled sweetly. "But that's not going to happen now that I have your blood and your venom in me." She pulled on his neck to bring his lips to hers. "You are injecting me with vitality." She chuckled. "In more ways than one."

His semi-hard erection swelled in an instant. "Perhaps we can skip breakfast, and I will inject you with some more of my vitality. I have plenty to give."

"Oh, I know." She kissed him on the lips. "But now that you've planted the idea of a Bloody Mary in my head, I crave it something fierce. Besides, I need to call Margo. If I don't, she's going to interrupt us in the middle of your vitality transfusion."

Reluctantly, he let go of her and took her hand. "What are you going to tell her?"

"A highly modified version of the story." She followed him back inside the cabin. "I can tell her about the treasure hunt for the amulet, but I can't tell her what it did because then I will have to explain Mey and her echoes and Jacki and her visions. Instead, I'll tell her that it was just a trinket Kalugal had planted ahead of time for us to find. The cartel thugs will be a group of robbers, and I won't tell her anything about the rescued women or about the monsters' well-deserved fate." Frankie frowned. "Although once we collect Margo in Cabo and she comes on board, she will learn the truth, so I need to be careful and not lie too much. I'll have to come up with a creative way of omitting the incriminating details while still staying close to the truth."

He nodded. "Good plan. What are you going to tell Margo about your injury? There is no trace of it left, so you can just skip it."

Frankie laughed. "The more important question is what we are going to tell Dr. Bridget. Can you claim that your godly venom is much stronger than that of the immortals and that it healed me?" She stopped walking and turned to him. "What if we tell her that you bit me over the wound? That would have delivered the venom's healing properties right where I needed them and sped up my recovery, right?"

Frankie hadn't even lowered her voice, so it was good that most of the ship's occupants were still asleep, and the corridor was deserted.

"That's not a bad idea. The only problem I can see is when someone else tries it, and it doesn't work. Bridget is a smart lady, and she will figure out that we lied."

Frankie shook her head. "She won't. Bridget knows only five gods, and that's not a big enough sample on which to base a scientific claim. Each Dormant is different, and each god has different powers, and that could include the potency of their venom. She will have to take our word for it."

"You are one smart lady, Frankie. It scares me a little that you know how to manipulate truth and lies so well."

"I will never lie or manipulate you." She gave his hand a squeeze. "If I do, you will know because you can peek into my mind."

"But I won't do that because it's an invasion of privacy. I will just have to trust you."

"That's the spirit." She smiled brightly. "Trust is the foundation upon which a good relationship is built."

4

KIAN

Kian was surprised to see Lokan and Carol at the large dining table his mother's Odus had set up.

It was supposed to be a family breakfast, and although Lokan was his cousin, he wasn't part of the inner circle like his brother was.

While Kalugal wasn't a member of the immediate family either, somehow, he had managed to insert himself into the family and clan leadership without putting much effort into it. He had done it with his intellect, charm, and natural leadership skills.

Kalugal's men worshiped him and liked him as a person, so perhaps it made him an even better leader than Kian.

Kian didn't doubt that he had the respect and loyalty of his clan, but he wasn't as well liked as his cousin, which was fine with him. Managing the clan affairs and keeping his people safe was much more difficult than what Kalugal had to deal with, and being liked was not a priority.

Besides, charm wasn't one of Kian's attributes, and neither was faking it.

Toven and Mia were also seated at the breakfast table even though they weren't part of the inner family circle. Annani had probably invited Toven because of his familiarity with the ancient Mesoamerican cultures. He might offer some insight into the amulet and its origins.

Syssi's parents were there as well, and as Syssi handed Allegra to Annani, Anita shook her head.

"You have her all of the time." She reached for her granddaughter. "I hardly get to see her."

Smiling, his mother kissed Allegra's cheek and then transferred her to Anita. "If you retired and moved into the village, you could see her whenever you pleased."

Syssi's mother chuckled. "Adam says that the day I quit, I'll die, and he's probably right. Knowing that I'm needed, that what I do improves and often saves people's lives, motivates me to keep going."

Annani nodded sagely. "I cannot argue with that. Having a purpose is essential to one's mental health, especially for immortals and gods."

"My grandparents keep busy while being retired," Mia said. "They have their hobbies and their friends, and they enjoy taking it easy."

"Nothing wrong with that." Anita stroked Allegra's hair, curling the soft strands around her finger. "Why didn't they come on the cruise?"

Mia shrugged. "My grandmother can't tolerate being on a ship. On top of being seasick, she gets terrible migraines. They decided to spend the ten days in their Pasadena home and enjoy time with old friends that they haven't seen in a while."

As the chitchat continued about things that Kian had no interest in, he scanned the faces of his family members, noting the changes in their expressions following yesterday's events.

With the wedding behind him, Dalhu looked like a new man. The stress he'd been under for the past several weeks was finally gone, and his marriage vows to Amanda had gained him approval from many who had been still suspicious of the former Doomer.

Lokan always looked stressed, which was understandable given the danger he was in due to his association with the clan and the undercover work he was doing for them.

Thankfully, his father had shipped him off to China, so he wasn't under constant scrutiny as he would have been if he'd remained on the island. Still, it had to be nerve-wracking to straddle the fence like that, and Kian wished he could just tell his cousin to cross over permanently, but he was the only spy they had in the Brotherhood, and they couldn't afford to lose that connection.

Kian doubted that Areana knew as much as she thought she did about Navuh's dealings, but even if she did, he didn't think she would have told Annani anything about them unless they included a direct threat to her sister's life. Regrettably, his aunt loved her psychotic mate and would never betray him.

"I still can't get over how gorgeous your dress was," Carol said to Amanda.

"When Lokan and I finally get married, I want your designer to make my dress."

Amanda pulled out her phone. "I'll get you her contact information right now."

"By the time we get married, the designer will probably be dead," Lokan grumbled under his breath. "Humans don't live that long."

Carol cast him an amused look. "Don't be such a pessimist. The Fates might resolve things for us sooner than we expect."

"What things need to be resolved?" Syssi asked.

"The island, our post in China, and the designer label that started as a cover for Lokan's work with the Chinese authorities but has become my life's passion."

Annani listened to the exchange with a small smile lifting her lips. "I do not see why any of these things should have an impact on your wedding ceremony. You can tie the knot right here on the cruise. We can squeeze you in for a lunchtime wedding."

Carol shook her head, causing her golden curls to flutter around her face. "I told Lokan that we can't get married as long as we are in danger. I want to feel safe when I pledge my life to this rascal." She nudged his arm playfully.

Annani's smile slid off her face. "The only place I feel safe in is my Alaskan home, but to be frank, I do not feel completely safe even there because safety is an illusion. The trick is to be vigilant and not to let fear paralyze you and prevent you from living your life."

5

ANNANI

Both of Kian's brows hiked up nearly to his hairline. "You don't feel safe in the village? That's news to me. Besides, since when have you been concerned about safety? Given your track record of shenanigans that have kept me awake at night, I assumed that you were fearless."

Annani smiled. "I am a goddess, so there is not much that can harm me, and the odds are in my favor, but since nearly my entire family got wiped out in a single act of terror, I know never to let down my guard. If I had not been vigilant back then, if I had underestimated Mortdh's irrational disdain for me and, by extension, for all females, I would not have fled in the nick of time, and I would have died along with everyone I knew and loved."

As Toven's sigh from across the table drew her attention, Annani turned to him. "I am sorry for bringing up a painful subject. Even five thousand years are not enough to blunt the pain of our loss."

He nodded. "It comes and goes. Sometimes, I manage to forget and enjoy the life I have with Mia, my children and grandchildren, and your entire lovely clan. But sometimes I'm crushed under the painful memories." He inhaled deeply. "I also carry the pain of entire civilizations wiped out of existence despite my best efforts to save them. I can't grasp the savagery, not in humans and even less so in Mortdh. As a god, he should have been above the ape-like savage impulses, but I guess that in his case, it wasn't innate but a form of insanity."

Kian chuckled. "No one thinks otherwise. Mortdh's insanity is a well-established fact."

Syssi put a hand on his arm. "We should change the subject. This is not good for the children."

She was right. Allegra and Evie were too young to understand what was being said, but Phoenix was older, and she was smart for her age. Listening intently to the conversation, the girl had worry in her eyes.

Annani waved a hand over the spread on the table. "We can continue talking after breakfast. When we are done, Okidu and Onidu can take the girls to the other room and watch them while Jacki shows us her amulet."

"Good idea," Jacki said. "I left Darius with Shamash in our cabin because I don't want my son to be anywhere near that thing when I take it out of the box." She turned to Amanda. "The same goes for your children."

Alena rubbed a hand over her rapidly growing stomach. "Perhaps I shouldn't be here when you bring it over. It might affect my baby, and I don't want to take the risk."

"I agree," Orion said. "We will either leave or join the girls in the other room."

"I'd rather leave." Alena turned to Syssi. "We can take the children with us."

Syssi hesitated for a moment before nodding. "Will you be okay watching over the three of them?"

Alena grinned. "Of course. It will be my pleasure."

"I'm very curious to see the amulet," Syssi's father said. "Would it be okay if I take pictures?"

Jacki scrunched her nose. "I'd rather you didn't. Some nutcase somewhere might see the photograph in one of your photography books, recognize the amulet for what it is and come looking for it. The thing has the ability to absorb the life force from the slain, and there are plenty of monsters out there that would slaughter thousands to imbue it with power."

"Uhm," Syssi cleared her throat. "We agreed to save the talking for later, remember?"

"Oops." Jacki covered her mouth with her hand. "I forgot. Let's change the subject to something happy and upbeat so I don't slip again."

When a long moment of silence stretched across the table, Annani's heart contracted. They were all searching their minds for happy topics to talk about and could not come up with a single thing. It was not because nothing good was happening in the world but because it was difficult to think positively after what had happened the day before. Annani had not heard all the details yet, and she had a feeling that things were even worse than what she was imagining.

Given how stricken Syssi looked under the fake smiles she was trying to cover her distress with, she might have talked with Jacki and gotten more information. Another possibility was that Syssi's empathic nature made her more sensitive to the suffering of others than anyone sharing the breakfast table with her.

"I have just the subject," Amanda said. "Wonder and Anandur's wedding tonight. Who wants to bet on Anandur wearing a garter under his tux pants and tossing it at the bachelors after the ceremony?"

Kian chuckled. "I'm not betting against it, and before you ask, he hasn't told me anything."

"You know what would be great?" Mia said. "If Wonder came dressed as Wonder Woman. After all, that was the inspiration for her name. It would be so cool."

As all eyes turned to Amanda, she lifted her hands. "Don't look at me. I'm sworn to secrecy. Besides, I want it to be a surprise. Wonder hasn't given me any instructions or asked for anything specific. She said that she trusted me to come up with stuff she would never even think of. She's very easy to please."

"She is," Annani agreed. "Back in Sumer, when she was still Gulan, she was a very gentle and amiable girl." She smiled. "I was the wild one, and my parents hoped that her easygoing nature would rub off on me."

"Did it work?" Jacki asked.

Annani laughed. "Not at all. I continued to come up with wild schemes, and poor Gulan was in a constant state of panic. I mean Wonder. She does not like to be reminded of her former life. For some reason, she is ashamed of having been my servant even though I never thought of or treated her as such. She was my best friend."

Gulan had been Annani's only friend. The palace guards she had played games with had included her in their playtime because she was the princess, and they had to do what she asked, not because they sought her company.

"There is no shame in being a servant," Syssi's father said. "And being the handmaiden of a princess is a very honorable position."

"Indeed." Annani sighed. "Perhaps it is more about her waking up from stasis as a different person than her years in my service."

"Tula is very different from her older sister," Carol said. "There is nothing timid about her, and she thinks very highly of her position as Areana's companion and confidant, and rightfully so."

Leaning back in her chair, Annani sighed. "I envy you for having seen my sister and Tula, but I do not envy you for what you had to go through to do so. I am not as brave."

Carol's eyes widened. "I don't believe that even for one moment. If you could have, you would have jumped at the opportunity to have a fabulous adventure."

"I am not sure," Annani admitted. "Your so-called adventure almost got you killed."

Syssi cleared her throat. "It seems like we can't have a conversation for longer than five minutes before it touches on a subject that shouldn't be discussed in front of the children."

Annani cast her a fond smile. "You are right that we should let the girls enjoy their innocence for as long as we can. At some point, though, we should stop shielding them from the ugliness of this world. They need to start building up their resilience or they will be paralyzed by the first crisis they face."

Syssi blushed, probably thinking that Annani was criticizing her for being soft, but that had not been her intention. Anita and Adam had not coddled Syssi when she was growing up. She was just a sensitive, soft-hearted soul.

6

JACKI

Once breakfast was over, Alena and Orion took the children to their cabin, and as the door closed behind them, Jacki leaned back in her chair with her coffee cup in hand and turned to Lokan. "Now, you can ask me whatever you want."

He arched a brow. "How did you know?"

She shrugged. "I don't need a paranormal talent to figure out what's on people's minds, and that includes immortals. You kept glancing my way, opening your mouth, and then closing it. Obviously, you wanted to ask me something."

"Yeah, I did, but Syssi kept reminding us that we shouldn't talk about upsetting things in front of the kids. Carol and I heard the main points of what you saw in your vision, but how did you know that it happened recently or that it happened at all? You could have seen the future."

"I just knew." Jacki leveled her gaze at her brother-in-law. "But that's not the real question, is it? You want to know how I convinced everyone of the veracity of my horrific vision, and then had them chase after the kidnapped women and tear the monsters who committed the atrocities to pieces with their fangs just based on what I told them, which could have been untrue."

Next to her, Kalugal shifted in his chair and squared his shoulders, ready to defend her, but Jacki didn't need his intervention.

"Yes," Lokan admitted. "I don't doubt what you saw or that those monsters were guilty of everything you said they were. The women you rescued are proof of that. My concern is that it was done based on a vision, and we all know that foretelling should be taken with a grain of salt."

"I'm not a compeller, and I didn't force anyone to accept my vision as truth. I'm not a convincing orator, either. I just say things as I see them without embellishing or diminishing anything. That's why I was believable when I described those horrific acts of cruelty. Still, Kalugal would not have ordered the attack without first peeking into the minds of several of the women and seeing exactly what I saw in my vision."

Annani lifted her hand to get everyone's attention. "If you are up to it, I want to hear it from you, Jacki. I heard a highly censored version from Kian, but I do not need to be coddled, and I want to know if there was anything in your vision about who ordered the massacre and the sexual assaults."

As horrible as that was, it hadn't been the worst of it, but evidently Kian had chosen not to tell his mother in order to spare her tender feelings.

Jacki wasn't as worried about the goddess's ability to handle the information as she was about Carol's.

Across the table, Carol was chewing on her lower lip and winding a curl around her finger, releasing it, and then winding it up again.

Jacki hesitated.

Carol was a survivor of torture and repeated sexual violation by a sadistic Doomer. She'd not only survived but had also become an undercover agent and gone on a highly dangerous mission. Still, Jacki had no doubt that she carried deep emotional scars.

"Carol, sweetheart. Perhaps it's better if you wait out on the balcony while I tell the Clan Mother what I saw."

The tiny blond shook her head. "Don't worry about me. After what I've been through, I'm no longer naïve or softhearted. I know the depths of depravity monsters can sink to."

As tears prickled the back of Jacki's eyes, she shook her head. "No, you don't. What I'm about to say is worse than anything you can imagine." Bile rose in her throat as the images played before her eyes, and she knew that verbalizing everything again would feel like acid was eating her from the inside, but hiding evil deeds to spare people's feelings was wrong.

The good people of the world needed to know because evil needed to be stopped and wiped off the face of the earth.

"I want to hear it," Carol said. "I'm a survivor, I'm brave, and I don't cower under the blanket, hiding from monsters. I kill them before they can get me."

"As you wish." Jacki sighed. "But don't say I didn't warn you."

When Jacki was done talking, all the males had their fangs fully extended,

Syssi, Nathalie, and Mia were sobbing, Amanda was crying quietly, with rivulets of mascara running down her cheeks, Sari's eyes blazed daggers, and the Clan Mother looked infinitely sad.

But Carol looked catatonic.

Jacki took in a deep breath and turned to Lokan. "I think Carol needs some fresh air."

"We all do." He helped his mate up and walked her out the open balcony doors.

"How do you do that?" Syssi blew her nose into a napkin. "How are you so strong? After what you told me yesterday, I couldn't sleep all night, and you didn't even tell me the worst parts. You didn't tell me about what they did to the children, the babies." As her sobbing intensified, Kian pulled her onto his lap and wrapped his arms around her.

Jacki closed her eyes and then immediately opened them as the horrific images flooded the space behind her closed lids. "I'm only as strong as I need to be to do the right thing."

"And what's that?" Amanda lifted a cloth napkin and wiped her mascara-stained cheeks.

"Rally the troops, rescue the survivors, and go to war. I did all three."

7

FRANKIE

"Good morning, Mistress Frankie and Master Dagor." Bob grinned, flashing his metallic teeth. They were just two convex strips of metal with grooves etched into them to mimic the look of the real thing. "What can I serve you today?"

"Two Bloody Marys and two bags of pretzels, please." Frankie leaned over the counter and scanned the various snacks. "Unless you have something more nutritious to offer."

"Peanuts are a good source of protein." Bob reached with one of his long arms to snatch them off the overhead conveyor. "I also have roasted edamame beans, another good source of protein."

"We will take both," Dagor said. "Two of each."

"Of course, master." Bob put four bags on the counter and then reached for two glasses to mix the Bloody Marys.

Frankie tore into the roasted edamame bag and shook some into the palm of her hand. "That should do it, right? Since it's nutritious and all that."

Dagor chuckled. "I'm not an expert on human dietary needs, but I doubt Bridget would approve."

Frankie shrugged and shoved another palmful into her mouth.

"Your drinks are ready." Bob pushed the two tall Bloody Mary glasses toward them. "Enjoy."

"Thank you." Dagor took the drinks and turned around to scan for a good place to sit. "Shade or no shade?" he asked.

He was wearing his sunglasses, so the bright sunlight wasn't a problem, and he wasn't concerned about skin cancer either. That wasn't the case for her, though.

Frankie had forgotten to put on sunscreen before leaving the cabin, and she needed to stay out of direct sunlight to protect her skin. Once she turned immortal, if she ever turned, she could do whatever she wanted and not worry about the consequences.

"Shade," she said.

"Thank you." Dagor rewarded her with a smile. "I prefer shade, too."

"So why didn't you say anything? It's not all about me, you know."

"I'm trying to be a gentleman." He walked over to a table with an umbrella opened and put the drinks down. "It's my job to take care of your needs to the best of my ability."

Huffing out a breath, Frankie sat down on the chair he'd pulled out for her. "It's my job to do the same for you. Next time you have a preference, please let me know. It might work for me or not, but at least I won't choose arbitrarily without taking your needs into consideration."

Dagor smiled. "Is that part of the list of things you wanted to talk to me about?"

She had forgotten all about it.

On the way to the ruins, she'd promised to give him a list of acceptable and unacceptable behaviors, but with all that had happened since, it was no wonder that it had escaped her mind.

"I don't really have a list," she admitted. "But if I had one, this would be on it. We need to learn as much as we can about each other, and the only way to do so is to be open about our likes and dislikes. We will have to figure out things as we go, and if you want, you can take notes."

Dagor was the type of guy who would actually do that. He liked everything neatly organized in the appropriate boxes, and anything that was out of place bothered him. She was willing to bet that he was a neat freak and added that to her own mental list of things she needed to learn about him.

"I keep it all up here." He tapped a finger over his temple. "So far, I have two items. One is to never leave you sleeping without letting you know in some form where I went and when I will be back. The other one is to express my preferences if I have them. Anything else that you can think of?"

"Many things, but since I can't think of them off the top of my head, we will have to address them as we go." Her gut clenched with what she was about to say next, but her expression was firm. "Hopefully, we will have plenty of time to do that on our trek through Tibet."

His eyes widened. "You want to come with me?"

She shrugged as if it wasn't a big deal. "You can't abandon your mission, but I can postpone my beta testing internship or perhaps assist in some way remotely." She grimaced. "Regrettably, I'm not a girl of independent means, and I need a way to earn a living while we are searching for the missing pods."

For a long moment, he stared at her as if she had grown a pair of horns. "You don't need to worry about money while you are with me, but finances are not the main problem with your very generous offer."

Frankie hadn't planned on blurting out her idea to Dagor before she had a concrete plan, and she blamed her impulsivity for that. "Finances are important to me because I don't want to be completely dependent on you for every purchase I make. That will just not do. But other than that, I see no problem with me joining you on the mission. Gabi is going, so it's not like you can't take civilians with you."

"You are still human, Frankie. And even if you start transitioning soon, it will be weeks before you are ready for a grueling trek."

So that was his problem. She was a weak human, and she would hold them back.

"I get it. You don't want me to slow you down. But maybe I can join you after my transition is complete and I'm back on my feet? I could fly out and meet you somewhere. I'm sure there are airports in Tibet."

"Not where we are going."

8

DAGOR

Dagor hated the uncertainty of their situation, and he hated putting Frankie in a position where she was planning to give up her dreams to be with him.

"Let's not talk about it now, okay? It can wait until your transition starts."

Her brow furrowed, and she assumed the stubborn expression he dreaded and loved at the same time.

On the one hand, it meant that Frankie was going to argue until she won, and he would have to accept things he didn't want to, but on the other hand, he loved her confidence and her ability to stick to her guns.

"We don't have the luxury of time." She huffed out a breath. "Besides, you are the one who needs everything planned out."

She'd got him there, but how could he make plans when it wasn't clear whether or not she could turn immortal?

What if she couldn't, though?

What if she remained human?

He was in love with Frankie. He couldn't just forget her because her lifespan was so short. It was better not to think about it just yet. Why worry about something that might not happen?

"I wish I could make a plan, but everything depends on you turning immortal."

Frankie narrowed her eyes at him. "So, what are you saying, that you will just leave me if I don't transition?"

"That's not what I'm saying at all. What I meant was that we can't plan for the future without knowing the outcome of your induction. Plans that will fit Frankie the immortal will not fit Frankie the human."

Deflating, she sank into the chair. "Yeah. The same things are going round on a loop in my head. Perhaps we can make two plans, one for each outcome."

That was actually not a bad idea.

"What happens with your job offer if you don't transition?"

"They erase my memories of gods and immortals, which will probably include this cruise and you." She winced. "Toven says that he's very good at that, and he can leave some of the memories and just change a few details. Maybe I would remember meeting you and falling in love, but not the fact that you are a god."

He nodded. "I get that part, but what about the job? Will they find you something else to do that is not in their village, or will they just leave you to find something else on your own?"

"I guess Toven can get me a job in one of the Perfect Match studios. Why?"

He smiled and reached for her hand. "If I know where you will be working, I can find you there, and even if they erase me from your memories, I can make you fall in love with me all over again."

Her eyes softened. "And then what? You will pretend to be human?"

"Yes. Hopefully, we will find the missing pods, so I will be free to spend time with you."

"For how long?" she whispered. "You're not going to age, and you can't keep thralling me every day to not notice that you look exactly the same years later."

"Thralling is not my only option. I can also shroud, but you are right. If I don't tell you the truth about me, I will have to thrall you every time we are intimate, and that means daily. I can't do that. You'll need to know who and what I am and accept me all over again."

"I'm sure I will, but I don't want you to suffer, and you will suffer if you have to watch me get old and die."

Dagor lifted his glass and emptied what was left down his throat. "It's my choice to make. The only choice you have is to either love me back or not. And don't think for even a moment about pretending to not want me just to save me heartache in the future."

She chuckled. "Am I that transparent?"

"To me, you are. You have a noble heart beating in your chest, and you think of the well-being of others before you think of your own."

"You think too highly of me." Frankie took another sip of her Bloody

Mary. "I'm not that selfless. What about our children, though? Will they be born Dormant or immortal?"

Dagor swallowed. "If we are blessed with children, they will be born immortal."

The thought of fathering hybrid children had been foreign to him only days earlier, but witnessing the wedding ceremonies and observing the two little baby girls at the family table had changed things for him, and what once had felt like 'hell no' had turned into 'hell yes' or at least 'hell maybe.'

"Oh, boy." She took another sip from her drink and then licked her lips. "Then you will need to hang around long enough for them to become adults so you can guide them on how to remain undetected."

"I plan on doing that regardless of whether we have children. I don't think I can live without you."

"Oh, Dagor." She leaned over and kissed him on the lips. "I love you too much to let you suffer when I die. I'll have to make you fall out of love with me."

"Not possible." He cupped her cheek. "You don't have it in you to be mean to me."

She arched a brow. "You wanna bet?"

"Sure." He clasped her hand. "What are you going to give me when I win?"

"What do you want?"

He leaned over and whispered the prize in her ear.

She laughed. "You are so naughty."

"Is it a 'yes'?"

"You got yourself a deal." She shook his hand. "What do I get if I win?"

"You won't win. Not this time."

9

SYSSI

Syssi sincerely considered asking one of the gods to remove the memory of what Jacki had told them, and if that made her a coward and a weakling, so be it.

She doubted she could continue functioning with that horror movie playing on repeat inside her head. She did not want to raise her daughter in a world where things like that could happen. But what were her options?

Move to a colony on Mars?

Suddenly, the gods' planet didn't seem that bad. Peace and security were worth sacrificing some freedoms for, right?

Not that it was an option. The gods thought of immortals and all other hybrids as abominations, and they were not welcomed on Anumati.

"Can I get you a glass of wine?" Kian asked quietly.

"I need something stronger than that, but I doubt it will help. What I need is a brain scrub to erase what I just heard."

"I can help with that," Annani offered.

Syssi shook her head. "I can't. I have to be strong."

Maybe she would take Annani up on her offer after touching the damn amulet and getting a dose of visuals to supplement what her mind had already supplied.

"I can be strong for the both of us," Kian murmured. "You don't need this crap to keep you awake at night."

"Yes, I do. I owe it to the victims."

"Dammit, Syssi. I need you to listen to reason. Please let my mother erase this ugliness from your mind and ease your burden."

She shook her head. "If all of you can handle this, I can as well. I have to."

Mia let out a long, shaky breath. "I can't handle this, and I will gladly accept Toven's help to erase the past twenty minutes from my mind. I know it's wrong, but I can't let this poison me from the inside. I want the bliss of ignorance."

But that was the problem. So many people were ignorant, most willfully so, because it was easier to believe the lies than acknowledge the ugly truth.

Syssi refused to be part of the uninformed masses, even if it meant sacrificing her peace of mind. "I'll take that drink." She lifted her head and scanned the room for the Odus. "Okidu, can you get me a giant margarita, please?"

"Of course, mistress." He bowed and rushed to the bar.

Amanda lifted her hand. "Make me one too."

"I'll get the whiskey." Dalhu pushed to his feet.

He had responded to Jacki's retelling the same way all the other males had, with glowing eyes and elongated fangs, but while Kian, Andrew, and David wrestled theirs under control, and Kalugal's, Toven's, and Lokan's had retracted halfway, Dalhu's were still fully elongated.

It was ironic that Syssi found Dalhu's rage reassuring.

The answer to violence shouldn't be more violence, but sometimes nothing else worked to eradicate evil and protect the innocent and the defenseless, and Syssi was glad to have the powerful warrior on her side.

Her father eyed the gods and immortals with fascination rather than trepidation, which was good, and her mother looked like she was on the verge of tears, but she did not allow them to fall.

Anita had always been an iron lady, the cornerstone of their family, and Syssi wished she had half of her mother's resilience and strength. She was also glad that her mother hadn't commented about her being overly sensitive like she used to when Syssi was a teenager.

They were nothing alike, and it had always been difficult to reconcile their different personalities.

Perhaps being a doctor had hardened Anita, or maybe she had chosen to become a physician because she had that hard core inside of her that Syssi lacked. It was no coincidence that Syssi hadn't followed in her mother's footsteps and had chosen to major in architecture with a minor in business. Neither field involved any human drama.

When Dalhu was done pouring whiskey for the guys and Sari, Okidu handed out margaritas to the rest of them, save for Mia. Even the Clan Mother accepted a glass with a salty rim and slowly sipped on it.

Taking the large glass with her, Annani leaned back in her chair and looked at Jacki. "You did not say anything about who was behind the attack other than the cartel thugs. They are known to be vicious, but usually not to such an extent. Did you notice anything that would indicate they were being directed by an outside force?"

Yeah, they were probably possessed by demons.

Syssi couldn't imagine a society that produced such monsters. It was beyond gang wars and drugs and even trafficking. Who were their mothers? Their fathers? Who had raised such twisted creatures?

"I didn't," Jacki said. "All I got were visuals of the attack. There might have been some clues, but I was too overwhelmed and shocked to notice anything else."

Annani nodded. "That is perfectly understandable, dear."

Syssi felt in her gut that touching the amulet would make her see more, but maybe it wasn't a good idea to do it with Carol in the room.

She and Lokan were still out on the balcony, but they would no doubt come back inside when Jacki brought the amulet to show them.

"Let's see that amulet," her father said. "I'm curious to see the thing that has caused so much trouble."

"The thing didn't do it." Jacki rose to her feet. "It was only a tool, and it helped us rescue the victims. Still, remember not to touch it with your bare hand. Use a cloth napkin."

"I don't have any psychic ability," her father said when Jacki ducked into the bedroom. "I can touch it as much as I want and not get any visions."

Her mother patted his arm. "It's better to be careful, Adam. You never know. Perhaps Syssi got her paranormal ability from you. She surely hasn't gotten it from me."

"I wish that was true." Her father cast her a reassuring smile. "But I'm not a Dormant."

What if he was, though?

They had never considered the possibility that her father could be a carrier of the immortal genes as well. Perhaps Dormants weren't as rare as they had initially believed, and the affinity Dormants and immortals felt for each other increased the chances of Dormant pairings.

Not that it mattered. Both her parents were way over the age of attempting to transition safely.

10

KIAN

"Ready for the big reveal?" Jacki opened the box and pulled out a cloth bundle.

"Very much so." Syssi's father pushed to his feet and walked over to look at it over Jacki's shoulder.

She put it on the dining table and carefully peeled off the layers of fabric without touching the object itself.

It was a big piece, definitely not something that would be comfortable to wear around the neck, but it was impressive, and Kian could imagine a male priest wearing it over his bare chest.

The opal in the center was the size of a large potato, and it most likely weighed two pounds or more. The color was magnificent even as it lay dormant on top of the fabric wrapping, and Kian was sure that if he dangled it from its chain, he would see even more colors as the light hit its polished surface. Most of it was orange, making it appear as if it contained fire, but there was also red, green, and yellow.

Holding a napkin, Adam reached for the amulet and lifted it by its chain. "It's heavy."

Jacki nodded. "It is."

As the amulet swung from Adam's fingers, the opal reflected the light as Kian had expected, and the colors seemed to swirl like there was something alive in it. A pulsating heart or a vein.

"Creepy," Andrew murmured, echoing Kian's thoughts.

"What's written on the edges?" Amanda turned to Toven. "Can you read that?"

The disgusted expression on his face indicated that he wanted nothing to do with the artifact, but he leaned a little closer, squinted, and then pulled out his phone and snapped a picture. "It's been a while, and I'm rusty. I'll try to decipher the writing from the photo, but I can guess what it says. It's something along the lines of beseeching the gods to accept the sacrifice, and in exchange, grant the wearer either prophetic powers or victory against their enemies. It's always the same. Blood and more blood." He leaned away.

"I don't sense anything nefarious from it," Syssi said. "Maybe it was drained after the vision?"

"That's possible." Jacki sat down, leaving the amulet in Adam's hands. "When I touched it, I felt as if I was being zapped by a bolt of lightning, and I let go of it immediately. I held it for no longer than a split second. The vision appeared right away, and in my head, it lasted a long time, but I was unconscious only for a few moments. Then, when I wanted to find the victims, I put it around my neck, and it was more of a hum than a zap, a steady flow of something that communicated in sensations of hot and cold. If I was on the right path, it felt warm, and when we veered off, it cooled down." She chuckled. "An ancient GPS."

"Then it's probably safe to touch." Leaning over, Syssi started to reach for it, but Kian grabbed her shirt from behind and tugged her back down. "Don't touch it without protecting your skin." He took his folded napkin and handed it to her. "Use this."

"Fine." She cast him a glare.

"In fact, there is no reason for you to touch it at all." He was still holding on to the back of her shirt. "You can see it perfectly well from where you are right now."

"Here." Adam walked around the table and laid the amulet in front of Syssi. "Now you can examine it to your heart's content without touching it."

"Thanks, Dad." She peered over the thing as if she was trying to decipher all of its secrets. "It's gaudy, but I don't sense evil. Not that I know what evil feels like."

"It gives off a sense of foreboding," Nathalie said. "When you feel anxious for no reason and think that you are going crazy, there is evil nearby."

As everyone turned to look at her, Kian wondered if there was anything to that. Nathalie had described how he felt on most days, so did it mean that evil was lurking nearby all of the time?

Yeah, it kind of did.

He had Doomers to worry about, missing Kra-ell twins that were so powerful they could enslave the entire planet, Kra-ell assassins that were after his mother and the twins, and the Eternal King and whatever he would do to Earth once he discovered that the human population had grown to eight billion people and that their technological advancement posed a threat.

"Is this something you learned from the ghosts?" Amanda asked Nathalie.

Nathalie nodded. "The first one, Tut. He said that evil was everywhere, hiding in plain sight and pretending to be something else. Evil is a great liar because it has no scruples, so it can be very convincing." She sighed. "As a kid, I thought that he was mean, and that he wanted to scare me so I would be dependent on him, but he was right."

"What kind of a name is Tut?" Sari asked.

Nathalie chuckled. "Tutankhamun, but I think he lied about it. There is no way Tut was an ancient pharaoh."

"Who knows?" Annani said. "He might be. Tutankhamun was an interesting fellow. Very smart and pragmatic even though he was just a kid at the time."

"You knew him?" Sari asked.

"Of course. I knew most of the world's great leaders."

11

SYSSI

As everyone's focus shifted to Annani, Syssi's remained on the amulet.

While the goddess regaled them with tales of ancient Egypt's religiopolitical climate at the time of the young pharaoh Tutankhamun and his predecessor Akhenaten, no one was paying attention to what Syssi was doing, and she might be able to touch it without anyone trying to stop her.

"The shift to a monotheistic religion nearly drove Egypt to economic ruin because its economy was based around the many temples of the different gods they worshipped." Annani sighed. "Akhenaten was too progressive for the times. The world was not ready for his lofty, elitist ideas. While he had gathered around him in his new beautiful capital city all the intellectuals of the time, which included all the priests from temples across Egypt, the common people of Egypt were left with no guidance, and things started falling apart. After Akhenaten's death, Tutankhamun reversed the move and restored Egypt to its former glory."

It was all fascinating, but Syssi was listening to it with half an ear while trying to control the trembling of her hand as she reached for the amulet.

Perhaps instead of taking it in her hand, she should only touch it with her finger? But which part should she touch, the opal or the casing?

Maybe she should stop being a chicken and just take it in her hand?

"Tutankhamun died at nineteen," Annani said. "But he managed to accomplish a lot in the ten years he ruled over Egypt."

Kian released an indignant huff. "A nine-year-old saved the country from economic ruin?"

"He was aided by his great-uncle, Ay, the real mastermind behind the restoration."

It was now or never. Kian was busy with his mother, and no one was looking at her. There would be hell to pay later, but she had to do it.

Closing her eyes, Syssi extended her hand and smacked her palm down on the amulet.

The vision was so instantaneous that it knocked her off her feet, and she felt herself falling backward, but she didn't hit the floor. Instead, she was floating over a scene and watching events unfold from above like she had done countless times before.

The main difference was the speed with which it had happened, and her full awareness of what was going on.

Syssi was both in the scene she was witnessing and in Annani's cabin on the ship.

Six males were gathered around a map in a dimly lit room, all armed to the teeth and looking dangerous. They were speaking Spanish, of which she understood only every fifth word, and then two of them switched to another language she didn't understand but recognized as the bastardized version of Sumerian that the Doomers spoke.

One of them approached the map and drew a red circle around one of the villages, and as he spoke, she suddenly understood what he was saying as if he was speaking in plain English.

"Make an example out of them so all the others tremble in fear and give us what we demand without a fight. We don't tolerate disobedience."

As the other four exchanged glances, Syssi hoped they would argue against the command or at least look uneasy, but when they turned to their co-conspirators, the four grinned with so much malice in their eyes that they looked more demonic than their masters.

"*Sí, señor.*"

The Doomer clapped the thug on the back. "Kill everyone, except for the pretty girls they refused to hand over. They are worth a lot of money to us. You can have your fun with them, but don't damage the merchandise too much. Just break it in." He laughed. "Surprisingly, virgins are not in high demand these days."

The vision winked out, and Syssi gasped, "Doomers."

"What about them?" Kian barked.

She was in his arms, and he was looking at her with fury in his eyes.

Oh, yeah, there would be hell to pay, but that was okay. Once he heard what she had to say, he would forget about being mad at her and get busy correcting the grave mistake they had made.

"Doomers were behind the attack. They control the cartel. If they come to investigate what happened to their monsters and find the remains, they will figure out immediately who disposed of them, and they'll come after us."

Only a bunch of hungry jaguars, lions, or immortals with fangs could have torn those monsters apart like that, but the big cats wouldn't have buried them.

It wouldn't take a genius to connect the dots and follow them to the only tourist group who had visited the ruins that day and then to the ship they had come from.

"Crap." Kian let out a breath. "What do we do now?"

"We turn around," Kalugal said. "We need to burn the bodies, or rather the body parts, before they find them."

Pushing out of Kian's arms, Syssi moved back to her chair and emptied the last of her margarita.

"Was it bad?" Jacki asked. "What did you see?"

"I saw six monsters planning a horrific attack and smiling about it."

"There were six of them?" Kian filled a glass with water and handed it to her.

"Two Doomers and four cartel thugs."

"How do you know they were Doomers?" Kian motioned for her to drink up.

She took a couple of sips and put the glass down. "Visions are strange. They spoke in Spanish to the thugs, and I understood a little of it but not enough to make sense of what they were saying. Then, the two Doomers switched to their own language, which I don't understand at all, but I know how it sounds. Then they spoke to the thugs again, and although it was back to Spanish, I heard it as if it was plain English. They ordered the thugs to make an example out of that village so no one would ever oppose them again, and they told them to take the pretty girls because they're worth a lot of money."

12

KIAN

Kian was doing his best to contain his anger, and yet he was doing a piss-poor job of it. Syssi was casting him fearful looks that cut him worse than anything she had revealed, but he couldn't bring himself under control.

It was her right to do whatever she deemed necessary to enhance her visions, and he could hate it as much as he wanted, but he couldn't stop her from doing that or be angry at her for using her Fate-given talent to help the clan.

Her latest revelation might save them a lot of trouble, provided that they made it to the burial site before the Doomers discovered what had happened to their henchmen.

"I need to tell the captain to turn around." He raked his fingers through his hair.

"Tell him we forgot someone," Jacki said. "He doesn't need to know why we are turning back, right? The less he knows, the better."

"I don't need to tell him anything. He will do as I ask." He pushed to his feet and offered Syssi a hand up. "Do you want to come with me?"

She hesitated for a split second. "Sure."

"I'm not mad," he said when they were outside the cabin.

"You could have fooled me. You still look mad."

"I'm angry because I hate when you put yourself in danger, but I also hate that I make it more difficult for you. You have every right to use your talent as you see fit as long as you don't hurt anyone else in the process. I just wish you didn't hurt yourself."

"I don't." She smiled and stretched on her toes to kiss his cheek. "Not really. I might seem fragile, and maybe I am, but I'm not a coward. What was the worst that could have happened? I would have seen something even more disturbing than what Jacki recounted? So what? If I couldn't live with it, your mother or Toven could have erased it from my brain."

He shook his head. "You know that it doesn't work like that. Remember the women we freed from the Doomers and took to Hawaii?"

"Of course. What about them?"

"Vanessa said that erasing their memories wasn't enough. They still remembered their trauma subconsciously despite the thrall, and the dissonance between what they felt but couldn't remember was detrimental to their mental health. They needed to work through it the conventional way."

Syssi let out a breath. "I didn't really plan on getting a memory wipe, but it was comforting to think that I had the option. Jacki must be made from solid titanium to handle what she saw so well. I'm grateful to the merciful Fates for sparing me the gruesome images and only showing me the demons at the planning stage. Perhaps the Fates, or whoever else is responsible for visions, know what each seer can tolerate and grant them glimpses of the past or future accordingly."

"That's possible." Kian stopped at the door to the bridge. "I might need you to court another vision."

Syssi looked at Kian, barely able to contain her astonishment.

Who was this man, and what had he done with her overprotective husband?

"Of course," she said quickly before he could change his mind. "What do you need me to find out?"

"We need to find where the Doomers are based and how many of them are involved with the cartels."

"I'll try, but you know how visions are. I might not get the answers to my questions."

"I know, but so far the Fates have shown you what you needed to see, so I trust that they will do the same now."

"I love you." She lifted on her toes and kissed him on his lips. "You're incredible."

A grin spread over his face, and he wrapped his arms around her, cupping her bottom. "I know, but it's always nice to hear. Tell me why I'm incredible."

"Well, there are the regular reasons, like the breadth of your shoulders, the shape of your lips, those tight glutes." She rubbed herself on him like a cat on a scratching post. "But what I admire most is your steadfast commitment to go against your instincts and not try to stifle me. I know how difficult that is for a caveman like you."

"You have no idea what a herculean effort that is." He reached for the door handle. "Let's take care of informing the captain of the change of plans, and then we'll go back to the cabin and try again."

Syssi nodded, but her stomach churned with unease at the thought of touching the amulet once more.

What if this time it showed her things she could never un-see?

13

ANNANI

After Kian and Syssi had left to talk to the captain, the conversation continued in hushed voices, but Annani didn't take part in it.

She was still trying to compose herself, and it was proving difficult.

Living through most of human so-called civilized history, she'd witnessed atrocities such as Jacki had described before, but that did not make it any easier to process. Especially since she had truly believed that humanity had been going in the right direction and that kind of evil was never to return.

She had been wrong.

Humans were still savages, too easy to incite into committing terrible crimes against others either by ideology, religion, greed, or rather all three woven into one hateful motivational force to destroy.

The Doomers were not responsible for all of it, but enough.

The thing was, she had a feeling that the ultimate responsibility was with the gods. They had engineered humans to be easily influenced so they could control them effortlessly, and that back door into human minds was what made it possible for evildoers to turn otherwise ordinary people into monsters.

Were the Eternal King and the Anumati establishment aware of that? Was that the reason they viewed hybrid children born of unions between gods and lesser species as abominations?

As half-human, immortals suffered from the same vulnerability to virulent ideology, and that was made clearly evident by the disciples of Mortdh.

She used to believe that there was hope for the Doomers and that there was a way to undo the brainwashing and turn them into decent people, and that was why she forbade her people to execute the captured ones and put them into stasis instead.

Once Navuh was taken down and replaced by a progressive leader, she hoped those Doomers could be rehabilitated. Without the constant brainwashing and indoctrination, there might be a chance for them.

But perhaps she had been wrong.

Maybe there was no salvation for their souls. Perhaps Navuh's propaganda created fertile ground, but the poisoning was done by their own evil deeds.

Not even Navuh would have ordered the gruesome murder of children. His goal was global domination, and he was ruthless in attaining that goal, but he wouldn't have bothered with annihilating a poor village in Mexico to make a point and terrify the local population into compliance.

Still, it didn't surprise her that Doomers were behind the cartels. Navuh needed money for his operations, and there was a lot of it to be had from drugs and trafficking. The Doomers responsible for the local operation were probably free to do whatever was needed to maximize those profits, and what had been done to that village was their autonomous decision.

Sowing terror ensured there was no resistance to their operations.

If captured, those Doomers did not deserve mercy. They did not deserve stasis and a second chance at life, but if she made an exception in their case, she would weaken her stance, and Kian would pounce on it, advocating for execution in most altercations with the Brotherhood.

Annani sighed. She could use some advice.

It was a shame that the first talk with her grandmother had not even been scheduled yet. The queen had vast experience and, given her machinations, she was also very smart. She might have some words of wisdom for her granddaughter.

The irony was not lost on her. Annani was one of the five oldest people on Earth, and yet she looked to someone even older for advice.

Perhaps Toven would have words of wisdom for her? After all, he was even older than she was. When there was a lull in the conversation, Annani caught Toven's eyes and presented her dilemma.

"End them," Kalugal answered for Toven. "And that's coming from me, as a former member of the Brotherhood. There are a few who are worth saving, but the ones Syssi saw in her vision are beyond redemption."

Toven nodded. "I agree. Ordering the torture and murder of children goes against every human and immortal instinct. Those capable of such acts are so diseased that there is no cure for them."

As everyone around the table echoed the same sentiment, Annani sighed.

"I do not often admit to having been mistaken, but I have to concede that it was naïve of me to apply my moral standards and my belief in the good that exists in all of our hearts to those who hold my beliefs in contempt and consider them a weakness to be exploited. Some Doomers might still hold on to a shred of decency, and those are the ones I want to save, but those who are proven to have none left need to be eliminated. Human lives mean nothing to them. Immortal lives mean nothing to them. Suffering means nothing to them. Therefore, they mean nothing to me."

14

KIAN

Kian could sense the change in the room as soon as he and Syssi returned.

He pulled out a chair for his wife. "Did something happen while we were gone?"

His mother nodded. "We had an interesting conversation about the merit of granting captured Doomers a second chance, and I arrived at the conclusion that, in certain situations, that is not advisable. The Doomers responsible for this attack do not deserve a second chance at life."

That was so unexpected that for a moment, Kian was stunned speechless. The Doomers had committed plenty of atrocities before, and his mother had always been adamant about not ending them if they were captured.

Thankfully, she had decreed that the lives of Guardians always came first, so killing Doomers in the heat of battle was okay.

Since most Doomers fought to the death, it wasn't often they were captured alive. It mostly happened when they were severely injured and could not fight any longer. That too didn't happen often, so even though Kian didn't agree with his mother's softhearted edict, he hadn't made too much effort to change her mind about it.

Still, over the centuries they had collected so many Doomers in their catacombs that they were running out of room.

He would like nothing better than to stop the inflow, but he doubted that his mother's resolve would extend beyond the Doomers responsible for the vicious attack on the villagers.

"That's a surprising and welcome change of heart, but I haven't decided what to do about the situation yet. My initial plan was to get rid of the evidence of our involvement by burning the bodies and hopefully avoiding direct confrontation with the Doomers. We are on vacation, we have a wedding to celebrate tonight, and I don't want to rush into things without giving it more thought."

"I agree," Kalugal said. "We don't know how many of them are out here. If it's only the two that Syssi saw in her vision, then we can easily get rid of them and continue on our merry way. But if there is a large group stationed here, we shouldn't go in seeking vengeance and get Guardians killed."

Given the determined expression on his mother's face, she didn't like that answer.

"I understand the need for caution, and I do not recommend rushing in without a plan, but we need to take out this cell of the Brotherhood, and we need to make it look like the locals did it."

That was an angle Kian hadn't considered. "That sounds good in theory, but how are we going to do that?"

His mother smiled. "You are the general, my son. You will find a way."

"Right." He raked his fingers through his hair. "I need to assemble my war council, and I hate that I need to do so during my damn vacation."

Next to him, Syssi shifted in her seat. "Maybe I should touch the amulet again to see how many of them are here?"

Every muscle in Kian's body tensed, and he clenched his jaw to keep himself from resisting. He'd been the one who had suggested that she try again, but now that he looked at the artifact that was still displayed on the table, he had second thoughts.

Resting on top of the fabric that Jacki had wrapped it in, it looked like a piece of costume jewelry, and if Kian hadn't seen how quickly it had thrown Syssi into a vision, he would have thought that it had nothing to do with it other than Syssi's belief in its power. But he'd seen her summon a vision before, and it had taken much more effort even when she did it in Allegra's room and somehow drew on their daughter's power.

But what if Syssi was just getting stronger and faster the more visions she summoned?

Maybe it had nothing to do with Allegra or the amulet?

He turned to her. "I want you to try something for me."

"What?"

"Try to summon a vision without touching the amulet. In fact, go over to the couch so you are not anywhere near it."

Syssi frowned. "Why?"

"I have a feeling that your powers have increased naturally and that you don't need anything to enhance them." He turned to Mia. "If you don't mind, I would like you to go out to the balcony while Syssi is summoning the vision. I don't want you enhancing her powers either."

"Of course." Mia put her chair in reverse.

Syssi lifted a hand. "Hold on, Mia." She turned to Kian. "I'm all for experimenting with my ability, but now is not the time for that. We need answers, and I need all the help I can get. Mia should stay and get even closer to me while I touch the amulet."

"Syssi is right," his mother said. "We do not have time to experiment."

"There is also the issue of fatigue." Amanda looked at Syssi. "We know that your prophetic ability diminishes with every try."

"That's true, but when I tossed a coin with Mia next to me, my accuracy didn't drop with each subsequent toss. I guessed every single one correctly no matter how many times I repeated it."

Mia nodded. "That's how Syssi discovered my enhancing powers."

Kian let out a resigned breath. "I see that I'm overruled." He pushed to his feet and positioned himself behind Syssi. "Go ahead. I'm right here to catch you if you fall."

15

SYSSI

Syssi had been sure that Kian would balk at the last moment, but she should have known that her husband would be true to his word.

She turned to Mia. "I wonder if touching you and the amulet at the same time would produce a stronger vision? Are you up for it?"

Mia shrugged. "I don't even know what I'm doing when I'm enhancing someone's power, but I know that I'm not going to see what you see, so yeah."

Toven looked worried. "I'm not sure about that."

"Why not?" Mia arched a brow. "It's not like I'm being taken into enemy territory, strapped to your back."

He winced. "That's different. I knew that I could protect you there. I can't protect you from the influence of this artifact or what it might reveal to Syssi."

"I'll be fine." She patted his arm before turning her chair around and driving over to where Syssi was standing. "Do you want to hold my hand?"

"Yes. Thank you." Syssi clasped Mia's small hand in hers and hovered the other one over the amulet, when it occurred to her that it wasn't safe for the girl.

The previous vision happened so fast that it had knocked her off her feet and she fell, but Kian had caught her. If Mia was in the way, she might get knocked over.

"Perhaps you should move a little to the side." She looked over her shoulder at Kian. "I trust you to catch me if I fall so I don't topple Mia."

"Of course." He put both of his hands on her shoulders. "Perhaps you can summon the vision while sitting on my lap. That way, you're not going to fall for sure."

She was seriously tempted to take him up on his offer, and the only reason she dismissed the idea was that she didn't want to add even more variables to her attempt.

"It's okay."

Taking a deep breath, Syssi put her hand on the amulet, but unlike the other time, nothing happened.

Baffled, she opened her eyes and frowned at the artifact. "It's not working. Maybe we've exhausted its power."

"Try to concentrate on your question," Jacki said. "Maybe it's weakened, and you need to pull it out of it."

Closing her eyes again, Syssi imagined the scene she'd witnessed before, with the two Doomers and four cartel thugs discussing the murder of innocents, and as the familiar swirl of an incoming vision started spinning in front of her, she surrendered to the sensation and let it pull her through the vortex.

Except, the scene she found herself in couldn't be farther from what she'd expected.

She was in the temple she had seen before, but this time both of the goddesses were there, the one with the silver hair and the seer, both glowing so brightly that it was impossible to discern their facial features.

Next to them, sitting on a cushion on the floor a few feet behind the seer, was a dark-haired goddess who didn't glow at all, and her face looked very familiar.

She was the feminine version of Aru, and she was using what looked like an old-fashioned quill to write in a large journal while the goddesses talked.

As the seer laughed at something the other one had said, the silver-haired goddess laughed too, and the two embraced.

They were obviously friends, and Syssi knew who they were. She also knew who the scribe was, and the pieces of the puzzle fell into place.

Did Kian know? And if he did, why hadn't he told her?

Also, why was she being shown this scene instead of what she'd asked for?

As the vision started fading and the vortex spat her out on the other side, she gasped, opened her eyes, and turned to look at Kian, who was holding her against his chest.

"That was short," he said. "What did you see?"

"Not what I set out to see." She pushed away from him and sank into her chair. "I think that the amulet is out of power."

"What about me?" Mia asked. "Did I help in any way?"

"Yes." Syssi smiled at her. "I think that I got the vision thanks to you, not the amulet. It was about the goddesses, not the Doomers or the cartel thugs."

Kian looked relieved more than disappointed, when he handed her a glass of water. "What was the vision about?"

She couldn't tell him in front of everyone, and she had a feeling that he already knew about Aru's connection to the seer and the queen but had chosen for some reason not to tell her.

"Oh, nothing." She waved a dismissive hand. "Before, I saw each of the goddesses separately, and now I saw them together in the temple, acting like the best of friends."

A sidelong glance at Annani proved her suspicion that her mother-in-law was in on the secret as well.

Syssi really didn't appreciate being kept in the dark like that.

"Perhaps I should give the amulet a try," Jacki said. "We need to know whether it's really out of power."

"Go ahead." Syssi waved a hand over the artifact.

"Wait." Kalugal hauled Jacki into his lap. "Now you can touch it."

Smiling, she kissed his cheek before turning back to the amulet.

Everyone held their breath as she lifted it by its chain and closed the palm of her other hand around it.

A long moment passed before Jacki opened her eyes and shook her head. "It's dead. There is no juice left in it." She turned to Kian. "I guess all we have left is our wits."

He grimaced. "What else is new?" He looked at the inert artifact. "So, what do we do with this thing now? Do you want to throw it in the ocean?"

Jacki looked at it for a moment before shaking her head and turning to Kalugal. "Add it to your collection of well-guarded treasures."

"What else is in there?" Kian asked.

Kalugal turned to look at him. "Mostly items that I'm still working on deciphering and a few things that were removed from sites without permission. Nothing in that collection would interest you."

Kian looked doubtful, but he didn't push the issue. "Would you like another cup of coffee?" he asked Syssi as he sat down.

"I would love a cup." Syssi smiled at Oridu, who rushed over with a fresh carafe. "Thank you."

She couldn't confront Kian in front of everyone about what she'd seen in her vision, but once the others left, she intended to bring it up with him and his mother.

16

DAGOR

"I should call Margo." Frankie pulled the phone out of her pocket. "Can you get us another round of drinks?"

Dagor smiled. "No more Bloody Marys for you. Water or coke, what do you prefer?"

"Coke and more peanuts, please."

"Yes, ma'am." He leaned to kiss her pouty lips. "I think being a beta tester for Perfect Match is a waste of your natural talents. You should be a negotiator."

In less than an hour, Frankie had mapped out their two possible futures, one if she remained human and the other if she turned immortal, and had successfully tackled and solved all of his objections.

She chuckled. "Right. You are easy to negotiate with because you love me. My talents didn't work on my former bosses."

"I don't know how they didn't all fall in love with you, but I'm happy they didn't."

Rolling her eyes, she waved him away. "Go. I need to make this call before Margo calls me, or I won't hear the end of it."

"Fine." He pushed to his feet and walked over to the bar.

"One cold Coke coming up," Bob said. "And a bag of peanuts."

"Were you eavesdropping?"

"Of course. I hear everything that's being said on my deck."

"That's creepy. Were you told to do that?"

"I was told to anticipate my clients' needs. How else am I going to achieve that objective if I don't listen to what they say?"

"Do you report what you hear?"

The robot tilted his head in a very human way. "Why would I do that?"

"It's called spying."

A brief moment passed with Bob probably scanning his database of knowledge for what it meant to be a spy. "I see. I was not told to spy. Should I?"

"No, you shouldn't." Dagor shook his head. "I need to talk to William."

"He's right over there." Bob pointed with his long metallic arm.

Dagor must have been so absorbed in the conversation with Frankie that he hadn't noticed William and his mate arriving on the Lido deck and sitting on the other side of the pool.

"I will. Can you give me one more coke?"

"Of course, master."

Frankie was still on the phone with her friend when Dagor returned to their table. He put her drink and the bag of peanuts down, kissed her on the cheek, and continued to the other side of the pool.

"Good morning," he greeted William and Kaia. "May I join you?"

"Take a seat." William pointed at the lounger next to him. "I see that Frankie is feeling much better today."

"Yes, she is." Dagor affected a sly smile. "My venom must have sped up her recovery. She woke up this morning fully healed."

"That's amazing," Kaia said. "I wish we could bottle it and use it as a miracle cure. The problem is that it only activates once it's injected into a body. I tried to collect William's venom and run tests on it, but what I found could not explain any of the effects it has. It's such a bummer."

William didn't look happy about her sharing that information, but Kaia ignored his frown. Instead, she lifted her head and looked in the direction of the railing. "The ship is turning around. Did we forget someone in Acapulco?"

"Maybe." William rose to his feet. "But I doubt it. Maybe it has to do with the women we rescued." He pulled out his phone and frowned at the display. "Whatever the reason, we should have been notified of the change in plans."

Sensing Frankie approaching, Dagor turned to look at her.

She was still clutching the phone to her ear and looked worried. "What's going on? Why are we turning around?"

As Dagor's and William's phones simultaneously buzzed with incoming messages, Dagor tensed. "Something is up." He pulled out his phone and read the message. "Please report to the dining hall for an emergency meeting."

"I got the same thing," William said.

"I didn't." Kaia stared at her phone and then looked up. "If only you guys are being summoned, it has to do with what happened yesterday, and there is trouble."

"I'll call you right back," Frankie said to her friend and ended the call. "I didn't get anything either, and I'm officially freaking out. I bet the damn amulet showed Jacki another village being attacked and more women being taken." She started shaking. "I can't believe that it's happening again."

"We don't know that." Dagor pulled her into his arms. "Maybe it's about something completely different. Wait until we find out what it's about. It might be something as simple as someone who has been accidentally left behind. I don't remember anyone taking a tally of who was on board before leaving the port."

She raised her eyes to him. "Will you let me know as soon as you do?"

"I'll send you a message. But in the meantime, don't freak out. Whatever it is, we can handle it. We have a ship full of highly trained Guardians and gods. No one stands a chance against us, not even if the entire cartel comes after us."

17

FRANKIE

Frankie watched Dagor and William walk out through the sliding glass door of the Lido deck and turned to William's mate. "What do you think is going on?"

Kaia had been the first to acknowledge that an emergency meeting meant trouble, but she didn't look concerned, which was reassuring.

"It probably has something to do with the cartel, but your boyfriend is right. You have nothing to worry about other than your friend not getting picked up from Cabo on schedule. You should call her and tell her that we will be at least two days late."

"Two days?" Frankie squeaked. "Margo is going to be so peeved."

That was putting it mildly. Margo was not quick to anger, but when she was pushed too far, it was better not to be anywhere near her.

"Yeah." Kaia gulped her drink before putting it down on the side table. "We left Acapulco yesterday evening, and we were sailing through the night. It will take at least until nightfall to get back unless it's urgent and the captain increases the speed. If he does, we can get there this afternoon, but that's still only a few hours saved. I don't know how long it will take them to solve whatever problem they encountered, but it will take at least half a day, and then we need to cover this distance again."

"You're right. It's gonna be at least a two-day delay, if not longer."

Kaia smiled. "I hope your friend is having fun in Cabo."

Frankie hoped so, too. Margo had sounded more upbeat the last time they had spoken, so maybe things were going well, and since the bachelorette party was supposed to last a week, she wouldn't have to wait alone the entire two days, just the last one.

That meant that Margo would have to book another night in the hotel, and that might be a problem. What if it was fully booked?

What if it was too expensive?

Lynda had paid for the flights and the rooms, and since it was an all-inclusive resort, they could eat and drink as much as they wanted as long as they didn't order premium alcohol.

"I need another drink." Frankie glanced at Bob before shifting her eyes to Kaia and the empty glass on the side table. "Can I get you something?"

"No, thank you." Kaia took out a pair of sunglasses from her tote and put them on. "I'm going to take a little nap. I don't need as much sleep as I did before the transition, but I still need more than William, and he kept me awake until sunrise this morning." A smile tugged on Kaia's lips. "Not that I'm complaining."

Frankie didn't know that the girl used to be a Dormant. She was just as beautiful as all the other immortal ladies, so it hadn't even occurred to her.

"When did you transition? Was it recent?"

"Yeah, although it feels like a lifetime ago." Kaia chuckled. "I crack myself up sometimes. A different lifetime, get it?"

"I guess so." Frankie smoothed a hand over her neatly combed-back hair. "Was it difficult? I mean, the transition?"

"Not really. It's not fun, and it's different for each transitioning Dormant. I itched all over, and that was pretty bad, but others had it much worse. The good news is that the clan hasn't lost a Dormant to transition yet, so you shouldn't be afraid. Also, having a god induce you improves your chances of a quick and successful transition. Seeing how you are already walking around and moving with ease the day after you were shot, I'd say that it's already happening."

It would be so nice if Kaia was right, but Frankie doubted that. "Aren't I supposed to develop a fever and lose consciousness?"

The girl frowned. "Fever is standard for all transitioning Dormants, and so are elevated heart rate and blood pressure, but not everyone loses consciousness. How old are you?"

"Twenty-seven, why?"

"The older the Dormant, the more difficult the transition, and in this regard, you are not considered young. Still, a god's venom might compensate for your age."

Frankie grimaced. "Thanks for making me feel old. Now I really need that drink."

"Enjoy." Kaia waved her off.

The girl needed to learn some social skills, but given that she was rumored to be a genius, that kind of went with the territory.

"Hello." Bob grinned at her. "What can I get you, Mistress Frankie?" He tilted his head. "Is it Francine or Francesca?"

"Both, and two more. My parents named me after my great-grandmothers, so my full name is Francine, Emilia, Francesca, and Fiona. My brothers used to tease me that I was triple F."

Bob assumed a frown, which didn't really work since his metallic skin didn't wrinkle, but it was close enough. "I have never heard that expression. What does it mean?"

"I'd better not tell you. Can I have a strawberry daiquiri?"

"Of course." The grin returned.

As Bob turned to get what was needed for her drink, it occurred to Frankie that he might know more about the change of the ship's course than the rest of them.

"Do you know why we have turned around?" she asked.

"We did?" He looked surprised, which worked pretty well with his mechanic eyebrows lifting and his camera eyes widening. "I was not aware of that."

"Oh, well. It was worth a try. I thought you were connected to the ship's mainframe or something."

In sci-fi movies, all the machines on board a spaceship were usually connected to the main ship's computer, so she assumed it was the same on cruise ships, but evidently Bob operated independently of the navigation and other systems.

He placed the drink on a napkin, added a paper umbrella, and pushed it toward her. "Enjoy."

"Thank you." Frankie took the glass and walked over to the table she and Dagor had sat at before.

A few more people had arrived while she'd been talking to Kaia, and several cast her curious glances, probably wondering how she was walking around after being shot the previous day.

In a way, it was odd for the immortals to notice her rapid healing.

Several of the Guardians had been shot as well, but their immortal bodies expelled the bullets and mended their flesh so quickly that it was as if it had never happened. So yeah, everyone knew that she was human, but she had thought that most of them wouldn't give it a second thought because they were so used to seeing people heal rapidly.

Evidently, she'd been wrong.

18

KIAN

"Hold on." Syssi put her hand on Kian's arm. "I need to talk to you."

"Is it urgent? I called an emergency meeting, and everyone will be waiting for me in the dining hall."

"They can wait a moment longer."

She waited until it was just them, his mother, and the Odus. "There was more to the vision that I didn't mention. There was a third goddess in the room with the queen and the seer that had no glow at all and looked like the female version of Aru." She arched a brow. "Is there something you are not telling me?"

The guilty look in his eyes was enough of an answer. "I'm sorry, but it wasn't my secret to tell. Aru was adamant about keeping his sister's part in this top secret, and I understood why. She's putting her life in danger."

"Doing what?"

When he hesitated, Annani let out a sigh. "Just tell her, Kian. Syssi already knows that the queen, the seer, and Aria are working together, and the rest is not as important. Besides, if you don't tell her what's going on, she will just have another vision about it. Apparently, the Fates want her to be part of our little conspiracy."

"There is nothing little about it." He reached for Syssi's hand. "Aru and his twin sister can communicate in the same way that Ella and Vivian do. Their telepathic connection is independent of time and distance. It's instantaneous. Aria works as a scribe for the Supreme Oracle of Anumati, who is also the queen's best friend. Aru told his sister about my mother, she relayed the information to the Oracle, who told Queen Ani that she has a granddaughter on Earth. The queen was overjoyed, and now she wants to talk to my mother through the twins. We didn't arrange the first telepathic meeting yet, but it should happen soon."

As Syssi's eyes darted to his mother, she smiled. "I am very excited. My grandmother wants to teach me about Anumati's history, its politics, and its social structure. I have no doubt that I will learn many fascinating things about the planet of the gods and how they became the creators of so many intelligent species throughout the galaxy."

"She wants to teach you how to be a queen," Syssi said. "Is she involved in the resistance?"

Kian nodded. "I think she is its leader. We will know more after my mother's first session with her."

"Can I attend?" Syssi looked at his mother with pleading eyes. "I can be your scribe, writing down everything Aru says so you could later go over the notes and study them. It's easy to forget important details while listening to lectures. I always took notes, and when I got home, I copied them to make a clean version that I could later study from for the test."

"I would love that." Annani leaned over and patted Syssi's hand. "But we need to ask Aru's permission." She sighed. "Usually, a task like that would be Alena's, but I cannot share this information with her."

"That's a problem." Syssi chewed on her lower lip. "We shouldn't keep this from the immediate family. It's too big of a deal, and eventually, it will have to come out. If we can trust your sisters and their mates with our lives, we can trust them with Aru and Aria's secret as well."

"I know." Kian groaned. "But even Aru's teammates don't know about his unique ability, so how am I going to convince him that it's okay to reveal it to my sisters and their mates?"

"Easy." Syssi grinned. "Tell him that I've seen the queen, the Oracle, and his sister in a vision, and I told everyone about it."

"But you didn't."

"Not yet."

"Please, don't tell anyone." He leaned over and kissed her cheek. "It was very difficult for him to tell me about his sister. We need to respect his wishes and keep it on a need-to-know basis."

"Fine." She leaned into him and hugged his waist. "I won't tell anyone."

"I need to run." He kissed the top of her head. "They are waiting for me."

Letting go of him, Syssi nodded. "I'll collect Allegra from Alena's cabin."

He hesitated at the door. "Do you want to come to the meeting?"

"Fates, no." She waved a dismissive hand. "I'm very happy to leave all the strategizing to you. Although, I want to remind you that the best people to consult are Dalhu, Lokan, and Kalugal. They know how Navuh operates, and they could guess how many people he would send for an operation like this."

19

DAGOR

Once Kian had explained his wife's vision and its repercussions, Dagor pulled out his phone and texted Frankie to let her know what was going on as he had promised.

The truth was that he was excited about a chance to finally meet the clan's enemies face to face, and casting a sidelong glance at Negal, he saw a similar spark in his friend's eyes.

Not that the Doomers would have time to socialize. Given the vehemence in Kian's voice, their life expectancy was very short.

"We have two options," Kian said. "If we get to the bodies before the Doomers discover them, we can burn the evidence and continue our journey without having to go out of our way to find the Doomers and do away with them. Or we can seek them out and eliminate them. Killing them won't solve the local cartel problem because the Brotherhood will just send replacements, and I'm not sure that we should get involved in a fight we cannot ultimately win. On the other hand, the next team might not be as monstrous as this one, and until the replacements arrive, the local population will enjoy a short breather. That being said, if the Doomers have discovered the bodies already, though, the first option is out, and we have to find them and eliminate them."

Dagor was fascinated by how the members of the Brotherhood were so different from the good people sitting in the dining hall with him. Genetically, they were the same people, so how had they turned out so wrong?

Their leader must be extremely powerful to corrupt their minds like that, but it was also possible that they were born defective. As a god, he was more familiar with the power of genetics than his new immortal friends, and to some extent, sycophantic traits could be bred in or out at the whim of the scientist.

Still, free will was not to be dismissed. People could channel their negative tendencies into doing good for society, and at the same time, it was possible to channel positive tendencies into evil deeds. It all depended on the ideology adopted by the individual or the expectations of their culture.

In a way, it was like the amulet. Its innate power was neither good nor bad, but it could be used for doing good or evil.

Thankfully, Anumati had outgrown that stage in its evolution, and not even the Eternal King could convince an entire population that murdering members of a different ideology was a righteous thing to do.

Even the Kra-ell, who were savages compared to the gods, had not wished to kill all gods out of hatred or some other deep-rooted resentment. They had just wanted to be granted equal rights.

What ideology could the Doomers' leader come up with that would justify the annihilation of Annani's clan?

Would William be able to explain that?

Dagor wasn't close to Kian like Aru had become, and so far, William was the only clan insider he had befriended.

As questions flew at Kian and were answered, Dagor wondered if he and his teammates should get involved. If they wanted to keep their association with the clan a secret, it wasn't a good idea for them to fight the Doomers alongside the immortals. If any of the enemy survived and managed to escape, the information leak could be catastrophic.

On the other hand, however, he and his fellow gods could provide valuable assistance.

The clan could easily handle the two Doomers that Kian's mate had seen in her vision, but what if there were many more of them? There could be thousands for all they knew. It wasn't likely, but it was possible.

Ultimately, it would be Aru's decision as the leader of their team, and Dagor had a feeling he would want to assist the clan.

"So, what's the plan?" Anandur asked. "Is it going to be a quick in-and-out mission, or should Wonder and I postpone our wedding?"

Kian grimaced. "That's another reason to just get rid of the evidence and get out, but I think it's wishful thinking on our part to assume that they didn't find out about it already. The Doomers were probably expecting the cargo of abducted women, and when it didn't arrive, they would have gone to investigate. It's very likely that they already know what happened and are investigating who was in the area yesterday. What they don't expect is for us to return, so at least they won't be lying in wait for us."

"That still doesn't answer my question," the redhead said. "Do we postpone the wedding or not?"

"We don't," Kian said. "For now. Hopefully, we will resolve the situation fast enough to still hold the celebration tonight." He scanned the room until his eyes landed on Toven. "We will probably need your assistance in compelling the Doomers to file a report explaining what happened to the cartel and their cargo in a way that will mask our involvement. I would hate to have to get rid of this ship."

Aru lifted his hand. "My teammates and I offer our assistance. We can help you fight, and we can also thrall the other immortals to do as you command."

"Thank you." Kian dipped his head in Aru's direction. "We will reconvene in my cabin later to discuss the plan. Our resources will have to be divided between the ship and the away team. Half the force will need to remain on board to protect the civilians and the women, and half will deal with the bodies and the Doomers."

20

FRANKIE

"I have bad news," Frankie said as soon as Margo answered the call.

"What happened? Did the ship really turn around? Did someone go overboard? Was someone left behind in Acapulco?" Margo fired off without waiting for an answer.

Usually Margo was a level-headed individual, but she was very protective of those she cared about, and since she saw the world as a dangerous place that was full of baddies who were out to get good people, she worried whenever things didn't follow familiar patterns.

"None of the above."

What the hell was she going to tell her? That they had buried the body parts of cartel monsters and were going back to burn them?

Margo would immediately build a conspiracy theory around it, but even she couldn't guess the truth.

"Then what happened?" Margo was practically shrieking in her ear.

"I can't tell you. It has something to do with Tom's mystery partners and some vicious competitors of theirs."

"Ugh, Frankie. Really? Stop with the bullshit and tell me what's going on, or I will imagine the worst."

Frankie doubted that. The worst had happened, and not even Margo could have imagined that. She'd been raised Catholic, but she'd never really believed in heaven and hell until now. Those monsters must have been hell-spawned to do what they did, and what had been done to them had not only been well-deserved but not enough.

"It's nothing the people here cannot handle. That's all I can say without violating my nondisclosure agreement, and all you need to know is that I'm not in any danger."

"Fine." Margo let out a breath. "I'll get it out of you when you finally get here."

If Toven compelled Margo to silence, then maybe she would be allowed to tell her friend the truth.

"Are you going to be okay staying there for two more days? How are Lynda and the other bridesmaids treating you?"

"They are done posturing and trying to make me feel inferior. Now they are just partying like there is no tomorrow and flirting with all the cute waiters."

"That sounds like fun."

"Nah, I'm bored, and I want out of here, but I'll survive two more days." Margo sighed. "I'll download a couple of books, sit by the pool, and read while sipping on margaritas."

"That actually sounds like even more fun than getting drunk and flirting with the staff, but I still feel bad about leaving you stranded."

"It's not your fault. Besides, Lynda is going to be so happy that I'm not bailing early after all, and that will save me a lot of grief down the line. She won't have anything to hold over me because I'm staying to the end of her lame bachelorette party."

"Yeah, there is that." Frankie took a sip from her strawberry daiquiri. "So, no cute guys in Cabo? What about the other guests? Any single guys?"

"There is a bachelor party with at least thirty guys here, but you know how men get when there are no women to tame their behavior. They are gross and spit out the most cringe-worthy pick-up lines. I turned my ring around so it looked like a wedding ring, and I told everyone who showed interest in me that I was married, but even that failed to deter some of them. Enough about me, though. I want to hear about you and Doug."

A smile lifted the corners of Frankie's lips. "I know that you are going to call me crazy, but I'm in love with him, and he loves me back. Our future together is still unclear, but we are working on a solution that will be acceptable to both of us."

There was a long moment of stunned silence on the other end. "You have known the guy for how long?"

"Three days, but when you know, you know, right? It's not like I fall in love with every guy I meet. Dagor is the first one that I actually care about. The others were just placeholders until my knight showed up."

And what a knight indeed. She still couldn't believe that a god was in love with her.

"Dagor?" Margo asked. "Is that Doug's nickname?"

"No, that's his real name. He introduces himself as Doug to Americans who have trouble pronouncing names they are not familiar with. Anyway, he's awesome, and you are going to love him. He's your type. A hot nerd."

Margo laughed. "How hot?"

"Scorching. We can hardly keep our hands off each other."

"Does he have a brother by any chance?" Margo asked.

"No, but his friend Negal is very handsome, too, and he has a very even-keeled personality. He's the dependable sort. But if you don't like him, there is another guy I have my eye on for you. His name is Max, and he's part of the security detail. He's flirty as heck and handsome in the boy-next-door kind of way—if the boy next door was six foot three, had the body of a professional wrestler and the face of a magazine model. Both guys are outstanding exemplars of masculinity, the good type, not the toxic one. You'll have a hard time deciding between them."

Frankie hoped that Margo and Negal would hit it off so their triad would all have gods for boyfriends, but if Margo chose Max, she had no problem with that either.

"Why choose?" Margo laughed. "I've been reading a lot of those reverse-harem books lately. It's fun to imagine having more than one guy, but I don't think I could do that in real life. I'm a one-man woman. Besides, who has the stamina to satisfy more than one man? I certainly don't."

Frankie stifled a giggle. Margo would soon discover that stamina was not a problem with immortal lovers. The venom was a miracle drug that was an aphrodisiac, euphoric, and analgesic all in one.

"Yeah, I'm not into polyamory either. Kudos to those who enjoy it, but it's just not me. I'm so happy that I found my one and only, and I can't wait for you to meet him."

"I can't wait either. I have to go, Frankie. Lynda is waving at me, and I'd better see what she wants before she throws a tantrum."

"Okay. I love you, and I'll see you in two days." *Fates willing.*

"Yeah. Be careful and stay safe."

"Always."

21

ANI

As Ani awaited her husband to join her for a rare, shared dinner in the grand dining room of the palace, she was not surprised that he was running late. El did not forgo a single opportunity to flaunt his royal privilege.

He never waited for anyone.

Everyone waited for him.

Ani did not mind. The tapestries adorning the chamber had been recently replaced with new masterpieces, as was done once a month from time immemorial, and she busied herself with admiring the artistry and craftsmanship.

The opulence of the room, with its grand size and shimmering chandeliers, was a fitting stage for the political theater often taking place around the ornate table, but it was rarely played out by her and El.

They did not dine together often, and when they did, it was to discuss affairs of the state. They were not a couple, not anymore.

In the past they had kept up the pretense, but after El had murdered their only son, Ani no longer bothered. She could not prove what he had done, so removing him from the throne had not been possible, and her fading into the background had not been an option either.

She had a job to do, and to do it, she had to pretend that she did not know El was responsible for his only legitimate son's demise, and she had to remain cordial to her husband. At first, it had been difficult, but thousands of years later, it had become second nature. They both played their roles as the rulers of Anumati together but apart.

Ani's role was limited, and she was not allowed to poke her nose into El's affairs or even question his decisions.

He was the king, and she was his official consort.

Nevertheless, she shouldered many responsibilities and represented families whose support was crucial to El's rule over Anumati. Also, she had nearly complete autonomy over her responsibilities, but she knew that El kept a close watch on her activities, and his spies were everywhere.

She had her own spies in his court, and he probably knew that as well, but he either did not care or could not figure out how anyone could spy on him while being compelled to reveal nothing of what they witnessed while in his service.

As the doors opened the king's guards entered first, taking their positions in the four corners of the room, and only then did El enter with all the pomp and ceremony of his station.

Her husband exuded power and commanded attention, but there was a calculated restraint in his demeanor, and not only because he was keenly aware of the delicate balance of power between them.

He had perfected the façade of the powerful ruler who was carrying the mantle of leadership for the sake of his people and not for personal glory, and every move he made, every expression on his face, reflected that.

What a master manipulator he was.

As much as she detested him, she admired his skill.

Ani rose to her feet and bowed. "Good evening, Your Majesty."

He dipped his head in greeting and motioned for her to sit back. "Good evening, Ani. I was delighted to receive your invitation to dinner. It has been much too long since we dined together. How have you been?"

"I have been busy." She offered him a measured smile. "The Supreme Oracle and I were discussing a new and exciting project that is of the utmost cultural and historical significance."

"Oh yes. It has been brought to my attention that you have visited the temple more often than usual. I was worried that you were experiencing the malady of ennui and sought solace from the Supreme Oracle."

Ani's gut clenched with sudden fear. If El could prove that she was losing her mind or sinking into depression, as many of the old gods did, he could put her in stasis for the long sleep.

Was he threatening her?

"Thank you for your concern, husband, but nothing could be further from the truth." She flashed him a bright smile. "I am championing so many new and exciting projects that I barely have a moment to rest, let alone suffer from boredom."

"I am glad to hear that." He leaned back so a servant could spread a napkin over his thighs. "So, tell me about this project that is of utmost cultural and historical significance."

No one could accuse El of not being attuned to her every word, but he was like that with everyone. Hypervigilant and always aware.

"The other day, I read some of the prophecies etched on the columns of the temple, and it occurred to me that they represented only a small fraction of the greatest prophecies throughout Anumati's history. Also, most of our citizens will never get a chance to visit the Supreme's temple and read them, and that would be a shame. We need a comprehensive, written collection that will be available to any citizen. The compilation would not only serve as a testament to our rich heritage but also as a guide for future generations of Anumatians."

El looked intrigued but also skeptical. "Recording what is etched on the columns is a good idea, but that is just a small fraction of the greatest prophecies. Most are lost in time or bear no resemblance to the original."

She dipped her head in acknowledgment. "My thoughts exactly. That is why I asked the Supreme Oracle to dedicate an hour a day to retrieving those prophecies from the vortex of time. We will have a scribe present to record what she says, but we will choose only the most significant prophecies to include in the compilation."

El's eyes darkened. "You know how unpredictable an oracle's visions are. Sofringhati might be the most powerful oracle ever born, but even she often spits out nonsense. She will have to be asked very precise questions to pull relevant prophecies from the past. Also, some of those predictions are not for public consumption."

"I am well aware of that. This is why I will be right there with the Supreme, asking the relevant questions and deciding which prophecies will go into the public record and which ones will go into a private one that will be kept in the royal archives and accessible only to you and me." She forced her expression to soften and reached for his hand. "I pray to the Fates that you and I would never succumb to the dreaded malady of ennui, but it is inevitable that one day we will, and those prophecies will serve to guide our successors."

The king's gaze hardened slightly, but Ani could see the cogs turning in his mind. She knew him so well that she could guess precisely what he was thinking even without the little tells that betrayed his excitement.

What if she discovered an ancient prophecy that was lost in time but could benefit him in some way?

What if she could warn him of potential threats to his throne?

Finally, he smiled. "It is a marvelous idea. Knowledge is power, and those lost prophecies could shed light on opportunities and threats we could not even imagine. It is crucial, though, that the knowledge is safeguarded. I want to review every new prophecy Sofringhati pulls out of the vortex of time and personally approve which ones are suitable for public consumption and which should remain private."

Ani nodded. "Of course."

As the servant placed a bowl of soup in front of the king, he thanked him graciously and turned to Ani. "Our reign has always been guided by the wisdom of our ancestors and the predictions of the oracles. It is our duty to preserve these insights for the citizens of Anumati."

Ani inclined her head in acknowledgment, hiding the triumph she felt from her husband's keen eyes. "With your permission, Your Majesty, I will announce the project at the upcoming gala."

He nodded. "It is very fitting to announce such a scholarly undertaking at a fundraiser for the new university. Well done, Ani."

Ani inclined her head. "Thank you, El."

22

FRANKIE

With nothing to do until Dagor returned, Frankie sat on a stool and leaned her elbows on the bar. "The strawberry daiquiri was really good, but I've exceeded my alcohol allowance for this morning. Can you make me a virgin version of it?"

"Of course, mistress." As usual, Bob looked as if serving her was the greatest joy of his day, and she wondered what about his expressions and voice created the effect.

Was it the rounding of his camera eyes?

Or was it the chirpy voice with which he replied?

When he was done preparing her drink, he added a pink paper umbrella, put the glass on top of a napkin, and pushed it toward her. "Would you like another bag of peanuts with your drink?"

"No, thank you. I've exceeded the daily allowance on those as well."

He arched a metal brow. "I was not aware that there was a limit. Are peanuts harmful when consumed in large quantities?"

"They can be if they are moldy, but that's not why I don't want any more. I've just had enough."

"I see." He turned his head and smiled at a group of teenagers heading his way. "Mistresses Lisa and Cheryl, and Master Parker. How lovely to see you again. Pink lemonades for the young ladies? And root beer for the gentleman?"

"Yes, please." Lisa sat on a stool next to Frankie. "Hi." She smiled. "How are you feeling?"

For a brief moment, Frankie was confused by Lisa's question, but then she remembered that she was supposed to be recovering from a gunshot. "Much better. Can't beat a god's—" she stopped herself before saying something inappropriate in front of the teenagers "—influence."

Lisa laughed. "You mean venom, and yeah, it's good to have a boyfriend with potent venom on hand." She leaned closer and sniffed. "You've started working on your transition, right?"

It was a little embarrassing to talk with Lisa about what it took to activate a Dormant, but the girl was over sixteen, and some of Frankie's cousins who were that same age were already sexually active.

Frankie had always been so small that people had assumed she was a kid even in college, so her first time had been when she was nineteen, but she was the exception rather than the rule.

"Yeah, we did, but I'm still not sure I'm even a Dormant."

Lisa leaned over and sniffed again. "You are definitely not entirely human. I think you've already started transitioning."

Frankie's heart leaped with excitement but was then gripped with fear. "Can you smell it?"

Lisa shrugged. "Not really."

"Then why did you sniff me?"

The girl turned to her friend. "It was Cheryl's idea. She asked me how I knew who was a Dormant and who wasn't, and I said that I didn't know, so she suggested that maybe it was the smell. But it's not. I just sense it, and I can't explain how."

"I don't have a fever," Frankie murmured. "Isn't that one of the first signs?"

Lisa shrugged. "I don't know. My mother passed out and was unconscious. I was freaking out, but it all ended well. Perhaps you should talk with her and some of the other transitioned Dormants."

"Yeah, I probably should. Maybe one of them didn't get a fever either."

It was so scary. What if she was transitioning already and didn't know it?

"Parker transitioned." Cheryl turned to the boy. "Did you get a fever?"

"I did, but it was nothing. I felt worse getting the flu when I was still human."

"How does it feel?" Frankie said. "Do you feel different after your transition?"

He nodded. "I'm fearless, which my mom keeps telling me is not good because immortals can still be killed. But I feel invincible."

"That must be awesome," Frankie murmured. "What about the prospect of living forever?"

He shrugged. "I don't really think about that, and when I do, I think of all the things I can do. I don't need to limit myself to one path in life. I can be a pilot, an engineer, a doctor, and a ballet dancer. I can be whatever I want."

Cheryl chuckled. "I've seen you dancing. You can forget about that one because you suck."

"For now." He leaned toward the girl until their noses were nearly touching. "But I can practice indefinitely until I get better."

As a wild idea popped into Frankie's head, she perked up. "Hey, you can dance with the stars."

He arched a brow. "What stars?"

"Like the television show *Dancing with the Stars,* when they take average Joes and Janes, pair them with great dancers, and they compete on television. There could be a Perfect Match adventure like that." She lifted a hand to her forehead. "Oh, wow. That could be amazing. I have to tell Toven about it." She leaned toward the kid and kissed his cheek. "Thank you for giving me the idea."

Looking flustered, he lifted a hand to the cheek she'd kissed. "You're welcome."

Frankie pulled out her phone and started typing a note with her ideas for the adventure. When she was done, she sent it to Mia, asking that she show it to Toven and ask his opinion.

The return text came back a few minutes later. *He thinks it's an awesome idea and asks that you develop the story further.*

"Yes!" Frankie pumped her fist in the air.

"I assume Toven liked it," Parker said.

"He did, and he wants me to develop it. It can be about two contestants falling in love despite competing for the grand prize. Like an enemies-to-lovers kind of story. They both need the prize money for something important, but then they fall in love, and each one tries to let the other win."

"I love it," Lisa said. "People can have a sexy adventure and learn ballroom dancing at the same time."

23

DAGOR

Dagor started typing a message to Frankie as he walked out of the dining hall. *We are done. Are you still on the Lido deck?*

Frankie: *I'm still here.*

Dagor: *I'm on my way.*

He needed a drink, and then he was taking Frankie to the cabin and making love to her until they arrived back at Acapulco.

Fates knew what they were going to find there, and he needed to load up on love and closeness.

The truth was he wasn't sure yet that his team would be asked to join. Kian was meeting with his war council in his cabin to formulate a plan, and he would let Aru know whether their team's assistance was needed or not.

Dagor was itching for a fight, but he also didn't want to leave Frankie alone. His first duty was to protect his mate, and although eliminating the enemy counted toward that goal, staying with her was the best way to keep her safe.

He found Frankie sitting at the bar with a fruity drink in hand.

"Hi." He leaned over her and wrapped her in his arms. "I missed you."

She chuckled. "You were gone for less than an hour." For some reason, her compact body felt tense against his chest.

He leaned back to look at her. "What's wrong?"

"Nothing." She sighed. "I had a great idea for a Perfect Match adventure, and Toven loved it. He asked me to develop it further, but I got stuck. I don't know what else to add."

"I wish I could help you, but I'm not very creative. Mia is a writer, right? Maybe she can assist you?"

"Mia is an illustrator of children's books, but she still knows more about creating stories than I do. I'll ask her."

Despite his sage advice, Frankie's shoulders still seemed just as tense as before. "What else is bothering you?"

She let out a breath. "Lisa said that I might be transitioning, but I don't have a fever, and I feel great. Everyone says that a fever is the first sign that the transition is starting. It's so annoying not to know what's going on with my body."

"Who is Lisa?"

"She's a Dormant who supposedly can tell who is a Dormant and who is not. I met her a while ago when she visited Mia, and later, she told Mia that Margo and I were both Dormants. She was just here and said that I might be transitioning, and I freaked out."

"Why? Isn't that what you want?"

"Yeah, but I want to know when it's happening, and I don't like that it's not happening the same way as it does for everyone else."

"Let's think about it rationally. First of all, Lisa might be wrong. Does she have a proven record of guessing correctly?"

"I don't know. According to Mia, Lisa guessed correctly one other time, but she hasn't had the chance to do it enough times to establish her talent."

"So, there is also a chance that she's right," Dagor said. "And because she has a special sense for those things, she senses them before any symptoms manifest."

"I think that's what scares me the most. I don't want to lose consciousness while shit goes down in Acapulco. Are you going to fight with the clan?"

"Not if you are transitioning. I'll stay by your side."

"Thank you." Frankie let out a breath. "That's very comforting to me. But I still don't want to lose consciousness and miss out on all the weddings and not be there when Margo comes on board so I can introduce her to Negal."

He arched a brow. "Is that your plan?"

"Well, yes. How cool would it be if all three of us had boyfriends who were gods? But if she doesn't like Negal, which could happen even though he's a great guy, I can introduce her to Max, but if I'm out of it, who's going to do that?"

That was an easy problem to solve. "I'll do it. I'll introduce Margo to Negal."

"What if she doesn't like him?"

Dagor grimaced. "Then I'll introduce her to Max. Happy?"

Instead of answering, Frankie wound her arms around his neck and pulled him in for a kiss. "I love you," she murmured against his lips. "You are the absolute best."

"I know, and so are you. So, did I address all of your fears and objections?"

"Almost. I will still miss the weddings. The Clan Mother comes up with a unique address to each couple, and I don't want to miss that or the vows."

He rolled his eyes. "I'll take photos of all the wedding gowns and record the ceremonies and the vows for you."

"What about the dancing? I wanted to dance at the weddings."

"Unless you want to do it while unconscious, with me carrying you to the dance floor, I can't solve that objection."

Frankie affected a pout. "You're a god. You're supposed to be omnipotent."

She was adorable, and he loved her so much.

"I don't know about the omni, but I'm certainly potent." He lifted her off the stool and into his arms. "We have seven hours until we reach Acapulco, and I know how I want to spend them."

Holding on to his neck, Frankie laughed. "I like your plan. But how are we going to get to Acapulco so fast? We've been sailing for nearly fourteen hours, and I doubt the ship can double its speed."

"Don't ask me how." He carried her through the sliding doors and continued to the elevators. "Kian said that's how long it's going to take, and I have no reason to doubt him. Still, seven hours is plenty of time."

24

KIAN

Kian wrapped his arm around Syssi and Allegra and kissed their daughter's warm cheek. "I'm sorry for taking over the cabin."

"There is nothing to be sorry about. I was heading to your mother's cabin anyway. Allegra is more than happy to spend the day with her grandmother, and all your sisters will be there to celebrate Wonder's bachelorette party. Callie, Carol, and Aliya will be there too, and Okidu will be there to help with the little ones, although I doubt his services will be needed." She chuckled. "I bet Allegra's feet will not touch the ground while all the ladies satisfy their baby fix."

His mother had insisted on hosting the party for her oldest friend, but he doubted Anandur would get to celebrate his last day as a bachelor.

Kian would keep him on the ship, and at least half of the Guardian force would remain to guard the civilians, but they wouldn't be celebrating with whiskey and cigars while their friends were fighting Doomers.

Hopefully the bodies hadn't been discovered yet, so it wouldn't come to that. The Doomers would start getting suspicious when their cargo didn't arrive, but they would likely assume that a competing cartel had stolen the women and killed off their henchmen. The only way they could know that immortals had been involved was if they discovered the body parts that looked like they had been shredded to pieces by wild beasts.

The question was whether they should pursue the Doomers even if it wasn't necessary, and Kian was conflicted about that. If they chose to fight the

Doomers, or if they were forced to do that, they would be lucky if the wedding happened at all.

"I hope we will not need to postpone the wedding. I would hate to disappoint Wonder. Anandur will pretend like it's not a big deal, but I know he will be disappointed as well."

"We do what we must." Syssi stretched on her toes and kissed his cheek. "Good luck, my love." She leaned away and looked into his eyes. "I hate war, and I don't want any of our people to get hurt, but these Doomers need to go, and I don't mean back to the island. Find them and eliminate them, even if it means postponing Anandur and Wonder's wedding. Give them hell."

Those were words he had never expected to hear from his gentle wife. Evidently, she'd now reached the same tipping point that he had gotten to centuries ago, and he regretted that she had been forced to do that.

He sighed. "We can't win this war, love. Navuh will just send a new team, and they will take revenge on the villagers."

Syssi briefly closed her eyes, and when she opened them, they shone with inner light. "I'm not qualified to give advice on these matters. You have good people on your team, and I trust you to come up with the best course of action for us and for the people living here. I don't want to make their lives even more hellish than they already are, but I can't stand the thought of the Doomers and their cartel cronies doing whatever they want, massacring and abducting people."

Welcome to my world, Kian thought but didn't verbalize. "Don't worry, my love. We will figure this out."

She cast him a forced smile, and he smiled back with just as much effort. "Enjoy the party."

The smile slid off her face. "It's hard to enjoy anything with this over our heads."

"I know, but we need to try. Otherwise, they win."

With a nod, Syssi opened the door and walked out.

Kian shook his head.

It was a sad world when even his peace-loving, sweet, empathic wife wanted him to unleash hell on these Doomers and their cronies. Not that the miserable state of affairs was news to him, but he would have liked to shield his wife from the ugliness.

The worst part was knowing that one day his daughter would have to deal with this crap. Kian was under no illusions that a utopian future awaited them where evil was eradicated, and everyone lived in peace and harmony. And that was even before considering the looming threat of the Eternal King.

Letting out a breath, he walked over to the bar, opened a new bottle of whiskey, and pulled out ten glasses. His war council included the usual suspects—Onegus and Turner to formulate a strategy, William to assist with technology, Andrew for his experience with counterintelligence and terrorist activity, and Toven because he might need the god's compulsion power. He'd invited Kalugal, Lokan, Rufsur, and Dalhu because they knew how Doomers operated.

Aru had offered his assistance, and Kian might still take him up on his offer, but he wasn't sure he wanted the gods to take part in the fight. He doubted that the Doomers would be able to distinguish them from the immortals just from looking at them, but given the reports on Negal's incredible strength and speed, these new gods were a different breed, and they would give themselves away as soon as the fighting started.

25

KALUGAL

Kalugal leaned back in his chair with his whiskey glass in hand. "My educated guess is that there is a team of twelve Doomers stationed in the area. That's the minimum size for operations abroad." He cast a glance at Lokan. "Is that still the case?"

Lokan nodded. "I'm not involved in these kinds of operations, but as far as I know, twelve is still the size of an average team. Don't forget that Navuh now has more warriors than he knows what to do with, so there is no reason to send out teams smaller than that."

"It was when I was still a member of the Brotherhood," Dalhu said. "But given how violent the area is and the various cartels competing for dominance, they might have sent a larger group. The next one up is thirty."

Kian let out a breath. "We can handle thirty Doomers. The question is whether they will mobilize their cronies to help them."

"That's not a problem." Kalugal waved a dismissive hand. "In fact, none of this is. I can take hold of their minds and freeze them, immortals and humans alike. I don't know why we are even here."

Kian smiled. "I like your confidence, but things are never as easy as that. The good news is that we know they are there, and we are prepared to take them on."

Turner lifted a hand. "We are getting ahead of ourselves. We can avoid a conflict if they haven't discovered the bodies yet. They know something is up because their shipment of women is missing, but their first assumption will be an attack by a competing cartel, not searching for bodies. They will investigate that first, and it might give us enough time to eliminate the evidence, which is the only thing that can point toward us. We can either burn the evidence or start a rumor about a satanic cult operating in the area. "

"We left more clues than just the torn-up bodies," Onegus said. "The tour trucks are riddled with bullets, and the tour company has records of renting out those trucks to tourists from a certain ship. Then there is Luis and another driver who were injured and are recovering."

"That's true." Kalugal put his empty glass on the table. "I thralled them to remember that we were ambushed by robbers and managed to escape by the skin of our teeth. It won't be difficult to connect the dots."

Turner made a noncommittal sound. "Why would they suspect tourists or call the local tour companies to ask questions? Perhaps it will occur to them after they've exhausted all the other options, but given how large this area is and how many players there are, it will take considerable time for them to start thinking in that direction."

Kalugal was surprised that Turner, the most cautious and calculating among them, was so dismissive of their blunder.

He blamed himself for not burning the bodies. He'd been busy with the traumatized victims, and it hadn't occurred to him that he could use gasoline from one of the trucks to douse the bodies and set them on fire.

"There is a simple way to find out whether they are onto us," he said. "I can call the tour company and ask whether anyone inquired about rentals the day before."

Onegus turned to him. "The Doomers would have thralled them to forget that."

"In most cases, my compulsion is strong enough to power through a thrall. I can also call Luis, but I will leave him for last."

"Why last?" Kian asked. "You should call him first."

"If they got to Luis, he might be compromised, and by calling him, I'll tip our hand."

"The same might be true of the receptionist in the tour company." Kian turned to look at Brundar. "Did you rent the vehicles to collect the women from the same place?"

"No."

"We should call that place as well," Kian said.

"Do you want me to do that?" Brundar asked.

"No, we need Kalugal to make the calls so he can compel the information out of whoever answers."

Turner shook his head. "We should wait until we get there and question those involved in person. Their phones might be compromised."

Kian cursed under his breath. "I don't want to get into the port blind. What if they are waiting for us?"

"We can handle them," Toven said. "If we have megaphones on board, Kalugal and I can freeze them all in place before they can fire a single shot."

"We have the noise cannon," William said. "We can use it to amplify your voice, but the cannon can distort that special quality that carries the compulsion."

"Regular megaphones will do." Kian pushed to his feet and walked to the bar. "So, is that our strategy? We get Yamanu to shroud the area, Toven and Kalugal freeze the scum, and we make target practice out of them?"

"I like that idea," Anandur said. "It's going to be over so quickly that I might even squeeze in a bachelor party before the wedding."

Onegus chuckled. "You forget the cleanup. That will take much longer."

When Dalhu uttered a growl, everyone's eyes turned to him. "I'd rather get up close and personal. Tearing them apart won't take much longer than shooting at them, but it's no fun when they can't fight back."

"The humans their henchmen violated, mutilated, and slaughtered couldn't fight back either." Kian returned to the table with a fresh bottle of whiskey. "I say it's fair to pay them back in kind."

26

KIAN

Kian found it difficult to keep the vehemence from his voice and even more so to keep it from his mind, but he couldn't fix all the world's problems no matter how much he wished to. Together with the Kra-ell, he had a force of about two hundred warriors, and that was barely enough to protect their three locations, let alone the innocents of the world.

He used to wonder if humanity was worth fighting for, and many times he had arrived at the conclusion that it wasn't, but he had a clan to keep safe, and when he'd become a husband and a father, there was no longer a question whether he would keep fighting.

He had no choice but to fight until his last breath.

"I think you should involve Aru and the other two," Toven said. "Not because we need them for this mission, but to solidify our alliance with them. If they fight with us against the Doomers, it will cement their loyalty to us."

Kian refilled everyone's glasses and sat down. "That's a good point. I'll call Aru."

Kalugal lifted his hand. "Before you do, I want us to consider calling the tour offices ahead of time. I know there is a chance someone could be listening on the line, but I can compel them as well."

Turner shook his head. "Not if they are recording all the conversations and listening to them later. I don't think your compulsion is retained in the recording."

Kalugal frowned. "I can't believe I've never tested it before. Let's do it now." He pulled out his phone. "Who should I call?"

"Not someone who is here," Kian said.

"Of course not. You can hear me." He smoothed a hand over his short beard. "The problem is that almost everyone I can call will do exactly what I ask them to, even without the element of compulsion. Jacki wouldn't, but she's immune, so she's not good for testing."

"Record a message and send it to Amanda," Kian suggested. "Ask her to call Anandur to tell him that Wonder had a change of heart and doesn't want to marry him."

"That's a good one." Kalugal glanced at Anandur. "There is no chance that Wonder would ever do that, right?"

Anandur crossed his arms over his chest. "Not in a million years. Wonder adores me."

"Get ready for a storm," Dalhu said. "Amanda will not find this funny."

Grinning like a fiend, Kalugal recorded the message and sent it to Amanda.

A moment later, his phone rang, and as he answered it, everyone braced for Amanda's outrage.

"What the hell, Kalugal? That's the cruelest prank ever. What were you thinking?"

"I'm sorry. We were testing a theory, and apparently, my compulsion power lost its potency when recorded and played back. And by the way, it was your brother's idea, not mine. I needed to ask you to do something you would never do unless you were under compulsion."

"You could have asked me to wear a dress made from polyester and come model it for you. Kian knows I would rather go naked than wear that. It gives me hives."

Kian chuckled. "And where would you have found such a dress on short notice? We needed to know right away."

"You have a point." She huffed out a breath. "Anything else I can help you with?"

"No, that's it," Kalugal said. "Please accept my apology for causing you distress."

"Apology accepted." She ended the call.

"Well, that idea crashed and burned." Kalugal put his phone back in his pocket. "We need to find some other angle. What if I can call and ask if anyone found a forgotten pair of sunglasses in one of the trucks?" He turned to William. "I'm sure you can reroute the call so it would appear as if it was coming from an Acapulco hotel. Not all the tourists arrive by ship. Some fly in, so there is no reason for the Doomers to suspect that their cargo is on a ship." He straightened in his chair. "We can have Roni hack into the hotel's surveillance cameras, and if Doomers show up asking questions, we will know that they found the bodies."

As all eyes turned to William, he shifted in his chair. "It's going to be difficult to do with the equipment I have on board, and if the hotel's camera feeds are not online, it's not going to work. The first thing Roni needs to do is find out which hotels have their security on the cloud, and then we will make that call appear as if it's coming from one of them."

Kian wasn't sure that it was worth the effort, given that they could easily overpower the Doomers and their hired monsters, but Kalugal seemed adamant about getting more information, and there was something to be said for that as well.

"Let's do it." He turned to William. "Call Roni and tell him what we need. I'm going to call Aru and ask him to join us."

27

WONDER

"What was that all about?" Syssi asked when Amanda ended the call.

With everyone talking about the ship turning around and going back to Acapulco, Wonder had been distracted and only heard snippets of the conversation. Amanda had said something about a cruel prank and polyester, which didn't make much sense.

"I can't believe these guys." Amanda snatched yet another margarita from Onidu's tray, her fourth if Wonder's count was correct. "Kalugal wanted to test whether his compulsion worked through a recording. Kian suggested me as the test subject, and Kalugal sent me a recorded message, commanding me to tell Anandur that Wonder got cold feet and didn't want to go ahead with the wedding."

Wonder laughed. "Anandur would have never believed it. He knows how much I love him."

"I know, but if that wasn't a recording, I would have been forced to make that call and sound like an idiot." Amanda plopped on the couch next to Wonder.

"What did polyester have to do with it?" Annani asked.

"I told him that he could have tested his hypothesis by telling me to wear a polyester dress and model it for the guys. There's no way I would have done it unless I was under compulsion." She smiled at Wonder. "Speaking of dresses, I'm dying to see your wedding gown. What did you end up doing?"

They had discussed incorporating Wonder Woman elements in the design, and Amanda had given her some pointers, but the dress was one of the few things that Wonder wanted full control over, and she had communicated with the designer herself. Most of the other decisions she had left in Amanda's capable hands.

In fact, Amanda had designed the dining hall decorations for all ten weddings and coordinated the menu with the kitchen staff. The female was a force of nature. Wonder had no idea how she'd managed all that on top of planning her own wedding.

"It's a very subtle nod to Wonder Woman. I have a gold tiara, and Callie is going to curl my hair and tease it so it looks like Wonder Woman's. I also have gold cuffs, and the dress has a gold bodice that looks a little like armor. And before you ask, I have no idea what fabric it's made from. It could just as well be polyester."

Amanda shivered. "I hope not."

"Real gold?" Syssi asked.

"Yep." Wonder took a sip from her margarita. "I wanted to get them at a costume shop, but Anandur wouldn't hear of it. He ordered real ones made for me."

"What about the dress itself?" Sari asked. "Any gold, red, and blue in it?"

Wonder shook her head. "As I said, the bodice is gold. That's as far as I was willing to go. Anandur wanted me to get a blue and red cape to put over the dress, but given how hot it is down here, a cape would have looked ridiculous."

"The venue is air-conditioned." Syssi put her glass on the coffee table. "But you are right. A few subtle nods to the character you took your name from are fun, but too much would have turned the wedding into a parody."

Wonder laughed. "That would have suited Anandur perfectly."

"Is he wearing anything interesting?" Alena asked.

"I have no clue. He wouldn't let me see, claiming that it was bad luck. I just hope he doesn't show up in fishnets and leather shorts."

Amanda nearly choked on her margarita. "Butt-less leather shorts."

Callie gasped. "He would not dare to show his butt to the Clan Mother."

Amanda was still shaking from laughter. "He would be facing her, so she wouldn't see his butt. I'm telling you, that's precisely what he's going to do."

Wonder groaned. "Fates, I hope he doesn't. I love his sense of humor, and he makes me laugh all the time, but this once, I want him to be serious and show up in a tux like any other groom."

"Boring," Amanda muttered under her breath. "Although I have to say that my Dalhu looked absolutely dashing in his tuxedo, so there is something to be said about traditional attire for the groom."

"Your dress was a showstopper," Syssi said. "Both of you looked amazing, and your vows to each other brought happy tears to my eyes."

Wonder winced. She'd worked on her vows for weeks and even asked Parker to help her, but the result still sounded like something a middle schooler would have written. She'd never known how to express herself in words and had always envied Annani for her natural oratory talent.

Her oldest friend had been born to rule, and the Fates had bestowed on her all the necessary talents, including the gift of saying the right thing at the right time, and sounding as if she had prepared ahead of time.

Wonder's Fates-given talent was superior physical strength, and at times like this, she felt ashamed for not contributing to the war effort. She should be preparing to fight along with the males and avenge the poor females who had been rescued, but even though she was physically built for war, mentally, she wasn't.

At least this time, she had a good excuse. She was the bride, and this was her day.

"By the way." Syssi shifted to face Annani. "I spoke to the kitchen staff and asked them to make more food this evening so our guests will get a nice meal during the celebration. I know it's not much, but it makes me feel a little less guilty about having fun while they are still grieving. "

Hearing Syssi say that made Wonder feel a little better about indulging while the victims suffered and the males were ready to go to war with the Doomers and the human monsters they had helped shape in their demonic image.

Leaning over, Annani patted Syssi's hand. "You would have gotten along beautifully with my sister. Areana ran a house for widows who had nowhere to go." She turned to Wonder. "Do you remember that?"

"Of course. Areana has a good heart. It's a shame that the Fates saddled her with a mate like Navuh. It's also a shame that my sister chooses to stay with Areana."

Annani arched one red brow. "What would you have Tula do?"

"Escape. We could have rescued her the same way we rescued Carol. Areana would have made up a story about Tula being depressed and committing suicide, the same way she did for Carol."

Now, that was a mission Wonder would have taken part in. To free her sister, she would have overcome her aversion to warfare and fought like a lioness.

28

ARU

Aru closed the cabin door behind him and was heading toward Kian's place when the familiar sensation of his sister opening a channel stopped him in his tracks.

Can you talk? Aria asked.

I'm heading to a meeting with the princess's son, so I don't have a lot of time. He leaned against the wall and pulled out his phone, pretending to scroll through his social media feed.

I'll make it short. The queen spoke with the king about recording the prophecies, and he loved the idea. We are on.

When? Aru smiled at an immortal walking toward the elevators.

The queen is going to make a public announcement at the upcoming fundraising gala and she will let us know then. It is safer for her and everyone involved if her activity is publicly known and endorsed by the king.

Smart. Anything else?

No, I just thought you would want to know that the first stage of the plan was successful. How are things over there? Are you getting to interact with the princess?

She is very excited about communicating with her grandmother. Other than that, I see her every night as she presides over the clan weddings. There is one every night.

I wish I could be there to see that.

I am glad that you are not. Earth is a savage place. Well, it is not fair to bundle everyone into the same group, but some elements are just barbaric beyond description.

They are worse than the most horrible predators in the most dangerous colonies because they torture and maim for pleasure. Animals do not do that.

That sounds horrible. I wish you did not have to be stuck there.

He let out a breath. *As I said, there are many good people here, and I am not in danger. It is just difficult to stomach the savagery, but I will tell you about it some other time. Kian is waiting for me.*

When you are free, open a channel and talk to me. I feel like you need to lighten your load.

That was one of the great things about having a twin. Aria always knew when he needed to offload, and she was resilient enough, so he did not need to sugarcoat things for her.

I do. Just do not tell the Supreme or the queen what I told you. I do not want them to change their minds about making Earth a hub for the resistance.

Aria chuckled. *The queen has not decided any such thing. It was your idea, and I did not hear either of the ladies saying anything about it. For now, all the queen wants is to get to know her granddaughter, and if she finds her worthy, to groom her for the throne.*

Yes, I know. But just do not say anything.

I will not. I promise. I love you, and I will talk to you later.

Same here, sister of mine. Aru closed the channel, pushed off the wall, and put his phone in his back pocket.

When he rang Kian's cabin doorbell, Anandur opened the door and grinned at Aru. "Your Highness." He bowed at the waist and waved with his hand, gesturing for Aru to come in.

"I'm not a royal or even a noble." He clapped the redhead on the back. "Are you ready for your nuptials tonight?"

"I am, but it's not certain that the ceremony will take place. I'm staying on the ship, but I won't get married with half of my friends fighting Doomers out there."

"Is there any news on that?" Aru sat down next to Turner, the clan's strategist.

"Nothing yet, but we are working on it." Kian rose to his feet and walked over to the bar. "Can I offer you some whiskey?"

"Always." Aru smiled at his host. "Thank you."

He wasn't much of a drinker, but Kian seemed to enjoy sharing his whiskey with his guests, and accepting the drink was an easy way to please his host.

Kian returned to the table a moment later and handed him a glass. "So, Aru, do you want to fight by our side?"

"Of course. I offered our help right away. What do you need me to do?"

"I'm not sure yet. If the Doomers show up in the port with a contingent of cartel thugs, we don't leave the ship. Kalugal and Toven can compel the Doomers and their cartel cronies to shoot each other or just freeze in place so we can take them out. Yamanu will provide the shrouding, of course. But if we need to go burn the bodies and go after the Doomers wherever they are hiding, we will need to split the force, with half remaining to guard the ship and half going out."

"Which group do you want us in?" Aru asked.

"I don't know yet." Kian regarded him with that intense gaze of his. "My Guardians tell me that Negal is as strong and as fast as the Kra-ell. Is that true for you and Dagor as well?"

Aru nodded. "The more recent generations of gods were given several enhancements that your grandfather's generation were not. We are stronger and faster, and we have better hearing and eyesight. We are also less sensitive to the sun and do not need protective eye gear. Simple sunglasses are enough."

Kian tilted his head. "Is that all the gods of your generation or just a select few?"

"Those are standard enhancements that everyone gets. Naturally, nobility and royalty get more and better enhancements."

"Like what?"

Aru leaned back with his drink. "They don't disclose that. It's considered rude to ask Anumatians about their genetic enhancements, and it's considered bad manners to show them off, so it's anyone's guess what anyone else has."

29

FRANKIE

"Let me look at you." Frankie pushed Dagor down on the bed.

He fell back only because he hadn't put up any resistance. "You're looking at me."

He reached for her, but she swatted his hands away.

"I never get the chance to just admire you because you are immediately all hands and mouth and tongue, and I forget my own name."

A smug smirk curving one side of his mouth, he lifted his arms and tucked his hands under his head. "I'm all yours. Do with me as you please."

Damn, it was sexy that a god was putting himself at her mercy.

No, that wasn't it. She should stop thinking of him as a god. He was just Dagor, the man she'd fallen in love with and who loved her back. It didn't matter that he wasn't technically a man, and it also didn't matter that he was immortal and that his blood could heal injuries. Well, it mattered, but that wasn't why she loved him.

"I love you." Frankie dipped her head and kissed his chest, where his shirt was parted at the top.

"I love you too, but you need to tell me when you want my hands on you because I'm not good at guessing."

She opened one more button and kissed the skin she revealed. "I like it that you ask." She popped the next one open and kissed that spot as well. "It's very sweet in a very dorky way." She continued unfastening all the buttons and spread his shirt. "I love your chest." She put her hands on his pectorals. "You are so broad and hard."

He chuckled. "There is another part of me that can be described with the same words, and it's very much in need of your attention."

"I bet." She looked at where the line of sparse hair descended from his navel and disappeared under the waistband.

Frankie had wondered about that before. The gods designed themselves to be incredibly pleasing to the eye, so if they had left body hair on their males, it was because goddesses found it attractive.

Dagor groaned. "Can I touch you now?"

She leaned up and kissed him lightly on the lips. "Patience, my love. We have seven hours, so there is no rush, and I want to take my time with you."

"You're torturing me."

"Oh, please." She rolled her eyes. "Don't be such a baby. Hold those arms over your head until I tell you that it's okay to touch me."

As she slanted her lips over his and slipped her tongue between his fangs. Dagor gasped and she felt his chest muscles contract under her.

It was difficult for Dagor to allow her to lead, to let her tongue lap at his while he wasn't allowed to touch her, and she appreciated his compliance with her wishes.

Holding on to his shoulders, she enjoyed the play of muscles under her hands as she teased and licked. He growled but responded only with his tongue, flicking it against hers and stoking her fire.

Her breasts were heavy, her nipples so stiff that they ached, and her core tingled with need.

She'd wanted to keep exploring, but the need inside of her was overpowering her resolve, and as fun as having Dagor at her mercy was, it was more fun when he took over.

There was always tomorrow to continue her explorations.

"You can touch me now," she murmured against his lips.

"Thank the merciful Fates."

She was under him between one breath and the next, naked within two heartbeats, and then he was kissing her breasts, his hot breath fanning over her nipples.

"Dagor." She threaded her fingers into his short hair. "I ache." She pushed on his head until his mouth was over her right nipple. "Kiss it."

"Bossy," he murmured over the stiff peak. "I don't hate it." He finally dragged his tongue over her aching flesh.

It was good, so damn good, but it wasn't enough.

Tugging on his hair, she hissed, "I said, kiss it."

He'd said that he didn't hate it when she gave him commands, right?

"So damn bossy," he murmured against her nipple.

When he pulled it into his mouth, she arched to get him to take more, and as he switched to her other breast, he cupped the wet one he'd just left.

"Dagor." She let go of his hair and pushed his shirt down his arms, needing to touch more of his skin.

If she could, she would have ripped it off him, and she had the silly thought that once she was immortal, she would do that just to see if she could. He shrugged it off, and the hand that released her breast traveled south to brush against her thigh.

As he smoothed his hand up her thigh, she rubbed her palms down his torso, and when she clasped his shaft over his pants, he groaned but kept sucking on her nipple.

When he finally brushed his fingers over her wet center, she quivered, and her hold on his erection tightened.

"You need to get naked."

Lifting his head, he looked at her with his glowing eyes and smiled, revealing his elongated fangs. "I like bossy Frankie."

"Good. Then do as I say."

"Yes, ma'am." He lifted off her and pushed his pants down his hips.

The man was male perfection.

Not a man. A god. An immortal.

The one she loved.

Her mate.

30

DAGOR

There was nothing more beautiful than Frankie in the throes of passion, wanton with desire, her eyes hooded, and her legs parted for him.

Kneeling between her spread thighs, Dagor slipped a finger inside her wet heat, and as she closed her eyes and moaned his name, it was all he could do not to pounce on her and impale her on his shaft in one go.

But Frankie was tiny, and he needed to make her ready.

Watching his finger going in and out of her, he added his thumb to the play, circling her engorged pleasure button.

"Yes. Oh, yes." She stiffened, and her back bowed as she climaxed.

He closed his fist around his erection, willing it to have patience until Frankie was ready for him.

Her sheath squeezed his finger, and her wetness coated it the way he needed it to squeeze and coat his shaft, but he kept pumping in and out of her and gently stroking her clit until her tremors subsided, and she pushed on his hand.

Her expression was still dazed when she rocked her hips and opened her eyes. "Get inside of me, Dagor."

He chuckled. "Still so bossy." He flipped them around so he was on his back, and she was straddling him. "If you want me, you'll have to take me."

"Challenge accepted, big guy." She looked at his erection with hungry eyes.

She gripped his shaft in her small, soft hand and began working it inside of her, and when she rose to sink farther down, Dagor's lips parted with a groan.

He hoped that seeing his fully elongated fangs wouldn't scare her.

The other times they had been intimate, she'd taken a much more passive role and hadn't had such an unobstructed view of them.

But when she opened her eyes, all he saw in them was desire and feminine satisfaction. It seemed that Frankie loved being in charge for a change, and he loved seeing her like that.

Her perky breasts danced as she rode him slowly, too slowly, and as much as he wanted her to have her moment, he needed her to start moving faster, or he was going to lose his sanity.

Gripping her hips, he pushed up hard, and when she moaned and braced her hands on his chest, he took it to mean that she was ready for him to take over.

"Fates, Frankie," he growled. "I can't get enough of you."

For several thrusts, he surged in and out of her, but then she began to ride him with gusto, and he let go of her hips to cup her breasts.

Frankie moaned when he squeezed and pinched, and when she was on the brink, she threw her head back and rode him even faster.

He could feel how close she was and that she needed something more to fall over the cliff. Letting go of her breasts, he clasped her ass with one hand and reached with the finger of his other to press on her clit.

"Come for me, Frankie."

"Yes. More."

His fingers dug into her ass; he held her in place as he rammed up into her and rubbed her engorged pleasure button harder.

The building expression of ecstasy on her face was a wondrous thing, and then she exploded, her sheath clamping around his shaft and squeezing tight.

With one swift motion, he flipped them around, pinned her head to the mattress, and had just enough presence of mind to lick her neck before sinking his fangs into her and filling her with his seed and venom at the same time.

She yelled, then shuddered around him, and then she was climaxing again, the small muscles inside her sheath milking him until there was nothing left.

His shaft softening only a fraction, he continued thrusting into her slowly until the last of her tremors subsided.

For a few long moments, Dagor feasted his eyes on Frankie's blissed-out expression, her long lashes fanning over her rosy cheeks. He would have happily stayed inside her until she woke up in a few hours, but he needed to clean up the mess they had made.

Reluctantly, he slipped out of her, and their combined juices rushed out, soaking the sheets under them.

Thankfully, he had brought an armful of bedding to her cabin so they wouldn't have to rush into the laundry every time they made a mess.

Dagor chuckled softly.

It paid to be an organized nerd who always planned ahead.

When he returned with several washcloths, Frankie was in exactly the same position he'd left her, and as he cleaned her with gentle strokes, she didn't even twitch a muscle.

Once he was done, Dagor gazed at Frankie's lithe, compact body and was overwhelmed with his feelings for her.

How had he fallen in love so quickly and thoroughly?

It was as if the Fates had designed Frankie especially for him. He wouldn't change anything about her except turning her immortal. Everything else just had to stay the same, or it would detract from her perfection.

31

ANNANI

Annani watched her old friend smile and chat with Callie, Carol, and her other guests, the smile never leaving her face for longer than a few breaths.

She rejoiced in Wonder's happiness, but there was a tinge of sadness over the childhood friend that was lost forever. Gulan's body might not have died in the earthquake that had swallowed her, but the female who had woken from stasis nearly five thousand years later was not the girl who had been Annani's servant and best friend.

At a different time in history, Gulan's old job description would have been a lady-in-waiting, and perhaps that title would not have grated on her as much as being called a servant had.

Apparently, Wonder had forgotten the deep friendship that had formed between them, or maybe she had never felt it as strongly as Annani had.

Gulan had chosen to shed her old identity and emerge as Wonder, the namesake of a comic's female superhero whose powers were about love, truth, and beauty. The character had been created during World War II as part of a team of superhuman beings who fought the Axis forces and various other villains. It was a most fitting name for Gulan. She was strong of body and character, and even though she detested violence, she had used her incredible strength to overpower and imprison Doomers, who had gone on a killing spree of women in the area she had lived in at the time.

The world could use a real Wonder Woman and her Justice League companions right now. Things were once again spiraling out of control, and the forces of evil were on the rise. Some were cloaked in good intentions, and others were not even bothering to do that.

Annani sighed. She was tired of the endless cycle of gaining some ground, only to lose most of it again. When things were going well, humans soon forgot how bad it used to be and allowed the forces of evil to take it away from them.

She could use her old friend to bolster her resolve, to encourage her when she despaired, but even living in the village had not brought them closer.

Wonder worked long days in the village café and spent her evenings studying a variety of subjects. She could not decide what subject she wanted to specialize in, but she knew for sure that she did not want to be a Guardian even though that was the role she had been born for.

Her friend's incredible strength made Annani wonder if Gulan's godly ancestors had some Kra-ell blood in them. To her great shame, she had never inquired who Gulan had descended from.

What kind of a friend was she, never to look into Wonder's lineage?

Back then, Annani had thought that getting to know Gulan's parents and her sister was enough, but it was not. She had acted as a princess would, feeling superior and being condescending without meaning to. It had been based solely on her birthright as a princess and heir to the throne.

Nowadays, it had more to do with the experience of having lived through five thousand years of history, while Wonder had lived only through just over twenty-three. While Annani experienced history firsthand, Wonder had learned about it from Annani's stories and from books.

It was not the same.

Despite the agelessness of her appearance, Annani carried the wisdom and nuances of her extended life, while Wonder had had only two decades to shape her as a person, most of them having been lived in a different world.

And yet, Annani had managed to maintain a spirit that was young at heart, a vivacity that animated her. In contrast, Wonder had always been more reserved and somber. She had been that way as Gulan in their shared youth back in ancient Sumer, and also as the woman she had become after her awakening.

"Remember our adventures outside the palace, Wonder? When I snuck out wearing your little sister's clothes?" Annani asked. "The days when we believed we could change the world if only we put our minds to it?"

Wonder smiled, a touch of wistfulness in her eyes. "You were so tiny that only Tula's clothes could fit you. And as for believing in our power to change the world, it was you, not me. I was happy to leave the world as it was if it could earn me a few peaceful days. You were fearless, and I was the opposite of that. Being your maid was the most stressful time of my life. I don't think I was as scared when I took three Doomers captive."

Annani winced. "You were not my maid. You were my best friend."

Wonder shook her head. "I was paid to guard you and keep you company."

"That is not what a maid does. Your job was a cross between a lady-in-waiting and a bodyguard." Annani chuckled. "You were the voice of reason and kept me grounded when my ideas were too wild."

Wonder rolled her eyes. "Tell me about it. Do you remember when you tried to convince me to sneak out of the palace and steal a boat? You wanted to visit the nearest city."

Annani laughed. "How can I forget? We got caught."

"Fortunately, it happened before we stole the boat. Your father would have been furious, and he would have blamed me for not reporting your shenanigans."

As they meandered through shared memories, each recollection bridged the chasm of time between their shared past and present. In Wonder's stories, Annani could see the young, reckless girl she once was.

She still retained some of that youthful exuberance and thirst for adventure, but she lacked the naïveté that had made her so hopeful as a girl.

Her daughters had been born in different epochs, different worlds, but none of them had ever been as naïve as their mother had been in her youth.

Alena was serene because she chose to be, not because she was oblivious to the ugliness around her. Sari was a born leader who cared mainly about keeping their clan safe and prosperous and less about the state of humankind. Amanda cared equally for her clan and the humans, but then she was the youngest and most sheltered.

"I propose a toast." Wonder lifted a full margarita glass. "To Annani, who has championed women's rights for thousands of years. You've seen societies change and evolve, and you've always been at the forefront, fighting for equality and justice, finally to achieve your goals in the twentieth century."

Annani sighed. "Women's rights have always been close to my heart. Seeing the progress over the centuries gives me hope, but there is still so much to do. It is disheartening that modern-day feminism often gets lost in political debates, while critical issues like trafficking do not get the attention they desperately need."

The mood of the group grew somber as they were reminded of the victims they had recently rescued, now being cared for on the lower deck of the ship.

"It's a harsh reality," Syssi said quietly. "The fight against trafficking and exploitation of women and girls is a battle that seems never-ending. But it's a battle we cannot afford to lose."

Amanda reached out, placing a hand on Syssi's arm. "The work we do makes a difference, even if we can't save everyone. This is why we continue to fight, why we continue to dedicate resources to a seemingly lost cause. We stand up for those who can't. Every life we save, every victim we rehabilitate and empower, is a step towards a better world."

Sari lifted her glass. "I'll drink to that."

32

DAGOR

The chime of a message notification echoed in the quiet cabin, pulling Dagor's attention away from the serene sight of the sleeping beauty in front of him. He reached for his device and read the message from Aru.

Please come to my cabin at your earliest convenience.

He had no problem guessing what the summons was about. They were joining the immortals in their fight against their enemies and the cartel thugs.

"Bring it on," he murmured. "I'm more than happy to rid Earth of a few more monsters."

He wondered why Kian hadn't gone on the offensive and eliminated his enemies on their island. He knew where it was, and he had the means to blast it to pieces. Nuke it if needed. One explanation was that there were innocents on that island that Kian was reluctant to kill, or maybe it was more about avoiding attracting attention. If Kian nuked the island, the humans would investigate.

Regrettably, the immortals were not susceptible to pathogens, so the Eternal King's usual modus operandi' when wanting to eliminate an entire population wouldn't work.

Glancing at Frankie, Dagor debated whether he should try to wake her up before leaving. Her breathing was calm and even, and there was a peaceful expression on her face. Blissful even. She'd been upset with him when he'd left the cabin while she'd been asleep, but waking her from such a deep and restoring slumber would be a shame. Still, he was determined not to make the same mistake twice.

He would tell her where he was going and why, and then she could go back to sleep.

"Frankie," he whispered.

When there was no response, he put his hand on her shoulder and gave her a little shake. "Frankie, I need to step out for a bit."

Not surprisingly, she was still soaring on the wings of venom-induced euphoria, too loopy to even flutter her eyelids open.

There was only one thing he could do, which was to leave her a note. She'd indicated that leaving a message on her phone was acceptable.

Pulling out his device, Dagor began to type a message.

Hey Frankie, I didn't want to wake you, but I need to step out for a bit. Aru just texted me, asking me to come to his cabin for a meeting, and I didn't want to leave without letting you know where I was.

Dagor was about to press send when he reconsidered and decided to add something romantic. The problem was that he knew next to nothing about romance, and he didn't have time to search the internet for romantic poems or ask one of the AI bots to write something for him.

With a sigh, he typed what he would have said if she were awake.

I'm not going to be gone long, but I know that I will miss you no matter how short the meeting is. I think I'm addicted to you in the best possible way. I love the way your body feels against mine, soft and yet solid. I love the sweet scent of your skin, and I love your smiling eyes. You are like a breath of fresh air in a stale world. I'll be back as soon as I can, and in the meantime, I will be thinking about you and counting the minutes until I can return.

He read over the message once and was satisfied with the result. It might not win any poetry contests, but it conveyed how he felt.

After sending the message, Dagor lingered a little longer, watching Frankie sleep, and then leaned down and placed a gentle kiss on her forehead.

Aru's cabin was on the top deck, next to the clan leadership, and as Dagor rang the doorbell, Negal opened up and motioned for him to come inside.

"It seems like we get to fight again." Negal grinned.

Dagor took a seat on the couch across from Aru. "I didn't get to fight in the previous altercation, and I'm very enthusiastic about having another opportunity to escort the vermin and their hired thugs to hell."

Anumatians didn't believe in the same hell that humans did. Their place of atonement was not a pit of fire where sinners burned for eternity. It was just a void of nothing, and being stuck there, endlessly reflecting on past lives and all the evil deeds committed through millions of years of existence, was scary enough.

Aru smiled but then quickly schooled his features. "Kian asked us to join them, not because they need our help. It's a way to cement our alliance."

"Makes sense." Dagor leaned back and crossed his arms over his chest.

The idea of solidarity with these immortals resonated with him. If he was to remain on Earth, he needed a community of people to call his own, and he liked the clan and what it stood for. He wouldn't mind becoming a member, but more importantly, he wanted that for Frankie.

If she turned immortal, she would need a community of immortals, and both of them could be happy living among these people.

Provided that Frankie turned.

Gabi had started transitioning days after she and Aru had first been intimate together. He'd heard that some of the Dormants had taken much longer to start transitioning, but they hadn't been induced by a god.

Frankie should have already started showing signs of transitioning.

But what if Lisa was right and Frankie was already on her way to becoming immortal without symptoms? Perhaps it had happened while she was recovering from her injury with the help of his blood?

"So. What's our assignment?" Negal asked.

"According to the former members of the Brotherhood, Kalugal, Dalhu, and Lokan, the Doomers rarely send out teams smaller than twelve, and that's probably the number of immortals we will face. But they are also very likely to be aided by a large cartel militia."

The mention of the cartel tightened the muscles in Dagor's jaw. "The humans are nothing," he spat. "The three of us could obliterate them on our own."

Aru chuckled. "Indeed. But even we can be brought down with enough bullets. The ship is well stocked with weapons, and I'm not talking about handguns. We are not trained in what they have, and we need to get in a few practice shots before we get to Acapulco to familiarize ourselves with the weapons. We don't know yet whether they will be waiting for us at the dock or if we will need to go after them. If it's the second option, half the force will stay on the ship to defend it, including Toven, who is the strongest compeller the clan has. We should decide who stays and who goes as well."

Dagor didn't need to think this through. "You need to stay."

Aru frowned. "Why? Don't you have faith in my fighting abilities?"

Dagor snorted. "We trained together. I know precisely what you can and cannot do. Your fighting skills are mediocre at best, but you can talk yourself out of tight spots. You are the one who's communicating with the commander, and you are good at spinning tales. If Negal or I have to explain why you are unavailable to answer his call, it won't end well."

"Good point." Aru rubbed a hand over his jaw. "I'll stay."

"When and where do we practice with the weapons?" Negal asked.

"I wasn't told yet. I'm waiting for further instructions."

33

FRANKIE

Frankie sensed that Dagor wasn't in bed with her even before she was fully awake. It was a feeling of something missing, something essential that she couldn't live without.

He could have been in the living room or maybe taking a shower, but she knew he wasn't anywhere in the cabin.

It was odd, to say the least. It was disconcerting.

She had lived for twenty-seven years without Dagor and hadn't felt like anything or anyone was missing from her life, but now, only a few days after meeting him, he had become so important to her, so vital, that she felt a sense of loss when he wasn't near.

Did all people in love feel that way?

It was scary to become so dependent on someone.

Opening her eyes, she confirmed that he really wasn't there. Some part of her hoped that she'd been wrong, and she would find him asleep next to her.

Dagor had promised to be with her until the ship reached Acapulco, and even when it did, it wasn't certain that he and his teammates would join the Guardians going to shore. He might stay with her.

There was no way seven hours had passed already, and the ship had arrived at Acapulco. Besides, given the swaying, the ship was still en route.

So where was Dagor?

Suddenly, panic seized Frankie. What if something had come up, and he'd left the ship early?

Perhaps Kian had decided that there was a faster way to reach Acapulco and he'd hired helicopters to take a team to shore?

Or maybe they had used the lifeboats?

Could it be that the smaller boats could get there faster?

Frankie had no clue.

Snatching her phone off the nightstand, she was relieved to confirm that less than two hours had passed since they had returned to her cabin, and there was also a message from Dagor.

Frankie smiled. He'd remembered what she'd told him about leaving while she slept. She clicked on the message, and as she read it, her smile grew wider with every word.

Dagor felt the same way she did. He was addicted to her, couldn't stand being away from her, and counted the seconds until they were together again.

Well, he hadn't used those precise words, but his meaning was clear.

The only thing missing to make things perfect between them was her turning immortal. Perhaps now that Dagor was busy, she could use the time to meet up with a few of the recently transitioned Dormants and ask them about their experience.

Frankie hit Mia's number. "Are you busy?"

"I'm working on an illustration, and Toven is in a meeting with Kian and the rest of the gang. Why? Do you want to meet up and do something together?"

"I would like to talk with some of the recently transitioned Dormants. Do you think you can call up your new relatives and we can meet on the Lido deck? We can talk over drinks."

Mia chuckled. "Let's see. There's Darlene and Cassandra, Toven's granddaughters, and Roni, who is Toven's great-grandson, but he's busy right now, hacking into hotels in Acapulco."

"Why?"

"I don't know. That's what Darlene told me. We can also invite Kaia, who is not related to Toven directly, and Karen, who is a Dormant like you awaiting transition."

"Really?" Frankie perked up. "How long has she been trying?"

Mia chuckled. "She hasn't started yet. Her situation is complicated. Gilbert, her partner, is a newly transitioned immortal, which means that his fangs and venom are not yet fully functional, so he can't induce her transition. She can wait five more months or so until he's ready, or she can do what Darlene did and use a surrogate."

Frankie frowned. "What do you mean by a surrogate? Are you suggesting that she takes another immortal into her bed when she's in a committed relationship? Don't they have like five kids together?"

"Three. Kaia and Cheryl are Karen's daughters from a previous marriage. But yeah, it's complicated. They need the surrogate only for the bite, but you can imagine how difficult it is to coordinate a thing like that."

"Yeah, I bet." Frankie chuckled. "It would have been easy if Karen and Gilbert were the adventurous types who didn't mind experimenting with multiple partners, but I guess they are not."

"I don't think immortals are capable of that," Mia said. "Darlene's mate had to be chained to the bed to prevent him from attacking the guy who volunteered to be the surrogate."

"Oh, wow. I'm surprised that the guy volunteered. Who was it?"

"I don't think you know him. His name is Max."

Flirty Max was just the type to volunteer for something like that. Now, she was definitely introducing him to Margo.

"I've met him. He's cool."

"Yeah. Max is a good guy, and it was nice of him to volunteer. So, when do you want to meet up on the Lido deck?"

"As soon as possible. Dagor is in a meeting with Aru, and I don't know how long it will take, but I don't want to miss any time with him."

"I get it. Let's meet up in twenty minutes?"

"Perfect. It will give me time to grab a shower and get dressed."

Mia laughed. "I'm not going to ask why you need a shower in the middle of the day."

"I could have just returned from a swim in the pool."

"Right. But you didn't."

"I did not."

Mia laughed again. "I'll see you in a bit."

Smiling, Frankie put the phone on the nightstand and got out of bed. It was nice having Mia so close, and it would have been nice to move into the village and see her every day, but if it meant not being with Dagor, the choice was easy.

Her mate came first for the simple reason that she couldn't stand being apart from him, and he couldn't be apart from her either.

With the clan satellite phone, she could call Mia whenever she wanted from wherever she was, and it would be almost as good as being next to her in person. The same wasn't true for Dagor. She needed him to be near, needed to touch him, smell him, kiss him, hear him murmur in her ear...

34

KIAN

"We can do it." William handed Kalugal a piece of paper. "Roni says that's the best hotel to route the calls through. It has hundreds of rooms, and despite what's going on with the cartels, it's about seventy percent booked. It also has a surveillance network covering all the public spaces, everything is accessible on the net, and Roni had no trouble hacking into their network."

"So, everything is ready for Kalugal to make the call?" Kian asked.

William nodded. "Roni is on standby." He chuckled. "This kid is incredible. He was ecstatic when I told him we needed his help. He said that he was frustrated about not being able to contribute because he's not a fighter, but this is something he can do better than most."

Kian could understand Roni's feelings all too well. If he could, he would have stormed the Doomers wherever they were and relished taking them down, but he was the leader of a community that depended on him, and he couldn't just gallop into battle whenever he felt the urge.

He had to stay behind and trust others to do their jobs. It wasn't different from having to rely on others to manage the clan's companies. Learning to delegate had been difficult, but he was getting better at it.

The life of an immortal was a continuum of endless learning experiences, and the same was true for the gods. Those who stopped learning succumbed to ennui.

"Okay, then." Kalugal rubbed his hands. "Which phone do I use to make the call?"

"This one." William handed him a device. "It's ready for you. But before you do, read the other comments Roni wrote down. He altered the hotel's records to show you staying there for the past week, and he also added ten rooms to your account that you supposedly booked yesterday." William smiled. "That was my idea. If the Doomers call to investigate, they will think that you rented the additional rooms for the rescued victims."

"Smart." Kalugal looked at the piece of paper. "I see that he booked it under the fake name I gave the tour company Luis works for."

William nodded. "Kevin Gunter and his wife Cecilia are staying in room 304. Roni says that there is a camera in the hallway directly across from the door to this room, and one of the exterior cameras is covering the window. If they come for you from either one, we will know. Calls to the landline in that room will be rerouted to the phone I just gave you."

"Excellent." Kalugal pulled out his phone. "I need to check the number for the tour company. By the way, how did Roni hack the hotel room's landline?"

William shrugged. "Call forwarding through the hotel's system. It's not complicated. All the numbers are listed in the hotel's database."

"Clever." Kalugal entered the number to the tour company into the new phone William had given him, activated the speaker, and leaned back against the couch cushions.

"*Buenas tardes*," a female answered. "How can I help you?"

"Hello, this is Kevin Gunter," he said with a heavy German accent. "Yesterday, my friends and I hired Luis and two other drivers to take us to the Tehuacalco ruins. One of my friends forgot his sunglasses in one of the vehicles, and he's wondering whether anyone has found them."

"I'll be happy to check for you, Mr. Gunter. Can you hold for a moment?"

"Of course." Kalugal smiled and put the call on mute. "I bet she's stalling so they have time to trace the call."

"It's possible," Kian agreed.

Several minutes passed before the woman came back online. "I'm sorry, Mr. Gunter, but no one has found any sunglasses."

Kalugal unmuted the call and affected a heavy sigh. "That's a shame. They must have fallen out during our tour of the ruins. If any of your tour guides finds a pair of Gucci sunglasses and brings them to your office, please call me at the Rivera Hotel. My wife and I will be staying here for another three days."

"Of course, Mr. Gunter. What is your room number?"

"It is not necessary for you to know the number to call me. The front desk will know where I'm staying and forward your call."

"As you wish, Mr. Gunter, but things are not as efficient here as they are in Germany. The person at the reception desk might ask me for the room number and refuse to forward the call based on the name alone." She chuckled, but it sounded forced. "They will need to look up the name in the computer, and that's one extra step they might not wish to do."

"For security reasons, I do not give out information about my lodging, *Fräulein*. I will call the front desk immediately after this and demand that they transfer calls to my room without asking for the room number. They will comply with my demand, or I'll escalate the issue to management."

"As you wish, sir."

"Thank you, *Fräulein*. Good day." He ended the call.

"Great performance," Kian said. "It was a good touch to refuse to give out your hotel room number. Made it sound more legit."

Kalugal smirked. "I know."

"So, what's next?" Kian asked.

"Roni is watching the feed from the hotel and waiting to see if anyone shows up," Onegus said. "If no one comes looking for Mr. Gunter, it's safe to assume that they haven't discovered the bodies yet. But if someone does show up, it might be because of the missing women we took and not necessarily because of the bodies."

Kalugal frowned. "Wasn't the whole idea to find out whether it was too late to eliminate the evidence of our handiwork or if we could still do that?"

"That was just one part of the plan," Kian said. "The second part was eliminating the Doomers who ordered the attack on the village. I know that it won't fix anything and that the Brotherhood will just send reinforcements, but I can't in good conscience let them live."

Dalhu nodded. "I agree on both counts. We need to take them out."

35

FRANKIE

"Thank you all for coming." Frankie pulled out a couple of chairs from a nearby table and added them to the one she and Mia had chosen. "I would buy you all drinks, but since they are on the house, it doesn't count toward repayment. All I can offer you is my sincere thanks."

Darlene waved a dismissive hand. "I'm so glad that this is behind me. I still remember how scary it was, and I'm happy to help in any way I can."

"Thank you." Frankie waved at Bob. "Can you come over and take our orders?"

"Yes, mistress, of course." He zoomed in from behind the bar. "What can I serve you, ladies?"

After they were done ordering their drinks and snacks, Frankie turned to Gabi. "Can you tell me about your transitioning experience? How long did it take to start after you and Aru started to work on it?"

"It just happened. Aru didn't know about Dormants. I knew I was one and what it meant, but I didn't know that Aru was a god. Anyway, my transition started on the third day." She smiled. "A god's venom is very potent."

Frankie felt the blood drain from her face. It was her fourth day with Dagor, and she'd even gotten a transfusion from him. She should have started transitioning already.

Perhaps she wasn't a Dormant after all.

She swallowed the bile that rose in her throat.

But wait a moment. They had used condoms at the beginning. The first time they hadn't was yesterday.

There was no reason to panic.

She let out a breath and turned to Kaia. "What about you? How long did it take for your transition to start?"

"Five days."

That was encouraging. "Was it difficult?"

"Not at all." Kaia glanced at her mother. "But it was slow for me. It took forever for my healing time to improve. I must be a very weak immortal."

"What does that mean?" Frankie asked. "I didn't know that there were weak and strong immortals."

"The more removed a Dormant is from the source, the more diluted their genes are," Kaia explained. "Kian is the son of a goddess, and therefore he is a strong immortal with an incredibly fast recovery time. I must be many generations removed from my godly ancestor, and that's why my healing time is much slower."

"There are exceptions," Darlene said. "I'm Toven's granddaughter, which makes me very close to the source, but my transition was pretty average."

After Darlene had shared the rest of her transition story and Bob had brought their drinks and snacks, Frankie turned to Karen. "Mia tells me that you are waiting for your husband's fangs and venom to be functional to transition."

Karen winced. "Gilbert and I are not married, but that's not important. We are fully committed to each other, and now that Gilbert is immortal, he's even more possessive and jealous than he was before. Everyone thinks that I shouldn't wait because of my age, but even though Gilbert and I have discussed several other options, neither of us is comfortable with any of them. Gilbert's latest idea was to ask one of the gods to volunteer his fangs. The advantages of that are clear. First of all, a god's venom is more potent, which will give me a better chance, and he can also thrall Gilbert and me, so it's not as difficult for us. But since Toven, Aru, and Dagor are already taken, that leaves only Negal."

"Not for long," Frankie said. "I plan to introduce him to my friend Margo, and if they hit it off like Dagor and I did, Negal will be taken as well. If you want to proceed with your plan, I suggest that you do that before we reach Cabo and Margo comes on board."

Karen groaned. "No pressure. No pressure at all." She briefly closed her eyes. "Is there any chance you could talk to Negal for us and explain what we need? It's so damn embarrassing. How the hell am I going to ask him such a thing?"

"I sure can," Frankie said. "Negal is a good guy. I have no doubt that he will be happy to do it."

Kaia shook her head. "You are not in high school, Mom, and you are not asking a friend to find out if a guy likes you. This is a delicate matter that should be addressed with the gravity it deserves by either you or Gilbert, but Gilbert is the better choice to approach Negal. The guy doesn't get embarrassed by anything."

"I'd better talk to Gilbert right away." Karen pushed to her feet and smiled apologetically at Frankie. "I hope you don't mind that I'm leaving so abruptly."

"Of course not." She waved her off. "Good luck."

Karen turned to leave but then turned back. "Do you know where we can find Negal?"

"He's in a meeting in Aru's cabin." Frankie pulled out her phone. "Dagor hasn't texted me yet, so they are still there."

Kaia looked up at her mother. "You can't bother them with your issues now, Mom. They are planning what to do about the Doomers once we get back to Acapulco, and the last thing they want to talk about is your transition. You should wait until tomorrow."

"I'm going to talk with Gilbert, and if he wants to approach Negal today, I'm sure the god will not mind sparing a few minutes to talk to him. All he needs to do is say yes or no. If he agrees, we need to make plans for tomorrow or, at the latest, the day after. That's all the time we have."

Now Frankie felt bad. "Perhaps I can wait a day to introduce Margo and Negal."

Karen shook her head. "Margo is your and Mia's best friend, and Negal is Dagor's. You can't postpone introducing them even if you want to. Besides, maybe it's good to put some fire under us so we finally get on with it."

36

KAREN

Karen didn't rush back to her cabin as she'd set out to do. Instead of the elevator, she took the stairs down to the third deck and used the time to think about what she wanted to say to Gilbert.

The truth was that he'd been the one pushing for her not to wait for him to grow out his fangs and venom glands.

In her opinion, her body wasn't going to age significantly in the four to five months it would take for Gilbert to be able to induce her transition, but it seemed like no one else shared her opinion.

Then, there were all the other changes Gilbert was experiencing. He was rewinding the clock, getting younger in front of her eyes, and his stamina would tire out an eighteen-year-old. His exuberance and energy had been exhausting when he was a nearly fifty-year-old human. Now that his body could keep up with his mind, Karen felt like she was left trying to catch up.

He claimed she was his one and only, but Karen had always known how important it was for partners in the relationship to have more or less equal footing on the scale of attractiveness. There were several measures that could compensate for one another, like looks, intelligence, and professional success, and she included full-time motherhood in that, but the aggregate score should be as similar as possible.

She and Gilbert had that equilibrium until he transitioned, but now the gap was widening by the day, and not just because he looked a decade younger than she did. His energy and reduced need for sleep meant that he could do more now than he could before, and he was using that time productively, including taking on more responsibilities with their children.

Karen felt outperformed, and she didn't like that at all. Still, was that reason enough to expedite her transition?

No, it wasn't.

But having a god's venom induce her was, and Negal was the only one still available, but not for long. She was on the older end of the range, and she needed all the help she could get to emerge immortal on the other side and not dead.

Karen had five children to think of, and if there was even the slightest chance that having a god induce her would make the difference in her survival, she owed it to her children to do everything in her power to secure his help.

With that realization solidified, Karen squared her shoulders and quickened her step. She'd already checked with Bridget that the clinic on board had all the necessary equipment, so that wasn't an issue. She would hate to miss the remaining weddings, but chances were that she wouldn't start transitioning until they returned to the village. It had taken Kaia five days to start transitioning, and she was nineteen. Karen expected that it would take at least twice as long for hers to start.

When she opened the door to their cabin, she was greeted by the usual chaos of her family. The twins were fighting over a toy, and Gilbert was chasing after Idina with a dress in his hand while their daughter was squealing with laughter and running around with nothing but her ladybug panties on.

Naturally, Gilbert could have caught her with ease, but it was a game they liked to play. Most of the time, Idina pretended that she didn't want to get dressed, and Gilbert pretended to be angry as he chased her with what he wanted her to wear. Sometimes, though, it was for real, and Idina refused to wear a particular item of clothing for this or that reason. When that happened, no game could convince her to change her mind, and Karen had learned just to go with the flow and let the girl wear whatever she wanted.

Was that bad parenting?

Maybe, but Karen was okay with not being perfect at everything. As a mother of five with a full-time job, she'd learned to compromise.

When Idina darted by her, she caught her around the waist and lifted her into her arms. "Stop running. You are making my head spin." She kissed her daughter's cheek and extended a hand to Gilbert for the dress.

"I need to talk to you," she said as she pulled it over Idina's head. "Remember what we talked about regarding the gods?"

He nodded.

"Aru and Dagor are out, and Frankie has just told me that she plans on introducing Negal to her friend when she comes on board in Cabo." She put Idina on the couch and gave her the remote. "Find a show you want to watch, sweetie."

Idina grinned like she'd just won a prize. "Thank you, Mommy," she said with the sweetest voice.

"You are welcome." Karen walked over to the kitchenette, with Gilbert following close behind her. "If Negal and Margo hit it off, there is a good chance that he will be out as well. We need to act now."

Gilbert ran a hand over his hair, of which there was much more now than there had been a month ago. "I need to talk to Negal."

Karen nodded.

"I'll get Eric and Max, and we will talk to him together. It will be easier to explain, and it won't sound like a creepy come-on."

"Good idea. Negal is in a meeting in Aru's cabin, and I don't know when it will be over. We basically have tomorrow night and perhaps one more to do it or miss our chance." She took in a breath. "If Negal doesn't work out, I'm waiting for you to be ready. The only reason to complicate things and do them in this convoluted manner is the added benefit of the god's extra-potent mojo. Frankly, if we can't get Negal, I don't see much benefit in involving another immortal who doesn't have that extra something. As for my advanced age, I don't think my body will change much in the next four to five months."

37

GILBERT

Thankfully, Darlene wasn't in the cabin when Gilbert explained to Eric what he needed to do and why it was urgent.

"How are we going to get Max?" Eric asked. "He's in a Guardians' meeting down in the dining hall."

"Can you text him? Maybe he can take a break?"

"We can do this without him. I was there, remember? I can tell Negal everything that happened." He grimaced. "Well, not everything, but the general gist of things."

"What if your testimony is not enough? Negal needs to hear it from the guy who did the biting and get pointers from him. It's not easy for an immortal to work himself up enough to produce erotic venom. Usually, they need to be near a female they are attracted to."

"Yeah, you're right." Eric rubbed his jaw. "Max did it without a female. He watched porn on his phone." He smiled. "I like the term you coined, erotic venom. What do you call the other type?"

"Combative venom."

"Not bad. You should put it on the clan virtual bulletin board. I'm sure it will catch on right away."

Gilbert didn't have the patience for this sort of idle chitchat. "Can you please text Max now?"

"Right." Eric pulled out his phone, typed a one-sentence message, and sent it.

"What did you tell him?"

"I asked if he had ten minutes for me."

"It will take longer than that to explain what we need."

Eric shrugged. "True, but there is a better chance of him answering in the affirmative when he thinks it will take only ten minutes and not an hour. Not that I think it will take that long. Twenty minutes at most."

As the phone pinged with an incoming message, Eric read it and smiled. "He asks when and where."

"Now, and here. We will explain what we need and then wait by Aru's door until Negal gets out. That's the part that might take longer than ten minutes."

"You should have said that before." Eric typed the message.

"I told you that Negal was in a meeting with Aru."

"Yeah, but you didn't tell me that you wanted to wait outside the door. Isn't that overdoing it?"

Gilbert released a breath. "I don't want to give him a chance to evade me. I need a yes or no answer before Frankie's friend gets here."

When Eric's phone pinged with another message, he looked at the screen. "He's on his way."

"I'd better pour us some whiskey." Gilbert walked over to the bar. "You have to give it to Kian. He's had all the cabins equipped with the best stuff."

"It's not coming out of his pocket." Eric shrugged. "The clan is paying for it."

"I'm not sure." Gilbert took out three small glasses and uncapped the whiskey. "But even if that's true, who makes all the money for the clan? If not for Kian, they wouldn't have all this money."

"True, although I'm sure Sari and her people contribute."

Gilbert pursed his lips. "Frankly, I don't know how it works. It might be that Sari takes care of her people, and Kian takes care of his."

"Then who's financing Annani's place in Alaska? It has to be a joint effort."

"Yeah, you're right."

When the doorbell rang, Eric opened the way for Max, and the two did the bro hug while clapping each other on the back.

Gilbert wasn't on such friendly terms with the Guardian, so he just offered him his hand. "Thank you for coming. I know that the timing sucks, and you are busy with preparations for the Acapulco mission, but this can't wait." He handed him a glass.

"I have time." The Guardian took a small sip. "But I need to watch the alcohol today. We have target practice scheduled for an hour from now, and it's not a good idea to hold an automatic while inebriated." He took another sip. "Damn, this is good whiskey. It's really hard to say no."

Eric snorted. "You have a hard time with saying no in general." He clapped him on the back. "You're too easy."

"Ain't that the truth." Max sighed. "So, what do you need my services for?" He leveled his gaze at Gilbert. "Are those the same services I provided for Eric and Darlene?"

"Close, but not the same. I want to ask Negal to help Karen and me the same way you helped my brother and his mate, and I think it will be good if he hears what's involved from you."

Gilbert had been worried that Max would be offended that he hadn't asked him to be the initiator, but if anything, the guy looked relieved. "Sure. I'll talk to him. Where is he?"

"Negal is in a meeting with the other two gods in Aru's cabin. I suggest we get up there and wait outside to trap him before he leaves to do something else."

Max nodded. "He and the other two are coming to the training. We can talk in the bar until the practice starts."

"Don't you think us cornering him by the door would be perceived as creepy?" Eric stuffed his hands in his pockets. "It might be off-putting for him."

"Which part?" Max cocked a brow. "The asking him to bite Karen while she and Gilbert are hot and sweaty, or the lurking outside the door, waiting for him to emerge?"

"I meant the second one, but you are right. The whole thing is creepy."

38

NEGAL

"Target practice is in an hour." Aru pushed to his feet. "We should grab something to eat first."

"Dining hall?" Negal glanced at Dagor.

"I'm going to check with Frankie. If she didn't eat yet, I'll meet you down there." He walked over to the door and opened it. "Hello, are you waiting for me?"

Negal and Aru exchanged looks. It couldn't be Gabi because Dagor wouldn't have sounded surprised or asked if whoever was out there was waiting for him.

Out of habit, Negal inhaled, sensing three immortal males out in the corridor.

"We are actually waiting for Negal," one of them said. "Is he coming out?"

Dagor moved aside, giving Negal and Aru an unobstructed view of the newcomers.

Negal recognized Max, who had headed the Guardians who'd joined the tour of the ruins. He'd fought alongside him until Frankie was shot. Then Negal had figured that she and Dagor needed someone to protect them on the way back to the ship, and he'd been the closest, so he'd jumped into the truck, but in the few moments that Max had seen him in action, the guy had seemed impressed.

Perhaps the Guardian wanted to ask about Negal's enhanced strength?

The other guy was Gabi's brother, Gilbert, and the one standing next to him was Eric, the middle brother.

"Hello, Max." He offered the Guardian his hand. "It's good to see you again." He turned to Gilbert. "Good to see you too, Gilbert, Eric."

Aru stepped out and frowned at Gilbert. "What's wrong? Is Gabi okay?"

"Gabi is fine. We need Negal for a few minutes, if you don't mind."

"What for?" Aru asked.

"It's a private matter," Gilbert said.

What could they possibly want from him? Did they have a relative they wanted to introduce him to?

Negal was enjoying his popularity among the clan ladies, and he had no wish to limit himself to just one.

Aru cast him a sidelong glance. "Do you want to go with them?"

"It depends." Negal cast Gilbert a broad smile. "What are you offering?"

"A drink on the Lido deck."

Negal was a little hungry, but he was curious to hear what Gabi's brothers wanted with him.

"Lead the way." He motioned for them to proceed.

"Don't forget that target practice is in an hour." Aru clapped him on the back. "You might want to grab something to eat first."

"I'll survive." Negal fell into step with Gilbert while Eric and Max trailed behind them. "So, what's the deal? Do you have a cousin you want me to meet?"

Gilbert shook his head. "Let's wait until we are sitting with drinks in our hands. This is not going to be an easy conversation."

"Now you're worrying me. Did I overstep some boundary I wasn't aware of with one of the clan ladies?"

He'd been cordial to a fault, and he'd only engaged with those who had actively come after him. He hadn't flirted with anyone or seduced them with his godly powers, or anything else that could be interpreted as questionable.

"Nothing like that. You did nothing wrong, Negal. I'm about to ask you for a huge favor that's going to make us both very uncomfortable."

Negal's gut twisted in a knot. Did they need him to give blood to someone?

Maybe one of the women down in the lower decks was in critical condition?

But how had they found out about it? Had they guessed that Frankie's recovery couldn't be explained any other way?

What was he going to do when they asked him?

Deny it?

Say that he had no idea what they were talking about?

Damn, what a mess.

The four of them made the rest of the way to the Lido deck in silence, found a table apart from the rest that offered some privacy, and ordered drinks from Bob.

"So, here is the situation." Gilbert put down his gin and tonic. "You know how female Dormants are induced, right?"

So that was what they wanted him for. "I'm sorry, Gilbert, but I can't. Your daughter is too young."

Gilbert frowned. "What are you talking about?"

"Isn't that what you need me for? To induce the transition of your daughter?"

"Cheryl?"

"Of course. Do you have another daughter who is almost of age but not yet?"

"No, but that's not what I want to ask you to do." Gilbert took a fortifying breath. "This is about my mate Karen. I'm a newly transitioned immortal, which means that my fangs and venom glands are still growing, and they are not functional, so I can't induce her. She's not young, and her best chance of transitioning is a god's venom, and you are the last god available. Naturally, I'm not suggesting that you have sex with my mate, only that you provide the bite."

He must have looked stunned because Max lifted a hand to get his attention. "I did that for Eric's mate, and it's not as complicated as it seems. The only problem we encountered was Eric demolishing the bed in a jealous fit. Bonded immortal males are very possessive of their mates, and we planned for that. We had him chained to the bed, but he pulled so hard on the chains that the bed fell apart."

Negal was starting to get the picture of how it was supposed to work. The couple would be engaged in the act, and they wanted him to bite the female when Gilbert was about to climax.

"Did it work?" Negal asked.

Eric nodded. "Max did a hit and run, but it worked."

"What do you mean by hit and run?"

Max lifted a hand. "I've got this. While Eric and Darlene were getting it on in their bedroom, I was in another room, getting in the mood. The doors were open, so I knew when to dash in, do my part, and dash out."

"Well." Negal rubbed the back of his neck. "That's definitely not something

I've ever done, but I'm willing to give it a try. After all, it's for a good cause, right?" He turned to Gilbert. "Are you sure that my venom is the best thing for your mate?"

"Yes. And there are other benefits." He swallowed. "You can thrall us not to see you, which other immortals can't do. Well, they can thrall Karen because she's still human, but not me, and I'm the one with the jealousy problem. Hopefully, that will make chaining me to the bed unnecessary. It will also make it easier for Karen."

"I can definitely do that," Negal said. "And even without the thrall no chains are needed. You are no match for me."

"He's right about that," Max murmured. "I've seen him in action." He looked at Negal. "You are as strong as the Kra-ell, right?"

Negal nodded. "After the rebellion, the gods decided to enhance future generations so we wouldn't be defenseless against the Kra-ell."

"Makes sense." Max emptied the rest of his drink down his throat and lifted the empty glass to signal to Bob that he needed a refill.

"One more thing." Gilbert cleared his throat. "Do you need a partner to get in a mood, or can you take care of it by yourself?"

Negal didn't like pleasuring himself when there were plenty of females available, but he wasn't a stranger to that form of release either. When they'd trekked through Tibet, there hadn't been any suitable partners.

Perhaps he could find a lady who wouldn't mind him leaving in the middle to bite someone else?

Nah, it was better to do it the way Max had. He could always seek a companion after he was done with his good deed.

"I can use my imagination to get in the mood. When do you want to do this?"

"Does tomorrow work for you?" Gilbert asked. "We can do it after Brundar and Callie's wedding. Our teenage daughter will be babysitting her younger siblings in another cabin, so we will have all the privacy we need."

"Good plan. I'll leave the party when you do and follow you to your cabin."

"Thank you." Gilbert offered him his hand. "Your help means a lot to me and my mate. Your venom is her best chance of survival."

39

DAGOR

"I'm finally done." Dagor clutched the phone to his ear. "Do you want to meet me for lunch in the dining hall?"

"Do we have time for a quickie?" Frankie asked.

Dagor's steps faltered. "That's worth skipping lunch for."

"I don't want you to go hungry. Not if you need to fight later. Can't we do both?"

"I have target practice in an hour."

There was a moment of silence. "That's plenty of time. We can have a twenty-minute quickie and then get lunch."

"If I bite you, you'll be out. I have a better idea. I'll stop by the dining hall, fill up two plates, and bring them up to the cabin. We will eat first and then make love."

"Works for me. I'll put on something sexy."

He groaned. "You're killing me, Frankie. Tell me what you are going to wear."

She laughed. "I'd better not, or you'll be sporting a tent while picking up the food."

"Right. By the way, do you know what Gilbert, Eric, and Max need Negal for?"

"Oh, wow. Karen really did it. But I can't tell you. You'll have to ask Negal."

"Why can't you tell me?" Dagor took the stairs down to avoid the crowd at the elevators.

"Because it's private, and they might be embarrassed about sharing the details. That's all I'm going to say on the subject."

"Fine. I'll get it out of Negal." He entered the dining hall and continued to the kitchen. "I'm going to hang up now so I can collect our food. Any preferences?"

"I don't know what they are serving today, but I'm not a picky eater. Whatever you bring is fine."

"See you soon." He ended the phone with a kissy sound that should have been embarrassing, but Dagor didn't care.

If Frankie loved it, he would be talking dirty to her and making kissy sounds in the middle of the war room.

Well, that might be a slight exaggeration. But anywhere else was fair game.

"Can I have two plates to go?" he asked one of the ladies working in the kitchen. When it was clear that she didn't understand what he'd said, he grabbed two empty plates and mimed putting food on them.

Smiling, she nodded. "*Da, ya ponimayu.*"

Dagor dipped his head. "*Spasiba.*"

He should have addressed her in Russian to begin with, but he'd been so preoccupied with thoughts of Frankie and what she would be wearing when he got to the cabin that he'd forgotten the kitchen staff came from Igor's old compound, and they all spoke Russian, and some also spoke Finnish.

When the two boxes of food were ready, he thanked her again and hurried out the door.

Thankfully, there was no line at the elevators going up, and he only had to wait for the cab to empty before getting in. No one stopped the elevator on its way to Frankie's deck either.

Once he was at the door, he rang the bell and held his breath as he waited for her to open up.

Would she be wearing stockings and garters and nothing else?

Or maybe just a see-through baby-doll?

He hadn't seen any such garments when he'd looked for something comfortable for her to wear after she'd fainted, but maybe she had a hidden stash somewhere. He hadn't looked in the nightstand drawers, and those were roomy enough to hide a number of flimsy, sexy outfits.

When Frankie opened the door, he was only slightly disappointed to see the short, colorful silk robe that left her long legs exposed but hid everything else of interest. She wasn't wearing stockings either, which meant no garters.

"Hello, beautiful." He leaned to kiss her pouty lips. "I like the robe."

"Oh, this old thing?" She batted her eyelashes playfully. "The sexy stuff is underneath." She moved aside to let him in.

When she closed the door behind him, he put the boxes on the entry table and reached for her. "Let me see."

"Na-ah." She batted his hands away. "No peeking until after we eat, or you will go hungry to your target practice, and I won't have you being outperformed by Aru and Negal and all the Guardians."

"I don't mind."

Usually, he was super competitive and minded very much, but he didn't mind losing if it meant seeing what Frankie had under the robe and hopefully peeling it off her with his fangs.

Not that it would make a difference to him. He had perfect aim.

"But I mind." She took the boxes and put them on the table. "Do you want a plate?"

"Not if you don't. I'd rather be done with lunch as soon as possible and get to unwrap my gift."

40

FRANKIE

The truth was that Frankie didn't have anything super sexy underneath her robe. It was just a nice little panties and bra set that she'd gotten on sale at Victoria's Secret, but it wasn't something that would cause Dagor's jaw to drop.

Hopefully, he wouldn't be too disappointed.

As Dagor wolfed down every last morsel in his box, Frankie picked at her food, careful not to overeat, even though everything was delicious. Intimacy on a full stomach wasn't fun.

When he was done, she pushed her box toward Dagor. "I'm full. You can finish it."

He didn't argue, and she enjoyed watching him eat everything.

"Would you like me to make you a drink?" she asked with a seductive smile.

"I'll make it." He rose to his feet and walked over to the bar. "What's your pleasure, beautiful?"

She loved it when he called her beautiful. He sounded like he truly meant it and wasn't just flattering her.

"Something sweet and simple, please. Perhaps vodka with cranberry juice and some ice cubes."

"Coming up."

She took the opportunity of him being preoccupied with the drinks to move to the couch. Tucking her legs under her, she leaned over the armrest.

Hopefully, the pose was sexy.

Holding a drink in each hand, he walked over to the couch, sat down next to her, and handed her the fruity drink. "Cheers." He lifted his glass and clinked it with hers.

"Cheers." She took a small sip.

Dagor had been generous with the vodka. A little too generous. Frankie liked her drinks on the lighter side.

He put his whiskey glass on the coffee table and smoothed his hand over her calf. "I want to unwrap my present."

"Go ahead." Her robe had parted, revealing her thighs almost all the way to her underwear.

Dagor's hand started a slow trek up her thigh, parting the rest of the robe until he reached her hot center and cupped it.

"I see that someone has been entertaining naughty thoughts. What were you thinking about, love?"

"You, of course."

"I know that you were thinking of me. I want to know what you were imagining." He slid his finger under the gusset of her panties and stroked her wet folds.

Frankie bit on her lower lip. "This."

"Really?" He slipped his finger into her and pumped it slowly in and out of her. "Or maybe it was this?"

"Yes, a lot more of this." She rocked on his finger, getting more of it inside.

There was something obscenely arousing about the way he was leaning nonchalantly against the couch cushions and fingering her.

His finger retracted and then lazily pushed back in. "I love how wet you get for me." He continued his slow fingering, getting her wetter and needier.

"And I love getting you hard," she teased.

"Oh, I am. I can hammer nails with how hard I am."

He withdrew his finger and came back with two. "Do you like this?"

Her eyes rolled back in her head. "Yes. Don't stop."

Leaning, he used his other hand to release the tie of her robe. "I've wanted to do that since the moment I entered the cabin."

As he parted the robe, exposing her body, his glowing eyes went to her breasts. She was wearing a white lacy bra that didn't do much to hide her nipples, especially the way they stood to attention under Dagor's hungry gaze.

Her panties were white lace as well, matching the bra. It was a bridal set that she'd bought on a whim because it was so pretty, and now she was glad she had because Dagor was practically salivating.

"This is very pretty." He pulled the bra cups down, exposing her breasts. "But what's underneath is even prettier." He leaned and took one of her nipples into his mouth.

His lips felt cold for a moment, but then he swiped his tongue over her stiff peak, and it felt hot.

"I'm glad you like it," she rasped.

He switched to suckling her other nipple and pinched the one he'd just left behind.

It was just the right amount of pleasure and pain, and as moisture leaked into her lacy panties, Frankie threaded her fingers into Dagor's hair. "Take me to bed."

He let go of her nipple and lifted his head. "Impatient, are we?"

"I have to be. We don't have time to take it slow."

He seemed to have forgotten the target practice he had in less than half an hour.

"Right." He shifted back, took her into his arms, and pushed to his feet while holding on to her.

She wrapped her arms around his neck. "I love how strong you are."

"I love you." His arms tightened around her.

As he laid her gently on the bed, Frankie pulled the robe off and tossed it aside. She was still wearing the panties, and the bra was still pushed under her breasts, but she was leaving those two items for Dagor to take off.

"Gorgeous."

Lowering his head, he kissed the skin on her inner thigh, working his way up with small nips and kisses until his mouth hovered over her center.

"Such pretty panties." He hooked his fingers in the elastic and tugged them down her legs, kissing and sucking her skin all the way down to the very tips of her toes and then back up.

By the time he reached her center, Frankie was panting with need, and the sight of Dagor's fully elongated fangs sent a shiver of excitement tinged with trepidation through her.

He could nick her with those monstrosities, and it would hurt unless he licked it with his magic saliva. Everything about him was magical, and she was the luckiest woman on the planet to have him fall in love with her.

Using just the tip of his tongue, Dagor parted her lower lips with soft strokes, and judging by the growling sounds he made, he was enjoying every moment of it.

Lucky. She was a very lucky lady.

Frankie arched up, shamelessly asking for more, but Dagor must have forgotten that they were in a time crunch and kept going at his unhurried pace.

"Dagor." She pulled on his hair. "Stop teasing me."

He treated her to another long lick. "I love driving you crazy with need."

He teased her mercilessly.

Frankie needed him to pay attention to her throbbing clit, but he was purposefully avoiding it, licking and kissing her folds and her slit but not where she needed him most.

"Dagor!" She pulled on his hair with a growl.

Chuckling, he flattened his tongue on her engorged nubbin, and she saw stars.

"Yes!" she screamed.

If not for his unyielding grip on her thighs, she would have shot up to the ceiling.

Her cry must have finally broken through to him, and as his tongue kept flicking over her clit harder and faster, she climbed toward the edge in seconds, and as he pushed two fingers inside her and closed his lips over that pulsating bundle of nerves, she detonated.

"Dagor!" Frankie screamed her climax.

Somehow, between one heartbeat and the next, Dagor got rid of his clothing, removed her bra, and lay on his side next to her quivering body.

"You are so beautiful to me, Frankie." His hand traveled up her ribcage, finding her breast and palming it for a moment before pinching her aching nipple.

His other hand joined the first, the pinching and plucking just shy of being painful, and just like that, she was nearing another climax.

Leaning over her, he kissed and nipped the side of her neck until he reached her earlobe. He nipped it a little harder and then licked the little hurt away.

How was he doing that with those huge fangs of his?

When he moved to her lips, she was once again delirious with desire, and when he slipped two fingers inside her, she exploded again, screaming his name into his mouth.

He kept kissing her through the aftershocks of her climax, and then he was hovering on top of her, the tip of his shaft poised at her entrance.

"I love you," he murmured.

"I love you too." She wound her arms around his torso, trying to reach his buttocks, but her arms weren't long enough.

Arching up, she got him to slide in a little further, and he took it from there.

He pulled back and surged in again, moving slowly at first, but that didn't last long. As he kept pumping hard and fast, the coil inside of her tightened once more, and as his shaft swelled inside of her, she knew that he was close.

As Dagor latched his lips onto the spot he was going to bite, Frankie tilted her head to the side and braced for the searing pain that she knew was coming.

His tongue swept over the spot, once, twice, preparing her, and then he bit down and climaxed at the same time.

41

KALUGAL

"Still nothing," William said. "Perhaps they haven't discovered the bodies yet."

Kalugal stood by the sliding doors of Kian's cabin, aimlessly gazing at the small waves the ship was gliding through. Hours had passed since he'd made the call to the tour company, but no one had come to question the hotel staff yet. No one suspicious looking had even crossed the lobby, and no one other than the housekeeper had entered the room Roni had put under his fake name. She would have been a suspect if they hadn't seen her cleaning the other rooms on that floor.

The rooms Roni had added as of yesterday hadn't been investigated either.

Still, Kalugal's gut was sending a warning message to his mind that things were not as they seemed, and that the shit was about to hit the proverbial fan.

He didn't have to rely solely on his gut either. It had been many decades since he'd last served in the Brotherhood, but he doubted things had changed substantially. When the cargo hadn't arrived, someone had been sent to investigate, and the breadcrumbs they had carelessly left behind were large enough for even the dumbest Doomer to follow.

They knew, and they were plotting something.

When the phone William had given him for the task rang, he wasn't surprised.

He activated the speaker. "Kevin Gunter speaking," he said, using his well-practiced German accent.

"Hello, Mr. Gunter." The voice on the other end was rough, and his accent was easily recognizable. "You have something that belongs to us, and we want it back."

"I do not know what you are talking about. Who is this?"

"Don't play dumb. We know what you did to our men and that you stole the cargo. You think you are some big shot who can come in, make a statement by shredding my men to pieces, and take what belongs to us, but you've made a big mistake by infringing on our turf. Since you are obviously a foreigner, you might be unfamiliar with who runs things in this area, so I'm willing to overlook the loss of my worthless men, provided that you return our property unharmed and untarnished to the same place you took them from. This is a one-time goodwill gesture that I will not extend again."

Kalugal's jaw tightened. The Doomer on the other end was talking about the women as if they were nothing more than cattle.

"Again, as I said, I do not know what you are talking about. Good day."

"Wait! We have Luis and his family. If you don't bring the women back by eight this evening, I will personally kill the four small kids, slowly and painfully, while my men will take turns having fun with Luis's wife and fourteen-year-old daughter. On second thought, his twelve-year-old son is a handsome boy. Perhaps some of the men would have fun with him as well."

Rage threatened to consume Kalugal, but he needed to continue the pretense and play into the Doomer's assumptions about him. It seemed that the guy wasn't sure that he was dealing with immortals, and Kalugal needed to keep it that way.

On second thought, it was more likely that the Doomer was only pretending to believe that he was dealing with a competing foreign cartel. He'd probably guessed who had torn his henchmen to pieces and taken the women. Other thugs wouldn't have cared about Luis and his family. They would have laughed at the demand to return the women in exchange for the tour guide.

Only someone who was decent and moral would respond to the threat. That did not apply to Doomers, mobsters, cartel bosses, and, regrettably, many others.

If the guy were a lone operator, Kalugal could have compelled the Doomer to release Luis and his family, but he wasn't, and the others would realize that something was wrong if the guy started acting too out of character.

"Perhaps we can come to an agreement. You know how the saying goes, it's not really stealing when taken from a thief."

"There will be no agreement. You will return the women and never come to this area again."

The plan was, no doubt, to ambush whoever came with the women, and since the Doomers knew they were dealing with immortals, they assumed that they would send a small force that they could easily overpower.

Kalugal affected a resigned sigh. "You know my name, but I don't know yours, and if we are to negotiate, I need a name."

"You can call me Bud, but there is nothing to negotiate."

It was obviously a fake name, but it didn't matter. Kalugal didn't need the vermin's real name because he would be dead soon.

"I can't make it by eight, Bud. The cargo has been moved and is more than half a day away." He switched to his compulsion voice. "The earliest I can do is meet you at the place you indicated at four in the afternoon tomorrow. You must agree to this. Until then, keep Luis and his family safe," Kalugal pushed with all the strength of his compulsion to ensure compliance.

If Bud was the commander of the group, Luis and his family would be safe.

"Be there exactly at four," Bud said.

"I will do my best, but in case I can't make it on time, should I call you on this number?"

"Yes, and don't bother trying to trace it. It's encrypted."

"I have no doubt."

As the call ended, Kalugal turned to Kian. "We need time to get organized. That's why I told him tomorrow at four."

"Obviously." Kian briefly closed his eyes. "What a clusterfuck." He opened his eyes and looked at Kalugal. "I detected the accent. Bud is a Doomer."

Kalugal nodded. "Not only that, but he also knows who we are. He pretended not to know, so we wouldn't guess who he was and would come unprepared."

From the corner of his eye, Kalugal saw Turner nodding. The guy's strategic mind was, no doubt, already working on a plan.

"I'm glad we have a full day." Turner pulled out his phone. "We need to get vehicles, drones, explosives, and, if possible, satellite pictures."

42

KIAN

Thank the merciful Fates for Turner. It seemed like he already had a plan, or at least the framework for one.

"What do you have in mind?" Kian asked.

"We are not going to the Acapulco port. We will find a spot several hours drive from there, use the rescue boats to get to shore and use ground transportation from there. If they know that we are coming with the ship, they will be waiting for us at the harbor, and they might be planning to attack it. Even if we are moored away from the dock, they could use speedboats and gliders to attack us. We can't count on the Mexican military or navy to come to our aid."

"I'm not worried about that." Kian crossed his arms over his chest. "Let them come. Toven and Kalugal can freeze them in place, and we have enough firepower on this ship to blow them out of the water."

Turner shook his head. "The best offense is to avoid confrontation where possible, especially when the enemy dictates the time and place. We need to take them by surprise."

"You are right," Kian said. "Please, continue."

"As I said, the Guardians will use the rescue boats to get to shore, and I'll arrange for armored vehicles to be waiting for us at a predetermined location."

"The less predictable we are, the better," Onegus said. "But they might anticipate our move."

Turner shrugged. "I doubt it. There is no way they know about me and my connections in Mexico. If you didn't have me, would you have been able to arrange for armored vehicles and the other equipment on such short notice?"

"Probably not," Onegus admitted. "Are you sure that you can get what we need?"

"Positive. I have a lot of connections in Mexico." Turner pushed to his feet. "I need to make a few phone calls and finalize the plan. I'll do it in my cabin and return as soon as I have everything mapped out."

"Thank you." Kian put his hand on Turner's shoulder. "I hate ruining your vacation."

Turner chuckled. "This is fun for me. I was afraid that I would be bored on the cruise."

"Well, then. I'm glad to supply you with entertainment."

He hadn't added that it was a shame people were suffering in the process. It wasn't Turner's fault. The guy liked solving problems. He didn't create them.

"What I wonder is why Bud didn't send a team to the hotel," Kalugal said. "That's the first thing I would have done."

"Maybe he didn't need to," William said. "He could have someone hack into the hotel's surveillance network the same way Roni did, but I doubt Doomers could have come up with that idea. That's not their style. He probably suspected that it was a trap or a decoy, and he either bribed or thralled the staff in the reception or the cleaning crew to check those rooms and report what they found. Naturally, they reported that no one had used the rooms, and Bud realized what we had done. We didn't consider that because the plan was to see if they would respond. Surprisingly, the Doomers were smart about it. The question is if they found out about the Silver Swan." He turned to Kalugal. "When you tampered with Luis's and the other drivers' memory, where did you have them pick you up?"

"I didn't alter that. They picked us up at the dock, but that doesn't mean that they know which ship we came from or even that we arrived on one. Many of the guided tours meet up at the dock. We could have come from any of the cruise ships and large yachts in the harbor, or we could have flown or driven in and stayed at one of the hotels or resorts. If I were in their shoes, a cruise ship would be the last place I would expect to find immortals."

"I hope you are right." Kian sighed. "I want to keep the damn ship. Not only did I remodel it twice, but it now has sentimental value attached to it."

Kalugal leaned back in his chair and crossed his arms over his chest. "Let's try to think like Doomers for a second. We didn't use firearms against the humans, so their remains don't contain any bullets. If the Doomers were thorough in their investigation, they would have realized that only a sizable group of immortals could have inflicted so much damage without weapons. They would assume that we came upon their henchmen by chance and were unprepared, which implies we were tourists. They would then search rental cars and tours for bullet-ridden vehicles. That's probably how they found Luis. I wonder why they didn't take the other two drivers, though."

"Luis was injured," Onegus said. "That made him a prime suspect."

"That might be," Kalugal agreed. "The next step would have been to search hotels, resorts, Airbnbs, and ships for Kevin Gunter. When Roni made the retroactive reservations under my name, it was probably after they had concluded their search. Bud knew that the information about my hotel stay was fake. Still, we could have been staying at a different hotel under a different name."

Kian let out a breath. "If they checked all the ships that were moored in the harbor yesterday, they would have found out that the Silver Swan's passengers boarded her at Long Beach. They also know that the clan is located somewhere in Los Angeles. It's not difficult to piece the two together."

Onegus didn't seem to share his opinion. "Half the ships in that harbor came from Long Beach."

Kian lifted a brow. "How many of them were privately owned?"

Onegus smiled. "That's the beauty of the way we do business. If anyone checks the records, the Silver Swan is not privately owned. It's the first passenger ship of a new luxury cruise line."

"I hope you are right. As I said, I would hate to have to get rid of it."

"Worst case scenario, you will change her name again." Onegus pushed to his feet. "I'm calling a meeting of the head Guardians. We will need Yamanu to shroud and Arwel to detect where Luis is held. They are not just going to bring him and his family to us. I hope you know that."

Kian nodded. "Unfortunately, I have to agree with you."

As Onegus started typing on his phone, Kian went through the list of Guardians in his head.

Yamanu's abilities would be needed to shroud the vehicles, providing them with the element of surprise. Kalugal wasn't a Guardian, but his formidable compulsion power was a game-changer. He would have to head the team going to meet with the Doomers. His ability to immobilize them and their cartel recruits could mean the difference between the success and failure of the mission.

Bhathian could lead the Guardians, and Max could assist him. The younger Guardian was showing a lot of promise, and Onegus was giving him more and more command positions to hone his leadership skills.

Kian's gaze drifted back to the balcony doors and the tranquil sea beyond them. Tomorrow would be stormy no matter how well they prepared, but at least today they could enjoy Anandur's wedding and even go through with the bachelor party no one had thought was going to happen.

The question was what would happen tomorrow and whether they would wrap up the whole mess in time for Brundar's wedding.

43

DAGOR

The sun's glare was mitigated by a smattering of clouds, and the air was pleasantly warm on the deck as Dagor, Negal, and Aru lined up for target practice.

The Guardians had set up makeshift targets—empty cans precariously balanced on the ship's railing.

Max handed them the same rifles the Guardians were holding. "This is an M4 Carbine. It's a lightweight, gas-operated, air-cooled, magazine-fed, selective rate, shoulder-fired weapon with a collapsible stock. It is the standard firearm issue for most U.S. military units." He sounded proud to be in possession of such advanced weaponry, and Dagor stifled the impulse to sneer at what these immortals considered top shelf. It was primitive compared to the weapons they had on Anumati, but it would do the job just the same.

Still, as he held it in his hands, he appreciated the lightweight design and the ease with which it handled. He had been trained in many weapons, including swords, hatchets, javelins, throwing stars, and some that had been invented on other planets, so mastering this relatively modern firearm would be a breeze.

"Do you know how to use this style of weapon?" Max asked.

"I can figure it out." Negal took aim and squeezed off a few rounds. A line of cans jumped off the railing, spinning into the air before splashing into the ocean. "Not bad for a beginner." Negal turned to Max with a smug grin on his face.

Aru stepped up next, took aim, and fired. The crack of the rifle was sharp, but he only hit one can. "Seems I'm a bit rusty." Aru shrugged.

The guy had always been a lousy shot, and there was no excuse for it, given that he was a god.

Dagor suspected that the reason for Aru's lack of aptitude with firearms was that he abhorred killing. It was odd since all troopers went through psychological screening, and those who were not suitable for combat were given administrative assignments. There might be something to Negal's suspicion that Aru had been given the leadership post for reasons that hadn't been disclosed to the two of them. Nepotism couldn't explain it, though, because an indefinite station on Earth was more of a punishment than a reward.

"Your turn, Dagor." Max motioned for him to take position.

He shouldered the rifle, feeling the familiar adrenaline rush of competition, took aim, and fired in quick succession.

Three cans clattered against the railing and tumbled overboard.

"Not bad." Max clapped him on the back. "You three seem to know your way around a rifle. Put new cans up, step back twenty feet to the line over there, and fire again. It's not as easy from forty feet away. Just try not to hit the railing. Kian will have our heads if we damage the ship. He'll tell us to fix it and repaint it."

"Don't worry." Negal took several empty cans from the cardboard box next to the railing and arranged them in a neat line. "I won't hit the railing or shoot into the water. Every bullet will hit the target." He cast Dagor a sidelong glance. "Two shots each; most cans wins."

"You're on."

"What about me?" Aru asked.

"Sorry, dude." Negal shook his head with a mock sad expression on his face. "You're not in the same league as Dagor and me. You need many more hours of practice."

"That's why we are here," Aru murmured under his breath.

"Fine," Negal relented. "If you want to be the designated loser in each round, be my guest. But remember what Max said about the railing."

As Dagor and Negal took turns again, Negal managed to hit the two cans with his two shots, which earned him approving nods from the Guardians.

Aru took aim but only managed to hit one. Thankfully, the other shot he fired landed in the water without damaging the railing. "Well, one is better than none."

Dagor felt the thrill of the competition, but the truth was that this wasn't a challenge for either him or Negal. He lined up his shot, exhaled slowly, and squeezed the trigger.

The first can flew off the railing.

He quickly realigned and fired again. The second can followed the first.

"Poor Aru." Negal shook his head. "Are you up for another challenge?"

"Bring it on."

"This is not a competition," Max grumbled. "This is practice. Aru, you need to keep firing from forty feet until you hit two in a row. Negal and Dagor, move back to the fifty-foot mark."

The practice continued with the Guardians offering tips and sharing laughs about this and that, and Dagor felt like he had been transported back to the training camp. He enjoyed the sense of camaraderie and the lightheartedness, but in the back of his mind he acknowledged that the reason for this target practice was anything but joyous.

The reason was the aftermath of a terrible tragedy, of a monstrous act against defenseless innocents. He didn't enjoy killing, but if he got a chance to kill those responsible for it, he would relish it.

As Dagor reloaded his rifle, ready for another round, Max called a halt to the practice.

"I have an announcement." His voice boomed to get everyone's attention. "There's been a change of plans. We're not going to Acapulco this evening. Kalugal received a call. The Doomers are holding Luis and his family hostage and demanding we return the women we rescued in exchange for their lives. The team in the war room is working on developing a strategy, but the gist of it is that we're going to stop at a different location along the coast, use a lifeboat to get to shore, and drive from there to the meeting point, which is where the bodies of the thugs were buried. Turner is organizing vehicles for us."

Dagor felt a knot of tension form in his stomach. He liked Luis, and he feared for his life and that of his family. Those people were beyond ruthless.

"When are we getting there, and what are we going to do about it?"

"I don't have the details yet," Max said. "Kalugal used compulsion to ensure the safety of Luis and his family until we get there. We don't know whether they've found out that we have a ship and that the women are on board, but in case they did, we don't want to bring the ship back and make it a target. We hope to surprise them and use compulsion to overpower them. I assume that Yamanu will shroud our team so the Doomers' human cohorts won't be able to see us. I don't expect it to be too difficult of a mission."

Dagor hoped Max was right.

He would do everything in his power to prevent Luis and his family from being added to the list of victims those monsters claimed.

The practice resumed, but the mood had shifted. It was no longer about sport and competition. Each shot Dagor fired was aimed at the enemy, and he did not miss a single one.

44

FRANKIE

When Frankie woke up, Dagor was gone, and there was no note from him either, but it was okay. She knew where he was. Still, it would have been nice to get a note with sweet love words.

Oh, well, she hadn't fallen in love with a poet. Dagor was an engineer through and through.

Stepping into the shower, she took her time washing her hair and conditioning it. Mia was coming later to style it for her, so maybe it was a little too early for that, but Frankie was sticky from lovemaking. Besides, Mia was an immortal now, with the sense of smell that came with it. Frankie had nothing to be embarrassed about, but if the roles were reversed, she wouldn't have wanted to smell Toven on Mia.

Following her transition there would be a lot of adjustments to be made, but she was ready to embrace them. What were a few inconveniences compared to living forever and being nearly indestructible?

Well, her family was still a problem she didn't know how to solve. If she was a Dormant, then her brothers were as well, and so was their mother, but her father probably wasn't, and leaving him behind in the human world was too painful to consider.

Perhaps she wouldn't transition after all, and agonizing about her father was premature.

Once she was done, Frankie wrapped a towel around her hair, rubbed her body dry, and padded naked into the bedroom even though the curtains were open. Who was going to see her?

The seagulls?

Chuckling, she pulled on a pair of panties and a loose, long T-shirt that she used as a nightgown. It was good enough for lounging in the cabin and watching some television.

She was just getting comfortable when the doorbell rang, startling her. It was too early for Mia, and Dagor knew the code to her cabin. Snatching the remote from the coffee table, Frankie switched to the door camera view, and when she saw it was Bridget, her heart started racing.

The doctor had probably come to check on her wound, and Dagor wasn't there to run interference. Could she just ignore her and not answer?

But then Bridget would call her, and she would have to lie that she had been asleep and let her in anyway.

Damn.

Walking up to the door, she plastered a smile on her face and opened it for the doctor. "Hey, Bridget. I didn't expect you." She patted the towel on her head. "Sorry about that. I've just stepped out of the shower."

"No need to apologize. I came uninvited." The doctor scanned her from head to toe with professional precision. "You look good for someone who got shot less than twenty-four hours ago. You seem to be doing remarkably well, but I want to make sure that everything is healing properly."

Right. Bridget probably suspected that something strange was going on and wanted to find out what was responsible for Frankie's rapid healing.

"Oh, it is. Remarkably so." She chuckled nervously. "Dagor has been taking such good care of me," she babbled, a bit too enthusiastically. "He bit me so many times that I probably have more venom in my veins than blood. In fact, I won't be surprised if I'm transitioning already. I don't have any symptoms, though. Is it possible to transition without developing fever?"

Bridget smiled. "Very young girls transition without any symptoms, but not adults. Not in my experience, anyway."

"Bummer." Frankie's heart sank, but she quickly rallied. "But at least it healed my wound because it's completely gone." She smiled apologetically. "Where are my manners? Please, take a seat." She waved a hand toward the couch.

"Thank you." Bridget put her black doctor's bag on the coffee table and sat down. "I didn't take that into consideration, but you are right. The venom has healing properties, and when delivered frequently, I guess it can speed up recovery quite dramatically."

"Lucky me." Frankie sat across from Bridget. "My boyfriend is a god with very potent venom, and he has been taking excellent care of me."

"Yes, it would seem so." Bridget tilted her head and looked at Frankie from under lowered lashes. "Given that Dagor is a god and the frequency of his venom injection, perhaps you are right about transitioning with no symptoms as well." The doctor seemed to be considering something for a moment. "We could test it. I could make a small cut on the palm of your hand and see how quickly it heals."

Frankie hesitated.

She didn't want to have the test done without Dagor being present. Besides, she was pretty sure that she wasn't transitioning, and she didn't want to have a cut on her hand.

Then again, Dagor could probably heal it with a few licks of his tongue, and if that didn't work, he could give her another tiny blood transfusion, although that was quite extreme for a little cut, so that probably wasn't a good idea.

Mostly, though, she didn't want to be disappointed by a negative result.

"I'm not ready yet." She smiled nervously. "We haven't been trying for long. We used protection before I got injured, so it's way too early for me to start transitioning."

"As you wish. Can I take a look at your wound before I go?"

Laughing, Frankie lifted her shirt. "What wound?"

Bridget shook her head. "Incredible. You've healed as fast as an immortal. Are you sure you don't want me to test you?"

Frankie shrugged. "It's the venom. I'm sure of that. Dagor and I managed to sneak in a little afternoon delight, so the latest injection is still in full force. Even if the cut heals faster than it should, it will be because of that."

"You are the boss of your own body, and you decide when and where." Bridget rose to her feet and took her bag. "I'll see you at the wedding tonight."

"Yes. And this time, you'll see me dancing the night away."

"I'm looking forward to it."

After the doctor left, Frankie sat down on the couch and reached for the remote, but instead of flipping through channels, her mind engaged in flipping through thoughts.

Perhaps she could run a little test by herself?

It wouldn't tell her anything because it was true that she just had a fresh injection of venom, and that would screw with the results, but she was curious, and she was never good with patiently waiting for things.

Padding to the kitchenette, she pulled a sharp knife out of the drawer and pricked the tip of her pointer finger.

"Ouch. That hurt." She put the finger in her mouth and licked the little drop of blood that had welled over it.

That wasn't going to tell her anything.

She pulled the finger out and watched as another drop of blood welled over the tiny wound she'd inflicted.

Well, so much for fast healing. It didn't seem to stop bleeding any faster than usual. The only difference was that it didn't hurt as it normally would.

Less than a minute later, it stopped bleeding, and it took another five minutes for it to disappear completely.

It wasn't the instantaneous healing of an immortal, but it was definitely faster than humans.

A wave of dizziness washed over her, and she pressed her hand to her forehead. "It's the venom. That's all. There is no way I'm transitioning."

But what if she was?

She needed to talk to Dagor, but he was in the middle of weapons practice and couldn't be disturbed.

She needed to talk to someone. Mia. She could call Mia.

Grabbing her phone, Frankie called her friend. "Hi, Mia, are you busy?"

"Not at all. Toven is with Kian, and I'm just doodling on my tablet. What's up?"

"Can you come over right now? You can continue doodling here, and then I will do your makeup, and you'll do my hair."

Mia chuckled. "It's still too early for that. I can come for a little bit and return later when it's time to start getting ready."

Frankie didn't want to inconvenience her friend. "Perhaps we can just talk on the phone. I don't want you to have to come here twice."

She could go to Mia's cabin, but Mia hadn't invited her, and she wasn't going to suggest it.

"Yeah, that will probably be better. Bridget gave me a lecture today about not resting enough. So, what did you want to talk about?"

Frankie chuckled. "Actually, it has to do with Bridget."

45

ANANDUR

Turner entered the makeshift war room, aka Kian and Syssi's cabin, with his laptop tucked under his arm and a cup of coffee in his other hand. "The transport is arranged. Armored vehicles will be waiting at the designated location." He put his coffee cup on the dining table.

"Good work." Kian eyed the cup as if he was contemplating the merits of caffeine versus the whiskey he'd been drinking since Kalugal's phone call with *Bud*.

"What's the plan?"

As Turner flipped his laptop open to look at his notes, Anandur wondered what had happened to his yellow pad. Usually, the guy wrote his action plan the old-fashioned way and only used the laptop for information gathering.

When Turner turned the laptop screen toward Kian, Anandur realized that he hadn't been looking at his notes but had pulled up a map of the coast of Mexico.

"We stop here, which is about two hundred nautical miles north of Acapulco. We lower a lifeboat and use it to get our force to shore. There is a road nearby, and that's where the vehicles will be waiting for us. I assumed forty passengers. Thirty-six Guardians, Kalugal, Dalhu, and the two gods. The transport is a mix of vans and SUVs that look like regular civilian vehicles but are bulletproof. We don't want to be detected too soon." He took a sip from his coffee. "They don't really expect us to return the women. They expect us to do precisely what we are planning, which is to take them out and release

Luis. Nevertheless, we will play along and pretend that the vans and SUVs are for transporting the women."

"Obviously, they are setting up a trap for us," Onegus said. "Losing the cargo looks bad for them. They probably don't want to report it to their commanders in the Brotherhood because failure will get them in trouble. But if they can show that they killed a bunch of clan members, losing the women will be forgiven. We are much bigger fish."

Kian nodded. "And if they hope to capture some of us alive, they might not booby-trap the area to blow us up, but we still have to assume that they would plan for a massive firepower advantage."

"I'm taking this into consideration," Turner said. "That's why I ordered bulletproof vehicles, but they may still have access to heavier caliber projectiles that would render the armor useless, or worse, RPGs. But keep in mind, they don't know about the assets we have, meaning a powerful compeller and an equally powerful shrouder, and they have no reason to assume that we would be well-armed because we did not use any weapons to take down the cartel thugs. In other words, chances are they underestimate us; they think that together with their cartel friends, they can overpower our inferior force."

"I agree." Kian took a sip from his whiskey. "Doomers prefer engaging face to face because they usually have an advantage in numbers. All they know is what Luis could have told them, which is the number of tourists he took to the ruins. A small group that included several females. They will assume that several immortals on vacation stumbled upon their goons, killed them, and rescued the women. They might even think that they are dealing with civilians. But in case their tactics involve heavier weaponry or explosives after all, what's the plan?"

Turner waved a hand at Onegus. "That's your part, chief."

Onegus nodded. "In addition to the vehicles, we are getting four surveillance drones. Before we enter the area, we scan it with the drones. If there is no one there, we will know that the place is booby-trapped, and we don't go in. When our force gets in front of the Doomers, Kalugal uses a powerful megaphone to freeze everyone, and the fun begins."

"We should first find and neutralize their scouts." All eyes turned to Dalhu, who rarely spoke up. "The standard operating procedure would have the commander send scout teams to observe and report on the approaching opposing force. We need to get to the scouts and eliminate them first."

"Actually, that may present an advantage for us." Kalugal's thoughtful tone indicated that he was thinking out loud. "We should capture and interrogate the scouts for intel. They would let us know what weapons and traps we would be facing. I can then compel them to report back whatever we want them to. This will amplify our element of surprise and help us navigate whatever the Doomers have prepared for us."

Kian and Turner nodded as one, and it was obvious both liked the info Dalhu shared and Kalugal's idea to capitalize on it.

Anandur sighed. "I wish I could join you. It has been a long time since I've kicked some Doomer butt." He glanced at Kian. "Is there any way you can assign bodyguard duty to someone else?"

Kian shook his head. "I could, but I won't. Your job is to keep your bride happy the day after your wedding, and she won't be if you run off to kill Doomers and cartel scum."

That was true. Wonder could take on any immortal in hand-to-hand combat and win, but she wasn't a fighter by nature. She was a gentle soul like Syssi and Alena. He still couldn't understand why the Fates had gifted her with superior strength when she clearly detested using it.

"Yeah, you are right." Anandur sighed. "I need to stay with my beautiful mate and guard my illustrious leader." He put the back of his hand on his forehead. "Oh, the hardship."

Onegus snorted.

"On a positive note," Kian lifted his nearly empty whiskey glass, "pushing the operation to tomorrow means that you get to have your bachelor party after all, and your wedding won't have to be delayed or postponed."

Anandur grinned. "That's the best news I've heard today. I'm looking forward to celebrating my last night of bachelorhood and then marrying the love of my life without worrying whether my groomsmen are going to make it in one piece and on time. But Brundar's wedding tomorrow might be affected." He turned to his brother. "I don't mind switching nights with you. Wonder might grumble a little, but she will come around."

"No," was Brundar's response. "I don't want a bachelor party, and I don't care about delaying my wedding. Killing the vermin comes first, and Callie agrees."

Knowing his brother, there was no point trying to argue with him.

"Well, I offered."

As the group continued discussing the finer details of the plan, Anandur glanced at Dalhu, who was sipping on a large glass of whiskey with a murderous expression on his face.

The guy needed to loosen up, and the bachelor party Anandur planned for himself was just what Dalhu needed.

Whiskey and cigars were great, but it wouldn't be his party if he didn't include something hilarious that everyone would be talking about for years to come. The thought of entertaining his friends, especially at times like this when everyone was gloomy and bemoaning the state of the world, brought a smile to his face.

Dressing up as a stripper for Kian's bachelor party had been a big hit, and people still talked about it years later. The Scottish sword dance at Bhathian's had left everyone in stitches. Those were tough acts to follow, and he wondered what he could do that would top those performances.

Perhaps he could challenge the guys to a dance-off? He could bring Bob to the party and have him dance for them. Or he could stick to his original plan, wear his Superman costume, and do his best Superman impression. Wonder had incorporated elements of Wonder Woman's costume in her wedding gown, but she claimed that they were just hints and made him swear that he wouldn't come dressed as Superman to their wedding. But since he'd already gotten the costume custom-made, and it was awesome, it would be a shame to let it go to waste.

46

DAGOR

As Dagor made his way to Frankie's cabin, his mood was much less upbeat than it had been when he'd left. The news he had to share was sure to upset her, and he wasn't looking forward to telling her about Luis and his family having been abducted and held hostage by the monsters.

He found her sitting on the couch in the living room, her expression brightening at his arrival but then quickly shifting to concern. "What happened?"

Joining her on the couch, he clasped her hand. "The Doomers have taken Luis and his family hostage. They're demanding we return the women we rescued in exchange. Kalugal compelled their leader to keep the family safe, so hopefully, they will be okay until we get there, which is tomorrow, not today. You should call Margo and tell her about the additional delay."

Frankie's brow furrowed. "We are not returning the women, right?"

"Of course not. Kalugal used compulsion to buy us extra time so we can prepare."

She shook her head. "I don't understand. Why didn't Kalugal just compel the guy to release them?"

"It's not that simple." Dagor sighed. "The person Kalugal spoke to is probably the leader, but we can't be sure of that. Whoever he is, though, he isn't alone. Kalugal can compel only those who hear him. The others wouldn't have been affected by it, and if the person he spoke to tried to release Luis and his family, the others would have realized that something was amiss and stopped him. Kalugal did the best he could under the circumstances, which is to hopefully ensure their safety until our arrival."

"Yeah, that makes sense." She leaned her head on his shoulder. "So, what now?"

"Kian and his war room team are working on a plan to take the Doomers and their cohorts by surprise, rescue Luis and his family, and get rid of the scum."

"That's not going to be easy." She lifted her head and looked into his eyes. "Are you going to join the mission?"

"Aru, Negal, and I can do things that the immortals can't, but it's up to Kian. We are not part of the clan, and we've never trained with the Guardians."

"I hope he doesn't call on you."

Dagor hoped he would, but he didn't want Frankie to worry. He gave her hand a gentle squeeze. "We want to help, and we can handle this easily."

"Just promise me to be careful, okay?" she said softly. "Even gods can be killed."

"I'm always careful, and I'm well trained." He gave her a reassuring smile and wrapped his arm around her shoulders, trying to ease her tension.

Letting out a breath, Frankie shifted to face him. "Bridget paid me a surprise visit earlier. I had no choice but to bluff my way through it."

"What did you tell her?"

"That you've pumped me full of venom, and that must have sped up my recovery." She chuckled. "The best lies are those closest to the truth. Anyway, I got carried away and suggested that I might be transitioning without symptoms, so Bridget offered to conduct a test and make a cut on the palm of my hand. "

He arched a brow. "Did you agree?"

Frankie shook her head. "I told her that you'd just given me a dose of venom, so even if I healed faster, it wouldn't be because my body was changing but because I still had a lot of venom in me. It seemed to convince her, and she let it go. But I was curious, so I pricked my finger to see how fast it healed." She lifted the finger to show him. "The results were inconclusive. I think it healed faster than normal, but what I'm sure of is that without the venom, it would still hurt."

"So, what's the conclusion from your experiment? Do you think you're transitioning or not?"

"I don't know." She chewed on her bottom lip. "I don't have a fever, and that's supposed to be the first sign."

Dagor reached with his hand to check her forehead, but her skin's temperature felt just right to the touch. "You are not warmer than usual. It might be the venom."

Frankie tried to hide her disappointment. "Yeah, that's what I thought."

"Hey." He cupped her face in his hands. "It will happen. We've only just started, and we will keep working on it."

She managed a small smile. "I know. I just hoped that maybe it was already happening."

47

WONDER

Wonder's bachelorette party had been going full swing since before lunch, and she was getting a little tired.

As the afternoon sun streamed through the cabin's glass doors, warming her face, she closed her eyes and tuned out the laughter and chatter.

"You should go rest a bit before the ceremony," Callie advised. "You look tired. Did you sleep at all last night?"

Wonder chuckled. "I was too nervous to sleep, and I don't know why." The thought of lying down only to be alone with her racing thoughts wasn't appealing. "I'm marrying the love of my life, and my best friend is presiding over the ceremony. I shouldn't have a care in the world."

Callie smiled. "You are an introvert, Wonder, and working in the café hasn't cured you of that. It stresses you out to think that all eyes will be on you."

That was only partially true. There were things that stressed her even more. What if Anandur did something to embarrass her in the name of fun? He loved clowning around, and she didn't want to be the stick-in-the-mud who spoiled the fun for him, but for once, she wanted him to be serious and give the ceremony its proper respect. Then there was the issue of the vows. She'd worked on them for weeks, but after hearing Alena's and Amanda's, she realized that what she'd produced was not on a par with theirs. It was tempting to let Callie help her write something better, but then it wouldn't be from her, and the vows were supposed to be deeply personal.

Wonder groaned. "My vows suck, and I'm afraid Anandur is going to do something goofy, but at least that way, everyone's eyes will be on him, so I won't be the center of attention."

Callie laughed. "I'm sure your vows are heartfelt, which is what really counts, and Anandur is not going to do anything too crazy with the Clan Mother watching."

"I hope not. I wish I could see him before the ceremony to make sure he's not wearing something outlandish."

"It's bad luck for the bride and groom to see each other on the day of their wedding," Callie said. "Now, how about a relaxing bath instead of a nap? It might help calm your nerves."

A bubble bath was the perfect excuse to get some alone time without offending her guests. "That sounds great."

Wonder pushed to her feet. "I'm going to take a bath, and while I'm gone, don't overdo it with the drinks."

A chorus of laughter and mock protests trailed her as she walked into the bedroom and were abruptly silenced when she closed the door behind her.

Letting out a breath, Wonder continued into the bathroom and closed that door behind her, too. She drew a bath, adding scented oils that filled the room with a calming fragrance, and as she sank into the warm water, she closed her eyes. With the heat seeping into her muscles, the tension that had built up throughout the day started to unwind.

As the water gently lapped against her skin, Wonder's thoughts drifted to Anandur. Her mate was adorable, and she loved him with every fiber of her being. She loved his sunny disposition, his strength, and the way he looked at her with love and unconditional approval. She made him happy, and he made her happy in return.

Wonder felt a surge of gratitude for the love she'd found not only with Anandur but with the entire clan.

Her new family.

A little over half an hour later, Wonder stepped out of the bath feeling relaxed, centered, and rejuvenated. She applied lotion to her face, wrapped a towel over her head, and put on a robe.

As she opened the door to the living room, Callie stopped mid-sentence and turned to her. "That was quick. Feeling better?"

"Much." Wonder scanned the room. "Where are Syssi and Amanda?"

"They went to check on the rescued women," Carol said. "Well, Syssi wanted to check on them, but since her Spanish is so-so, Amanda joined her as an interpreter." She glanced at her watch. "I think it's time to get on with the second part of the festivities. We need to get you ready, girl." She pushed to her feet. "I need to see your wedding dress. Callie told us that it's unlike any dress we have seen, and I'm bristling with curiosity."

Wonder waved a hand toward the bedroom. "Follow me and take a look."

"Yay!" Carol clapped her hands.

The wedding dress was spread over the bed, and it was a stunning amalgamation of traditional white and elements inspired by Wonder Woman's costume.

"Oh, my goodness, Wonder, it's absolutely perfect!" Carol exclaimed.

Callie had already seen the dress, so she just smiled and nodded.

Aliya got closer and smoothed her hand over the chiffon. "It's very pretty." She lifted her gaze to Wonder. "Mine is more modest."

"I'm sure it's gorgeous."

"Yeah." Aliya's eyes sparkled. "I know that it's considered bad luck, but Vrog helped me pick it. He loved it."

Wonder smiled, her eyes tracing the intricate details of the dress. The bodice was made from gold fabric, and it flowed into a graceful skirt. The accessories included a real gold tiara and a pair of thick cuffs that had been custom-made. Those were the only part of the outfit that Anandur had been privy to because he'd ordered them.

"You're going to look like a goddess," Carol gushed. "Anandur won't be able to take his eyes off you."

"Isn't it a bit too much?" Wonder looked at Callie. "Maybe I should forgo the tiara?"

Her friend's eyes bugged out. "Are you kidding me? This thing is real gold and made for you. I designed your hairdo around it."

"Then I guess it stays." Wonder lifted the tiara and ran her fingers over the delicate carvings. "I'm going to feel like an imposter princess."

"You are a princess." Annani glided into the bedroom. "Every bride is a princess on her wedding day, and you, my dear, will look regal. I cannot wait to see you in this outfit with your hair and makeup done, walking up to the dais surrounded by your bridesmaids." She smiled. "We did not have that custom in Sumer, so we did not include it in our musings about our future weddings."

Wonder blushed at the thought. As a girl, she'd fantasized about marrying Esag, Khiann's squire. She'd been devastated by his refusal to break his engagement to be with her, but in retrospect, he had saved her life by breaking her heart. If she hadn't run away, she would have died with everyone else in their city.

She was grateful to Annani and the Fates, who had guided her to suggest Tula as a maid to Areana. Her sister had accompanied Mortdh's bride to his stronghold in the north, which had saved her life.

48

FRANKIE

As Dagor's phone buzzed with an incoming message, he read it with a raised brow. "That's a surprise. I'm invited to Anandur's bachelor party." He looked at Frankie. "I'm not a close friend of his. Why would he invite me?"

"Maybe he likes you?"

"Anandur likes everyone."

Frankie knew that Anandur was the name of one of Kian's bodyguards, but she wasn't sure which one he was. Given Dagor's last comment, though, it had to be the redhead. "Anandur is the tall one, right? The blond who looks like a statue of an angel doesn't like anyone, so it can't be him."

"That's Brundar, who's surprisingly Anandur's brother. He's getting married tomorrow, provided that we are done with the mission in time for his wedding." He chuckled. "I'm sure he's not going to invite me to his bachelor party." Dagor put his phone on the coffee table. "I don't want to go to Anandur's either."

"Why not? It will be good for you to mingle a little and make new friends." He needed more people to talk to other than Negal, Aru, and her. "Check with Negal and Aru if they've gotten an invitation. It will be less awkward for you if they are there."

"That's not the reason I don't want to go. I don't like the idea of leaving you alone."

"That's sweet." She leaned over and kissed his cheek. "But I'll be fine. I need to call Margo and let her know about the delay. And then I have to start getting ready for the wedding. It will take me at least an hour to just do my makeup, and I'm doing Mia's makeup, too. She's coming over to do my hair."

"In that case, I might go if Negal is going too."

As Dagor's phone buzzed with another message, Frankie had a feeling it was either Negal or Aru asking him the same question.

"It's Negal," Dagor said. "He's asking whether I got an invitation and if I'm going." He lifted a brow. "Am I going?"

"Yes. Text him that you are."

"Yes, ma'am."

When Dagor was done texting, Frankie pulled him in for a scorching kiss.

"If that was meant to incentivize me to go, it failed," he murmured against her lips. "I'd rather stay with you than hang out with a bunch of dudes."

"Go." She playfully pushed him. "But just so you are mentally prepared, tonight, you are taking me to the dance floor. I'm fully healed, Bridget already knows, so there is no need to keep pretending. I plan on wearing one of my form-fitting evening gowns and sky-high heels. Be ready to be wowed."

"Oh, I am." He kissed her back.

Frankie waited until the door had closed behind Dagor before reaching for her phone, but she didn't call Margo right away.

How was she going to explain the additional delay without revealing too much?

Well, she'd just have to wing it.

"Hi," Margo answered. "So, which dress are you wearing for tonight's wedding?"

"The red one."

"Oh, wow. You are going in with all guns blazing."

Frankie winced. "Yeah, I'm dressing to impress. I have a bit of bad news, though. We're going to be another day late."

"What happened?" Margo's voice was laced with concern.

Frankie bit her bottom lip, searching for a plausible explanation. "Uh, there were some complications with docking in the Acapulco harbor." She hoped her improvised excuse sounded believable. Actually, it was true to some extent, just not the whole truth. But Margo wasn't easily fooled, and she could smell bullshit a mile away. Of course, Frankie didn't improve the situation when she decided to embellish the story. "Apparently, you can't just show up with a ship and drop anchor. You need to reserve a spot, and they don't have anything open until tomorrow."

"My bullshit detector is flashing red. What's the real story, Frankie?"

Damn. She could never lie to Margo, not in person and not over the phone.

Frankie sighed. "I wish I could tell you, but I can't."

There was a brief silence before Margo spoke again. "Lynda's bachelorette party is wrapping up tonight, and everyone's flying home in the morning. Maybe I should just call it quits and head back as well. I still have work, you know."

"Please, don't. The cruise is still ending on schedule. The crew can't extend beyond that, and you're not expected back at the office until after the cruise anyway. Just book one more night at the hotel. It'll be worth it, I promise. We will have so much fun, and besides, you won't believe the selection of hot, single guys. It's like a hottie buffet."

Margo laughed. "You should have opened with that. I'll book one more night."

They chatted a bit more about Lynda and her bridesmaids and how Margo's relationship with her future sister-in-law had improved over the past couple of days.

Frankie glanced at her watch and sighed. "I wish I could talk with you more, but I need to start getting ready. You know how long it takes me to put makeup on for an occasion like this."

"Knock them dead, girl, and have that boyfriend of yours take pictures of you in the venue. I want to see you in your dress."

Frankie winced. "I'm not allowed to send out photos of anyone or anything other than myself." No one had told her that, but she'd been told that all of her communications would be monitored. If she tried to send photos of people she shouldn't, they would just not go through. "That's why I didn't send you pictures of Dagor and his friends. Tom's partners are super secretive about everything, and I don't want to risk our future employment with Perfect Match for some pictures."

If everything went well and she transitioned, she wouldn't be taking the job offer, but Margo would.

"So have him take a picture of you before leaving the cabin. I'm sure that's okay."

"I will." Maybe.

49

ANANDUR

Anandur couldn't suppress his grin as he headed to his bachelor party, decked out in his embellished Superman costume. He'd added a pair of black, devilish horns and smeared red makeup over his face. It was a nod to the demon illusion he often used to intimidate his enemies, although it had been a while since he'd gotten to use that bad boy.

Kian no longer took an active part in skirmishes, and there hadn't been many of those lately, either. The only time Anandur still saw action was when he occasionally took part in rescue missions. Perhaps the next time he went out on one of those, he would do his demon stunt just to keep up the skill.

"Hello, my Justice League friends." Anandur made his grand entrance, flinging his cape back and thrusting his chest out.

The cabin erupted in cheers and laughter.

Kian handed him a glass full of whiskey. "We were placing bets on what you were going to wear. I won."

"Awesome costume." Bhathian regarded him with a frown. "I hope that's not how you are going to show up to your wedding?"

"I wish." Anandur took a sip from the whiskey. "If I do, my bride will just walk away. She made me promise to wear a tux, but I'll do something to dress it up. Wearing a boring penguin suit is not my style."

Scanning the room, he spotted Kri, who technically should have been a bridesmaid because she was Wonder's friend too, but she'd been his friend longer, and when he'd asked her to be his groomsmaid she'd been more than happy to accept. She had on a tux, her long blond hair was braided, and her pretty face was free of makeup as usual. She looked sharp.

"Superman with horns and a demon's red face." Arwel laughed. "Now that's a combination Hollywood hasn't tried yet."

Anandur laughed. "Maybe I should do like Stallone, write a script and sell it on the condition that I get to star in the movie. It's going to be a blockbuster."

"Good idea." Kri clapped him on the back. "But it will sell better if you take Wonder with you. They'd snatch her up in a heartbeat."

"I know." He grinned. "She's the real Wonder Woman." He lifted his glass in a toast. "To my lovely Wonder, to love, and to new beginnings."

His brother clinked glasses with him and offered him the rarest of gifts—a smile. "I'm happy for you. Wonder completes you."

Anandur affected a gasp and put a hand over his chest. "Wow, Brundar. That's the most romantic thing I've ever heard you say. Thank you."

His brother shrugged. "You only get married once."

"True." Anandur took a sip of his whiskey. "That's a good reason to make the most of the celebration, but I would have liked to join you guys tomorrow. If I showed up dressed like this, it would petrify the humans."

Bhathian shook his head with a grin. "Or make them die of laughter. Besides, the plan is for Kalugal to freeze them, so they will be petrified anyway."

Anandur feigned a pout. "That's no fun. What if you unfreeze them one at a time, after disarming them, of course, and then let them wrestle for their lives?"

"That's not a good idea," Arwel said. "We'd obviously win, and then we would have to put them in stasis because the Clan Mother doesn't allow us to execute them."

Anandur lifted his glass but then lowered it. "Actually, this one time, the Clan Mother has agreed to make an exception because of their monstrous cruelty, and she's not only allowing us to end them permanently but actively encouraging it. My problem is that death by venom is too merciful for monsters. I don't want them to die with a smile on their faces. I want them screaming in pain."

Anandur was glad to see nods all around. "Ripping their hearts out of their chests while they're frozen is better, but doing that while they are fighting for their lives and losing would be even more satisfying. I want them to experience the terror and pain they inflicted on those villagers."

The brutality of his words was not lost on his friends, but they all shared his view that the heinous acts committed by their enemies demanded justice.

Anandur cast a sidelong glance at the gods he had invited to his party and was glad to see similar expressions on their faces. He would have hated it if they'd started spouting nonsense about finding the good in people and giving them another chance. Or worse, trying to somehow justify their horrendous actions. It would have been lunacy, but reading news from the human world, he'd learned that there was no shortage of lunatics, either delusional or paid to spout things that no decent, intelligent person should ever accept or believe.

"Well, that was a fun topic for a bachelor party. Not." Kian chuckled. "I suggest that we forget about the mission until tomorrow and focus on celebrating the joyous occasion tonight." He stepped forward with a bottle of fine whiskey in one hand and a box of premium cigars in the other. "Time for a toast."

He poured whiskey into the line of fresh glasses on Okidu's tray and then waited for his butler to pass them around. "To love and the bliss of matrimony."

As glasses clinked and the sounds echoed around the room, Anandur downed the whiskey in one go, enjoying the smooth, fiery liquid warming his throat.

Kian flipped open the box. "Come and get your cigars, gentlemen and lady, but please light them up on the balcony and make sure that the doors are closed before you do."

Kri leaned over the box. "Which one do you recommend for a novice?"

"The Short Story," Kian said as he handed Kri a diminutive cigar. "They are very good despite their smaller size."

"Okay." She took the offered stick and headed out to the balcony.

After everyone was outside with a cigar in hand, Okidu made the rounds offering cutting services and lighting the cigars for them, and the pleasant smell of the sea breeze was replaced with the rich aroma of tobacco.

Anandur watched Kri puff on hers with surprising ease. Michael, the only one in their group who hadn't taken a cigar, shook his head at his mate. "I thought that you didn't like the smell of cigarettes."

"I don't, but cigars smell good."

Anandur caught Michael's eye and smiled. "Come on, Michael, light up. It's a tradition. You'd better get used to it. We do this at every bachelor party."

Michael grimaced but took the cigar Kian offered him. "You guys are a bad influence."

Anandur grinned. "You want to be a Guardian, right?"

Michael sneered. "I am a Guardian."

"Not yet, you're not. You are a Guardian in training. Light up."

"If I do, are you going to finally graduate me to full-fledged status?"

The kid was good, but he wasn't ready yet. "I wish I could, but you need more training."

"Fine." Michael handed the cigar to Okidu for cutting and lighting. "One more step on the journey toward full status." He took a puff and immediately started coughing.

"This is not a cigarette," Kian said. "Don't inhale. Just hold the smoke in your mouth and then release it."

As the cigars burned and the whiskey flowed, the mood in the room gradually shifted. The jokes resumed, laughter rang out, and stories were shared, each tale more embellished than the last, with Anandur's being the most outlandish of them all.

It was as if they were determined to squeeze every drop of joy out of the evening, because tomorrow, they would be busy killing monsters, which would be satisfying but add more taint to their souls.

Evildoers did not only destroy the lives of their victims, their victims' families, and their whole communities, but they also forced the good guys to become killers.

Anandur understood perfectly well why Wonder didn't want to be a Guardian even though she was stronger than most of the males puffing cigars out on Kian's balcony.

She didn't want to be a killer.

To this day, his beautiful, gentle mate had nightmares about killing the males who had set out to violate her and then end her. She had probably saved the lives of countless women who would have fallen victim to those males, and yet she couldn't shake the guilt for taking their lives.

Anandur had gotten over that a long time ago, perhaps because the natural aggression of males made it easier for them, or perhaps it got easier the more times one killed. He was nearly a thousand years old, and he had ended the lives of many, which had probably saved multitudes of innocents.

He had no regrets.

With a sigh, he took another puff of his cigar, letting the rich smoke fill his mouth. Tonight was about living in the moment, about laughter and camaraderie. Later, he was going to marry the love of his life in front of his friends and family.

Things didn't get much better than that.

50

DAGOR

"I'm ready to go." Dagor extinguished his cigar in the ashtray. "I still need to change into my tux."

It would take him a minute, but he was anxious to get back to Frankie and see her all decked out.

"Yeah, me too," Negal said. "I need to take a shower to wash off the cigar stench."

"Shhh." Dagor put a finger on his lips. "You're insulting our host," he whispered.

"Right." Negal rolled his eyes while saying out loud, "I need to wash off the lovely aroma of cigars."

Chuckling, Dagor glanced at Aru, who was in the midst of an animated discussion with Kian.

When Dagor signaled that he and Negal were leaving, he waved them off. "Don't wait for me."

Negal pushed his hands into his pockets. "Did you hear Aru? He said that tearing out the hearts of those Doomers was barbaric. According to him, Anumatians have evolved from such savagery."

Dagor let out a low chuckle. "Yeah, 'evolved.' Anumatians destroy entire populations without even setting foot on their planets, and that's somehow more civilized?"

Negal nodded. "That's precisely what crossed my mind when he said it. It's a convenient way to distance ourselves from the reality of what we do. If we don't see it, touch it, or smell it, then it's somehow okay. That's such hypocrisy."

Dagor's thoughts drifted back to the horrors inflicted by the Doomers' henchmen. The images Jacki's words had painted were forever etched into his mind, fueling rage and a burning desire for justice. "What they did to those villagers was horrific. Nothing less than a barbaric response seems fitting."

Negal remained silent for a moment. "It's a fine line," he finally said, "between justice and vengeance, between civilization and savagery. But the way I see it, you need to respond in kind. It's better to sow such intense fear in your enemies that they won't dare repeat their evil deeds than to act civilized and let them believe that you are weak. That will only encourage more violence and more suffering and will force you to eventually do what you should have done to begin with. Aru must have led a sheltered life before he joined the Galactic Peacekeepers."

Dagor laughed. "Peacekeepers. What a joke that is. We are the overseers, the enforcers, but the noble bleeding hearts back home prefer the nice-sounding term Peacekeepers. The whole universe is full of hypocrisy."

"I guess we'll have to find our own balance," Negal said quietly. "Do what needs to be done, but not lose ourselves in the process. I can perform barbaric acts without becoming a savage. I know why this needs to be done, and I think that the trick is not to relish it."

"That's not easy, my friend. The need for revenge is a powerful force."

They parted ways in the elevator when Dagor exited on Frankie's level, and Negal continued to the upper deck.

He was about to enter the code when Frankie opened the door, and seeing her, he took a step back.

"You look... stunning," Dagor finally managed to say.

Her eyes sparkled with delight at his reaction, and her smile widened. "Thank you. I was hoping that would be your response." She stepped aside to let him in.

"I'm glad I didn't disappoint you." He couldn't take his eyes off her.

Every detail was flawless, from the hair that was styled to perfection to the way her red dress hugged her figure. It was more than her physical beauty that captivated him, though. It was the confidence and joy she exuded that truly made her shine.

He wanted to pull her into his arms and kiss the living daylights out of her, but he knew better. If he ruined all the work that she'd put into looking the way she did, Frankie would give him hell.

He rubbed a hand over his jaw. "I need a few minutes to shower and change."

"Take your time." She smiled. "There is no rush. Do you want me to pour you a drink in the meantime?"

"No, thanks. I had enough whiskey at the party. I'm going to stick to water and juice for the rest of the night."

"As you wish." She walked over to the bar, sashaying her hips. "I'm making myself a gin and tonic."

Stuck looking at her shapely ass, he was rooted in place until she looked at him with a raised brow.

"I'm going." He tore his eyes away from her and forced his feet to take him to the bathroom.

After a quick shower, Dagor changed into his tux, and as he combed his hair, he caught himself humming and smiling at his reflection in the mirror.

It was the Frankie effect.

She brought a sense of excitement and happiness to his life that he hadn't known he was missing. Adjusting his bowtie in the mirror, he took a deep breath and squared his shoulders.

"You look good," she said as he entered the living room, her eyes roaming over him. "Really good."

"Thank you." He extended his arm to her. "Shall we?"

"We shall." As Frankie took his arm, her touch sent a familiar thrill through him, and he wondered whether it would always be like that.

Dagor offered a prayer to the Fates to give him a chance to find out by allowing Frankie to transition.

When they entered the festively decorated dining hall, Frankie gasped. "Look at this. It's Wonder Woman themed."

The tablecloths alternated between red, white, and blue, and a gold sash was draped over their middles. The chair covers were similarly color-themed, with a gold bow tied at each. A gold eagle symbol inside a red circle was projected onto the ceiling.

It was a lovely tribute to Wonder Woman, honoring Anandur's bride-to-be.

Toven and his mate entered right behind them and paused to join in admiring the decor.

"They really went all out with the theme," Mia commented, her eyes taking in the festive decorations. "It looks very patriotic."

"Right." Dagor swept his gaze over the room. "I just realized that the colors also represent the United States flag."

Soft music played in the background, and Dagor wondered whether it also had anything to do with Wonder Woman.

As Toven and Mia continued to their table, Dagor and Frankie joined Aru, Gabi, and Negal.

"You look amazing," Gabi told Frankie. "Where did you get this stunning dress?"

Frankie chuckled. "From my cousin Angelica, who got it in a thrift store. It's supposed to be some famous designer's, but the label was cut off, so it might have been a story the store owner told my cousin."

"It's absolutely stunning."

"Thank you." Frankie beamed.

Dagor loved that she was so confident and comfortable in her own skin that she didn't feel the need to impress anyone with anything other than the power of her personality and her exuberance. She wasn't embarrassed about wearing a borrowed dress that came from a thrift store.

She was proud of it.

In fact, he loved everything about her, from her tiny feet clad in sky-high heels to the tip of her head and the elaborate coif that Mia had twisted her hair into.

"Let's make a toast." Dagor reached for the bottle of champagne, uncorked it, and poured the bubbly into everyone's glasses. He raised his and waited until everyone at their table followed. "To the lovely couple getting married tonight, to my friends, old and new, and to Frankie, who brings light and joy into my life."

51

ANANDUR

The moment Anandur had been awaiting was finally here.

He stood at the entrance to the dining hall, flanked by his seven groomsmen and one groomsmaid, dressed in a smart tuxedo and a white dress shirt, which would make Wonder happy. But he wasn't wearing a bowtie, and the shirt wasn't buttoned all the way to the top, so the Superman T-shirt he was wearing underneath was showing.

"You couldn't help yourself, could you?" Kri murmured. "Button that shirt up and hide that thing. Wonder will be upset."

"No, she won't." Anandur grinned. "She will be tickled. You look great, Kri. I love the gold bowtie. It's a nice touch."

"Thank you." She adjusted the tie. "Michael's is blue."

Each of his groom's-persons had chosen a bowtie that was either red, white, or blue to honor his bride, and Kri was the only one who had thought of adding gold to the ensemble.

Brundar looked sharp with his white-blond hair unbound and cascading down his back. Kian looked like a god, which was nothing new, and Onegus was grinning like he was the one getting married. Bhathian was straining the seams of his tux, and he looked miserable, confined in the restricting garment. Arwel had his shoulder-length hair gathered in a ponytail and looked pained, probably because he was picking up the emotions of the rescued women all the way from the lower deck where they were housed.

Yamanu looked great with his black hair gathered in a long ponytail, and Michael was looking at Kri with unabashed admiration.

It had been a tough choice between Michael and Max, and the reason Michael had won was simply because of being Kri's mate. The kid wasn't even a full-fledged Guardian yet, but he showed great promise and most importantly, his heart was in it.

As the music that signaled the groom's entrance started playing, Anandur and his entourage walked toward the dais where Annani was waiting.

Smiling at his guests, he took in the decorations and was impressed by how well they had turned out. It had been all Amanda's doing, and he owed her a big thank you for making the night special for him and Wonder.

Clad in her white ceremonial robe that was edged with gold, Annani radiated warmth and love but also unmistakable power. Her glowing skin made her look majestic and ethereal, which, as it turned out, was even more spectacular than they had believed. Not all gods glowed in the dark, only the nobility did, and the stronger the glow, the more royal the status.

To him, though, the Clan Mother looked like an angel, her smile reaching across the room and touching his heart. It was a smile that conveyed love, pride, and acceptance.

The chatter and music in the room seemed to fade into the background as Anandur walked toward the dais and his great-great-grandmother, who was the heart of their community.

As he took his place, Anandur scanned the smiling faces of his clan members, and the positive energy sent his way filled him with joy. His gaze drifted across the room, eventually finding his mother seated at the family table.

The look on her face was one of immense pride and affection, and her warm smile seemed to say, "I am so happy for you."

Naturally, his mother loved Wonder.

Everyone did.

His gentle, beautiful, graceful mate. In a few moments, she would walk in, surrounded by her bridesmaids, and she would smile at him from across the room.

He hoped she would be amused by the Superman shirt peeking from under his dress shirt. She'd wanted him to just wear a plain tuxedo and look dignified for a change, but she knew him well enough to expect something mischievous.

If he had done nothing special, she would have been disappointed.

Standing at the foot of the dais, Anandur felt an unexpected wave of emotion sweep over him. Given that he and Wonder were each other's fated mates, he had viewed this night just as a joyous event to celebrate their union with the clan, but now, as the reality of the moment settled upon him, he realized that it was so much more than just a fun party.

This was a binding of souls, a public declaration of his and Wonder's eternal commitment to one another. It was a testament to the love that had grown and flourished between them, a love that was now going to be made official in front of their community. It was an acknowledgment of their bond, a celebration of their unity, and a promise for their shared future.

52

WONDER

Wonder hadn't seen her bridesmaid's dresses until tonight, and now that the eight of them flanked her four on each side, she wasn't sure whether she should be mad at Amanda for going overboard with the dining hall decoration and the dress designs or thank her for being so bold.

One thing was for sure: no one was going to forget this DC Universe-themed wedding, so maybe it was a good thing, given that there were ten of them taking place.

Each of her bridesmaids had a different dress that matched her personality in addition to being Wonder Woman-themed.

Carol's was a long, flowing red gown with a subtle gold waistband and gold trim along the neckline. It was Grecian-style, the one-shoulder strap adorned with a golden W emblem. It was bold and pretty, like the female wearing it.

Vivian wore a navy-blue chiffon dress with a V-neck and an A-line silhouette. The skirt was sprinkled with silver stars, mimicking Wonder Woman's star-spangled look. It was conservative and demure, matching Vivian's motherly character. Her daughter Ella wore a knee-length, metallic gold dress with a fitted silhouette and a sweetheart neckline. The dress was more daring and modern, fitting the young female who had recently changed her hair color from pink to blue.

Wonder had gotten close to the two during her study sessions with Parker.

Vivian had taken on a maternal role in her life, and Ella had become like a sister to her, but Wonder still wished that Tula could be there to celebrate her wedding.

Callie, her future sister-in-law, had chosen a wrap dress in a vibrant red color, edged with gold piping, and Aliya's dress was a simple navy sheath complemented by a gold headband.

Mey's dress had a red bodice and a flowing, blue, high-low skirt. The transition from red to blue was accented with a gold belt that was supposed to symbolize Wonder Woman's lasso, but Wonder doubted anyone would figure out what it meant to convey. Jin's dress had a gold sequined bodice, representing Wonder Woman's armor, and it was paired with a sleek navy pencil skirt. Eva was dressed in a long, deep blue Grecian-style gown with a flowing skirt and a detachable gold arm cuff.

When the moment arrived and the bride's song began playing, Wonder took her first step into the event hall, flanked by her bridesmaids. Keenly aware of every eye in the room turning towards her, her heart raced with excitement and nervousness, but as she beheld the smiling face of her groom, the anxiety vanished, and only the excitement remained.

Anandur looked dashing in his elegant tuxedo, and a wave of relief washed over her that he had chosen the traditional attire over the Superman costume he had brought aboard. His wild red hair, usually untamed, was slicked back neatly, giving him a distinguished look that only heightened his natural charisma. He looked every bit the hero Guardian she knew him to be, and the sight of him made her heart swell with love.

As their eyes met, she saw in his gaze a radiant happiness that mirrored her own, and the love she felt for him surged through her, so intense and profound that her heart felt like it was swelling within her chest.

Amusement lifted her lips as she imagined the swelling turning physical, overcoming her tight bodice, and causing a wardrobe malfunction.

She certainly didn't need that to make her wedding day even more memorable than it already was. Shaking off the absurd notion, Wonder smiled back at Anandur and lifted her gaze to Annani.

The contrast between Anandur's towering figure and Annani's petite form was striking, but despite the goddess's small stature, she commanded the space with her formidable presence. It was a remarkable sight—the goddess and the Guardian, standing at equal levels, their heights balanced by the dais.

Annani had always been larger than life, and as Gulan, Wonder had felt invisible under the goddess's immense shadow. Compared to Annani, she felt small and insignificant. What were her impressive stature and her physical strength compared to the goddess's power, indomitable spirit, and unwavering determination?

Today, though, as she stood in front of the dais holding Anandur's hand, Wonder realized how far she had come and how much she had grown. She was no longer Gulan, the servant girl who had been tasked with protecting and serving the princess. She was now Wonder, a new person with no limits and nothing holding her back.

Her gaze shifting to Annani, she regarded the goddess who had been a constant in her life, the princess she had idolized as a young girl and still revered.

Despite her diminutive stature and her delicate appearance, Annani was fierce and courageous and had a relentless drive that defied the odds. She had faced adversities that would have daunted most, and yet she had persevered, and her vision for a better future remained clear.

Reflecting on Annani's journey, Wonder was struck by the enormity of what her oldest friend had achieved. Annani was more than just a leader of her clan; she was a guardian of humanity, shielding mankind from Navuh's toxic influence.

No one could compare to Annani, and Wonder shouldn't either. She had her own journey, her own path to follow, and her story hadn't been written yet. She might have been born nearly five thousand years ago, but she'd lived only twenty-three of them, and she had a lot to learn.

She felt a surge of gratitude toward her old friend for officiating at her wedding and for being a symbol of the resilience and hope that Wonder aspired to embody in her own life, of courage, compassion, and steadfastness in the face of adversity.

With a role model like Annani and with the love and support of Anandur and her new clan family, Wonder was stepping into a future filled with endless possibilities, and instead of feeling overwhelmed, she felt empowered.

She made a silent promise to herself to strive to be as courageous, as resilient, and as dedicated to her beliefs as the goddess. In her own way, she would carry forward the torch of hope and justice, standing alongside those she loved and fighting for a better world.

53

ANNANI

This night held a special place in Annani's heart, almost rivaling the emotional intensity of her daughters' weddings. Wonder, or Gulan as she was once known, was still her closest friend despite the thousands of years separating them. Seeing her standing next to her prophesied mate and looking so profoundly happy was deeply moving.

As she gazed at the couple before her, Annani's mind wandered to the prophecy of an old human seer who had foretold of Gulan's destined love thousands of years ago.

In a distant land and time, you will find true love with a gentle giant of a man.

What a succinct description of Anandur that was.

A gentle giant of a man.

At over six and a half feet tall and with broad shoulders that could barely fit through a standard door opening and massive muscles all over, he was a giant, and although not many would call him gentle, Annani knew that he had a heart of gold and cared deeply about his brother, his clan, and now his mate.

The soothsayer's prophecy for Areana had also been accurate.

A heavy burden rests on your shoulders, and you have a most important task. Your gentle soul and soft heart will guide you on your path. I see a child in your future, a son born to you and the rogue. Stay strong and true to yourself and teach him right from wrong.

It was easy to see that the rogue was Navuh, and the son was either Lokan or Kalugal. The soothsayer should have said sons, not son, but perhaps teaching Kalugal right from wrong was more important than teaching Lokan because the younger brother was so much more powerful than the older, and if he had stayed with the Brotherhood and become his father's right-hand man, Annani shuddered to think of the consequences. Navuh was smart, but Kalugal was brilliant, and combined with his compulsion power, he was extremely dangerous.

And yet, he'd grown up to be a decent male, a good husband and father, and a fair leader of his men. All of that was most likely thanks to his mother's influence.

The near-perfect accuracy of those prophecies was so evident that it stirred within Annani a flicker of hope for her own prophesied reunion with Khiann, her long-lost love so cruelly taken from her by Mortdh.

Silently, she recited the seer's words from memory.

Do not despair, Princess Annani. Not all is lost. True love cannot die. Its fire cannot turn to ice. Your beloved's love floats in the ether, ready to be reborn. Khiann will find a way to come back to you in some form. Seven children will be born to you, all different, but his spirit will shine through their eyes, warm and bright. And one day, many years from now, he will come to you, and you will know him at first sight. I saw it all with my blind eyes, my lady, and everything I see with my second sight comes to pass.

The possibility that Khiann might reincarnate as an immortal, or perhaps even as a god on Anumati, lingered in her thoughts. The recent arrival of gods from Anumati had opened up a realm of possibilities Annani had never considered before. Could her Khiann be waiting for her there?

The notion that she might find him again if she one day took the throne, as her grandmother planned, was both tantalizing and daunting. Even if she was keen on usurping her grandfather, the Eternal King, it would take many thousands of years to achieve, and she wanted her Khiann back now.

Annani pushed these personal reflections aside.

Tonight was not about her and her lost love; it was about Wonder and Anandur. They deserved her full attention.

Focusing back on the couple, Annani allowed the significance of their union to guide her words. This was a celebration of a bond that transcended time and space, a union of two souls destined to be together.

"Today, we witness not just the joining of two individuals, but the celebration of a destiny fulfilled. Wonder and Anandur, your journey to this moment is a testament to the strength of love and the power of fate."

Annani paused, looking at each of them in turn, ensuring her words reached not just their ears but also their hearts. "In each other, you have found a mirror for your strengths, a balm for your weaknesses, and a partner for your journey through life. May your love be a beacon that guides you through every challenge and a sanctuary that brings you peace in times of turmoil."

Annani looked upon Wonder and Anandur with affection as she raised her hands. "Before all gathered here and the eternal embrace of the Fates, I bestow upon you my blessings. May your love be as deep and unending as the oceans, always finding its way back to the shores of each other's hearts. May it be as steadfast as the mountains, unshakable in the face of trials and tribulations. May your union be blessed with understanding and patience, with laughter and joy, with courage and strength. May you always find in each other a haven of peace and a wellspring of happiness. May the bond that unites you grow stronger with each passing day, weaving a tapestry of shared memories, dreams, and aspirations. May you have the wisdom to navigate the journey of life together, hand in hand and heart in heart."

She took a deep breath, her final words imbued with a profound sense of hope and joy. "And may the Fates smile upon you, guiding you through the journey of life, filled with love and fulfillment. May you always find strength in your unity, and may your love be a guiding light for all who witness it."

Annani lowered her hands, her eyes sparkling with unshed tears of joy. "By the power vested in me, I now pronounce you joined in the bonds of fate and marriage. May your journey together be as boundless as the sky and as luminous as the stars."

As the room erupted in applause and cheers, Annani watched as Wonder and Anandur turned to look at their friends and family with happiness and love shining in their eyes.

Officiating over Wonder and Anandur's wedding provided Annani with a deep sense of fulfillment. The coming together of two souls that were meant for each other was a reminder of the beauty and power of love, a force that transcended time, space, and the trials of fate.

54

ANANDUR

As Annani concluded her blessing, a new surge of emotion swept through Anandur, and he teared up a little, but that was okay. Everyone would just think that he was goofing around, but Wonder would know better.

He turned to his bride, wrapped his arms around her, and poured all his love and passion into the kiss to outshine all kisses.

In the background, the room erupted into a cacophony of hoots and applause, but as absorbed as he was in holding and kissing his mate, Anandur heard it as if it was coming from a great distance. Still, he could feel a wave of warmth and joy emanating from their guests and enveloping Wonder and him.

As he pulled back from the kiss, he caught sight of his brother smiling—a genuine, heartfelt smile that was such a rare sight to behold that it imprinted itself in Anandur's memory.

Two down and plenty more to go, he promised himself.

Who would have known that the stoic Brundar was a romantic at heart?

Now that Anandur knew the secret to unlocking his brother's smiles, he was going to get many more out of him.

Up on the dais, Annani laughed, the magical sound pulling Anandur from his musing. "That was a kiss to remember," the goddess said, her tone full of mirth. "To loosely quote a movie that has become a favorite of mine, *The Princess Bride*—since the invention of the kiss, there have been a handful of kisses that were rated the most passionate, the most pure of all, and this one left them all behind."

As the crowd erupted in a new volley of hoots, cheers, and applause, Wonder blushed and offered Anandur a shy smile.

The Clan Mother lifted her hand to shush the guests. "Wonder and Anandur, as you stand here before your family, friends, and the Fates themselves, ready to embark on life's most beautiful journey, it is time to pledge your vows to each other."

Anandur hoped he could remember the vows he had so carefully worded and memorized. Taking a deep breath, he waited for the applause to subside, and as the room settled into an expectant hush, he looked into Wonder's eyes and took her hands in his.

"Wonder, my love. From the moment you knocked me out with your taser, threw me over your shoulder, and put me in a cage, I knew you were special. In fact, that was probably when I fell head over heels in love with you."

As a burst of laughter echoed through the crowd, Wonder's blush deepened, but she smiled, encouraging him to go on.

He gave her hand a gentle squeeze. "Never before had I met a woman who could quite literally kick my butt, and I must say, I was thoroughly impressed. You've intrigued me, challenged me, and brought a whirlwind of joy and excitement into my life. You are my rock, my anchor, my everything."

A few chuckles sounded in the background, and someone whistled.

"I promise to cherish every moment with you, in laughter and in tears, in triumphs and challenges. I vow to be your strength when you feel weak and to be your mentor when you need guidance in this modern world you have awoken to, helping you overcome the challenges it throws your way. But most of all, I promise to always make you laugh, to fill our days with joy, and our nights with the warmth of my love. I pledge to be your partner in every adventure that awaits us."

He paused, his heart brimming with emotion. "I vow to love you, to respect you, and to grow with you for as long as we both shall live, which, hopefully, is forever. You are my heart, my soul, and my fierce Wonder. I am forever yours, completely and irrevocably."

As he concluded his vows, the room burst into applause, but Anandur's focus remained solely on Wonder.

Moist with tears, her eyes sparkled with love and adoration.

"I love you," she whispered. And if that was the extent of her vows, it was good enough for him.

55

WONDER

Wonder remembered her first encounter with Anandur vividly. It had been in the alley behind the club where she worked as a security guard, and the moment that had sealed her fate was probably when he'd smiled at her, giving her a two-fingered salute. Initially, she had thought he was checking her out but soon realized that he was reading her T-shirt, which read "bouncer" for the club. She had wondered then if he was also a bouncer or perhaps a policeman, but he was neither. He was something far more extraordinary—an immortal Guardian—but it would be a while before she found out that he was one of the good guys and not one of the evil ones whom she'd intercepted trying to drain human females of their blood.

He had seemed different from the start, so nice and friendly, but as he followed the behavior pattern of the others, disappointment had washed over her. Appearances could be deceptive, and nice-looking males were often the most dangerous, capable of luring in unsuspecting victims.

Determined not to let her guard down, Wonder had followed him into the alley, hoping that he was different, that he wasn't intent on killing the woman he was taking back where no one could see him.

As she'd peeked time and again, gauging the situation to see if she needed to intervene, she'd been envious of the woman and her obvious pleasure, but when Anandur flashed his elongated fangs, she could wait no longer and had pounced, tasering him until he'd collapsed in a heap. The woman had screamed, and Wonder had quickly thralled her into silence, a necessary but crude intervention.

Straightening the woman's clothes, Wonder had sent her back to the club and turned her attention back to the male.

Anandur had been still twitching from the taser's effect, fighting it with all his might, so she had knocked him out with the butt of her taser gun. After stripping him of his clothes to ensure that he had no tracking devices on him, she'd dumped them in a dumpster and had hoisted him over her shoulder. She knocked him out again before stuffing him into her car, and then dumped him in the gorilla cage, like she had done with the others she had caught.

Now, as she stood beside him on their wedding day, Wonder couldn't help but smile at the irony. The man she had once apprehended and viewed as a potential threat was now the love of her life, her fated mate.

Life was full of unexpected turns.

Her eyes never leaving his, Wonder's heart swelled with love. "It is true that when we first met, I knocked you out and treated you as a threat, but deep inside, I knew you were not the enemy. You shone too bright to be evil, but I couldn't take any chances. I imprisoned you, hoping that you would prove to me that you were good. In my gut, I must have known even then that you were my destined partner, my fated love, and in short order, you convinced my mind that my gut and my heart had been right."

A chuckle rippled through the crowd, and Anandur's smile broadened, his eyes twinkling with amusement and love.

"In you, I found not only a formidable warrior but a kind and loving soul. You've turned my world upside down in the best possible way. You've challenged me, supported me, and loved me unconditionally. You accepted me for who I was and stood by me through thick and thin, even when I insisted on following distant whispers all the way back to the place that I had awoken in."

Wonder paused, her eyes prickling with unshed tears. "Anandur, my love. I promise to cherish every moment with you, in laughter and in tears, in triumphs and challenges. I vow to stand by your side and be your partner in every adventure life throws our way."

Her voice grew softer, more intimate. "Even the most formidable warrior needs to come home to find comfort and support, and I promise to always be there for you as your sanctuary, your confidante, and your best friend." Wonder smiled. "And I solemnly swear to occasionally let you win when we spar, just to keep things interesting."

They never did spar, but she had known their guests would love the comment, and to prove her right, laughter filled the room.

Anandur's grin widened. "You're on, love."

"Most of all," Wonder continued, "I promise to love you with every fiber of my being for as long as we both shall live. You are my heart, my soul, my Anandur. And I am forever and irrevocably yours."

As she finished her vows, the room erupted with more applause and cheers, but for Wonder, the only person in the world at that moment was Anandur.

56

FRANKIE

Frankie dabbed at her eyes with a napkin, blotting the tears that had pooled in their corners.

The three wedding ceremonies she had witnessed had been so beautiful, each with its own unique and touching story, and she couldn't help but wonder what was special about her own love story with Dagor.

What would their wedding vows be about?

She'd met a god, thought that he was hot, and the rest was history?

The most unique thing about their relationship was that Dagor was a god, but even though that was most extraordinary, it wasn't something to wax poetic about.

Upon further reflection, though, she realized that within a very short span of time they'd had experiences most people didn't share in a lifetime.

They'd found a mysterious amulet, rescued a group of women who'd been abducted and were on their way to be sold into sexual slavery, and had killed their abductors.

It had been so traumatic to just listen to the sounds of battle between the Guardians and the cartel monsters that the memory of Dagor protecting her with his own body and absorbing the bullets that could have killed her was blurry. She had been terrified of the sounds of gunfire, the screams, and the shrieks, feeling helpless, huddling on the floor of the truck with Dagor on top of her.

He'd jerked every time he'd been hit, but there had been nothing she could do to help him. When a bullet had passed through his arm into her side, it had soon robbed her of consciousness, but before she'd passed out, she'd seen the panic in Dagor's eyes as he tried to stem the bleeding by pressing on the wound.

Frankie would never forget it.

Her next coherent memory after that had been waking up in the ship's clinic. Then he'd given her his blood to expedite her healing even though it was a big secret that Kian had forbidden the gods to reveal.

The secret was safe with her, and even if she never turned immortal and was somehow allowed to retain her memories of this incredible world she'd been invited into, she would take the gods and immortals' secrets to her grave.

Sadly, though, it meant that even if she transitioned and one day stood in front of the goddess with Dagor by her side, she couldn't share all that he had done for her with others.

Still, there was plenty she could say that didn't violate Kian's orders. Besides, she had known Dagor for only a few days, and she had no doubt that their life together would provide many more wonderful stories to incorporate into her wedding vows.

Next to her, Dagor was deep in thought, perhaps contemplating the same things she was, and as she reached over and gently squeezed his hand, he turned to her and smiled.

Smiling back, she waited for the music to start and the newly mated couple to take the dance floor. "Did you know about how Anandur and Wonder met?"

He shook his head. "I don't know any of these immortals well enough to know their personal stories. In that regard, you and I are in the same boat." He chuckled. "That was unintentional but fitting."

"I'm on a boat—" Frankie sang without completing the line.

She was a lady, and she didn't use vulgar language out loud. Only on the inside, and not that often either.

Her mother had a strict rule about cussing in the house that her brothers often had gotten in trouble for breaking, but Frankie had internalized her mother's words instead of rebelling against them.

The message was simple. If she wanted people to respect her, she'd have to respect herself first and view herself as someone who was worthy of respect. That being said, many people, including her brothers, thought that cussing earned them respect, so there was that.

Dagor laughed. "I've heard that song, but it took me a while to understand what was funny about it."

"Yeah, my brothers kept singing it and earning slaps over the back of their heads from our mother. She doesn't allow language like that in the house."

Dagor's expression turned serious. "I would like to meet your family one day. Do you think it's possible?"

Her breath caught in her throat. "Why not?"

He waved a hand over his face. "This might be difficult to explain."

Frankie cupped his clean-shaven face. "You could grow a beard. It can hide your perfection. Or we can just tell my parents and my brothers that you are the son of a famous model and a movie star, whose names need to stay confidential because you were their love child."

He looked at her with such intensity in his blue eyes that she was taken aback. "What's wrong?"

"If you are a Dormant, so are your brothers, your mother, your aunts and uncles on your mother's side, and all of their children. The immortality genes pass from a mother to her children. You might have an entire tribe to bring to the clan."

"Yeah, I know. It had occurred to me." She swallowed. "It's amazing and terrifying at the same time. How the heck am I going to explain this to my family? And what about my father? He's probably not a Dormant."

His eyes softened. "First, you need to transition, and then we will worry about the best way to do this."

"Yeah, that's what I told myself when the thought crossed my mind. There is no point in worrying about something that might not be relevant if it turns out that I'm not a Dormant."

He lifted her hand to his lips. "I have faith in the Fates. You will transition."

57

NEGAL

As Dagor and Frankie left the table to go dancing, Negal scanned the neighboring tables for available ladies he could ask to dance.

He was a hot commodity on this cruise, with so many lovely females vying for his attention that he was having a hard time choosing between them.

When he caught Karen looking at him, though, he knew it wasn't because she was interested. The moment their eyes met, she smiled nervously and averted her gaze.

Her unease was understandable, given what her mate had asked him to do. Come to think of it, he should establish a rapport with her before they proceeded with their plan for tomorrow night.

Pushing to his feet, Negal walked over to the table and flashed a friendly smile at Gilbert before turning his attention to Karen. "May I have this dance?" he asked, offering her his hand.

Karen hesitated, her eyes flickering towards Gilbert. The silent exchange between them was brief, and when Gilbert gave a subtle nod, Karen smiled, placed her hand in Negal's, and stood up.

"I thought we should get to know each other a little," he said.

She cast him a puzzled look. "I'm sorry. What did you say? I can't hear anything over this loud music."

He'd forgotten that her human hearing was limited compared to all the immortals on the dance floor, but if he spoke any louder, everyone there would be a party to their very private conversation.

Instead of answering, he gave her hand a gentle squeeze and steered her toward the glass doors leading to the balcony. "On second thought, I could use some fresh air. It's gotten stuffy in here." He paused with his hand on the door handle. "It's quieter out there."

Karen glanced back at Gilbert, seeking his approval, and upon receiving an affirming nod, she smiled up at Negal. "I would love some fresh air, too."

As they slipped out onto the balcony, the cool night air was indeed a relief from the stuffiness of the crowded dining hall.

Leaning against the railing, Negal wasn't sure what to do with his hands to seem as unintimidating as possible. If he crossed his arms over his chest, he might look threatening, but if he put his hands in his pockets, he would give her the impression that it was not a big deal for him.

It wasn't, but this was a delicate situation, and it was a big deal to her. Her life was on the line.

Suddenly, it occurred to him that he could improve her chances of success by giving her a small blood transfusion.

Anyway, he planned to thrall her and Gilbert to ignore his presence, so if he added a blood injection during the bite, neither of them would be any the wiser.

He spread his arms behind him and gripped the railing. "It occurred to me that we haven't spoken about what's coming. I only talked with your mate, and I noticed that you were nervous."

She chuckled. "Am I so easy to read?"

"Perhaps not usually, but tonight you were obvious, which is understandable. Your mate approached me and asked for my assistance, and I agreed. But then it occurred to me that I didn't check with you whether you are okay with this. He should have brought you along."

Karen let out a breath. "Frankly, it was I who asked Gilbert to talk to you. I'm very grateful to you for agreeing to do it." She chuckled nervously again. "I bet this is not going to be fun for you."

"It's not a hardship either. In fact, I feel honored to be asked to assist in your induction. "

Her expression softened. "That's very nice of you. You're a good guy, I mean god."

He laughed. "Guy is fine. It's a general term I'm comfortable with." Negal glanced at the starry sky and pondered the timing of their plan. "Perhaps we should move our arrangement to tonight." He shifted his eyes to her. "We thought that the mission would happen today, which was why we settled on tomorrow, but now that the mission has been moved, the reverse is true. Besides, the wait time will just intensify your anxiety."

Karen's eyes widened. "I think tomorrow would be better. I need more time to prepare. I'm not quite ready yet."

Negal smiled. "Sometimes it's best to just pull the Band-Aid off, as you humans like to say. We don't know how tomorrow's mission will go. It might delay us another day."

"Oh boy." Karen moved to lean against the railing next to him. "No pressure." A wry smile played on her lips. "It's a good thing that I'm a female. Otherwise, I would have suffered from performance anxiety and failed at the task."

Her attempt at humor made him laugh. He appreciated her effort to lighten the mood. "I can thrall you to relax and basically ignore my presence for the rest of the night starting now. You won't even be aware of me being there."

Karen turned to face him. "That might work. If I don't have to be consciously aware of... well, the process, it might be easier to go through with it."

Pleased with her easy acquiescence, Negal nodded. "I promise to make sure it's a seamless experience for you."

Karen took a deep breath. "Okay, tonight it is."

As the balcony doors opened and Gilbert stepped out, Negal wasn't surprised. He'd wondered how long the guy would hold off before jealousy and concern for his mate would prompt him to join them.

He briefly entertained the thought of using his thrall to ease Gilbert's mind because Karen's stress was probably being amplified by his unwarranted jealousy.

"I hope I'm not interrupting." Gilbert's eyes shifted from Karen to Negal.

"You're not," Negal assured him. "We were discussing moving our plans to tonight instead of tomorrow because of the change in scheduling for the mission."

As Karen stepped closer to Gilbert and took his hand, her gesture seemed to calm him somewhat, but the underlying tension was still palpable. "Negal made a good point about my anxiety building with every passing hour. He said that it's better to just rip the Band-Aid off and be done with it."

Gilbert hesitated for a brief moment before nodding. "I only want what's best for you, and if you want to do it tonight, that's fine with me."

"We'll need to ask Kaia to take the kids to her and William's cabin for the night," Karen said with a slight tremble in her voice.

Negal contemplated reaching into her head and calming her nerves, but he then remembered that human minds were fragile, and he should keep the thralling to a minimum. "Let me know when you're ready." He pushed away from the railing. "I'm going to ask one of those lovely ladies to dance, but I'll be immediately at your disposal whenever you call for me."

"Thank you." Karen offered him a tight smile. "I greatly appreciate your help."

58

KAREN

As they returned to the dining hall, the loud music hit Karen like a physical wall, making any attempts at conversation difficult.

Talking with Negal outside had been surprisingly calming and reassuring, in part because he was so nice and considerate but mainly because he wasn't even slightly attracted to her. His willingness to contribute his venom to her transition was purely altruistic, and he had absolutely no interest in her.

Karen sighed.

Getting old and becoming invisible to young men and gods didn't feel good. It wasn't that she was interested in anyone other than Gilbert, but feeling desirable was a big part of her identity as a woman, and lately, she'd been losing that part of herself.

It was good that she was about to transition and regain her youthful attractiveness.

As Negal walked over to one of the tables and asked an immortal female to dance, Karen sat down and scanned the tables for Kaia and William, finding them on the dance floor.

It was amusing to watch their mismatched dancing moves, with Kaia waving her arms over her head as if she was in a rock concert, and William swaying in place like a scarecrow in the wind.

Following her gaze, Gilbert saw them, too. "I'll go talk to Kaia."

Karen caught his arm as he started to get up. "Let them have fun. I'll go to the cabin and tell Cheryl to move the kids to Kaia and William's cabin. I'm sure they won't mind, given the reason for the sleepover. Wait until they sit back down and just let them know what's going on. I want them to enjoy themselves for as long as they wish, and Cheryl and the kids will probably be asleep by the time they get back."

Gilbert let out a breath. "Do you want to get something to eat? The line at the buffet is not long."

She put a hand over her belly. "I don't think I could take a single bite, but you go ahead. I'll be waiting in our cabin."

"Are you sure?"

"Yeah." She patted his arm. "I need to organize the kids, tidy up a bit, and then take a few moments to myself." She gave him a peck on the cheek, noting how hard he was clenching his jaw. "Relax. It's going to be okay. Negal finds me about as attractive as this chair, so you don't need to be jealous."

"That's absurd." Gilbert looked at her with incredulity in his eyes. "Any healthy heterosexual male would find you attractive."

"Thank you." She smiled. "That's sweet of you to say, but I'm no spring chicken, and I'm a mother of five children." She gave him a slight push. "Go, get something to eat. You'll need your energy tonight."

As he finally did as she asked, Karen let out a breath and refilled her glass with white wine.

It was a scary step, but she'd been preparing for it for weeks.

She had already spoken to Bridget, ensuring that the clinic was adequately equipped to monitor her in case it was needed.

Bridget and the nurses were busy tending to the victims who needed more medical attention than anyone had anticipated, and Karen didn't wish to add to their burden, but it was what it was.

Bridget understood and approved.

Glancing around at the joyous celebrations, Karen felt a pang of regret at the thought of missing some of the weddings. Each ceremony was a beautiful testament to love and commitment, something she had always cherished, but her successful transition took precedence.

Downing the glass of liquid courage, Karen pushed to her feet and looked at her mate, who stood in line at the buffet. She smiled and waved and then turned around and walked toward the exit doors.

Negal intercepted her just as she was about to exit the hall. "Is everything alright?"

"Yes." She gave him a reassuring smile. "I'm going up to our cabin to help my daughter move the little ones to Kaia and William's room. Gilbert is at the buffet," she added.

"I'll join him for a meal and come up with him when he's ready." Negal hesitated before adding. "Do you need me to thrall you now to make it easier for you?"

She shook her head. "Let's wait until everything is in place. The twins might be fussy and want their mommy, and then the whole thing would have to be postponed until tomorrow anyway. I don't want to have to be thralled more than necessary." She lifted her hand to her temple. "There is no point in living forever if this is not working right."

"You are a smart woman, Karen." He made a move as if to kiss her cheek but then grimaced and leaned away. "This is going to be more difficult than I thought."

She frowned. "Why?"

"Don't take it the wrong way, but your scent is," he rubbed a hand over the back of his neck, "how should I say it, unpleasant to me."

Karen's eyes widened, and her first instinct was to smell her armpits, but then she remembered what Casandra had told her about fated mates getting addicted to each other and their scent changing to deter other immortals from trying to seduce them.

That shouldn't be happening to her, though. She was still human, and she hadn't even been injected with anyone's venom. She'd never been bitten, and the reality of it happening tonight made her shiver, and not in a good way.

"What do you smell?" she asked.

"Gilbert." He grimaced. "His scent is all over you."

"Oh, I see. Will you be able to overcome it when the time comes?"

He nodded. "I won't breathe through my nose until I have my fangs in your neck."

Another shiver rocked Karen's body. "Can you please make it so I won't feel the bite?"

His eyes softened. "Are you scared?"

"A little."

"It only hurts for a second, and then there is bliss. But I'll make sure to muffle the pain with my thrall."

"Thank you."

59

GILBERT

When the loud music was replaced with a pleasant melody to complement dinner, Kaia and William joined the line at the buffet, and Gilbert took the opportunity to tap Kaia's shoulder.

"I need a word with you," he murmured.

"What's up?" She followed him to a quiet spot next to the kitchen entrance.

"There's been a change of plan. Instead of it happening tomorrow, it's happening tonight." He didn't have to spell it out. Kaia knew what he was talking about. "Karen went up to our cabin to help Cheryl move the little ones to yours. I hope it's okay."

"Of course." Kaia cast a glance at William. "But what's the rush? Even if Negal hooks up with Frankie's friend, that doesn't make them fated mates, and he can still offer his venom services. I don't know why Mom freaked out like that."

Gilbert took a deep breath. "Perhaps she had a gut feeling about it. In any case, I'm glad that it's finally happening, and Negal is perfect for the job. He's kind, polite, and your mother believes that he doesn't find her attractive, which I think is bullshit, but I'm glad she thinks that. It will make everything easier. Besides, after the cruise, Negal is leaving with Aru and Dagor, and it could be months before he's back."

It was beyond awkward to talk to the girl he had raised as his daughter about his sexual relationship with her mother, but it was unavoidable, given that he needed her help.

Kaia nodded. "That's why I didn't say anything. If she's ready, go for it. I wish you both the best of luck."

Gilbert placed a hand on her shoulder. "Thanks, Kaia. And thank William for us, too."

"I will." She kissed his cheek and returned to her spot next to William in the line for the buffet.

Scanning for Negal amidst the sea of guests, Gilbert spotted him at the bar, talking to Aru.

"Negal," Gilbert motioned for him to step aside. "I need a word with you."

The god said something to his team leader and walked toward Gilbert with a drink in hand. "How are you holding up?" he asked.

Surprisingly, Gilbert felt much calmer than he'd expected to feel under the circumstances, and he wondered whether Negal had already thralled him without telling him.

"I'm doing well. Thanks for asking." He looked around, making sure that no one was paying attention to them. "I'm heading upstairs. I'll give you a call once everything is set."

Negal clapped Gilbert on the back. "Don't start anything before I get there. I need to thrall you both before you two get busy."

"Of course. Is there anything I need to prepare for you in the other room? Something to get you going?"

The only thing he could offer was a lingerie catalog, so he hoped the god would say that he didn't need anything or that he would take care of it himself.

Negal laughed. "I might not look it, but the Fates blessed me with a vivid imagination. I don't need external stimuli."

"That's good." Gilbert gave him a tight smile. "How about a bottle of wine or perhaps Snake Venom? You know, the beer the immortals love so much."

"I'll be fine." Negal squeezed his shoulder. "Go to your mate and offer her some wine to soothe her nerves."

"Thanks, Negal. You're a good guy."

The god chuckled. "Karen said the same thing. I guess that's what happens when you are mated for as long as the two of you have been. You form the same opinions about people and use the same phrases."

Gilbert wasn't sure whether it was meant as a compliment, but he took it as such.

"That's what a good partnership is like. I wish for you to get as lucky as I did with finding a great partner. Life is blessed when you have someone wonderful by your side. Someone you are happy to wake up next to each morning and return to at the end of each day."

The god sighed. "I have given up hope of ever finding that someone special. I'm not as young as my teammates, and I've been all over the galaxy before getting assigned to patrol this sector. If I haven't found her by now, I never will." He affected a nonchalant smile. "Not that I made a big effort to look for her. It either happens or it doesn't. I'm quite satisfied with my bachelor status and having the freedom to sample a variety of lovelies wherever I'm stationed."

60

KAREN

On the way to the cabin, Karen's mind raced with the thoughts of what she was about to do. She was no longer worried about the awkwardness of having Negal bite her while she was having sex with Gilbert.

If she wasn't aware of it while it happened, she could live with the fact that it had afterward. With that settled in her mind, the worry of survival returned.

If it was only about her, she wouldn't have thought twice about it, but she had five children, and only one of them was an adult with a mate of her own. The other four needed their mother, and losing her would devastate them in ways that she was all too familiar with.

After losing Kaia and Cheryl's father, Karen had functioned on autopilot because she had two little daughters to take care of, and her girls had been suffering in ways that they couldn't even fully express at such a young age. Things had gotten a little easier with time, but that wound had never really mended, not even after meeting Gilbert and falling in love with him.

Immortality wasn't going to cure it either. If she survived, she would carry the pain of loss for eternity.

With a sigh, Karen entered the code to the cabin and opened the door.

As she'd expected, Cheryl was in front of the television with the twins sleeping in the crib and Idina sprawled on the couch, clutching her blanket in one hand and her favorite doll in the other.

"You're back early," Cheryl said without shifting her gaze away from the television. "What happened? Someone spill wine on your dress?"

Instinctively, Karen looked down to examine her gown and then shook her head. "No, I came to tell you that you and the little ones are spending the night at Kaia's and to help you move them. Gilbert invited a couple of friends over after the party."

She hated lying to her daughter, but Cheryl was too young for Karen to share the truth about tonight with.

Kaia had promised not to tell her younger sister anything about the plan, and Karen hoped she'd kept her promise, but given the knowing look in Cheryl's eyes, she knew exactly what was about to transpire.

"Are Kaia and William back in their cabin?"

"No, but they know you'll be there when they are done partying for the night."

Cheryl yawned. "I watched the ceremony on television. It was hilarious before it became boring, so I switched to something else."

They had taken all the kids to the first wedding, but the twins had been fussy, and Idina turned into a terror, so Gilbert had offered Cheryl five hundred dollars for each night she stayed to babysit even though he could have hired one of the human staff to watch over the kids for much less than that.

Cheryl was more than happy to babysit for that outrageous amount and watch the weddings on the ship's closed-circuit broadcast.

"Are they still broadcasting?" Karen took off her high-heeled shoes.

"Yeah. But it's boring. People eating and dancing."

"That's what weddings are all about."

"Nah, they are about the ceremony and the vows. I think it's cool that the Clan Mother makes every ceremony unique." Cheryl yawned. "So, how are we going to carry the little ones over to Kaia's cabin? Do you want to put them in their strollers?"

"You can wheel the twins' crib, and I'll carry Idina."

Cheryl nodded. "First, help me pack a bag for them."

As they organized everything the kids would need tomorrow morning, Cheryl put the bag inside the crib and pushed it toward the door.

"Do you remember the code to Kaia's cabin?" Karen asked as she crouched next to Idina.

"Naturally." Cheryl opened the door. "The code is Kaia's birthday. I'll leave the door open for you."

"Thanks."

As Karen scooped Idina into her arms, she opened a pair of sleepy eyes. "Is everything okay, Mommy?"

Karen dipped her head and kissed Idina's warm cheek. "Everything's fine, sweetheart. You're going for a sleepover in Kaia's cabin, and tomorrow morning, you'll have fun with your big sister."

"Yay." Idina yawned. "Will you come to have fun with us, Mommy?"

"I will, sweetie." Karen carried her to the next cabin over and walked straight to the bedroom where Cheryl had already prepared the bed.

Cheryl covered her little sister with a blanket and kissed her forehead. "She's so adorable when she's asleep. I wish she was that cute when she's awake." She smiled at Karen. "Can you stay for a few minutes so I can get my things?"

"Of course."

As she waited for Cheryl to return, Karen looked at the sleeping faces of her children and wondered for the umpteenth time whether she was doing the right thing. Despite giving her transition the best possible tools for success, there was still a small chance that her gamble wouldn't pay off, and she might leave her children motherless.

On the other hand, nothing in life was guaranteed, especially for a mortal, and Karen would rather grab destiny by the horns and drive it to where she wanted it to go rather than be jostled through life by its whims.

"*Qué será, será.*"

61

GILBERT

Gilbert tried not to dwell on what was about to transpire as he made his way to the cabin.

It was better that way.

He couldn't afford to be overwhelmed by irrational jealousy or fear for Karen's life.

As he opened the door, he was greeted by the familiar aftermath of his kids' chaos. There were toys strewn about, a few scattered pieces of clothing, and half-empty sippy cups on the coffee table.

"Given how much I'm paying Cheryl to babysit, she could've at least cleaned up," he murmured as he started picking up stuff off the floor.

"She would have if I didn't practically shove her out the door." Karen came out of the bedroom with a large bag and started picking up things on the other side of the room. "I think she knows what's going on."

He arched a brow. "Do you think Kaia told her?"

Karen shrugged. "Cheryl is just too smart for her own good. I bet she had it figured out, but thankfully, she had enough tact not to say anything and pretended to believe my story about inviting friends over after the wedding."

"It's the truth, just not the whole truth." He threw the items he'd collected into the bag and took it from her. "How are you holding up? Are you okay?"

"Yeah." She let out a breath. "*Qué será, será.*"

"That's the spirit." He pulled her into his arms and kissed her forehead. "Negal suggested that I pour you a glass of wine to soothe your nerves."

She chuckled. "That's not a bad idea. You know what I like."

Karen wasn't a big drinker. She had the occasional glass of wine, and when she was in a mood to celebrate, she liked a Moscow Mule, with just a tiny bit of vodka and a lot of ginger beer.

"I do, but this time, I'm going to pour double the vodka in your Mule. You need it to take the edge off."

She smiled up at him. "I'm not going to argue."

When he was done mixing the drink for her, he added ice cubes and handed it to her. "Here you go."

"Aren't you going to make one for yourself?"

He shook his head. "I'm doing mental gymnastics to not let myself get overwhelmed with unwanted feelings, and I need to stay sharp until Negal gets here and takes us both out of our misery. It would be nice to forget that he's about to intrude on our intimacy."

"He can't intrude if he's invited." Karen took a long sip of her drink and sighed. "This is so good. Thank you."

"You're welcome. I mixed it with love."

"I know you did." Karen reached for his cheek and cupped it. "So, how are we going to do this? I mean technically."

"Well, I think you should be on top." He swallowed. "Wearing a dress. I don't want him to see you naked even if you do think that he's not attracted to you."

"He's not." Karen frowned. "He said that my scent is unpleasant to him because I smell of you, but you haven't bitten me yet, so I don't know how that's possible. From what I was told, it's the repeated venom injections that affect the body odor."

"That's both reassuring and worrisome." He puffed out his chest. "The ape in me is very happy that I marked you with my scent, but now I'm worried that Negal won't be able to bite you because he'll be repulsed by the smell."

Karen's cheeks turned a deep shade of red. "He said he would hold his breath and do it quickly." She grimaced. "I'm so glad that I'm not the male in this relationship, or I wouldn't be able to get it up." She eyed him from under lowered lashes. "Will you?"

Gilbert threw his head back and laughed. "Do you have to ask? Since my transition, I have had the libido of an eighteen-year-old. My problem is getting it to go down, not up."

That was true, and she felt guilty for not being able to keep up with him. It was just one more reason to stop pussyfooting around and just do it. "Let's grab a shower and scrub really well. Hopefully, the aroma of the soap and generous spraying of perfume will overpower the scents Negal finds objectionable."

Gilbert winced. "In that case, we should shower separately. Otherwise, I won't be able to keep my hands off you, and we will have to get another shower. I don't think it's fair to Negal to keep him waiting."

"Right." She stretched on her toes and kissed him lightly on the lips. "See you in ten minutes."

He nodded. "I'll text Negal and tell him to be here in fifteen."

After taking a quick shower in Cheryl's bedroom, Gilbert put on a pair of nylon pants and a T-shirt. He straightened the room and covered the bed with the decorative cover that Cheryl had taken off. Negal would hopefully use the armchair in the corner, but just in case he wanted to use the bed, Gilbert planned on changing the bedding tomorrow.

When Karen emerged from their bedroom, her hair was wet, and she had a long nightgown on that would do well for what they had in mind but was too sexy, in Gilbert's opinion. It was made of satin, sleeveless, with only thin straps holding it up, and even though it wasn't form-fitting, it draped over Karen's body in a most enticing way.

"You look beautiful." He rubbed a hand over his jaw. "Too beautiful."

"Oh, stop it." She rolled her eyes and waved a dismissive hand, but he caught the small smile tugging on one corner of her lips.

As the doorbell rang, Gilbert cast another reassuring smile at Karen before opening the door.

"Hello, Negal. Thank you for doing this for us. Can I offer you a drink?"

"No, thank you. I've had enough for tonight." Negal walked in and smiled at Karen. "I'll start with you. Where would you like to do it?"

She looked confused for a moment, but when understanding dawned, she motioned to the couch. "You mean the thralling, right? I know what to expect."

As she sat down and Negal joined her, Gilbert sat across from them on an armchair.

"Here is what I'm going to do," Negal said. "I'm going to thrall you to relax and focus entirely on Gilbert. You will be dimly aware of my presence, but you will not be disturbed by it in any way. I'll be like a distant thought in your mind. Sound good?"

When Karen nodded, Negal looked into her eyes for a few moments, and when he was done, she pushed to her feet, cast Gilbert a seductive smile, and walked into their bedroom.

"I really need to learn how to do this," Gilbert murmured as he took her place on the couch.

"I'm going to do exactly the same to you," Negal said. "Ready?"

"One moment." Gilbert lifted his hand. "Before I forget that you are here, I wanted to ask if you would like to use the other bedroom or stay here in the living room."

"It doesn't make a difference to me. What's your preference?"

"The living room, if you don't mind. My children sleep in the other bedroom. I tidied it up, but I didn't have time to change the bedding."

"No need to go to all that trouble. This is going to be over very quickly."

"Thank you. You're making it all remarkably easy for us."

The god grinned. "I'm glad. Now, look into my eyes."

One moment, Gilbert was aware of looking into Negal's eyes, and the next, he was confused and didn't know where he was or what he was about to do. After shaking off the momentary fugue, he remembered Karen's seductive, come-hither smile. She had put on a sexy nightgown for him, and he couldn't wait to take it off her.

Something in the back of his mind reminded him that the nightgown had to stay on, but he couldn't remember why.

Oh, well. He could work with that.

Pushing to his feet, he turned toward the bedroom.

He found Karen sitting on the bed with her arms spread to the sides, her hands braced on the mattress, and her legs crossed under the long skirt of her nightgown.

"Hi, handsome," she greeted him with a throaty lilt in her tone. "I've been waiting for you."

As Gilbert's erection tented his nylon pants, Karen laughed and beckoned him forward. "I see that someone is eager to say hello."

62

NEGAL

Negal took the syringe he'd prepared ahead of time out of his pocket and put it on the coffee table. He didn't know how long his blood would remain viable after extraction, which meant that he had to do it at the last moment before biting Karen.

It wasn't going to be easy to do that when he was about to shoot his load, but he was determined to give the mother of five the best chance of survival he could.

Removing his tux jacket, he hung it on the back of a dining chair and sat on the couch in the living room. Next, he yanked the bowtie off and popped open several buttons of his shirt.

He leaned back and let his thoughts drift back to Anumati and the many goddesses he had bedded. Not all of them had stuck in his memory, but he remembered a select few who could get him excited just by thinking about them.

There had been overwhelming passion and vigor in those most memorable encounters, and yet he had never felt fully satisfied. He'd come close a few times with Evanitta, the one goddess whom he had hoped to mate, but even she had been distant. There had been no true intimacy between them, and their connection had been primarily physical.

If not for the great works of art in film and literature depicting fated love and the unbreakable bond between fated mates, Negal wouldn't have known that anything was missing. Perhaps he would have been satisfied with the physical pleasure and never missed the melding of the souls he'd witnessed so rarely among his acquaintances.

On Earth, though, his experiences had been different.

Earth had been a revelation to him, showing him facets of intimacy and relationships that were absent in his life back home.

Even though human women couldn't possibly match the physical perfection of goddesses or keep up with his stamina, they compensated by being livelier, for lack of a better term, or perhaps more playful and less stifling.

There was something to be said for shorter lifespans.

Negal had memorized the names of those who had left a strong impression on him, and he rifled through the archives in his mind for an exciting memory to get him aroused and ready to deliver the bite.

There was Emily, a petite brunette with a quick wit and infectious laughter. Sophia was a tall redhead who was a talented and passionate artist. Jasmine, with the most incredible ass and smiling eyes, was an ambitious businesswoman. Lina, a voluptuous, naughty nurse with a great laugh.

Each of these women had left an impression on him and helped him understand what it meant to be human. Their uniqueness and individual strengths and vulnerabilities had given him a richer experience than he had ever known back on Anumati.

He finally settled on Rachel as an inspiration for his solo pleasure session. The biologist was perhaps the least beautiful of the women he had been with, but she'd captivated him with her exquisite mind and curiosity about the universe that he'd been happy to indulge, pretending to ruminate when he had actually been describing real phenomena.

Rachel was tall, thin, and modestly endowed, but she had a devious mind. Just thinking of her made him harder in an instant.

With a groan, Negal reached into his pants and gripped his swollen erection.

At first, he stroked it leisurely, his hand moving up and down without applying much pressure. It was like saying hello, a gentle communion before even the first kiss, just to let things warm up a little.

The image of Rachel sitting on the counter in her kitchen, her shirt bunched up over her small breasts, her nipples dark and stiff from the treatment he'd given them only moments ago, her legs spread wide, and her fingers threaded in his hair as he licked and sucked.

So wanton, so sexy.

The sound of her moans reverberating in his head, he cranked things up with his hand, his grip tightening as he moved up, squeezed the head, and then went down in a corkscrew motion.

After Rachel had orgasmed all over his tongue, he'd gripped her ass and impaled her on his shaft in one powerful thrust, and she'd come again with a scream that had reverberated through the small kitchen of her Lisbon apartment.

Given the sounds coming from the bedroom, things were getting heated in there, and as he swiped his tongue over his fangs, Negal tasted venom.

He was ready, in more ways than one, and when he heard Karen scream her orgasm, his own was triggered, barreling up his shaft with a nearly unstoppable force, but he couldn't let it happen—not until he fulfilled his task.

Squeezing the top off with a vice-like grip, he bit down on his lower lip, nearly slicing through it, and the pain was enough to halt the eruption.

Blood dripping down his white shirt, he hiked his pants up, stuffed his aching shaft behind the zipper, and reached for the syringe.

Gritting his teeth, he tore the package open and made a fist before sticking the needle into his vein.

The vial filled so quickly that he had to yank the needle out, and then he was spraying blood and had to lick the puncture wound closed.

Syringe in hand, he rushed toward the bedroom and the woman he was about to help induce into immortality.

63

GILBERT

As the aftershocks of Karen's climax subsided, she collapsed on top of Gilbert's chest. He wrapped his arms around her, holding her tightly while his heart still raced from his own orgasm.

"I love you," he whispered into her neck.

Panting, she didn't answer, and he felt a surge of anxious anticipation that felt familiar and justified, but when he tried to think of what he was waiting for, the thought slipped away.

There was a surreal, dream-like quality to the postcoital bliss, and as Negal quietly entered, Gilbert's mind couldn't process his presence. The god felt distant, like a shadow at the edge of Gilbert's consciousness.

As the specter's hand reached out, cradling Karen's head, Gilbert tensed, sensing that something monumental was about to happen. But it felt like part of a dream, and a veil separated the ghost of the god from reality.

Then, the ghost of Negal tilted Karen's head to the side, exposing the delicate skin of her neck and licking the spot.

Gilbert felt a surge of fear and possessiveness gripping him. Everything inside of him rebelled against what was coming, but he was paralyzed, held by invisible chains that were nonetheless unbreakable.

The god hissed, flashing a pair of monstrous fangs, and struck, piercing Karen's skin.

Gilbert expected her to scream in pain, but she only groaned softly. And then she was climaxing again while the fangs were still embedded in her neck.

He felt like his brain was about to explode through his scalp because he needed to stop what was happening but couldn't move.

It seemed like forever before the god retracted his fangs, licked the spot clean, and then was gone between one blink of Gilbert's eyes and the next.

Karen was still climaxing, her sheath gripping his rapidly hardening shaft, and soon, he was coming again.

When both their bodies stopped trembling, Gilbert held her tightly to his chest.

Suddenly, his thoughts cleared, and he knew precisely what had happened. Negal had thralled him and Karen, so they hadn't been fully aware of anything outside the bubble encompassing the two of them.

It was done. Negal had provided the venom necessary for Karen's transition.

Paralyzing panic flooded Gilbert, a choking sensation and nausea that he hadn't felt since he'd become immortal.

Karen was his world, the center of his universe, and the thought of anything happening to her was unbearable. If she didn't make it, he would find a way to end his own life. But he couldn't. They had three little ones to raise, and Cheryl was still a young girl. He would have to wait for their children to be fully grown and suffer through existing without Karen until they had families of their own and were well settled in their lives.

It was a morbid thought that he had to push to the back of his mind and put a blockade in front of it. For Karen's sake and the sake of their children, he had to remain optimistic.

A god's venom activating Karen's godly genes increased her chances of survival dramatically, and Gilbert was beyond grateful to Negal.

Still, the jealous monster living inside his head had him checking that Karen's nightgown was still on, draped over them both and hiding where they were still connected.

"Mine," he whispered against her neck, and tightened his hold on her. "Only mine."

Karen didn't answer, probably because she was floating on the euphoric cloud that the god's venom induced. Gilbert hoped she was enjoying the trip, but more than that, he hoped that everything would turn out well, Karen would successfully transition, and they would have many years ahead of them to explore a future filled with endless possibilities.

For now, though, he focused on the fragile woman in his arms.

Listening to her slow and steady breathing, feeling the warmth of her body against his, he beseeched the Fates to keep his mate safe.

64

DAGOR

"This was fun." Frankie removed her shoes as soon as they entered the elevator. "I love dancing, but my feet are killing me."

Suddenly, she was so tiny next to Dagor, barely reaching the top of his chest, and his protective instincts were triggered even though it didn't make any sense. The high-heeled shoes didn't make Frankie stronger or more resilient, although he had to admit that dancing for over two hours without taking a break was impressive for a human. It had been tiring even for him.

Frankie was probably exhausted.

"You should have taken the shoes off and danced barefoot."

Casting him a sultry smile, she stretched on her toes and kissed his cheek. "I knew you would bite me later and make my little footsies all better," she whispered.

The guy standing behind them chuckled, and the woman next to Dagor grinned.

If they were alone in the elevator, he would have lifted her into his arms and started on the fun, but there were four other people riding up with them, and he wasn't about to give them a show.

Clearing his throat, he leaned down and offered quietly, "How about a foot massage?"

"Ooh, that would be wonderful."

As they exited on Frankie's deck, two of the females who had been riding with them exited too, and he had to wait until they entered their cabin to lift Frankie and kiss her like he'd wanted from the moment she'd made the comment about his bite.

He carried her to the bedroom and set her down on the bed. "Do you need help peeling this dress off?"

She turned and offered him her back. "You can get the zipper for me, but before you get any ideas, I need to shower first. I'm sweaty, and I need to wash all the makeup off before getting in bed."

"How about a relaxing bath?" he suggested as he pulled the zipper down. "I can scrub your back."

"That would be lovely."

He leaned down and kissed her forehead. "I'll start the bath for you."

"You are spoiling me, Dagor, and I love it." She let the dress fall to her waist, revealing the lacy bra underneath that was the same red color as the dress.

Swallowing, Dagor rushed into the bathroom before he could be tempted to do away with the pretty bra and deprive Frankie of the bath she wanted.

As the tub filled with warm water, his thoughts wandered to her transition. He knew it was still too early to start worrying about it working, but he couldn't help it.

They didn't have a lot of time, and it was crucial that she transition before the end of the cruise. If she didn't, she might give up.

What if he could expedite the process with another transfusion?

The other time hadn't done what Kian had been afraid it would do, but perhaps when combined with his venom and his seed, the addition of the blood transfusion would do the trick?

Then again, what if giving her more of his blood would be detrimental to her health?

He needed to consult Aru.

Standing by the bathroom door, Dagor watched the steam rise from the water as the idea of accelerating Frankie's transition solidified in his mind. There was no harm in doing that, and the only downside was that if it didn't work, they would both be devastated.

"Trust in the Fates," he murmured.

Turning back to Frankie, he saw her seated on the edge of the bed, wearing only her bra and panties and rubbing her feet. She looked tired but happy, and he dreaded spoiling her mood by voicing his concerns.

Perhaps it would be better not to tell her his plan yet and let her enjoy the aftermath of the party while soaking in the tub.

"Your bath awaits, my lady." He executed a deep bow. "Should I carry you?"

She smiled at him with love shining in her eyes. "Not tonight, my love. I want to take off my makeup before I get into the water, and it will take a while."

He didn't know why she needed to wash her face before getting in the tub, but he wasn't going to question her beauty routine. Apparently, there was much more to it than just applying color to her cheeks and painting her eyelashes black.

"Can I help?"

"A girl needs to keep a few secrets." She batted her eyelashes, which he'd just noticed were thicker than normal.

He lifted his hands in the sign for peace. "I'll leave you to it, then, and get out of the tux."

She pushed to her tiny feet, stretched on her toes and kissed his cheek. "Give me fifteen minutes to do my nightly routine, and then you can come in if you want."

He kissed the tip of her nose. "Take your time and soak those poor feet of yours."

When she closed the door behind her, he walked into the living room and wrote a text to Aru.

Is it safe to give Frankie another transfusion to expedite her transition?

Aru's response came a moment later. *Probably, but make sure it's a small quantity.*

'Probably' was not as good as a yes, but it was better than a no.

Dagor needed a syringe, and he knew where to get it.

After changing into a pair of jeans and a T-shirt, he made his way to the clinic.

The ship was quiet, with most of its occupants either still in the dining hall enjoying coffee and desserts or back in their cabins. Dagor didn't want to bump into anyone and have to explain where he was going and why, so he took the stairs instead of the elevator.

Reaching the clinic deck, he continued to the storage room and slipped inside. The cabinet where he had found the syringes before was locked, but he knew now where the nurses kept the key.

Securing the syringe, he closed the cabinet and turned to leave, but stopped to fill his pockets with a few toiletries just in case anyone wondered what he'd been doing sneaking into the storage room in the middle of the night.

65

FRANKIE

In the bathwater's soothing warmth, Frankie let her mind drift, and her body relax, the tension slowly ebbing. She had half-expected Dagor to join her, but as the minutes ticked by and the bathroom door remained closed, she wondered what he was doing.

She'd needed a few minutes to take off her false lashes and wipe off the layers of makeup, but once that had been done, she wouldn't have minded his offer to massage her feet and scrub her back.

A flicker of concern crossed her mind. After the lecture she'd given him about always letting her know where he was, he wouldn't just leave without saying anything.

As more time passed, her concern deepened into worry. Maybe something had happened? She knew the ship was safe, but Dagor's sudden disappearance was troubling. He would have told her if something was going on and he had to go. He wouldn't just leave her in the bathtub.

Her mind began to race with possibilities. Was there an emergency? Had something gone wrong with the plan regarding the Doomers? Maybe the teams assigned to rescuing Luis had been called to depart immediately?

The thought sent a chill down her spine.

Nah, she was probably freaking out for nothing. He might be in the living room watching television or listening to music. If she had her phone with her, she would have called him, but she'd left it in her purse, which was on the bed, next to her discarded dress that she'd forgotten to hang back in the closet.

With a deep sigh Frankie leaned back in the tub, trying to calm her racing thoughts, but her eyes kept darting to the bathroom door, hoping to see it open and Dagor walk in.

When it finally happened, Frankie's head snapped up, and her heart skipped a beat. "What took you so long? I was worried about you."

He arched a brow. "You asked for fifteen minutes, and that's precisely how long I was gone."

She pouted. "It felt like longer. Now get undressed and join me in the tub. I'm taking you up on your offer to scrub my back."

Smiling, he sat on the edge of the tub. "You didn't ask me where I was."

She frowned. "I didn't even know that you left."

"So why were you worried?"

She let out an exasperated breath. "Never mind that. Where did you go?"

"I went down to the clinic to get another syringe."

Her gut twisted into a knot. "Why?"

"I think that another transfusion could help expedite your transition." He pulled out a couple of small, wrapped soaps from his pocket and then the syringe. "Only if you are comfortable with it, of course. It's up to you."

Frankie hadn't considered that before, but now that he was offering, it made sense to her, and she wasn't about to refuse the offer unless there were risks she wasn't aware of.

"Are you sure it's safe to give me another transfusion?"

"I asked Aru, and he said that it probably is, which means that he's not sure. But then he's not a doctor."

Chewing on her bottom lip, Frankie nodded. "There is probably nothing left in my system from your first transfusion, so it's probably safe to do another one. I don't think it can do any harm, and the worst that can happen is that it won't do anything." She smiled nervously. "But my feet will not ache tomorrow for sure."

Dagor regarded her for a moment before tearing the packaging open and pulling out the syringe. "One last chance. Yes or no?"

"Yes."

She couldn't suppress a small wince when the needle pierced his skin. It was one thing to know intellectually that Dagor was capable of healing quickly and quite another to watch the needle sink into his vein without the usual preparations like an elastic band to swell the vein. She hoped that this deviation from what she knew as standard procedure wouldn't cause any complications.

As he drew a small quantity of his blood, she wondered what it would look like under a microscope. Would there be millions of nanobots floating in it, tiny genetic machines that cured and repaired and facilitated transition in carriers of the godly genes?

She offered him her arm, trying to keep still, but her heart was pounding in her chest, and she felt queasy. When the needle pierced her skin at the spot where she previously had the IV, she felt a slight sting, but it was nothing compared to the emotional weight of the moment. She watched as Dagor gently pressed the plunger, his eyes locked on her face, searching her eyes for signs of discomfort or distress.

The sensation was odd, a slight warmth spreading from the injection site, but nothing more dramatic than that.

Dagor disposed of the syringe by putting it back into its torn wrapping and tossing it into the trash container under the sink.

"You'll need to dispose of it better than that," she said. "If anyone comes to clean the cabin, they'll see the bloodied syringe and might report it."

"You're right." He pulled his T-shirt over his head and tossed it on the counter. "I'll take care of it tomorrow."

Her concerns flew out the window as her eyes roamed over the perfection of his body. "Take your pants off and get in the tub with me." She scooted to the side. "I need to thank you for what you just did for me." She gave him a sultry smile.

Dagor pushed his pants down, revealing how excited he was about her offer of gratitude even before finding out what she had in mind.

"I did it for me as much as I did it for you." He stepped into the tub and got behind her back. "I want you with me forever."

66

DAGOR

Morning light filtered through the parted curtains, casting a soft glow across the bed and the woman sleeping peacefully beside Dagor.

He'd been awake for a while, watching Frankie. Most of the time she seemed peaceful, with a faint smile on her lips, but from time to time a frown furrowed her forehead, and she stirred in her sleep.

Was she having bad dreams?

"Good morning," she murmured, her eyes fluttering open as she turned to face him. "What time is it?"

"It's still early." He leaned to plant a soft kiss on her lips. ""How are you feeling?"

"Good." Her smile widened. "In fact, I feel wonderful." She wound her arms around his neck and drew him closer. "You gave me a lot of yourself last night."

He chuckled. "Yeah, I did."

He'd given her his blood once, his venom twice, and his seed four times. If that wasn't enough to induce her transition, he didn't know what else he could do other than keep doing that every night until it happened.

"When do you need to leave? Do we have time to have breakfast together?"

He glanced at his watch. "I have a little over an hour."

"That's plenty of time." She stretched her arms over her head. "Let's eat in the cabin. I'm too stressed and worried to make small talk with people in the dining room. I want you all to myself."

He'd had other ideas about spending the morning, but Frankie seemed to need reassurances, and the best way to do it was to give her more information about the mission. The worst thing would be to leave her guessing.

"We both need to shower." He kissed the tip of her nose. "The rigorous activities of last night have left their mark."

"You go first." She yawned. "I want a few minutes longer in bed."

After a quick shower, he got dressed and started on the coffee. By the time it was brewed, Frankie emerged from the bedroom wearing a loose T-shirt and a pair of shorts that were almost indecent.

"I hope you don't intend on wearing that out of the cabin while I'm gone."

Smirking, she tilted her head. "Why? I'm much more covered in this than I am in my bikini. Are you telling me that you don't approve of me going swimming while you're away, either?"

Dagor had a feeling that he should tread carefully or find himself in trouble. "Of course, I don't mind you swimming in your skimpy bikini. It's just that those shorts are too sexy because they tickle the imagination, and I want you to wear them just for me."

"Good save." She sat down on the chair he pulled out for her. "But for future reference, the only types of comments I'm willing to accept in regard to my attire are how good I look in it."

"Noted." He poured them both coffee and handed her a cup. "You look very sexy in those shorts."

"Thank you. I appreciate the compliment."

"The bottoms of your ass cheeks peek from underneath the frayed hem, and all I can think about is nibbling on them. I bet the same thought will cross the mind of every unmated guy who sees you, and there aren't that many mated immortals on this ship."

She rolled her eyes. "Fine. I won't send you off to battle worrying about my ass being on display. I didn't plan on wearing them outside the cabin anyway." She lifted her chin. "This is my staying-inside lounging outfit. I like to dress more elegantly in company."

That was a relief for more reasons than one. The most important was that Frankie wouldn't be tempting all the other single males with her sweet bottom peeking from the too-short shorts, and the other one was that she felt comfortable enough with him to slouch.

Dagor pulled out a box of crackers from the cabinet and a tray of assorted cheeses from the fridge. "Is this good enough for breakfast?"

She shrugged. "If it's good enough for you, it's good enough for me. I'm not the one heading out to battle and needing good nutrition to fuel my body."

"That's not true." He put the items on the table and went back to get plates. "You are about to fight the most intense battle of your life. Your transition."

"Fates willing," She lifted both hands with fingers crossed. "Although after you gave me your blood, I'm not worried about me. I'm worried about you."

He put the plates on the table and sat down. "Maybe you will feel better once you know what the plan is."

Her eyes widened. "Are you allowed to tell me?"

"I don't see why not." He pulled out a bunch of crackers and put them on her plate. "The ship will get as close as it can to shore about two hundred nautical miles north of Acapulco. We will take one or two lifeboats to shore and then drive to the location. Turner has arranged for bulletproof vehicles to await us, along with surveillance drones. We will stop several miles before reaching the place where we engaged the cartel and send out drones to scout the area. We are taking every precaution to protect ourselves from being ambushed, which is most likely what they are planning."

She shook her head. "I didn't even think of the possibility of an ambush. Just shows you how little I know about these things."

If anything, his explanation seemed to make her even more anxious.

Dagor reached out with his hand, brushing a strand of hair from her face. "You have nothing to worry about. I'm a god, and I can take hold of the minds of humans and immortals." He didn't add that he couldn't do that to a large group of people.

If they were all human, he and Negal together might have been able to do it, but the twelve immortals complicated things.

Her chin wobbled. "You're not impervious to bullets."

"I took two dozen bullets in my back, and it was nothing. It wasn't pleasant, but I was in no real danger. I possess strengths and abilities that far surpass those of the immortals and even Toven."

Frankie's eyes widened. "I knew you were more powerful than the immortals, but Toven? How?"

This wasn't a good time for a lesson in Anumati's history, but he'd promised to tell her more about himself, and he could condense the events that had taken place over thousands of years into a few minutes.

"Remember what I told you about the pods and the people inside of them?"

She nodded. "The Kra-ell, whoever they are."

"There are two species of intelligent beings on my home planet. Those who call themselves the gods and the Kra-ell. The Kra-ell are traditionalists who refused genetic alterations and followed a simpler way of life that was not based on technology. There is more to it than that, but I don't have time to dive into the entire history of our planet. At some point, the Kra-ell rebelled, demanding equal rights, and since the gods hadn't expected to have to defend themselves in their homes, they were not prepared. The Kra-ell were physically stronger and had had eons of tribal wars to develop their fighting skills. The gods had to resort to unconventional means to defend against the Kra-ell. They modified a class of robotic household servants, the Odus, transforming them into formidable killing machines. Long story short, the robotic servants were decommissioned after the rebellion and their manufacturing was outlawed. It was part of the peace agreement between the gods and the Kra-ell. To compensate, new genetic modifications were included for the new generations of gods. I was among those who received enhancements to increase our strength and speed to give us an edge against the Kra-ell. These enhancements make me more powerful than most gods, including Toven."

"So, you're like... supercharged?"

Dagor chuckled softly, appreciating her attempt to ease the tension. "Something like that, yes. I have abilities that are beyond the ordinary, even by the standards of my world."

"Oh, wow, that's so hot." She fanned herself jokingly, her eyes twinkling with mischief. "I'm one lucky girl. I can now boast that my boyfriend is stronger than Mia's."

"You might not want to do that. Toven is royalty, and I am not. He has a glow, and I don't."

"Yeah, the Clan Mother glows, too, but that's just a gimmick. It doesn't do anything. You have super strength."

"True, but Anumati's society is hierarchical despite purporting to be a democracy with equal rights and opportunities for all. At the top are the royal families, which have the strongest luminosity; below them are the nobles, who are distant relatives of the royal families who retained some glow; and at the bottom are the commoners, which is where I fall."

"What about the Kra-ell?"

"They have their own society and their own hierarchy. The Kra-ell queen is usually the strongest compeller, which is a hereditary trait, so the throne basically stays in the family even though any other Kra-ell female can challenge the queen."

Frankie listened intently, her gaze never leaving his face. "That's so fascinating. When you return from the mission, you must tell me more."

"I will." Dagor squeezed her hand. "Rest. Watch some movies to take your mind off the mission or spend time with Mia. I'll be back before you know it."

"Promise?" She gripped his hand, tears brimming in her eyes.

"I promise." He leaned over and kissed her lips, her nose, her cheeks, her forehead. "I love you, and I'll be back."

67

KALUGAL

Kalugal stood on the outdoor promenade, the cool ocean breeze whipping around him as he waited for his team to assemble.

He gazed at the lifeboats and contemplated how many were needed. Each was capable of carrying one hundred and fifty people, so one lifeboat was enough for their team of forty, but the idea of deploying two boats seemed like a good tactical move. If the Doomers somehow found out about them disembarking north of Acapulco and sent someone to investigate, they would assume that a much larger force was coming their way.

The ship was not full to capacity, so the remaining lifeboats would suffice for all the passengers if the unthinkable happened and the Doomers managed to sink the ship or a catastrophic storm appeared out of nowhere.

Kalugal very much doubted that was a possibility, but it was always better to err on the side of caution.

It had been a long time since he'd gone on a mission. The altercation with the cartel thugs hadn't been planned, but it had felt damn good to deliver justice and save the women, and it had given him a taste for more.

He'd been a businessman for so long that he had forgotten what it was like to be a warrior, and he had never been a warrior for justice before. The thrill of the fight had been dormant in him, overshadowed by financial strategies and corporate negotiations.

Kalugal had no illusions about being a savior, and he was well aware that one small operation like the one they had stumbled upon would not cure the world of its evils. He'd thought that InstaTock was a better way to influence minds and encourage them to think critically by providing pertinent information, but that had been naïve as well. People rarely bothered to dig deeper beyond the slogans fed to them by various instigators, and the more negative and harmful thc slogan, the more viral it became. For those who wished to destroy humankind and Western civilization in particular, social media was the perfect breeding ground for malignant ideologies.

The spoiled brats who had never known any real hardship couldn't recognize evil even when it was staring them in the face with a loaded gun pointed at their foreheads. They parroted the malignancies they were fed, thinking that they were righteous when they were the absolute opposite of that.

Positive messages were ignored, trivialized, or twisted to mean the opposite of what was conveyed.

Kalugal let out a sigh. Perhaps nothing ever really changed because humans were so short-lived and had such short memories. Lessons of the past were forgotten, and the same mistakes were repeated time and again, bringing misery, death, and destruction.

Rinse and repeat.

"Hello, cousin." Kian walked over with Dalhu, with the brothers trailing a few feet behind them.

Dalhu was armed to the teeth and looking formidable.

"I've never fought by your side before," Dalhu said. "I'm eager for the opportunity."

"Don't get too excited. After I freeze them all, there won't be any fighting to do, but be ready to have lots of blood on your hands." Kalugal grimaced. "Tearing out hearts is messy."

Anandur chuckled, and Brundar arched one blond brow.

Dalhu grinned. "I'm a painter. Mess doesn't bother me."

The banter stopped when Bhathian arrived with Max and a contingent of Guardians.

They were all heavily armed, except for Kian who was staying behind, and Anandur and Brundar, who weren't joining the mission because they had to guard him.

Kalugal knew that Kian would have gladly allowed them to join the party, but his esteemed aunt insisted that her son always have two bodyguards by his side whenever he was away from the protective walls of the village.

"I wish I could join in." Anandur glanced longingly at the group of armed Guardians. "Wonder said that she was okay with me going on the mission."

"That's very considerate of her, but your brother is getting married tonight." Kian put a hand on the redhead's shoulder. "And his bride won't be happy if you come to the wedding with blood and gore stuck under your fingernails that no amount of scrubbing can clean."

"Callie won't mind," Brundar said.

Anandur cast a questioning look at Kian, but his boss didn't seem in the mood to relent. "It's a shame that Brundar is not getting a bachelor party. I had so many fun ideas."

Brundar shook his head. "I don't want a bachelor party. I've said it at least twenty times."

"You can still have one," Kalugal said. "Your brother and your boss are staying on board, and I'm sure you have many friends among the Guardians who are staying to protect the ship and can celebrate with you while being vigilant about safeguarding it."

Kalugal wasn't sure that Brundar had any friends, but pretending to think that he did was the polite thing to do.

"I don't want a bachelor party, period." Brundar cast him a glare that would have scared a lesser male.

Anandur sighed. "My brother has trouble enjoying anything other than being with his mate and killing bad guys. If you want to make him happy, take him with you."

Kalugal could have sworn that Brundar's lips curved in a shadow of a smile as he turned to Kian. "For once, Anandur is right. Can you assign someone else to your security detail?"

Kian hesitated for a split second before nodding. "It's your wedding tonight. Are you sure that Callie will be okay with that?"

That earned Kian an even deadlier glare than the one Kalugal had been treated to. "My mate knows who she's bonded to. As long as I show up to the ceremony, she'll be fine."

Kian nodded. "Then go. I'll get a replacement."

"Thank you." Brundar bowed his head, which Kalugal had only ever seen him do in the presence of the Clan Mother.

Anandur looked incredulous. "This is so unfair. I got turned down twice, and he gets to go after asking once?"

Kian shrugged. "If you want to go so badly, I can find a replacement for you as well."

The redhead crossed his arms over his chest. "Now, I don't want to go on principle. I'm staying."

Kian didn't seem affected by the theatrics, probably because he was used to them.

Bhathian, who had been listening to their exchange, walked over to Brundar. "You should get armed."

Brundar patted his chest. "I have all I need right here."

68

DAGOR

As the winch detached from the lifeboat Dagor braced for impact, but as the vessel hit the water, it was minimal. Nevertheless, he and his companions got sprayed with ocean water.

When the other boat hit the water moments later, they were sprayed again.

"Damn," Negal cursed next to him. "Now I will have to smell the ocean on myself until we get back."

"It's not that bad." Dagor lifted his T-shirt and sniffed at it. "You've gotten spoiled."

"I have," Negal admitted. "It has been a long time since I've had to endure any hardship, and I don't miss it. I like wearing clean clothes, sleeping in a comfortable bed, and getting regular showers."

"I hear you," the Guardian sitting on Negal's other side said. "That's why I love our current mode of operations. We go in, free the victims, and take care of the scum who's holding them in one way or another, and the whole thing takes no more than six hours, including the drive to and from the mission. I never have to go to bed without showering."

"Do you go on missions every day?" Negal asked.

As the two continued talking about the rescue missions the clan engaged in on a regular basis, Dagor checked his gear once again, ensuring everything was in place. The weight of the weapons was unfamiliar, but it was somewhat comforting even though he didn't expect to make use of them. They were primitive compared to what he'd been trained on, crude even.

His strength, his speed, and his enhanced senses would most likely suffice, and he doubted he would need more than that to fight a few immortals and a horde of humans.

Even though the rebellion was a thing of the past and no one expected another Kra-ell insurgence, the powers that be had decided to ensure that the new generation of gods was built as efficient killing machines. He had never thought in those terms before getting drafted, but during training, it had been drilled into the minds of the new recruits. They were a protective shield for Anumati's society in case the gods' home was ever attacked again, either by the Kra-ell, who were their neighbors, or unknown outside forces. Their enhancements were insurance. The decision to enhance the physical strength of the next generation was made to ensure that they never got caught again with their pants down, as the human saying went.

There were only about twenty people in each boat, which was a fraction of what they could carry, but it was done to create the perception of a much larger force in case the Doomers and their cartel goons discovered their mode of transportation. Besides, as a rule, two were better than one in case one got damaged, or some other unforeseen event took place.

The truth was that Dagor was impressed with the level of planning that had gone into the mission.

It was always better to spend the time preparing and accounting for all contingencies than going in with a half-baked plan and fighting harder and longer than necessary. If everything went according to Turner's plan, the actual battle would be over in minutes.

The big question was whether the enemy had brought the hostages to the site or was hiding them somewhere else. The contingency for that was to capture the Doomers' leader and interrogate him to reveal their location.

It was also important to find out what these Doomers knew and whether they had reported the incident to their superiors on the island.

The sea was calm, but the waves breaking at the shore bounced the boat around. The boat slowed as it approached the designated landing spot, and the team readied themselves to disembark.

When they got within wading distance, Dagor and Negal followed the Guardians' example and strapped their rifles high across their chests before jumping into the water that reached below their waists.

After dragging the boats to shore, they put some effort into camouflaging the vessels so they wouldn't be visible from the highway, which was only a few hundred feet away, and then walked to where the vehicles were parked discreetly, hidden from casual view but easily accessible.

As the team divided among the vehicles, Dagor joined the lead car. He double-checked the earpiece he had been given, and then the convoy set off, leaving the shoreline behind.

His thoughts turned to Frankie.

He had left her safe and sound on the ship, and he already missed her. Even the thrill of the upcoming battle wasn't enough to overshadow the tight feeling in the pit of his stomach where an invisible tether connected him to her.

The farther he got from her, the stronger the pull got and the tighter the knot in his stomach felt.

Dagor had to remind himself that what he was doing was important. They were about to confront the Doomers, rescue the hostages, and bring justice to those who had caused so much harm.

69

KALUGAL

Kalugal signaled for the convoy to come to a stop five miles away from the rendezvous point with the Doomers. It was time to deploy the spy drones, which were an essential part of their reconnaissance strategy. He couldn't help but marvel at the technology that Turner's contractor had procured for them on such short notice.

These drones were unlike those he had seen the clan use before. They were smaller than the palm of his hand, designed to look like some kind of a bird, and their operation was impressively stealthy.

"Look at this." He put one on his palm. "Have you seen anything so advanced?"

The question was directed at Bhathian, but Dagor responded with a chuckle. "I guess Kian didn't tell you about our drones. You wouldn't detect one even if it was perched on your shoulder. They are the size of a mosquito."

Kian had mentioned something about the gods' technology, but since he'd also said that it was impossible to take it apart and reverse engineer it, Kalugal had lost interest.

"Good for you." He smiled at the god. "Did you bring anything with you on board?"

Dagor shook his head. "We didn't bring any of our equipment, and I've been lamenting that decision since the whole mess with the cartel started. Our disruptor would have disabled their weapons and communicators, which would have given us a clear advantage." He glanced at the Guardians standing around them. "We have enough power to easily win this battle and free the hostages, but it would have been less messy with better tools."

"Indeed." Kalugal cast him a smile. "Next time you join the clan on a cruise, bring everything you have. Trouble always follows wherever they go."

The god tilted his head. "They? Aren't you part of the clan?"

"Yes and no. I like to think of our community as a coalition. Annani's descendants are the clan, while my people and I are not connected to each other by familial ties. My men and I came together as a group that sought similar goals, which was freedom from the oppression of the Brotherhood and a peaceful life away from wars and conflicts." Kalugal let out an exaggerated sigh. "And yet here we are, fighting alongside the clan to correct wrongs and do good."

Bhathian cleared his throat. "The history lesson can wait. We need to release the drones."

"Absolutely." Kalugal took the remote from the Guardian. "Let's see how these things work."

As the drones took to the sky, their engines emitted a low hum that was barely discernible. With the natural sounds of the surrounding forest, even the keen hearing of immortals would struggle to detect them.

Kalugal watched the drones ascend and then switched to the display on the remote, which provided a bird's-eye view of the area.

"Now we wait," he murmured, his eyes fixed on the monitor displaying the drone footage. "They will each do just one flyby. Less chance of them being noticed."

Peering at the screen from behind Kalugal's shoulder, Yamanu let out a breath. "I hope they didn't have time to set up traps on all the accessible paths. Our advantage is that they don't know which direction we are coming from. "

Kalugal turned to look at the Guardian. "We are not in a rush, and we can progress slowly to make sure there are no makeshift traps on the way."

Yamanu let out a breath. "It's very easy to set up detonations along the way, and even with our keen eyesight, we might not see the wires strewn across the road in time."

When the drones reached the meeting point, Kalugal whistled. "Well, that's something I didn't expect."

It was impossible to tell the Doomers from the cartel thugs, but together, there were at least a hundred fighters there. But the most alarming part was not the number of adversaries but the weaponry they possessed. Among the standard firearms, Kalugal spotted two jeeps with armor-piercing machine guns mounted in the back.

"They have at least a hundred fighters," he muttered. "And armor-piercing weapons. They probably have RPGs as well."

Yamanu, who had been watching over Kalugal's shoulder, let out a breath. "This changes things."

Kalugal nodded, his gaze still fixed on the screen. "We need to adjust our tactics and approach in stealth, taking them by surprise."

"We need to ditch the vehicles and approach on foot," Bhathian said.

Dalhu nodded. "As we discussed, they will have sentries posted about two miles out in all directions. Four teams are the standard, but since they only have twelve immortals, there might be fewer. In any case, the sentry teams will probably have one immortal and one or two humans each."

Evidently, Dalhu remembered the standard procedures better than Kalugal, but then it wasn't surprising. The guy had left the Brotherhood five years ago, while it had been many decades since Kalugal had escaped his father's stronghold.

"We need to do the same," Bhathian said. "We need to dispatch four teams to take out the sentries first so we can make it the rest of the way without being spotted. We get within hearing distance, you use your megaphone, and it's all over."

70

DAGOR

Dagor stood to the side, listening in on Kalugal's strategic huddle with his leadership team as they discussed the battle plan.

No one had thought to ask for his or Negal's advice, but the immortals didn't seem to mind that they were listening. Did that mean that they were interested in their input?

Clearing his throat, Dagor stepped forward. "If I may, I can offer a slight improvement to your plan." It was a big one, but he was downplaying it, not wishing to sound condescending or to offend.

Kalugal nodded. "Go ahead."

"You don't need four teams. Negal and I can go ahead and take out all the sentries. We are faster, stronger, have sharper senses, and we can shroud ourselves to become invisible. We can achieve the objective faster and with less chance of complications."

Kalugal's eyes rounded with appreciation. "Why didn't I think of utilizing your superpowers before? I can shroud myself from immortals, too, but I can't pull off a disappearing act. I can only make myself look like someone else."

Dagor eyed him with curiosity. "You have godly powers despite being a hybrid. How come?"

Kalugal's compulsion ability was so strong that few of the gods back home could compete with it, and only those that came from the same royal line as the Eternal King at that. And now he had revealed that he could also shroud himself from other immortals.

Kalugal smirked. "I'm special. I am the descendant of two powerful gods. That's why inbreeding was so popular among our people." He winked. "When genetic manipulation wasn't available to us, it was the method of choice to produce more powerful offspring."

"Which gods were your ancestors?" Dagor asked.

They knew that Kalugal was a descendant of the Eternal King through Mortdh, but who was the other one?

"That's a story for another time," Kalugal said. "Now, we need to focus on the task at hand. Since you two can pull a disappearing act, you're on."

That was easier than Dagor had expected. "Good."

Next to him, Negal grinned like he had just won a game of Barkada. "We can do more than that," he whispered so low that only Dagor could hear him.

He nodded. "If I may, I have another idea for improving our chances of success."

"I'm listening eagerly," Kalugal said.

Dagor cast a quick look at the other members of the leadership team to make sure that he wasn't stepping on anyone's toes, but they all seemed as eager as Kalugal to hear what he had to say.

"Both Negal and I can conceal one more person in addition to ourselves. Once we dispatch the sentries, we can come back to collect you and another person. We can get you right in front of the Doomers without them being any the wiser. Once you freeze them, the rest of the convoy can arrive to help with the cleanup."

A smile bloomed on Kalugal's face. "That's perfect, Dagor. Thank you. We don't even need to waste time on the sentries. You and Negal can sneak me and one more warrior past them right in front of the Doomers. The element of surprise will be complete."

Bhathian shook his head. "We need to take out the sentries. When you freeze those at the meeting point, the sentries will be too far away to hear you, so they will not be frozen, and they could cause plenty of damage to our convoy, which will still need to reach you. The sentries might activate booby-traps to blow up our vehicles. They might have armor-piercing bullets, RPGs, and Fates know what else. Eliminating them is a must."

Max nodded. "After the sentries are dealt with, we will follow slowly behind and check for traps. When you reach the Doomers and their patsies and freeze them, we will not be far behind."

Kalugal groaned. "What if taking out the sentries reveals our hand? I'm sure that they have to report to their cohorts every few minutes."

Dagor lifted his hand to get their attention. "That's a good point, which necessitates another change of plan. We need to take you with us, and instead of taking the sentries out, you will compel them to keep reporting that nothing is happening. We will take them out on our way back."

Kalugal grinned. "That's brilliant. Thank you, Dagor."

Negal pushed his hands into his pockets. "We can achieve our objectives much faster if Dagor and I carry you and the other guy on our backs. We can cover twice the distance in half the time."

Kalugal shook his head. "I draw the line on being carried."

Negal shrugged. "As you wish. But we can cut the time in half that way."

"Thanks, but no thanks." Kalugal squared his shoulders. "When the stories about today are told, I don't want them to include you carrying me on your back." He turned to Max. "Coordinate with the convoy to hold back until we give the signal that the scouts have been dealt with."

"Understood," the Guardian nodded.

Kalugal turned to Bhathian. "If anything changes back here, let us know right away. We need to adapt. The situation could evolve quickly."

"Of course." Bhathian looked offended. "This is not my first rodeo."

"I know." Kalugal clapped him on the back with a smile. "I like to reiterate things, even those that you might think everyone knows. That way, there is no room for confusion."

"Who do you want to take with you?" Bhathian asked.

Kalugal turned to Dalhu. "Do you want to come?"

"Of course." The guy grinned as if Kalugal had offered him a prize, which, in a way, he had.

Dalhu seemed to be spoiling for a fight, but if everything went according to plan, there wouldn't be much fighting to be done.

71

DALHU

"So, here is how it's going to work," Negal said as the four of them collected their equipment. "We will scout the area and locate the sentries. Then we will come back for you."

When Kalugal nodded, Negal continued, "Dagor and I are not the best of shrouders, and shrouding others along with ourselves drains our ability. After we locate all the pairs, the four of us will get in position to take the first one, but Dagor and I will approach them first while shrouding only ourselves, which is much less draining for us, and incapacitate them. You will stay behind until they are ready for you. Then you come, and you do your thing with the compulsion."

Dalhu was disappointed. "Then what do you need me for? You can take just Kalugal."

Negal smiled. "Precautions. What if we encounter someone who is immune to compulsion? Or if we walk into an ambush? Dagor and I can probably handle that on our own, but you seem like a capable warrior, and having you with us might save the day."

Dalhu had a feeling that the god was just being courteous, but he wasn't going to argue. He was itching for action, even if it involved nothing more than running through the forest.

As he found out a short time later, though, keeping up with the gods was not easy. The dense forest around them was both a blessing and a curse. It provided cover, but the uneven terrain and the thick undergrowth made it challenging to move quickly and silently.

Dalhu was no stranger to physical exertion, but keeping pace with the gods was proving to be a herculean task. After more than an hour of running at breakneck speed, every breath he drew was a labored gasp, and his lungs were burning with the effort.

If they didn't slow down, the sentries would be alerted to their presence by his and Kalugal's huffing and puffing.

"Slow down," Kalugal finally whispered. "We don't need to run at top speed. We have plenty of time."

Kalugal's whisper was music to Dalhu's ears. The gods seemed to move with supernatural ease, and despite the speed at which they were running, their steps barely disturbed the forest floor.

He admired and envied their agility and strength, and those were not the only attributes of theirs that were superior to his and Kalugal's.

Even though the gods were at least a hundred feet ahead, they'd heard the whisper, which attested to their superior hearing. With all the ambient noise of nature around them, Dalhu doubted he could have heard a whisper from such a distance.

Dagor was the first one to switch from a run to an easy jog, and Negal reluctantly followed his example.

"Let's walk for a little bit," Kalugal whispered. "Dalhu and I need to catch our breath."

As they transitioned to a walk, Dalhu's chest heaved as he drew in deep, steadying breaths. When he and Kalugal were no longer huffing and puffing, the sounds filling the silence were the chirping of insects, the rustle of leaves, and the distant calls of animals.

Negal smirked. "We offered to carry you on our backs."

"There is no need for that," Kalugal said. "You were just going too fast."

Dagor, the more serious of the two gods, frowned. "Perhaps you should rest while Negal and I scout ahead. We can find where the sentries are and come back for you after we've dealt with them."

Kalugal cast Dalhu a sidelong glance. "What do you think?"

"I think it's a smart use of resources."

Dalhu might not have the godly abilities of Dagor or Negal, but he had his own strengths to bring to the table. He was a skilled warrior and a quick thinker, and he had a personal stake in the success of this mission. He might recognize some of those Doomers from his time in the Brotherhood, and if they belonged to the group of those he had vowed to one day eliminate, this mission would kill two birds with one stone, pun intended.

"Very well." Kalugal walked up to a tree and sat down, leaning against its trunk. "Go ahead."

Dalhu joined him, unstrapped his water canteen, and took a long swig.

"These gods are such show-offs," Kalugal murmured as he pulled out his own canteen. "They act so superior."

"They are superior." Dalhu grimaced. "Therefore, it doesn't count as showing off."

Kalugal took a sip of water, his gaze still fixed on the spot where Dagor and Negal had disappeared. "I know, I know. It's just hard to accept that they are better than us. We're supposed to be the elite, the best of the best. And then these gods come along, and suddenly, we're playing catch-up. When it was only Annani and Toven, it was okay. They are our royalty. But these are simple guys. Commoners."

Dalhu cast Kalugal a sidelong glance. "I'm a commoner compared to you, but I can still beat you on the sparring mat. You are a commoner compared to the Clan Mother and Toven, but you are a powerful compeller and a successful businessman. Each of us brings our own strengths to the table."

A hint of a smile tugged at the corner of Kalugal's mouth. "You're right, of course. I'm a prideful, competitive guy, but I admit that I'm grateful for their help."

72

DAGOR

"Just as Dalhu anticipated, there were four sentry pairs," Dagor reported. "Each one seems to have one immortal and one human. The Doomers stationed them about a mile away from the meeting place, though, not two. They are covering all the accessible pathways."

Kalugal nodded. "What about surveillance equipment? Did you detect any?"

Negal shook his head. "Unless it was very well hidden, we didn't see or hear anything, but that doesn't mean there isn't any. We are good, but without our equipment, we can't be sure." He sighed. "We shouldn't have left it behind."

"It was supposed to be a vacation," Dagor reminded him.

Now that they knew where the sentries were located, there was no reason to keep whispering.

"Are they within shouting distance of each other?" Kalugal asked.

"They are about an hour's walk away." Negal smirked. "At your speed, not ours. When we are within earshot of them, we will stop. Dagor and I will go first, subdue and gag the first pair, and only then will you and Dalhu emerge. After you compel them, we will remove the gags. We will do the same with the other three pairs."

Kalugal nodded. "Good plan."

"Let's do it." Dalhu strapped his rifle over his chest.

As the group set out, moving quietly through the dense underbrush, Dagor's senses were on full alert.

When they were close to the first sentry pair, Dagor held up his hand, signaling everyone to stop.

The forest around them was a symphony of sounds, but Dagor and Negal were as silent as shadows, their footsteps muffled by the thick undergrowth.

It was possible to shroud sounds as well, but Dagor had found that he couldn't make himself perfectly invisible and soundless at the same time. Perhaps as he grew older he would develop the ability to do both, but for now, he had to rely on his training for the silent approach.

Evidently, he and Negal were doing a good enough job because both the human and the immortal seemed oblivious to them. The two spoke in low tones, and then the immortal laughed at a crude remark made by the human.

Dagor's stomach turned over at the blatant disregard for human life and dignity evident in their conversation. He focused on the immortal and motioned for Negal to aim at the human.

Negal wasn't happy about getting the easier target, but they could switch targets with the next sentry pair.

With another hand signal, Dagor initiated the attack, and they struck in perfect coordination. Dagor lunged at the immortal, clamping a hand over his mouth to stifle his scream and twisting his arm behind his back to immobilize him.

Negal tackled the human sentry just as swiftly, with a hand covering the man's mouth while his other arm secured a firm grip.

The human's eyes widened in shock and fear.

It was satisfying to watch the two freak out because they couldn't see their assailants, only hear and feel them. The immortal was most likely aware of shrouding, but since most of the immortals couldn't manipulate the minds of other immortals, he had no idea what was happening to him.

Working quickly, they gagged their captives using strips of cloth they had brought along, tying them securely around the mouths of the sentries. Next, they hogtied their limbs, using fortified rope they'd brought from the ship to use on the immortals. With that done, he and Negal released their shrouds.

As fun as it was terrorizing the two, it was a waste of energy to keep up the shroud for any longer than necessary.

"Nice job." He high-fived Negal.

A low-pitched bird call was the signal for Kalugal and Dalhu to come forward.

As Kalugal approached the subdued sentries, Dagor watched intently, ready to intervene if necessary. He had seen compulsion at work before, or rather its effect on Frankie when Toven had compelled her to keep immortals and gods a secret from anyone outside the ship, but witnessing Kalugal's power was fascinating.

Kalugal knelt before the human sentry first.

The man's eyes widened with fear and confusion, but as Kalugal's deep, commanding voice washed over him, they glazed over. The sound of compulsion was potent, almost tangible in the air, and Dagor could see the human's body slackening as Kalugal's influence took hold.

"Please release him," he told Dalhu. "He won't move from this spot or say a word other than everything is fine, all is quiet, or there is no one here."

After Dalhu did as Kalugal had instructed, the human sat up, leaning against a tree with a line of drool forming in the corner of his mouth.

"He looks like a zombie," Dalhu murmured.

Turning his attention to the immortal, Kalugal repeated the process. The immortal initially tried to fight the compulsion, but he was overcome in seconds. His eyes became blurry, and the tension left his muscles.

"You can untie him as well," Kalugal told Dalhu.

When Dalhu positioned the immortal next to the human, Kalugal smiled evilly.

"What's your name?" he asked the immortal.

"Badsor."

Negal chuckled. "It sounds like a bedsore."

"Badsor." Kalugal used his commanding tone. "Put your thumb in your mouth and suck on it."

The guy's eyes bulged out, but he did exactly as he'd been ordered.

"Good." Kalugal crossed his arms over his chest. "Take off your boots and socks and suck on your big toe."

The veins on the guy's neck swelled as he tried to fight the compulsion, but his hands obeyed immediately, untying the laces, removing the boots and the socks, and then contorting to put his big toe in his mouth.

Negal laughed. "Can I take a picture?"

"Go ahead." Kalugal waved a hand as he turned to the human and gave him similar instructions.

When the human had his toe inside his mouth and was drooling all over the dirty digit, Kalugal uncrossed his arms. "You will keep sucking on your toes until it's time to report to your superiors that there is nothing going on and that everything is quiet."

Dagor watched the display of Kalugal's formidable abilities with a mix of fascination and discomfort. He was not affected by the compulsion, but he knew that there were gods capable of taking control of the minds of other gods.

The Eternal King was the most powerful compeller in the history of Anumati, and it was very likely that his granddaughter was a formidable compeller as well, but so far, he hadn't seen the princess using her power on anyone.

Hopefully, she wouldn't use it on him or his friends.

"We are done here," Kalugal said. "On to the next pair."

73

KALUGAL

Once all the sentries had been taken care of, Kalugal activated his earpiece. "The coast is clear. You can start moving."

"That's not a report," Bhathian grumbled in his ear. "I need details."

Rolling his eyes, Kalugal activated the earpiece again. "Negal and Dagor located four sentry pairs within a one-mile radius of the meeting place. They caught and subdued them, and I compelled them to keep reporting that everything was fine and nothing was happening. The four of us are about to continue, with Dagor and Negal shrouding me and Dalhu. Once I'm in front of the demon horde, I will pull out my trusty megaphone, order them to freeze, and let Dalhu loose. He's been itching for some action. So, if the rest of you want to join in the fun, you'd better hurry up."

"We are on our way," Bhathian said. "But don't let Dalhu loose before we get there. We need the leader of the Doomers alive for questioning."

"Even if Luis and his family are found?"

The contingency was to capture the leader in case they were not there, and leverage was needed to get them released.

"Yes. Kian wants us to bring the leader to the ship for questioning."

"I don't know how wise that is," Kalugal said. "Leadership positions in the Brotherhood go to the older members of the order. The leader might recognize me even though I left a long time ago, and even if he doesn't remember me, he will recognize Lokan for sure. Getting rid of him as soon as possible is the safest strategy."

"Don't worry. He's not leaving the ship alive. You and Lokan are safe."

Kalugal didn't trust reassurances that weren't backed by an iron-clad plan. "I'd rather err on the side of caution. I want to know exactly what Kian plans to do with the Doomer."

"I give you my word that the bastard won't live after we are done questioning him. I'll personally see that he's dead."

Kalugal was sure Bhathian had every intention of fulfilling his promise, but the law of unintended consequences was a bitch, and shit happened.

"Just make sure that he's subdued the entire way. I don't want the bastard to have a chance to escape."

"I will. We will knock him out with venom if necessary."

"Thank you. I appreciate it." He ended the conversation and turned to Dagor. "When do you want to start shrouding?"

"We should start now. It will take us fifteen minutes to get to the meeting spot, and both Negal and I can easily shroud for that long."

Kalugal waved a hand. "Then let's do it."

As Dagor and Negal's shrouding enveloped them, rendering their small group invisible to the outside world, it was an eerie sensation.

Seeing Dalhu and the two gods disappear was a very disconcerting experience.

Kalugal knew they were there, but he couldn't see them, and he could barely hear them. Would he feel it if one of them touched him?

"You will need to drop the shroud when we are in position, or they won't hear me. Please touch my shoulder if you got it."

"I'm not shrouding for sound," Dagor said. "Negal and I are trained to move nearly soundlessly, but from now on, we shouldn't communicate verbally."

Kalugal felt the god's hand on his shoulder. "I was afraid that I wouldn't feel that. Can you keep your hand there? I don't want to accidentally veer off the path and walk away from you."

The hand on his shoulder tightened a fraction in confirmation.

As they progressed, Kalugal found himself adjusting to the sensory deprivation this new mode of operation created. It was a strange dance, moving in sync with an invisible partner, especially since Kalugal wasn't the trusting type.

The only person in the world he trusted implicitly was Jacki. He would follow her blindly wherever she led him. But Dagor wasn't even a friend, and relying on him was a struggle.

74

DAGOR

As their group made its way through the last mile separating them from their enemy, the dense foliage around them rustled gently in the breeze. The canopy of trees swayed, casting shifting patterns of light and shadow on the ground, and the sunlight filtering through the leaves played tricks on the eye, creating an almost surreal atmosphere.

Occasionally the distant call of a bird pierced the air, adding a layer of authenticity to the scene, with the subtle hum of cicadas and the occasional buzz of a mosquito providing a backdrop to the anxious anticipation.

As they entered the clearing and Dagor's eyes fell on the immortal and human scum, his jaw clenched. They looked so nonchalant, lounging in their roofless jeeps, chatting and laughing as if they and their comrades hadn't committed the most heinous crimes just days before.

Scanning the treetops surrounding the clearing, he expected to find goons hiding in their canopies, but there were none. Evidently, the leader of the thugs was confident in their numbers and their firepower and did not think that posting hidden snipers was needed.

Dagor would have loved to finish the job the other immortals had done and tear them apart with his fangs, but their firepower was too formidable. The armor-piercing bullets could do massive damage, and while he was incapacitated for even a few brief moments, they could end him by beheading him or tearing out his heart.

It had to be done the way they had planned.

Squeezing Kalugal's shoulder, Dagor let him know that he was about to drop the shroud.

Kalugal activated the megaphone, put it next to his mouth, and nodded.

Dagor dropped the shroud.

"Don't move a muscle," Kalugal said, the compulsion in his voice reverberating through Dagor so strongly that he was frozen in place for a moment as well. "And don't say a word."

The shock on the faces of the Doomers was a sight to behold. Their sudden shift from arrogance to fear was a vindication that Dagor savored. It was a reversal of fortunes. The hunter becoming the hunted.

He relished the stunned and terrified expression on the males' faces, the knowledge that they were going to die.

A smile tugged on the corner of his lips.

The poetic justice of the situation was not lost on him. These were the monsters who had thought themselves invincible, untouchable, but now they faced the inevitable consequences of their actions.

"Payback is a bitch, vermin," he murmured under his breath. "How does it feel to be helpless in front of a superior force? How does it feel to know that you are about to die?"

His whisper had been too low for the Doomers to hear, but Dalhu stood right next to him. The guy turned to him and put a hand on his shoulder. "Patience, my friend. Retribution is moments away."

Dagor nodded.

"Members of the Brotherhood of the Devout Order of Mortdh," Kalugal's voice boomed through the megaphone. "Come forward," he commanded.

Eight males broke the ranks and walked toward them.

"Stop ten feet in front of me," Kalugal ordered.

Dagor observed the rage on their faces with pure satisfaction. It was like balm for his soul.

He would enjoy killing them slowly.

They halted precisely ten feet away. The distance was negligible for someone like Dagor, who could close it in the blink of an eye. But it wasn't the physical space that mattered, it was Kalugal's complete control over them.

Their eyes burned with hatred and frustration, a reflection of their impotence in the face of overwhelming power. Dagor could almost taste their fury, and it thrilled him.

The thought of prolonging their suffering, of savoring their fear and desperation, was tantalizing. Dagor imagined the various ways he could inflict pain, each more satisfying than the last. It was a dark, exhilarating thought that danced in his mind, an unpleasant reminder of his predatory nature, but at this moment, he embraced the side of himself that he normally sought to stifle.

There was not an ounce of pity in his heart for these people. Earth would be a better place without them to taint its soil.

75

KALUGAL

Kalugal scanned the faces of the Doomers, but he didn't recognize any of them. They must have been born after he had run away because there was no recognition in their eyes either, only intense hatred and fear.

Good.

The rumble of vehicle engines announced the arrival of the rest of their team, the graveled ground crunching under their tires until they stopped some distance behind him.

Kalugal didn't turn to look. "Who is the leader of this operation? Raise your hand," he commanded.

When the hand of one of the eight shot into the air, Kalugal ordered, "Take two steps forward."

The guy looked like a robot whose legs were operating independently from the rest of his body.

It was so comical that Kalugal had a hard time keeping his menacing expression. "Tell me where Luis and his family are being held!"

There had been enough compulsion in his voice to topple an army, and he got several answers at once.

"The van," one Doomer said.

"In the back," another said.

"In the van in the back," the leader spat.

Kalugal thought that he recognized the voice of the one who had called him, the one who'd said his name was Bud, but he wasn't sure. Still, it was easier to refer to him as Bud than the leader.

When Bud opened his mouth again, Kalugal lifted a hand. "Shut up. You are not to speak unless I tell you to."

He motioned for Negal to step forward. "Go get Luis and his family."

Negal hesitated. "If they heard your command, they will be just as affected as the others and unable to move. I can carry two or three at most, and there are more of them."

Kalugal didn't want to chance releasing anyone else from his immobilizing compulsion. Even using the megaphone to tell Luis to move wouldn't work because there might be another Luis among the humans. It was a popular name.

He could send Dagor and Dalhu along with Negal, or he could wait for the Guardians to get out of the vehicles and send them instead.

"You don't have to carry them," Dagor said. "You can just drive the van over here, and the Guardians will take them to safety."

"Good idea," he said. "Do what he said."

Kalugal offered a prayer to the Fates for the family to be found safe and sound. Until they were in the hands of the Guardians behind him, he didn't intend to do anything and was content with keeping the enemy frozen and waiting.

The longer he made them suffer, the better.

Negal broke into a jog, weaving between the vehicles on his way to the back where the lone van was parked.

Bhathian and Max took up position next to Kalugal.

"Can we get to work?" Max asked.

"Not yet." Kalugal watched Negal throw the van door open and hop inside. "I want Luis and his family to be out of here before we start."

He waited anxiously until he heard Negal in his earpiece. "They are all here, and they are alive."

Kalugal released a relieved breath. "Thank the merciful Fates."

Negal hadn't said unharmed, just alive, but Kalugal hadn't expected them to be unharmed. He just prayed that the harm had been limited to being terrified or getting roughed up. Hopefully, Luis's wife and teenage daughter hadn't been violated.

The sound of the van's engine revving up broke the tense silence, and Kalugal watched as Negal skillfully maneuvered the vehicle towards them, somehow managing not to drive over anyone even though the plan was to kill them all anyway.

Perhaps Negal was looking forward to killing them up close and personal?

Kalugal could understand that. It was how he'd felt when he'd killed those who held the kidnapped women. But then another thought crossed his mind. Perhaps there was a soul or two worth saving from this Sodom and Gomorrah?

Some of the humans looked as young as sixteen, and perhaps they didn't have the blood of innocents on their hands. If so, he would spare them. He would ask the Guardians to enter each of the humans' minds to decide who lived and who died.

As the van pulled up close, he motioned for the Guardians to approach the van and assist with the extraction.

As the van's driver door opened, Negal jumped out and jogged around to slide the passenger door open. He and several Guardians carried the family out of the van and into the vehicles behind them.

Given that their eyes were closed and their bodies were limp, Kalugal assumed that Negal had thralled them to sleep. It should have occurred to him to tell the god to do that, but it hadn't, and he was glad that Negal had taken the initiative.

Luis and his family had been traumatized enough.

Once the family was out of harm's way, Kalugal turned to Max and Bhathian. "Now, we can proceed with our plan, but I don't want us to kill indiscriminately because it will make us no better than them. Look into their minds and kill only those with the blood of innocents on their hands."

Bhathian arched a brow. "What if some of the Doomers didn't kill with their own hands but commanded the humans to do it?"

"Then the blood of innocents is on their hands as well. Though I doubt you will find even one Doomer worth saving."

Kalugal wondered if that was true for him and Dalhu as well and preferred not to dwell on it. He'd never killed innocents intentionally, but some might have been unintended casualties in the wars his father had sent him to fight.

"You heard Kalugal," Bhathian addressed the Guardians. "If you find anyone who deserves another chance, spare him. The leader is to be taken in for questioning."

76

KIAN

Kian had been receiving typical military-style succinct progress briefings from Bhathian, so when his phone rang with Kalugal's ringtone, he was glad to finally get the complete account of events from his cousin.

"Hello, Kalugal. How are things going out there?"

"I thought you knew. Bhathian said that he reported to you."

"He did, but all I got were bullet points. I know that Luis and his family are alive and safe, but Bhathian didn't say anything about their physical and mental state. Did you check on them?"

"I did. Negal had the foresight to thrall them to sleep when he got them, but we had to wake them up so I could release them from the compulsion not to move. Luis's wife couldn't stop crying, and his daughter was curled into a ball and trembling. The younger children were a little better, but they were also terrified and traumatized. The bastards kept threatening them with all the terrible things they planned to do to them. If not for the compulsion I put on Bud to keep them safe, I don't want to think what would have been done to them. Anyway, I thralled them to calm down and rest when they get home."

That was good, but Kian wondered what would happen when Kalugal's thrall faded. Hopefully, Luis could get counseling for his family. Acapulco was a modern city, which should imply that it had well-equipped hospitals operated by well-trained physicians, but Kian had no idea if mental health specialists were easily accessible and covered by health insurance.

"Bhathian said that you got the leader and disposed of most everyone else."

"I didn't want to order everyone killed indiscriminately in case there was an innocent among them, so I played the biblical God and tasked Dagor, Negal, Dalhu, and several of the Guardians to find some that were worth saving among these modern Sodomites and Gomorrahites. They found two teenagers who had been recently recruited and hadn't taken part in the atrocities."

Kian grimaced. "Those two are monsters in training. Their teachers are gone, but new ones will come, and if you leave them alive, they will become as bad as the others."

"They won't because I did a number on their minds. They now believe that a powerful Colombian cartel is moving in, and that it's taking out all the competition. The Colombians killed all the members of the cartel they belonged to, including the leaders, and left them alive as a cautionary tale. If they stay out of trouble, the Colombians won't kill them, but they are coming for anyone who dares operate in the area. My main objective was to ensure Luis and his family's safety so they could go home without fear of retribution, but it will work to keep these teenagers out of trouble as well."

Kian shook his head. "What does one have to do with the other?"

"It has nothing to do with the imaginary Colombians, but I made up another story for Luis. I'll tell you about it when I get back. I'm bringing Bud as you have requested, but I don't understand why you want him on the ship. We can question him out here and be done with it. We are making a big pyre with all the bodies, and I would love to throw his on top after I've played with him a little. Or a lot. He's the one who gave the order to massacre the villagers in the most brutal way imaginable to scare everyone in the area into compliance."

"I want to interrogate him at my leisure and then execute him." Kian smiled. "Even my mother approves."

"That's a big change in her attitude. I wonder why now. I'm sure the Doomers have done worse in the past."

"Perhaps, but these are different times, and it was shocking that such cruelty and barbarism still exist. Things were supposed to become more civilized, and we believed that the Brotherhood was becoming more sophisticated. We knew they were dealing in drugs and trafficking, and both are bad, especially the trafficking, but to order the horrific slaughter of an entire village is just so demonic that even my mother doesn't believe these Doomers are capable of redemption." Kian sighed. "I wish she had realized this years ago, and that it didn't have to take this catastrophe to drive the point home that some people are beyond redemption and need to be eliminated. Being soft-hearted toward perpetrators of evil ultimately leads to more innocents suffering and dying."

There was a long moment of silence, and then Kalugal released a breath. "If left unchecked, evil will spread like cancer and kill everything in its wake. The problem is that good people who champion and revere life can't comprehend what evil is and what it wants. They can't understand the thirst for death and destruction, so they try to rationalize evil deeds."

"What can we do, cousin? You are the mastermind with global domination ambitions. Can you think of a way to eradicate evil for good?"

Kalugal chuckled. "Contrary to what you think, I don't have delusions of grandeur. There are things that even I can't achieve. But if you want, I will be more than happy to discuss this with you over whiskey and cigars. Brundar has already celebrated his bachelor party by cutting out hearts and other organs that I won't mention, so you and I can enjoy a quiet hour on your balcony before his wedding tonight."

"That sounds delightful, but I need to interrogate the prisoner first, and I'll need your help to compel him to talk. If we have time after that, I'll gladly share with you a glass of whiskey or two and a cigar."

77

FRANKIE

"I have good news." Mia put the phone down. "Toven said that everything went more or less according to plan, none of ours got hurt, and Luis and his family are safe."

Frankie released a long, relieved breath. "What do you mean by more or less?"

"He didn't say." Mia frowned. "Why are you still sweating? Dagor is obviously fine."

"I'm not sweating." Frankie wiped the back of her hand over her forehead and slumped against the couch cushions. "Well, not anymore now that I know no one got hurt. What about Luis and his family? Are they going to be alright? It must have been horrifying for them."

"I don't know." Mia turned her chair around and drove to the kitchenette. "Do you want something to drink? I can make you another vodka with cranberry juice."

Frankie shook her head. "No, thanks. All this stress has made me a little dizzy. I don't know how the Guardians' mates handle it when they go on their rescue missions. I know that it's really hard to kill immortals, but it's not impossible. I would have gone crazy with worry."

"Yeah, me too." Mia poured cranberry juice into two glasses. "It's easier when you are part of the action. When I went on a mission with Toven, it was stressful, but in a good way. I felt like a badass."

Frankie's jaw slacked. "How the hell did you go on a mission? Did he carry you on his back?"

"Actually, that's exactly what he did on one of the missions." Mia put one of the glasses in the cup holder attached to her chair and held the other one as she drove back to the living room. "I've been on more than one."

Frankie shook her head. "Who are you, and what did you do with my timid best friend?"

Mia smiled. "I've never told you this, but I have a very special paranormal talent. I'm an enhancer. I make other talents stronger, and on several occasions, Toven needed me to fortify his compulsion ability. Two of the missions were nothing special because there was easy access for my chair, but one of them was in a remote region in Karelia, and he had to carry me. That was the stressful one because we were in enemy territory, but it was probably the most excitement I've had in my life, and that's including my Perfect Match adventure."

"Un-freaking-believable." Frankie felt her head spinning. "I want you to tell me all about it." She took a sip from the sweet juice, but it only made her feel nauseous, so she put it back on the coffee table. "I don't know what's wrong with me. I'm nauseous and dizzy, and everything I try to eat or drink makes it worse. I really don't handle stress well."

Mia frowned. "Are you sure it's stress? Maybe you are transitioning?"

"I don't have a fever."

"You are sweating, and the air conditioning is on." Mia maneuvered her chair to get closer. "Let me feel your forehead."

"I don't have a fever," Frankie insisted but leaned her forehead into Mia's extended palm to humor her.

"You're a little warm." Mia pulled her phone out of its holder. "I'm calling Bridget."

Frankie swallowed. "I can't be transitioning yet. It hasn't been long enough."

Except, she'd received a booster, so maybe she was.

Dagor had given her a blood transfusion last night, and that was in addition to the venom. It was very possible that she was transitioning.

"There is no harm in calling the doctor and asking her opinion, right?"

Panic constricting her throat, Frankie nodded.

What if she lost consciousness before Dagor returned?

What if she was out cold for the rest of the cruise?

She'd been looking forward to telling Margo about all the wonders of the immortal world and introducing her to Dagor, and now she would miss all that. Margo would be so disappointed.

Mia put her phone back in the holder. "Bridget says that you should come down to the clinic."

Frankie had been so up in her head that she hadn't even heard Mia speaking with the doctor.

"What did you tell her?"

"That you were nauseous, dizzy, and felt a little warm to the touch. She said she needs to run some blood tests on you to rule out a reaction to the blood transfusion."

As panic rose in Frankie's chest, her head swam, and bile rose in her throat.

How did Bridget know about Dagor's blood transfusion? Had she guessed?

"Don't look so scared." Mia patted her knee. "I don't think it's an allergic reaction to the transfusion. It didn't happen in the first twenty-four hours, and the chances that you are reacting to it now are very slim. I'm sure it's the transition."

"Oh, right." Frankie let out a breath. "That transfusion. I forgot about it."

Bridget had referred to the one she had administered to replenish Frankie's lost blood. She didn't know about Dagor's.

Mia looked at her with worry in her eyes. "Your fever seems to be getting higher. We should get you to the clinic before you pass out."

78

DAGOR

Dagor wiped his hands on his pants and grimaced. As soon as they got back to the beach where they had left the boats, he was going to dunk into the water and wash all the grime away.

It had been a lot of work to get rid of all the bodies, old and new.

This time, they had made sure that no trace remained. The vehicles, the rifles, and the ammunition were going back with them to be donated to Turner's contractor, who had supplied them with the transport and the drones.

Next to Dagor, Negal sat with his arms crossed over his chest, his eyes closed and a smile on his face.

"What are you so happy about?" Dagor asked.

Negal opened his eyes and looked at him. "I enjoy a job well done. We cleaned up the area for these people, at least for a little while. New goons will fill the vacuum, but not immediately."

Dagor grimaced. "I'm glad that killing makes you happy."

Negal's smile got even broader. "Why? Are you sad for those monsters?"

"Not at all. I'm sad that monsters exist and that good people have to dirty their hands with their tainted blood to make life bearable for those who can't defend themselves."

"I'm with you on that." Dalhu turned around to look at them. "But I also enjoyed the killing." He turned back to look at the road ahead.

Dagor had no doubt. After the particularly gruesome way he'd killed four of the eight Doomers, the guy looked calmer and more relaxed than he had ever seen him before.

What Dagor wanted to do was call Frankie, and now that he had calmed down a little from the rush of the battle, he felt centered enough to do that, but he was in a jeep with three other people, and it would be awkward.

Maybe texting her would be better.

Pulling out his phone, he turned sideways so Negal couldn't see the mushy love words he was about to type.

Hello, my love. I'm on my way back. It will take us about three hours, maybe a little longer, and I'll be counting the minutes until I can hold you in my arms. After I shower first, that is. You don't want to know what I'm covered with.

He hit send before it occurred to him that it wasn't romantic to mention that he was dirty and covered in gore.

When she didn't return his text right away, his gut clenched with worry, but then the three dots started dancing, indicating that she was typing a message.

When several minutes passed with the dots blinking but no text, he wondered what was taking so long. Was she writing and then erasing what she'd written?

Finally, when the message appeared, he let out a relieved breath.

I'm so glad that you are coming back to me. I was worried, but then Toven told Mia that none of ours got hurt, so I knew you were okay. I have a surprise for you. It's a good one. Something both of us have been waiting for. I love you.

"No way!"

"What?" Negal asked. "What's going on?"

"I don't know for sure, but I think Frankie is transitioning."

"Congratulations." Negal clapped him on the back. "What did she say?"

"That she has a surprise for me."

Negal's smile faltered. "It might be something else, you know."

"She said that it's something we have been waiting for. What else can it be?"

"Maybe her friend flew in by helicopter," Dalhu said. "Just ask her."

"She won't tell me. She wants it to be a surprise."

"Just ask her." Negal pushed on his back. "How are you going to survive the next three hours, not knowing for sure?"

His friend was right.

Dagor typed. *I know that you probably don't want to tell me news like that in a text, but I have to know, or I'll go crazy. Are you transitioning?*

The answer came a moment later. *Yes. Maybe. Bridget thinks I am, but it's not a sure thing.*

Dagor had no doubt that Frankie was on her way to becoming immortal, and he finally let the floodgates of his love open and fill his heart to bursting. He felt so buoyant that he expected to start floating above the seat.

His hands trembled as he typed back. *Thank the merciful Fates, my prayers have been answered. I love you so much.*

79

FRANKIE

Frankie lifted the back of the hospital bed to a sitting position. "Are you sure you need me here?" she asked Bridget. "I'm perfectly fine."

Well, she was fine except for the nausea, the dizziness, the elevated blood pressure, the faster-than-usual heartbeat, and the mild fever. But she didn't feel faint, and she didn't expect to lose consciousness.

"You're doing well now," Bridget said. "But that can change rapidly, and you have no one to watch over you in your cabin. If you slip into a coma, no one will know."

"I can watch over Frankie," Mia offered without much conviction in her tone.

"That's okay." Frankie gave her a thankful smile. "I'll just wait for Dagor to return. He can watch over me."

Bridget shook her head. "I prefer that you stay in the clinic where I can monitor your vitals even if I'm not here. I can see the readouts from the blood pressure and heart monitors on my tablet while I'm doing other things."

"Look on the bright side," Mia said. "At least you're not hooked up to a catheter and an IV. You can use the bathroom and drink coffee." She cast a sidelong glance at Bridget. "She can drink coffee, right?"

"Water is always better, but a few sips of coffee won't kill you." The doctor winked at Frankie.

"Ugh, Bridget. Is that what doctors consider a joke?"

Bridget shrugged. "A bit too morbid for you?"

"Yeah." Frankie rolled her eyes. "I'm transitioning, and I might die."

Mia gasped. "Fates forbid, Frankie. Don't talk like that."

Bridget smiled. "You'll be fine. Thanks to Dagor's venom, you are doing better than most transitioning Dormants. I was worried because of your fainting spells, but it must have been something that the venom cured as well."

It was a combination of venom and blood.

"I'm so lucky," Frankie murmured. "I didn't think it would happen to me."

Mia reached for her hand and clasped it. "I was sure of it. It wasn't a coincidence that the Fates brought you and Dagor here so you could meet."

Frankie chuckled. "Does Toven have a third nickname that starts with an F and ends with an E? Because he's the one who made it happen."

"Kian had something to do with it as well," Bridget said. "The Fates don't work in a void. They move chess pieces to arrange the board for the game they have in mind."

A knock on the door had Frankie's heartbeat spike, and the monitor beeped a warning before the door opened, and Dagor rushed in, looking like he'd just showered with his clothes on and didn't bother to dry off.

"You're awake," he whispered. "I was afraid that by the time I got here, you would be unconscious."

A smile spread over her face. "You've been texting me every fifteen minutes to ask if I was still awake. I answered the last text about ten minutes ago."

He smiled sheepishly. "I didn't want to push my luck."

Bridget patted Dagor's wet shoulder. "We will leave you two alone." She motioned with her head for Mia to follow.

"I'll see you later." Mia gave her hand a little squeeze before letting go.

When the door closed behind them, Dagor walked over to the bed and took her hand. "I want to kiss you, but I don't want to drip water all over you."

As it was, he was making a puddle on the floor.

"What did you do? Swim to the ship?"

She wouldn't put it past him. He was so strong that he could probably swim faster than the lifeboat's engine could propel it.

He chuckled. "I dunked in the ocean before getting on the lifeboat, and when I got on board, I used a hose to wash off the seawater. I just needed to see you right away, and I didn't want to waste time on a shower."

That was so sweet.

Leaning over, she reached for his shirt and pulled him to her for a scorching kiss. When she got dizzy, this time from oxygen starvation, she let go and sucked in a breath. "I love you, Dagor, and now we can be together forever. I'm never letting you go."

His eyes blazed blue light as he regarded her with such fierce love that it took away what breath she had left in her lungs.

"I'm not letting you go either. I know it's selfish of me, but I'm taking you up on your offer to accompany me on my mission. The good news is that we have all the time in the world, and after my mission is over, I will implore Toven to let us both become testers for the Perfect Match adventures so you won't have to give up on your dream."

Happiness filling her heart, Frankie laughed. "A better use of our talents will be for me to do the testing and you to work on the code."

He leaned over and kissed her softly. "Only if we work in the same building and can see each other whenever we want. I don't want to ever be separated from you."

Frankie's heart swelled with love. "I can't wait to start this new chapter with you. We will have so many adventures together."

"Fates willing."

He leaned down and took her lips in a kiss so passionate and filled with so much love that it left all other kisses behind.

COMING UP NEXT
DARK HORIZON TRILOGY
Children of the Gods Series Books 80-82

Read the enclosed excerpt.

INCLUDES
80: Dark Horizon New Dawn
81: Dark Horizon Eclipse of the Heart
82: Dark Horizon The Witching Hour

Coming up next in the
PERFECT MATCH SERIES
The Valkyrie & The Witch

To read the first three chapters, JOIN the VIP club at ITLUCAS.COM.

After breaking up with my boyfriend, I vow never to date a physician again and avoid workplace romances like the plague. Seeking an escape from bad memories and hospital politics, I apply for a job at the Perfect Match Virtual Fantasy Studios, where I hope to explore fantastical scenarios and beta-test new experiences.

I have no intention of entering a new relationship anytime soon, but it is difficult to ignore Kayden, a fellow trainee who's good-looking and charming but regrettably has aspirations of becoming a physician.

Hoping never to get paired with him to beta test an experience, I choose the Valkyrie adventure. It seems like a safe bet to avoid a guy like him, who would never select an experience where the female is the kick-ass heroine and the man only gets a supporting role. However, the algorithm has other plans in store for us. It seems to think that we are a perfect match.

Join the VIP Club

To find out what's included in your free membership, flip to the last page.

DARK HORIZON EXERPT

1

MARGO

Sunset in Cabo San Lucas was magnificent, and Margo had made sure to watch it every day since her arrival at the resort. The bright azure sky transitioned into an array of rich colors, with deep oranges, fiery reds, pinks, and purples reflecting over the pool's surface in a spectacular mirror-like effect. But as the sun dipped lower, so did the temperature, and the day's heat was replaced by the cool evening air.

Shivering, Margo draped a large pool towel over her bikini-clad body and cast a sidelong look at Lynda, who was collecting her things.

"Leaving already?"

"It's getting cold." Lynda wrapped a towel around herself and tucked the corner to secure it. "Are you coming inside?"

"I'm going to stay a little longer." Margo took off her glasses and put them on the side table. "I'm almost done with this book, and I have to know how the story ends."

Well, it was a romance, so happily ever after was guaranteed, but how the couple overcame the obstacles to get there was what made it interesting. So yeah, real life didn't come with guaranteed happy endings, but if Margo wanted real life, she could watch the news.

Not that all those who reported the news could be trusted to deliver objective truths either, and the view of the world that most of them broadcast was projected through the prism of their own agenda, but it definitely didn't promise happy endings. On the contrary, according to most of the media, the world was full of hate and strife and was about to end soon for one reason or another.

Perhaps they were right, but in either case, Margo preferred to spend her free time reading stories that ended in 'happily ever after.'

Lynda pursed her lips, which was a sure sign that she was going to deliver a lecture on all the ways Margo was disappointing her. "All you did during my bachelorette party was read, read, and read some more." She waved her hand for emphasis. "I've been sitting out here long after my friends left, hoping to have a nice chat with my future sister-in-law, but I should have known that you'd have your nose glued to your phone, reading."

Lynda scoffed at eBooks. She rarely read anything other than fashion magazines—the paper versions.

"I thought you were napping." Margo was well aware that Lynda hadn't been dozing off. She'd been watching the buffed-up lifeguard from behind the safety of her dark eyeglasses.

There was nothing wrong with that, but after what she witnessed during the bachelorette party, Margo wasn't sure that Lynda was faithful to Rob. Not that she was going to say anything to her brother. He would only accuse her of hating Lynda and trying to come between them.

The truth was that she wasn't fond of Lynda, but she didn't hate her either. The woman did have some redeeming qualities. Besides, Margo wasn't the one marrying her, and if Rob was happy with her, she was happy for both of them.

"I wasn't napping," Lynda huffed. "I was resting to conserve my energy for partying later tonight. Unlike you, I'm here to have fun and enjoy my bachelorette party." She pouted.

That pouty expression was what made Rob jump to fulfill Lynda's every demand, and it was also what Margo hated the most about her.

She assumed what she hoped was a pleasant expression. "I've had lots of fun with you and your friends. We drank, we sang karaoke, and we went dancing. It's been an awesome vacation." She smiled. "I'm so glad that you invited me."

That was a lie.

Margo would have been much happier if she hadn't been invited. Lynda hadn't paid for anything, and attending her week-long bachelorette party had eradicated Margo's meager savings. Also, calling the experience fun was an exaggeration. While Lynda and her friends had gotten drunk and flirted with the waiters and the lifeguards, Margo had mainly lounged by the pool, drinking virgin cocktails and catching up on her reading.

"Well, you are Rob's sister, so of course I had to invite you." Lynda sighed while collecting her bag from the back of the lounger. "It's our last night here, so I suggest that you take a break from your reading and join us on an outing." She slipped the strap of her oversized Louis Vuitton over her shoulder. "We are going to the Mandala, which is the most famous club in Cabo." Her eyes sparkled with excitement. "It's a must-see destination, and you can't skip it. You have to come."

"You girls enjoy." Margo cast her a fake apologetic smile. "As you know, I have a problem with loud music. My ears keep ringing for days, but I can join you for drinks later if you are still up for it when you return."

Lynda shook her head. "At this rate, you are going to stay single forever. You don't like any of the men that Rob and I introduce you to, you don't like nightclubs, and you work in an office with a bunch of other women. How are you going to meet any guys?"

"Online dating services." Margo put her glasses back on. "That's what everyone does these days." Except for her, but she wasn't going to admit that to Lynda.

"Oh well." Lynda tossed her artfully frosted tresses over her shoulder and put her feet into her Gucci three-inch-heeled slides. "Call me if you change your mind." She sauntered away.

Closing her eyes, Margo let out a relieved breath.

Everyone kept trying to set her up with someone as if being single was a terminal disease.

Margo went out on occasional dates, and sometimes she pretended she was out while staying home and turning her phone off just so people would leave her be. She even lied to her besties about her so-called dating life, complaining about the imaginary men she was supposedly seeing, who were all turning out to be disappointing.

The truth was that she hated dating. Her mother suspected that she was asexual or preferred members of her own gender, but Margo had proved her mother wrong by showing her the collection of her book boyfriends.

Margo just preferred fantasy over reality, and the heroes of her novels were all magnificent supernaturals. Suspending disbelief that they were as fabulous as the authors described them was easier when she didn't have to compare them to her underwhelming experiences in the real world.

Perhaps maturing too quickly and looking like a woman when she was still a child had something to do with it. At age thirteen, she had found that older men openly lusted after her and had made crude remarks which at the time had frightened and repulsed her, and she had never really gotten over that.

It wasn't rational, and she knew logically that there were plenty of nice men out there who weren't perverts, but it was a struggle not to think about what was going through men's minds when they looked at her and what they were planning to do to her.

Her mother had pressured her to get therapy, but Margo didn't like sharing her inner demons with strangers. She'd read self-help books and enough romance novels to fill up a library, and if that hadn't helped, she reasoned that nothing would.

She wasn't like other young women her age, who were obsessed with finding suitable partners, but she had learned to hide it. Going to bars with Mia and Frankie, Margo had flirted with guys like a pro, but she had never given any of them her phone number or taken any home. The only ones she'd actually gone out with had been friends or acquaintances of friends who had been vetted beforehand.

"Hey, pretty lady."

Margo tensed and opened her eyes, but the guy wasn't talking to her. He was talking to a leggy brunette with a huge hat on her head that hid her entire face from view.

The sun was almost all the way down, so the hat was no longer necessary, but it was an elegant accessory, and the woman looked like someone who paid attention to her accessories even more so than Lynda, and that was saying something.

Her sister-in-law was obsessed with designer labels.

Margo let out a breath and turned her phone on, going back to the eBook she'd been reading before the interruption. Still, she couldn't help but overhear the conversation going on two loungers down from her.

The woman was trying to make the guy leave her alone, but he was obnoxiously persistent.

"I can't join you at the bar," the woman said. "Please, leave. I asked you twice already."

"Just tell me your name, and I'll leave," the guy said.

Yeah, right. If she told him her name, he would ask another question, and when she answered that, another, and so on.

Some men didn't know when to quit.

"You are making me uncomfortable," the woman said. "My boyfriend is the jealous type, and if he sees you talking to me, he will get mad. Please go."

She was probably making up the story about the boyfriend, just like Margo had done countless times before, but the guy was either drunk or obtuse and refused to get the hint.

"Your boyfriend doesn't scare me." He thumped his hairy chest. "If you want a real man, dump the asshole and come with me. I'll show you a real good time, and I won't leave a precious jewel like you alone by the pool."

Margo turned on her side and gave the dude a bright smile. "You should do as she says. Marcello is a beast, and he's crazy. He will beat you up just for looking at Kitty."

"Oh?" The guy turned his attention to her. "What about you, missy? Do you also have a jealous boyfriend?"

"I'm happily married." She discreetly turned her ring around and lifted her hand to show him her fake wedding ring. "Patrick and I are expecting our second child." She rubbed a hand over her flat belly. "I hope it's a boy this time. What do you think about the name Solomon? I want my son to be smart, and King Solomon was supposedly the smartest man ever born."

Mindless chatter about children was a sure way to chase off even the most persistent flirts, but the guy was either smarter than he looked or good at detecting lies because he lifted a brow. "And where is this husband of yours?"

"Home with our daughter. I'm here with my sister-in-law, celebrating her last days as a single woman."

A convincing lie always had an element of truth in it.

The dude shook his head and pushed to his feet. "Slim pickings today." He walked away without saying goodbye.

"Thank you for the save," the woman under the large hat said. "Can I show my gratitude by buying you a drink?"

"Sure." Margo put her phone away and took off her reading glasses. "I'm Margo."

The woman chuckled. "I'm not Kitty. I'm Jasmine, or Jaz for short." She removed her enormous floppy hat, revealing a face that took Margo's breath away.

Jasmine was stunning.

"Is that your real name?" she blurted out. "Because you look too much like the princess from the Aladdin movie for the name to be a coincidence."

Black glossy hair tumbled in thick waves down Jasmine's shoulders, and her warm, olive-toned skin was so perfectly smooth that it seemed to be made of glass. Her almond-shaped eyes were deep brown with amber flakes floating around the pupils, their shade so striking that Margo suspected they were colored contact lenses. The high cheekbones, the straight nose that was slightly hooked at the end, and the full lips that were covered in berry-colored lipstick made Jasmine perfect for the role of an Arabian princess.

Her new friend laughed. "Believe it or not, but that's my real name. After the midwife placed me in my mother's arms, she took one look at my face and named me Jasmine."

Margo lifted a brow. "You looked like this as a newborn?"

"I can show you a picture." Reaching into a large tote bag, Jasmine pulled out her phone and frowned. "I'm so sorry, but you'll have to excuse me. I need to make a phone call first. I'll show you the picture after I'm done."

"The jealous boyfriend?"

Jasmine didn't smile. "Yeah. His name is not Marcello, but you must have some psychic powers because the rest of your description fits." She rose to her feet. "Can you watch my stuff while I take care of this?"

"Sure."

As Margo watched Jasmine walk away, the discomfort in her gut was a sure sign that there was a story there, and it wasn't a good one.

2

NEGAL

After scrubbing all the dirt and gore from his body, Negal stepped out of the shower and checked his nails to make sure they were clean. It was a bitch to get all the dirt and blood from under them, and he'd had to use a brush. He'd worked on them until they bled, but that wasn't a big deal for a god.

The skin healed immediately.

The clothes he had worn on the mission, though, were beyond salvageable, and he'd put them in a trash bag, but he wasn't sure what to do with the bag. The ship didn't have regular cabin service, and if he wanted clean towels and other supplies, he had to get them himself, which he might do after going down to the clinic and checking whether Dagor needed anything.

Dressed in a fresh pair of jeans and a black T-shirt, his hair washed and combed back, Negal finally felt like he was presentable enough to show up at the clinic.

Dagor, on the other hand, hadn't bothered to get properly cleaned up in his rush to see Frankie. He had jumped out of the lifeboat and had swum the last few feet to the ship. By the time the rest of them had gotten on board, he had used a hose to shower while fully clothed and had run to see the woman he loved.

It was very romantic and very unlike the crusty Dagor, but then love changed people, and in Dagor's case, it was for the better.

Hopefully, Frankie was okay. During their journey back to the ship, Dagor had called her every fifteen minutes, and she'd answered every time, so apparently, she wasn't slipping in and out of consciousness like Gabi had.

As Negal opened the door to the front room, the nurse smiled at him. "Can I help you?" Her smile was flirty, and he was about to put on the charm, but then the inner door opened, and Dagor stepped out.

Negal turned to him. "How is Frankie doing?"

"She's doing great." Dagor grinned. "Do you want to come in and see for yourself?"

Negal's eyes widened. Aru hadn't allowed them to see Gabi during her transition, so this was a very unexpected invitation.

"Are you sure she will be okay with me coming in?"

"Yeah. Toven and Mia were here not too long ago, and Frankie was very happy to see both."

"Okay then." Negal waved a hand. "After you."

When they passed through the front office, the nurse gave him an appreciative once-over, and he returned the favor with a smile and a wink.

He had to admit that being the most coveted male around was undeniably enjoyable.

Back on Anumati, Negal was a nobody. Just another guy from a family of modest means who hadn't had overly lofty aspirations. Serving in the interstellar fleet, he was content to slowly advance in the ranks, and the height of his ambition was to one day become a team commander. All positions above that required higher education that was nearly inaccessible for someone of his lowly status.

"Negal," Frankie beamed at him from the patient bed. "It's so nice of you to come visit me."

She looked so good that he had to wonder why the clan doctor was keeping her in the clinic.

"Hi, Frankie. I'm so glad to find you awake. How are you feeling?"

She shrugged. "Except for some fever and occasional nausea, I feel great. I was expecting to suffer much worse during my transition." She waved a hand at the lone chair in the room. "Please, take a seat. I want to hear what you've been up to."

Negal froze.

Did she know about his contribution to Karen's transition into immortality?

It was supposed to be a secret. Karen and Gilbert had asked him to supply his venom to aid in her transition, which was an uncommon thing for a bonded couple to even consider, let alone request. The venom bite was a very intimate act with strong sexual connotations, and Gilbert, who was a newly transitioned immortal, was even more possessive of his mate than he had been before that. But desperate times called for desperate measures, and Negal's godly abilities had been greatly beneficial to the successful completion of the procedure. Still, it wasn't something the couple wished to become fodder for clan gossip.

How had Frankie found out about it?

"What's the matter?" She tilted her head. "You look like you forgot something."

He shook his head. "I didn't. I just don't want to take Dagor's seat."

"It's fine." His friend clapped him on the back. "Sit down and chat with Frankie while I get us coffee. Gertrude doesn't mind as long as I bring her a cup as well."

So that was the nurse's name. Perhaps on his way out, Negal could flirt with her and make arrangements for tonight. The cruise was half over, and after that, there would be no more lovely immortal females vying for his attention.

His team was heading to Tibet to search for the missing Kra-ell pods, and it might be a long time before he found a suitable female to spend a few hours of pleasure with.

Negal wasn't looking forward to it, but he had a duty to perform.

He sat down on the chair and steepled his fingers over his knees for the simple reason that he didn't know what to do with them.

Frankie regarded him with a knowing smile. "You still haven't told me what you've been up to lately, and I don't mean the mission you've just come back from." She grimaced. "As glad as I am that those bad guys were dealt with, I don't want to hear the gruesome details. I'm much more interested in your love life."

He frowned. "What did you hear?"

She chuckled. "That you're very popular with the clan ladies."

Negal let out a breath. Maybe she didn't know about Karen after all and was just fishing.

"Indeed. I'm the only available bachelor on this cruise, so of course I'm popular. I could have warts all over my face and still get more attention than I could ever hope for."

"But you don't have warts. You are a god, and you are absolutely perfect." Frankie pulled out her phone. "Do you mind if I take a picture of you?"

"Why do you want to?"

"I want to show it to my friend Margo." She turned on her side and leaned closer to him. "I'm not supposed to take pictures of anyone on the ship, but we are inside a clinic that has no windows and looks like any other medical facility out there. No one will be able to recognize it, so I hope that whoever is monitoring outgoing calls, texts, and emails will let this one slide."

He really didn't want Frankie to show his picture to her friend and get her hopes up for nothing because he wasn't interested.

Wincing, Negal shifted on the uncomfortable chair. "Are you trying to play matchmaker?"

She rolled her eyes. "Obviously. Mia, Margo, and I are best friends, and two of us are mated to gods. It's only fair that Margo mates a god as well, and you are the only one left."

Negal groaned. "I don't want a mate. I'm perfectly happy being a bachelor and enjoying the attention of the single clan ladies." He leaned closer to Frankie, so they were almost touching noses. "Who are immortal and have the stamina to match. With all due respect to your friend, I don't want to waste the last days of the cruise on a human."

Frankie recoiled as if he had insulted her mother. "You are such a bigot, Negal. I was human until this morning, and yet Dagor chose me. Margo is beautiful, smart, and has the heart of a tiger." She leaned away from him and started scrolling on her phone. "Here. Take a look." She shoved the phone in his face.

Not wanting to antagonize her further, Negal took the phone and looked at the photo of a pretty blond human. She might be beautiful by human standards, but she was quite ordinary when compared to goddesses or even immortal females. That being said, there was a fierceness in her eyes that spoke to him. "I see what you mean by her having the heart of a tiger." He handed Frankie the phone back. "She looks formidable."

Frankie frowned. "That's it? That's all you have to say about her?"

"What did you expect me to say? That I fell in love with her at first sight?"

"Well, yeah." Frankie pouted. "I heard one of the immortals talking about falling in love with the picture of his mate before ever meeting her." She sighed. "Well, that was disappointing. Perhaps I should show Margo's picture to Max." She looked at him with a slight smirk, lifting one corner of her lips. "Perhaps he will react like I hoped you would."

"Max is an excellent choice for your friend." Negal pushed to his feet and dipped his head. "I wish you an easy and successful transition." He turned to leave.

"Wait. What about that picture?"

Taking a deep breath, he turned back to her. "What for? I'm not interested in dating your friend. You should take a picture of Max and send it to her."

"Ugh, Negal. You are such a party pooper."

"I'm sorry." He dipped his head again and walked out.

Outside her room, he found Dagor delivering a cup of coffee to the nurse.

"Leaving so soon?" his friend asked.

"Yeah. Frankie wanted to take a picture of me and send it to her friend. Can you please talk to her and ask her not to try to set me up with anyone?"

Dagor grimaced. "Why won't you give it a try? You might find Margo attractive."

Behind Dagor, the nurse cleared her throat. "Do you really want to have this conversation in front of me?"

Damn. Negal had plans for that nurse. Turning his best smile on her, he lifted his hands in mock surrender. "I'm sorry. I didn't come here expecting matchmaking." He lowered his hands. "I much prefer to court ladies of my own choosing."

3

PETER

Peter sat on the Lido deck and watched the sunset with an Old Fashioned in his hand, swirling the dark liquid around the large ice cube in the middle. It was getting cooler, which was a welcome respite from the day's heat.

He was a little miffed about not having been chosen to join the Guardian force that had dealt with the Doomer and cartel infestation. It would have been a nice break from thinking about Kagra and what had gone wrong in their relationship.

Things had been great between them during the joint Guardian and Kra-ell mission to China, the sex was phenomenal, and for a while Peter had thought that they had something special, but she had made it clear in so many words that he had been merely a passing curiosity. Kagra had wanted to experience what it was like to be with an immortal, and Peter had been conveniently available and willing.

Had she found him lacking compared to the males of her own race? Was that the reason she'd dumped him?

The Kra-ell males were faster, stronger, and could properly challenge her in the cruel Kra-ell mating rituals.

It was ironic that despite his proclivity for dominant bedroom games, he couldn't give her what she needed. Compared to the males of her species, he was too gentle, but he'd naively hoped that she would find his style of love-making revelatory.

Oh, well. When it wasn't meant to be, it wasn't meant to be, right?

It was her loss. He was wittier, funnier, and much better mate material than her fellow Kra-ell.

Still, despite the self-pep talk, the sting of rejection lingered.

Whatever. He was tired of mulling over the mysteries of love and the unpredictable nature of relationships.

Evidently, he was more clueless than he'd believed.

"Can I please have a mojito?" An unfamiliar female voice caught his attention.

It was heavily accented and a little nasal, which meant that it belonged to a human, and he had never seen one of the human servers on the Lido deck. It wasn't that they weren't allowed, but they preferred not to mingle with the immortals any more than they had to while serving in the kitchen and the dining hall and keeping the ship tidy.

Given their experience with the Kra-ell, that was perfectly understandable.

These humans were used to having been exploited by the powerful aliens, being treated as serfs at best and slaves at worst. The females had been given very little choice regarding accepting invitations from the male Kra-ell. Once they had produced a hybrid offspring or gotten beyond a certain age, they had been released from that obligation, but it must have been a miserable existence. Logically, they might acknowledge that their rescuers were different than their former masters and that no one would take advantage of them, but he could understand why they were wary of yet another kind of alien overlord.

Turning to look at the female, Peter recognized her as one of the servers from the dining room. Her blue hair and the piercing in her left eyebrow were her calling cards. He didn't like either, but he liked the rest. She was pretty, even beautiful, for a human, with smiling eyes and a mouth made for kissing. Her tiny T-shirt left her midriff exposed, and her waist was so small that he could encircle it with his hands. Low-hung jeans hugged her rounded hips and delectable bottom.

For a brief moment he considered flirting with her, a playful smile forming on his lips, but then he remembered where she had come from and changed his mind. During her time in the Kra-ell compound, she must have been subjected to the whims and desires of the powerful Kra-ell, and she might feel trapped.

The last thing he wanted was for the woman to assume that she had to suffer his advances the same way she had been forced to submit in the Kra-ell compound. He didn't want her to feel obligated to please him or to be caught in a situation where she felt powerless.

He had never asked Kagra about her own experience under Igor's rule. She had also been a victim and had suffered worse than the human females, so when she hadn't volunteered information about that time, he'd respected her choice to put the past behind her. It was better not to draw out pain that was best forgotten.

With a sigh, Peter shifted his eyes away from the woman and continued gazing at the horizon while sipping on his Old Fashioned.

"Is this seat taken?" the blue-haired server asked, standing with her mojito next to his table.

There was an abundance of empty chairs scattered across the outdoor bar, so it was clear that her interest was in him and not the other vacant chair next to his table.

"Not at all, please, have a seat." He waved a hand at the chair. "I'm Peter."

She flashed him a friendly smile. "I'm Marina." She put her drink down on the table and offered him her hand.

Leaning over, he took her slender fingers in the tips of his and resisted the urge to lift her hand to his lips. Instead, he gave it a gentle shake and let go.

"It's such a beautiful day, don't you think?" Marina gracefully settled into the chair across from him.

"It is. That's why I'm sitting up here and enjoying the view." He deliberately shifted his gaze to the ocean so she wouldn't think it was a come-on line.

"That's what I thought as well." She affected a sigh. "And I also thought that it was a shame to drink alone on such a lovely day."

Was she flirting with him?

She sounded a little nervous, so maybe she was, and if so, she was doing it in surprisingly good English. Most of the humans from the former Kra-ell compound spoke Russian and Finnish, and very few spoke English at all, let alone so well.

"You're absolutely right." He smiled to put her at ease. "Your English is excellent, by the way."

"Thank you." She grinned. "I've been studying for several hours every day." She crossed her legs. "My shifts at Safe Haven left plenty of free time, so that's what I dedicated most of it to. When the offer to work on the ship came, I saw it as a great opportunity to practice my new skills." She leaned a little closer, her perfume tickling his nostrils. "The community members in Safe Haven are a little standoffish. We basically keep to ourselves, and they keep to themselves. Still, I'm very grateful to them for inviting us to join them. It's a very nice place to live." She chuckled. "The problem is that we don't get to meet new people, so it gets a little boring."

Peter was pretty sure that she was flirting with him, but he wasn't going to assume anything. If Marina was interested, she would have to do more than hint.

He leaned in a bit just to indicate that he wasn't averse to the idea. "Your people keep to themselves here as well. You are the first human I've seen on this deck."

She shrugged. "It's mostly a language barrier thing. They are all taking classes, but the older ones don't learn as quickly."

"That's a relief." He leaned back. "I was concerned that your people were afraid of us."

"Some are," she admitted. "But I think it's stupid. Your people liberated us. You gave us choices, and you are kind and polite to us. You are nothing like the Kra-ell. It's like night and day."

He was relieved.

"I'm glad that you feel that way. Are you enjoying the cruise so far?"

Marina's expression shifted slightly, and she let out a small sigh. "Honestly, it's mostly work, and as you know, we've been on this ship before, so it's not a novelty either, but the pay is good so I can't complain." She shrugged, her blue hair shimmering in the waning sunlight. "The weather is also much nicer this time around. Sailing through the Arctic wasn't much fun."

"Can I ask you something?"

She smiled. "Of course."

"Why the blue hair?"

4

MARINA

Marina leaned back in her chair, her gaze fixed on Peter. "It's my banner of freedom, my autonomy, my right to do with my body as I please and to paint my life any color I choose."

She'd been observing Peter since the voyage began, not only because he was handsome in a way that stirred something inside of her, but also because he looked lonely and sad. Even when sitting among friends and sharing laughs with them, his eyes had remained clouded and his expression defeated.

He was ripe for the taking, the perfect candidate to help her escape the drudgery of Safe Haven and her mind-numbingly boring job as a maid.

She had spent a lot of time observing the immortals in order to choose the right one, and approaching Peter had been a daring and calculated move.

Hopefully, focusing her attention on him wouldn't be a mistake like choosing to settle at Safe Haven had been. This time, she wasn't letting her emotions make the decisions for her.

She'd voted with the others to move there instead of to the immortals' village out of fear. Like the others, she hadn't wanted to exchange one type of tyranny for another, and just like them, she'd been convinced that humans could never be more than slaves to these powerful immortals.

The Kra-ell had been cruel masters, but she had learned what to expect from them, how to stay out of trouble, and how to minimize her exposure to the meanest amongst them. At the time of the vote, she hadn't known much about the immortals. All she had known about her rescuers was that they had defeated the formidable Kra-ell, which meant that they were even more powerful and scary than her former masters.

Over time, though, she had begun to change her mind about them. Every one of the Guardians posted at Safe Haven had been polite and kind. She'd thought they had been instructed to act that way, but she experienced the same on the ship. Everyone she'd interacted with had treated her like a person, with smiles and kind words. No one had looked down their noses at her, been impatient with her, or snapped at her.

The fortress of fear that had started eroding at Safe Haven had crumbled entirely during the cruise.

"I get it," Peter said. "I can't imagine how difficult it must have been." He took another sip of his drink before putting the empty glass down. "Were you born in the compound, or were you abducted?"

"I was born there." She lifted her hand to tuck a stray strand of hair behind her ear. "And before you ask, both of my parents are human. I'm not part Kra-ell, for which I'm thankful."

He winced. "Not all of them are bad. Igor was terrible, but even the males in his close circle weren't all horrible people. They were his victims, compelled to obey him just like everyone else."

Oops. She must have stepped on a toe. Or whatever the phrase was when someone said something they shouldn't have.

Evidently, Peter was a Kra-ell sympathizer.

"I know that. We watched the televised trial. Lusha did a great job defending them. She made us proud even though she has Kra-ell blood in her."

Lusha's quarter Kra-ell part was dormant, but it had been enough for her to get privileges that pure humans hadn't gotten in the compound. She'd been allowed to attend university and had become an attorney. Marina and others like her had been home-schooled, and their job prospects were limited.

"Lusha did an amazing job," Peter agreed. "Do you know that Jade is now mated to one of us?"

"I heard that. But so what? You are powerful immortals, and you defeated the Kra-ell who enslaved her and killed the males of her tribe. Mating one of you was a step up for her."

"She and Phinas fell in love."

Peter looked like he really believed that, but she doubted a female who had never spared her own daughter a kind look was capable of love.

Perhaps these immortals were a little naive when it came to the Kra-ell, thinking that they were like them.

"I heard that you entrusted the Kra-ell with safeguarding your village in your absence. Do you really trust them to do that?"

Peter nodded. "Jade saved Kian's life, and she's proved herself loyal many times over. Kagra, too."

His voice had hitched a little when he said Kagra's name. Were the two involved? Was being separated from her the reason he looked so lonely and sad?

If so, Marina had bet on the wrong guy.

Affecting a smile, she looked at him from under lowered lashes. "Is there something going on between you and Kagra?"

"Not anymore." He lifted his empty glass to signal to the robotic bartender. "Do you want another drink?"

So that was why he had looked so sad. He was getting over a breakup, which made him even more ripe for the taking. Now, she definitely wanted one more drink so she could keep talking to him.

"Yes, please." Marina emptied the rest of the mojito down her throat. "More of the same. The mint is very refreshing."

After Bob brought them their drinks, Marina leaned back with hers in hand. "So, what happened between you and Kagra?"

"Nothing worth mentioning." His eyes flashed as he sipped on his drink. "It was just a fling, and we both moved on."

Marina had a feeling that there was more to it, but if that was a touchy subject for him, she was perfectly fine with leaving it alone. "Very well. I won't ask about her. Tell me a little about yourself."

Peter regarded her with his intense dark eyes as if trying to read her mind. "What do you want to know?"

"You are a Guardian, right? I've seen you sharing a table with several males whom I recognized from the liberation of the compound and later the sea voyage."

"Yes, I am."

"Do you enjoy what you do?"

"Most days, I do. I've tried a few things throughout my life, but nothing has brought me as much satisfaction as being on the force and saving innocents from bad people, so I came back."

He was perfect. The guy was a protector, and that was precisely the type of male she needed. Someone who would want to take care of her.

"Can you tell me a little about what you do as a Guardian, or is it a secret?"

"It is a secret, but you are going to get your memories wiped after the cruise is over, so it doesn't matter."

That wasn't good. Her plan was to make the immortal fall in love with her, or at least care deeply for her, and invite her to live with him in the village.

"Why would they want to erase our memories? There is no need for that. We are under compulsion to keep the existence of Kra-ell and immortals a secret."

He shrugged. "I'm not the boss, and it's not my decision, so perhaps I'm wrong about that. It's just what they usually do to humans they employ after the job is done."

She let out a breath. "I hope you are wrong because I don't want to forget you."

It was almost jarring to see the change that her words evoked in him. Suddenly, there was desire in his eyes that hadn't been there a moment ago.

Leaning over the table, Peter reached for her hand. "Are you flirting with me, Marina?"

She gave him a coquettish smile. "What if I am?"

DARK HORIZON TRILOGY

INCLUDES

80: Dark Horizon New Dawn

81: Dark Horizon Eclipse of the Heart

82: Dark Horizon The Witching Hour

NOTE

Dear reader,

I hope my stories have added a little joy to your day. If you have a moment to add some to mine, you can help spread the word about the Children Of The Gods series by telling your friends and penning a review. Your recommendations are the most powerful way to inspire new readers to explore the series.

Thank you,

Isabell

Also by I. T. Lucas

THE CHILDREN OF THE GODS ORIGINS

1: Goddess's Choice

2: Goddess's Hope

THE CHILDREN OF THE GODS

Dark Stranger

1: Dark Stranger The Dream

2: Dark Stranger Revealed

3: Dark Stranger Immortal

Dark Enemy

4: Dark Enemy Taken

5: Dark Enemy Captive

6: Dark Enemy Redeemed

Kri & Michael's Story

6.5: My Dark Amazon

Dark Warrior

7: Dark Warrior Mine

8: Dark Warrior's Promise

9: Dark Warrior's Destiny

10: Dark Warrior's Legacy

Dark Guardian

11: Dark Guardian Found

12: Dark Guardian Craved

13: Dark Guardian's Mate

Dark Angel

14: Dark Angel's Obsession

15: Dark Angel's Seduction

16: Dark Angel's Surrender

Dark Operative

17: Dark Operative: A Shadow of Death

18: Dark Operative: A Glimmer of Hope
19: Dark Operative: The Dawn of Love

Dark Survivor

20: Dark Survivor Awakened
21: Dark Survivor Echoes of Love
22: Dark Survivor Reunited

Dark Widow

23: Dark Widow's Secret
24: Dark Widow's Curse
25: Dark Widow's Blessing

Dark Dream

26: Dark Dream's Temptation
27: Dark Dream's Unraveling
28: Dark Dream's Trap

Dark Prince

29: Dark Prince's Enigma
30: Dark Prince's Dilemma
31: Dark Prince's Agenda

Dark Queen

32: Dark Queen's Quest
33: Dark Queen's Knight
34: Dark Queen's Army

Dark Spy

35: Dark Spy Conscripted
36: Dark Spy's Mission
37: Dark Spy's Resolution

Dark Overlord

38: Dark Overlord New Horizon
39: Dark Overlord's Wife
40: Dark Overlord's Clan

Dark Choices

ALSO BY I. T. LUCAS

PERFECT MATCH

ALSO BY I. T. LUCAS

Vampire's Consort
King's Chosen
Captain's Conquest
The Thief Who Loved Me
My Merman Prince
The Dragon King
My Werewolf Romeo
The Channeler's Companion
The Valkyrie & The Witch
Adina and the Magic Lamp

TRANSLATIONS

DIE ERBEN DER GÖTTER

Dark Stranger

1- Dark Stranger Der Traum
2- Dark Stranger Die Offenbarung
3- Dark Stranger Unsterblich

Dark Enemy

4- Dark Enemy Entführt
5- Dark Enemy Gefangen
6- Dark Enemy Erlöst

Dark Warrior

7- Dark Warrior Meine Sehnsucht
8- Dark Warrior – Dein Versprechen
9- Dark Warrior - Unser Schicksal
10-Dark Warrior-Unser Vermächtnis

LOS HIJOS DE LOS DIOSES

EL OSCURO DESCONOCIDO

1: EL OSCURO DESCONOCIDO EL SUEÑO
2: EL OSCURO DESCONOCIDO REVELADO

3: EL OSCURO DESCONOCIDO INMORTAL

EL OSCURO ENEMIGO

4- EL OSCURO ENEMIGO CAPTURADO

5 - EL OSCURO ENEMIGO CAUTIVO

6- EL OSCURO ENEMIGO REDIMIDO

LES ENFANTS DES DIEUX

DARK STRANGER

1- Dark Stranger Le rêve

2- Dark Stranger La révélation

3- Dark Stranger L'immortelle

The Children of the Gods Series Sets

Books 1-3: Dark Stranger trilogy—Includes a bonus short story: **The Fates Take a Vacation**

Books 4-6: Dark Enemy Trilogy —Includes a bonus short story—**The Fates' Post-Wedding Celebration**

Books 7-10: Dark Warrior Tetralogy
Books 11-13: Dark Guardian Trilogy
Books 14-16: Dark Angel Trilogy
Books 17-19: Dark Operative Trilogy
Books 20-22: Dark Survivor Trilogy
Books 23-25: Dark Widow Trilogy
Books 26-28: Dark Dream Trilogy
Books 29-31: Dark Prince Trilogy
Books 32-34: Dark Queen Trilogy
Books 35-37: Dark Spy Trilogy
Books 38-40: Dark Overlord Trilogy
Books 41-43: Dark Choices Trilogy
Books 44-46: Dark Secrets Trilogy
Books 47-49: Dark Haven Trilogy
Books 50-52: Dark Power Trilogy
Books 53-55: Dark Memories Trilogy
Books 56-58: Dark Hunter Trilogy
Books 59-61: Dark God Trilogy

MEGA SETS

CHECK OUT THE SPECIALS ON
ITLUCAS.COM
(https://itlucas.com/specials)

FOR EXCLUSIVE PEEKS AT UPCOMING RELEASES & A FREE I. T. LUCAS COMPANION BOOK

Join my *VIP Club* and gain access to the VIP portal at itlucas.com

To Join, go to:
http://eepurl.com/blMTpD

Find out more details about what's included with your free membership on the book's last page.

TRY THE CHILDREN OF THE GODS SERIES ON AUDIBLE
2 FREE audiobooks with your new Audible subscription!

PERFECT MATCH SERIES

Vampire's Consort

When Gabriel's company is ready to start beta testing, he invites his old crush to inspect its medical safety protocol.

Curious about the revolutionary technology of the *Perfect Match Virtual Fantasy-Fulfillment studios,* Brenna agrees.

Neither expects to end up partnering for its first fully immersive test run.

King's Chosen

When Lisa's nutty friends get her a gift certificate to *Perfect Match Virtual Fantasy Studios,* she has no intentions of using it. But since the only way to get a refund is if no partner can be found for her, she makes sure to request a fantasy so girly and over the top that no sane guy will pick it up.

Except, someone does.

> **Warning:** This fantasy contains a hot, domineering crown prince, sweet insta-love, steamy love scenes painted with light shades of gray, a wedding, and a HEA in both the virtual and real worlds.
>
> Intended for mature audience.

Captain's Conquest

Working as a Starbucks barista, Alicia fends off flirting all day long, but none of the guys are as charming and sexy as Gregg. His frequent visits are the highlight of her day, but since he's never asked her out, she assumes he's taken. Besides, between a day job and a budding music career, she has no time to start a new relationship.

That is until Gregg makes her an offer she can't refuse—a gift certificate to the virtual fantasy fulfillment service everyone is talking about. As a huge Star Trek fan, Alicia has a perfect match in mind—the captain of the Starship Enterprise.

The Thief Who Loved Me

When Marian splurges on a Perfect Match Virtual adventure as a world infamous jewel thief, she expects high-wire fun with a hot partner who she will never have to see again in real life.

A virtual encounter seems like the perfect answer to Marcus's string of dating disasters. No strings attached, no drama, and definitely no love. As a die-hard James Bond fan, he chooses as his avatar a dashing MI6 operative, and to complement his adventure, a dangerously seductive partner.

Neither expects to find their forever Perfect Match.

My Merman Prince

The beautiful architect working late on the twelfth floor of my building thinks that I'm just the maintenance guy. She's also under the impression that I'm not interested.

Nothing could be further from the truth.

I want her like I've never wanted a woman before, but I don't play where I work.

I don't need the complications.

When she tells me about living out her mermaid fantasy with a stranger in a Perfect Match virtual adventure, I decide to do everything possible to ensure that the stranger is me.

The Dragon King

To save his beloved kingdom from a devastating war, the Crown Prince of Trieste makes a deal with a witch that costs him half of his humanity and dooms him to an eternity of loneliness.

Now king, he's a fearsome cobalt-winged dragon by day and a short-tempered monarch by night. Not many are brave enough to serve in the palace of the brooding and volatile ruler, but Charlotte ignores the rumors and accepts a scribe position in court.

As the young scribe reawakens Bruce's frozen heart, all that stands in the way of their happiness is the witch's bargain. Outsmarting the evil hag will take cunning and courage, and Charlotte is just the right woman for the job.

My Werewolf Romeo

The father of my star student is a big-shot screenwriter and the patron of the drama department who thinks he can dictate what production I should put on. The principal makes it very clear that I need to cooperate with the opinionated asshat or walk away from my dream job at the exclusive private high school.

It doesn't help matters that the guy is single, hot, charming, creative, and seems to like me despite my thinly-veiled hostility.

When he invites me to a custom-tailored Perfect Match virtual adventure to prove that his screenplay is perfect for my production, I accept, intending to have fun while proving that messing with the classics is a foolish idea.

I don't expect to be wowed by his werewolf adaptation of Red Riding Hood mesh-up with Romeo and Juliet, and I certainly don't expect to fall in love with the virtual fantasy's leading man.

The Channeler's Companion

A treat for fans of *The Wheel of Time*.

When Erika hires Rand to assist in her pediatric clinic, she does so despite his good looks and irresistible charm, not because of them.

He's empathic, adores children, and has the patience of a saint.

He's also all she can think about, but he's off-limits.

What's a doctor to do to scratch that irresistible itch without risking workplace complications?

A shared adventure in the Perfect Match Virtual Studios seems like the solution, but instead of letting the algorithm choose a partner for her, Erika can try to influence it to select the one she wants. Awarding Rand a gift certificate to the service will get him into their database, but unless Erika can tip the odds in her favor, getting paired with him is a long shot.

Hopefully, a virtual adventure based on her and Rand's favorite series will do the trick.

The Valkyrie & The Witch

After breaking up with my boyfriend, I vow never to date a physician again and avoid workplace romances like the plague. Seeking an escape from bad memories and hospital politics, I apply for a job at the Perfect Match Virtual Fantasy Studios, where I hope to explore fantastical scenarios and beta-test new experiences.

I have no intention of entering a new relationship anytime soon, but it is difficult to ignore Kayden, a fellow trainee who's good-looking and charming but regrettably has aspirations of becoming a physician.

Hoping never to get paired with him to beta test an experience, I choose the Valkyrie adventure. It seems like a safe bet to avoid a guy like him, who would never select an experience where the female is the kick-ass heroine and the man only gets a supporting role. However, the algorithm has other plans in store for us. It seems to think that we are a perfect match.

Adina and the Magic Lamp

In this post-apocalyptic virtual reimagining of Aladdin, James, the enigmatic prince, and Adina, the fearless thief, navigate the treacherous streets of Londabad, a city that echoes London and Ahmedabad and fuses magic and technology. In the face of danger, the chemistry between them ignites, and the lines between prince and thief, royalty and commoner blur.

FOR EXCLUSIVE PEEKS AT UPCOMING RELEASES & A FREE I. T. LUCAS COMPANION BOOK

JOIN MY *VIP CLUB* AND GAIN ACCESS TO THE VIP PORTAL AT ITLUCAS.COM
TO JOIN, GO TO:
http://eepurl.com/blMTpD

INCLUDED IN YOUR FREE MEMBERSHIP:

YOUR VIP PORTAL

- READ PREVIEW CHAPTERS OF UPCOMING RELEASES.
- LISTEN TO GODDESS'S CHOICE NARRATION BY CHARLES LAWRENCE
- EXCLUSIVE CONTENT OFFERED ONLY TO MY VIPS.

FREE I.T. LUCAS COMPANION INCLUDES:

- GODDESS'S CHOICE PART 1
- PERFECT MATCH: VAMPIRE'S CONSORT (A STANDALONE NOVELLA)
- INTERVIEW Q & A
- CHARACTER CHARTS

IF YOU'RE ALREADY A SUBSCRIBER, AND YOU ARE NOT GETTING MY EMAILS, YOUR PROVIDER IS SENDING THEM TO YOUR JUNK FOLDER, AND YOU ARE MISSING OUT ON **IMPORTANT UPDATES, SIDE CHARACTERS' PORTRAITS, ADDITIONAL CONTENT, AND OTHER GOODIES.** TO FIX THAT, ADD isabell@itlucas.com TO YOUR EMAIL CONTACTS OR YOUR EMAIL VIP LIST.

Check out the specials at
https://www.itlucas.com/specials

Printed in Great Britain
by Amazon